George H. Cantwell

You Ask!-I'll tell!

George H. Cantwell

You Ask!-I'll tell!

ISBN/EAN: 9783337373733

Printed in Europe, USA, Canada, Australia, Japan

Cover: Foto ©Andreas Hilbeck / pixelio.de

More available books at **www.hansebooks.com**

"YOU ASK!—I'LL TELL!"

A

HOME AND BUSINESS COMPANION

OF

ALL THINGS

OF

EVERY-DAY LIFE.

EMBRACING

EVERY ONE HIS OWN DOCTOR—EVERY ONE HIS OWN SURGEON—EVERY ONE
HIS OWN DRUGGIST—EVERY ONE HIS OWN LAWYER—EVERY ONE HIS
OWN COOK—HOUSEHOLD MANAGEMENT—THE ART OF CARVING—
THE ART OF DRESS-MAKING—THE ART OF FANCY NEEDLE
AND WAX FLOWER WORK — ETIQUETTE — TOILET — HOME
AMUSEMENTS—PARLOR AND OUT-DOOR GAMES—A
TREATISE ON THE HORSE.

A BOOK

FOR THE FATHER—MOTHER—SISTER—BROTHER—LOVER—LAWYER—DOCTOR
—MERCHANT—MECHANIC—FARMER—MARINER—YOUNG AND
OLD—MALE AND FEMALE.

BY

GEORGE H. CANTWELL, M. D.

RIVERSIDE PUBLISHING CO.

PREFACE.

THE EDITOR, in congratulating himself upon the completion of this work, gratefully acknowledges the favors and courtesies extended to him by the PROFESSIONAL and SCIENTIFIC GENTLEMEN whom he has had occasion to consult. And, equally, to those Authors whose works have (by their consent) furnished much valuable information, he offers his sincere thanks. Especially does he express thanks to Madame Kellogg, who has personally prepared a most instructive treatise on the art of dressmaking, illustrated with the plans and diagrams so successfully employed for instruction in her classes. Ladies who are fortunate in the use of this book will be under many obligations to the Madame for her plain and comprehensive hints on dressmaking.

The many books published—whether *Cookery Books, Family Doctor,* or *Law books; books on Dress, Furniture, Etiquette, Amusements,* or *Needlework—* have none of them met the popular want, inasmuch as not more than one-tenth of the contents were useful in the household (however valuable to the expert). Their pages were encumbered with a mass of impracticable matter, which increased the volume so much, that what should have been contained in one book was made to fill several ; thus not only increasing the cost, but rendering it as difficult to find the identical item required as to find a needle in a "haystack."

The object of the present work is to furnish a large number of needles, and to place them in a needle-case, having a place for each needle, and each needle in its place, so that it may be found the moment it is wanted ; to furnish the digested contents of many books in one volume at the minimum cost—just as Professor Liebig, in the preparation of his extract, condenses an ox into the space of a small jar, retaining the essence, thereby reducing the cost and adding to the convenience.

While portions of this book are the results of a careful and comprehensive

vii

research of our best writers and most scientific men, it is not a mere compilation, but in plan and detail is the product of the Editor's own mental application. A large proportion is original, in this view, that it has NEVER BEFORE BEEN PUBLISHED, but has accumulated from contact with sagacious and practical people, and now reduced to form ESPECIALLY FOR THIS WORK.

In the appendix may be written or pasted additional receipts which are found worthy of careful preservation for ready reference ; this is a feature which the systematic housewife will fully appreciate.

The reader may depend upon everything in these pages as being PRACTICAL, having been proved by ACTUAL TRIAL AND CONSTANT USE. Two of the receipts presented were obtained at a cost of fifty dollars, in cash, for each, and many others at a cost varying from five to twenty dollars, for each, and were all *proved before being admitted here.*

It is not claimed that this work is perfect ; but the Editor has spared no pains to make it *useful.* IT IS RELIABLE ; and he feels confident that no work hitherto published contains so much general and valuable information, in such a condensed and useful form, or for many times its cost.

None but those who have actually engaged in the preparation of a work of this kind can estimate the amount of labor involved, and the many difficulties to be overcome before it can be completed.

In claiming for this work the title of "A HOME AND BUSINESS COMPANION OF ALL THINGS OF EVERY-DAY LIFE," the Editor thinks the public will endorse it, and sustain him in the assertion, that for whatever you want to know, ask the book and it will tell.

"Knowledge is power." It is treasured up in a reservoir from whence all may draw—to make domestic use of which, it requires to be brought to our homes. We here offer a portable reservoir of that *knowledge-power*, and if by drawing from it the mother is enabled to lighten her household cares ; to run the machinery of domestic life so that there shall be no creaking ; to care for her children, that they may be healthy, virtuous and wise—the boy to be active, manly, generous and intelligent—the girl to be the joy of the household, industrious, unselfish and refined—the father to guide and control the whole domestic economy ; that all may work together in harmony with the laws of nature ; the business man to manage and conduct his affairs successfully and avoid law suits ; then will the Editor feel that he has succeeded in his undertaking.

CONTENTS.

FOR INDEX, see end of Book.

	PAGE
HOME MANAGEMENT	11
QUACKERY	13
SLEEP—VENTILATION	15
INFANT MANAGEMENT	19
EVERY ONE HIS OWN DOCTOR	23
CHILDREN'S DISEASES	23
THROAT DISEASES	31
SKIN DISEASES	33
BRAIN AND NERVE DISEASES	39
TEETH AND EAR DISEASES	52
CHEST DISEASES	57
HEART DISEASES	61
STOMACH AND BOWELS	65
KIDNEY DISEASES	75
FEMALE DISEASES	79
FEVERS	83
RHEUMATISM	88
ABSCESSES AND SORES	92
BURNS AND SCALDS	97
WOUNDS AND FRACTURES	99
EYE DISEASES	112
EVERY ONE HIS OWN DRUGGIST	119
PROPERTIES OF MEDICINE	122
GLOSSARY OF MEDICAL TERMS	139
EVERY ONE HIS OWN SURGEON	136
BANDAGES	138
SUBSTITUTES FOR SPLINTS	140
CUPPING AND LEECHES	141
HOW TO PRESERVE HEALTH	143
BATHING AND CLEANLINESS	144
TAKING EXERCISE	146
TEMPERANCE AND MODERATION	148
EFFECT OF INTERMARRIAGE	152
PREVENTION OF ACCIDENTS	155

	PAGE
ADVICE TO SWIMMERS	156
STRENGTH OF MEN	157
EVERY ONE HIS OWN COOK	159
WHERE TO FIND JOINTS	161
RULES FOR MARKETING	163
BAKING, ROASTING AND BROILING	174
THE ART OF CARVING	218
HOW TO PICKLE, CAN AND PRESERVE	225
PREPARATION OF VEGETABLES	230
PASTRY AND CAKES	242
CONFECTIONERY AND ICES	257
HOW TO MAKE DRINKS	262
BREAD MAKING	271
MAKING HOME COMFORTABLE	275
HUSBAND AND WIFE	299
THE USE OF LANGUAGE	307
RULES OF ACCENT	314
HOW TO WRITE PROPERLY	320
LAWS OF ETIQUETTE	324
BALLS AND PARTIES	331
THE TOILET	343
DOMESTIC AND FARM RECIPES	351
EVERY ONE HIS OWN LAWYER	376
LANDLORD AND TENANT	379
PARTNERSHIP AND WILLS	382
WEIGHTS AND MEASURES	387
HOME AMUSEMENTS	392
THE ART OF NEEDLEWORK	415
THE ART OF DRESSMAKING	447
TREATISE UPON THE HORSE	459
APPENDIX	469
INDEX	485

HOME MANAGEMENT.

SIGNIFICATION OF THE WORD HOME—WHY QUACKS SHOULD BE AVOIDED
—PRACTICAL SUGGESTIONS ABOUT FOOD, EXERCISE, SLEEP, VENTILA-
TION, AND THE CARE OF INFANTS.

HOME.—This word has a comparatively narrow signification in this
country: it is not often used, and then
to denote a "dwelling-place." The
English attach a far deeper meaning
to it. To them it means *the place where
the heart is* — the one place on earth
where, above all others, the affections
are centred — father, mother, brother,
sister, are all concentrated in that little
word. To make our dwelling-place a
HOME, it must be made attractive; it
need not be fashionable — it must be
neat; do not shut out the *sunshine* — it
may fade the carpet, but it will preserve the health of the inmates, and
give an air of cheerfulness all through
the house. Don't be afraid of a little
fun, lest a hearty laugh shake down
some of the musty old cobwebs there.
If you want to ruin your sons, let them
think that all mirth and social enjoyment must be left on the threshold
without, when they come home at night.
When once a home is regarded as only
a place to eat, drink, and sleep in, the
work is begun that ends in gambling-
houses and reckless degradation.
Young people must have fun and relaxation somewhere; if they do not
find it at their own hearthstones, it will
be sought at other and perhaps less
profitable places. Therefore let the fire
burn brightly at night, and make the
homestead delightful with all those
little arts that parents so perfectly understand. Don't repress the buoyant
spirit of your children. Half an hour
of merriment, round the lamp and fire-
light of a home, blots out the remembrance of many a care and annoyance
during the day; and the best safeguard
they can take with them into the

world is the unseen influence of a
bright little domestic sanctum.
Encourage your children to bring
their companions home with them occasionally — say once a month; allow
them a cheerful room, well lighted and
warmed. Encourage them in vocal
and instrumental music, in parlor
games and other innocent recreations.
And although it is well to look in upon
them sometimes — to know them — do
not remain, to be a restraint upon
them, but let them enjoy themselves in
their own way. The fact that you take
an interest in them, and try to make
them happy, will be sufficient to keep
them from becoming too boisterous,
and will teach them moderation and
self-control.

Let cheerful conversation be encouraged, and the children invited to
join in and ask questions. Children
hunger perpetually for new ideas.
They will learn with pleasure from the
lips of parents what they deem drudg-
ery to study in books; and even if
they have the misfortune to be deprived of many educational advantages, they will grow up intelligent, if
they enjoy in childhood the privilege
of listening daily to the conversation
of intelligent people. We sometimes
see parents, who are the life of every
company that they enter, dull, silent,
and uninteresting at home among their
children. If they have not mental activity and mental stores sufficient for
both, let them first use what they have
for their own households. A silent
house is a dull place for young people,
a place from which they will escape if
they can. How much useful information, on the other hand, is often given

in pleasant family conversation, and what unconscious, but excellent mental training in lively social argument, cultivate to the utmost all the graces of home conversation.

Instead of swallowing your food in sullen silence, or brooding over your business, or severely talking about others, let the conversation at the table be genial, kind, social, and cheering. Don't bring disagreeable things to the table in your conversation, any more than you would in your dishes. The more good company you have at your table the better. Hence the intelligence, refinement, and appropriate behavior of a family which is given to hospitality. Never feel that intelligent visitors can be anything but a blessing to you and yours. And in your own conversation, never lose sight of the fact that the first essential thing is *truth* — the next, *good sense* — the third, *good humor* — and the fourth, *wit*.

Boys are more boisterous than girls; it is natural to them, and should not be unduly restrained, or it may crush out that fine manly spirit and elasticity which enables the man to surmount all difficulties.

"Ma, were you ever a boy?" said a bright-eyed little boy when reproved by his mother for too much sportiveness; "Were you ever a boy?"

This was a boy of the right stamp — having the ring of the true metal.

Boys and girls should be brought up together as companions; in this way boys are more gentle, pure minded, and conscientious than those educated wholly with their own sex.

So girls brought up with boys are ever more vigorous in thought and action, less vain and frivolous, than when under the care of women alone. Boys and girls in schools together are more healthy and refined in all their associations than either sex alone.

In domestic happiness, the wife's influence is much better than her husband's; for the one, the first cause—mutual love and confidence — being granted, the whole comfort of the household depends upon trifles more

immediately under her jurisdiction By her management of small sums, her husband's respectability and credit are created or destroyed. No fortune can stand the constant leakages of extravagance and mismanagement; and more is spent in trifles than women would easily believe. The one great expense, whatever it may be, is turned over and carefully reflected on ere incurred; the income is prepared to meet it; but it is pennies imperceptibly sliding away which do mischief, and this the wife alone can stop, for it does not come within a man's province. There is often an unsuspected trifle to be saved in every household.

It is not in economy alone that the wife's attention is so necessary, but in those niceties which make a well regulated house. An unfurnished cruet-stand, a missing key, a buttonless shirt, a soiled tablecloth, a mustard-pot with its old contents shaking hard and down about it, are really nothings; but each can raise angry words and cause discomfort. Depend upon it, there is a great deal of domestic happiness about a well-dressed mutton-chop, or a tidy breakfast table. Men grow sated of beauty, tired of music; are often too wearied for conversation, however intellectual; but they can always appreciate a well-swept hearth and smiling comfort.

A woman may love her husband devotedly—may sacrifice fortune, friends, family, country for him — she may have the genius of a Sappho, the enchanted beauties of an Armida; but, melancholy fact, if with these she fails to make his home comfortable, his heart will inevitably escape her. And women live so entirely in the affections, that without love their existence is void. Better submit, then, to household tasks, however repugnant they may be to your tastes, than doom yourself to a loveless home. Women of the higher order of mind will not run their risk; they know that their feminine, their domestic, are their first duties.

A good appetite is essential to a

good digestion, but a snow-white table-cloth is a great promoter of a good appetite. — No one can eat in comfort if any member of the family appears at the table in slatterly dress; with un-kempt hair; showing a breadth of black under the finger-nails; with a hawking and a spitting and a blowing of the nose, and their tremendous associations.

But the spotless napkin, the most splendid roast, and faultless concomitants all, what do these amount to, if sadness is written on the face of the wife; if an angry scowl gleams from the corrugated brow of a morose husband, or a dissatisfied look comes from a child's eye, and the meal is partaken of in ominous silence? Away with such unloveliness! there is no sunshine in such a household, and the members of that family, if they grow up at all, will become the refrigerators, the bane of every company into which they may be thrown in after life.

Rather let the family table be the place of glad reunions; as much looked forward to as the promised coming of a cherished friend; let courtesies more than courtly be ever cultivated; let smiles wreath every face; let calm satisfaction sit on every countenance; let light hearts, and cheery words, and obliging acts, and watchful attentions be the order of the day; these are the promoters of a healthy digestion; and these are they which largely help to make happy homes, and good hearts, and generous natures.

The home being thus a happy place, one of the requirements of health is established, and here let us say that the one great requirement upon which all others rest, is common sense,—this is the great safeguard to health, and the best physician; it teaches us to protect ourselves from all quackery, and to accept and practice the laws of health. "Prevention is better than cure."

QUACKERY.—According to Johnson, a Quack is "a boastful pretender to arts which he does not understand; one who proclaims his own medical ability in public places; or an artful tricking practitioner in physic." And this gives us a sufficiently clear definition of the art practised by such a pretender to medical knowledge. The advertising Quack of bygone times was a travelling mountebank, who, from a stage in some public place, vaunted the hidden virtues of his nostrums, and his own power to cure all diseases to which flesh is heir. Nostrum vendors of the present day do not so present themselves to a credulous public; as a rule, they keep behind the curtain, and flood the columns of the newspapers, and all other mediums of advertisement, with their mendacious statements of wonderful cures effected by their invaluable remedies. Never, perhaps, was Quackery so rampant and ubiquitous as in this so-called enlightened 19th century; it would almost seem as if people wished to be duped, so eagerly do they clutch at each new panacea introduced with a great flourish of puffery, and a cloud of lying witnesses in the shape of forged testimonials. So great is the consumption of "patent medicines," whose government stamp appears like a certification of marvellous efficacy — whose high price is almost looked upon as an evidence of occult virtue. Quackery is sometimes confounded with Empiricism; but there is this difference between them — the former either adopts a concealed mode of treatment, or pretends to be possessed of a remedy applicable to every form of disease, and every individual case; the latter is founded upon the principle that, as certain medicines are known to have cured certain diseases, it will be right and safe at all times, and under all circumstances, to administer those remedies, whenever the diseases, against which they have been successfully employed, appear again.

An empiric must be an instructed man, a Quack need not; he may be, and often is, utterly ignorant of the nature and real operation of his much-vaunted remedy, composed, as he would have the public believe, of rare and costly ingredients, and of

universal efficacy. Nothing but un-
blushing effrontery is here required,
and a carelessness of consequences
that would be ludicrous were it not
highly criminal.

Dr. Letheby, in concluding a series
of valuable articles on the mischievous effects of Quack Medicines, writes
thus on Quack advertisements : — "If
any of our readers have ever been
the victims of Quackery, we venture
to say that it was through the medium
of a cunningly-devised advertisement;
for this is at all times the great decoy
of the Quack. He knows its power,
for he can count its results by thousands; and he spares no pains to use
it with advantage. He studies it as
he would a science; and he pays as
much attention to the skilful practice
of it as many do to the exercise of a
noble art. Indeed, the cunning and
ingenuity of the quack are ever on
the alert to find new means of de-
veloping the resources of the all-pow-
erful puff. At one time it comes forth
in the shape of a learned lecturer,
' who, at the request and earnest solici-
tation of many friends to humanity,
has condescended to enlighten the
world, by giving a course of six lectures on the entire principles of his
system.' In the details of this course,
everything is alluded to that can by
any possibility excite the morbid feelings of those to whom the lectures
are addressed ; there are, for example,
skeletons, drunkards' stomachs, diseased hearts, consumptive lungs, and
other things of a like character ; and
not unfrequently, a hint is given that
there is some probability of a sort of
sparring-match between the lecturer
and a real doctor, who has been invited to attend. This artifice has the
effect of bringing together a large
audience, and of producing to the
lecturer very happy results.

"At another time, the puff appears
in the form of an ingenious account
of a new medicine, and of all the
diseases which it will infallibly cure.
These are generally enumerated in
nearly the same order — the category

beginning with flatulency, and ending
with thoughts of self-destruction.
"To this is, generally, added a ster-
eotyped account of the nature and
effects of the medicine on the blood
and humors. Morison is particularly
apt at this : indeed he may be called
the founder of the *humorous puff*.
"The simplicity of this style is so
exceedingly popular, that almost every
new claimant for the honors and
profits of quackery adopts it.
"Then, again, there is *the testimonial
puff*, which has always been very successful as a decoy ; and it wants but
little management beyond that of
keeping it up. Indeed, there are men
who live by writing these puffs and
selling them at so much per dozen.
The styles of the various classes are
always the same ; and they may be subdivided into the *debauchée* puff, the
humanity puff, the *sedentary* puff, and
the *professional* puff.
"The *puff professional* is always in
the familiar style.
"Another sort of puff is that in
which the advertiser abuses Quackery,
and disclaims all connection with the
unprincipled parties who thus impose
on the credulity of their victims.
"Last of all comes the most vicious
and abominable of all species of advertised quackery — that which is to
be found in the by-places of every
considerable town. The announcements to which we refer profess to be
an account of the practice of some duly
qualified medical man, who will undertake to cure disease with certainty,
with secrecy, and at a small charge.
Many an unwary victim has been
lured to the den of these impostors
by their specious announcements, and
after having been almost ruined in
health and in pocket, has found
himself for years afterwards the subject of the grossest extortion. That
secret which the advertiser professed
to keep, is a source of revenue to him,
and we need not say how it is abused.
We would warn the unwary from
such dangers, as we would from the
plague ; and no language is severe

enough to condemn the practices to which we refer.

"In conclusion, it must be manifest to our readers that the tricks of Quackery are at all times no other than the tricks of imposture. The idea of curing disease or of benefiting mankind has no place in the mind of the Quack; and even if it had, it is associated with too much ignorance to be of use. The one single object which he has in view is that of getting money by deception, and he cares not how it is accomplished, or at what cost it may be to the life and health of the community."

FOOD.—To be healthy we must eat wholesome food, which, to be digested and absorbed into the system, must be well masticated (or chewed), and not swallowed in a hurry, but slowly, in order that a full flow of saliva may take place, and the food become well moistened with it before it passes into the stomach. This will prevent the necessity of drinking much at meals, which is an unwholesome habit, and especially if much cold water is indulged in while eating, for this will check the flow of gastric juice, and indigestion will follow. This same result will occur if too much food is eaten, which is apt to be the case when one eats in a hurry. Cheerfulness is a great help to digestion. Some kinds of food contain more nutrition than others, and are more easily digested (the tables giving the amount of nutriment, and the time required to digest the several articles of food, will be found in another part of this book), but, as a rule, food which is best enjoyed is best digested.

EXERCISE is also necessary to health; an idle man will rust out sooner than an industrious one will wear out. The laboring man generally gets exercise enough, and in his case we will merely suggest that when one set of muscles have been kept in work all day, it will rest him more to call into use for half an hour those muscles which have been unused, than it would to sit or lie still for that time. Persons of sedentary occupations should have some regular plan of exercise: riding horseback — playing ball — billiards — calisthenics are all good, but perhaps the best is *walking;* it brings the whole body into motion, and can be indulged in by all classes, rich and poor, though, to be beneficial, it should be pleasurable, and, to this end, a good, intelligent companion is desirable.

In selecting methods of exercise, every individual should be guided by his own individual tastes. It is better to change frequently from one exercise to another. It is well even to consult our whims and our varying moods. Above all things, we should strive to prevent our exercise from becoming a dry, hard, mechanical routine. The heart should go with the muscles.

SLEEP.—There is no absolute standard for the amount of sleep required; seven or eight hours is generally necessary — some require more, others less. To regulate the amount of sleep, it is a good plan to get up as soon as you wake; do not sleep in the daytime; and do not go to bed before your usual time. Continue this, and in a few days Nature will accommodate herself to the case, and you will not wake until she has taken the amount she demands. Old people need more sleep than the middle aged — nine or ten hours not being too much for them. Growing children also require more sleep, and it is wise not to waken them in the morning if they do not of themselves wake early enough: let them go to bed earlier the next night. It is an old saying that "one hour's sleep before midnight is worth two hours after." It is none the less true now, and every year adds to its force.

VENTILATION.—The sleeping room should be large and well ventilated. We spend more hours in it than in any other room; it should, therefore, be the most cheerful; and yet how often is it considered that any room will do to sleep in. If the room is small, the door should be left open, or lower the window half an inch from the top. *A room where the sun cannot* *reach at some part of the day is unfit for a human being to sleep in.*

A New York merchant noticed, in the progress of years, that each successive bookkeeper gradually lost his health, and finally died of consumption, however vigorous and robust he was on entering his service. At length it occurred to him that the little rear-room where the books were kept opened into a back yard, so surrounded by high walls that no sunshine came into it from one year's end to another. An upper room, well lighted, was immediately prepared, and his clerks had uniform good health ever after.

A familiar case to general readers is derived from medical works, where an entire English family became ill, and all remedies seemed to fail of their usual results, when, accidentally, a window-glass of the family room was broken, in cold weather. It was not repaired, and forthwith there was a marked improvement in the health of the inmates. The physician at once traced the connection, discontinued his medicines, and ordered that the window-pane should not be replaced.

A French lady became ill. The most eminent physicians of her time were called in, but failed to restore her. At length Dupeytren, the Napoleon of physic, was consulted. He noticed that she lived in a dim room, into which the sun never shone ; the house being situated in one of the narrow streets, or rather lanes, of Paris. He at once ordered more airy and cheerful apartments, and all her complaints vanished.

From these facts, which cannot be disputed, the most common mind should conclude that cellars, and rooms on the northern side of buildings, or apartments into which the sun does not immediately shine, should never be occupied as family rooms or chambers, or as libraries or studies. Such apartments are only fit for stowage, or purposes which never require persons to remain in them over a few minutes at a time. And every intelligent and humane parent will arrange that the family room and the chambers shall be the most commodious, lightest, and brightest apartments in his dwelling.

Feather Beds are going out of fashion. This is a step in the right direction, for they are enervating and positively unhealthy. The best bed, and the most healthy, is a curled hair mattress. For additional warmth, it is well to spread a comforter, or a blanket doubled, upon the mattress, under the sheet. Good hair mattresses are rather expensive ; thirty pounds weight make a fair one, thirty-five pounds a better, and forty pounds quite a good one. Husk from corn makes a good mattress. It requires to be well picked before using. Dried leaves from the maple or beech make a clean, healthy bed for the poor.

If a spring bottom is placed under the mattress, and a good conscience on top of it, good and refreshing sleep may be expected.

Position for Sleep. — It is a good plan on first getting into bed to lie on the left side, and after to change to the right side, which is the most natural position ; sleeping with the arms extended above the head, or with the mouth open, generally causes disturbed sleep, even if it is not absolutely injurious.

Night Dress. — A long, easy fitting night dress should always be worn to sleep in, first removing the garments worn during the day.

Dr. Winslow wisely says, there is no fact more clearly established in the physiology of man than this, that the brain expends its energies and itself during the hours of wakefulness, and that these are recuperated during sleep. If the recuperation does not equal the expenditure, the brain withers — this is insanity. Thus it is that, in early English history, persons who were condemned to death by being prevented from sleeping, always died raving maniacs ; thus it is also that those who are starved to death become insane — the brain is not nourished, and they cannot sleep. The practical inferences are three : — 1st. Those who think most, who do most brain work, require most sleep. 2d. That time "saved" from necessary sleep is infallibly destructive to mind, body, and estate. Give yourself, your children, your servants — give all that are under you, the fullest amount of sleep they will take, by compelling them to go to bed at some regular hour, and to rise in the morning the moment they awake; and within a fortnight Nature, with almost the regularity of the rising sun, will unloose the bonds of sleep the moment enough repose has been secured for the wants of the system. This is the only safe and sufficient rule; and as to the question how much sleep any one requires, each must be a rule for himself — great Nature will never fail to write it out to the observer under the regulations just given.

In his remarks to invalids on this important subject, Dr. Hall says : "The more you can sleep, the sooner you will get well. Sleeping in the daytime, if before noon, will enable you to sleep better the following night. Go to bed at regular hours with an empty stomach. Get up as soon as you wake of yourself, but do not be waked.

"The great regulator of sleep is exercise; it is the best anodyne in the universe, and the only one that is always safe, always efficient, and always wholesome and natural. If you cannot take much exercise, take a little, and from day to day gradually increase the amount."

Being waked up early, and allowed to engage in difficult or any studies late and just before retiring, has given many a beautiful and promising child the brain fever, or determined ordinary ailments to the production of water on the brain.

Let parents make every possible effort to have their children go to sleep in a pleasant humor. Never scold or give lectures, or in any way wound a child's feelings as it goes to bed. Let all banish business and every worldly care at bedtime, and let sleep come to a mind at peace with God and all the world.

The human body falls asleep by degrees, according to M. Cabinis, a French physiologist. The muscles of the legs and arms lose their power before those which support the head, and these last sooner than the muscles which support the back; and he illustrates this by the cases of persons who sleep on horseback or while they are standing or walking. He conceives that sense of light sleeps first, then the sense of taste, next smell, and, lastly, that of touch.

Dr. J. C. Jackson, celebrated as a water cure practitioner in Western New York, says : "As a habit and fashion with our people *we sleep too little*. It is admitted by all those who are competent to speak on the subject, that the people of the United States, from day to day, not only do not get sufficient sleep, but they do not get sufficient rest. By the preponderance of the nervous over the vital temperament, they need all the recuperating benefits which sleep can offer during each night as it passes. A far better rule would be to get at least eight hours' sleep, and, including sleep, ten hours of incumbent rest. It is a sad mistake that some make, who suppose themselves qualified to speak on the subject, in affirming that persons of a highly-wrought, nervous temperament need — as compared with those of a more lymphatic or stolid organization — less sleep. The truth is, that where power is expended with great rapidity, by a constitutional law, it is regathered slowly ; the reaction, after a while, demanding much more time for the gathering up of new force, than the direct effort demands in expending that force. Thus, a man of the nervous temperament, after he has established a habit of overdoing, recovers from the effect of such overaction much more slowly than a man of different temperament would, if the balance between his power to do and his power to rest is destroyed. As between the nervous and the lymphatic temperaments, therefore, where excess of work is demanded, it will always be seen that, at the close of the day's labor, whether it has been of muscle or thought, the man of nervous tem-

perament, who is tired, finds it difficult to fall asleep, sleeps perturbedly,
wakes up excitedly, and is more apt
than otherwise to resort to stimulants
to place himself in conditions of pleasurable activity. While the man of
lymphatic temperament, when tired,
falls asleep, sleeps soundly and unin-
terruptedly, and wakes up in the morning a new man. The facts are against
the theory that nervous temperaments
recuperate quickly from the fatigues to
which their possessors are subjected.
Three-fourths of our drunkards are
from the ranks of the men of nervous
temperaments. Almost all opium-eat-
ers in our country — and their name
is legion — are persons of the nervous
or nervous-sanguine temperaments.
Almost all the men in the country who
become the victims of narcotic drug-
medication, are of the nervous or nervous-sanguine temperaments.

Dr. Cornell, of Philadelphia, in the
Educator, gives the following opinion
corroborative of the above as an explanation of the frequency of insanity.
He says: "The most frequent and immediate cause of insanity, and one of
the most important to guard against,
is the want of sleep. Indeed, so rarely
do we see a recent case of insanity
that is not preceded by want of sleep,
that it is regarded as almost a sure
precursor of mental derangement. Notwithstanding strong hereditary predisposition, ill health, loss of kindred or
property, insanity rarely results unless
the exciting causes are such as to produce a loss of sleep. A mother loses
her only child; a merchant his fortune; the politician, the scholar, the
enthusiast may have their minds powerfully excited and disturbed; yet, if
they sleep well they will not become
insane. No advice is so good, therefore, to those who have recovered from
an attack, or to those who are in delicate health, as that of securing, by all
means, sound, regular and refreshing
sleep."

A great deal of sickness may be prevented by knowing just what to do at
the first premonitory symptoms. Many

persons would take a simple remedy
immediately, if they only knew what
that remedy was. But they will not
send for a physician until they are
nearly prostrated by the disease; and
again there are numerous little ailments causing great annoyance and
much suffering, — little "pains and
aches" that do not actually require
the services of a doctor, — the remedy
for which is generally known, but just
at the moment it is needed the exact
name of it, the proportion, or how it
should be taken, is forgotten, and
though not knowing where to turn to
for the information, the disturbance is
allowed to run on until it becomes serious, and perhaps quite difficult to
cure.

It frequently happens in country
places, that persons, in sudden attacks
of illness, find themselves beyond the
early reach of a physician. To all
thus situated, the following pages are
submitted, not claiming for the remedies presented that they are "sure
cures," or possess "fabulous virtues,"
but they are those which have been
found most successful in the practice
of the profession, and have been especially adapted for family use by an
eminent physician. If the directions
given are carefully followed, much suffering and anxiety will be avoided. If
the symptoms are severe, or the nature
of them not understood, consult a good
physician at once; remember that delays are dangerous, and in nothing
more so than in sickness. And when
you consult him, be careful to follow
his instructions not only in the matter
of medicine, but also in diet, exercise,
etc. If he gives directions on these
subjects, he has a reason for it, and
they should be complied with. It is
the experience of all physicians that a
non-observance of these rules, in many
cases, not only retard, but in some
cases actually prevent a recovery from
sickness.

INFANTS.—As ours is a book especially designed for the mother and the
nurse, the treatment of children is one
on which we shall naturally be ex-

pected to dwell at considerable length. We shall, therefore, take the first stage of infantile existence as our starting point, and, in as brief and clear a manner as possible, explain the various operations and processes, means and measures, which are, or may be, necessary for bringing a child safely through the difficulties and dangers of babyhood. How great are these dangers is shown by the well-ascertained fact that nearly half the children born in this country die before they reach the age of five years; this is a fearful rate of mortality, and it would seem to indicate that, notwithstanding our high state of civilization, there must be something very defective in the general run of our infant management: indeed, it has struck us as not unlikely that the too common practice of mothers in the upper, and sometimes in the middle classes of society, of delegating to others that most tender and delicate of the mother's duties, viz., suckling the child, *may* possibly have something to do with this high rate of mortality among infants, and we would impress upon such of our readers as are mothers, or likely to become such, that nothing but the most urgent necessity should induce them to forego the performance of this most pleasing and sacred duty. Even if the child have all the aids and appliances that wealth can procure — a healthy wet-nurse, and the most careful possible of *hired* superintendence — it can never have the same advantages, and the same chances of escaping the dangers which beset its early career, as if it drew nourishment from the mother's breast, was nursed in the mother's arms, and watched over by the anxious carefulness of the mother's heart. There are cases we know, and many, in which the child must of necessity be deprived of these advantages, and confided to the care of those who are not its natural guardians; but there are many more cases in which there is no real necessity for such deprivation — only " the usages of polite society require it." Far " more honored," we would say, are such customs " in the breach than the observance." Mothers! suckle your infants, if God has blessed you with the means of doing so; if you have health and strength, and can by any possibility do it, watch over your tender nurslings, and bind them to you so closely by the cords of natural affection, that no after change, or circumstance of life, shall be able to loosen those blessed ties. But this is a digression into which we ought not, perhaps, to have been tempted, and from which we must return to the more practical part of our subject.

Infant Management.—Directly the little creature has entered upon the stage of exis⁺ence, and has been washed and dressed by the experienced hands of a careful nurse; after the first feeble cry has been uttered—that cry that so thrills the mother's heart — it will be well content to be quiet for a while, wrapped in warm flannel, and placed in the maternal arms, or, if that may not be, between the blankets, or in the nurse's lap; there will be a calm breathing, and a flush of life spread over the tiny face; and the eyes, which have only once yet looked upon the world will be closed in sleep. It is probable that, for many hours, the infant will be thus calmly sleeping, as motionless as Chantry's chiselled children; one can only tell it lives by the heaving of the chest and the color in the slightly-parted lips and small lineaments; but at the end of some hours, sooner or later, there will be a slight restless motion, as the pulse of life grows stronger in the veins, and the demands of nature for sustenance are just beginning to be felt. The mother has, ere this, probably, sufficiently recovered her strength to be able to take the child to her bosom, and holding it there in a loving embrace, she counts every tiny pulsation with a delight which only a mother can experience. But she cannot yet satisfy the want of which the infant is but half conscious, for unlike the lower animals, which can suckle their young directly they are born, the lacteal fluid will not flow from her breast until the end of the second, or sometimes, even the third day. It is concluded by some that the mouth of the infant should not be applied to the breast until that period; but Dr. Marshall Hall says: "Let this application be made as soon as the fatigue of labor is perfectly over, if the mother is doing well. The child's mouth is softer than that of the nurse. The secretion of the milk will be greatly excited, and the milk secreted will be equally gently removed. There will then be no milk abscess—no milk fever in many cases in which these must otherwise occur. If the infant be not early applied, the breast becomes swollen, and the nipple drawn in; and nursing becomes at once difficult and painful to the mother, and a source of fretfulness to the infant."

It is very common for a nurse to give to an infant, a few hours after it is born, a very little thin, perfectly smooth oatmeal gruel; this affords the necessary nutriment, and excites a gentle action of the bowels, and has the effect of relieving them of a thick, dark-colored matter, technically called *meconium*, which they contain at birth; a drop or two of Castor Oil is also given, with or without the gruel; this, perhaps, is scarcely necessary, but there is no valid objection to it; therefore, if it is the nurse's usual practice, she need not be interfered with in the matter. If, at the end of the first day, no sustenance can be obtained from the mother's breast, a little lukewarm fluid, composed of cow's milk and water, in equal proportions, and slightly sweetened with lump sugar, should be given in a feeding bottle, with a prepared calf's teat, or a nipple of India-rubber fitted to it; by this the child's mouth becomes accustomed to the natural mode of obtaining nourishment; when this kind of food has once been given, it should be continued about every two hours or so, a very small quantity at the time — letting the child, before each feeding, endeavor to obtain it from the mother's breast first; as soon as it can do this, of course all artificial food

should be put aside—that is, if the flow of milk is sufficient; if not, the breast and the bottle may be used alternately, for a while. "The mother's milk and the mother's warmth are the proper sources of nutriment and heat to her own infant; it should lie on no other breast and in no other arms." And certainly, for the first six or eight months of infantile life, no other than the natural nutriment is required, provided the supply of this be good, and sufficient in quantity; should this not be the case, the question of artificial food will have to be considered, unless a wet-nurse is engaged, against which there are many objections, both economical and moral.

To every mother, then, is to be committed the care of her own infant, in its largest, broadest sense. She is the first to submit herself to all those rules of diet, medicine, exercise, and quiet which are essential to insure her own good health. She is then to supply her own infant with milk, and with warmth, and for this latter purpose, she should lay it by her own side in the night. She should, in the third place, become the superintendent of its health, detecting the first signs of indisposition, and seeking immediately for the remedy.

Nor does the mother's office terminate even here. But she will go on to superintend the development of its mental powers, its dispositions and its affections.

One of the most fruitful sources of disease, in the early days of infantile life, is improper management in relation to diet, and a large proportion of the suffering and mortality which occurs during this period, arises from this cause alone; and he points out very clearly and forcibly the necessity there is of nursing upon a regular plan to insure the present and future health of the child.

"Milk ought to be the diet of infants for a certain time, and *it alone* will be sufficiently nourishing for nineteen out of twenty children — perhaps ninety-nine out of a hundred.

Fewer children would perish, if so fed, than are destroyed by rushing into the opposite extreme of feeding them with more viscid food; the use of farina or farinaceous foods for all infants under the age of nine months, and even in many beyond that, lays the foundation of future disease—the powers of assimilation in an infant not being suited for such food. Milk alone is the natural food, and this should be pure, not skimmed, nor previously reduced by water—unless in the country, where the milk is particularly rich, and then it may be reduced with one-third of water; in warm weather the milk should be placed in the coolest place that can be found; and should there be the slightest tendency to acidity observed, it should be at once rejected; sweetening with sugar in such a case would but increase the evil." As to the *temperature* of the food: "Our great aim ought to be to follow as much as possible in the footsteps of nature; and as we may observe that 96° or 98° Fahr. is the temperature of the mother's milk, so should we give it to the infant; and for the purpose of regulating this, as well as the state of the atmosphere, a thermometer should be kept in every nursery. The milk should not be boiled, but a bowl or pitcher containing it may be placed in boiling water, and so the required heat retained."

In warm weather an infant might be taken out of doors when about a fortnight old; in winter it would not be prudent to expose it before it is at least a month or six weeks old, and then only if the day is fine, and for not more than twenty minutes; if an east wind prevails, the child should be kept in-doors. Sleep should never be encouraged in the open air, nor should the glare of the sun be allowed to fall on its face; of course, the morning chill and evening damp should be avoided. When the infant does go out, let it be in the nurse's arms, *not in a perambulator*, that modern invention for the benefit of gossiping nurses, and for the destruction of infant life.

With regard to the *Diseases of Infants*, we may observe that the most frequent of these are—1, disorders of the stomach; 2, disorders of the bowels; 3, exhaustion; 4, febrile affections; 5, exanthematous diseases, or those which are attended with eruptions of the skin; 6, affections of the head; 7, diseases of the thorax, or chest; 8, affections of the abdomen, or belly.

Disorders of the stomach generally depend on improper diet; or they may be secondary, and the effects of a disordered or confined state of the bowels. They are often detected by acid or fœtid eructations and breath, or by the unusually frequent regurgitation or vomiting of food.

Disorders of the bowels can never be mistaken or overlooked by an attentive nurse, the evacuations, in their number and appearance, being the perfect index to these disorders.

It must never be forgotten, that whenever the system has been exposed to sources of exhaustion, this condition may become, in its turn, the source of varied morbid affections which are apt to be ascribed to other causes, and treated by improper, and therefore dangerous, measures. If the infant has had diarrhœa, or if it has been bled by leeches; or if, without these, its cheeks are pale and cool; and if, under these circumstances, it be taken with symptoms of affection of the head, do not fail to remember that this affection may be the result of exhaustion. This important subject seems to have been generally misunderstood.

Fever is sooner detected. In every such case it is advisable not to tamper nor delay, but to send for the physician, and watch the patient with redoubled care and attention.

Especially examine the skin, hour after hour, for eruptions. It may be measles or scarlatina, etc. It will be especially desirable to detect these eruptions early, and to point them out to the physician. Above all things, let not a contracted brow, an unusual state of the temper or manner, unusual drowsiness or wakefulness, or starting, and especially unusual vomiting, escape you.

Be alive to any acceleration or labor, or shortness of the breathing, or cough, or sneezing, or appearance of inflammation about the eyes or nostrils. These symptoms may portend inflammation within the chest, whooping-cough, measles. Pain of the body, with or without vomiting; or diarrhœa, with or without a morbid state of the bowels, or of the discharges, ought also to excite immediate attention. One caution should be given on this subject: some of the most alarming and fatal affections of the bowels, like some affections of the head, are unattended by *acute* pain or tenderness; their accession, on the contrary, is insidious, and it will require great attention to detect them early.

Another view, and another mode of the classification of the diseases of infants, full of interest, full of admonition, is — 1, as they are *sudden ;* or 2, as they are *insidious;* or 3, as they are, in the modes of accession, intermediate between these two extremes.

Of the sudden affections, are fits of every kind, croup, and some kinds of pain, as that of colic; of the second class are hydrocephalus, or water on the brain, and tubercles in the lungs or abdomen, constituting the two kinds of consumption. Fits, again, are cerebral, and arise from diseases within the head, or from irritation in the stomach and bowels, or from exhaustion ; or they are evidence of, and depend on, some malformation or disease of the heart.

Domestic treatment should never be trusted in such terrific affections as these; not a moment should be lost in sending for the medical man.

If anything may be done in the meantime, it is — 1, in either of the

two former cases to lance the gums; 2, to evacuate the bowels by the warm water injection, made more active by the additon of brown sugar; 3, and then to administer the warm bath. An important point, never to be forgotten in the hurry of these cases, is to reserve the evacuation for inspection, otherwise the physician will be deprived of a very important source of judgment.

In cases of fits arising plainly from exhaustion, there need be no hesitation in giving 5 drops of Sal Volatile in water; light nourishment may be added; the feet must be fomented, and the recumbent posture preserved.

In fits arising from an affection of the heart, the symptom is urgent difficulty of breathing; the child seems as if it would lose its breath and expire. In such a case, *to do nothing* is the best course; all self-possession must be summoned, and the infant kept perfectly quiet. Every change of posture, every effort, is attended with danger.

Sometimes the attacks assume the character of croup; there is a crowing cough, and breathing; or there is difficulty of breathing, and then a crowing inspiration. The former case is generally croup; the latter is, in reality, a fit dependent on a morbid condition of the brain or spinal marrow, although it takes the appearance of an affection of the organs of respiration.

In either case it is well to clear the bowels by means of the slow injection of from a quarter to half a pint of warm water, with or without brown sugar; indeed this is the most generally and promptly useful of all our remedies in infantile diseases. To this the warm bath may always be added, if administered with due caution. For instance, it should not be continued so as to induce much flushing or paleness of the countenance.

EVERY ONE HIS OWN DOCTOR.

PROPER TREATMENT FOR CHILDREN'S DISEASES—HOW TO RELIEVE AND
CURE THE MANY ILLS THAT FLESH IS HEIR TO—SICKNESS WHICH MAY
BE PREVENTED BY AVOIDING THE CAUSES.

TEETHING. — In all the affections of infancy, whether sudden or otherwise, the suspicion should fall upon the condition of the gum and of the teething, and therefore it is desirable that the mother should make herself acquainted with the use of the gum-lancet.

In many cases of convulsions, and other infantile affections, the use of this instrument affords the simplest, quickest, and readiest means of affording relief. In any case of this kind, should there appear to be danger from delay, let the mother carefully pass her finger along the child's gum, and if it appears to be unnaturally tumid at any particular part, let her apply the instrument there. If the affection be a fit, it may be used whether any part of the gum is hard and swollen or not, simply as the easiest mode of relieving the system by blood-letting. A gum-lancet should always be kept, but should this not be at hand, a common lancet or a sharp pen-knife will do. Make a free incision along the course of the gums, down to the teeth, or socket, if there be none; have the child's head held perfectly still, and be careful to guard against pushing the instrument too far back, so as to wound the throat. The operator should remember that perhaps the child's life depends upon the due performance of this duty, and nerve herself for the task.

There are many diseases to which infants are liable, which are very insidious in their advance, and present at first no very marked symptoms; but the watchful eye of the mother, or of a careful nurse, can generally detect the approach and progress of such — the countenance, manner, gestures, and motions of the child; the peculiarities of its cry; the state of its secretions and excretions; all afford indications of this, or anything new or strange in either of these, is sufficient to give the alarm and excite inquiry. If there is a falling off in the looks, color, and flesh of the child, there is reason to apprehend the formation of tubercles in the lungs — the harbingers of consumption.

The medicines and remedial means which must be kept for nursing, are few and simple. Rhubarb, Magnesia, and Manna for aperients, with Castor Oil; a few Senna leaves also, for infusion, may be useful. Ipecacuanha Powder and Wine, as an emetic; and for cordials, Brandy and Sal Volatile, the former, for exhaustion generally; the latter, when this is connected with pain and irritation of the bowels. What shall we say about anodynes, but simply to warn against their use? Except under the direction of the medical man, they should scarcely ever be given; nevertheless, it may be prudent to have at hand a small bottle of Laudanum, of which, in violent and excruciating pain, a single drop may be given. If a carminative, Dill Water is the best, to be combined, where there is much flatulency, with Fœtid Spirit of Ammonia, this, with a little

Carbonate of Soda, for acidity of stomach; Aromatic Confection for loose bowels; and Poppies and Camomile for fomentations, may complete the stock of medicines, which should be kept under lock and key, and only administered by the mother, or a nurse who can safely be trusted. But the warm bath, the injection, and the tooth-lancing, are the safest remedies; therefore, let the apparatus necessary for these be always at hand and ready for use. We have thus, as we hope, indicated with sufficient clearness how to preserve the health of our infant, or detect the signs of disease, and to meet it when it comes.

THRUSH.—This disease is common with infants who are fed improperly, or upon artificial food; it consists of an eruption of small white or ash colored ulcers, on the inside of the mouth and edges of the lips, not unfrequently extending to the throat and fauces; it is caused by irritation of the bowels, and generally gives rise to excoriations about the anus and nates. When these symptoms appear, nurses say it is "going through" the child, and indicate a speedy termination of the disease. Under ordinary circumstances, and if sufficient attention be paid to it, Thrush is not a dangerous affection; but if neglected, and sometimes if not, it assumes a gangrenous character, the ulcers increase in size and become livid; it is then much to be feared.

Treatment.—As this disease is nearly always attended with diarrhœa, some anti-acid and astringent mixture should be given, after, perhaps, one dose of Rhubarb and Magnesia; the Compound Chalk Mixture of the Pharmacopœia, with a few drops of Laudanum should the irritation be very great. To the eruptions of the mouth should be applied, with a camel hair brush, a little Honey and Borax, in the proportion of 6 drams of the former to 2 of the latter; or, in aggravated cases, a lotion composed of Nitrate of Silver, 1 scruple dissolved in 1 ounce of water. Dust over the excoriated nates and anus with Hair Powder, or dap

them with Goulard Water, two or three times a day. If the child is at the breast, great attention should be paid to the diet of the nurse; if not, the food must be at once simple and nutritious, milk forming the chief part of it: if the disease assumes a gangrenous character, there will be great exhaustion, and Beef Tea and Tonics will be required; for young children something like this:—Dilute Nitric Acid, 1½ minims; Syrup of Orange Peel, ¼ an ounce; Infusion of Calumba, 1 dram; Water, 3 ounces; take a dessert spoonful twice or three times a day.

CROUP.—This is an inflammation of the larynx and trachea, causing a difficulty of breathing, and a rough hoarse cough, with a sonorous inspiration of a very peculiar character, sounding as if the air was passing through a metallic tube: it most usually attacks children of from one to five years. The first signs are merely those of a common cold or catarrh; then comes on a dry cough with hoarseness and wheezing; at night there is restlessness and rattling in the throat, after which the croupy crow and sound above spoken of give unmistakable warning of the disease, which goes on increasing in intensity for a day or two, or perhaps several days, before there is a really alarming paroxysm, which mostly occurs about midnight. The child, after tossing restlessly about, endeavoring in vain to sleep, will start up with a flushed face, protruding eyeballs, and a distressing look of terror and anxiety; there is a quick vibrating pulse, and agitation of the whole frame, which presently becomes covered with a profuse perspiration: as the struggle for breath proceeds, there is clutching of the throat as though to force a passage, the arms are thrown wildly about, the respiration becomes more labored, the rough cough more frequent, and the characteristic Croup rings out like an alarm note. There is expectoration of viscid matter, but so difficult is it to be got rid of, that the effort appears to threaten strangulation; gradually the symptoms become weaker, and eventually the child falls into the sleep of exhaustion. It will probably wake up refreshed, and during the day may appear pretty well; but at night again, probably there will be a recurrence of the attack with aggravated symptoms, convulsions, spasms of the glottis, causing the head to be violently thrown back, in the effort to obtain a passage for the air through the windpipe; there is a fluttering motion in the nostrils, the face is puffed and of a pale leaden hue; a film comes over the sunken eyes, the pulse becomes feeble and irregular; there are more gasping convulsive efforts to continue the struggle, but in vain, the powers of life at length succumb, and the patient sinks into a drowsy stupor, which ends in death. Such is the frequent course of this painful disease, and the changes from bad to worse are so rapid that there is little time for the operation of remedies, that is, when the paroxysms have begun.

Treatment.—Confinement to the house in case of threatened Croup is always advisable, unless the weather should be very warm and open, and then exposure after sundown should be avoided; a dose of Calomel, about 3 grains, should be administered, and followed by nauseating doses of Tartarized Antimony, of which 1 grain may be dissolved in an ounce of warm water, and a teaspoonful of the solution given every quarter of an hour, until the effect is produced; should the bowels be confined after this, give Senna Mixture, or a Scammony Powder. Mustard and Bran Poultices to the throat. Leeches, if the patient is of a full habit, and the breathing is very labored; and a spare diet are the other remedial measures.

In the paroxysms, the most prompt and vigorous measures must be adopted to give any chance of success: bleeding in such quantity as to diminish the vascular action on the surface of the wind-pipe, and to relax the muscles; strong emetics to cause full vomiting, which often has a most beneficial effect;

warm baths, and blisters applied from one ear to the other. Calomel combined with Ipecacuanha Powder, or Tartar Emetic, should be given every four hours or so, and if the danger is extreme, counter irritation by means of Mustard Poultices applied to the calves of the legs, etc. In leeching for Croup, one leech for each year of the child's age is the general rule to be observed, and the best part is over the breast-bone, where pressure can be applied to stop the bleeding if required; over the leech bites, apply a blister should one appear necessary. If the above powders should cause too violent an action on the bowels, add to them a little Chalk with Opium. Should the child appear likely to sink from exhaustion, after vomiting has been produced, stay the emetics, and give Liquor of Acetate of Ammonia 20 drops, with 5 or 10 drops of Sal Volatile, or the same of Brandy in a little water, or Camphor Mixture; a little White Wine Whey may also be administered. *Of course, the first endeavor in an attack of Croup should be to obtain medical assistance;* but if this cannot be procured, there must be no temporizing — resort at once to the remedies most ready to the hand, using them according to the best knowledge and discretion available.

Let the contagious nature of Croup be ever borne in mind, and especial care taken to keep apart those affected with it from any other children in the family or house. Let it also be remembered that the great agents in producing it are cold and moisture, and, the greatest of all, the east wind, and that those who have once been attacked by it are peculiarly liable to a recurrence of such attack.

Croup is most likely to be fatal when inflammation commences in the fauces, and this, if discovered in time, may be stopped by the application of a solution of Nitrate of Silver to the whole surface within sight, and to the *Larynx*.

Spasmodic Croup, or Child Crowing, as it is often called, exhibits much the same symptoms as the Croup; it is not, however, of an inflammatory character, but is symptomatic of some other disease commonly coming on as a result of irritation caused by hydrocephalus, teething, worms, etc.; the medical man only can judge of the probable cause, and he will use such remedies as are most applicable to the peculiarity of each case. The following mode of treatment has been found efficacious in many cases of Croup; it is simple and easy of application:

"A sponge, about the size of a large fist, dipped in water as hot as the hand can bear, must be gently squeezed half dry, and instantly applied under the little sufferer's chin over the larynx and wind-pipe: when the sponge has been thus held for a few minutes in contact with the skin, its temperature begins to sink; a second sponge, heated in the same way, should be used alternately with the first. A perseverance in this plan during ten or twenty minutes produces a vivid redness over the whole front of the throat, just as if a strong mustard-plaster had been applied; this redness must not be continued long enough to cause a blister. In the meantime, the whole system feels the influence of the topical treatment; a warm perspiration breaks out, which should be well encouraged by warm drinks, as Whey, weak Tea, etc., and a notable diminution takes place in the frequency and time of the cough, while the hoarseness almost disappears, and the rough ringing sound of voice subsides, along with the difficulty of breathing and restlessness; in short, all danger is over, and the little patient again falls asleep, and awakes in the morning without any appearance of having recently suffered from so dangerous an attack. I have repeatedly treated the disease on this plan, and with the most uniform success. It is, however, only applicable to the very onset of the disease; but it has the advantage of being simple, efficient, and easily put in practice, and its effects are not productive of the least injury to the constitution."

An ordinary croupy cough is re-lieved by Castor Oil and Molasses, mixed together in equal quantities, and given in teaspoonful doses.

Whooping - Cough. — This well-known disease is chiefly, but not wholly, confined to the stages of infancy, and it occurs but once in a life-time. It may be described as a spasmodic catarrh, and its severity varies greatly; sometimes being so mild as to be scarcely known from a common cough, at others, exhibiting the most distressing symptoms, and frequently causing death by its violent and exhausting paroxysms.

The first symptoms of this cough are those of an ordinary cold; there is probably restlessness and slight fever, with irritation in the bronchial passages; this goes on gradually increasing in intensity for a week or ten days, and then it begins to assume the spasmodic character; at first the paroxysms are slight, and of short duration, with a scarcely perceptible "whoop," but soon they become more frequent and severe; a succession of violent expulsive coughs is followed by a long-drawn inspiration, in the course of which the peculiar sound which gives a name to the disease is emitted; again come the coughs, and again the inspiration, following each other in quick succession, until the sufferer, whose starting eyes, livid face, swollen veins, and clutching hands, attest the violence of the struggle for breath, is relieved by an expectoration. To weakly children, Whooping-Cough is a very serious malady — to all it is frequently a sore trial, but to them it is especially so ; therefore, great care should be taken not to expose them to the danger of catching it. That it is contagious there can be no doubt, and although some parents think lightly of it, and imagining their children must have it, at one time or another, deem that it matters little when, and therefore take no pains to protect them against it ; yet we would impress upon all our readers, who may have the care of infants, that a heavy responsibility lies at their door. It is by no means certain that a child will have this disease; we have known many persons who have reached a good old age and never contracted it; and it is folly and wickedness, needlessly, to expose those placed under our care to certain danger.

Like fever, Whooping-Cough has a course to run, which no remedies, with which we are at present acquainted, will shorten; the severity of the symptoms may be somewhat mitigated, and we may, by watching the course of the disease, and by use of the proper means, often prevent those complications which render it dangerous, and this brings us to the consideration of the proper mode of

Treatment. — The first effort should be directed to check any tendency to inflammation which may show itself — to palliate urgent symptoms, and stop the spasm which is so distressing a feature of the case. To this end, the diet must be of the simplest kind, consisting for the most part of milk and farinaceous puddings; if animal food, it must not be solid, but in the form of Broth or Beef-tea; roasted Apples are good; and, for drinks, Milk and Water, Barley-water, weak Tea, or Whey. Care must be taken to keep the bowels open with some gentle aperient, such as Rhubarb and Magnesia, with now and then a grain of Calomel or Compound Julep Powder, if something stronger is required. An emetic should be given about twice a week, to get rid of the phlegm — it may be Ipecacuanha Wine or the Powder. To relieve the cough, the following mixture will be found effective: — Ipecacuanha Powder, 10 grains; Bicarbonate of Potash, 1 dram; Liquor of Acetate of Ammonia, 2 ounces; Essence of Cinnamon, 8 drops; Water, 6½ ounces: Dose, a tablespoonful about every four hours. 20 drops of Laudanum, or 1 dram of Tincture of Henbane, may be added if the cough is very troublesome, but the former is objectionable if the brain is at all affected.

For right restlessness, 2 or 3 grains of Dover's Powders, taken at bedtime, is good; this is the dose for a child three years old. Mustard Poultices to the throat, the chest, and between the shoulders, are often found beneficial; so is an opiate liniment composed of Compound Camphor and Soap Liniment, of each 6 drams, and 4 drams of Laudanum. *Roche's Embrocation* is a favorite application, and a very good one; it is composed as follows: — Oil of Amber and of Cloves, of each ½ an ounce; Oil of Olives, 1 ounce; a little Laudanum is perhaps an improvement. This may be rubbed on the belly when it is sore from coughing. Difficulty of breathing may be sometimes relieved by the vapor of Ether or Turpentine diffused through the apartment. In the latter stages of the disease, tonics are generally advisable. Steel Wine, about 20 drops, with 2 grains of Sesquicarbonate of Ammonia, and 5 drops of Tincture of Conium, in a tablespoonful of Cinnamon Water, sweetened with Syrup, is a good form; but a change of air, with a return to a generous diet, are the most effectual means of restoration to health and strength.

Squinting, stupor, and convulsions are symptomatic of mischief in the brain; in this case leeches to the temples, and small and frequently repeated doses of Calomel and James's Powders, should be resorted to. Fever, and great difficulty of breathing, not only during the fits of coughing, but between them, indicate inflammation in the chest, on which a blister should be put, after the application of two or three leeches. In this case, the rule must be low diet, with febrifuge medicines, such as Acetate of Ammonia, Tartarized Antimony in Camphor Mixture, and Calomel and James's Powders. For a slight attack of Whooping-Cough, mix equal quantities of Castor Oil and Molasses; give a teaspoonful whenever the cough is troublesome; it will generally afford relief at once.

Concerning the Whooping-Cough. —Mr. James Craig, of Newcastle-on-

Tyne, in England, has published a paper, in which, after adverting to the fact that twelve thousand two hundred and seventy-two persons died from Whooping-Cough in 1862, he states that during a recent visit he noticed in the most respectable Swedish journals a statement to the effect that Whooping-Cough can be cured by inhaling the air from the purifying apparatus in gas-works. One of these writers says, "This knowledge we have had from two or three mouths. I know a family where three children were cured by three visits to the purifying-house. Our most distinguished physician for the diseases of children, Professor Abelin, has found the remedy equally effective on a patient of his own family. I have seen a boy from three to four years of age be cured by six visits, the first three only lasting ten to fifteen minutes; the latter, on the contrary, thirty to forty-five minutes." Mr. H. M. L. Blackler, of London, confirms this statement, and adds that the practice of sending children to gas-works to inhale the gas from newly opened purifiers has been adopted in France for two years past; and he says, from information obtained at various works which he frequently visits, he infers that the cure for Whooping-Cough is perfect. "It often occurs that as many as a dozen children are brought to the gas-works at one time, and the managers have now come to regard this new custom as part of the daily routine of business."

Physicians in Hartford, Conn., have adopted with marked success this new method of treatment for curing children afflicted with Whooping-Cough. The juvenile patients are taken on a tour of inspection to the city gas-works, and while intently engaged in witnessing the various processes employed in manufacturing their evening's artificial illumination supply, they breathe the not very pleasant air of the gas-house. In some way, not very clearly understood, the inhaling of this air is found to cure or greatly alleviate the complaint. This ingenious method of benefiting the youthful mind and body simultaneously has become immensely popular in the place, the people at the gas-works asserting that during the last twelve months no less than three hundred cases have been experimented upon, the results, generally, being of a most favorable character.

To Prevent Squinting.—Sometimes there is a tendency in children to squint; it shows itself for a few moments, occasionally only, at first, and can scarcely be noticed. The habit, for in most cases it is a habit, although an unconscious one, is generally taken from having seen some cross-eyed person, and if not broken off will become permanent. Make two small paper tubes, about three-quarter inch diameter and two inches long. Make the inside of these tubes black, and apply them to the eyes in a similar way as a pair of spectacles. The only way then to see an object is to look straight, and both eyes will be directed to the light, and the tendency to look crossways removed.

Cholera Infantum is greatly prevalent in cities in hot weather; it is one of the most fatal diseases of children, occurring generally while teething.

Cool pure air is one of the best remedies. Let the room be large and dry, and in fine weather take the child into the open air; if the child is weaned, let its food be arrow-root, tapioca, and milk; keep the pores of the skin open by a tepid bath, or by sponging the body with warm water. Let the drink be Gum-water or some other mucilageous liquid: this, *if promptly attended to at the commencement of the disease,* will generally be sufficient. If the vomiting continue, mix 1 dram of Camphor in 1 ounce Sulphuric Ether, and give 10 drops every half hour. As soon as the vomiting stops, give Syrup of Rhubarb and Potassa, or put 2 drams of Powdered Catechu and ½ dram bruised Cinnamon in half pint of boiling water, cover it over and steep for an hour. Give a teaspoonful every three or four hours, according to age and severity of the case.

COLIC.—At times children suffer intensely from these pains; if it arises from costiveness, which may be known by the belly being hard and swollen, give an injection of warm soapsuds; if from wind on the stomach, give ½ teaspoonful of Peppermint Water, or a small portion of Bicarbonate of Soda in a little sweetened water.

Frequently a hot flannel applied to the belly (or warm the hand by the fire, and apply it with gentle friction to the stomach,) will give quick relief.

FITS arise from different causes, but generally indicate disturbance of the brain. Fits are the sign of disease rather than a disease in themselves, and of course the treatment should have reference to the cause. If a child, previously healthy, is suddenly taken with a fit, place it in a warm bath, and at the same time apply a sponge dipped in cold water to the head: this will draw the blood from the brain and soothe the system, and if scarlet fever or measles are the cause, it will bring them out.

MEASLES.—This is a contagious eruption, commonly affecting children, and the same individual but once.

The first *symptoms* of Measles are shivering, succeeded by heat, thirst, and languor; then follows running at the nose, sneezing, cough; the eyes water and become intolerant of light; the pulse quickens, the face swells; there are successive heats and chills, and all the usual signs of catarrhal fever. Sometimes the symptoms are so mild as to be scarcely noticeable, sometimes greatly aggravated; but in any case, at the end of the third day, or a little later, an eruption of a dusky red color appears, first on the forehead and face, and then gradually over the whole body. In the early stage of this eruption, there is little to characterize it; but after a few hours it assumes the peculiar appearance which, once seen, can never be mistaken; the little red spots become grouped, as it were, into crescent-shaped patches,

2

which are slightly elevated above the surface, the surrounding skin retaining its natural color. On the third day of the eruption it begins to fade and disappear, being succeeded by a scurfy disorganization of the cuticle, which is accompanied by an intolerable itching. The febrile symptoms also abate, and very quickly leave the patient altogether; but often in a very weak state, and with a troublesome cough. Between exposure to the infection and the breaking out of Measles, there is usually an interval of fourteen days, which is called the period of incubation; so that it is not uncommon, where there are several children in a family, for the cases to succeed each other at fortnightly intervals.

Treatment.—Generally speaking, for simple Measles, little medicine is required; give the patient plenty of diluent drinks; let him have a spare diet, and a moderately warm and well-ventilated room; keep the bowels gently open; if a roasted apple or a little Manna in the drink will not do this, give a mild saline aperient, something like this:—Ipecacuanha Wine and Sweet Spirits of Nitre, of each 1 dram; Tartrate of Potash 4 drams; Solution of Acetate of Ammonia, 1 ounce; Syrup of Poppies, 2 drams; Cinnamon or Dill Water sufficient to make 4 ounces: Dose, a table or dessert spoonful, three or four times a day; should this not be sufficiently powerful, substitute Sulphate of Magnesia for the Potash, and add 4 drams of Tincture of Senna. Where there is much heat of the skin, sponging with tepid vinegar and water will commonly relieve it, and also the itching. When the eruption has subsided, and the desquamation of the skin commenced, a tepid bath will materially assist this process, and get rid of the dead cuticle. On the third or fourth day after the subsidence of the eruption, a powder of Calomel, with Rhubarb, Jalap, or Scammony, according to the habit and strength of the patient, should be given; care should be taken to protect the patient against change of weather, and to restore the strength by a nourishing diet. Attention should be paid to the cough, and the proper remedies given if required.

Sometimes the eruption of Measles disappears suddenly, then there is cause for alarm; the patient should be directly put into a warm bath, and have warm diluent drinks; if the pulse sinks rapidly, and there is great prostration of strength, administer Wine Whey and the following draughts:— 10 drops of Aromatic Spirits of Ammonia, or 5 grains of the Sesqui-carbonate in ⅓ an ounce of Camphor Mixture, with a drop of Laudanum, every four hours; should the prostration be very great, weak Brandy and water may be given. The state of the chest, head, and bowels should be closely watched for some time after the patient is convalescent, as disorders of these organs are very likely to occur.

SCARLATINA is but another name for Scarlet Fever, although, popularly the former is considered a milder and less dangerous disease than the latter. It is scarcely possible to mistake this eruptive fever for any other; almost invariably we have first sore throat, with shivering, headache, and loss of appetite; probably there may be sickness and vomiting, with heat of skin, quick pulse, and great thirst. In about forty-eight hours from the commencement of the attack, we have an eruption of red spots on the arms and chest, these gradually become more thickly planted and widely spread, until they pervade the whole of the body, making the skin appear of one uniform scarlet tint, that is over the body generally; in the extremities it is more in patches, the skin being perceptibly rough to the touch. On the second day, generally, the tongue presents the appearance of being covered with a white film, through which the papulæ project as bright red spots, as we see the seeds on a white strawberry; then the white creamy looking film comes away grad-

ually, and leaves the tongue preter-naturally clean and red. On the fourth or fifth day the eruption begins to fade, and by the seventh or eighth has entirely disappeared, and with it the febrile symptoms. Then commences the desquamation of the cuticle, which comes away in scales from the face and body, and in large flakes from the extremities. It is during this process that the greatest danger of contagion is to be apprehended, and until it is completed, the patient should be kept apart from the rest of the family: it may be hastened by tepid bathing and rubbing. Sometimes, with scarlet fever, there is little real illness; the patient feels pretty well, and in a few days would like to leave the sick chamber; but it is always necessary to be cautious in gratifying such a wish, both for the sake of the invalid and of others; after an attack of this fever, as after measles, the system is peculiarly susceptible of morbific influences, and a chill taken at such a time may cause the most alarming results.

Sometimes we have a great aggravation of the symptoms above described; the throat gives the first warning of the attack; there is stiff neck, swelling of the glands, the lining of the mouth and fauces becomes at once of an intense crimson color; there are ash-colored spots about the tonsils; the general eruption is of a deeper color, and spreads more rapidly than in the simple kind. This form of the disease is professionally termed *Scarlatina anginosa.* Then again we have the malignant form, with the rash in irregular patches of a dusky hue, which sometimes recedes and appears again. There is intense inflammation of the throat at the very outset, with general enlargement of the salivary glands; the neck sometimes swells to a great size; there is a sloughy ulceration of the throat, from which, and the nostrils, through which it is difficult to breathe, there comes an acrid discharge, causing excoriation of the nose and lips, and sometimes extending to the larynx and trachea, as well as to the intestinal canal, causing croup, vomiting, and purging. The poisonous secretion enters into the circulation and vitiates the blood; sometimes the sense of hearing, as well as of smelling, is entirely destroyed by the acrid matter coming in contact with, and inflaming, the mucous membrane. With this form of the disease it is extremely difficult to deal, and the patient often sinks beneath it in spite of the best medical advice and assistance.

Treatment. — At first, mild aperients only should be given, with diluted drinks and a spare diet; the patient should have plenty of fresh air; the head should be kept cool by means of ice in a bladder, the hair being cut off or shaved. The following is a good febrifuge mixture : — Carbonate of Ammonia, 1 dram ; solution of Acetate of Ammonia, 2 ounces ; Water of Camphor Mixture, 6 ounces : a dessertspoonful to be taken every four hours, for a child, (a tablespoonful for an adult.)

If the throat swells much externally, and there are headaches, apply from 2 to 4 leeches ; should the weakness be great, a Blister or a hot Bran Poultice must suffice. To gargle the throat, dissolve 1 dram of common salt in ½ a pint of water ; with children who cannot gargle, this may be injected against the fauces, or up the nostrils, by means of a syringe or elastic gum bottle. When the inflammatory action has ceased, and the skin is peeling off, it is necessary to take good stimulant and nutritious food, with tonics, such as Iron and Quinine, unless they cause bad head symptoms, in which case they must be discontinued, and the diet chiefly depended on. With regard to the more malignant form, but little more is to be done ; the depressing effect of the contagious poison upon the whole body, and upon the nervous system especially, is so great as to defy all active treatment. If we can save such patients at all, it must be by the liberal administrations of Wine and Bark to sustain the flagging powers until the deadly

agency of the poison in some measure passes away. When the patient is not killed by the violence of the first contagion, the system is reinoculated with the poisonous secretions from the throat; Wine and Bark must be diligently and watchfully given, the throat injected or gargled (as above directed), and the most vigilant care observed for some time, should convalescence fortunately ensue.

A dropsical affection is one of the most frequent results of Scarlet Fever. This seldom occurs, if the warm bath is daily used as soon as the skin begins to peel off. After the dropsy has set in, give the warm bath twice a week, and encourage perspiration by the Compound Tincture of Virginia Snake-root, from 10 to 20 drops (according to the age of the child), in a little warm herb tea.

QUINSY.—This kind of inflammatory sore throat generally commences with cold chills, and other febrile symptoms ; there is fulness, heat, and dryness of the throat, with a hoarse voice, difficulty of swallowing, and shooting pains towards the ear. When examined, the throat is found of a florid red color, deeper over the tonsils, which are swollen and covered with mucus. As the disease progresses, the tonsils become more and more swollen, the swallowing becomes more painful and difficult, until liquids return through the nose, and the viscid saliva is discharged from the mouth ; very commonly the fever increases also, and there is acute pain of the back and limbs. Sometimes, when the inflammation has reached a certain height, it gradually subsides, and the tonsils diminish with it, although they commonly remain for a considerable time unnaturally large ; at others, there is a formation of abscess in one or both tonsils, and the patient suffers the greatest agony and distress, appearing often upon the point of suffocation ; and this continues to be the case until the abscess bursts, or is opened to allow the matter to escape.

Treatment. — When the case is not

severe, it may be treated, in the early stages, like *Catarrh ;* but when it is, more active measures will be required. An emetic, followed by a strong purgative; a blister outside the throat, and warm bran or linseed poultices; a cooling regimen with acid water, or pieces of rough ice put into the mouth and allowed to dissolve; leeches at the side of the throat if it swells much; inhaling the steam of hot water through an inhaler or an inverted funnel; and the continuation, every four hours or so, of a saline aperient; these will be the proper measures to adopt. When the abscess has burst, and the inflammatory symptoms have subsided, a generous diet will be necessary, with tonic medicines. If the tonsils continue swollen, they should be rubbed outside twice a day with stimulating liniments; Turpentine and Opodeldoc, equal quantities, will be as good as any; and the throat gargled with salt and water, a teaspoonful of the former put into a tumblerful of the latter. When there is chronic soreness of the throat, with hoarseness and cough, there is commonly also a relaxed and elongated uvula, which closes the passage when the patient lies down, and causes a sensation of choking. In this case a gargle made with Salt and Cayenne Pepper (about a tablespoonful of the former, and a teaspoonful of the latter, in a pint of boiling water) should be tried; the throat should be kept uncovered, and sponged with Vinegar twice a day. If these means are unsuccessful, it may be necessary to have part of the uvula cut off: this must be done by a surgeon, as must also the application of caustic, sometimes to be made when the throat has a granulated appearance.

DIPHTHERIA comes on, in many instances, very suddenly, like cholera, influenza, and erysipelas, without any warning symptoms; in others, there is soreness of the throat, like tonsillitis, or of the naris, like catarrh; or there is pain in the deglutition, like pharyngitis, or cynanche maligna; shiverings are very irregular.

The specific *cause* of the disease is atmospheric, as in cholera, influenza typhus, and potato rot. Debility, cesspools, malaria, and all nuisances predispose to it; and all irregularities of regimen, cold drink when heated, sudden changes of temperature, and overexertion, are exciting causes.

The principles of *treatment* are antiseptic and tonic, stimulant and nutritious. The capillary system should not be engorged with fluids, neither should anything evaporating be applied to the skin. Blisters inflame and ulcerate; leeches debilitate and their bites slough; and strong purgatives cannot be borne. Temperate, dry, and well-ventilated bed-rooms are a desideratum; a Calomel purgative, varying in strength with the age of the patient. In children, where there are symptoms of laryngitis, a rapid exhibition of the Chloride of Mercury, such as a grain or two every hour until the breathing is easier; then every three or four hours until the false membrane is loosened, and the bowels evacuate green stools, or vomiting commences. It has been found that children who are teething have the most inflammatory symptoms. Decoction of Bark, with Hydrochloric Acid, varying the dose of the latter from one minim to ten every four hours, in from a teaspoonful to two tablespoonfuls of the former. Gargle with Chloride of Sodium and Vinegar, a tablespoonful of each in a teacupful of hot water; also inject this up the nostrils when they become obstructed; this relieves the breathing, destroys the fetor, and allows the ulcers to heal.

Apply a stick of Nitrate of Silver to every part where the false membrane or exudation can be seen; when the disease spreads beyond the caustic case, a probang and a clean sponge saturated with a strong solution of Nitrate of Silver will answer.

Rub the external fauces with Compound Iodine Ointment night and morning, and, where erysipelas may appear, apply the Stick Caustic, and lay on a plaster of strong Mercurial Ointment.

Keep all about the patient sweet and clean, and give a nutritious diet—such as mutton, milk, rich gruels, and beef-tea; and a warm Negus-compound of Port Wine and Water, equal quantities, with Sugar and Lemon. All the drinks should be taken warm.

The following treatment is said to be very effectual in croup:—Take a common tobacco-pipe, place a live coal in the bowl, drop a little tar upon the coal, draw the smoke into the mouth, and discharge it through the nostrils.

Sore Throat.—This is commonly a symptom of inflammatory fever, and is often the result of a simple cold; some persons are peculiarly liable to it, and experience great difficulty of swallowing from relaxed *Uvula*. Sometimes in Sore Throat there is simply inflammation of the mucous membrane, and when this is the case it will, probably, pass away in a day or two, with a little careful nursing and aperient medicines. Should it extend into the air-passages, causing cough and catarrhal symptoms, it becomes a more serious business, and medical advice should at once be sought. In the meantime a Saltpetre gargle should be used, or Sal Prunella balls, one being put into the mouth occasionally and allowed to dissolve; hot bran poultices may also be placed about the throat, which, at a later stage, may be rubbed with a liniment of Oil and Hartshorn.

There is an erysipelatous form of Sore Throat which is highly dangerous, and requires very active treatment: a strong gargle of Lunar Caustic must be used in this case, or the inflamed part must be pencilled with the Caustic in the stick; if it extends to the larynx and air-passages, this frequently proves fatal. This is a distinct form of disease from Diphtheria, which has proved so fatal.

Small-Pox.—This, like Scarlet Fever and Measles, belongs to the class of eruptive fevers; it attacks persons of

all ages, but the young are most liable to it. At no particular season of the year is it more prevalent than at any other, nor does climate appear to be influential in averting or modifying its visitations. When it occurs naturally, the premonitory *symptoms* are those of other fevers of its class; there are usually cold chills, pains in the back and loins, loss of appetite, prostration of strength, nausea, and sometimes vomiting; with young children, there are sometimes convulsions. About forty-eight hours after these symptoms set in, an eruption of hard, red pimples begin to overspread the face and neck, gradually extending downward over the trunk and extremities. Each pimple is surrounded by the peculiar dull red margin termed areola, and has a central depression on the top, containing lymph; at this period the eruption is decidedly vesicular, but it becomes afterwards pustular; this change takes place on about the fifth day of its appearance, when the central depression disappears, suppuration takes place, and the vessels are filled with matter, which shortly after oozes out and dries into a scab. In about ten days this falls off, and leaves a pale purple stain like a blotch, which gradually fades, unless the disease has penetrated so deeply as to destroy the true skin, in which case a pit, or, as it is usually called, a "pock-mark," remains for life.

The primary fever of this disease lessens as soon as the eruption appears; but after this has left the face, and travelled downward, attacking successively the lower parts of the body, a secondary fever sets in, which is more severe than the first, and not unfrequently assumes a typhoid character.

Small-pox may be either *distinct*, sometimes called *discreet*, or *confluent*: in the former case, the pustules are perfectly distinct from each other; in the latter, they run into each other. This latter is the most dangerous form of the disease, the fever being more intense and rapid, and having no intermission; it goes on increasing from the first, and frequently, by its violence, in nine or ten days so exhausts the system, that coma, delirium, and death ensue, preceded by convulsions, hæmorrhages, bloody stools, dysentery, and all the train of symptoms which indicate that a virulent and fatal poison has entered into the circulation.

By all this it will be evident that Small-pox is not a disease to be trifled with. As soon as the premonitory fever comes on an emetic should be administered, and followed by a purgative of a tolerably active nature; then keep the patient on spare diet (certainly no meat), and give plenty of warm diluent drinks; keep the bowels moderately open by means of saline aperients; let the patient have plenty of fresh air, and sponge the skin with cool or tepid water, as may be most agreeable, to diminish the heat of the body. Sometimes there is not energy in the system to develop the pustules with sufficient rapidity; in this case, nourishment and stimulants should be given in the form of broths, wine, whey, etc.; warm or mustard foot-baths should also be resorted to, and to allay irritability, a 10 grain Dover's Powder may be administered at bedtime, or a ¼ of a grain of Morphine, in Camphor Mixture. A good nourishing diet will be required in the secondary stage of the fever, and if it assumes a typhoid character, the treatment should be the same as that of typhus fever. Frequently the face is much swelled, and the eyelids closed; in this case, rub the latter with Olive Oil, and bathe the whole with Poppy fomentation. If the throat is sore, use a gargle of Honey and Vinegar, 1 tablespoonful of the former, 2 of the latter, added to a ½ pint of Water or Sage Tea. If there is much headache, cut the hair close, apply mustard poultices to the feet, and a spirit lotion to the head· to reduce itching, apply to the eruptions a liniment composed of Lime water and Linseed Oil, equal quantities; to check diarrhœa, give

Chalk Mixture, with 5 drops of Laudanum in each dose; if perspirations are too copious when the eruptive fever has subsided, take acidulated drinks. Smearing the eruptions with Mercurial Ointment, or puncturing each pustule, and absorbing the pus with wool or cotton, has been recommended to prevent the deep pitting which is so great a disfigurement to the face.

There is no disease more certainly and decidedly contagious than this; after imbibing the poison, a period of twelve days generally elapses before the commencement of the fever, and during this time no inconvenience may be experienced. Besides breathing the effluvia arising from a person attacked, Small-pox may be communicated by inoculation with the matter of its pustules, and the resulting disease being of a milder character, this method was formerly much practised to guard persons from a spontaneous attack; since, however, the introduction of Vaccination by Dr. Jenner, this practice has been abandoned. This disease is frequently epidemic, and the statistics of its different visitations show that the mortality of those attacked who have not been vaccinated is 1 in 4, whilst of those who have, it is not 1 in 450: a strong argument this for *vaccination*.

To Prevent "Pitting" in Small-Pox.—The application consists of a solution of india-rubber in chloroform, which is painted over the face and neck when the eruption has become fully developed. When the chloroform has evaporated, which it very readily does, there is left a thin elastic film of india-rubber over the face. This the patient feels to be rather comfortable than otherwise, inasmuch as the disagreeable itchiness, so generally complained of, is almost entirely removed, and, what is more important, "pitting," once so common, and even now far from rare, is thoroughly prevented wherever the solution has been applied.

If the above remedy is not at hand, paint the face twice a day with glycerine, this will likewise prevent pitting

VACCINATION. — Whether vaccination is a protection in all cases, and through life, is a question of great importance. Probably the mild form of vaccina does not last through life. Most physicians advise to re-vaccinate once in about seven years.

ITCH. — All classes are liable to this disease, but it is most common among persons who neglect personal cleanliness. This little creature (*acarus scabrei*), in its natural size, is so minute as to be scarcely visible to the naked eye. The most prominent symptom of the disease is a constant and intolerable itching; it never comes on of itself, but is always the result of contact with an affected person. It first shows itself in an eruption of small vesicles filled with a clear watery fluid, occurring principally on the hand and wrist, and in those parts most exposed to friction, such as the spaces between the fingers, and the flexures of the joints, etc.; after a time it extends to the legs, arms, and trunk, but it rarely appears on the face. The insects are often found in the vesicles, but not always; hence some have doubted whether they are really the cause of the disease, although it is generally supposed that they are.

The Itch is never got rid of without medical treatment; but to that it will always yield, provided proper cleanliness be observed. Sulphur is the grand specific for it; it may be applied in the form of ointment, prepared as follows: Flowers of Sulphur, 2 ounces; Carbonate of Potash, 2 drams; Lard, 4 ounces: to be rubbed well in wherever the eruption appears, every night and morning; washing it off with soap and flannel, before each fresh application. The most effectual plan is to anoint the whole body, from the nape of the neck to the soles of the feet, and out to the ends of the fingers; put on socks, drawers, flannel wrapper, and gloves, and so remain in bed for thirty-six hours, repeating the anointing operation twice during that time; then take a warm bath, and wash the whole person with soap and flannel. In mild cases, a sulphureous vapor bath, taken twice in twenty-four hours, with soap and warm water washing, will generally be sufficient. In obstinate ones, it may be necessary to resort to alterative aperients, a spare diet, with ointment, warm baths, and a lotion, made as follows: Dissolve 4 ounces of Sulphate of Potash in a quart of water, and add ½ ounce of Sulphuric Acid; to be applied warm, with a sponge, before the fire. According to an announcement made to the French Academy of Medicine, by M. Bonnet, Benzine rubbed on the affected parts will cure Itch in five minutes; the patient has only to take a warm bath after it, and lo! he is clean. In France, also, an ointment composed of 2 scruples of Naphthaline to 1 ounce of Lard has been found an effectual remedy for this troublesome disease; but we hold that there is nothing like sulphur.

RINGWORM has its seat in the roots of the hair, and is believed to be attended by the growth of parasitic fungi; its predisposing causes are any derangement of the general health from ill or undue feeding, breathing impure air, drinking bad water, uncleanly habits, scrofula. Its immediate or exciting cause is generally contact with those affected with it, or using combs or hair-brushes which they have used.

Treatment. — Take a piece of white paper, fold it in the form of a funnel, light the wide end, and hold it so that the smoke coming out of the small end will come against a plate. This moist black applied to the Ringworm will cure it, or if this is not convenient, apply creosote with a camel's hair pencil.

Mr. Erasmus Wilson remarks, "that improper food is a frequent predisposing cause, and that he has observed it in children fed too exclusively on vegetable diet," recommends in the way of *treatment* that as soon as the irritation appears to be subdued by soothing means, such as warm poultices, etc., an ointment composed of 1 dram of Sulphate of Zinc to 1 ounce of Simple Cerate, using also a Sulphate of

Zinc lotion. The head, from which the hair has been previously removed, by shaving or close cutting, should be washed with soap once a day, and after being dried, anointed with Pomatum so as to keep the scalp moist with oleaginous matters. Dr. A. Thomson says "that the application which he has found most beneficial is a solution of 1 dram of Nitrate of Silver in ½ an ounce of Diluted Nitric Acid. The diseased circles, after the scalp has been shaved, to be pencilled over with the solution, and in ten or fifteen minutes afterwards the parts should be well sponged, first with tepid water, and then covered with pledgets of lint dipped in cold water, and the evaporation diminished by covering the wet linen with oiled silk." He also says, "that in India an ointment composed of a dram of Powdered Nut Galls, a scruple of Sulphate of Copper, and an ounce of Simple Cerate, is said to prove most beneficial."

Salt Rheum—Tetter—Shingles— popular names for diseases of the skin, which are a variety of *Herpes.*

The eruption, which consists of vesicles in distinct clusters, upon inflamed bases, that extend a little beyond the margin of each cluster, is generally preceded by such constitutional symptoms as loss of appetite, headache, cold chills, sickness, and accelerated pulse. Sometimes there is heat and pricking in the skin, and a sensation as though hot needles were thrust into it; or there may be a deep-seated pain in the chest. At times, however, the patient has no warning of this kind, and he is first made aware of the affection by the appearance of red patches, with small elevations, clustered together; these gradually enlarge, and become clear and glassy, being filled with a colorless lymph, which first turns milky and then concretes into scabs. As the crusts fall off, and the eruption disappears at one part, it frequently shows itself in the immediate vicinity, and so gradually creeps all over the skin; sometimes there is a free discharge and ulceration. In

some cases the clusters of eruption begin at the loins, and extend downward to the thighs and legs; very commonly they form a sort of band round the waist, and hence, probably, the name given to the disease. From the twelfth to the fourteenth day is the time at which the scabs, if a cluster, may be expected to fall off, leaving the skin beneath red and tender, with little indented rings, where the vesicles have been. Generally the disease runs its course in about three weeks; it is not contagious, and may attack the same person more than once. Young persons between twelve and twenty-five years of age appear to be most subject to this disease, which, however, sometimes attacks aged people. Summer and autumn are the seasons when it most prevails; the cause of it is not very clear; probably it may arise from sudden changes of temperature, and chills when in a heated state. For

Treatment — We should recommend aperients to keep the body gently open, with a light and nutritious diet; effervescing draughts, made with Bicarbonate of Potash instead of Soda; if, as is sometimes the case, there is much pain, take Dover's Powder at bedtime, from 5 to 10 grains, according to age; bathe the eruptions with Goulard Water, and dress them, when discharging, with Zinc Ointment, spread upon lint; or a compound infusion of Gentian, 4 ounces, and Iodide of Potassium, ½ ounce, mixed, one teaspoonful taken after each meal, and 2 scruples of Naphthaline and 1 ounce of Lard spread on linen, and applied to the diseased skin twice a day, will do excellent service. Old persons generally require tonics to improve the general health.

ERYSIPELAS. — We will first say a few words as to the cause of this inflammatory affection of the skin, which often commences very suddenly, and spreads with a rapidity truly alarming, especially when, as is often the case, it first makes its appearance on the head, face, or neck, and so involves some of the most delicate and susceptible organs of the human frame. Vicissitudes of cold and heat causing peculiar conditions of the atmosphere, may be named among the most common *causes* of this disease, which frequently appears to originate in the slightest puncture or scratch of the skin, as also from wounds or sores; it is very contagious, and its appearance in a hospital ward is greatly dreaded, as wounds and amputated parts which, up to the time of this visitation, have been going on extremely well, frequently assume an inflamed, probably a gangrenous character, which leads to a fatal termination of the case. In a house where a confinement is taking, or is likely to take place, Erysipelas should be carefully guarded against, as there is undoubtedly a close connection between that and child-bed fever, which is so frequently fatal. On systems debilitated by any disease, whether acute or chronic, this inflammatory affection appears to seize with peculiar avidity, and to spread through the tissues of the skin most rapidly; it is when extending beneath this that it constitutes what professional men term *phlegmon*, meaning literally to burn — then it is that purulent matter forms, the parts slough, or mortify, and gangrene ensues. No unprofessional person should attempt to tamper with this condition of things; there must be a free use of the lancet to let out the morbid matter, and the most prompt and decisive line of action adopted; if a limb is so affected, or any part that can be excised, its removal will probably be necessary to give the patient a chance for life.

Among the predisposing causes of Erysipelas may be also mentioned want of cleanliness, insufficiency or bad quality of the food, and irregularity of living; there may be hereditary and constitutional predisposition, and where this exists, the inflammation is very easily excited, strong mental emotion, or a fit of inebriety, being sometimes sufficient to bring on an attack; it often co-exists with or immediately follows some fevers, in which it may be presumed that purulent

matter enters into the venous circulation.

The *symptoms* of an attack are usually of a febrile character, such as shivering, headache, furred tongue, accelerated pulse, and often derangement of the stomach for a day or two previously; then there is a tingling and burning sensation, with stiffness and pain at some particular part, followed by a discoloration of the skin, and a slight elevation of the surface; the red or purplish tint is confined at first to one spot, but soon extends itself, and includes the limb or part affected; frequently this is the head, which, with the face, becomes so swollen and disfigured that the patient cannot be recognized; the eyelids puff out and entirely close the eyes, and each avenue to the senses is for a time closed. In very bad cases delirium and coma come on, and death ensues from effusion on the brain; sometimes the patient dies from suffocation, the glottis being closed, on account of the internal swelling of the throat; and all this may take place in a few hours, so rapid is the progress of the disease. In the milder forms, the patient may be tranquil; until the swelling subsides, there will be a little wandering of the mind probably, more particularly at night, and uneasy restlessness from the pain and inconvenience of the swelling. As the redness extends from the part first affected, that part becomes paler, the swelling there subsides, and sometimes vesicles, like those caused by a scald, appear on the surface; if the inflammation is merely superficial, it is neither very troublesome nor dangerous; but when it becomes *phlegmonous* — that is, dips down and affects the deeply-seated tissues — there is great cause for alarm; when this is the case, the color is generally very florid, the tingling and the burning sensation severe, and the surface hard and firm to the touch. The young and sanguine are most likely to be affected in this way; those of a feebler habit more commonly suffer from the *edematous* form of the disease; in this, the parts affected are of a paler red, and softer and inelastic, so that they pit on pressure.

Treatment. — Rest, mild diet, and gentle laxatives, such as Salts and Senna, or Rhubarb and Magnesia, to subdue the fever; then, in mild cases, apply to the inflamed skin Powdered Starch, Magnesia, or Arrowroot; in more severe cases, wash the surface with soap and water, and well dry it, then apply Caustic. To do this, moisten the skin with clear water, and apply Nitrate of Silver, being careful to go an inch beyond the inflamed part on every side, to stop the spread of the inflammation. After this, a lotion of Lunar Caustic, made by mixing 1 scruple of Nitrate of Silver in 1 ounce of water, may be applied with a camel's hair brush over the whole inflamed surface.

The powers of the system are generally reduced. Tonics, such as Iron, Quinine, or Wine are required.

Grubs or Worms on the face, generally called *Acne* or *Spotted Acne.* The tumors which arise from this disease occur chiefly in the face; they contain a thick, cheesy matter, which it is difficult to get rid of, on account of its consistency, and the small opening afforded for its egress.

Acne has four distinct forms of development:—1st. Simple Pimple, which is its mildest form, and is almost confined to persons between the ages of fifteen and thirty, at which period of life it is very prevalent. It may be considered as a form of inflammation set up by nature to rid the system of the superfluous matter accumulated in the follicles;—first appear red spots on the skin, accompanied by itching and irritation; these gradually swell into unsightly pustules, which in a short time discharge their contents; the inflammation then subsides, and the skin resumes its usual appearance. If proper attention is not paid to these pimples, and dirt is suffered to get into them, the disease assumes its second form, Spotted or Maggot Pimples, on account of the little black specks, like the heads of maggots, which present themselves.

When several of the follicles become inflamed together, and a hardening of their bases ensues, we have, thirdly, Stone Pock, as it is commonly called; and if the pimples become very red, or coppery, then it is called, fourthly, Rosy-drop, Carbuncle-face, Brandy-face, Copper-nose.

Treatment. — The great object is to obtain a free discharge of the offending matter, and to remove the cause by exciting the tissues of the skin to a healthy action; hence frequent washing is desirable, and friction applied gently, so as not to break the pustules, and cause them to run one into another, producing wounds difficult to heal. A sponge and warm water, in which has been dissolved a small quantity of Bicarbonate of Soda, and afterwards a soft thick towel, are the best cleansing adjuncts; and for a lotion to cool the inflamed parts and allay irritation, take Goulard's Extract, or Liquor of Acetate of Lead, 1 dram, added to 8 ounces of Elder-flower, or Rose-water; or else, to the same quantity of the latter, add Glycerine, $\frac{1}{2}$ an ounce; Chloride of Zinc, 12 grains. Dip a piece of lint into either of these lotions, and moisten the pustules therewith frequently. When the disease is obstinate, and especially if it assumes this red appearance, it is well to apply Collodion with a camel-hair brush to the eruptions occasionally, and to use a stronger form of the last of the above lotions, with a dressing at night of stimulating ointment, composed of Ointment of Zinc, and of Nitrate of Mercury, in the proportion of 1 dram of the former to 1 ounce of the latter, with 4 drops of Creosote added. Care should be taken to keep up a proper action of the liver and kidneys, that the skin may have only its own work to do in removing the impurities of the blood. The system should be strengthened by tonics, and a generous but not over full diet; it is best to avoid fermented liquors. The following is a good mixture: — Spirit of Nitric Ether, 2 drams; Liquor of Potash and Ipecacuanha Wine, of each 1 dram; Syrup of Rhubarb, ½ an ounce; Infusion of Gentian, 7 ounces: take two tablespoonfuls two or three times a day, and one of the following pills every second or third night: — Compound Rhubarb Pill, 2 scruples; Mercurial or Blue Pill, 12 grains; make into 12 pills.

Bilious, or Sick Headache, is, perhaps, the most common of any; it generally begins in the morning, and is often relieved by a strong cup of tea or coffee. It is caused by a defective action of the digestive organs. The pain usually commences on one side of the head just over one of the eyes; if it continues long it is diffused over the whole head, accompanied by a sickness at the stomach, and sometimes vomiting, and extreme languor and depression of spirits: singing in the ears, dimness of sight, confusion, and great restlessness, are often its attendants. Evacuating the bowels, either with or without medicine, relieves the most urgent symptoms, but it is generally desirable to take some active aperient. On going to bed at night, take a 5-grain Blue Pill, and in the morning, a Seidlitz Powder. Generally there will be no Headache the next day, but it will probably return as severe as ever in a few weeks, its recurrence in some cases being at almost regular periods. It can generally be traced to some error in diet, such as taking food that is indigestible, or in too large quantities, or stimulating drinks, with insufficient exercise. Very often it arises from some derangement of the biliary secretions, either as to quantity or quality, or defective assimilation, sometimes from the habitual abuse of purgatives, which enfeebles the tone of the alimentary canal. "Under these latter circumstances it is," as Dr. Elliott observes, "a most intractable complaint." Very commonly a simple dose of Rhubarb and Magnesia, with about 30 drops of Sal Volatile, will remove a common Sick Headache; but when there is nausea, and vomiting or purging does not come sponta-

neously to remove it, the former should be excited by an emetic, composed of 1 grain of Tartarized Antimony and 20 of Ipecacuanha, and after this has acted, a Rhubarb and Blue Pill. Persons subject to this kind of Headache should carefully abstain from fat meats, pastry, butter, and rich food generally.

That which we have just been describing is one of the forms of *Sympathetic Headache,* sympathy with a disordered stomach being the immediate cause; sometimes an excess of alkali, at others of acid in the alimentary canal, will produce this: in the former case, a vegetable acid, such as Vinegar, will afford relief; in the latter case, in which there is likely to be heart-burn and acid eructations, a dose of Sal Volatile, or of Carbonate of Soda, or Potash, will be the best remedy. In all these cases, it seems likely that the blood circulating in the brain is both mechanically and chemically affected by the defective action of the assimilative and secretive organs of the stomach. We sometimes find that the postponement of the customary evacuation of the bowels, for ever so short a time, will cause a Sympathetic Headache, and that this will be relieved directly the evacuation has taken place — a clear proof of the intimate connection there is between the head and the stomach.

Congestive Headache. — So called because it proceeds from a congested state of the vessels of the brain; arising either from an over-fulness of blood, or a weakness of the organ, or from an excessive nervous irritability, which frequently upsets the balance of the circulation. Whichever of these may be the case, there is nearly always a dull pain over the whole of the head, which is worst at the fore and hind parts. When it arises from an over-loaded condition of the vessels, there is usually a bloated countenance, with full red eyes, and a dull inanimate expression; here we find, on inquiry, a sluggish liver, and inflammation of the brain, tending to apoplexy or paralysis.

Leeches to the temples, or cupping on the back of the neck; cold applications to the head, with spare diet, mercurials, and active aperients, will be the proper treatment.

A weak brain is generally a consequence of some long standing discharge which has debilitated the whole system, and in this condition of things, if from any cause there is a more than common flow of blood to the brain, there will be Headache, with a pale, sallow countenance, and a languid pulse; frequently swelled feet, excessive fatigue on the slightest exertion, with palpitation of the heart, and increase of pain in the head. Here measures of depletion would be improper; we must soothe and sustain by means of sedatives and tonics, such as Conium and Quinine, either in the form of pills or mixture, as follows :— Take of Extract of Conium, 24 grains, Sulphate of Quinine, 12 grains, make into 12 pills and give 1 three times a day, or Sulphate of Quinine, 12 grains, Sulphuric Acid, diluted, 12 minims, Tincture of Conium, 2 drams, Infusion of Gentian, 6 ounces; take a tablespoonful three times a day. Good nourishing food will be required in this case, and stimulants, such as Ale and Wine, in moderation. Where the Headache proceeds from nervous irritability, the mode of treatment must also be soothing and strengthening; but in this case we must avoid stimulants as much as possible; tonics are best here, with plenty of fresh air and exercise, and all that tends to invigorate the frame.

Rheumatic Headache is commonly caused by exposure to cold, especially a draught of air; the pain is chiefly confined to the back and front of the head, and is felt most at night when the patient is warm in bed; it is a remittent shifting pain, shooting from point to point, following the downward course of the jaw, whose muscles are commonly implicated.

Take a light diet, wear warm clothing, avoid exposure, wet feet, or dampness. When the local pain is great, apply hot fomentations, or a mustard poultice, to the back of the neck.

Periodic Headache, Brow-ache, Brow-ague, or Neuralgia of the Head, as it is variously called, is an intermitting pain, which comes on at periods more or less regular, and is confined to the brow. It will nearly always yield to full doses of Quinine, especially if combined with Conium.

Organic Headache, resulting from actual disease of the head itself, is rare, and when it does occur, only a palliative mode of treatment can be adopted. Sedatives, such as Opium and Conium, may, for a time, relieve the almost intolerable anguish, but they will not touch the disease itself.

We have now adverted to the *Bilious* or *Sick Headache*, sometimes called the *Sympathetic* or *Dyspeptic;* also to the *Congestive*, the *Rheumatic*, the *Periodic*, and the *Organic Headaches*, these being the principal classes into which *Cephalalgia*, as it is sometimes called, can be divided. Let us in conclusion enumerate the distinct and specific *causes* to which pain in the head may be assigned: Rheumatic Inflammation of the Pericranium, or of the Mucous Membrane of the Frontal Sinus; Mental excitement; Strong or long continued impressions upon the senses of Hearing, Sight, or Smell; Excessive Impetus of Blood to the Head; Impeded return of the same; Congestion or Inflammation of the Brain; Suppression of Bile, Perspiration, Urine, etc.; Organic Disease of the Head; Sympathy with the Stomach, and Constipation; Frequent use of Narcotics or Stimulants; Intestinal Worms; Changes in the Atmosphere, and Neuralgia.

Delirium Tremens is generally the result of excessive and continued indulgence in intoxicating drinks; it consists of an exhausted condition of the nervous system, and is accompanied with more or less of mental disorder. The taking of opium for a considerable period will also sometimes produce this state of nervous exhaustion, which is called Brain Fever; the French term it *Delirium et mania è potu.* There is a similar disease, called *D. Tramalicum,* which sometimes occurs after serious accidents and operations. The symptoms of Delirium Tremens are great restlessness and irritation by day, and by night want of sleep, or uneasy slumbers, haunted by frightful dreams, causing the patient often to scream out in terror; the mind is haunted by suspicions of those around, and although generally more collected than in other forms of Delirium, appears at times to be possessed of demons, which torment the patient with wild visions of seas of flame advancing to overwhelm him, and belts and rings of fire encircling him, and threatening destruction; legions of mocking spirits, too, come around him; he is tormented with unquenchable thirst, and the stings of a guilty conscience goad the poor inebriate almost to madness; he shrieks and raves, prays and curses all in the one breath; and when he sinks exhausted, finds no solace in sleep, which refuses to visit his hot and aching eyes, and agonized and trembling frame. As the disease advances, the mind becomes more and more disordered, the temporary Delirium probably passes into actual insanity; then ensue convulsions, probably epilepsy or apoplexy, leading to a death-like stupor, which is but the prelude to death itself.

What can be done in such a case? The *treatment* must, of course, be of a soothing character: Opium, in full doses, either in the form of Morphine or Battley's Solution, should be administered; if, as is sometimes the case, the stomach is too irritable to retain liquid medicine, give the Gum Opium, in a pill, a grain and a half as a first dose, to be followed by half-grain doses every hour or so; a drop of Creosote on a lump of sugar, may also be given, to stay the sickness, or an effervescing draught with a drop of Hydrocyanic Acid in it. As the liver is generally more or less affected in this disease, a little Calomel should be got down, about three grains placed on the tongue, if pills cannot be taken; if they can, make six with the above quantity of Calomel and half a dram of compound Colocynth pill; take two first, and one every two hours after, until they operate. Some recommend combining the Opium with these; if this is done, it is best to add a grain and a half of Morphine to the above formula.

If these efforts are successful, and the nervous excitement is subdued, there will be great prostration of strength; the great object will then be to restore the tone of the stomach, and to enable the patient to overcome that craving for alcoholic stimulants, which is sure to send him back into the paths of intemperance if it is indulged; a Bitter Infusion of Camomile is perhaps the best, but Carbonate of Soda, or Potash, in six or eight grain doses, should be given, with a small portion of alcohol, it may be Brandy mixed with yolk of an egg, beaten up raw, er with arrowroot, some bitter ale, and good nourishing food.

A Drunkard's Cure. —Some months ago, a gentleman advertised that he had discovered a sure specific for the cure of drunkenness. He would not divulge the secret of what compounds he used, but furnished the medicine at so much per bottle. He did not have so many applicants for cure as he expected, considering the extent of the disease. In fact, the more malignant cases did not seem anxious for relief. They rather appeared to enjoy their malady. A few, however, placed themselves under treatment, and some were cured — whether by taking the medicine or by not taking strong drinks, we are not prepared to say. One of the cured ones had faith in the medicine, rigidly carried out the directions of the doctor, and now has not the least taste for intoxicating drinks; whereas, one year ago, he was an inebriate, and could not get along with less than from a pint to a quart of whiskey per day.

He said that he had, at some trouble and expense, procured the recipe for the preparation of the medicine, which he had published for the benefit of suffering humanity. It is as follows: Sulphate of Iron, 5 grains; Peppermint-water, 11 drams; Spirit of Nutmeg, 1 dram, mix in a pint of water. This preparation acts as a tonic and a stimulant, and so partially supplies the place of the accustomed liquor, and prevents that absolute physical and moral prostration that follows a sudden breaking off from the use of stimulating drinks. It is to be taken in quantities equal to an ordinary dram, and as often as the desire for a dram returns.

APOPLEXY.—This is deprivation of life or motion by a sudden stroke, or blow; it is one of the most awful and appalling modes of sudden death; in an instant a healthful and vigorous man is smitten down—one who has exhibited no signs of disease—who has perhaps received no premonitory warning, lies before us motionless and stark.

Apoplexy may be either *cerebral*, proceeding from congestion or rupture of the brain, or *pulmonary*, proceeding from hæmorrhage into the parenchyma of the *lungs*. The first is its more common form.

The *causes* of Apoplexy are either predisposing or exciting; among the first may be named—1st, *Sex*: men are more liable to it than women, because they are more subject to its exciting causes.—2d, *Age*: it is very rare in childhood, rare also in youth, most common between the ages of forty and seventy, rare much beyond the latter age. — 3d, *Bodily conformation*: the man of sanguine and plethoric temperament, with large head, short neck, and full chest, is most liable to its attack, although one of the opposite state and condition of system is sometimes smitten down by it.—4th, *Mode of Life*: persons of sedentary habits, who live luxuriously, are its frequent victims. — 5th, *Sup-*

pression of Evacuations or Eruptions, as the piles, perspiration, healing of a seton, or a wound. — 6th, *Mental Anxiety*: such as a long continuance of harassing fears, business perplexities, grief, or any violent emotion, or passions. All these are predisposing causes of Apoplexy, to which it has been said that the studious are more liable than others; but this is an error, as the history of lawyers, judges, and philosophers, ancient and modern, is sufficient to show. Persons of advanced age, who take rich and stimulating diet in more than sufficient quantity, and whose intellectual faculties are exercised but little, are those most frequently carried off by this embodiment of the Greek idea of the "skeleton at a feast." The most powerful *exciting causes* of Apoplexy, then, are intemperance, whether in eating or drinking, as well as violent exertions of the mind and body; whatever, in short, tends to determine the blood with an undue impetus to the brain, or impedes its return from it, is an invitation to this dreadful destroyer to step in and arrest the vital current in its flow, as the breath of frost stays the water of the river.

Treatment. — This, of course, must vary considerably, in accordance with the pathological condition of the brain of the person attacked, and with other circumstances which only those accustomed to the treatment of disease can judge of. The *immediate* measures to be adopted when a fit of Apoplexy comes on, which may be known by the patient falling down in a state of insensibility or stupor, out of which it is impossible to rouse him by any of the ordinary means; the face is generally flushed, the breathing difficult and stertorous, the upper lip-margin is projected at each expiration, the veins of the head and temples protrude as though overfilled, the skin is covered with perspiration, and the eyes are fixed and bloodshot: sometimes, however, the face is pale, with a look of misery and dejection, and the pulse, instead of being full and hard, is weak and intermitting; in the former case, as soon as the patient has been placed in a sitting position, with the legs depending, everything about his neck removed, and the air freely admitted, a vein should be opened in the neck, or arm, and the blood allowed to flow until the pulse is greatly reduced; a pallor in the face, and a generally relaxed state of the muscle, shows that fainting is about to ensue: In the latter case it is always necessary to relieve the neck from all pressure, to place the body upright and admit air — but beyond this the treatment must be different; cold water should be dashed in the face, strong spirits of Ammonia applied to the nostrils, and the feet placed in a warm bath, with a little mustard, and every means taken to arouse the patient from his state of lethargy. As soon as this is so far effected that he can swallow, give ½ dram of Aromatic Spirits of Ammonia in 1½ ounces of Camphor Mixture, as a stimulant draught; but it is only when the pulse is feeble and fluttering that the stimulant may be administered; this is the exceptional case of Apoplexy. Most commonly the symptoms are those first described, and if relieved at all it must be by free bleeding, and other measures of depletion. Purgatives must be got down soon as possible; 10 grains of Calomel placed on the tongue, and washed down with a black draught, or 2 or 3 drops of Croton Oil may be rubbed on the back of the tongue, and a lavement composed of 2 tablespoonfuls of common salt, with a little oil or butter, and a pint of warm water; or a tablespoonful of soft soap mixed with the same quantity of warm water; or an ounce of Spirits of Turpentine rubbed down with the yolk of an egg, and a pint of thin gruel; one of these should be repeated every two hours until the same decided effect is produced. Other means of relieving the system may be taken should these fail, such as blisters behind the ears to the nape of the neck, or calves of the legs: should the head be very hot, let it be shaved, and a cold lotion be ap-

plied to it—Water and Vinegar, or Acid Water, will do best. Should the attack be soon after a full meal, administer an emetic, a scruple of Sulphate of Zinc, with a grain or two of Tartar Emetic; something like this should always be given when Apoplexy arises from the effects of opium or spirits. Cupping on the temples, or opening the temporal artery, is sometimes resorted to in obstinate cases, and in Pulmonary Apoplexy; after the most violent symptoms are relieved by copious bleeding, nauseating doses of Tartar Emetic, frequently repeated, or Digitalis, to reduce the action of the heart, have been found useful. In all cases, after the crisis of the disease is over, and when the patient has become convalescent, it behooves him to be very careful, as a slight indiscretion may bring on a fresh attack.

We have said that Apoplexy comes without warning, but this is not strictly true. However sudden the attack itself may be there are certain premonitory symptoms which no prudent man will disregard: among these may be named, a sense of fulness in the veins of the head, and a feeling of pressure in the head itself, with occasional darting pains, giddiness, vertigo, partial loss of memory, and the powers of vision and of speech; numbness of the extremities, drowsiness, and a dread of falling down; irregularity in the action of the bowels, and involuntary passage of urine. These all indicate that some internal mischief is going on, and if their warning is attended to the threatened attack may, perhaps, be avoided. Persons, whose full habits of body and modes of life predispose them to this disease, should, when such warnings reach them, live sparingly, avoid stimulants, especially fermented and spirituous liquors, take regular and moderate exercise, sleep on a firm pillow with the head elevated, and nothing round the neck to impede the act of breathing. Keep the bowels regulated by an occasional dose of Colocynth and Calomel Pills, and saline purgatives. Those of a spare habit should take light, although nourishing, diet, a little beer or wine, if they have been accustomed to it, and it does not affect the head; spirituous liquors and hot spices should be avoided, and great bodily fatigue or nervous excitement of any kind.

PARALYSIS.—The total loss or diminution of motion, or sensation, or both, in any part; it is termed and often called *Palsy*. There are several kinds of palsy or paralysis, such as the *Paralysis agitans;* the Shaking, or as it is sometimes called, from the peculiarity of the patient's gait, the Dancing Palsy; *Hemiphlegia*, when one side of the body only is smitten; and *Paraphlegia*, when it is the lower half which is more or less deprived of its nervous power; but in all cases it is the brain which is the seat of disorder; and if this is confined to one of its hemispheres, the attack, if it does not include both sides, is most likely to fall on the opposite side of the body. The rupture of a vessel in the brain is one of the most common causes of Paralysis, and this may occur without there being any decided apoplectic symptoms; a slight transient faintness and confusion of ideas may precede the attack, or it may come on during sleep, so that the patient may only be made aware that he is paralyzed by his inability to speak plainly, or to move a limb or one side of his body. Sometimes the attack is gradual, and occupies a considerable time — days, weeks, and even months elapse before the loss of nervous energy becomes complete; and this helplessness may be produced by a succession of slight shocks, as it were, or by the gradual stealing on of an apparently torpid condition; this latter is more commonly the case when the disease arises from a decided state of general debility, which in time involves the brain, until the structure gives way, and softening is the consequence. Literary men, and all who have much head work, are especially liable to that condition of the brain which

causes Paralysis, and so are hard drinkers, and others whose lives or habits necessitate a frequent state of cerebral excitement; with such the progress of the disease is probably rapid; if of full habit, they will, it is likely, die quickly of apoplexy; if of spare, they will sink into a state of mental and bodily imbecility; in either case they may be subject to epileptic fits.

It is all nonsense to talk of a cure of Paralysis. Palliatives may be tried, and, in some cases, with a certain measure of success. There may be a partial restoration of power to the helpless leg or arm; the speech may become less thick, and the face less perceptibly drawn on one side; but we never yet saw a case of complete recovery, nor one in which there was not, sooner or later, a renewal of the attack. True, some paralyzed persons live to a good old age, and are enabled to enjoy themselves and perform the duties allotted to them; but seldom, if ever, do they become like unto their former selves; there is a little dragging of the foot in walking, the hand cannot grasp so tightly, nor the arm be lifted so quickly and readily in obedience to the will as formerly; there will, also, probably be a little hesitancy or thickness of speech, and the two sides of the face will not quite correspond.

In the above observations we have already hinted at some of the *causes* of this seizure, one of the chief being pressure upon or disease of the brain or spinal cord. When confined to the lower part of the body, there may be reason to believe that the defect of power is in some cases but functional; in this case the cause may be long exposure of the lower limbs to wet and cold, self abuse, excessive indulgence in venery, inflammation of the bowels or kidneys, effusion in the spinal cord from a blow or burn or other injury; disease of the womb or of the urethra may also give rise to it. Palsy of either of the limbs may be caused by pressure, and general Palsy by the action of lead or mercury upon the system; therefore those who work in these metals are peculiarly liable to be so affected, such as button-gilders, glass silverers, plumbers, etc.

The most dangerous form of this kind is when it affects the muscles of respiration, in which case it rapidly proves fatal. Among the premonitory *symptoms* of Paralysis may be named headache, confusion of ideas, loss of memory, impaired vision, drowsiness and partial stupor, with, frequently, numbness and pricking or tingling sensation in the limb or part about to be attacked. With persons of a full habit, there will be heat and flushings in the face, and most of the signs of an approaching fit of apoplexy; then follows indistinct articulation, loss of power, and the other marked and unmistakable indications of an actual attack.

The proper *treatment*, in the case of a patient of a full habit, will be bleeding and cupping in the neck and strong purgatives, about 5 grains of Calomel, followed by Senna Mixture, or Croton Oil Pills, every four hours, until they operate freely; when there is faintness and confusion of intellect, give a teaspoonful of Sal Volatile in a glass of water, and repeat it in an hour if required; no alcoholic stimulant must be administered; put the feet and legs in a hot mustard bath, and place the patient in a warm bed, with the head and shoulders well raised. Follow up the cupping in the neck with a blister, and after that put in a seton if required; after they have once acted well, keep the bowels gently open with Rhubarb or Castor Oil; let the diet be spare, and the quietude of the patient as perfect as possible. After the acute stage of the disease has passed, local stimulants should be used, and the affected parts well rubbed with the hand, or a flesh-brush. Electricity and Galvanism may also be employed, where there is no reason to suspect structural disorganization. In paraphlegia it is often very difficult to get the bladder to act· and, when it

does, the urine flows from it involuntarily; great attention should be paid to this, and stimulant diuretics given; the Tincture of Cantharides in ½ dram doses is, perhaps, the best that can be used.

In some cases, much relief has been afforded by the use of Sulphur Baths and Chalybeate Waters. Mercury, which is strongly recommended by some, is but a doubtful remedy. Strychnia has proved serviceable, but should only be given under medical superintendence. Repeated moxæ along the course of the spine, and small blister on the insides of the legs and thighs are recommended by Dr. Graves.

In Palsy of the face, if it is caused by a blow, a few leeches behind the ear, and at the angle of the jaw, may prove beneficial; if cold is the cause, hot fomentations and stimulating liniments should be applied; as also in Palsy of the hands, fingers, or other extremities, with Electro-Magnetism, persevered in for a considerable time. In all cases of Chronic Paralysis, it should be borne in mind that the nervous system requires arousing and stimulating to a due performance of the functions necessary to life; in nearly all there is a sluggish action of the bowels, which are often obstinately constipated, and require the strongest purgatives to keep them at all open; it is sometimes better to employ enemas, than continue giving drastic medicines. The paralytic patient frequently enjoys pretty good general health, and eats largely, and this increases the above difficulty, especially if it be a heavy person, with little power of self-movement. When confined entirely to bed, sores and sloughing ulcers are not uncommon — (an air or water bed greatly obviates the danger of them.)

SUNSTROKE is an affection of the Brain, caused by the rays of the sun striking upon the head. It frequently begins with headache and dizziness, and the patient falls senseless. — Take the patient into the shade, apply cold water to the head, and proceed as directed for Apoplexy.

HYDROPHOBIA.—This is the well known canine or dog madness, whose chief symptoms are spasmodic contractions of the larynx, preventing the patient, although thirsty, from swallowing any kind of liquid; one of the most dreadful and fatal visitations that can affect humanity. It has been known to medical writers from the days of Hippocrates downwards, and described under a great variety of names, all having reference to the difficulty of swallowing, or to the horrible fear which possesses the patient, as expressed in the old names *aero-phobia* and *panto-phobia*, dread of air, and dread of all things. It is generally distinguished as *Rabiosa*, with madness, and *sine rabie*, without madness. From Dr. Watson's "Lectures" we copy the following description of this fearful malady, which in man is produced by inoculation with the saliva of an animal, generally a dog, infected with it. When a person has been bitten by a rabid animal, the wound, if treated in the ordinary manner, will generally heal readily enough; but "after an uncertain interval, which lies for the most part between six weeks and eighteen months, the following *symptoms* begin to be noticeable. The patient experiences pain, or some uneasy or unnatural sensation in the situation of the bite. If it becomes healed up, the scar tingles or aches, or feels cold or stiff, or numb; sometimes it becomes visibly red, swollen, or livid. The pain or uneasiness extends from the sore or scars toward the central parts of the body. Very soon after this renewal of local irritation,—within a few hours, perhaps, but certainly within a very few days, during which the patient feels ill and uncomfortable,—the specific constitutional symptoms begin; he is hurried and irritable; speaks of pain and stiffness, perhaps about his neck and throat; unexpectedly he finds himself unable to swallow fluids, and every attempt to do so

brings on a paroxysm of choking and sobbing, of a very distressful kind to behold; and this continues for two or three days, till the patient dies exhausted."

Does it follow, then, that all persons bitten by a rabid dog or other animal, must die? is there no hope for them? assuredly we would not promulgate such a doctrine as this. In the first place, a very small proportion of those who are so bitten have the disease at all; and this partial immunity has sufficed to establish a false reputation for many of the nostrums vaunted as infallible remedies. If the bitten person becomes not mad, the nostrum has saved him; if he dies raving, it has not been rightly administered, and so the faith of believers remains unshaken, and quackery is triumphant. It has been calculated that the proportion of persons bitten who suffer from the disease is about one in twenty-five.

Treatment. — As no positive cure has been discovered for this terrible disease, all efforts must be merely preventive; directly the bite has taken place, a free excision of the wound should be made, taking care that every particle of flesh that the saliva has touched be removed; then thoroughly wash the wound with tepid water, keeping up this application for a considerable time: some recommend stimulating dressings to the part, but the advisability of this is very questionable; better to let the wound heal than to keep the system in a state of irritation. If there is any doubt about the poison being all removed, a strong solution of Lunar Caustic should be applied, or the Caustic itself; this is as likely to be as effective as the actual cautery, which some recommend. Mr. Youatt says he never saw the Lunar Caustic fail, and it may be used at any time before the disease manifests itself, although the longer it is delayed the less chance there is of success.

St. Vitus's Dance. — This distressing malady is characterized by grotesque jerks of the body, etc., resulting from the futile efforts of the will to restrain the involuntary muscles; in the convulsions the flexor and extensor muscles internally are alternately in strong action.

Treatment. — Remove all causes of excitement, anger, or fear. Let books and study be forbidden, and require some sort of cheerful outdoor exercise daily. Regulate the diet; let it be plain and nutritious, but not stimulating; let the bowels be kept in order by some gentle physic. The shower- or sponge-bath should be used daily, and for the nervous system, 24 grains of Iron by Hydrogen, 1 grain of Sulphate of Morphia, 5 grains Extract of Nux Vomica; mix and make 30 pills, and take 1 pill twice a day.

NEURALGIA. — A painful affection of the nerves : when it occurs in those of the face it is termed *face-ague* or *tic-doloreux;* when it affects the great nerve of the leg, it is called *sciatica:* other parts, such as the fingers, the chest, the abdomen, etc., are also liable to this agonizing pain, one of the most severe and wearing to which the human frame is liable ; the exact nature of it is not very clear; that is to say, the origin of the disease, for although its immediate seat is a nerve, or set of nerves, yet there must be some originating cause. It can frequently be traced to some decay, or diseased growth of the bone about those parts through which the nerves pass; and in some severe cases it has been found to depend upon the irritation caused by foreign bodies acting upon those highly sensitive organs. The only *symptom* of Neuralgia, generally, is a violent darting and plunging pain, which comes on in paroxysms; except in very severe and protracted cases, there is no outward redness nor swelling to mark the seat of the pain, neither is there usually constitutional derangement, other than that which may be caused by want of rest, and the extreme agony of the suffering while it lasts, which may be from one to two or three hours, or even more, but it is not commonly so long. Tenderness and

swelling of the part sometimes occurs, where there has been a frequent recurrence and long continuance of the pain, which leaves the patient, in most cases, as suddenly as it comes on; its periodic returns and remissions, and absence of inflammatory symptoms, are distinctive marks of the disease. Among its exciting *causes,* we may mention exposure to damp and cold, especially if combined with malaria; and to these influences a person with a debilitated constitution will be more subject than another. Anxiety of mind will sometimes bring it on, and so will a disordered state of the stomach, more particularly a state in which there is too much acid.

As for *treatment,* that of course must depend upon the cause ; if it is a decayed tooth, which, by its exposure of the nerve to the action of the atmosphere, sets up this pain, it should be at once removed, as there will be little peace for the patient until it is : if co-existent with Neuralgia there is a disordered stomach, suspicion should at once point thereto, and efforts should be made to correct the disorder there. If the patient is living in a moist, low situation, he should at once be removed to a higher level, and a dry gravelly soil. Tonics, such as Quinine, and Iron, should be given, and a tolerably generous diet, but without excess of any kind. In facial Neuralgia, blisters behind the ears, or at the back of the neck, have been found serviceable; and, if the course of the nerve which appears to be the seat of mischief can be traced, a Belladonna plaster, or a piece of rag soaked in Laudanum and laid along it, will sometimes give relief; so will hot fomentations of Poppies and Camomiles, or Bran Poultices sprinkled with Turpentine. In very severe cases ¼ of a grain of Morphine may be given to deaden the nervous sensibility, and induce sleep, which the patient is often deprived of at night, the pain coming on as soon as he gets warm in bed. Sir Charles Bell's remedy for obstinate cases of Neuralgia, was 1 or 2 drops of Croton Oil, mixed with

1 dram of Compound Colocynth Pill, divide into 12. Weakly persons, however, must not venture upon taking this powerful remedy.

An application of Chloroform on lint has sometimes proved very effectual in relieving severe Neuralgic pains, and so has an ointment composed of Lard and Veratrine, in the proportion of 6 grains to the ounce. A mixture of Chloroform and Aconite has been recommended for facial Neuralgia, the form of preparation being 2 parts of Spirits of Wine, or Eau de Cologne, 1 of Chloroform, and 1 of Tincture of Aconite, to be applied to the gums of the side affected, by means of a finger covered with a piece of lint, or soft linen, and rubbed along them; the danger of dropping any into the mouth being thus avoided. When the pain is connected with some organic disease, as a decayed tooth, or chronic inflammation of the gums, or the sockets, or superficial necrosis of the bone, substitute Tincture of Iodine for the spirit in the above formula. We would caution our readers strongly against the careless inhalation of Chloroform as a remedy for Neuralgia, which appears to be growing into practice; several deaths have resulted from it, the method being to pour a little on a pocket-handkerchief, without much regard to quantity, and hold it to the mouth until the required insensibility is produced. This remedy should never be administered except under the supervision of the medical adviser.

Persons at all liable to this painful affection, should be extremely careful not to expose themselves to wet or cold; above all, not to sit in draughts, a very slight cause will often bring it on when there is the least tendency to it.

Hiccough or Hiccup. Of this compound word it has been suggested that the first syllable, *hic*, may have reference to *hitch* or *catch; hiccup* is the general pronunciation. This is a convulsive catch of the respiratory muscles, causing spasmodic contraction of the diaphragm, with a partial closure of the larynx; generally, it is but trivial and transient, causing no permanent inconvenience; but, sometimes, when it occurs in the latter stages of acute disease, it is very alarming, indicating a giving way of the nervous system.

Young females of an hysterical tendency sometimes suffer from obstinate Hiccough. We have known it to continue for weeks with but little cessation, except during the hours of sleep, and, occasionally, breaking in upon them. Long fasting, or the sudden introduction of some strong stimulant into the stomach, will often cause a common Hiccough, for which cold water, continually sipped and swallowed, will often prove a remedy, but nothing is so likely to remove it as strong excitement of the mind. Acupunctuation has been recommended as a remedy, but we have never seen it tried, and much question the desirability of its application. Most antispasmodic medicines are likely to be of service, and we have seen the following given with good effect: — Carbonate of Soda, 1 dram; Sulphuric Ether, 3 drams; Tincture of Ginger, 2 drams; Tincture of Gentian, 4 drams; Camphor Mixture, sufficient to make 8 ounces. Take two tablespoonfuls every two or three hours. Sometimes hot applications to the upper part of the chest and the throat will relieve the symptoms; but, if all these should fail, a surgeon had better be consulted, especially if the patient is in a weak state.

The simple form of Hiccough is readily cured by taking a teaspoonful of Carbonate of Soda in a little cold water.

FAINTING. — This is a state of total or partial unconsciousness, occasioned by diminished action of the heart, causing a less rapid circulation of blood through the brain. The causes of it are various, and sometimes very peculiar, such as a particular smell; that of a rose, for instance, has been known to occasion it; certain objects presented to the sight; surprise, joy, fear, or any sudden emotions; loss of blood, or anything which tends to debilitate the system by diminishing the vital energy.

The first sensation of fainting to the patient himself is generally a singing in the ears, then the sight becomes confused, and all the senses deadened; a clammy sweat breaks out over the person, the countenance becomes deadly pale, and the limbs refuse to support the weight of the body, which sinks to the earth as helpless and motionless as a corpse; indeed, the condition so closely resembles that of death, that it is difficult to distinguish it therefrom. This is a complete faint; frequently the fits are only partial and very limited in duration; but whether so or not, the best *treatment* is to place the patient in an horizontal position; free the face, neck, and upper part of the chest from all incumbrances; let the fresh air play freely upon them, and sprinkle the former with cold water; holding to the nostrils from time to time some volatile stimulant, such as Hartshorn or Ammonia; as soon as swallowing can be accomplished, administer about 30 drops of Spirits of Wine, or Sal Volatile, in water.

Persons subject to fainting should not go into crowded rooms where the air is bad, should not become excited, or wear light clothing. Cold bathing, a nutritious but not a stimulating diet, and vegetable tonics, will help to cure the tendency.

NIGHTMARE.—A sense of weight and oppression at the chest, felt at night, and generally preceded by a frightful dream, in which the sleeper fancies himself on the edge of a precipice, or struggling for his life with some enemy in the form of a fiend or dreadful beast, from which he makes desperate but fruitless efforts to escape. The cause is, generally, indigestion; it may be owing to distension of the stomach by flatulency, or lying in a cramped and uneasy position; sometimes it is occasioned by great mental disquietude or irritation, or over fatigue. The best remedies are plenty

4

of outdoor exercise, a well regulated diet, light suppers, taken early in the evening, and no studying for an hour or two before retiring. Avoid costiveness, lie on your side, and do not raise the hands above the head. Shaking a person while suffering from Nightmare will waken them out of it.

Somnambulism, or Sleep-walking. —It is not very uncommon for persons to fall into this curious state, which appears to be one between waking and sleeping. It is one of those psychological phenomena which, like mesmerism, is as yet very imperfectly understood. Somnambulists are thought by some to be endued with a kind of clairvoyance, or inner sight, which is diffused over the whole body, but is especially seated at the epigastrium and the finger-ends. Notwithstanding which, however, the sleep-walker is liable to dangerous falls, and other accidents; it is, therefore, necessary that he should be carefully watched and guarded; above all, he should be never rudely nor suddenly disturbed when in this state, as a fright or shock of any kind may be attended with very serious results.

As a preventive, wind once or twice around the patient's leg, on retiring, a thin, flexible copper wire, long enough to reach the floor; or, a copper chain of No. 8 wire, three or four feet long, with one end of it held in the hand and the other end passed to the floor, is a more convenient application, and quite as effectual. It will also sometimes prove valuable in inducing sleep to those who are nervous and wakeful. The chain should be removed after the patient is asleep, as too long a continuance is injurious.

COLDS can scarcely be spoken of as a disease, although it is the prolific source of many diseases, and a large proportion of the cases which the family doctor is called in to treat are termed colds, under which generic term, if we may so speak, are included *Catarrh, Influenza,* bronchial affections, and the incipient stages of *Bronchitis.* As to the results of a cold, were we to particularize these, we might include fevers, rheumatic affections, and half the diseases to which the flesh is heir. In this climate, more especially, with its sudden changes of temperature, and variations in the condition of the atmosphere, persons are very liable to "catch cold," as it is called, and, generally speaking, far too little care is taken to guard against this liability, and the effects of a "slight cold" when it is contracted.

The *symptoms* of a cold are familiar to most persons, for there are few who have not experienced them ; as a general rule the *treatment* should be avoidance of exposure to out-of-door atmospheric influences, unless the weather be very fine and mild ; warm diluent drinks and diaphoretics at night to promote perspiration, with the use of the foot-bath. The saying runs, " feed a cold and starve a fever," but this is not always the safe course ; if there is an absence of febrile symptoms, which is rarely the case, a warm nourishing diet may be the rule, and medicines may be pretty nearly dispensed with, but if these symptoms are present the system must be reduced by low diet and aperient medicines. A high medical authority has recently recommended *a total abstinence from liquids;* he says :—" To those who have the resolution to bear the feelings of thirst ,for thirty-six or forty-eight hours, we can promise a pretty certain and complete riddance of their colds ; and, what is perhaps more important, a prevention of those coughs which commonly succeed them."

If a cold settles on the outer covering of the lungs, it becomes pneumonia, inflammation of the lungs, or lung fever, and in many cases carries off the strongest man to the grave within a week. If cold falls upon the inner covering of the lungs, it is pleurisy, with its knife-like pains and its slow, very slow recoveries. If a cold settles in the joints, there is rheumatism with its agonies of pain, and rheumatism of the heart, which in an instant sometimes snaps asunder the cords of life

with no friendly warning. It is of the utmost practical importance, then, in the wintry weather, to know not so much how to cure a cold as how to avoid it.

Colds always come from one cause, some part of the body being colder than natural for a time. If a person will keep his or her feet warm always, and never allow himself or herself to be chilled, he or she will never take cold in a lifetime ; and this can only be accomplished by due care in warm clothing and avoidance of drafts and exposure. While multitudes of colds come from cold feet, perhaps, the majority arise from cooling off too quickly after becoming a little warmer than is natural from exercise or work, or from confinement to a warm apartment.

COUGH.—A convulsive effort of the lungs to get relief of phlegm or other matter ; it may be a symptom of *Bronchitis*, or *Catarrh*, or *Croup*, or *Influenza*, or *Laryngitis*, or *Phthisis*, or *Pleurisy*, or *Pneumonia*, or *Relaxed Uvula*, also *Whooping-Cough*.

We can here lay down but a few general principles with regard to the treatment of simple cough without reference to the peculiar disease of which it may be symptomatic ; and first let us observe that it may be either what is properly, as well as medically, termed *dry* or *moist*. In the former case, Opium and its preparations are advisable ; in the latter they should not be used ; the irritation will be best allayed by Henbane or Hemlock, either the Tincture or Extract, with demulcents, as Barley-water, Linseed-tea, etc., and Liquorice, either the Root boiled, or Extract ; it is well also to add from 5 to 10 drops of Ipecacuanha Wine to each dose ; inhalation also of the steam from boiling water will generally be found beneficial — and especially if some medicinal herb, such as Horehound or Coltsfoot, be infused in it. In moist coughs, there should not be so much fluid taken, and the use of demulcents must be somewhat restricted. Opiates may be administered, but not too freely, either separately or in cough mixtures ; Paregoric Elixir, in which the Opium is combined with Benzoic Acid and Oil of Aniseed (expectorants), and Camphor (antispasmodic), is perhaps the best form of administration; a teaspoonful in a glass of water generally allays the irritation and frequent desire to cough which arises from it. In cases where there is difficulty of expectoration, some such mixture as this should be taken : — Compound Tincture of Camphor, 4 drams ; Ipecacuanha Wine, and Oxymel of Squills, of each 2 drams ; Mucilage of Acacia, 1 ounce ; Water, 4 ounces : mix and take a tablespoonful when the cough is troublesome ; for old people 2 drams of Tincture of Benzoin, commonly called Friar's Balsam, may be added to the above ; and if there should be much fever, 2 drams of Sweet Spirits of Nitre. For all kinds of cough, counter-irritants should be applied, such as blisters and warm plasters, rubbing in of stimulant ointments, on the chest and between the shoulders; those parts also should be well protected by flannels next the skin, dressed hair-skin, and other contrivances of the kind. For coughs which are more particularly troublesome by night, it is best to give the Opium, Henbane, or Hemlock, as the case may be, at bedtime, in the shape of a pill; of the extracts of either of the latter, 5 grains may be given ; of the first, 1 or 2 grains of the Gum, or ¼ of a grain of Morphine. A long experience of their efficacy among a large number of dispensary patients enables the writer to recommend, with confidence, the following pills : — Take of Compound Squill Pill, 1 dram; Ipecacuanha Powder, and Extract of Hyoscyamus, of each ½ dram, mix and make into 24 pills; take one or two on going to rest. Great relief is afforded by the use of a warm foot-bath and warm gruel, with a 10-grain Dover's Powder after the patient is in bed, then plenty of covering to encourage perspiration. Coughs should never be neglected, they are so frequently symptomatic of organic disease ; if they do not yield to simple remedies, let medi-

cal advice be sought, whether the patient be old or young.

CATARRH.— An inflammation of the mucous membrane of the nostrils, or bronchial passages, causing an increased afflux of the matter secreted therein. There are two distinct kinds of this disease, viz., cold in the head ; and epidemic catarrh, commonly called *Influenza.*

The *causes* are exposure to cold or wet, epidemic poison, which, as the result of over stimulus to the nerves, produces congestion of some portion of the mucous membrane, and generally, more or less, of inflammatory fever in the whole system.

The *symptoms* are a dull, heavy pain in the forehead, redness of the eyes, fulness and heat of the nostrils, followed by the distillation of a thin acrid fluid from those parts; hoarseness, frequent sneezing, and soreness of the trachea; difficulty of breathing, cough, and loss of appetite, with a sense of chilliness, and a general feeling of lassitude : the pulse, towards evening, becomes considerably accelerated, and more or less of fever ensues as the disease proceeds; the mucus, at first, thin, colorless, and expectorated with difficulty, gradually becomes thicker, of a yellow color, and more easily brought up; after a few days it diminishes in quantity, and soon ceases altogether, if proper care be taken, and the right remedies used; and this brings us to the

Treatment—Which will be low diet, plenty of diluents, such as Barley-water or thin Gruel, acidulated with a little Lemon Juice, or Cream of Tartar; if there is much difficulty of breathing, and much inflammation, bleeding, general or topical, must be resorted to, with diaphoretic and aperient medicines, and Calomel in 3 grain doses; a blister to the chest if the desired relief is not afforded by these means, and the promotion of perspiration by Dover's Powder, 10 grains, at bedtime ; the use of the foot-bath, warm drinks, and plenty of clothes on the bed; an infusion of

Linseed and Liquorice Root may be given where the cough is very troublesome, and the chest sore; and if the rest is much disturbed, a draught containing ⅛th of a grain of Morphine, 2 drams of Liquor of Acetate of Ammonia, and ½ a dram of Ipecacuanha Wine, with an ounce of Camphor Mixture, should be administered at bedtime instead of the Dover's Powder. Catarrh in children may be distinguished from measles by the mildness of the febrile symptoms in the former, and the absence of many characteristic marks of the latter. The disease is seldom attended with fatal consequences, except in elderly persons, or those far advanced in pulmonary complaints and greatly debilitated constitutions; it often proves the first stage of bronchitis, and commonly causes great constitutional derangement, and renders the system liable to the attacks of other diseases. Sometimes, after it has continued on a person for a longer period than usual, the inflammation of the mucous membrane affects that of the *bladder*. A snuff made as follows is very effectual for catarrh in the head: 1 dram of Crystals of Nitrate of Silver dissolved in a teaspoonful of warm water, and mixed with 3 drams of Lycopodium; put in a dark place, and let it dry, then rub it into a powder with the finger: take a pinch of this once a day, drawing it up the nostrils well into the head.

TEETH.—True, bony teeth are found only in the higher or vertebrated animals: there are three kinds, Molars, Bicuspids, and Cuspids. The following cut exhibits more clearly.

These three sorts of Teeth, which we may call grinders, tearers, and cutters, represent three classes of Teeth

among the lower animals; that man has them all we may take as an evidence that he is intended to be an omnivorous feeder.

Although the Teeth form so prominent and distinguishing a feature of all the full-grown individuals of the higher forms of animals, yet most of these animals, including man, are born without any Teeth at all. When the child is born, the jaw is covered with gums, but underneath the gums are little cavities in which the Teeth are formed; and as they go on growing, they at last press upon the gum, and causing it to absorb, finally break through it. This process is called *dentition*. It is frequently a source of disordered health to children, especially if anything occurs to prevent the absorption and ready yielding of the gum to the pressure of the tooth below. The absence of Teeth during the period of human infancy evidently indicates that the food required at that period does not need their employment. It is a well-known fact, that the food of the infant is its mother's milk; but it is too often forgotten that, till Teeth are developed, Nature does not intend the child to take food that requires preparation by Teeth in order to its digestion. The practice of feeding young children with solid food, is the cause of great destruction of life; and even sops should only be sparingly administered, in cases of necessity, till the first Teeth have appeared.

From what we have before said, it will be seen that in the adult man there are thirty-two Teeth, but if we examine the jaw of a child after it has "cut" all its Teeth, and before it is six years old, we shall find that it has but twenty. Nor are these teeth increased in number by the addition of others; but whilst this first set of Teeth are performing their duties, an entirely new set is growing underneath them, in precisely the same way as they did at first. Gradually the fangs of the first set of teeth are absorbed, in consequence of the pressure of those beneath, and they fall out, or are easily removed, and make way for the others. The order in which the Teeth appear — as well as the time — is subject to considerable deviations, but the following periods will be found to be about the time.

First, or Milk Teeth.

2 lower middle incisors,	4th to 8th month.
2 upper "	4th to 8th "
4 lateral incisors,	7th to 11th "
4 anterior, or 1st molars,	12th to 18th "
4 eye, or canine teeth,	16th to 22d "
4 back molars,	19th to 38th "
20	

In some children, the whole of the Teeth may be cut by the end of the third year, whilst, in others, the process of dentition may be prolonged to the fifth year.

Order of Appearance of the permanent Teeth.

4 first molars, one on each of the two sides of the two jaws,	6th to 7th year.
4 middle incisors, two in each jaw,	7th to 8th year.
4 lateral incisors, a little later than the last,	7th to 8th year.
4 first bicuspids,	8th to 9th "
4 last bicuspids,	10th to 12th "
4 eye, or canine Teeth,	11th to 13th "
4 second molars,	12th to 14th "
4 back molars, or wisdom Teeth,	18th to 30th "
32	

The irregularity of Teeth produces an accumulation of tartar at their base, which causes an absorption of the gum, and eventually the Tooth drops out without decay. These irregularities arise from inattention to the Teeth, during second dentition; but if proper care is taken at that period, all undue growth may be guarded against.

The Teeth should be kept clean. There are two sources of impurity to the Teeth. The first is from a deposit of tartar upon them near the gum; and the second is from portions of food adhering to them after meals. The accumulation of tartar is a frequent source of disease in the Teeth and gums, and precautions should be taken to prevent its adherence to them. The best plan is that of cleaning them with the brush night and morning. Dentifrices are frequently employed, and, perhaps, when simple, they are of service. All chemical products, however, should be avoided. Anything which acts chemically upon the Tooth will open the way to speedy decay. The simplest dentifrice, and one of the best, is a mixture of prepared Chalk and well powdered Camphor. The Chalk acts as a scouring material, whilst the Camphor stimulates the gums, and counteracts the decomposition of any small particles of food that may lurk among the Teeth. The purer the water that is employed for washing the Teeth the better. To cleanse away portions of food adhering to the Teeth, the toothpick should be used. Metallic toothpicks are objectionable; those made of bone or quills are to be preferred.

When Teeth are found to be decayed, immediate attention should be paid to them. They more frequently indicate serious derangement of the health than is imagined. Where Teeth are already decayed, they cannot be restored to their pristine integrity, but the decayed part may be removed, or the whole Tooth may be extracted. The sooner this is done the better; for decay has an undoubted tendency to spread, and nothing is so disagreeable to other people as the breath of a person tainted with the faint odor of decomposing Teeth.

Decay of the Teeth frequently comes on from long-continued indigestion, from exposure to cold, from a scrofulous habit of body, from eating and drinking very hot or very cold articles of diet. Now, in all diseases, prevention is better than cure.

Persons should take care to avoid those states of the system, and those causes which are known to be favorable to the production of decayed Teeth.

TOOTHACHE. — For this distressing and very common malady almost every one has a "sure cure," the peculiarity of which is, that it does little or nothing to mitigate the anguish of the sufferer to whom it is recommended, which anguish is commonly caused by the exposure of the interior pulp, containing the nerve and blood-vessels, to external influence, by decay of the outer portion of the Tooth. Among the remedies which we have to suggest, as having found them pretty generally successful, are Creosote, Chloroform, and Laudanum; separately or in combination, they may be tried all ways; the mode of application is to saturate a small piece of lint or wadding, and introduce it into the hollow of the Tooth, keeping it there as long as it may be necessary; should there be no available hollow, put it as close as possible to the seat of pain. Many of the other remedies recommended we have known to afford relief occasionally; such as inhaling the vapor from Henbane Seeds put on a hot piece of metal; chewing a piece of Pellitory Root, or using the Tincture; putting a piece of Sal Prunella in the mouth and allowing it to dissolve; applying a drop or two of the Oil of Cloves, or Cinnamon, on lint; or thrusting into the hollow Tooth a piece of wire previously dipped in strong Nitric Acid; this application, if properly made, destroys the nerve, but it must be very carefully done, so that the Acid does not touch the other teeth or the mouth. An aching Tooth may oftentime be stopped, and remain serviceable for years; but this must not be done while the nerve is in an inflamed state, as in this case the pressure will but increase the anguish. Where a Tooth is so far gone as to be very troublesome, it is best to have it out; the pain of the operation is sharp, but short, while the constant ache, ache, destroys alike health and spirits, and unfits one for all the active duties of life.

HEARING. — This word signifies the faculty or sense by which sound is perceived; it is reckoned among our external senses, its particular organ being the *Ear;* in our article on which we have explained how certain mo-

tions or vibrations of the air, striking upon the tympanum, or drum, so excite the auditory nerve, whose fine reticulations or febrillæ are spread over the interior of the organs, as to cause them to communicate to the brain, a sensation by which the mind obtains the ideas awakened by the sounds. All this is very wonderful, and past human comprehension ; we know that it is so, but we cannot tell how this communication between mind and matter can take place; we see the machinery of the organs, and we are cognizant by certain results of its being put into operation. We know that if we utter certain words in the ear of a friend or foe, the thoughts or ideas which we intended those words should convey, are conveyed to his mind, and he speaks and acts accordingly ; but our chain of reasoning upon cause and effect wants some links to make it complete. We are sure that we do *hear* and are *heard*, but we cannot tell *how* this hearing is effected. It is one of the mysteries of our being, and there are many such to teach us humility and our dependence upon God. See remarks on the causes of the deprivation of Hearing and the means of its recovery.

DEAFNESS may proceed from any injury inflicted on the delicate organs of the ear by loud noises, violent colds, inflammation or ulceration of the membrane of the auditory passages; hard wax or other substances interrupting the transmission of sounds; either over dryness or excessive moisture in the parts; want of tone in the general system from debility; among one of its frequent causes, is some defect in the structure of the organ itself, which no medical treatment can obviate; in this case there is generally dumbness as well.

The *treatment* will depend to a considerable extent on the cause; if there is an accumulation of hardened wax, or any defective or diseased action in the secreting glands of that substance, a few drops of a saturated solution of Common Salt, or of Ox Gall and

Balsam of Tolu, one part of the former to three of the latter, may be dropped into the ear, while the head is held on one side, night and morning; or applied on a piece of wadding inserted by means of a probe; before each application, the ear should be syringed out with warm milk and water, or soap and water. If there is a thin acrid discharge accompanying the deafness, apply a blister behind the ear and keep it open for some time with Savine Ointment. When deafness proceeds from cold in the head, diaphoretics, the warm foot-bath, and flannel wrappers, must be the remedies; if from debility and consequent loss of tone, drop stimulants into the ear, electrify or galvanize, and give tonics; this will be the treatment also if it proceeds from defective energy of the optic nerve.

EARACHE may proceed from abscess in one or more of the passages, or it may be altogether neuralgic. In children it is not uncommon during the period of dentition, and is especially severe in cutting the permanent teeth; grown persons sometimes suffer from it when producing their wisdom teeth; it is often brought on by exposure to cold or draughts; there is not often much constitutional derangement, although the pain is sometimes excruciating, unless it is long continued.

Treatment. — In children, during dentition, lancing the swollen gums will often afford relief, especially if an aperient be given, such as Rhubarb and Magnesia combined with a little Ginger, as in the Gregory's Powder; elder children may have a little Laudanum dropped into the ear, and take Compound Senna Mixture, repeated until the bowels are freely opened; should these remedies not prove effectual, a fomentation of Camomiles and Poppies should be applied, and a warm poultice afterwards; the heart of a roasted onion applied warm to the external orifice will sometimes afford relief. If the case is very obstinate, two or three leeches behind the ear, followed by a blister, may be tried, with an Anodyne Saline Aperient something like this: — Acetate of Morphine ½ a grain, Solution of Acetate of Ammonia 3 ounces, Sulphate of Magnesia 1 ounce, Water or Camphor Mixture 5 ounces; mix and take two tablespoonfuls every four hours. When Earache is caused by an abscess, and is attended with much swelling and severe pain, hot fomentations and poultices will be the treatment, syringing the external passages with warm water, and, after the abscess has discharged, with a Solution of Sulphate of Zinc, in the proportion of 8 grains to the ounce of plain, or Rose Water, attention being paid to the bowels. With some persons any derangement of the general health will cause the formation of these abscesses, and in such cases the treatment must be rather general than local. Earache, no doubt, often proceeds from derangement of the digestive organs, and may be relieved by active purgatives and emetics. When it is strictly neuralgic, Quinine, or some preparation of Iron, will be the most appropriate remedy, with stimulating liniments rubbed in behind and about the ear.

Noises in the Ear, like the distant sound of bells, roaring of the sea, hissing and singing, etc., are often indicative of a determination of blood to the head; with some, mere derangement of the digestive organs will cause these noises; when accompanied by a certain degree of deafness, they are generally occasioned by an accumulation of wax in the external passage, or a partial stoppage of the Eustachian tube by cold. When the noises become chronic, or long continued, bathing the head regularly every morning with cold water will sometimes remove them; if cold be the cause, or disordered stomach, they will pass away with the temporary ailments which occasioned them; if too great a fulness of the veins of the head, cupping, leeching, or abstraction of blood by means of the lancet, with a depletive course of treatment, must be adopted.

Polypus of the Ear is by no means an uncommon form of the fungoid growth which sometimes occurs in several of the internal tissues. It is of a jelly-like consistence, and a whitish-yellow color, and is attached to the membraneous lining of the ear; there are also granulations of fungus which sometimes shoot up from the membrane, and are distinguished by their reddish hue from polypi; these may generally be removed by being held firmly with a pair of forceps, and then gently twisted and pulled at the same time; this should only be done by a properly qualified person, as much mischief may result from the unskilful application of the forceps to so delicate a part; sometimes, when the polypus is in the external passage, and not far up, it may be destroyed by astringent applications, such as the Muriated Tincture of Steel, or Burnt Alum, applied with a camel-hair brush.

Wax in the Ear.—When this substance becomes too hard, or accumulates too much, there will be a sense of contraction, with cracking or hissing noises, and generally deafness to a considerable extent; in this case the ear should be syringed with warm soap-suds, the instrument used being a proper one for the purpose, holding about 4 ounces, and having but a small tube or pipe which does not fill the whole passage, but allows the escape of the back water, for catching which a hand basin should be held close against the neck. As many as a dozen syringefuls may be injected at one time. A strong lotion should be put into the ear-passage over night and kept there by means of cotton wool or wadding; Almond Oil and Laudanum, in the proportion of 2 ounces of the former to 1 of the latter, is a good application in this case, as in many other kinds of ear disease; it will also frequently stop Earache resulting from cold and other causes.

INFLUENZA.—It has lately been very much the fashion to call any kind of cold which is accompanied with catarrhal symptoms, Influenza; but this, in nine cases out of ten, is a misnomer; the true disease seldom occurs except as an epidemic, attacking many persons at once; it comes on quite suddenly, and its symptoms are those of a general fever; there is great prostration of strength, generally showing loss of appetite, heat and thirst, cough and difficulty of breathing, owing to the air valves and bronchial passages being clogged with mucus; there is also running at the nose and eyes, weight across the brow, with throbbing pain, and great depression of spirits. The febrile symptoms do not commonly last more than four or five days, sometimes but one or two, but the cough generally remains for a considerable time, varying according to circumstances, such as exposure to cold or wet, predisposition to cough, etc.

With the strong and healthy this is not a dangerous disease, but aged or weakly persons are frequently carried off by it. In the former case but little medical treatment is required. Keep the patient in bed, and let the temperature of the room be warm and equable; open the bowels with a gentle aperient, such as Rhubarb and Magnesia, or Senna Mixture, and follow this up with weak Wine Whey, or some warm diluent drink, in a pint of which a grain of Tartar Emetic and a dram of Nitrate of Potash has been dissolved; give a wineglassful of this about every four hours. It is not generally safe to practice much depletion, but where there is great difficulty of breathing, and irritation of the throat, a few leeches may be applied just above the breast-bone, in the hollow of the neck. Stimulating liniments may also be applied to the chest, and Mustard poultices, but blisters are scarcely to be recommended. Hot fomentations may also be useful, and medicated inhalations, such as a scruple of powdered Hemlock or Henbane, sprinkled in the boiling water from which the steam ascends into the throat. The fresh leaves of the above plants may be used, or a dram of the Tincture, if these cannot be procured. When the fever is subdued, if there is still cough and restlessness, a 5-grain Dover's Powder may be given at bedtime, or ⅛th of a grain of Acetate of Morphine, with a 5-grain Squill Pill, for the cough, if required. If there is great feebleness, tonics must be administered; Infusion of Calumba, Cascarilla, or Gentian, with Carbonate of Ammonia; 1 ounce of the former with 5 grains of the latter, three times a day, with a mildly nutritious diet — Broths, Arrowroot, Sago, and a small quantity of Wine. Such is an outline of the course to be pursued in most cases of Influenza which really require medical treatment at all; generally warmth, rest, and good nursing will do all the business. Should the cough be very obstinate, and resist all efforts to remove it, change of air will generally prove effectual, and this is beneficial in most cases.

BRONCHITIS—Is one of the above-named forms of disease which claims a prominent notice at our hands. It may be succinctly described as inflammation of the lining membrane of the passages of the throat, through which the work of respiration is carried on. It will be evident that an inflamed state of these passages must, besides the local irritation caused thereby, seriously interfere with the vital functions.

Bronchitis may be either *acute* or *chronic;* the former stage may commence immediately after exposure to cold; most usually the lining membrane of the eyelids, nostrils, and throat are first affected, and then the inflammation extends downwards into the chest. The earlier symptoms are running at the nose, watering of the eyes, frequent sneezing, and all the distressing symptoms of what is generally known as *Influenza*, which see. The fever generally runs high, there is extreme lassitude, with headache, and probably a troublesome cough, with expectoration of mucus : with adults this, the most active stage of the disease, frequently assumes a very danger-

ous character, and prompt measures are required to arrest its progress. If the febrile symptoms continue to increase in intensity, and the breathing becomes difficult from the clogging of the tubes with mucus, there is great reason for apprehension. The patient should, as a matter of course, be confined to bed ; warm diluent drinks, such as Linseed-tea, or Barley-water, with a slice or two of Lemon in it ; gentle aperients, if required ; foot-baths and a Mustard Poultice applied to the chest.

It is especially during the spring months, and when there is a prevalence of east wind, that Bronchitis attacks young and old, often hurrying the former to a premature grave, and making the downward course of the latter more quick and painful ; with aged people, in such cases, there is commonly a great accumulaton of mucus in the bronchial tubes, which causes continued and violent coughing in the efforts to expel it, which efforts are often unsuccessful ; thus the respiration is impeded, the blood, for want of proper oxygenization, becomes unfit for the purposes of vitality, and death, often unexpectedly sudden, is the consequence. Such bronchitic patients must be carefully treated — no lowering measures will do for them, but warm and generous diet ; Opium cannot safely be ventured on. Warm flannel next the skin, a genial atmosphere, inhalation of steam — if medicated with Horehound, or some demulcent plants, so much the better — a couple of compound Squill Pills at night, and during the day a mixture, composed of Camphor Mixture, 6 ounces, with Tincture of Squills, Wine of Ipecacuanha, and Aromatic Spirits of Ammonia, of each 2 drams, with perhaps 2 drams of Tincture of Hops — take a tablespoonful every three or four hours. Such is the most rational mode of treatment ; and this, and others to which we have alluded, are some of the forms in which bronchial disease manifests itself. In all these forms, the condition of the digestive organs requires great attention ; the cough, especially when it assumes a spasmodic character, depending frequently upon the state of the stomach; so much so, that, when the stomach is empty, a little food taken during a violent fit of coughing has been known to stay it immediately.

The following is said to be an excellent remedy : — Take common Mullein Leaves, dry and rub fine, and smoke them three or four times a day in a new pipe, taking care to draw the smoke well into the throat.

CONSUMPTION is a wasting away of the body, resulting generally from disease of the lungs. It stands at the head of the diseases of our climate. The State of New York alone loses about twenty thousand persons a year by this terrible disease.

The formation of tubercles on the lungs may arise from various causes; where there is predisposition, the most trifling exposure to cold or damp, the least deviation from the rules of health, will frequently develop the disease; and even where there is not, it requires but little to set it up; and this is the case, not only in America, but all through Europe.

Among the most general of the predisposing, or exciting *causes*, may be mentioned, in addition to the hereditary taint spoken of, a scrofulous habit of body, a peculiar formation of the chest, compressing the space appropriated to the lungs, so that they cannot have free play; this is sometimes the result of artificial compression, against which we cannot raise our voice too loudly or too often. Inflammation of the lungs, catarrh, syphilis, king's evil, small-pox, measles, or any disease which has a tendency to impair the quality of the blood or weaken the system, may be classed among the causes of Consumption; as may certain employments which necessitate the breathing of an atmosphere loaded with impurities, causing irritation of the pulmonary passages, which is likely to extend to the lungs themselves, and initiate tubercular disease. Previous to the invention of magnetic guards for the mouth, which attract the minute particles of steel dust, and prevent their entering, needle grinders seldom attained to the age of forty years; and it is now found that hair-dressers, bakers, millers, masons, brick-layers, laboratory men, coal-heavers, chimney sweeps, dressers of flax and hemp, and workmen in leather warehouses, are all especially liable to pulmonic disease. A slight cough, resulting from a cold caught by sitting in a draught, or getting wet, or wearing damp linen, will, if neglected, often become worse, and eventually lead to Consumption. So too will scrofula, with which a large proportion of the ill-fed, ill-clad, and worse-housed lower classes are affected. It has been noted, that soon after scrofulous eruptions have disappeared from the surface of the skin, symptoms of Phthisis have shown themselves, a clear indication that the disease had retreated to the lungs, which would appear to be its internal stronghold.

The *symptoms* of Consumption, although they vary somewhat with the cause of the disease, yet have a general similarity in their character. There is at first languor and a sense of debility. On the slightest exertion the pulse becomes accelerated, and the breathing difficult; there is often a short, dry cough, which increases in strength and frequency. At first there is little or no expectoration, but gradually this comes on, and eventually becomes copious, the thick mucus being after a while streaked or tinged with blood. There is gradual emaciation of the body and loss of strength; then come night-sweats, disturbed rest, and a hectic flush, or spot on the cheek — constant thirst, and a cough which seems to gather strength, in proportion as the frame, which it racks and tears, becomes more and more attenuated.

There is at first a sense of tightness on the chest; then, as the respiration becomes more labored, succeed sharp, cutting pains, particularly under the sternum, or breast-bone, and at the time of coughing; very commonly the mind partakes of the weakness of the body, and sinks into a desponding state, or has sudden alternations of hope and fear, clinging, however, frequently to the latter until life is extinct. The termination of the sad scene is commonly brought about by the rupture of one or more of the blood-vessels of the lungs in a fit of coughing; hæmorrhage ensues, and the patient sinks exhausted, to add another to the long catalogue of victims to Consumption.

If taken in the earlier stages, the progress of the disease may probably be arrested; and, with great care, where there is known to be hereditary predisposition, it may possibly never be developed at all; but when the tubercles are formed, and suppuration has commenced, the cough become distressing, and the expectoration considerable — although by the application of certain remedies, a removal to a mild climate, and a careful guarding against all adverse influences, the progress of the disease may be for a time arrested, and so the life prolonged, yet it is not often that a permanent cure is effectual.

For diet, those articles should be chosen that contain phosphorus, lime, soda, and iron. Inhalation of medicated vapor into the lungs is highly recommended, but as each case requires an inhalant adapted, it should be left to the physician to prescribe it. The cough may be relieved by the following prescription : 1 ounce Tincture Bloodroot, 1½ grains Sulphate of Morphia, ¼ ounce Tincture Digitalis, ½ ounce Wine of Antimony, 10 drops of Oil of Wintergreen. Mix; take 30 drops 3 times a day.

Cod-Liver Oil, a tablespoonful taken before each meal, has shown, in many cases, very remarkable and satisfactory results. The *Medical Reporter* says that a consumptive patient, now under treatment, is taking cream, with better effect than was experienced under the Cod-Liver Oil, previously tried.

Eat the pure, sweet cream, abundantly, as much of it as the stomach will digest well.

Night Sweats.—1 dram Compound of Oxide of Zinc, and ½ dram Extract of Conium ; make 20 pills, and take 1 or 2 every night. The sponge bath is also good for this purpose.

DIARRHŒA.—The best remedy for this attendant upon Consumption is 20 or 30 grains of Tris-nitrate of Bismuth after each meal.

For the Cough. — 1 ounce Syrup of Tolu; ½ ounce Syrup of Squills; 2 drams Wine of Ipecac; 3 drams Paregoric ; 1½ ounces Mucilage of Gum Arabic; mix, and take a teaspoonful occasionally.

PLEURISY.— This, which is the most common form of the above-named diseases, may be *caused* by exposure to cold, blows, falls, or anything which gives rise to inflammation in other parts; those of a full plethoric habit are chiefly subject to it.

The early *symptoms* are generally cold chills, shivering fits, and rigor, which is followed by acute pain in the side, a flushed countenance, difficulty of breathing, dry cough, and full, hard, and frequent pulse. Pain is nearly always present, generally in a particular spot under one of the breasts, but sometimes at another part of the chest, or on the shoulder, the armpit, or under the collar-bone; it is greatly increased by pressure, coughing, and deep inspiration ; the patient, therefore, breathes thick and short, suppresses coughing as much as possible, and fears to exert himself, or to lie down. Sometimes the inflammation causes a sticking of the Pleura, and adhesion of the membrane covering the lungs, and that which lines the chest; at other times there is an effusion of fluid into the cavity

Treatment. — Copious bleeding from the arm should be at once resorted to if the patient can bear it, to be continued at intervals until the pain and difficulty of breathing is relieved. Leeches, or cup; ing, and a warm poultice to the seat of pain ; a large blister after the latter comes off if necessary ; a full dose of Calomel immediately after the bleeding; and then Tartar Emetic about every two hours, beginning with ½ a grain and increasing it to 2 grains; if this produces vomiting and purging, lessen the dose again, and add 6 drops of Laudanum to each. When the urgent symptoms are relieved, give Calomel and Opium Pills, 2 grains of the former to ¼ grain of the latter, every four hours, until the gums are affected; or if this causes watery evacuations, give Grey Powder in 3-grain doses, or rub in a dram of Mercurial Ointment every two hours; the diet must be low, and perfect quiet maintained; the temperature of the room kept up to about 60° Fahr., and the patient somewhat elevated in the bed. Should symptoms of exhaustion arise, the difficulty of breathing increase, and coma or delirium be threatened, recourse must be had to stimulants, such as Beef Tea, with Wine, etc. The following mixture may also be given: Sesquicarbonate of Ammonia and Laudanum, of each ½ a dram, to Camphor Mixture 6 ounces; take a tablespoonful every one, two, or three hours, as required.

Pneumonia, or Lung Fever.—So similar in every respect are the symptoms and treatment of this form of lung diseases to those described under the head of *Pleurisy* (see PLEURISY), that we need only refer our readers to that article for information.

ASTHMA.— This is a disease of the lungs, whose main characteristic is laborious breathing, which comes in paroxysms, and is accompanied by a wheezing noise. The attack commonly occurs in the night, the patient having gone to bed in a listless, drowsy state, with a troublesome cough, oppression at the chest, and symptoms of flatulency; towards midnight probably the breathing becomes more labored, the wheezing sound louder, and the patient is obliged to assume an erect posture, to prevent suffocation. Sometimes he starts out of bed, and rushes to the window for air; or he sits with his body bent forward, his arms resting on his knees, with a flushed or livid face, if it be not deadly pale, gasping and struggling for breath, in a condition painful to behold; the pulse is weak and intermittent, with palpitation of the heart; sometimes there is vomiting, with involuntary emission of the urine, which is of a pale color, and relaxed bowels. The attack will probably last for a couple of hours or more, when the severe symptoms will gradually remit, with an expectoration of frothy mucus, and a tranquil sleep follows. For some days there will be felt a tightness of the chest, and the slightest exertion brings on a difficulty of breathing; there will be slighter paroxysms, and, after a longer or shorter period, another severe one.

Humid Asthma is that in which the attack terminates with expectoration; when it does not, this is called *Dry Asthma;* persons so afflicted have generally disease of the heart or lungs. When they have not, it is called *Spasmodic Asthma,* and to this persons are sometimes subject who, when the attack is past, may appear quite vigorous and healthy.

The *causes* of Asthma are hereditary predisposition; dwelling in a cold or moist atmosphere, or being subject to sudden changes of temperature; inward gout, intense study, or great mental anxiety; suppression of accustomed evacuations; irritation of the air-cells and lungs by atmospheric impurities; irritation of the stomach, uterus, or other viscera.

Treatment.— The objects to be attained in this are, first, to moderate the violence of the paroxysms; second, to prevent its recurrence. Where the patient is of a full habit, not advanced in years, and the disease is of no long standing, bleeding may be resorted to, especially if the face is flushed, and the pulse moderately strong. But this must not be attempted if the disease has become chronic, and the patient is elderly, especially if the face during the attack is preternaturally pale and shrunk. In either case gentle aperients should be administered, and anti-spasmodic mixtures and injections; a blister on the chest will often afford much relief. The following is a good formula for the mixture: — Tincture of Assafœtida and Sulphuric Ether, of each 2 drams; Tincture of Opium, 1 dram; Peppermint Water, 6 ounces; mix, and take a ·tablespoonful every hour. If the expectoration is scanty and difficult, add to this Tincture of Squills, 2 drams; Wine of Tartarized Antimony, 1 dram; or make the vehicle, instead of Peppermint Water, Mixture of Ammoniacum, that is, about 2 drams of the gum rubbed down with 6 ounces of water. The best aperient is Castor Oil, given in Peppermint, or weak Brandy and Water. Where there is reason to suppose the stomach is overloaded, an emetic, composed of 1 grain of Tartarized Antimony, and 1 scruple of Powder of Ipecacuanha, in half a tumbler of warm water, should be given. The enema thrown up may consist of 2 drams of Gum Assafœtida to a pint of thin gruel. Tincture of Lobelia Inflata is good in obstinate cases, dose 1 dram; and also Tincture of Nicotiana, or Tobacco, in nauseating doses; inhaling the fumes of the leaves of this plant through a pipe, and also of Stramonium, is sometimes of service, and the good effect of either will be assisted by a cup of hot coffee, putting the feet in warm water, or using the warm bath.

To prevent the return of a paroxysm of Asthma, avoid the exciting causes, keep the bowels gently open with Rhubarb or some other mild aperient, and strengthen the tone of the stomach by bitter infusions, such as Camomile or Gentian; if there is tightness of the chest, put on a blister, and take an emetic now and then to clear out the phlegm from the bronchial passage; take at bedtime 10 grains of Dover's Powder, or the same of compound Squill Pill, with a little warm gruel. For the rest, take light and nourishing diet, avoiding everything difficult of digestion; wear warm clothing — flannel next the skin — have regular and

moderate exercise, change of climate if possible, should the situation occupied be damp, or bleak and exposed. Do not indulge in sensual or intemperate habits.

Hay-Asthma. — Also called Hay-Fever, or Summer Bronchitis, is a disease which occurs about the time of the hay harvest, and appears to be caused by the pollen of some wild plants getting into and inflaming the bronchial passages. This theory is supported by the fact that those who live in situations where there is little or no vegetation do not suffer from it. A difficulty of breathing, and a burning sensation in the throat, are the chief characteristics of this affection, on which no remedies seem to exercise a curative effect; a removal to a different locality is most effectual.

Sometimes Chloride of lime, placed in different parts of the sleeping-room, has a good effect. Tincture of Lobelia in 30-drop doses gives some relief.

Diseases of the Heart. — These may be divided into—1st, Functional or Nervous; and 2d, Structural, or Organic. Chief among the former we have *Palpitation, Syncope* or *Fainting*, and ·*Angina Pectoris.* In a structure so complex, and formed of such different tissues as the Heart is, one might expect that it would be subject to many diseases of both a general and a partial character; and, accordingly, we find there are few persons who have not had to complain of symptoms which were indicative of Heart affection of some kind, although few, perhaps, really have what may be properly called Heart *disease.* Strong emotions of the mind, derangements of the liver or stomach, will often cause flutterings and palpitations, an increase or decrease of arterial action, and other symptoms, which would seem to indicate that there was something very wrong with the great organ and centre of circulation; but these symptoms, in a great majority of cases, are merely sympathetic; and very commonly, when a person is said to die of "a broken heart," there is no organic disease to justify the popular verdict.

Among the principal organic diseases to which the Heart is subject, we may notice first, *Pericarditis*, or *Inflammation of the Pericardium*, which may be induced by exposure to damp and cold, and other causes which affect the serous membranes of the body generally. The *symptoms* are tenderness over the region of the Heart, amounting, when pressure is made, to sharp, cutting pains, so that the patient cannot lie on the left side; most commonly the pleura, or investing membrane of the lungs, is involved in the mischief, and in this case, there will be acute pain on coughing or drawing a deep breath; sometimes, however, there is little or no acute pain, only a sense of heaviness and oppression: generally the pulsations are accelerated, often so much so as to constitute flutterings or palpitation: they may be regular or intermittent; although it is not easy to feel this, if, as is frequently the case, there is much effusion into the pericardium; this may be detected by the bulging out of the skin of the thorax over the seat of disease: of the nature of the effusion—whether it be merely thin bloody serum, or thick with coagulated lymph, or fibrous, or containing cartilaginous or osseous deposits—can only be determined by auscultation employed by a skilful person. Pericarditis is one of the most frequent and worst features of acute *Rheumatism*.

CARDITIS, or Inflammation of the Heart, sometimes occurs, and here, although the principal seat of mischief is the muscular tissue of the organ itself, yet its investing membrane is generally implicated more or less, and the same *symptoms* are presented as those just described, although it is likely to be in an aggravated degree. It would be useless to prescribe any general plan of *treatment* in these cases, as this must depend very much upon the peculiarities which they present, and the temperament and condition of the patient. Of course, if inflamma-

tion is quite apparent, low diet and aperients must be the rule; leeches may be applied over the cardiac region, if there is much pain, and especially if accompanied by a pricking or burning sensation; but the lancet should never be used, except by the medical man, who alone can judge of its propriety. Perfect rest, and an avoidance of all excitement, should always be enjoined in this and other cases of Heart disease.

ENDOCARDITIS, or Inflammation of the lining membrane of the Heart, is commonly an attendant of the two former diseases, or of inflammation of the internal coat of one or more of the principal veins: its chief symptoms are fever and anxiety, with bulging of the præcordial region; it requires, like the others, as a rule, rest and antiphlogistic treatment.

Atrophy of the Heart sometimes accompanies a state of general debility; it is a consequence of a deficiency in the supply of blood, and will be pretty sure to terminate in death.

Hypertrophy of the Heart, is the result of an excess of nutrition; the nutritive process here appears to go on more rapidly than the absorbent. Fresh matter is deposited before the old is removed, and hence there is an increase in bulk, which interferes with the proper performance of the *organic* functions. Hearts have been known to increase in this way to more than double their proper size and weight. Hypertrophy is usually divided into three kinds, viz.: *simple, eccentric*, or *aneurismal*, and *concentric*. The first is the least common; in this the *parietes*, or divisions, are thickened, without any diminution in the capacity of the cavities; the second, most frequent, has the parietes thickened, and the cavity proportionably enlarged; the third, has the cavity diminished, in proportion to the thickening of the walls. Any one of these forms of Hypertrophy may affect a single cavity, or the whole Heart. If the left ventricle is attacked, apoplexy and hæmorrhages sometimes ensue. In this disease, the pulsations are for the most part regular and strong, often visibly raising the bedclothes; the chest is bulged out on the left side, and the sound on percussion dull. Rest, abstinence, sedative medicines, and more or less depletion, according to the circumstances of the case, are the proper remedial measures. It is only by perseverance in this course that any good can be looked for.

Dilation of the Heart, is sometimes caused by excessive exertion and strong excitements of any kind; in this case it would seem to be the result of increased action. The whole substance of the organ, or one or more of the cavities or smaller orifices, may be dilated, the walls being merely extended without any increase of substance. In this case, the muscular parietes being thinned and feeble, there will be a want of vigor in the circulation, the muscular compression and extension will be weak and irregular, and the valvular action incomplete, so that the blood will frequently escape out of its proper channels, and these hæmorrhages, although trifling in themselves, will so reduce the patient that he will, probably, be carried off by one of them. Abstinence from the exciting causes of the disease, rest, and nourishing diet, with strict attention to the general state of the health, are the means to be taken in this case.

Disease of the Valves, so commonly follows Endocarditis, if of long continuance, that it may almost be considered as a chronic form of that disease; it is a thickening of the internal lining of the Heart, especially at the valves; it becomes not merely thickened uniformly, but is the seat of warty excrescences, and even cartilaginous and osseous formations of considerable size, extending into the cavities of the Heart. In old persons, and especially those addicted to a generous mode of living, we most frequently meet with ossification, the effects of which are sanguineous and serous congestion, difficulty of breathing, apo-

plectic seizures, and other symptoms of embarrassed circulation.

Nervous, or Spasmodic affections of the Heart, are met with most frequently in women who are suffering from anæmia, chlorosis, hysteria, etc., and in men of a quick, irritable temperament naturally, or rendered so by the free use of stimuli, or an unrestrained indulgence of the passions, and irregularities which seriously interfere with the working of this delicate piece of machinery, whose stoppage must cause instant death.

Palpitation of the Heart has been experienced by most persons who have run themselves out of breath, or by any violent exertion caused a great increase of action in the respiratory and circulatory organs. In a healthy and proper state, we are not generally sensible of the regular *beat, beat,* of the pulse, which goes on night and day, whether we sleep or wake, and tells that the great organ of vitality is duly performing its office; but when, from any cause, these beats become unusually frequent, and forcible, we both feel and hear them, in a very troublesome and distressing manner; and especially is this the case when the bodily strength has been reduced, and the nervous sensibility increased by sickness; sometimes the pulsations are loud and clear and regular, at others they are faint and intermittent; now a distinct throb or several, and then a tremulous flutter, or a quick beat.

When there is violent throbbing of the Heart, which may be felt by a hand pressed upon the chest, while the patient is himself unconscious of it, there is reason to apprehend organic disease; but when there is such acute consciousness as we have described, there is generally only functional, or nervous derangement, without any structural change.

A disordered stomach may be the cause, although there may be no other symptoms of this: we have known cases in which a very slight irregularity in the mode of living has produced Palpitation of the Heart, and that, too, in an otherwise healthy person. In some, almost any strong nervous stimulant will produce it, and we recollect one instance in which it always came on after a cup of tea, and was never troublesome when this beverage was not taken: we mention this to show that Palpitation is not always, nor indeed commonly, symptomatic of Heart disease, and need therefore cause no unnecessary alarm, although its frequent recurrence should set the patient inquiring as to what is the real cause. Young women with whom there is derangement of the menstrual functions, in whom the blood is watery and poor, wanting the red corpuscles; the listless, the pallid, the hysterical, in these we meet with Palpitation in its most aggravated forms; as also in the indolent, the susceptible, and the delicate; those who dwell on morbid fancies, and excite the imagination with sensual thoughts, or horrible pictures—to such every beat of the pulse seems like a call from the world of spirits, every flutter and palpitation like a brush from the wings of the angel of death, or the whispering voice of an accusing conscience. In these cases the only treatment likely to be of service must be directed towards removing the predisposing and exciting causes, and establishing a more healthful nervous condition—gentle exercise, tonics, change of air and scene, an endeavor to occupy the mind in some useful and moral pursuit, a well regulated and generally frugal, although sufficiently nourishing diet, and a strict avoidance of all that can excite or stimulate either mind or body. By this means Palpitations, not connected with organic disease, may generally be got rid of. If the patient is of a full habit, and has a tolerably strong pulse, bleeding or cupping may perhaps be resorted to with advantage; but this should be cautiously done. In such, too, a course of gentle purgatives may be necessary; they should not be salines,

but of a cordial nature, something like this:—Pill of Aloes and Myrrh, and Compound Galbanum Pill, of each ½ a dram; divide into 12 pills, and take one at bedtime. Compound Infusion of Senna and Decoction of Aloes, of each 3 ounces; Spirits of Sal Volatile, 1 dram; Compound Tincture of Cardamums, 2 drams; Tartrate of Potash, ½ ounce; mix, and take two tablespoonfuls occasionally.

HEARTBURN is a sense of uneasiness at the pit of the stomach, from whence it ascends, with acid eructations and a burning heat, into the throat. Sometimes it is accompanied by faintness, nausea, and vomiting, and commonly by what is termed Water-brash, and the mouth becoming filled with a limpid fluid from the stomach, the upper orifice of which is called cardis, from its being the seat of the Heart; it is especially liable to be disturbed by any irritating causes, and such disturbance we term *Heartburn* or *Cardialgia*. Anything which deranges the functions of the stomach will be likely to cause this—indigestible food, especially butter and cheese, or fat and oil of whatsoever kind; so also will strong mental emotion and pregnancy, in the latter months of which there is usually more or less Heartburn. The best remedies are alkalies, combined with mild aperients, such as Magnesia, or Tartrate of Soda and Rhubarb. If there is much flatulency, Gregory's Powder, in ½ dram doses, is good; and where the pain is great, about 5 drops of Laudanum may be taken with each dose. In obstinate cases, a leech or two, or a succession of small blisters, to the pit of the stomach, will probably be useful; but the main thing is a well regulated and simple diet, and avoidance of the offending substances; no ale, beer, nor wine, but a little brandy and water at dinner; gentle exercise, and the treatment directed under the head of Dyspepsia.

The Pulse.—As the Heart is the great central organ of circulation, and sympathizes with all the changes which take place in the system at large, it follows that the Pulse must be an important guide to those whose investigations are directed to the discovery of the ailments which cause functional and other derangements. All should, therefore, make themselves acquainted with the language of the Pulse, which may easily be felt by the fore and middle fingers, pressed slightly on the upper and under side of the wrist, about an inch above the lower joint of the thumb, where the pulsating artery lies. The beats may then be distinctly counted, and a little practice will render the detection of any irregularity or difference of force easy. With a healthy man, in the prime of life, there will be about seventy-two beats in a minute, that is supposing him to be quiet and unexcited. Any great bodily exertion, or mental emotion, will render the pulse more rapid. With children, where there is a great activity both of body and mind, the arterial action will be accelerated. We give the above as a general average. Age has a great influence in the frequency of the pulse. M. Quetelet gives the following as a scale of averages : — At birth, 136 per minute; at 5 years old, 88 ; at from 10 to 15 years, 78 ; at from 15 to 25 years, 69 ; at from 25 to 30 years, 71 ; at from 30 to 56 years, 70.

LIVER.—This is the largest glandular apparatus in the body, and one of its most important offices is to secrete the bile. Having this important duty to perform, it is of the utmost consequence that the Liver should be kept free from disturbing agencies, so that it may be in a proper condition for the discharge of its functions. The evil to which it is most liable is a disturbance of its circulation, causing either active or passive congestion, both of which are by no means uncommon conditions of the organ ; in the former case, there will be an increase in the flow of bile ; in the latter case, probably a decrease, or an altered state of the secretion. Sometimes an inflammation of the organ occurs; this is most common in hot climates ; it is called, in scientific lan-

guage, *Hepatitis;* in this disease we have suspension of the secretion altogether, and a softening or hardening of the substance of the Liver, or the formation of abscesses, according to the degree and nature of the disease.

Active Congestion of the Liver may be a consequence of an irritated state of its tissues, owing, probably, to the retention in the blood of the materials which ought to have been taken up by the kidneys, the skin, or some other excretory organ ; or it may be owing to the pressure of too much carbonaceous matter in the food; or there may be some local cause, some organic disease of the Liver itself. Either of these will tend to an excessive secretion of bile, and cause what are called bilious disorders of the stomach.

Passive Congestion of the Liver is usually the result of some mechanical impediment to the due supply of blood to the organ, or to its return from thence ; the mischief may be an impeded action of the heart, or a defective operation of the functions of the lungs ; or it may be caused by continued pressure upon the seat of the Liver, such as results from leaning at a desk, or remaining in a stooping position ; persons of sedentary habits are likely to be affected in this way. It may be merely what is called " a sluggish Liver ;" there is a diminution in the quantity of the bile, but no alteration of its quality. In the more severe forms of Passive Congestion, however, the bile, after its secretion has been suspended for a time, becomes acrid and plentiful, causing, when it passes into the intestines, much constitutional disturbance.

The *symptoms* of Congestion are generally great uneasiness in the right side, and a dull, heavy pain near to the shoulder-blade of that side ; if *active*, as before observed, the bile will be plentiful, coloring the evacuations, and producing often a bitter taste in the mouth, and leading sometimes to *Jaundice*; if *passive*, there is also the same uneasiness and pain in the region of the Liver, with a diminished flow of bile, or a changed condition of it, as before described; and after a while there is probably *acute inflammation* set up, which generally seizes on the substance of the Liver, and involves the whole, or only a part of it; most commonly the former is the case.

In the acute stages of inflammation there is pain in the right side, which is increased on pressure, or when a deep breath is drawn; there is usually, too, quick breathing, often a cough, but not always either of these. Nearly always there is pain in the right shoulder, and more or less of yellowness of the eyes, and, indeed, of the whole skin; occasionally absolute jaundice; the urine is high colored, and the fauces either pale and clayey, or tinged with greenish-yellow bile; vomiting, too, is sometimes a symptom.

Treatment of acute Liver inflammation should be active measures of depletion to prevent the formation of abscesses. If the system will bear it, there should be Cupping or Leeching over the seat of the organ, to be followed up with Hot Bran Poultices, and afterwards by a Blister, the latter to be several times repeated, if required; the bowels should be freely opened, and the system reduced by Calomel combined with Colocynth, or some other active purgative, to be followed by a saline aperient mixture, as under: Epsom Salts, 6 drams; Liquor of Acetate of Ammonia, 1 ounce; Tartrate of Potash, 2 grains; Wine of Colchicum, 1 dram; Camphor Mixture, sufficient to make 6 ounces; 1 ounce to be taken every four hours. The Calomel to be kept up for some time in small doses, combined with Opium, if the pain is violent. When there is reason to believe that suppuration has taken place, the treatment must be altered, and nourishing food and tonics given with mineral acids, such as the Muriatic with Gentian.

For Chronic Inflammation of the Liver : — Leptandrin, 1 dram; Podophyllin, 1 scruple; Apocynin, 1 scruple; Extract Nux Vomica, 6 grains; Castile Soap, 1 dram; make 30 pills,

take one every night; a continued use of this, and daily sponging the chest and bowels with water, in which a little Nitric and Muriatic Acid has been mixed, following up the same with vigorous friction over the parts, will gradually result in a cure

Inflammation of the Spleen.—The symptoms of this disease are much the same as Inflammation of the Liver, except that the spleen is on the left side, while the liver is on tne right side. The treatment for this disease, both in its acute and chronic form, should be the same as for Inflammation of the Liver

JAUNDICE. — A disease proceeding from an obstruction of the flow of bile in the liver, and characterized by a yellow color in the skin.

The peculiar effects which we notice in Jaundice are occasioned by the absorption of bile into the circulation, owing to some impediment to its passage in the usual way from the liver. The most common obstructions are *Gall-stones*, tumors which press upon the duct; or spasm, causing constriction of the same, may also be the cause; and sometimes strong mental emotion. In this disease we notice that the white of the eye acquires a yellow color, varying from the slightest tinge to that of gold; the whole of the skin of the face, too, and sometimes of other parts of the body, assumes the same tint; the stools become white and chalky - looking, and the urine, and sometimes also the perspiration, is tinged with bile.

A loathing of food, sour stomach, bad taste in the mouth, disinclination to move about, sleepiness, especially after dinner, and often a giddiness when stooping, are peculiar features.

Of itself, this is not a dangerous disease; but, as symptomatic of organic mischief going on somewhere, it should be viewed with fear, and have immediate medical attention.

Treatment.—Begin with an emetic, then take equal parts of Wild Cherry Bark, Bayberry Bark, Barberry Bark, Prickly Ash Bark, and Horse Radish

Root, say 1 ounce of each, well bruised, and steep all night in 4 pints of Cider: take a little of it after each meal; the more vegetables and ripe fruits the better. Acid drinks should be used. Nitric and Muriatic Acid mixed with Water will do well; and the same mixture for a sponge bath every morning is invaluable in this complaint, especially if vigorous friction precedes or follows it. An occasional warm bath is a great help. This treatment, if persevered in, will eradicate it from the system.

Inflammation of the Stomach.—There is generally pain after eating, and sometimes the meals are vomited up; urine is scanty, and high colored. *Treatment.*—Leeches to the pit of the stomach, followed by fomentations, cold iced water for drink, bowels to be evacuated by clysters; abstinence from all food except cold gruel, milk and water, or tea. Avoid excesses, and condiments.

Indigestion — Dyspepsia generally begins with pain in the stomach soon after eating; an irregular appetite; after a large meal there is pain and nervousness, restlessness, and sometimes vomiting, or belching up of sour wind; a clear fluid, called water-brash, rises, and runs from the mouth; a feeling of emptiness and great weakness at the pit of the stomach, a bad taste in the mouth, headache, heartburn, and sometimes palpitation; the bowels are irregular, sometimes the food passes off in an undigested state.

The great cause of Dyspepsia is the food not being well chewed, but eaten too fast; this generally leads to eating too much, so that the stomach is overloaded, and digestion cannot proceed, because it cannot be well churned, neither can the gastric juice permeate the compacted mass. To this may be added drinking largely, especially cold water, at meals, so that the food is washed down instead of being well-chewed and mixed with the saliva. *Treatment.* — The bowels must be regulated, kept open. This can often

be done by eating food of a laxative nature, such as bran bread, etc., but generally some gentle medicine is required. Mix 4 ounces sweet Tincture of Rhubarb, and 2 drams Bicarbonate of Soda, and take a tablespoonful after dinner. The acidity of the stomach may be removed by taking a teaspoonful of Carbonate of Magnesia in a little water when required. Plenty of out-door exercise is necessary, and it should be of such a character as to engage the mind. The brain *must* have rest. Care and anxiety *must* sometimes be laid aside.

Water-Brash is a term applied to a discharge of thin watery fluid from the mouth, when the stomach is empty. It comes up about ½ an ounce at the time, with acid eructations, but without much straining, sometimes to the extent of a pint. It is a symptom of irritable and neuralgic indigestion, or a form of *Dyspepsia*, and also of some of the more malignant diseases of the stomach. Persons who take much oatmeal are peculiarly subject to this affection. Why they are so, has not yet been clearly ascertained. *Treatment.* — Bismuth, a full dose, will generally afford relief; if there is pain, Morphine should also be taken, or some other anodyne. After the water has ceased to flow, some stomachic should be given, with a mineral acid. A mixture like this will be best:—Infusion of Cascarilla, 6 ounces; dilute Sulphuric Acid, 3 drams; Tincture of Cardamums, 2 drams: take a sixth part twice a day. Attention should be paid to the action of the liver before administering these remedies; perhaps a little mild mercurial, such as Blue Pill, or Grey Powder, had better be given in any case, about a couple of doses, combined with Rhubarb.

Vomiting, or Nausea. — A term commonly applied to sickness of the stomach, a loathing or tendency to reject, without actual vomiting. The sensation of nausea is usually referred to the stomach, and is no doubt commonly due to causes connected with that organ only; yet very frequently the feeling is sympathetic, having its origin in the brain or the nervous system. Thus we know that a severe blow on the head, a dislocation, or other injury to any part of the body, attended with severe pain, will occasion Nausea; so will horrible and disgusting sights and sounds and odors, or anything which affects the brain through the medium of the senses. The Nausea of pregnancy, too, appears to be purely sympathetic, and the action of emetics must be attributed rather to their influence on the nervous system, than directly on the stomach; for it has been found that they act as well when injected into the veins as when swallowed. So we find that gall-stones in the kidneys, tumors in the womb, and many other diseased conditions of the various organs, give rise to a feeling of sickness — all showing that this feeling is, in many cases, merely sympathetic. The relaxed state of the nervous, and consequently of the muscular system, which attends Nausea, is favorable to the performance of certain surgical operations, such as the reduction of dislocations, ruptures, or constrictions. Hence surgeons, previous to such, often produce it artificially by the administration of tartar emetic.

The proper *remedies* for Nausea, of course, will depend upon the causes. If it proceeds from affection of the brain, but little can be done to relieve it; if from disorder of the stomach, free vomiting, which may be easily excited by warm water and a little Ipecacuanha, or merely tickling the fauces with a feather, or a brisk purgative, will afford relief; if occasioned by some nervous shock to the system, a glass of Sherry Wine or a little Brandy, or some other nervous stimulant. In any case, effervescing draughts made with Carbonate of Soda and Lemon-Juice will be grateful, and probably effectual; if other means fail, a Mustard Plaster to the pit of the stomach may be tried; or Creosote, in drop doses, rubbed down

with a little Sugar or Gum; or a mix-ture like this—Hydrocyanic Acid, 12 drops; Acetate of Morphine, 1 grain; Carbonate of Soda, 1 dram; in Water, 6 ounces: take a tablespoonful every three hours. A drop of the above acid, or of Creosote in Soda Water, is also likely to be of service. A reclining position is best for the patient; and perfect quietude, both of body and mind, especially when the affection has a nervous origin.

Inflammation of the Bowels.— Leeches, blisters, fomentations, hot baths applied to the belly, the warm bath once in two days; the diet should be arrowroot, gruel, or sago; after this mutton broth, boiled chicken, etc., fresh air and gentle exercise as soon as the strength will permit; to move the bowels, make a clyster of 1½ pints of Gruel, a tablespoonful of Castor Oil, one tablespoonful of Salt, and a lump of Butter, mix and inject slowly: one-third of this is enough for an infant.

COLIC.—The *symptoms* of Colic, in general, are a painful distension of the lower region of the belly, with a twisting round of the navel, and very commonly vomiting, costiveness, and spasms. Among the most frequent causes may be named worms, poisonous or unwholesome substances, long undigested food, redundancy of vitiated bile, internal gout and rheumatism, intense cold, hard or acid fruits, or vegetables.

The *treatment* must depend greatly upon the cause; thus, in *Bilious* Colic, where there is loss of appetite, bitter taste in the mouth, great thirst, fever, costiveness, and vomiting, with spasmodic pains, mercurials and purgatives must be administered, with effervescing draughts, fomentations, and friction. If the symptoms become violent, and inflammation of the intestines appears likely, bleeding by the lancet or leeches may be resorted to, especially if the patient be young and plethoric. In *Flatulent* Colic, where there is costiveness, pain, soreness, and griping of the bowels, rumbling, and distension, with inclination to vomit, and coldness of the extremities, the administration of aromatic cordials, with opiates and purgatives, warm applications to the stomach, and antispasmodic clysters ejected every three or four hours; bleeding, as above, if inflammation is threatened. In *Hysteric Colic*, where there is nausea, spasms, costiveness, and great dejection of spirits, the proper course will be laxatives, if required, with Spirits of Ammonia, Sulphuric Ether, and, after the bowels have been evacuated, Camomile Tea, or other bitter infusion, with a little anodyne. Turpentine clysters have also been found useful.

Although Colic is properly a painful affection of the colon, *without* inflammation or fever, yet it is frequently accompanied with febrile and inflammatory symptoms, and often results in *inflammation of the bowels*. It may generally be distinguished from actual inflammation by the spasmodic contraction of the abdomen, the absence, or trifling degree of fever and insensibility to pressure, and also by the state of the pulse.

For *Lead*, or *Painters' Colic*, so called because it formerly prevailed in cider counties, where leaden vessels were much used in the manufacture of the beverage, the same general remedies may be used as for other forms of colic: for the Palsy, arising from the absorption of lead, which is generally confined to the wrists, galvanism, friction, and shampooing, with Bath, or other chalybeate waters. Those engaged in the manufacture of lead, or in occupations in which one or other of its preparations are frequently handled, may generally escape its baneful effects by strict attention to cleanliness; they should never take their meals where they work, or with unwashed hands. Let them eat fat meat, and butter, and acidulous drinks, especially those rendered so by Sulphuric Acid. From the first attack of Lead Colic, patients generally recover; but unless they change their occupations, or observe the above precautions with scrupulous care, the attacks are repeated, each time with greater violence, and they become, eventually, miserable cripples.

CONSTIPATION. — Habitual confinement of the bowels, which is produced from want of tone in the muscular coat of the stomach, or a tendency to absorb the fluid elements of the fœces, so that they are left in too solid a form for the muscles to act upon. The latter is more commonly the case.

Treatment. — The observance of a regular period of evacuating the bowels, which is most proper in the morning after breakfast. The use of mild aperients, brown bread instead of white. There should be an entire change in the dietary for a few days while taking opening medicine. Leptandrin, 1 dram; Podophyllin, 1 scruple; Apocynin, 1 scruple; Extract Nux Vomica, 6 grains; Castile Soap, 1 dram: mix, and make 30 pills, take 1 pill every night. Sometimes an injection of cold water once a day, for a week or two, will cure costiveness without medicine.

PILES. — The troublesome disease so called, consists of tumors situated on the verge of the anus, or fundament, which tumors are formed by distension of the veins at the extremity of the rectum, or lower bowel; they are usually about the size of a bean, sometimes much larger, and are caused by the distension of the veins with congested blood. When there is an action of the bowels they are forced down, and if there is much constipation and straining, or much exertion necessary, so as to irritate and inflame the parts, they are likely to be greatly distended, so that they cannot be pressed back again; in this case they become very large and painful, and eventually perhaps burst, to the great relief of the patient; or they may run into abscesses, and, it may be, lay the foundation of a fistula.

Piles may be either "blind" or "bleeding;" the latter is the case when the veins within the bowels become much swollen, of a red color, and uneven surface, having their walls so thin that the slightest effort to relieve the bowels causes them to bleed freely. The former is when the swellings become filled with a fibrinous deposit from the blood, so that they form tumors and excrescences outside the anus; sometimes these, although inconvenient, are not very troublesome otherwise. If the cause which produced them be removed, they will be likely to remain quiescent for a time; but strong purgative medicines, a cold, or too much exertion, may stimulate them into activity, then they become inflamed and very painful; then we have what is called "A Fit of the Piles." Persons with torpid livers, or with whom the venous circulation is sluggish, are those most subjected to Piles, which are no doubt the result of passive congestion of the veins about the rectum; but it will usually be found that the disease will not become fully developed unless there is also habitual constipation. The *treatment* should therefore be both local and general; the first directed to remove all obstacles to the proper action of the liver, and to cleanse the large bowels of matters which may press upon the veins, and impede the return of the blood from the lowest bowel, which is the seat of the disease. To this end we should give mild aperients, combined with alteratives, beginning with pills like these: Rhubarb, 1 dram; Ipecacuanha, ½ a dram; Blue Pill, 1 scruple: make into 24 pills, and take 2 every night until the motions become soft and sufficiently frequent, then 1 every other night. A stimulant will also be required, and Confection of Black Pepper is perhaps the best; or Ward's Paste, which is composed of Sulphur, Copaiba, Balsam, and Spices; about a teaspoonful of the former, or from 10 to 15 grains of the latter, may be taken night and morning. Should the bowels not be moved sufficiently by these means, take Confection of Senna, commonly called Lenative Electuary, 3 ounces; Sulphur, 1 ounce; Jalap and Cream of Tartar,

of each 2 drams, and Ginger, 1 dram, with Syrup enough to make it up into a soft Electuary. Dose, a teaspoonful twice a day, or only every night, if too active.

The *local* treatment consists in injecting 2 or 3 ounces of cold water into the bowel just before the passing of a motion; this partly empties, and contracts the distended veins, and facilitates the passage of the fœces. Care should also be taken to press back within the sphincter ani, or muscular ring which guards the entrance of the bowel from the anus, every Pile which protrudes, as if suffered to remain outside, it will, by the pressure of the above muscle, become strangulated and inflamed. When the Piles are in this latter condition, they should be fomented with hot water, by means of a sponge, every four hours or so, and the recumbent position should be maintained as much as possible; leeches, also, may be applied to them, with a linseed poultice to encourage the bleeding. If there is inflammation of Piles within the sphincter ani, make an injection thus:—Dissolve in 8 ounces of boiling water, Acetate of Lead and Opium, of each ½ a dram, and of this lotion, when cool, throw up into the bowel with a small syringe just ½ an ounce, by measure, after a motion, but not more than twice in twenty-four hours; and only in cases where the bleeding is profuse, should this powerful application be used. For internal Piles, also, leeches may be applied with advantage; they can be applied externally, and followed by warm fomentations, or a hip-bath. When Piles first show themselves, before there is much inflammation, or after this has subsided, an astringent ointment should be applied with the finger, as far as it can be thrust, night and morning. The Compound Gall Ointment is best for this purpose, or one prepared thus: Gallic Acid, 1 dram; Powdered Opium, ½ dram; Goulard's Extract (a saturated solution of the Subacetate of·Lead), 10 drops; Lard, 1 ounce.

DIARRHŒA.—Looseness of the

bowels. This is a very common disorder, arising from a variety of *causes*, foremost among which may be mentioned suppressed perspiration, a sudden chill or cold applied to the body, acid fruits, or any indigestible food, oily or putrid substances, deficiency of bile, increased secretion of mucus, worms, strong purgative medicines, gout or rheumatism turned inwards, etc.

The *symptoms* are frequent and copious discharges of feculent matter, accompanied usually with griping and flatulency; there is weight and uneasiness in the lower belly, which is relieved for a time on the discharge taking place; there is nausea, often vomiting; a pale countenance, sometimes sallow; a bitter taste in the mouth, with thirst and dryness of the throat; the tongue is furred and yellow, indicating bile in the alimentary canal; the skin is dry and harsh, and if the disease is not checked, great emaciation ensues.

The *treatment* must depend in some degree on the cause. The removal of the exciting matter, by means of an emetic, or aperient medicines, will, however, be a safe proceeding at first. If the Diarrhœa be caused by obstructed perspiration or exposure to cold, nauseating doses of Antimonial, or Ipecacuanha Wine, may be given every three or four hours, the feet put into a warm bath, and the patient be well covered up in bed. When the case is obstinate, resort may be had to the vapor bath, making a free use of diluents and demulcents. Where there is acidity of the stomach, denoted by griping pains and flatulency, take Chalk Mixture, with Aromatic Confection, and other anti-acid absorbents or alkalies, such as Carbonate of Potash, with Spirits of Ammonia, and Tincture of Opium, or some other anodyne; if from putrid or otherwise unwholesome food, the proper course, after the removal of the offending matter, is to give absorbents, in combination with Opium, or if these fail, acid and an anodyne. The following is

an efficacious formula: Diluted Sulphuric Acid, 2 drams; Tincture of Opium, ½ a dram; water, 6 ounces: take a tablespoonful every two hours. When the looseness proceeds from acrid or poisonous substances, warm diluent drinks should be freely administered, to keep up vomiting, previously excited by an emetic; for this purpose thin fat broth answers well; a purge of Castor Oil should also be given, and after its operation, small doses of Morphine, or some other preparation of Opium.

The following prescription was used by the troops during the Mexican war with great success:

Laudanum ....ounces 2
Spirits of Camphor............. .... " 2
Essence of Peppermint................... " 2
Hoffman's Anodyne...................... " 2
Tincture of Cayenne Pepper...........drams 2
Tincture of Ginger.....................ounces 1

Mix all together. Dose: a teaspoonful in a little water, or a half teaspoonful repeated in an hour afterward in a tablespoonful of brandy. This preparation will check Diarrhœa in ten minutes, and abate other premonitory symptoms of cholera immediately. In cases of cholera, it has been used with great success to restore reaction by outward application.

When repelled, gout or rheumatism is the cause, warm fomentations, cataplasms, blisters to the extremities, and stimulant purges, such as Tincture of Rhubarb, to be followed by absorbents with anodynes. If worms are the exciting cause, their removal must be first attempted, but drastic purgatives, often given for the purpose, are dangerous; in this case, Turpentine and Castor Oil, 1 dram of the first and 6 of the last, may be recommended. The Diarrhœa which often occurs in childhood during teething, should not be suddenly checked, nor at all, unless it prevails to a hurtful extent; if necessary to stop it, give first a dose of Mercury and Chalk, from 2 to 4 or 6 grains, according to age, and then Powder of Prepared Chalk, Cinnamon, and Rhubarb, about 2 grains of each every four hours. Diarrhœa sometimes attacks pregnant women, and, in this case, its progress ought to be arrested as quickly as possible. In all cases of looseness of the bowels it is best to avoid hot thin drinks, unless given for a specific purpose; the food, too, should be simple and easy of digestion; Milk, with Cinnamon boiled in it, thickened with Rice or Arrowroot, is good; vegetables, salt meat, suet puddings and pies are not; if there is much exhaustion, a little cool brandy and water may be now and then taken. When Diarrhœa is stopped, astringent tonics, with aromatics, should be given to restore the tone of the stomach.

This disease may be distinguished from *Dysentery* by being unattended by either inflammation, fever, contagion, or that constant inclination to go to stool without a discharge which is common in the latter disease, in which the matter voided is sanguineous and putrid, while that in Diarrhœa is simply feculent and alimentary.

DYSENTERY.—Inflammation of the mucous membrane of the large intestines, causing frequent evacuations of a peculiar fœtid matter, consisting of a large proportion of mucus, generally more or less mixed with blood. *Flux*, or *Bloody Flux*, according as the discharges are free from, or deeply tinged with, the sanguineous fluid, are common names for this disease, which some French writers term *Colite*.

The *causes* of the inflammatory action may be a specific contagion; great moisture in the atmosphere succeeded by sudden heat; putrid or otherwise unwholesome food; noxious vapors and exhalations; ulceration of the colon, resulting in spasmodic constriction.

The usual *symptoms* are cold shiverings and other febrile signs. There may be at the outset unusual costiveness, with flatulency, severe griping, and frequent inclination to go to stool: then comes loss of appetite, nausea, and vomiting, an increase of the febrile heat, copious evacuations as above described, which reduce the strength, and cause great emaciation.

The proper *treatment* will be first with regard to the accompanying fever; if it be of the inflammatory kind, and the patient can bear it, there must be blood-letting, antiphlogistic medicines, and low diet; but very commonly the fever assumes a putrid character, in which case it must be treated as *Typhus*. If it becomes *intermittent*, tonics must be resorted to, as prescribed under that head. With more immediate reference to the disease itself, the seat of which is the intestines, an emetic consisting of 20 grains of Ipecacuanha Powder and 1 grain of Tartarized Antimony, followed by copious drinks of warm water, should be given as soon as the vomiting ceases, a powder, composed of 1 scruple of Powdered Rhubarb and 2 grains of Calomel, or a full dose of Castor Oil, or some refrigerant cathartic, such as Epsom, or Glauber's Salts. Ipecacuanha alone, in doses not sufficiently large to produce vomiting, say 5 grains, frequently given, often acts well as a cathartic in Dysentery. After this administer emollient glysters about three times a day, with Laudanum about a dram in every third one, or glysters of Mutton-broth and Arrowroot. For drinks, which should be cold, or nearly so, give solutions of Gum Arabic, or Milk, decoctions of Linseed, Salop, or Barley, or thin Arrowroot. If these do not stop the Flux in twenty-four hours or so try the following mixture:—Tincture of Opium and Nitrate of Potash, of each 1 dram; Antimonial Wine 2 drams; Mint Water, to make 6 ounces: take a tablespoonful every two or'three hours. When the disease has yet more advanced, and the frequency of the stools appears to proceed chiefly from a weakened and relaxed state of the bowels, tonics and astringents should be given—Arnica Bark, Calumba, Cascarilla, Catechu, Logwood, Kino, Quassia, are among the best; Lime Water is also good, and an acidulous mixture composed thus :—Diluted Nitrous Acid 2 drams, Laudanum ½ dram, Water 6 ounces ; take a sixth part every four hours. This also will be found efficient — Tincture of Catechu, Confection of Opium, and Aromatic Confection, of each 2 drams, Cinnamon Water, 6 ounces ; take two tablespoonfuls every four hours. Where there is much debility, Brandy and Water may be given ; but neither this nor Laudanum will do for the febrile stages.

Persons residing in warm climates are especially subject to Dysentery. Those who are recovering from its attacks should be careful to avoid exposure to cold or damp, or any sudden atmospheric changes ; to be regular in their mode of living, and to go warmly clothed, as they are very liable to a recurrence of the attack.

Cholera Morbus is often preceded by heartburn, a sour taste in the mouth, and flatulency ; there is vomiting and purging of a decidedly bilious character ; griping and distension of the stomach, cramps, and ultimately convulsions ; clammy sweats, difficulty in breathing, an anxious expression of face, constant hiccough, and if relief is not quickly obtained, death.

Treatment. — 3 drams of Spirits of Camphor ; 3 drams of Laudanum ; 3 drams of Oil of Turpentine ; 30 drops of Oil of Peppermint. Mix, and take a teaspoonful in a glass of weak Brandy and Water for diarrhœa, and a tablespoonful in weak Brandy and Water for cholera.

Lose no time in sending for medical attendance when attacked, and inform the doctor of what has been taken.

Medical men assert, and experience shows, that this is an excellent remedy and well worth being kept on hand by every family.

Asiatic or Malignant Cholera, with which we first became acquainted in this country in the autumn of 1831, is a more severe form of the disease than either of the above ; it very commonly comes on without any premonitory warning whatever, and the patient is a corpse in a few hours.

Cold perspiration, with prostration of strength, vomiting, and purging, but not of bile in this case, but a thin, colorless, odorless fluid, like rice-water ; then come the dreadful cramps, seizing on the calves of the legs, the thighs, the fingers, the toes, and all muscular parts ; the body is bent, the limbs twisted, the face becomes cadaverous and corpse-like, with sharp and contracted features, sunken eyes, with a dark circle round them, blue lips, and a tongue of leaden hue ; the look wild and . pitiful, the breathing hurried and difficult, the voice low and husky, the form seems to shrink and dwindle visibly, the pulse, at first small and weak, becomes rapidly more so, until its feeble beatings can scarcely, if at all, be detected ; a smell, like that of a charnel-house,. is exhaled from the body, which loses its natural warmth, as more withered and ghastly becomes the face ; and the arms and hands, wrinkled like those of a washerwoman, with livid finger-nails, fall helplessly at the side, and the weak, wailing voice sinks to a whisper in its frequent calls for drink, to quench the intolerable thirst. To the last, there appears to be a wandering kind of consciousness, but no power to express a wish or will ; there is utter indifference in that forlorn look which the sufferer occasionally casts around, and no ray of pleasant recognition lights up the eye when it rests upon familiar faces. Then comes the perfect insensibility of collapse, and soon the feeble flickering light of life is quenched ; unless, as is sometimes the case, re-action sets in ; then the pulse begins to flutter, like a bird escaping from the snare, the skin to get warm again, the dim eyes to brighten, the face to assume a more natural hue, the flaccid muscles to become more tense, the pulse is again perceptible, and it may be seen at a glance that the crisis is past, and the vital energies of the patient have rallied, and are likely to carry him through this imminent danger.

With regard to the *treatment* of

Cholera, there is much disagreement among medical men, and so rapid is the progress of the disease, that there really is little time for the operation of remedies. At times, when it is likely to be prevalent, particular attention should be paid to the state of the bowels, and the slightest tendency to looseness should at once be checked. Chalk Mixture, with a little Aromatic Confection added, taken after each loose motion; add 5 or 10 drops of Laudanum to each dose, and take milk and farinaceous diet; avoid unripe fruits, hard puddings, pastry, and any indigestible food; live temperately, but not too abstemiously, so as to weaken the system; be careful as to the purity of the water drunk, and to avoid chills, or whatever tends to lower the standard of health. If the bowels are confined, do not take saline aperients, but such as are of a warm, stimulating character, such as Rhubarb, combined with Magnesia, mixed in Cinnamon or Peppermint Water. If the more severe symptoms above described come on, obtain medical help immediately, if possible; should it not be so, use every effort to keep up the temperature of the body by hot applications, apply friction to the muscular parts most affected with cramps; hot Bran Bags, with Turpentine sprinkled over them, are good, Mustard Poultices and strong Liniments. Let the patient gratify his intense thirst with copious draughts of cold water, in every quart of which has been dissolved 1 drain of Common Salt, the same of Chlorate of Soda, and 20 grains of Chlorate of Potash; administer every quarter of an hour, by placing it upon the tongue, a powder containing 1 grain of Calomel and 1 grain of Opium; and about every half hour a draught, with 20 drops of Sulphuric Ether, or 5 drops of Chloroform, with 10 drops of Laudanum, or Camphor Mixture.

Some physicians recommend warm stimulating drinks, such as Brandy and Water, with cataplasms of Opium and Camphor, blisters to the stomach, and antispasmodic clysters.

Nothing can show more clearly how little is really understood of the real nature of this terrible disease, than the diverse opinions entertained with regard to the proper remedial measures: it is indeed the pestilence that walketh in darkness, and whether contagious, as some contend, or infectious, as others, or both, as seems likely, it warns us to be prepared for the summons that may come at any moment.

WORMS. — There are several kinds of these troublesome parasites which infest the intestinal canals of man. Those most generally found there are the *Ascarides*, small Thread Worms, varying from the eighth of an inch to one and a half inches in length; they are mostly in the rectum, or last gut. The *Lumbrici* are long round Worms, from two or three to ten or more inches in length; they are of a yellowish-white or brownish-red color, and are usually found in the small intestines. The *Tænia*, or Tape-worm, occupies mostly the upper part of the intestinal tube, but is occasionally found in every part of it. There are two sorts of Tænia: one, the commonest, frequently grows to an enormous length (as much as thirty or forty feet), and generally comes away entire; the other passes off in one or more joints, which resemble pumpkin seeds.

As may be expected, from the highly organized and sensitive parts which they occupy, Worms cause great constitutional derangement, resulting in all kinds of bad symptoms, more especially affecting the stomach and head; hence we have in these cases variable appetite, sometimes deficient, at others absolutely voracious; pains in the stomach, fœtid breath, nausea, headache, vertigo and giddiness, irritation about the nose and anus; frequently cough and disturbed rest, and a disordered state of the bowels. In children, we have a hard and tumid belly, with slimy stools, and sometimes convulsive fits. Occasionally in adults, as well as children, Worms give rise to epileptic fits, and cause great emaciation.

An excessive use of fruit and vegetables, or sugar, or any other highly nutritive substance, favors the generation of Worms, which most frequently infest those of a relaxed habit, with weak digestive organs; the greater indulgence in sweets, and too common abstinence from salt, appears to be the main reason why children are most troubled with them.

Worms are more common in some countries and districts than others, and it has been noticed that they are particularly so in parts where much milk and cheese are taken. It has been asserted that a habit of eating meat in a partially raw state will be pretty sure to produce them.

Treatment. — This must be of a tonic and strengthening character; such medicines as tend to invigorate the system are the best, and especially those which act upon the stomach and intestines; Salt, preparations of Iron, Sulphur, and Camphor, are those which may be principally depended on, in conjunction with an avoidance of vegetable and saccharine food. About 1 ounce of common Salt dissolved in nearly ½ a pint of water, and taken in the morning fasting, once a week for some little time, will generally bring away any kind of Worms, if the plan is followed out, especially if a pill containing 1 grain of Calomel and 3 of Extract of Colycinth, be taken at bedtime the previous night. At the same time should be taken a strengthening mixture, composed of Sulphate of Iron, 12 grains; Infusion of Quassia, 12 ounces; Tincture of Ginger, 2 drams. Dose, two tablespoonfuls twice a day. Or else, Sulphate of Iron and Quinine, each 12 grains; dilute Sulphuric Acid, 24 minims; Cinnamon Water, 12 ounces: dose as above.

For Tape-worm, Castor Oil and Spirits of Turpentine is often given; about ½ an ounce of the latter, and 2 drams of the former, is the dose. It should be taken fasting, and may be repeated two or three times, at intervals of two or three days or so. Pomegranate Bark is a very old and useful remedy for this kind of worm: the mode of administration is to boil 2 ounces of the bruised bark in 1½ pints of water down to a pint, the whole of which is to be taken in the course of the morning, fasting, in four draughts, with intervals of half an hour between each. Should this not be effectual the first day, it may be repeated two, three, or even four times. Another remedy is the Oil of Male Fern. Rue, Tansy, Tin Filings, Tobacco, and a variety of other substances, have likewise been recommended, but those mentioned appear to be the most efficacious. For the species called Lumbrici, the bursting pods of the *Cowhage* are no doubt useful; and for the small white Thread Worm, so frequently infesting the last gut of children, about ¼ pint of Limewater should be injected once a day, and an active aperient pill, or powder, or a dose of Castor Oil, be given once a week. Should this not effect the desired object, inject a solution of Salt in Water, or a strong decoction of worm seed.

Although Salt is recommended as a remedy for Worms, yet salt meat is not good for persons so troubled: plenty of it should be eaten with fresh animal food, and the few vegetables that may be taken; but it is better to avoid these altogether for a time, as well as fruit, and live chiefly upon bread and farinaceous puddings.

Diseases of the Kidney, or renal diseases, as they are sometimes called, are generally difficult of treatment; the most common are those which result in the formation of *calculi*, or stone, which is sometimes retained in the pelvis, where, by constant deposition, it increases so as to completely fill that, and the calices which open into it, causing a stoppage in the flow of the secretion, and a most dangerous state of constitutional derangement. Generally, however, the stone passes through the ureter into the bladder, producing in its passage violent spasmodic pains in the loins, with nausea, and generally hæmorrhage, etc. With this we commonly get inflammation of the Kidneys, from which abscesses and other morbid alterations are likely to result. From chronic inflammation appears generally to arise that alteration in the structure of the kidneys known as *Bright's Disease*, the chief characteristics of which are the deposition of a pale yellowish substance in the interstices of the organs, leading to a granular or tuberculated form of the surface, and a decreased vascularity of the whole organ, whose diseased condition is indicated by a dull, heavy pain in the loins, a hard pulse, and a secretion of so large a quantity of albumen in the urine, that it coagulates on being heated, or with the addition of nitric acid. This condition of the Kidneys is sometimes the result of hard drinking; it sometimes follows scarlet fever, and usually produces dropsy, in which case we have a bloated expression of countenance. Suppression of urine may be the ultimate result of obstruction of calculus in the ureter, or it may occur as an idiopathic disease; in either case it is a condition of great danger. In common with other organs, the Kidneys are also subject to various morbid growths and depositions, such as cancer, fungus, hæmatodes, melanosis, tubercle, etc.; but the diagnosis of all chronic affections of these organs is very difficult, owing to the similarity in their symptoms: the dull, heavy pain in the loins, dropsy, and sometimes hæmaturia, being common to all. We can, therefore, scarcely venture to indicate any particular line of treatment. A medical man should be consulted as soon as possible when there is reason to suspect all is not right with this important organ, to which, we may just observe, that injury often results from long-continued and violent exercise on horseback; also from collections of hardened stools in the colon, as well as from retrocedent gout, a blow, or violent exercise of any kind.

For Inflammation of the Kidneys, an infusion made from Buchu Leaves, Queen of the Meadow, Foxglove, or other diuretics, may be taken. The bowels should be kept open by some gentle medicine, such as Senna Tea or Magnesia.

Bright's Disease. — This is a particular disease of the kidneys — the distinguishing mark of which is the presence of the serum of the blood in the urine (which coagulates on the application of heat; there may be only sufficient to cloud the fluid, or enough to form nearly a solid mass). The causes of this disease, which was first described by Dr. Bright (hence its name), are various. It may be severe cold, repressed perspiration, or immoderate use of ardent spirits; and it not uncommonly follows Scarlet Fever. It is usually accompanied by febrile symptoms, and dropsical swellings of the face and extremities, and eventually of the body also. The best *treatment* is cupping in the loins, hot baths, and purging with Calomel and Jalap. A mixture as under should also be given: Sweet Spirits of Nitre, 2 drams; Liquor of Acetate of Ammonia, 1 ounce; Camphor Mixture, 7 ounces: take two tablespoonfuls three times a day. Low diet, and an avoidance of alcoholic stimulants.

Inflammation of the Bladder may be either acute or chronic; in the former case it is likely to be the result of a catarrh, which, after affecting the mucous membrane of the throat, nose, and chest, acts upon that of the urinary organs. If not from this, it may proceed from some accidental or local cause. But however this may be, the symptoms are much the same. There is severe pain and a sense of tightness in the lower part of the abdomen, with a constant desire to pass urine, which comes out cloudy or milky, and deposits pus or mucus at the bottom of the vessel; there is often, too, a feeling of sickness, and generally more or less fever.

The *treatment* in this case will be to give at once about 5 grains of Calomel, following it up with a Rhubarb draught, or some other mild aperient;

the application of leeches to the lower part of the abdomen, with the use of a warm hip-bath, to encourage the bleeding, the bath to be continued daily, or twice a day, if necessary; the use of diluents, such as Barley Water, or Linseed Tea, and abstinence from all stimulating drinks whatever. These means, with a rigidly abstemious diet, and rest in a recumbent position, will generally reduce the inflammation in the course of a few days. Should they not, and should the patient be of a full habit of body, bleeding from the arm may be resorted to, and such other measures of depletion as may be necessary. The following is a good formula for a mixture: Nitrate of Potash and Tincture of Henbane, of each 2 drams; Liquor of Acetate of Ammonia and Mucilage of Acacia, of each 1 ounce; Camphor Mixture, 10 ounces: take 2 tablespoonfuls every four hours. Injection of the bladder with warm water, or some emollient fluid, such as Infusion of Linseed, is sometimes resorted to with good effect. The suppression of urine, and consequent distension of the bladder, will sometimes cause inflammation of that organ; or it may proceed from a calculus of considerable magnitude lodged within it. If the inflammation be chronic, leeches are seldom required; in other respects the treatment must be much the same as that above recommended. When this treatment does not afford relief, and the urine retains its acid quality, which may be known by its turning litmus paper red, 2½ grains of Calomel, with 3 grains of Opium, should be taken three times a day; if the urine is alkaline, and deposits mucus of a brownish color, the patient should take with each dose of the above mixtuie 15 minims of Wine of Colchicum; this is Sir R. Brodie's plan of treatment. Great care should be taken, when the patient is recovering, as to the diet and mode of living; a very slight excess in eating or drinking, or violent exertion, may bring on a relapse. It is well to take, for some little time, one of the following pills

twice a week : — Blue Pill, 12 grains : Ipecacuanha Powder, 3 grains; Acetous Extract of Colchicum, 6 grains : mix and make into 6 pills. An aperient draught of Compound Infusion of Senna, or of Rhubarb and Magnesia, should also be taken occasionally. If there is much debility, with griping and flatulency, a tablespoonful of Brandy in a glass of Soda Water will be a good accompaniment to the daily dinner.

Irritation of the Bladder. — It sometimes occurs during the latter stages of gonorrhœa that the patient is annoyed by a frequent desire to void his urine; gradually this desire becomes more urgent and continuous, returning as often as every ten or fifteen minutes; there is great pain during the passing of the water, and heat, extending up to the neck of the bladder; if this state of things continues the urine will be tinged with blood, and will deposit bloody mucus; this indicates *ulceration* of the organ, arising from the irritated state of the mucous membrane. The proper *treatment* in this case will be, to keep the bladder in a state of rest by the insertion of a short flexible catheter, retained in its place by a bandage carried between the thighs, through which the urine may escape as it collects. To allay the pain and irritation, Opium, in 1 or 2 grain doses, should be administered, and a suppository, composed of 5 or 6 grains of the same, introduced into the rectum; the bowels must be kept open by Castor Oil; and a blister applied to the pubes to produce counter-irritation, is likely to afford relief. A recumbent position should be maintained, warm hip-baths used, and an abstemious diet preserved, avoiding malt liquor and all kinds of stimulants. There is a plain distinction between this form of urinary disease and stone, or calculus, in the circumstance that, whereas with them the pain is most excruciating when the bladder is empty, it is most so with this when it is full. An irritable state of the bladder may be brought on by other causes than that above indicated — such as a too long retention of urine, excessive indulgence in venery, or spiritous liquors, etc. — but in all cases the treatment should be much the same, varied, of course, according to the constitution of the patient, and the exigencies of the particular case.

Paralysis of the Bladder may be caused by fever; it sometimes occurs in persons of advanced age, as well as in those affected with a paralytic affection; the organ loses its voluntary power to expel the urine, which must be drawn off by means of a catheter; general and uterine stimulants must be administered, especially blisters to the loins, and a pill, composed of 5 grains of Chio Turpentine, and a ¼ of a grain of Powdered Cantharides, given twice a day, is a mode of treatment which has been found effective. It has been observed that the urine, which on the introduction of the catheter to the patient in a horizontal position would not flow, has done so when he has been placed erect; a circumstance attributed to the pressure of the viscera upon the bladder.

DIABETES is characterized by a large discharge of urine, containing eventually, if not at first, a large proportion of saccharine and other matter. There is gradual emaciation, voracious appetite, great thirst, weakness, and disinclination to motion; the alimentary process is improperly performed, and thus the food taken does not yield its proper amount of nourishment, and constitutional derangement is the consequence.

Treatment. — The diet should be entirely animal food — all vegetable substances to be avoided — the bowels to be kept quietly open with pills of Aloes and Soap, emetics and diaphoretics occasionally administered, perhaps the compound Ipecacuanha Powder, 10 grains at bedtime, is the best; alkaline drinks, such as Soda Water, may be given with advantage, and blisters and issues applied to the regions of the kidneys, covering the skin with flannel, anointing it with

Camphorated Oil, using the warm bath and the flesh-brush, are also good, as are Chalybeate and Sulphurated Waters. Tonics, astringents, and stimulants will be of service, especially preparations of Iron with Tincture of Cantharides; if in the summer, sea-bathing, and anything which may serve to invigorate the system. Such is an outline of general treatment; of course, constitutional peculiarities require special and appropriate remedial measures, and of these only the professional adviser can judge.

Incontinence of Urine. — This is very common among children, and may be ascribed, generally, to weakness; although, in some cases, it is owing to want of care in the nurse or mother. It sometimes occurs in grown persons, especially in males, after an operation for stricture, or some disease of the urinary organs; and in females after childbirth; it may, then, be attributed to some mechanical defect which allows the urine to pass off as fast as it is secreted.

In children, the change occurring at puberty generally cures this complaint. Before this age, children should be used to make water just before going to bed, and give them but little drink. It is also a good plan to take the child out of bed late at night to make water: this, with some decided scolding if they should wet the bed, will often break up the habit, for it is generally only a habit. In adults, it arises from debility, or disease of the bladder.

The sponge bath, with friction after, should be used daily, an infusion of the *Trailing Arbutus* should be drank occasionally. Tincture of Buchu, or Tincture of Cantharides, in small doses, will be useful.

GRAVEL. — Crystalline sediments deposited in the bladder from the urine; when amorphous, that is, shapeless, irregular, and reducible to powder, they may be either red or pink, consisting chiefly of Lithate of Ammonia; or white, into the composition of which the Phosphates largely enter. When crystallized, they may be also red, or white, the former consisting of crystals of Uric or Lithic Acid, and the latter of Triple Phosphate of Ammonia and Magnesia. Although the deposits in Gravel vary considerably in their form and color, and to some extent in their character also, yet the nature of the disease is essentially the same. If the deposited particles remain stationary in the bladder for a length of time, others gather around them until they form a hard solid mass, which has to be broken down or crushed before it can be removed.

The *symptoms* of an attack of Gravel are constipated bowels, restlessness, and dry skin, with pains in the loins, commonly on one side, where it descends, following the course of the urethra; the thigh and leg feel numbed; and sometimes in the male the testicles are drawn up. There is frequently sickness, and an urgent desire to make water, which is passed with difficulty, and is high-colored and turbid, depositing a sandy powder, which is sometimes red, at others white, or a mixture or alternation of the two colors, with occasionally a bloody tinge. Derangement of the digestive organs is common in such a case; there will probably be constipated bowels, with acid eructations with great restlessness, and a sense of weight at the pit of the stomach.

Treatment.—1 quart of hard wood ashes, ½ gill of soot (from the chimney), mixed with 6 pints of water, stir it occasionally for a day or two, then let it settle, and filter it. Take a teaspoonful three times a day, or half a teaspoonful of fluid Magnesia, or 20-drop doses of Liquor Potassa.

Tonics should be taken to improve the tone of the stomach—½ dram Fluid Extract of Gentian, or the same quantity of Tincture of Peruvian Bark, 3 times a day. Take no acids either in food or drink; plain nourishing diet in moderate quantities. Open-air exercise, and a sponge bath, followed by friction, are among the best remedies.

MENSTRUATION. — The func-

tions of the uterus, by which the menstrual, catamenial, or monthly discharges take place. These generally commence between the fourteenth and sixteenth years of age, although we have known them to begin as early as eleven or twelve. A considerable period may elapse between the appearance of the first and second menstrual discharge; but, when they are properly established, their recurrence, at regular periods, may be calculated on with great certainty, unless some functional or other derangement of the system interferes with them. Ordinarily a lunar month of twenty-eight days is the intervening period, but with some females the discharge occurs every third week. The fluid discharged resembles blood in color, but it does not coagulate; the quantity is from three to five ounces, and the process occupies from three to five days. The quantity, however, and duration of the emission, varies greatly in different females, and unless the former is either very scanty or excessive, these do not appear important particulars; but the regular recurrence of the issue is important to health. This should be borne in mind, and due care taken not to suppress the discharge by exposure to cold or wet, or by violent exertion of any kind about the time when it may be expected. It is desirable that young females should be properly informed by their mothers, or those under whose care they are placed, of what may be expected at a certain age, or they may be alarmed at the first appearance of the Menses, taking it to be some indication of a dangerous disease or injury, and, perhaps, by mental agitation, or a resort to strong medicines, do mischief to themselves. If the Menses do not appear at the usual age, or for some years after, no alarm need be felt, provided there is no constitutional derangements which can be attributed to this cause. Some women never menstruate, although they may be married and have a family. Most commonly with suppressed Menstruation, which we understand the term *Amenorrhœa* to signify, there is, if not actual disease of the parts more immediately involved in the process, a weakly and unhealthy state of the system. When there is such suppression, discharges of blood will sometimes occur from the nose, mouth, and gums, or from the stomach and bowels: nearly always there will be unnatural heats and flushings, headache, tendency to faint, and hysterical symptoms. At the regular periods when the Menses ought to appear, there will be great excitability, and an aggravation of the above symptoms; with those of full habit, there will be a strong, bounding pulse, with acute pain in the head, back, and limbs; with the feeble and sickly, extreme languor, tremblings, shiverings, and pale visage.

In the first case, the *treatment* will be spare diet, free purging with saline aperients, cupping in the loins, and vigorous exercise between the periods. In the second, nutritious diet, with Wine or Bitter Ale; tonic medicines — some form of Iron is the best, in combination with Quinine; gentle aperients, such as Castor Oil, or Compound Rhubarb Pill, and the use of the hip-bath, the latter especially, for a few days before the menstruating period; every other night the bath should be made more stimulant by the addition of a little Mustard, and, on every occasion, active friction with dry coarse towels should be used; a lavement, containing 2 drams of Spirit of Turpentine, may also be useful; and a leech or two applied to each thigh, on the upper part, as near to the situation of the uterus as may be. All this should be done in a case of *acute suppression*, that is, where the secretion of the Menses has taken place, but derangement of the general health, or perhaps some mechanical obstacle, prevents its appearance; if the latter is the case, of course, surgical aid is necessary.

Chronic Suppression may result from the acute, or from defective nutrition of the organs; from the early termination of menstrual functions, or from the weakness occasioned by a profuse discharge of "whites" from the uterus. In this case there is generally pains in the head, sides, and back, loss of appetite, giddiness, sallow complexion, with a dark line round the eyes, generally torpid bowels, with other dyspeptic symptoms. It is sometimes difficult to distinguish between this and the early stage of pregnancy; in both there is a large abdomen, but in the latter usually the breasts are flat, in the former full and plump, but the doubt will not long remain — the morning sickness, the increasing size of the abdomen, and the other unmistakable signs of pregnancy, if it be that, will dissipate it in a month or so.

In a case of chronic suppression, if there be no indications of disease which call for special treatment, and if the age of the patient be such as to warrant a reasonable expectation that emmenagogue remedies may be of service, they should be resorted to.

In this case, too, the warm hip-bath should be used about the proper period of Menstruation, and it would be well to give some uterine stimulant, such as Ergot of Rye, of which about 5 grains, with 2 grains of Aloes, and a drop of Essential Oil of Juniper, made into 2 pills, or mixed up in a powder, would be about the dose to be taken each night at bedtime, with a draught of Pennyroyal Water; or a mixture composed of Spirit of Turpentine, made into an emulsion with Yolk of Egg, Sugar, and Essence of Juniper, about 6 drams of the first and 1 of the last, in a 6-ounce mixture; 1 ounce to be taken three times a day. These means of promoting the discharge in any case must not be prolonged much beyond the menstrual periods, between which all possible means must be taken to strengthen the system; good diet, plenty of active exercise, the use of the shower-bath, or cold or tepid sponging; Steel Mixture, with Aloes and Iodine, in one or other of its forms; these are the proper remedies.

When the menstrual period comes round again, use the means above directed, and continue thus to alternate the treatment until success crown the efforts, or the case becomes altogether hopeless. If the Amenorrhœa proceeds from a want of energy in the uterine organs to secrete the red discharge, as is often the case after frequent miscarriages, child-bearing, or inflammation of the womb, as well as after leucorrhœa, or "whites," there will probably be the usual signs of Menstruation, followed by a white discharge only, and accompanied by acute pain at the bottom of the back, vertigo, and hysteria. Weakly young women, before accession of the Menses, and elderly ones, at the time of their cessation, or "change of life," as it is commonly called, are often so affected. In such a case we should prescribe hot baths and tepid injections, pills of Sulphate of Iron and Aloes, with Balsam of Copaiba, 10 or 20 drops in milk, three times a day; or Powdered Cubebs, from a scruple to half a dram; good diet, and a recumbent position as much as possible during the periods. If the patient is of a full habit, apply leeches, 10 or 12 over the sacrum, to be followed by a blister, with restricted diet, and, for a time, avoidance of sexual intercourse.

Sudden Suppression of the Menses may arise from exposure to cold or wet, from extreme mental distress, and several other causes; it is generally accompanied by violent headache, severe pain in the loins and abdomen, difficulty of breathing, and shivering. In this case the patient must take warm diluent drinks, saline aperients, till the bowels are freely opened, have hot Bran Poultices applied to the lower part of the abdomen, immerse the feet and legs in hot water, rendered stimulant by the addition of Mustard; if the pain is extreme, take an opiate draught every four hours, and have a lavement, with 1 dram of Turpentine, and ½ a dram of Tincture of Opium thrown up; she must also be kept as quiet as possible.

Painful Menstruation is the rule with some females, but the exception with most; it does not seem to be in any way connected with the quantity of the discharge, and it may attend both the secretion and the emission; or but one or other of the processes, and but partially, coming on in paroxysms, or continually, during the whole process; the matter discharged is often thick and membraneous, and sometimes has in it clots and streaks of blood. The cause of this is not very clear. It has been observed to occur after strong mental emotions, a cold caught during the menstrual period, a fright or other shock to the system, and would seem to indicate an irritable state of the womb. In this case we must resort to warm hip-baths and friction, fomentation of the parts, diluent drinks, saline aperients, opiates, and a spare diet; injection of warm water high up into the vagina, etc.

It is necessary at each monthly turn to do something in these cases to quiet the pain: for this purpose, 20 drops of Laudanum, in a wineglass of tepid water, thrown into the bowel, will be highly serviceable.

WHITES is a symptom of disease, rather than a disease itself. Local treatment will be of little avail in cases of long standing, unless the general health be attended to. To keep the bowels gently open, take Compound Rhubarb Pill, 5 grains, as often as required, and to strengthen and cool the system, a mixture like the following:—Sulphate of Iron, 12 grains; Diluted Sulphuric Acid, 1 dram; Sulphate of Magnesia, 4 drams; Peppermint, or Cinnamon Water, 12 ounces: take two tablespoonfuls twice or thrice a day. In obstinate cases, there should be an injection into the vagina of a solution of Alum and Sulphate of Zinc, 3 drams of the former and 1 dram of the latter, to a pint of water; 3 or 4 ounces to be thrown up, while the patient lies with the hips rather elevated; this position to be retained for some time, with the parts covered by a napkin or sponge, so that the fluid may be kept in. If there is itching and irritation of the parts, it may be allayed by an injection composed of Carbonate of Soda, 2 drams, in a quart of Bran Tea or Poppy Decoction. If the simple Alum and Zinc injection proves ineffectual, add a dram of Powdered Catechu to each pint, or use decoction of Oak Bark as a vehicle for the above Salts. When there is much debility, with suppressed or scanty menstruation, preparations of Iron as the above mixture, with Compound Steel Pills, or some compound of Canada Balsam, 3 grains, and ½ a grain of Quinine, or the latter substance ½ a dram, with dilute Sulphuric Acid, 1 dram, in 6 ounces of Gentian or Cascarilla : a tablespoonful to be taken twice or thrice a day. Should there be profuse menstruation, nothing is so likely to be effectual as the Iron and Acid Mixture, with or without the Sulphate of Magnesia, according to the state of the bowels. Mustard poultices to the lower part of the back, or stimulant liniments, rubbed well in every night, for a time, will often prove useful.

Milk Fever. — An aggravated form of the excitement which takes place at the onset of lactation ; its first symptoms are increased heat of the system, preceded by shivering, and sometimes accompanied with vertigo and slight delirium ; these are followed by severe headache, thirst, dry tongue, quick pulse, throbbing of the temples, and intolerance of light.

The *cause* may be a cold, or over-heating the apartment, too stimulating a diet, or any obstruction to the flow of milk from the breast.

The *treatment* should be spare diet, perfect tranquillity, subdued light, cooling drinks, and saline aperient medicines ; the head should be kept somewhat elevated, and bathed with cold water or evaporating lotions : if the symptoms should become worse in spite of this, apply half-a-dozen or more Leeches to the head, and put the feet in a warm Mustard bath. Most lying-in women have more or less of this fever, which is no doubt an effort of nature to rouse the hitherto dormant mammary organs to secrete a proper quantity of milk ; if, however, it is not checked, the arterial action runs too high, and no milk at all is secreted.

Inflammation of the Breasts. — It may occur at any period between early and advanced womanhood, but most commonly it does occur within a week or two of childbirth, and is the result of some obstruction in the flow of milk, or change in its normal character ; such a change will be sure to occur if the milk is suffered to remain long in the breast ; therefore, should the infant be unable to relieve it at all, or insufficiently, artificial means must be taken to do so.

When the premonitory symptoms of mammary abscess (broken breasts) are observed, recourse should at once be had to remedial measures. Let the breast be well yet gently rubbed with a soft hand, into the palm of which is poured fresh Olive or Almond Oil : the friction should be continued for about ten minutes, and repeated every four hours or so. Goose-grease and other fatty substances are recommended, but simple 'Oil is best, the friction being the principal agent for good. Between the intervals of this, the breast should be kept covered with a tepid water dressing, having over it oiled silk to prevent evaporation. Care should be taken during this treatment to keep the bowels gently open, and to keep under the febrile symptoms. Leeching the breast in case of threatened abscess is sometimes resorted to, but its utility is very questionable ; at all events, it should never be so unless under proper direction ; there may be cases in which it is advisable. A mammary abscess will frequently continue discharging for a considerable period, and during this time the patient should be supported by a nourishing, although light, diet. Stimulants are generally to be avoided, but sometimes they are really necessary. A warm Bread Poultice is best for the abscess ; it should be changed about every four hours, and covered with oiled silk; when the discharge has nearly ceased, simple tepid water dressings may be substituted. The breast, during all this time, should be supported by a soft handkerchief tied round the neck; an application of Collodion Oil over the part has sometimes been used; it forms a thin coat which, contracting as it dries, affords the necessary support, if the breast is not very large and heavy; if some amount of pressure is required, strips of strapping crossing each other will effect this object. After all danger of inflammation is over, a more generous diet may be allowed; a grain of Quinine, in a little Sherry Wine, two or three times a day, or half a pint of Porter. Should the breast remain hard, friction with Soap Liniment should be resorted to; a dram of Compound Tincture of Iodine to each ounce will render it more effectual.

Sore Nipples. — Very painful and distressing cases of *Sore Nipples* frequently occur after child-birth; sometimes they cannot be avoided, but frequently they arise from too great an anxiety on the part of the mother, who is constantly meddling with them, applying the mouth of the child, and resorting to all sorts of expedients to draw them out. A judicious nurse will prevent this, and also take care to guard the breasts as much as possible from those constant alternations of wet and dry to which they are exposed. Nipple shields of ivory or glass, with India rubber teats, may be readily procured, and should be used when the nipples are too sore and tender to bear the application of the infant's mouth: in this case, the milk must be drawn from the breast by one of the contrivances above mentioned, and given to the child in a feeding bottle. Glycerine has been found a good application for chapped or otherwise sore nipples; it must be applied with a camel hair brush, first wiping the part dry with a soft piece of linen; if obtained pure, there will be little or no smell in it to annoy either mother or child; Collodion is also useful, but it causes considerable smarting. If, as is sometimes the case, there be suppuration, warm bread poultices must be applied, and after them tepid water dressing. A little borax or alum dissolved in soft water is often used.

Change of Life generally occurs between the ages of forty and fifty years; the symptoms are great irregularity, both in the quantity and times of the usual discharges, sometimes entirely disappearing for four or five months, then coming again, and sometimes with an immense flow. Constipation of the bowels, and palpitation of the heart, a changeable appetite, and general unrest, timidity, dizziness, and bad feelings in the head are peculiar symptoms.

If this period be safely passed, a healthy old age generally follows, but great care is required, and the advice of a good physician should be obtained, for disease may have been laying dormant in the system, and as the customary discharges are stopped, may now develop itself.

The diet should be plain and nutritious, but not stimulating. Exercise in the open air, and the sponge bath, must not be neglected. The bowels should be regulated by some gentle medicine. If there is a tendency of blood to the head, cupping, or leeches, and some cathartic medicines will be proper, but should only be given under the advice of a physician.

FEVER.—The characteristic marks of Fever are an increase of heat, an accelerated pulse, a foul tongue; often cold chills and shivering, headache, sore throat, great thirst, and an impaired state of the functions generally.

The *causes* are various; among them may be named exposure to cold, heat, or wet, fatigue, long-continued watching, or mental anxiety, intemperance, unwholesome or insufficient food, breathing impure air, and all the bad local influences to which the lower classes, especially of large cities, are too often exposed, and the excesses and irregularities to which these classes are addicted. Most of the forms of Fever are epidemic, and their prevalence at or after periods of scarcity and privation, of unusual heat, or excessive moisture, render it impossible to doubt that there are certain states of the atmosphere, and conditions of the system, which render the latter peculiarly predisposed to febrific influence; and this is the case with all epidemic diseases, for many of which we look for an increase at particular times and seasons; thus, in the spring, measles prevail generally to a greater extent than at any other part of the year; Scarlet Fever is most common in the autumn; and Typhus towards the close of summer, which, especially if it be cold and wet, is the season most productive of all kinds of fever.

Typhoid Fever. — We generally look for the typhoid symptoms at about the end of the second week of the Fever, and as soon as they appear, we commence strengthening the system for the great trial it must sustain, by all the means in our power, having, however, a due regard to local congestions, and other complications, which may present themselves. If the brain is not too much affected, we at once resort to stimulants, such as Brandy or Port Wine, the latter mulled, with a grain or two of Quinine in each dose of half a wineglassful two or three times a day. If there is much cerebral excitement, we give Ammonia, the Carbonate, 5 grains, or Aromatic Spirit, 10 drops, in 1 ounce of Decoction of Bark, three times a day; also Beef Tea in small quantities frequently. It is the rule, in most diseases, to wait for a clean tongue and moist skin before we administer tonics and stimulants; but, in this, we should often lose our patients if we did so. Very commonly we administer these even when we know Pneumonia or Bronchitis are present, overlooking the lesser for the greater danger. Besides which, it is by no means clear that the stimulant method of treating Pneu-

monia is not the most successful — at all events we have found it so. Sulphate of Quinine, 1 grain, with 10 drops of dilute Sulphuric Acid, in 1 ounce of Infusion of Roses, is a good form of tonic; its acidity, too, renders it pleasant and refreshing to the fever-stricken. When the debility is extreme, Brandy and Port Wine, in equal proportions, ½ a wineglass together, may be given.

It is sometimes necessary to give nutrients and stimulants in very small quantities — the power of swallowing being nearly lost — a teaspoonful of Port Wine, thickened with Arrowroot, every quarter of an hour or ten minutes; or of Beef Tea, with a little Brandy in it. In this case, too, a Beef Tea clyster may be used with advantage. When, as is often the case, there is paralysis of the bladder, so that the urine does not pass off, a catheter must be used. It is necessary to pay particular attention to the back and other parts of a typhus patient, as troublesome bed-sores frequently occur. The use of the water-bed will generally prevent this. As the typhoid symptoms disappear, and convalescence becomes fairly established, the greatest mischief is to be apprehended from an indulgence of that craving for solid food and stimulant drinks which is experienced by the patient. He longs for Chops and Steaks, Oysters and Ale; he is sick of Arrowroot and Beef Tea, and all kinds of "slops," and becomes quite angry that he cannot have some change of diet. He wants something solid to eat, now that he has an appetite for it; but a judicious nurse will deny him this gratification for a time. Light puddings of Arrowroot, Ground Rice, Sago, Semolina, or Tapioca, may be first ventured on; and when the tongue is quite clean, and all febrile symptoms have disappeared, a beginning of meat diet may be made with a small slice of chicken; and if this agrees with the stomach, there may be a gradual advance to stronger meats, with wholesome white kinds of fish for an occasional variety. It is likely that tonics may be required for a considerable time after the patient is convalescent; and, as soon as there is sufficient strength for the journey, it is desirable that he should have a change of air, especially if the same local influences are still in operation by which the disease was first induced. We should have mentioned above, that in cases of Fever of a low, malignant kind, fresh Yeast, in teaspoon doses, given every three or four hours, has been found very beneficial, and that, through the whole course of the disease, disinfectants, such as the Chloride of Lime or Zinc, should be freely used.

Fever and Ague. — An intermittent fever, characterized by cold fits succeeded by hot; very prevalent in damp, marshy districts. Between the paroxysms, or periods, there is a perfect intermisson when no fever is present, and the patient feels only the lassitude resulting from debility, and can often go about his ordinary employments, if they be not too laborious. Agues have been divided in accordance with the paroxysmal periods, into—1. *Quotidian*, or daily, having an interval of twenty-four hours between the attacks; 2. *Tertian*, or third-day, having an interval of forty-eight hours; 3. *Quartan*, or fourth-day, having an intermission of seventy-two hours between each attack: and 4. *Erratic*, when the return of the fever goes beyond the latter period, and is commonly irregular in its recurrence. The paroxysms of Ague are divided into three tolerably regular stages: — 1st, the *Cold Stage*, when the chill creeps over the system, the color departs from the lips, the face becomes deadly pale, and the whole frame shivers and trembles as though smitten by a frosty wind, the pulse becomes slow, and the veins seem filled with ice; there is generally nausea and faintness, and an utter prostration of strength: the patient has no power to stay the convulsive trembling of his every limb and joint, and which continues for a longer or shorter interval, as the case may be, and is succeeded

by — 2. The *Hot Stage*, when the warmth of the body gradually returns, at first irregularly, by transient flushes; then by a steady, dry, burning heat, which rises much above the natural standard; the lips resume their color, the cheeks are flushed, the tongue is parched and white; there is a sense of fulness in the head, and flying pains in the loins, back, and other parts of the body, accompanied sometimes by a twitching of the nerves, and a difficulty of respiration; there is great thirst, and the urine is highly colored, and burns as it is voided; the pulse is quick, strong and hard, as in more sustained fevers. Then comes — 3. The *Sweating Stage*. At first a slight moisture breaks out upon the face and neck, and this is succeeded by a profuse general perspiration; the temperature of the body falls gradually to the natural standard, the pulse softens and diminishes in frequency, the respiration becomes more full and free, the pains depart; there is a desire to evacuate the bowels, and all the animal functions are restored to their proper order. Very seldom does the disease leave the patient at once, but retires slowly, as though loth to be beaten; most probably the quotidian becomes a tertian, then a quartan, and then again erratic, before it finally discontinues its attacks, which also become gradually lighter and of shorter duration, until they cease altogether.

Ague attacks, almost indiscriminately, persons of all ages and conditions of life, more perhaps those of the middle age than any other, and men more than women. If poor people are generally more aguish than rich, it is simply because they are more exposed to its

Exciting Causes. — The principal of which is marsh *miasma* or *malaria;* that is, the effluvia arising from lands that have been flooded, and afterwards exposed to the heat of the sun, which draws up the moisture in the form of vapor, laden with deleterious gases, from decomposed animal and vegetable substances. Not always does the person inhaling this experience the attack of Ague at once; the disease seems to be, as it were, latent in the system, and to be called into activity by a particular state or condition of the body, or by some other circumstances favorable to its development, such as wet or cold weather, exposure to night air, over-anxiety, want of rest or food, or aught which tends to debilitate the system. It has been contended by Dr. Snow that merely atmospheric agents do not communicate Ague, but that it enters the system by the alimentary canal, by means of the marshy and stagnant water drunk by those who live in low-lying districts. It may be so to a certain extent, but not altogether; it is by the lungs chiefly we are inclined to think that the poison enters. And what are its *effects* upon the internal economy? It causes a distension of the liver and of the spleen, the former being called *gall-cake*, and the latter *ague-cake :* the proper circulation of the blood is interfered with ; it accumulates in the veins of the viscera generally; the functions of the liver and the alimentary canal are disturbed, and the consequences are such as we have endeavored to describe.

Treatment.—Ague may generally be considered as a curable disease — in dry and temperate climates especially. The more regular forms of attack are the least dangerous. When it comes at irregular periods, as it sometimes does, with great violence, and when the patient is prostrated by some other sickness, it is likely to prove fatal, especially if of long standing. Sometimes a mere change of residence to a more dry and airy locality, with proper attention to diet, will suffice to check it ; and should these measures not succeed, there is little danger in allowing it to run its course, unless the patient should be weakly, in which case medicines should at once be resorted to.

It is not often that a first attack of Ague can be anticipated : and during the paroxysm efforts must be directed to alleviate the severe symptoms, to shorten its progress, and avert the danger of internal congestion. In the cold stage, we should apply artificial warmth, such as hot-water bottles, or a mustard bath, to the feet, mustard poultices to the pit of the stomach, friction of the back with stimulating liniment — say Soap Liniment and Spirits of Turpentine, equal parts — and the use of the hot-air bath in extreme cases. Negus, Tea, Gruel, Barley-water, or any warm diluent drinks, may be given; and should the fit prove long and severe, a draught, consisting of Tincture of Opium and Æther, or Compound Spirit of Ammonia, of each half a dram, to an ounce of Camphor Mixture or Peppermint Water. When the hot stage comes on, the body should be sponged with cold water; and cool drinks, such as Lemonade — if iced, so much the better — be given. Should no Laudanum have been previously administered, a half dram dose, without any stimulant, but with a dram of Liquor of Acetate of Ammonia, may be given, unless there is congestion of the veins of the head, or delirium, in which case leeches, or cupping on the temple, should be resorted to, and the opiate avoided. In the sweating stage, the patient should be kept as tranquil as possible; moderate the perspiration, and, if the exhaustion is great, administer a little weak spirits and water. When the fit is over, dry the surface of the body with warm towels, put on clean, well-aired linen, and have a warm bed ready for his reception. During the intermission of the paroxysms, a mixture like the following may be taken :—Sulphate of Quinine, 12 grains; diluted Sulphuric Acid, 24 minims; Camphor Mixture, 6 ounces. Mix, and take two table-spoonfuls every four hours. Should this not prove effectual, or should it cause, as Quinine sometimes does, a throbbing in the head, it is best to try Solution of Arsenite of Potash, 5 minims, three or four times a day, in any convenient vehicle; the dose may be gradually increased to 10 minims; but the action of this remedy must be carefully watched, as too much of it may act prejudicially on the system. Should there be tremors, griping pains in the stomach and bowels, or itching of the face and eyelids, let it be at once discontinued. Large doses of Quinine, say 10 grains, will sometimes arrest an attack of Ague, if taken just as it is coming on, and so, sometimes, will anything making a strong impression on the mind; such as fear, hope, joy, anger, etc. Sulphate of Zinc is a good remedy for Ague; 3 grains of it made into a pill, with Confection of Opium, may be taken 3 times a day, the dose to be increased a grain every day, until it reaches 10 or 12 grains. No fluid should be swallowed for some time after the dose, or it may cause vomiting. Finely powdered Charcoal, 20 grains, in Brandy and water, every three or four hours, has been recommended by good authorities, and so have 10-grain doses of Calomel, formed into pills with mucilage, or molasses. Bitter infusions, such as Quassia, and Gentian, or Camomile, are no doubt serviceable in this disorder, during the progress of which, purgatives should be given occasionally — 3 to 5 grains of Calomel at night, and a draught of Rhubarb and Magnesia in the morning, is the best. By this course the disease will be arrested, but the germs of disease still remain in the system, and it is necessary that these shall be eradicated, or in fourteen, twenty-one, or twenty-eight days there will be a recurrence of the disease.

The daily use of small doses of Quinine, for at least forty days, when, if there has been no new exposure to the cause of the disease, it will be entirely eradicated from the system; for this purpose we have found the following a valuable prescription:

Quinine Sulphate, 32 grains; Syrup per Chloride of Iron, 2 drams; Simple Syrup, 4 ounces. Dose: Teaspoonful three times per day.

Yellow Fever is another disease arising out of biliary derangement. It is sometimes called *Balum Fever*, or *Black Vomit*, and is a remittent fever, accompanied with yellowness of the skin, and vomiting of a black or dark brown fluid; these two symptoms are its invariable accompaniments, and they are attended with all the usual marks of fever in a high degree. This disease belongs to the West Indies, and other hot climates, and is extremely fatal. It first comes on with weakness and pain in the limbs, headache, heat in the eyes, parched mouth, the tongue is browned and furred, with red edges; there is a hard, quick, and full pulse, a dry hot skin, the bowels are confined, and the urine small in quantity and high colored, commonly tinged with bile. In from twenty-four to forty-eight hours the fever reaches its height, and the powers of life sink beneath its fury; the pulse becomes almost imperceptible or intermittent, the breathing labored and difficult; there is a distressing hiccough, continual vomiting of the black matter, and bleeding from the nose, mouth, and other passages, and very shortly exhaustion and death.

A milder form of Bilious, or as it is sometimes called, *Gastric Fever*, prevails in this country, the treatment of which varies but little from that prescribed in *Typhus*. In this the mischief is almost wholly confined to the alimentary canal; the head is but little affected, and the febrile symptoms do not run high, therefore it is best not to administer violent remedies. If, as is commonly the case, there be diarrhœa, let it go on for a little time, as by this means the system becomes relieved of its superfluous bile; it must, however, be carefully watched, and checked, if the motions exceed three or four daily; if the motions should be very offensive, finely powdered vegetable charcoal may be given, 10 or 15 grains, twice a day, in water. After the first week the diarrhœa should be stopped, and to this end an injection of Starch or Gumwater, with Laudanum (20 or 30 drops for an adult), had better be tried before recourse is had to medicines. Should this not succeed, Chalk Mixture, with a little Aromatic Confection, with 6 drops of Laudanum in each dose, three times a day; or the following:—Diluted Sulphuric Acid, 3 drams, Laudanum, 2 drams, water, 6 ounces; mix, and take 1 ounce every three or four hours, or after each loose motion. Should these not have the desired effect, try these powders, one every six hours:—Powdered Opium and Rhubarb, of the former 1 grain, of the latter 12 grains; Bicarbonate of Soda, 12 grains; divide in six. If, on the contrary, there is constipation of the bowels, administer a clyster of thin gruel with salt, or brown sugar, administering also Castor Oil, or some mild aperient, should the operations be sufficiently copious. Should there be obstinate vomiting, give Soda Water, or a simple effervescing draught; if these fail, try Hydrocyanic Acid, in drop doses, in plain water, or either of the above drinks; a blister to the pit of the stomach may also be applied should other measures be necessary; and as a last resort, 6 grains of Calomel may be placed upon the tongue, and washed down with a little plain water. To restore the tone of the stomach and assuage thirst when the diarrhœa is stopped, give acidulous drink of some kind. This is a good formula:—Nitro-Muriatic Acid, 10 drops, Lump Sugar, 1 ounce, water, 1 pint; half a tumbler to be given every three or four hours. For restoring the strength of the convalescent patient, give Chicken Broth, Beef Tea, Wine, and Bitter Ale; if the abdomen becomes swollen and indurated, let it be well rubbed night and morning with a liniment composed of Turpentine and Sweet Oil in equal quantities; in this case the gruel enema may be used with Castor Oil and Turpentine, of each about a tablespoonful. The recumbent position should be maintained throughout the attack.

RHEUMATISM. — This is a painful disease, which affects the muscles and joints of the human body. It chiefly affects the larger joints, as the hips, knees, and shoulders, and is generally attended with swelling and stiffness; when accompanied by fever it constitutes *Acute Rheumatism*, or *Rheumatic Fever*. Some pathologists make the following distinct varieties of the disease:—1st, *Articular Rheumatism*, occurring in the joints and muscles of the extremities; 2d, *Lumbago*, occurring in the loins, and mostly shooting upwards; 3d, *Sciatica*, occurring in the hip-joint, with emaciation of the nates.

Acute Rheumatism generally commences with a feeling of weariness, shivering, and a quickened pulse, accompanied by redness, heat, and pain, in or around one or more of the larger joints; sometimes several are affected at once, but usually they are attacked in succession — this method of going from one joint to another being a marked characteristic of the disease; sometimes the first joint is relieved when the attack is felt in another, but not always; sometimes the whole of the larger joints become implicated, and then the smaller ones, and finally the heart, in which case there is generally a fatal termination to the patient's sufferings. The fibrous tissues of the body appear to be the media by which the Rheumatic affection is communicated from one part to another. The disease, it is likely, is constitutional, depending on a morbid condition of the blood; one of its symptoms is considerable heat of the skin, and a profuse sour-smelling perspiration; generally the urine is high-colored, and deposits a sediment like brick dust. In one of the acute forms of the disease there is puffiness around the part attacked, with distinct red lines running from it, and, subsequently, œdema; with this there is, generally, a high degree of inflammatory fever, with a furred tongue, and very copious acid perspirations; this is the form in which the heart is most likely to be affected. In the other and more common form, the fever is not so violent, and moderates as soon as the joints begin to swell; this form is generally called Rheumatic Gout.

The similarity between Gout and Rheumatism renders it probable that the same cause may originate both. There is, however, a marked distinction in the circumstance, that in Gout the poison, which is in the system, separates itself from the blood, and is deposited in the form of chalk-stones; in the latter it appears to be thrown out in that peculiar acid so remarkable in the perspiration.

Cold and moisture would seem to be the principal exciting causes of Acute Rheumatism, probably by checking perspiration, and so preventing the poisonous principle from passing off by the skin, so that it is retained, and circulates in the blood. Violent exercise and over-exertion will sometimes bring on an attack of this disease, which, like Gout, is hereditary in some families. Persons between the ages of fifteen and forty are most subject to it, but where there is the above-mentioned predisposition it often shows itself in the young.

The *treatment* of the acute form should be prompt and active, the inflammatory fever having first to be subdued; purgatives and general bleeding, if the patient is of full habit, but not the latter otherwise. Dr. Graves says that in this disease, "Blood-letting should be practised with great caution, and its effects carefully observed: take away five or six ounces of blood, and if the pain be lessened and the sweats diminished, you are encouraged to bleed more boldly."

About 3 grains of Calomel at night, and a Black Draught in the morning, to be repeated every four hours until the bowels are freely opened; plenty of warm diluent drinks, and confinement to bed with warmth to promote perspiration. Apply to the inflamed parts a lotion composed of Spirit, Vinegar, and Water, one part of each of the former to two of the latter, with the chill taken off; if the pain is very great at the joints, Leeches may be applied. When the inflamma-

tion is in some measure subdued, recourse may be had to the grand specific in diseases of this class, viz., Colchicum, 15 drops of the wine of which may be taken every four hours, with ½ a dram of Sweet Spirits of Nitre, ½ an ounce of the Liquor of Acetate of Ammonia, and 1 ounce of Camphor Mixture; at bedtime a scruple of Dover's Powder, with 2 grains of Calomel, until the mouth becomes slightly affected, when the latter must be omitted; should the action of the Colchicum on the bowels be too strong, reduce the dose by one-half, or omit it altogether, and give ½-grain of Tartrate of Potash, with 5 grains of Nitrate of Potash, in Camphor Mixture, every four hours. Should the joints continue swollen and purple, blisters may be applied after the Leeches, and when the bites are healed, friction with Mercurial Liniment, and an air-tight covering over cotton carded wool, should be applied.

In less acute cases, where the urine is acid, and deposits the before-mentioned sediment, a mixture like this may be taken in conjunction with saline aperients: Bicarbonate of Potash, 2 drams; Infusion of Gentian or Calumba, 6 ounces: take 1 ounce three times a day until the deposit ceases; or substitute for the Bicarbonate, the Liquor of Potash, 1 dram. Also dissolve a little Nitrate of Potash in Barley-water, and take a wineglassful now and then as a restorative to health. When the disease appears to be nearly subdued, take Hydriodate of Potash, 1 dram, in Decoction of Sarsaparilla, 8 ounces, a wineglassful twice a day.

When Rheumatism has become chronic, it is generally very intractable; it is most capricious in its visitations, sometimes affecting one joint, sometimes another, and generally leaving the part attacked swollen and tender; to this it will frequently return, sometimes causing thickening of the joint and permanent lameness; sometimes the symptoms resemble those of Acute Rheumatism, and require leeching, spare diet, and a similar line of treatment; but this is not generally the case: a tolerably generous diet, with nervous stimulants and stimulating applications being mostly necessary for the chronic forms of this troublesome and painful disease, in which, excepting Colchicum, nothing appears to exercise such a specific action as Guaiacum, which may be taken in the form of powder or tincture. Besides these two remedies, Ginger, Mustard, Sulphur, Turpentine, Compound Powder of Ipecacuanha, and Cod Liver Oil, have all been found beneficial. Indeed, there is perhaps no disease for which so many different "cures" are recommended; nor is there one which more obstinately retains its hold on the system, and defies all attempts to dislodge it. Anything which promotes free perspiration is likely to be beneficial; warm bathing and friction; sulphureous, hot-air, and vapor baths have been found of great service, and the patient must not be disheartened if they do not succeed at once, or if the disease returns after they have, as it appeared, subdued it; he must continue the remedies for a long time, and return to them again and again if necessary. Seldom or ever is Rheumatism quite got rid of, when once it has taken a hold of the system.

LUMBAGO. — A rheumatic affection of the muscles of the loins. This, as many of us well know, is an extremely painful affection; the pain being aggravated by any action which brings the muscles involved in the disorder into play. Like Sciatica, it is but a modification of Rheumatism; nevertheless, it requires, in some measure, a peculiar *treatment.* When accompanied by fever and much pain, which is aggravated by the warmth of the bed, leeching or cupping is advisable, with aperients and diaphoretics; 3 grains of Calomel at night, with about 10 grains of Compound Ipecacuanha Powder, and a Senna Draught in the morning, following it up with this mixture: Solution of Acetate of Ammonia, 1½ ounces; Wine of Colchicum, 1 dram; Sweet Spirits of Nitre and Simple Syrup, of each 2 drams; Cam-

phor Mixture, 4 ounces; take a fourth part about every four hours. The Dover's Powders should be continued every night — not the Calomel; about a couple of doses of this, at intervals of a week or so, will be found sufficient. Warm applications to the loins will afford great relief; one of the best is a large Bran Poultice, applied quite hot, all over the loins. Dr. Graves recommends a stream of hot water, directed with considerable force against the part; it is beneficial not only on account of the heat, but also for the mechanical impulse which it gives. When there is no fever with the Lumbago, the best medicine is Volatile Tincture of Guaiacum, 1 dram, in Cinnamon Water, three times a day, with the Dover's Powder at night, and friction with Soap Liniment and Tincture of Aconite, or Opium, about a dram to the ounce; or apply a Belladonna Plaster, keeping the bowels freely open with a Colocynth Pill occasionally, or a draught of Senna, or Compound Decoction of Aloes; Decoction of Sarsaparilla, with Iodide of Potassium, may be also given with advantage. In obstinate cases, Acupuncture, Electricity, and Galvanism, have each and all been successfully applied. The following is a good form for a liniment to be used in such cases: Strong Liquor of Ammonia, Tincture of Opium, Spirit of Turpentine, and Olive Oil, equal quantities; rub in warm, night and morning.

SCROFULA. — This is a disease characterized by a chronic swelling of the absorbent glands, which tend slowly to imperfect suppuration. One popular name for it, is the King's Evil. It is characterized by want of power, or tone, in the system. Its most prominent symptoms are the formation of indolent tumors in various parts of the body, but most commonly in the neck, behind the ears, and under the skin; after a while these suppurate, and discharge a thick cheesy matter. A scrofulous person has generally a puffy, unhealthy appearance about the face; the upper lip is thick and tumid, the belly prominent; there is frequent discharge from the eyes, nose, and mouth; a predisposition to catarrh and swelled tonsils, often causing a huskiness in the voice. The digestive functions are imperfectly performed, consequently the bowels are irregular; the skin is seldom free from some kind of eruption, and there is listlessness and want of energy about the whole manner and appearance of the person so affected. Scrofula is among the commonest of hereditary taints — the children of scrofulous parents are seldom free from it, and we find such especially among the lower classes — pallid, puffy, dull and inanimate creatures, with a dry, harsh skin, grievously full of blemishes, and a mind almost a blank. Sometimes, though but rarely, and under favorable circumstances, we find a scrofulous child whose want of bodily power and activity seems to be compensated by a remarkably quick and intelligent mind; but this is quite the exception to the rule; and very often, in such cases, it may be accounted for by the extra care and attention bestowed upon the development of the mental powers of those who are deficient in muscular energy.

Scrofula commonly first shows itself between the ages of three and seven; but not always in those early stages of life. Sometimes in those who have the taint, it may lie dormant until after the age of puberty, waiting, as it were, for some incitement to call it forth. A slight cold, unwholesome food, bad air, or a variety of other causes, may have this effect. Very few persons, however, really die of Scrofula — the ascertained proportion is about eight in one hundred thousand; but scrofulous persons often die of diseases which attack and overcome them, more readily and easily, on account of the vitiated and weakened condition of the system. Children who are brought up by hand, or even by a wet nurse, are more liable to Scrofula than those suckled by the mother; and especial care should be taken that all such are well fed and

cared for, warmly clothed, well supplied with pure fresh air, and kept from all influences which might tend to develop the tendency of a scrofulous condition, which in all probability they have.

Treatment.—Give nutriment, adapted to age, but not over-feed. Give plenty of animal food, with a moderate proportion of vegetables and fruit; plenty of milk, a little beer and wine. Assist the digestive powers, if necessary, with mild aperients, Rhubarb and Grey Powders: give tonics, Steel Wine and Quinine (alternately, week by week, with Cod Liver Oil), occasionally changing the above for some other tonic. Decoction of Sarsaparilla, with Iodide of Potassium, is likely to be serviceable; or Iodide of Iron, in the form of a syrup. There should also be sea-bathing once or twice a week; and if the glands of the neck are much swollen, they should be brushed over with Tincture of Iodine, or rubbed with Iodine Ointment.

SCURVY. — The characteristics of this disease are great debility, a pale complexion, with bloated skin, and livid spots about it here and there; soft, spongy gums, with offensive breath; swellings on the legs, and hæmorrhages from the mouth, nose, and bowels; the stools and urine are very fœtid; and, as the disease proceeds, the livid spots on the skin enlarge and deepen in color, until they resemble bruises, from the effusion of blood into the cellular tissues; the skin also becomes dry and rough, and of an uniform dusky hue; the debility increases, there is great difficulty of breathing, constipation of bowels, and disinclination to take any kind of nourishment, so that eventually, unless the disease yields to medical treatment, the patient dies of exhaustion.

Such is the inevitable course of a bad attack of Scurvy. Of course, lighter ones are constantly occurring, and severe ones in which the proper remedies are employed in time to arrest the progress of the disease, the origin of which is intimately associated with fatigue, cold, moisture, and impure air, and chiefly with a deprivation of vegetable food, and eating too exclusively of salt provisions. From this it must be evident that a liberal diet of fresh meat and succulent vegetables should be at once resorted to. Let the patient have plenty of open-air exercise and tepid bathing; drinking saline and chalybeate waters will be serviceable; and if vegetables cannot be procured, a portion of Lime or Lemon Juice should be taken daily. Mild aperient medicines will also be required, and, in many cases, tonics; preparations of Soda are the best, with bitter infusion. It has been ascertained that in this disease the blood is deficient in potash, therefore this substance should be among the remedies administered — either the Bi-carbonate, Chlorate, or Tartrate will do; a dram dissolved in a pint of water should be taken daily. Commonly Scurvy, if not very bad, can be secured by dietary measures alone. In the epidemic which prevailed in the prisons of Perth, in 1846, the addition of milk, and in some cases, meat, to the usual allowance, arrested the disease. Malt liquor is good for those affected with Scurvy; of Lemon Juice, ½ pint should be given every day, pure or diluted with water; this appears to be almost a specific, few cases resisting its influence.

INFLAMMATION. — There are few diseases that do not present, at some period during their course, inflammatory symptoms, and in some they may be regarded with satisfaction rather than alarm, as indications of a healthy action; thus, in wounds and ulcers we would rather have redness, swelling, and a considerable degree of pain, than the livid, purplish look, and dull, dead sensation, which shows that there is a want of vitality. The reparative processes of nature in the animal frame are mostly the result of inflammation, which, however, becomes exceedingly dangerous when it runs high, and baffles the skill of the medical man to subdue it.

An attack of Inflammation may terminate in any one of three ways — viz., by *resolution, suppuration,* or *mortification*. By the first, which is most common, we understand a gradual subsidence of the swelling, a diminution of the heat, pain, and redness, and an abatement of the fever — in short, a gradual return to the natural state and condition of the part affected; the second termination is when the inflammatory action goes on to the formation of pus; then we have a red, shining swelling, growing more and more so, and becoming soft in the centre, from whence, in due time, either through an artificial or natural opening, the matter makes its escape; the third, the least common and most dangerous termination, is *Mortification*. The first of these is, of course, the most desirable to be brought about, and where it cannot be, effusion of the watery part of the blood is pretty sure to follow; internally, we see this in pleurisy and water on the brain; externally, in blisters, burns, and scalds.

ABSCESS is a collection of pus, or purulent matter, in a cyst or cavity formed in any of the tissues of the body.

Causes. —Inflammatory action of the adhesive kind, induced by a blow, or prick, or the introduction of something poisonous, or otherwise irritating. The cells of the membrane become filled with adhesive matter, a mere drop at first, but as ulceration proceeds, this increases in quantity, the surrounding parts are gradually absorbed, the solids converted into a fluid state, more active inflammation is set up, causing acute pain, restlessness, loss of appetite, and of consequence, great constitutional derangement. The absorption does not proceed with equal rapidity on all sides, but has a tendency towards the surface of the body; by this we learn that matter has no corroding property — to act upon the tissues, among the more remote and permanent consequences, may be mentioned a general weakening of the system, and often lasting injury to the parts affected. Abscesses are of two kinds — *acute* and *chronic;* the former may last from three to six weeks, beginning to discharge usually at the end of the first period: the latter, which is commonly seated in some internal part, such as the liver, may continue for several months, its duration depending very much upon the remedial means resorted to, situation, constitution of the patient, etc.

Symptoms. — Heat, and tenderness of the part affected, is the premonitory symptoms of acute Abscess. It is commonly confined at first to a small spot, which becomes red and painful to the touch: very soon a distinct throbbing may be felt, which is a sure indication of the formation of matter; then the parts begin to swell, and the skin exhibits a shining, semi-transparent appearance, sometimes being tinged with purple; this becomes more marked and decided as the tension increases, with the increase of the matter beneath, until it gives way of itself, or is opened by some sharp instrument, and the pus flows out, at first of a cream-like color and consistence, often turgid and tinged with blood; thus it continues for a week or more, then gradually becomes clearer and thinner, until it is quite watery, or ceases altogether. During this process, before the matter has found a channel of escape, the pain becomes more and more complete, until it is almost unbearable, giving the patient no rest night or day; then ensues the constitutional derangement, and often febrile symptoms, which must be relieved by means of cooling aperients.

Fomentation with water as hot as it can be borne, and hot bread or linseed poultices, should be resorted to in the first stages of an acute Abscess: strong drawing and irritating applications are often made use of, but this only increases the anguish without doing good; indeed it is both cruel and hurtful. The poultices should be frequently changed, in order to keep up the requisite degree of warmth; they should be carefully adjusted so as not to press unduly upon the tenderest part, and, when the pain is very severe, poppy heads should be boiled in the water with which they are mixed, and this poppy decoction should also be used for the fomentations. If, as is often the case, the Abscess should be in the hand or lower part of the arm, that limb should be supported by a sling made of a silk handkerchief, or some other soft material, so as to keep it from hanging down; adjust it so as to have the upper part of the arm as nearly perpendicular as may be, and the bend of the elbow at right angles with it. To keep the system cool and allay the fever which generally more or less attends active inflammation, the patient should take, every other night or so, an aperient pill, composed of Compound Extract of Colocynth, 4 grains, Calomel, 1 grain, and two or three times a day, a tablespoonful of the following mixture: — Sulphate of Magnesia, ½ an ounce, Carbonate of Magnesia, 1 dram, Wine of Tartarized Antimony, 2 grains, Camphor Mixture, 6 ounces; should this mixture cause griping in the bowels, add thirty drops of Essence of Peppermint; if it acts too violently, reduce the quantity of Sulphate of Magnesia to one-half, and take a pill every third night only. When the anguish prevents rest at night, this draught may be taken at bedtime: — Acetate of Morphine, ¼ of a grain, Liquor of Acetate of Ammonia, 1 dram, Camphor Mixture, 7 drams.

After the discharge of purulent matter has ceased, the poultices may be discontinued, and moist rags kept applied for some days, after which the edges of the wound may be drawn together by strips of adhesive plaster, over which it is best to place a dressing of Turner's Cerate or Spermaceti Ointment. If the wound is deep and large, it may be some weeks before it fills by granulation, but otherwise the healing process proceeds rapidly, unless there is a want of vital energy in the system, or a diseased state of the part immediately affected; in this case bad sloughing ulcers result, which are very difficult to heal. For their treatment, see *Ulcers.*

A physician will generally open an Abscess, when it is sufficiently ripe, rather than wait the slower process of the breaking of the skin, and by doing this he often saves the patient much suffering and constitutional derangement; but no person unacquainted with the anatomy of the part should attempt this. To do it effectually, the cut should be bold and deep, and exactly in the right place; an unpracticed hand will probably leave the largest reservoir of matter untouched, and so render another incision necessary, and effect no good purpose by the pain inflicted. Where the integument which covers the seat of the Abscess is hard and thick, it is nearly always necessary to open it, and only the skilled practitioner can judge of the proper time for doing this; therefore his aid should in all such cases be solicited, as in those of deeply seated and internal Abscesses, which generally assume a *chronic* character. With regard to the treatment of these, no specific directions can be given — it must depend much upon the character of the tissues which they affect. As a general rule, the patient's strength must be supported by a good and generous diet, and the administration of tonic and cordial medicines, taking care to keep the bowels moderately open. Stimulating plasters made of Burgundy Pitch, Gum Ammoniac with Mercury or Galbanum, are applied with advantage to the abdomen, or other seat of the affection, as are poultices of oatmeal with vinegar, or yeast, or water impregnated with salt. For Abscesses in the neck, Astley Cooper recommends incision with a sharp knife, pressing the matter well out so as to excite adhesive inflammation, and dressing the wound with bread poultices, moistened first with Sulphate of Zinc in solution, and afterwards with Spirits of Wine, giving good light nourishment, and carefully regulating the bowels.

For the relief of the hectic fever, night sweats, and other constitutional disturbances, caused by both acute and chronic Abscesses, but more especially the latter, preparations of bark or iron, mineral acids or Cod-Liver Oil may be given during the period of copious discharge; and especially immediately after it, when the powers of nature are most sorely taxed to supply the waste and reconstruct the destroyed tissues, is nourishing food and strengthening medicine required.

Ulcer, Ulceration. — A solution of continuity in any of the soft parts of the body, either open to the surface, or to any internal cavity, and attended with a secretion of pus or some kind of discharge, is an Ulcer; and the process of forming this is Ulceration.

In Ulceration the lymphatics are as active as the arteries, and absorb the pus as soon as it is formed, causing thus a disappearance of the natural structure without, as in the case of abscess, anything to supply its place. It is by this destructive process going on between an abscess and the skin, that the latter is laid open to the surface. Wounds in the flesh, if at all deep, are very likely to pass into Ulcers; thus, instead of healing, as it is called, by "the first intention," they remain open, discharging pus or matter, and presenting a granulated surface; this we should call a healthy Ulcer, or one tending to heal. If, on the contrary, there is no appearance of filling up with red granulations, but the hollow rather deepens, and the disorganized tissue comes away in a black or bloody discharge, this is an unhealthy, or sloughing Ulcer, and if not changed in its nature will penetrate more and more deeply, and will either reach some vital part or kill the patient by exhaustion. Where there is not sufficient energy and vitality in the system to resist the process of destruction in the tissues, and build up anew the destroyed parts, a wound is likely to become an Ulcer, and this will assume the latter condition; hence the necessity of giving all the assistance possible to the vital powers, by nutritious food, and tonic and stimulating medicines.

Persons in whom, from age or other cause, the circulation has become sluggish, are those most liable to Ulcerations, and that of an unhealthy kind. This may take place in any part of the body, but it most commonly occurs in the legs, which are farthest removed from the great course of circulation. *Ulcerated Legs* are among the most difficult cases that a surgeon has to deal with: he will first insist upon perfect rest, and keeping the limb in a horizontal position as much as possible. When the Ulcer is very foul and dark-looking, warm poultices will have to be applied to bring away the slough; when this is accomplished, and there is a tolerably clean surface, discharging only pus, a simple water dressing may be sufficient for a time. Should the Ulcer improve under such treatment, this may be continued until the healing takes place. If, however, the granulations, which will begin to fill up the hollow, appear large, pale, and flabby, and not small and red, as they should do, an astringent lotion will be necessary; this may be either of the Sulphates of Copper or Zinc, or Acetate of Lead. Lotions are far better than ointment, as they are more cleanly; the rags wet with them have to be often renewed. If it is really necessary for the patient to get about, in which case the limb should be bandaged, it is, perhaps, best to keep a dressing of Zinc Ointment applied during the day, and wash the unhealthy granulations, when the bandage is removed, with a Nitrate of Silver or Sulphate of Copper lotion. It is often desirable, even where rest can be taken, to use the roller bandage, which should be applied from the toes upwards in the manner directed under the head of *Bandages*. Previous to this application, the wound, besides the dressing, should be covered with strips of Soap or adhesive Plaster (the former is the best), applied so as to overlap each other some distance above

and below the ulcer. If Zinc Ointment does not seem to agree well, try Turner's Cerate, or the Cerate of Lead; in some cases Red Precipitate Ointment, considerably diluted, answers very well. Venice Turpentine, Resin Ointment, and other drawing and irritating applications, are sometimes recommended, but they are decidedly injurious. These are a few hints for general treatment, but individual cases present peculiarities which call for numerous modifications. The constitutional treatment will require great attention; the strength must be supported, and any tendency to inflammation must be kept down by cooling medicines. If there is great pain, so as to prevent sleep, 5 grains of Pill Soap and Opium, or of the Extract of Hyoscyamos, may be given at bedtime. Sometimes an Ulcer on the leg opens into one of the large veins, and a serious loss of blood ensues: in this case the limb should be elevated above the body until the hemorrhage can be stopped by pressure and astringent applications.

In cleansing an Ulcer, too much care should not be taken to remove all the pus or matter; it is better to leave some of it on, to protect the tender surface against irritation. If the Ulcer, when bandaged, feels hot and painful, saturate the bandage with cold water, and keep it wet for a time; a piece of oiled silk over all will prevent rapid evaporation, and greatly assist in this object. It is not always judicious to heal an Ulcer too quickly; if of long standing, it is likely to be an outlet for morbid matter, which, if retained in the system, might cause serious functional derangement, if not fatal disease, such as apoplexy.

BOILS. — These painful inflammatory swellings mostly occur in young and vigorous persons, so much so indeed as to be generally looked upon as a sign of robust health. Now and then, however, we find them breaking out upon the weak and delicate; in any case, they are symptomatic of some derangement of the system, which takes this means of relieving itself of that which is superfluous, or dangerous to its internal economy. They should be regarded as warnings that some change in the diet or mode of life is necessary to the preservation of complete health ; those who neglect such warnings often suffer the consequence in an attack of severe illness, or an eruption of a more painful and dangerous kind. See *Carbuncle*.

The seat of the Boil is the true skin and the subjacent cellular membrane. A small, angry-looking spot on the outer skin first appears ; this gradually enlarges into a swelling with a whitish conical centre, surrounded by a hard inflamed base ; sooner or later this is sure to suppurate and discharge pus and blood, and a fibrous mass called a core. Until this latter is ejected, the abscess will not heal. It often lies deep, and causes great pain before coming away. Warm water bathing, and poulticing with Linseed Meal, is the proper treatment at first ; Resin Ointment, or Venice Turpentine, or some other drawing application of an irritating nature, is often applied, but it causes unnecessary pain, and effects no object that the poultice would not. As soon as the prominent part of the swelling becomes soft, a cut should be made with a knife or lancet through the skin beneath which the core lies ; this permits the escape of the confined matter, and relieves the pain. The poultices should be continued until the core is drawn out, soon after which the healing process will commence ; this may be facilitated by a dressing of simple ointment, or pure hog's lard will do.

Boils and Carbuncles have recently been successfuly treated with Opium, of the aqueous extract of which a thick solution has been painted on any suspicious spot ; this forms a coating which must be renewed three or four times a day : twenty-four hours' application is said to be generally sufficient to arrest the spread of the inflammation. A plaster composed of equal parts of Soap, Opium, and Mercury, spread on thick leather, is then placed on the spot, having a hole in the centre for the escape of any matter ; if painful, a poultice must be applied. If, in spite of this treatment, the Boil will have its course, strong Nitric Acid is said to be the best application, using it freely two or three times, taking care to remove the slough before each application, supporting the margin with plaster and poulticing freely. The beneficial effects of the opium is said to depend upon the soothing influence which it exerts upon the capillaries, small arteries, and nerves ; its immediate effect is to lessen the throbbing, heat, and redness. The use of the plaster is to give support to the inflamed vessels, and to protect the surface from the atmosphere.

Boils often follow each other in rapid succession. They are very painful and troublesome, but not in themselves dangerous ; they seldom run into ulcerations and deep-seated sloughing sores unless neglected. Persons who are obliged to go about their daily avocations with them will do well to apply, during the day, a piece of lint saturated with Olive Oil, and kept on with strapping. For internal treatment, those of a full habit should take 3 or 4 grains of Blue Pill two or three times a week, with a Senna Draught each morning after ; they should also be abstemious in their diet, and avoid stimulants. Delicate persons should take a Compound Rhubarb Pill every alternate night, or a draught composed of Rhubarb and Magnesia, 10 grains of each, in Cinnamon Water ; these should have generous diet. Decoction of Sarsaparilla, ½ a tumblerful twice a day, and tepid baths, may be of service to such.

CARBUNCLE is essentially the same affection as the boil, but differing in magnitude and in its situation. It is usually located in the back of the neck, or the shoulders, in the interval between them, or the loins ; a very common situation for it is immediately below the occiput, on the very top of the neck, where the integument is thickest.

The *causes* of carbuncle are essentially similar to those of *boils* (which see) ; external irritation of some kind is generally the immediate cause; although there must also be a predisposition to carbuncular inflammation, arising from a particular state and condition of the system, generally an excess of fibrin, or inflammatory, matter, in the blood.

The first *symptom* of the disease is pain, followed by a hard, red swelling; very soon the surface of the tumor assumes a livid tint, and a soft, spongy feel ; small ulcers form on the skin, and, from their numerous orifices, which give the surface a sieve-like appearance, flows out a thin, pasty discharge, which is characteristic of the disease. These openings quickly break into one, and then the discharge thickens as the dead cellular tissue begins to escape ; to enable this to do so freely, an incision down to the very base of the tumor is made, and then crossed by another ; the hemorrhage attendant on this is commonly very considerable, as well as beneficial, in reducing the inflammation. Such is the mode of *treatment* usually adopted in carbuncle: Warm Bread or Linseed Meal poultices are applied, both before and after the cutting ; and, if the bleeding is excessive, Port Wine, or decoction of Oak Bark, with a little spirit, may be used to moisten them. The poulticing should be changed about every eight hours, and continued until the morbid matter is all discharged, and the wound is nearly filled with healthy granulations ; when these have risen to the level of the surrounding skin, the wound may be dressed with the ointment of Nitric Oxide of Mercury, or Red Precipitate ointment, as it is more commonly called. The constitutional treatment in this case should first be of an antiphlogistic kind; aperient, and febrifuge medicines, and low diet ; but as soon as the carbuncle has been opened, and the discharge becomes copious, the patient's vigor

must be sustained by good Beef-tea, Wine, and other nourishing condiments. Sometimes there is great prostration of strength, and as much stimulant is required as in typhus fever ; Bark, Opium, and Ammonia are commonly given to relieve the pain and arouse the nervous system. Persons of a full habit of body are those most subject to carbuncles, which are frequently fatal if they are situated high up in the neck, because they are usually attended with inflammation of the membranes of the brain. When on the back or loins, although frequently of enormous size, they are not so dangerous.

Burns and Scalds. — There are no more frequent, distressing, and dangerous accidents than those which result in the above ; they cause great pain, often amounting to agony, local injuries of a most serious character, and permanent constitutional derangement, even if death does not immediately or quickly ensue. The first rule to be observed in the event of the clothes catching fire, is to avoid running away for assistance, as the motion will only fan the flames, and increase the evil. Presence of mind in the sufferer is rare on such an occasion, but the best plan is to lie down and roll on the floor, screaming of course for assistance. Whoever comes should snatch up a rug, or piece of carpet, or other woollen article, and envelop the person in it; this will be sure to extinguish the flame, then cut the clothing away from the burnt parts, taking care to use no violence where it adheres, nor to break any blisters which may be raised. The great object is now to exclude the air from the blistered or raw surfaces; it is usual to cover them with flour and then wrap them in wadding or cotton wool. A good application is either of the above substances saturated in Limewater and Linseed Oil, equal parts mixed : this is extremely cool and soothing, and it greatly assists the healing operation: it should not be disturbed for some days, unless the discharge should

7

be great, and the wounds painful, in which case a fresh application of the same should be prepared, and put on immediately on the removal of the other. Whiskey, Brandy, or some other strong spirits, and even Turpentine, are recommended by some; but we question if they are so efficacious as the above remedies, and the anguish which they cause at first is a serious objection to their use. The Wadding or Cotton Wool covering is sometimes applied quite dry, with good effect; and where the tissues are not deeply or extensively injured, a lotion composed of an ounce and a half of Vinegar to a pint of Water is a good application, as is also a saturated solution of Carbonate of Soda. The flour dredging is that which is the most readily available, and it is perhaps as good as any; it should be applied immediately, and repeated as often as moisture is perceived issuing through the crust which it forms over the burnt parts; if these have fresh sweet oil brushed over them with a feather, previous to the application of the flour, it will adhere better. That which is most to be apprehended in severe burns is the great constitutional depression which often follows the excitement and severe pain; especially is this the case with children, and when the seat of this injury is the chest or abdomen, or other vital part; hence the effects should be closely watched, and stimulants administered, if there are such symptoms as shivering, pallor of countenance, sinking of the pulse, or coldness of the extremities: Ammonia, Wine, or Spirits, must then be given in doses sufficient to arouse the failing powers, without too much exciting the brain. If there is excessive pain, a slight opiate should be administered to allay the irritation of the nervous system, which, however, frequently receives so severe a shock as to lose its sensibility for a time; and when this is the case there is great reason to apprehend a fatal result. A burn, if properly treated, and unless very severe, will generally do

well, and require little after-dressing; but if the blisters are suffered to break, and the true skin beneath becomes inflamed by exposure, matter will be secreted, and troublesome ulcerations formed : Bread-and-water poulticing will be the best treatment in this case, with Goulard Lotion, if there is much inflammation, or an ointment composed of Extract of Goulard, 1 dram, mixed with 1 ounce of fresh lard; this should be applied spread on soft linen.

When the burn is deep, after the flour has been on for some days, poultices as above should be applied until the coating of flour all comes away, and the wound looks clean and clear; after which the simple water dressing will be best, and when nearly healed the Goulard Ointment as above.

When parts immediately contagious are involved in the burn, care must be taken to interpose dressings, or they may become permanently united.

After the more immediate constitutional effects of a severe burn have passed off, it will be necessary to be careful as to the patient's diet; which should be sufficiently nourishing and stimulative, especially while discharge is going on; taking care, however, to reduce it if febrile symptoms should set in. So constantly are these painful accidents occurring, and so frequently does it happen that the care of a medical man cannot be obtained for them, that it behooves all heads of families to make themselves acquainted with the best remedial measures. When they are very severe, every possible effort should be made to obtain medical aid; if they are but slight, this may well be done without. It should be borne in mind that the principal aims in the treatment of such cases are, first, the protection of the injured parts from atmospheric influence ; secondly, to keep down inflammatory action, both local and constitutional ; and thirdly, to soothe the nervous irritation which may arise, and to sustain the system should too great depression take place.

WOUNDS AND FRACTURES.

INJURIES BY LACERATION, BRUISING AND PUNCTURE—SYMPTOMS WHICH
BETOKEN DANGER—DISLOCATION DESCRIBED—A TREATISE ON SPRAINS,
RUPTURE AND INFLAMMATION—THE PRESERVATION OF EYESIGHT.

WOUNDS.—A recent solution of continuity in any soft part of the body, occasioned suddenly by external causes, and generally attended with hæmorrhage at first, is a wound. It may be one or the other of six kinds. 1st, an *Incised Wound*, made by a sharp instrument, effecting a simple division of the fibres. 2d, a *Lacerated Wound*, one in which the fibres, instead of being cleanly divided by a sharp instrument, are torn asunder by violence; the edges in this case are not straight, but jagged and uneven. 3d, a *Contused Wound*, one made by a violent blow from some blunt instrument, or unyielding surface. This resembles the preceding. 4th, a *Punctured Wound*, one made with a narrow-pointed instrument, as a sword or bayonet. 5th, a *Poisoned Wound*, such as the bite of a viper, mad dog, etc., or a slip of the lancet in dissecting bodies in a state of decomposition. 6th, *Gunshot Wound*, one caused by a bullet, or other hard substance, propelled from a musket.

The *treatment* of Wounds must, of course, depend very much upon their character. If it be a clean cut or chop, we should first stanch the blood, by bathing it with cold water, cleaning away any extraneous matter with a soft sponge; then bring the edges of the Wound together so that they shall unite evenly, and fix them so, with strips of adhesive plaster; a space being left between each slip for the escape of any blood or matter which may form. Should the Wound be of any great magnitude, so that the edges gape when unconfined, they should be drawn together by means of two or three stitches; in making which, a threaded needle (a curved one) should first be passed through the flesh, inwards, about a ¼ of an inch from the edge of the Wound, then on the other side outwards; the ends of the thread are then to be brought together and tied tightly. The stitches should be an inch or more apart, and must not be drawn or dragged together with great force, or they may cut through the parts, nor must they remain in too long, or they may cause irritation: from two to four days will be sufficient for them to answer every useful purpose; between them strips of adhesive plaster should be placed, and if a limb, a roller bandage should cover the whole. If the plaster is not readily procurable, a piece of linen may be bound round, and smeared with white of egg. Should the Wound become painful and throb, and the patient feel chilly and uneasy, it is likely that there is matter forming which requires a way of escape. In this case remove the plaster by washing it with a sponge dipped in warm water; then either put on a warm poultice, or lint, dipped or saturated with warm water, with a piece of oil skin over it, to prevent rapid evaporation. This mode of operation should be continued until pain and inflammation cease, and nothing but healthy pus is discharged. If any, simple strapping with adhesive plaster will then do.

A *stab* which goes deep is more difficult to heal than a surface incision, because, even if it does not injure an

99

important organ, it may lead to the formation of matter amid the under tissues, when the wound is closed at the top, and for this a way of escape must be made.

A Lacerated Wound caused by a hook or blunt instrument, should be first sponged clean, the torn portions laid in their natural positions as nearly as possible; then the edges of the Wound brought together by strips of sticking-plaster, putting over the whole a thick layer of lint dipped in cold water, and bandaging just light enough to keep the dressing secure; the lint should be kept moist.

In Bruised Wounds there is generally more sloughing of the injured parts; to remove which, warm poultices are necessary, otherwise they may be treated like clean cuts. When the sloughing is over, and healthy granulations begin to form, apply water dressing, and adhesive plaster, as above.

Punctured Wounds, from thorns or splinters, often lead to serious results. If the offending substance can be drawn out, by means of a needle, or a pair of tweezers, it should be done; if not, poultices will assist in removing it, and keeping down the inflammation, which is sure to arise from its presence among the tissues. There will most likely be a small abscess formed; and when this is opened, and the matter discharged, the thorn or splinter will most probably come with it, or may be removed. Sometimes from this apparently slight cause Lock-jaw may follow, or an irritative fever as the result of the inflammatory action, the treatment must be based upon the supervening symptoms, generally leeches, active aperients, and the same as that for inflammation will be required.

Wounds from a Fish, or Crochet Hook, are not generally very difficult to heal unless the system is in an unhealthy condition, in which case a mere scratch will suffice to set up inflammatory action; the great difficulty is the first, that of extracting the in-strument, which, on account of its barbed point, cannot be drawn out in the ordinary way: a slight incision will, therefore, be necessary; if the hook has no handle, or one that can be taken or cut off, the best plan is to depress the blunt end so as to cause the barbed point to penetrate the integument upwards, and make its way out; then take firmly hold upon the point, and through the flesh opening made by it draw out the whole of the hook; if this cannot be done, a slight cut, as far as the point has penetrated, will be necessary; and then a little careful manipulation will free the hook; afterwards strapping and cold water dressing should be applied, or a poultice, if there is much inflammation.

For Wounds and Lacerations of the Scalp.—Surgeons are now pretty generally assured that the best treatment is to free the torn piece from dirt or foreign bodies, and restore it as quickly as possible to its natural situation, no cutting away of any part (as practiced formerly) is now advised, and sewing is scarcely ever necessary; let the hair be cut or shaved off round the wound, draw the edges together with strips of adhesive plaster, and apply over it cold water dressing.

POISONING. — A Poison is a substance which, when taken internally, is capable of destroying life without acting mechanically on the system.

In apoplexy, epilepsy, some diseases of the heart and brain, and rupture or distension of the stomach, we have the same symptoms as those of narcotic poisoning. It behooves us, therefore, to make close inquiry into the cause of the dangerous symptoms, and not adopt remedial measures too hastily, although we know that promptitude in adopting the right measures is of vital importance. Hence we see how desirable it is that one skilled in the diagnosis of disease should be at once summoned in a case of suspected poisoning; if the aid of such cannot be procured at once, it is better to adopt such means as a limited knowledge will suggest than to let the patient perish for want of help. It is popularly believed that there are certain antidotes for particular Poisons, but this is not the case; there are, therefore, three great principles to be kept in view all through the course of treatment: 1st, to remove the poisonous matter from the stomach as soon as possible; 2d, to protect the coats of the stomach against the action of the Poison, by involving it in some viscid substance; 3d, to act upon the substance chemically so as to effect a change in its nature — to render it inert or innoxious.

Treatment. — Send for a physician immediately; if a stomach-pump is at hand, use it, if not, give an emetic of Sulphate of Zinc, or take Warm Water, with Mustard in it; or tickle the throat with a feather, or in some way cause vomiting; do not let the patient sleep for twelve hours after taking Poison, even if you have to use violent measures to keep him awake. When the physician arrives he will direct the treatment.

FRACTURE. — One of the commonest accidents, to which all are liable, is a fracture of one or other of the bones, which is often produced by a slight fall, or some other trifling accident, especially in very cold weather, when the bones are more brittle than at other times; and yet very heavy falls frequently occur without a fracture of any part of the osseous system, that being the result of some sudden concussion, or violent strain upon a part of the frame which is unable to bear it, consequently snaps short off; breaking more longitudinally, generally, in this case than in splinters. According as a fracture has a *transverse*, *longitudinal*, or *oblique* direction, in relation to the axis of the bone, it is distinguished by these terms. It is also called *Simple* when the bone only is divided, without external wound; *Compound*, when there is the same kind of injury, with laceration of the integuments. When Fractures occur in, or near, the middle of the long

bones, such as those of the leg, thigh, arm or forearm, they are readily detected, even by the eye and hand of one unskilled in anatomy: there is always great pain and loss of power over the portion of the limb below the Fracture, which will hang loosely, and may be moved in almost any direction, without reference to the proper action of the joints; the broken ends of the bone, too, will be quite perceptible to the feel, and there will be a grating sound when they are moved about. In many parts, however, as near the joints, and where there is much muscle, the symptoms are not so plainly marked, and it is often extremely difficult for even a surgeon to make out the exact position of a Fracture, even if he has sufficient assurance that such is the nature of the injury; and this difficulty is increased by the swollen and inflamed state of the parts.

The desirability of obtaining professional assistance in all cases where there is a likelihood of a Fracture having taken place, must be so evident to our readers, that we need scarcely insist on it.

DISLOCATION is the removal of the articulating portion of a bone from that surface to which it is naturally connected. This removal is generally effected by violence, and the primary object of remedial measures is to bring the point of articulation, or union, back to its natural position. When the muscles are only extended, and there is no laceration, or severance of a ligament, and no fracture of either of the bones, there is little difficulty in reducing common dislocations, if taken in hand shortly after their occurrence; but if the bones are suffered to remain long displaced, so that the muscles become accustomed, as it were, to their new position, there is sure to be permanent distortion, and most likely lameness of some kind. The displaced bone, at its new point of contact with other bones, forms a connection therewith, and finds there a basis for its future movements and operations, it requiring as much force to remove it from thence as it did from its more natural position.

Dislocations may be either complete or incomplete; in the first, the articular surfaces remain partially in contact, which can only occur in the foot, knee, and ankle; in the last, there is an entire separation; it is simple when there is no wound communicating with the joint, and externally with the air, and it is compound when there is such a wound.

Nearly all the bones of the human body are liable to displacement, but some are much more so than others — such are those of the hip, the ankle, the shoulder, the elbow, the lower jaw, the fingers, and toes, and in these joints the detection of the dislocation is tolerably easy, even to the unprofessional person; but with many other parts it is extremely difficult of detection; therefore, a surgeon should always be called in when an accident has occurred in which there is likely to be such a result.

The *symptoms* of a dislocation having taken place, are loss of power in the limb or member, which becomes fixed in one position, any attempt to move it causing extreme agony; there is also a sensation of numbness in the part, and the patient feels sick and faint, probably on account of the severe pain; an examination of the joint also will show a deformity.

Treatment. — It is useless in such a case to apply fomentations or stimulant liniments; attempts should at once be made to "reduce" the Dislocation, as it is called; until this is done there will be no relief for the patient, and the longer it is delayed the more difficult will the operation be, because the muscles, which are at first relaxed by being drawn out so far as to allow the joint to slip out of its socket, or from its point of articulation, resume their former rigidity, and exert a greater power in opposition to the efforts of the operator.

Whenever there is a doubt as to the nature of the injury which has happened, it is always best to wai. the arrival of a surgeon before making any violent efforts to reduce what is supposed to be merely a Dislocation, but may in reality be that in combination with a fracture, or an injury of quite another kind; but when the case is tolerably clear, no time should be lost in effecting the reduction. This may be done by drawing down the limb or members until the ends of the dislocated joints are brought as nearly together as possible; then if the pressure is relaxed, the muscles will generally draw them into their proper position, and hold them there; care should be taken to keep the upper bone of the two which it is desired to connect firmly fixed, so that in pulling the lower, the downward or outward, as the case may be, does not follow it, and so prevent the necessary extension of the muscles. If the Dislocation is in the humerus, or shoulder, a very common part, pass a sheet or strong towel round the body of the patient, and fasten the ends to a staple in the wall, or some other fixed support; then take another towel, and making what is called a "clove-hitch," slip it over the elbow, draw it tight, and give the ends to two or three strong assistants, who must pull gently, yet firmly and steadily, for some minutes, while the operator, with his knee beneath the armpit, endeavors, by raising and depressing the bone as it is drawn out, to direct it so that, when it has attained a point of extension beyond the edge of the socket from which it has been displaced, it will slip back into it. A dislocation of the shoulder may be either forwards or backwards; although the latter is a rare case, it may be known by the swelling at the shoulder-blade, the flatness of the outside, and incapacity of movement; the reduction may be effected in the same way as above described. After it is accomplished, it is most prudent, in either case, to keep the arm confined to the side for some days by means of a bandage, as it may be thrown out again by the slightest attempt to use the limb

Dislocation of the Collar Bone may occur at either end, but it is difficult for a non-professional man to detect this, and if such an injury is suspected, it is best to summon surgical aid, compressing the parts until it arrives with a crossed bandage. This accident, however skilfully treated, usually results in some permanent deformity.

Dislocations of the Elbow are the most difficult to understand and to reduce of any, on account of the complication of joints at that part, where, it must be remembered, three bones meet, viz., the arm-bone, and the two bones of the forearm, the second of which may be dislocated by itself, backwards or forwards, and the last only backwards, carrying the radius with it; two lateral displacements of the bones of the forearm also sometimes occur, and lastly, and rarely, a displacement in which the cartilaginous surface of the humerus rests between the radius and ulna. It must be evident that a thorough knowledge of the anatomy of the parts is required for the reduction of either of these, therefore we need not enter into a description of the means to be used.

Dislocation of the Spine is the most serious that can happen; in this case, death is sure to ensue, and it usually takes place soon after the accident, which happily is of very rare occurrence; but little can be done to remedy this mischief, and that little must be under the direction of the professional adviser.

Dislocation of the Ribs sometimes, though rarely, takes place, and this is very difficult of detection; the treatment is the same as that of a *Fracture*.

Dislocation of the Pelvic Bones and Os Coccygis.—These are both of extremely rare occurrence, immense force being required to effect either of them; they cannot be treated by other than a surgeon, and have generally a fatal result.

Dislocations of the Wrist Joints are generally caused by the hand receiving the weight of a heavy fall;

it may be of three kinds, all of which may be distinguished from a sprain by the unnatural bony projections, either in the front or back, as the case may be, in contradistinction to the soft swelling only, which is set up by the latter. The mode of reduction is this: let the patient's arm be grasped firmly, just above the elbow, by an assistant, while the operator, supporting the forearm with his left hand, takes hold of the patient's hand with his right, and the two exerting their force in opposite directions, produce the extension necessary to replace the joints in their natural position. After the reduction a roller bandage should be applied round the wrist, and a splint bound before and behind the forearm, passing on either side down as far as the metacarpal bones.

Dislocations of the Fingers and Toes are of rare occurrence, and when they do happen, it is generally between the first and second joints; they may be easily known by the projection of the dislocated bones, and reduced without much difficulty, if done soon after the accident; the wrist, during the operation, should have a slight forward inclination given to it; this will relax the flexor muscles.

Dislocation of the Jaw.—A blow upon the chin when the mouth is opened widely, will sometimes cause this, as will yawning or gaping very deeply; by it the patient is placed in a very awkward position, with mouth set wide open, and no power to close it or to articulate words. This kind of dislocation may be either complete or partial; in the latter case the mouth is not opened so widely as in the former, and it may be known by the chin being thrown on one side, opposite to that of the displacement. There is not usually much difficulty in reducing a dislocation of the lower jaw — the upper cannot be dislocated; the plan is to wrap a handkerchief round each thumb, and placing them in the inner angles of the jaw, the coronoid processes, as they are termed, endeavor, by forcing it backwards and downwards, to restore it to its proper position. Success will generally attend the effort, if only a moderate degree of force be used, especially if it be by a skilful hand. Some put a transverse piece of wood into the patient's mouth to serve the purpose of a lever, but this is a rough method of operating, and no really skilful surgeons resort to it.

BRUISES. — Make cold applications immediately: ice, cold iron, or cold water will do; this, if applied immediately, will prevent discolorations of the skin. After the inflammation has subsided, apply liniments with the hand, and gentle friction.

Sprains or Strains is an accident very likely to occur, especially in the wrist and ankle bones, and is productive of extreme pain, sometimes causing faintness and vomiting. There is, generally, effusion of blood beneath the enlargements, hence the discoloration of them, observable in these cases; commonly, also, there is rapid swelling, which renders it difficult to ascertain whether a discoloration or fracture has not taken place; therefore, if the injury is severe, a surgeon should be consulted. Not only are Sprains excessively painful at the time of their occurrence, but they are likely to lead to permanent injury, especially if neglected, and in this case they are more difficult to cure than either dislocations or fractures. Dr. South says: — "It would be better to break a limb than sprain a joint, the former, in ninety-nine cases out of a hundred, being cured in the course of a few weeks, if the skin has not been broken, while the effects of the latter may, at best, remain for weeks or months, as weakness or stiffness of the joint."

In the treatment of Sprains, perfect rest of the injured part is essential. We do not mean to say that they are never cured without this, but never so speedily and completely; and, without it, there is always great danger of bad after-consequences; therefore, the patient, as soon as it has been ascertained that there is nothing more than a Sprain, should take to his couch or

sofa, and remain perfectly quiescent, especially if the injury is in the ankle or knee, or any part of the leg, in which case the limb should be kept in a horizontal position, with warm moist flannels applied to the joint by day, and a warm bread-and-water poultice at night; should this not reduce the swelling and subdue the pain in the course of twenty-four hours, leeches may be applied and repeated two or three times if required. When the tenderness has, in a measure, subsided, a piece of lint dipped in vinegar, or diluted acetic acid, may be laid over the part; this will, probably, bring out a pustular eruption of the skin, and divert the low inflammation from the ligaments, at a time when stimulating friction could not be borne. When the pain has entirely ceased, and the joint has resumed its usual appearance, great caution is necessary in using it, as irreparable mischief often results from doing so too much or too early. If it continues swollen, it should be bound up with straps of soap plaster, or a roller. But before binding, plenty of friction, with Soap Liniment and Turpentine, should be tried, and a stream of cold water poured from a considerable height.

If the injury is in the elbow or wrist-joint, the arm should be sustained in a sling, and never suffered to hang down. Persons of full habit will require active purgatives, especially if the inflammation runs high; and if the pain is very severe, so as to prevent sleep, an opiate may be taken at bedtime; 10 grains of Dover's Powder is, perhaps, the best, or 5 grains of Extract of Hyoscyamus, if Opium cannot be taken.

WART. — This is an excrescence from the cutis or outer skin, or a horny tumor formed upon it; it is not generally so painful as it is disagreeable and unsightly, coming nearly always upon the hands, or some other conspicuous place. The best treatment is to touch it with some Caustic, or Escharotic. Nitrate of Silver is the most effectual, but this turns the skin black, which is, in many cases, very objectionable. Caustic Potash will answer the purpose, so will Acetic Acid, if of extra strength, and Nitric Acid. The application should be made daily, and the decayed part pared off, or cut with scissors. If it can be conveniently done, a ligature of silk tied tightly round the base of the Wart will cause it to decay, and eventually drop off. Some of the acrid vegetable juices, such as those of Celandine and Spurge, are popularly used as a cure for Warts.

CORNS.—There are few persons who have not suffered from these troublesome excrescences, which arise from a thickened state of the outer, or scarf skin, caused generally by the pressure or friction of tight, or ill-fitting shoes; the sensible, that is the true skin, feeling the pressure, endeavors to protect itself by throwing up a sort of defence, which assumes a conical form, having the apex within pressing upon the tender skin, and often causing intolerable pain, and sometimes inflammation to such an extent as to form an abscess at the point.

In the *treatment* of Corns, the first object should be to remove the exciting cause; comfortable, well-fitting boots or shoes should be substituted for those of an opposite character, and the Corn, after the foot has been soaked in warm water, to soften it, should be pared carefully away, particular care being taken not to wound the more sensitive part. When the outer surface is removed, there will be perceived in the centre a small white spot, which should be carefully dug out with a pointed knife or pair of scissors. When this too is removed, cover the seat of the Corn with a small circular piece of thick soft leather spread with Soap or Diachylon plaster, leaving a small hole in the centre, corresponding with that from whence the root of the Corn has been taken. Should any of this latter remain so as to cause irritation, apply to it, every second or third day, a piece of Lunar Caustic, scraped to a point, and slightly

moistened. Some persons apply strong Acetic, or other acid; but this is not so effectual, and more likely to cause inflammation, which will be best allayed by a warm poultice of bread crumbs, moistened with Goulard Water, the foot being held up as much as possible, and the system kept in a cool state with saline aperients, etc.

Soft Corns, which form chiefly between the toes, are often very painful and troublesome; let them be cut away as close as possible with a pair of scissors, and then dressed with rags wet with Goulard Water, or a solution of Sugar of Lead. Ivy leaves form, for such, a cool pleasant protection from friction; they should be put on fresh every day.

Beneath the corner of the nail of the great toe a peculiar kind of Corn sometimes occurs; it should be cut, or scraped out with the finger-nail, and Caustic applied as above directed. Mere callosities of the skin on the hands and fingers are not Corns, although often called so; they have no roots and are not painful, therefore it is best not to interfere with them, for if removed others would come in their places, while the friction is kept up, in which they originate.

BUNIONS.—This painful and annoying kind of swelling is the result of inflammation of a small bursa, situated just over the joint, at the ball of the great toe; the pressure of tight shoes is generally the exciting cause, and all such pressure should be at once removed. During the first stages, one or two leeches should be applied to the swelling, with warm fomentations and bread poultices. A permanent enlargement of the part is generally the result, and this must be studied in taking measure for the boot. An application of Caustic will sometimes reduce it considerably; it should be kept covered with Burgundy Pitch, or Soap Plaster, spread upon soft leather, or a circular piece of the fungus called German Tinder.

Ingrowing Toe-nail.—There is usually a fungoid growth in and about the part of the toe where the nail enters, and this must be destroyed by the free application of Caustic; then, if the nail be scraped thin, the edge may probably be lifted out, so that a small piece of scraped lint, or carded cotton, can be placed under, and prevent its penetrating again, so as to irritate and keep up the inflammation. Most surgeons recommend the entire removal of the nail, or of that half of it to which the ingrowing edge belongs, but a cure can often be effected without this. Apply a poultice of Slippery Elm, mixed with a little weak lye; on removing the poultice, press a little lint under the edge of the nail, repeating this daily, and cut off the nail when so raised with a sharp knife, keeping some lint under the edge of the nail until the toe is healed. Then, to prevent a recurrence, scrape the nail quite thin in the middle, or cut a notch the shape of a saw-tooth in the middle of the nail, which will then become narrower by contraction, and thus free itself from the flesh.

CHILBLAINS.—An inflammatory affection of the skin, generally confined to the extremities, and especially the fingers and toes. Exposure to sudden alternations of heat and cold usually give rise to these troublesome visitations, which are rather characterized by itching and irritation than pain. Persons of scrofulous habit and languid circulation, are most subject to them, as are children and aged persons. It is a popular fallacy, that to keep the surface of the skin in a state of unnatural warmth, by hot bottles and woollen socks by night, and fur linings and feet warmers by day, is the best way to prevent Chilblains; but this only serves to keep up a constant perspiration, and so weakens the tone of the system, and increases the liability to them. A nightly foot-bath of cold, or for aged persons of tepid salt and water, with plenty of friction with a rough towel, and exercise during the day, will be most likely to keep Chilblains from the feet; and for the hands, a careful rubbing so as to

get them thoroughly dry after every washing or dipping in water, and an avoidance of all unnecessary exposure to severe cold, are the best preventive measures. It is a good plan to have a pan of oatmeal always at hand, and to rub them well over with that after they have been wetted and wiped as dry as possible; this will absorb any moisture left by the towel, and have a softening and cooling effect.

Should Chilblains come, as sometimes they will, in spite of all precautions, let them be gently rubbed every night and morning with some stimulant application. Alcohol, Brandy, Spirits of Turpentine, or Camphorated Spirits of Wine, are all good for this purpose; but the application which we have found most efficacious is a lotion made of Alum and Sulphate of Zinc: 2 drams of each to half a pint of water, rubbed in warm; it may be made more stimulating by the addition of 1 ounce of Camphorated Spirits. When the Chilblains are broken, there must be a different course of treatment; the ulcers formed are often difficult to heal, especially in weakly and ill-conditioned persons; there is generally a great deal of inflammation, which must be subdued by means of bread-and-water poultices applied cold, and afterwards by cooling ointments, such as the Cerate of Acetate of Lead, or Spermaceti Ointment, with 40 drops of Extract of Goulard added to the ounce; should there be a disposition to form proud flesh, the Ointment of Red Precipitate should be used.

CANCER is a malignant disease—one of the most fearful with which medical science has to contend. It has two principal forms of development, called *hard* and *soft*. All parts of the skin are liable to its attacks, but those which appear to be more so are, the integuments of the face, the female breast, the uterus, and the organs of generation in both sexes. It sometimes affects the hands, and occasionally, from certain local causes, the male scrotum. When Cancer attacks the face, or any exposed part, it commonly begins with a small indurated spot, resembling a tubercle or wart; there is no appearance of inflammation, nor is there particular sensitiveness. This condition of things often continues for a very considerable time — sooner or later, however, ulceration sets in, and although it probably is long before it penetrates deeply, there may be matter secreted, which drying, forms a scab over the seat of the disease. By-and-by, sharp, shooting pains will be felt, the intervals between them, at first long, diminishing by degrees, until they become almost constant. There is a gradual, although slow, enlargement of the tumor, which is at first movable, but becomes afterwards attached to the skin and adjacent tissues; the ulceration spreads and deepens, and eventually becomes an open sore, with thick, hard, jagged edges, and a soft centre, eaten, as it were, into irregular hollows; the discharge is thin, bloody, and irritating to the surrounding parts; there is inflammation and hardening of the absorbent glands about the seat of disease, and the whole of the tissues appear to be invaded by a cartilaginous kind of growth, which spreads among and through them, like the creeping roots of some parasitic plant. It sometimes happens that there is an extensive sloughing of the whole diseased mass, which comes away, leaving a healthy wound, which heals by granulations, and happy is it for the patient when such is the case. Most commonly the disease creeps on like a secret miner, investing the very citadel of life, the heart, if it be situated near it, or some other vital organ, and after a term of, it may be years, the patient sinks exhausted by the pain and continual drain upon the system.

We have here briefly traced one of the forms in which cancerous disease is developed, proceeding as we have seen from scirrhous, or occult, to open, or true Cancer, as it is sometimes called: the first stage is distinguished by induration, coldness, insensibility, and deficiency of color, all indicating a low state of vitality; the characteristics of the second stage or condition are tenderness, soreness, presence of color, often approaching to a purple tint, bloody and serous discharge, cutting and throbbing pain, evidences of activity and progression.

Although mostly confined to the glands and to certain parts, as the female breast and womb, the stomach, the liver, and the testicles, yet there are few organs or tissues of the body which may not become the seat of this truly malignant disease; thus we find it sometimes seizing on the brain, the eye, the lip, the cheek, the nose, or the tongue, and it may perhaps have made considerable progress before its presence is suspected, coming like a mere pimple or hardening of the skin. Those attacked by it are mostly beyond thirty years of age, and are frequently persons of a scrofulous habit; there can be no doubt that it sometimes proceeds from hereditary taint; that it has been produced by contact, although it can scarcely be called a contagious disease. It may be excited into activity by the sudden application of cold, or by a blow, or by great anxiety or trouble of mind. Some irritating substances seem to have the power of producing it; soot certainly does, hence the prevalence in sweeps of *Cancer of the Scrotum*, of which we shall presently speak more fully. Women are more subject to it than men, and married more than single women; statistics completely refuting the theory that celibacy favors the development of the disease, which most usually takes place about the time when the menstrual discharge ceases, as though the healthy balance of the system had been hitherto kept up by this periodic discharge, and was now destroyed.

With regard to the often mooted question, Is Cancer curable? although quacks and empirics may declare that it is, true science makes no such positive assertion. Quackery says, — it can be cured without the knife; but this we do not believe, and so rarely with, that the exception but strengthens the rule. Are palliative measures then all that should be resorted to? our readers would ask: nay, there is a chance of preserving life, which is dear to all, for some years at all events; therefore, if circumstances admit of it, and the patient is desirous that it should be so, let the trial be made, and made as it only can be, by the aid of the highest surgical skill.

Considerable difference of opinion exists as to the *treatment* of persons suffering under this disease. While some would keep them on a diet barely sufficient to support life, others, among whom is Sir Astley Cooper, say that a good nourishing diet is required; and this would seem to be the more rational course, certainly so in the later stages, when the free discharge and constant pain wear out the strength and reduce the system; stimulants, of course, must be avoided as much as possible, especially those of an alcoholic nature. The above authority does not believe in the possibility of curing Scirrhous Cancer; all applications and medicines he considers therefore as merely palliatives, and this is the view taken of them by most really scientific men. It will be evident, therefore, that the avoidance of all which may tend to excite the disease to activity is a paramount object, for the attainment of which, perfect rest of body and mind, as far as this is compatible with a due performance of the functions of vitality, should be enjoined; the biliary and other secretions are to be carefully watched, and such medicines administered as may be necessary to keep them in a healthy state. Gentle aperients should be occasionally given, and those of an alterative nature are to be preferred; such as 5 grains of Plummer's Pill, at bedtime, and a Rhubarb draught in the morning; drastic purgatives, such as Jalap, Scammony, etc., are to be avoided, and also, as a general rule, salines. With regard to local applications, in the earlier stages, trial may be made of

Iodine rubbed in in the form of ointment, which has, on some few occasions, been found capable of dispersing hard swellings supposed to be cancerous; a plaster composed of Mercury and Ammoniacum has also been recommended; stimulating applications are decidedly objectionable, although they are sometimes used. When the tumor has passed into the soft state, or the sharp, shooting pains have commenced, it is time to begin the administration of sedatives; Hemlock is that generally recommended; the soft extract given as pills in 5 grain doses, or the Inspissated juice, ½ a dram, or the powdered leaves, from 3 to 10 grains; this, or Henbane, or the two in combination, are serviceable, both internally and applied as poultices. Opium in its several forms is also given, but it has a tendency to confine the bowels; Belladonna and Stramonium, too, may be tried should the above not have the desired effect, but it should be only under the direction of a medical man. Bichloride of Mercury given in combination with Tincture of Bark, Decoction of the same, or of Sarsaparilla, is sometimes administered; of the latter named root, the Extract or Decoction is a favorite remedy. Gentian, and Quinine, and the various preparations of Iron, Iodide of Potassium, Cod Liver Oil, Infusion of Malt, the mineral acids, especially Nitric, and Arsenic, in the form of Fowler's Solution, have all their advocates, and all their peculiar advantages depending upon constitutional and other differences. Some use the Phosphate of Iron, made into a paste with water, as a local application; or a Solution of the Muriated Tincture of Iron; some Arsenical Ointment; some evaporating Spirit Lotions; some Limewater and Linseed Oil; and some warm poultices. But again, says Sir Astley Cooper, "it is all nought; cold or hot, they are alike useless; the best dressing for the ulceration is prepared thus:— 1 ounce of Soap Cerate, 1 dram of Extract of Belladonna, melt and mix;" if there

Is much inflammation, he does not object to the use of Leeches. When the discharge is offensive, add a little Solution of Chloride of Lime, or Soda, to the lotion. We need scarcely enlarge upon the absolute necessity for extreme cleanliness; the wound, when it is discharging, must be frequently dressed, and the patient's linen often changed, or the fetor will become intolerable.

In some cases of Scirrhous Cancer, pressure has been applied with a certain amount of success; shields of sheet-lead of various thickness, or tin plates, have been placed over the tumor, over these, strips of adhesive plaster, and then linen compresses and roller bandages. In open Cancer, the wound has been filled with powdered chalk, and thickly dusted with starch powder, covering the more irritable surface with gold-beaters' skin. In this mode of treatment, care is taken to have the plaster and bandages evenly applied, and the cavities so filled up that pressure on the part be firm and even, without partial stricture. But we might fill a volume were we to enter fully into all the various modes of treating Cancers, the real or pretended remedies for which are indeed too numerous to mention here; a qualified practitioner only can judge of the means best adapted for particular cases.

If the Cancer be in the womb, a horizontal position should be maintained; the lotions can only be applied as injections, and no dressing on the immediate seat of the disease is possible, although a solution of Iodine, or other preparation, may be applied, by means of a camel-hair brush; leeches to the loins and groins may be applied if there is much inflammation, the warm hip-bath used daily, and opiate injections administered, with a suppository at night. There should be abstinence from sexual intercourse, and perfect quiet. If the cancerous ulceration be on the tongue, it should be brushed over several times a day with a camel-hair pencil dipped in the following composition: Borax and Hemlock, powdered, of each 1 dram; Honey, 1 ounce; it is well also to apply to the surface, once a day or so, a brush dipped in Muriated Tincture of Iron.

When the ulceration is on the face, the same application may be used, or Arsenical Solution of Potash, or Lime-water with Calomel—the Black Wash as it is called. In this situation, Cancer is sometimes confounded with *Lupus;* but whereas the former at its commencement is hard and colorless, the latter is soft and of a bright red color; the Cancerous tubercle, too, is single, but in *Lupus* there are usually two or more spots.

An operation for Cancer should be performed in the indolent stage of the tumor; that is, while it is hard and movable, before it has become attached to the surrounding tissues, from which it will be difficult, if not impossible, to extirpate it, when the disease has passed into the ulcerated state, and the absorbent glands have become affected. In operating thus, in the early period of the disease, there is a chance that the whole of the tumor may be removed, especially as is recommended, if a considerable portion of the healthy substance be cut away with it; but it generally happens that the patient's mind is not made up until the symptoms become really alarming, and the suffering great. Then, when the operation is performed, the parts may unite, the wounds may heal, and all for a time appear to go on well, but sooner or later, the disease will be pretty sure to show itself again, and this time its progress will be more rapid than at first.

Canker of the Mouth. — This is a gangrenous inflammation of the mouth; it begins in small blisters on the inside of the cheek, or on the tongue, which soon become little ulcers, which are very painful, and sometimes spread both wide and deep.

Treatment. — First clear and regulate the bowels by some gentle cathartic medicine. Rhubarb and Magnesia, or a Compound Cathartic Pill, one taken every night for some time, should also be used; the mouth should be washed frequently with Sage Tea and Vinegar, or a tea made of the leaves of the Black Currant, or Roots of Blackberry, should be freely drank. Dissolve 1 dram of Crystals of Nitrate of Silver in ½ a wineglass of water, and apply to the ulcers with a camel-hair pencil as required.

POLYPUS is a tumor generally occurring in the nose, but sometimes in the womb, or the ear, and so named from an erroneous idea that it had many roots or feet; it is the result of an excessive growth of the mucous membrane, and sometimes assumes a malignant character. It may be either of a soft texture, so as easily to tear and bleed, or firm and fibrous, or even almost cartilaginous. The color is commonly a yellowish-gray, and it has little or no sensibility, although it causes much pain by its pressure upon the surrounding parts, stoppage of secretions, etc. It is attached to the surface from which it springs by a narrow neck like a footstalk. When in the nose, it interferes with the breathing, so that the patient sleeps with the mouth open. In this situation it may sometimes be destroyed by the persevering use of astringent applications, such as the Tincture of Steel applied with a camel-hair brush, twice a day, or a little Burnt Alum taken like snuff. In the womb, Polypus can only be treated by a surgeon, as here, and indeed elsewhere, an operation is generally required for its removal,—ligatures, scissors, or forceps being used for the purpose. The operation, if skilfully performed, is not a dangerous one, and it is necessary, for, although a Polypus is commonly of slow growth, it is at all times very inconvenient, and often it increases very rapidly, and assumes a malignant character.

WEN.—An encysted tumor, whose seat is the cellular membrane of any part of the body. It is movable, has a pulpy feel, and varies in size, but seldom exceeds that of an egg. With regard to the *treatment* of Wens, Dr. Graham observes that, although it is not often any advantage arises from the use of local applications, yet sometimes a strong stimulant applied frequently to the surface will disperse them, when small and recently formed; and of all stimulants, electricity appears to be the most efficacious. Those who wish to try it may have sparks from the battery, and slight shocks passed through it daily A very strong solution of salt and water is likewise a powerful stimulant in some cases of Wens, and has been known to bring them away by causing the cyst to open and discharge its contents. The surface of the Wen must be bathed with this solution very frequently every day. No benefit can be expected in less than a fortnight, and sometimes not sooner than a month or two. I am disposed to think this remedy worthy of more attention in these cases than it has yet obtained. The great advantage attending it is, that it gives no pain or inconvenience of any kind. The operation of removing Wens by the knife is attended with much less pain than is generally supposed.

Varicose Veins are not uncommon in the legs of stout elderly females, and may be met with in those of all ages and both sexes. In this affection there is enlargement of the vessels, which stand out from the surface of the limb like cords; like which, too, they often assume a knotted appearance. This affection may be attributed to obliteration, or deficient action of the valves of the Veins of the leg, or some other cause of obstruction of the flow of blood upward, through those of the abdomen. Pregnancy, habitual costiveness, liver disease, abdominal tumors, may be all mentioned as exciting causes. The pressure of a truss, or belt also, or of garters too tightly tied, may bring on this varicose condition of the veins, especially in persons whose occupation necessitates much standing. Great care should be taken to avoid a scratch or contusion of the swollen part, or a wound may be produced which is likely to result in an ulcer very difficult to heal. The part should be supported and protected by a bandage, or elastic stocking. If the former, it should be very carefully and evenly applied; but a well-fitting stocking of elastic web is the best and most convenient.

Iodine Ointment should be well rubbed over the part affected every night, using considerable friction, and in the morning shower cold water upon it.

Rupture, or Hernia, is a protrusion of some part of the abdominal viscera, but principally the intestines. There are four chief varieties of Rupture:— 1st, Inguinal, which is in the groin, above the fold. 2d, Femoral, which is below the fold of the groin. 3d, Navel, or Umbilical. 4th, Ventral, occurring at the side, or middle of the belly, below the navel. The first of these is the most common form of Rupture; next in frequency is the second; the third is not uncommon with children at birth. This also sometimes affects stout elderly persons, especially females who have borne many children. It has been clearly established that about one out of every five men is ruptured; in women, the proportion is not nearly so great, as their avocations generally involve less muscular exertion. With them, the femoral form is most common.

Symptoms and Treatment. — A swelling, at first very small, shows itself in one or other of the situations above named. It is not painful, nor are there signs of inflammation about the spot; if it recedes on pressure, or on a recumbent position being assumed, the patient may be pretty sure that it is a Rupture; if, on pressing it back, there is a gurgling noise, it contains intestine only, but when omentum also is projected, there will be a solid, doughy kind of feel. Persons are often ruptured for some time without being aware of it. They will, perhaps, ex-perience uneasy sensations about the pit of the stomach, a kind of dragging, with slight nausea; on their having occasion to make some great exertion, that hitherto undiscovered lump will become more prominent, and force itself upon the attention, and there may or may not be sickness and vomiting until it is returned into the abdomen, which it generally can be with a little careful manipulation. The object, then, is to secure such an amount of pressure over the orifice of escape as to prevent its protruding again; and this can only be done by a truss of some kind. *The patient is never safe without one;* and, as it is of the utmost consequence, both to the comfort and safety of the wearer, that the instrument should be exactly suited to the case, it is best to resort at once to an experienced surgical mechanist for a supply of this essential article. First, the part should be sponged night and morning with cold water, and if it gets chafed or abraded, it should be dusted after each sponging with Starch powder or Flour. A regular action of the bowels is essential to the safety of ruptured persons, as the violent medicines necessary to relieve a state of costiveness will be likely to increase the Rupture to a dangerous extent. Castor Oil, or some other gentle aperient, should be taken as often as may be necessary to insure a daily motion without much straining.

One of the tendencies of this affection is to cause a deficient action of the bowels, and when these are much confined, and there is a sense of constriction about the middle, and vomiting of feculent matter, an examination should always be instituted, to ascertain if Rupture has not originated this train of symptoms. It may happen with ruptured persons who do not wear a truss, and also with those who do, if the instrument is not quite suited to the case, that the protruding gut or omentum may become so large that there is much difficulty in getting it back, or reducing the Rupture, as we should say; if the patient cannot, by lying down on his back, and gently pressing it up through the aperture, accomplish this, the aid of a surgeon should be obtained, if possible: should it not be, a warm bath may be first tried, keeping the patient in until he feels faint, so as to relax the muscles. He should, during this time, repeatedly renew the efforts above directed. If this fails, apply pounded ice, in a bladder, to the part, or a freezing mixture, composed of Table Salt, Saltpetre, and Sal Ammoniac, in equal proportions, with a little water added, just enough to make it liquid. If neither of these can be readily obtained, intense cold may be produced by means of wet rags laid over the swelling, and evaporation encouraged by a continual stream of air from a pair of bellows directed upon the rags, which should be frequently rewetted.

Sometimes the return of the Rupture may be accelerated by a reversal of the position of the body, placing it on an inclined plane with the head downward. Bleeding to faintness while standing up, and then lying down, has sometimes succeeded, but, of course, only a surgeon could attempt this. Should all means fail, we have what is called *Strangulated Hernia*, and an operation is necessary; this is always attended with considerable danger. When Rupture of the groin occurs with young children, nothing can be done for the first three months or so but to keep the child as much as possible in a recumbent position, and sponge the part frequently with cold water; at the end of the above period a light truss may be worn, with every prospect of a cure, if proper attention is paid to the case. When a person about forty years of age becomes ruptured, there is little chance that a cure will be effected, although by constant pressure on the part, with an avoidance of violent exertion, the size of the Rupture may be greatly reduced.

Diseases of the Eye. — The Eyeball itself is liable to be affected by *Acute, Chronic, Purulent,* and *Strumous Ophthalmia,* the first of which is con-fined to the conjunctiva, or outer-covering of the front of the eye; its chief symptoms are a smarting sensation, and a feeling like that caused by the presence of dust; there is also considerable stiffness, and the whites become tinged with red, owing to the veins being suffused; on a close examination, the red vessels may be distinctly traced, and it may be observed that they move with the surface, showing that the inflammation is but superficial.

Treatment. — Warm bathing of the Eye, combined with an active mercurial treatment, should first be tried. If the habit of the patient is such as to bear this, 5 grains of Blue Pill at night, and a Saline or Black Draught in the morning, continued for three successive days, or alternate days, may be given; if not, the mercury must be taken in a milder form, as in the Grey Powder, and combined with Rhubarb, say 3 grains of the former and 8 or 10 of the latter, every other night; the diet should be low, and light excluded as much as possible from the inflamed organ. Should the warm bathing not produce a good effect in a couple of days or so, use the following lotion: Wine of Opium, 1 dram; Sulphate of Zinc, 8 grains; Acetate of Lead, 16 grains; Rose, or plain Distilled Water, 8 ounces; dip a piece of linen in this lotion, and bind it, not too tightly, over the eye, letting part of the fold hang down so as to cover it well; keep this moistened. Should it be necessary to resort to other measures, drop into the eye, from a quill or small glass tube, a Solution of Nitrate of Silver, the strength about 4 grains to the ounce of Distilled Water, 2 or 3 drops three times a day, and apply leeches. When this disease continues long, the inflammation extends deeper, and it becomes *chronic,* which has all the symptoms of the *acute* form of disease, except the feeling as of dust in the eyes; the latter of the above measures will generally reduce it; or should not the Nitrate of Silver drops succeed, use Wine of Opium alone in the same way, and a lotion made with Green Tea, and about one-sixth of its bulk of Brandy, or other strong spirit.

Either of the above forms of Ophthalmia, especially the two latter, may result in ulceration of the Cornea, which, in its more dangerous form, is caused by extensive inflammation of the Cornea itself; in its less dangerous form, by the little pustules already spoken of. In the former, the treatment cannot be too active and energetic, as there is little chance of saving the eye by other than the strongest methods; Calomel and Opium, Blisters, Leeches, etc., will no doubt be employed by the physician. No one else can detect the niceties of the case sufficiently well to treat it properly.

Rheumatic Inflammation of the Eye has its seat in the middle or sclerotic coat; it is characterized by intense pain, which becomes more severe towards night, when it is generally accompanied by fever, and constant aching of the bones of the orbit; in this case it may be seen that the inflammation is deeply seated, by the immobility of the red veins, when the lids are moved about; the treatment here will be like that of Acute *Rheumatism.*

Inflammation of the Iris is characterized by intolerance of light, but not the spasmodic closure of the eyelids before mentioned; the whole colored part of the eye loses its clearness, and sometimes has on it white or yellow spots; a pink zone invests the cornea, and seems to give a tinge to the whole front of the ball. This is a very rapid and violent form of Eye disease, and bleeding, mercurials, and strong purgatives must be resorted to if they can possibly be borne; 2 grains of Calomel with a ¼ of a grain of Opium, given every six hours until soreness of the mouth is produced, and if it does not open the bowels freely, Black Draughts every morning, very low diet, and blisters behind the ears, are the orthodox remedies, and the best.

Of that opacity of the crystalline lens called *Cataract,* we have spoken under

its proper head. There is another disease which, without any such opacity, or paralysis of the nerves, produces blindness. It is characterized by unusual dilation of the pupil, which contracts but sluggishly, and has generally a greenish-brown hazy appearance; this is not very amenable to medical treatment. Counter-irritants, such as Blisters, may be tried, with Mercurials and Iodide of Potassium, but there is little chance of preserving the sight, which has usually become impaired before the above symptoms declare the nature of the disease, which is often mistaken for Cataract; the mischief in this case seems to be deep in the vitreous humor, the cloudy appearance of which can only be seen when the eye is looked straight into.

Inflammation of the Choroid is known by its accompanying dull heavy pains, and by bulging and discoloration of the white portions; this, like *Dropsy of the Eye,* which occurs in the aqueous and vitreous humors, causing enlargement and loss of sight, cannot be treated by other than a skilful surgeon, and seldom by him with success. The aid of such must also be sought for Cataract of the Eye, the only cure for which is the entire removal of the ball, an operation by no means dangerous, and easily gone through by the aid of Chloroform.

It should be borne in mind that when Lead or Mercury, in any of their forms of combination, are applied to the Eye for any length of time, they are likely to produce Opacity of the Cornea, and consequent dimness of vision; and even without this result, the white, by the use of Nitrate of Silver, may become permanently stained of an olive color.

We have now to speak of those Eye affections which relate rather to the appendages than to the globe itself; although, from the intimate connection existing between all parts of this complex organ, no one part can be morbidly affected without the rest partaking, to some extent, in the mischief.

8

STYES are little inflammatory tumors which frequently make their appearance on the edges of the Eyelids of children; they rarely affect grown persons, and, although troublesome, are not at all dangerous locally, nor prejudicious to the general health; they run the same course as boils, which, in reality, they are; generally speaking, they require no medical treatment, but when very large and painful, a Hot Water Fomentation will prove beneficial; when once the matter has escaped, they heal very quickly; a simple dressing of Spermaceti Ointment is sometimes required, but not often.

The edges of the Eyelids are sometimes very red and stiff, in consequence of the inflammation of the small follicles or ducts which open there; the best remedy is a little Red Precipitate Ointment rubbed into the roots of the lashes, when the lids are closed on retiring to rest; this may be repeated every night until no longer required. A little Grey Powder, combined with Rhubarb, should be given, and the patient kept quiet and somewhat low. When inflammation has been going on in the Eyelids for a time, their insides, when inverted, will often present a rough granular appearance; in this case they should be gently rubbed over with a smooth piece of Dry Sulphate of Copper; the lid should be kept open after the application until the Eyeball is syringed with warm water, to remove from it any of the solution caused by the flow of tears acting on the Sulphate; there will probably be great smarting of the Eye, and increased redness of the white portion, which must be suffered to subside before the application is repeated, which it will, most likely, have to be many times. Low diet, and Mercury with Rhubarb, as recommended in the last case, are also required in this. Sometimes the hairs on the lids grow inwards, and cause great irritation of the balls; Collodion brushed over the lids will, as it dries, cause contraction of the skin, and so draw the hairs out-

ward, but this is only a temporary relief, and the application must be frequently repeated; surgical aid must be sought for the case, which is called *Trichiasis.*

Entropium and **Extropium** are turning in and turning out of the edges of the Eyelids; in the first case the lashes rub against and inflame the ball; in the second, the inside of the lid is exposed, and becomes sore and inflamed. Only a skilful operator can effectually deal with these two forms of Eye disease, although some relief may be afforded in the former of them by the Collodion application above described. *Ptosis* is a dropping of the upper eyelids in consequence of palsy arising from disease of the nerve which supplies the levator muscle; sometimes the dropping is partial, sometimes entire, so that the whole eye is covered. This is a symptom of organic disease, which may be of a trivial and temporary character, or extensive and permanent; no domestic treatment can be of any service in the case. Small *encysted tumors* and red spots, called *nævi*, frequently appear about the Eyelids, and also little abscesses, the latter especially after erysipelas, small-pox, or any other inflammatory diseases which affect the cellular membrane, which is very loose about the Eye. The latter may be pricked with a common lancet, when there is no doubt about their character; but the former should not be meddled with except by experienced hands. Diseased conditions of the apparatus for the conveyance of tears from the lachrymal sac to the nose, sometimes occur; only a surgeon can attempt to remove the obstructions, and remedy any defects which may be discoverable in the organs.

As to SQUINTING, OPTICAL ILLUSIONS, or SPECTRA, NEAR and SHORT SIGHT, our readers will find full particulars in relation thereto under their several heads. We have now gone through most of the diseases to which the Eye and its appendages are subject in as full and we trust satisfactory, a manner as our space would permit.

A few remarks on the appearance of the Eye as symptomatic of disease, may be useful in conclusion.

A BLOOD-SHOT EYE may indicate either inflammation, or congestion, or extravasation of blood in the organ itself, or catarrh, or influenza, but measles especially.

CONTRACTED PUPIL, if it be not the result of local disease, shows that some serious mischief is going on in the brain; there may be compression, or watery effusion; this is not unfrequently the result of taking large doses of opium.

DILATED PUPIL occurs in amaurosis, and several diseases of the brain; small doses of Opium will frequently produce this; and the outward application of Atropine, or Belladonna, will nearly always do so.

INTOLERANCE OF LIGHT we have already spoken of as a symptom of Strumuous Ophthalmia; in severe headaches, fevers, and inflammation of the brain it is also met with.

PROMINENCE OF THE EYEBALLS may result from dropsy of the eye itself, but it is often symptomatic of some obscure disease, affecting the *Brain* or *Heart.*

SMARTING OF THE EYE occurs in acute Ophthalmia, and in that stage of measles in which these organs are particularly affected.

SQUINTING, although commonly a chronic condition of the muscles of the Eye, is, when it comes on in the course of active disease, indicative of mischief in the brain, which may terminate in *Apoplexy.*

WATERING OF THE EYES is, when acute, symptomatic of Influenza; when chronic, of some obstruction to the flow of tears through the nasal duct.

YELLOWNESS OF THE WHITES of the Eyes precedes and accompanies Jaundice, and indicates an improper action of the *Liver.*

SIGHT. — It is only necessary for us here briefly to remark of this faculty of seeing, that, like the other senses, it conveys no clear information to the mind, until it has been well exercised and tested by comparison: thus the person born blind, to whom the faculty is for the first time given, recognizes not the objects he looks upon, although touch, taste, or smell may have previously made them known to him.

The image now first painted on his retina may convey a different impression to his mind from that which an examination of the same object by another sense than Sight had conveyed, and he can only arrive at a true conception by studying and comparing. The blind man in Scripture, to whom our Saviour gave sight, saw men as trees walking; he had known there were men before, and he had known that there were trees; could tell when he came in contact with one or the other, but he could not tell what they were like; now he had a new power of *testing* his former experience, and correcting his feeble impressions. The infant, when it first opens its eyes to the light, looks upon a world of wonders, and can form no correct idea of any object which it sees, until it has also touched and handled, tasted, or smelled it. The moral of all this is, that Sight, like every other faculty, requires careful education, and the pitch of perfection to which it can be educated is truly surprising. Very seldom is it sufficiently and properly exercised. Most men walk about this beautiful and wonderful world as if they had a veil before their eyes; vision is to them but a half faculty, a dull, almost inert sense. But such should remember, that he is best able to serve himself and his fellow-creatures, and to appreciate the power and goodness of God, who improves and exercises to its fullest extent every power and faculty which God has given to him for the enjoyment of life.

To Preserve the Eyesight. —1st, avoid straining the eyes by reading small print, or looking at minute objects.

2d. Avoid reading or writing much in the dusk of the evening.

3d. Do not continue to look at glaring objects.

4th. Hold the object you are looking at, a considerable distance from the eye.

5th. Sit in such a position that the light may strike upon the object from behind, over the shoulder.

6th. Do not read while riding, or in any place where there is jolting. This is particularly injurious to the eyes, because, from the constant shaking, the object cannot be kept the same distance from the eye — therefore, cannot accommodate itself to it.

On this topic, Dr. Clark gives some excellent admonitions. He says:

"Frequently some imprudence in youth during the student period, while the body is in a state of immature development, results in a permanent disability of the eyes. A few nights of successive study, or days of constant application, during a period of physical debility; a day with the microscope, viewing an eclipse; a few hours' reading in the cars, or any continued exercise of the organs of vision without sufficient rest, will frequently give a shock to the nervous apparatus of adjustment, from which the eyes never fully recover.

"When, after reading, writing, sewing, or the like, there is an obscurity or confusion of objects, or if there is a feeling of fatigue in the eyes, or if black motes and sparks and flashes of light appear, or if objects appear to be surrounded with a halo, it is time to stop. No man can afford to continue the employment of the eyes upon near objects. Absolute rest of the eyes and mind are requisite — or, what will often do better, an entire change of employment. By giving the eyes timely rest, and guarding carefully the general health, the asthenopic may accomplish much eye labor."

Rules for Judging when the Eyes Require the Assistance of Spectacles. — (1.) When we are obliged to remove small objects to a considerable distance from the eye in order to see them distinctly. (2.) If we find it necessary to get more light than formerly; as, for instance, to place a light between the eye and object. (3.) If on looking at, and attentively considering a near object, it fatigues the eye, and becomes confused, or if it appears to have a kind of dimness or mist before it. (4.) When small printed letters are seen to run into each other, and hence, by looking steadfastly on them, appear double or treble. (5.) If the eyes are so fatigued by a little exercise that we are obliged to shut them from time to time, so as to relieve them by looking at different objects. When all of these circumstances concur, or any of them separately takes place, it will be necessary to seek assistance from glasses, which will ease the eyes, and in some degree check their tendency to become worse: whereas, if they be not assisted in time, the weakness will be considerably increased, and the eyes be impaired by the efforts they are compelled to exert.

Felon, or Whitlow.—An inflammation at the end of one of the fingers or thumbs, very painful, and much disposed to suppurate. The effusion may be immediately under the skin, or deeper among the tendons, or it may press on the periosteum; this last is the worst and most malignant form; it is consequently called *Felon*. The excessive pain and irritation which attend a Whitlow, is due chiefly to its situation under the nail, and the thickened skin at the end of the finger or toe, which, from its unyielding nature, confines the inflamed part, and prevents the quick discharge of the matter formed.

Whitlows generally arise from pricks or bruises, or other injuries of a local nature; but with some they occur so frequently as to prove that they are, in a measure, constitutional.

Treatment. — The chief point is to soothe and soften the part affected by the free use of warm fomentations and poultices, to render the nail and skin supple, and favor the formation and discharge of the matter. When there is much inflammation, a leech or two may be applied to the swelling; and

If the pain causes deprivation of rest, a Calomel and Opium Pill, containing a grain of each, may be taken at bedtime, and a gentle aperient draught in the morning. If the abscess does not burst of itself, after the above measures, it should be opened with the lancet; the nail should be pared away as thin as possible, and any loose portions of it removed. Warm poulticing should be continued a couple of days or so, after the Whitlow is opened, and then a dressing of Simple Cerate should be applied, changing it about every eight hours; if this treatment should not suit, use Turner's Cerate, or try Water dressing. A small blister is sometimes necessary to promote an increased discharge, and give a salutary stimulus to the diseased parts; it may be kept on about twelve hours, and the raw surface, when it comes off, dressed with Spermaceti Ointment. When the Whitlow is seated among the tendons, there is excruciating pain, but little swelling of the affected finger, although there may be of the hand and wrist, and perhaps of the whole forearm; this requires a free incision made very early, and only a surgeon can treat the case.

It is not advisable to apply caustic to any fungus or proud flesh which may arise in these cases; they will disappear if the wound can be stimulated to healthy action.

Bone Felon. — The *London Lancet* says: "As soon as the disease is felt, put directly over the spot a fly blister, about the size of your thumb-nail, and let it remain for six hours, at the expiration of which time, directly under the surface of the blister, may be seen the felon, which can instantly be taken out with the point of a needle or a lancet."

Another remedy, very efficacious, is take rind of fat pork (if rusty the better), mix gunpowder with it, and apply as a poultice. Let it remain on for sixteen or twenty hours. The last hour or two will be painful, but on removing it the Felon will be gone, and the patient relieved.

Bleeding at the Nose. — Persons of a sanguine temperament and full habit of body are most subject to this disease, we were about to say; but perhaps it ought rather to be regarded as a salutary provision for the relief of the overcharged system. If it does not run to a weakening extent, it is very questionable whether it should be interfered with. Those who are troubled with vertigo and headache, arising from a fulness of the veins and a tendency of blood to the head, know how much better and lighter they feel after a good bleeding from the nose; and there can be no doubt that many a fit of apoplexy has been averted by it, and many an attack of inflammatory fever, or inflammation of the brain. This bleeding may arise from several causes, among which may be named violent exercise, great heat, blows on the part, the long maintenance of a stooping posture, and a peculiar smallness of the vessels which convey the blood to the brain, rendering them liable to rupture. It may come on without any previous warning, or be preceded by headache and a sense of heaviness, singing noises in the ear, heat and itching of the nostrils, throbbing of the temporal artery, and accelerated pulse. When it comes on too frequently and continues long, so as to cause faintness, and especially if the person subject to it be of a weakly habit or advanced in years, it should be stopped as soon as possible. The stoppage may sometimes be effected by immersing the head in cold water, free exposure to cool air, and drinking cool acidulous liquids. The body of the patient should maintain an erect position, with the head thrown somewhat back, a key or other cold substance be applied to the spinal cord, vinegar be snuffed up the nostrils, or an astringent wash injected with a syringe. It may be composed as follows: Alum and Acetic Acid, of each 2 drams, Water, 6 ounces; or 3 drams of the Muriated Tincture of Iron in the same quantity of Water. Or, if these fail, the nostrils may be plugged with lint dipped in a strong solution of the Sulphate of Copper; or the lint first moistened, and then dipped in finely powdered Charcoal. When the bleeding has stopped, there should be no haste to remove the clotted blood from the nostrils; let it come away of itself. Do not blow the nose violently, nor take stimulants, unless there be excessive faintness, in which case a little cold Brandy and Water may be taken. Where there is a full habit of body, cooling medicines, low diet, and leeches to the temples, may be safely advised, with perhaps occasional bleeding from the arm.

Extraordinary as it may appear, a piece of brown paper folded and placed between the upper lip and the gum, will stop bleeding of the nose. Put a piece of paper in your mouth, chew it rapidly, and it will stop your nose bleeding.

Frost Bite.—The effect of severe cold is to weaken the circulation, the ex- tremities become blue, or livid, and if severe cold is long-continued, the circulation stops; this is Frost-bite. Drowsiness comes on, then sleep, and death.

Treatment.—The best plan is to place the limb, or part frozen, in cold water, for some time; and as feeling begins to return, let the water be made a little warmer very gradually. If the person frozen be gone so far as to become insensible, and apparently dead, undress him and cover him with snow, except the mouth; or in ice-cold water. Let him remain so for a few minutes, then rub with cold wet cloths; as the body becomes thawed, or supple, use dry cloths, and place the body in a cold bed, and rub with warm hands, continuing this treatment for some hours. If life appears, put a little Spirits of Camphor on the tongue, then rub the body with spirits and water, and give Brandy and Water to drink.

EVERY ONE HIS OWN DRUGGIST.

MEASURES.—Liquid medicines are measured by the following table :—

60 minims	are contained in	1 fluid dram.
8 fluid drams...		1 fluid ounce.
16 fluid ounces..		1 pint.
8 pints............		1 gallon.

And the signs which distinguish each are as follows :—c. means a gallon ; o, a pint ; *fʒ*, a fluid ounce ; *fʒ*, a fluid dram ; and ℥, a minim, or drop. Formerly drops used to be ordered, but as the size of a drop must neces- sarily vary, minims are directed to be employed now for any particular medi- cine, although for such medicines as Oil of Cloves, Essence of Ginger, etc., drops are frequently ordered.

IN ORDER THAT WE MAY MEASURE MEDICINES ACCURATELY, there are graduated glass vessels for measuring ounces, drams, and minims.

WHEN PROPER MEASURES ARE NOT AT HAND, it is necessary to adopt some other method of determining the quantities required, and therefore we have drawn up the following table for that purpose :

A tumbler............	usually contains about	16 ounces.
A teacup............		6 "
A wineglass..........		2 "
A tablespoon..........		4 drams.
A dessertspoon......		2 "
A teaspoon..........		1 "

These quantities refer to ordinary sized spoons and vessels. Some cups hold

Process of Making Medicines.—

SOME SUBSTANCES require to be pre- pared in a particular manner before they can be powdered, or to be assisted by adding some other body. For ex- ample, Camphor powders more easily when a few drops of spirits of wine are added to it ; Mace, Nutmegs, and such oily aromatic substances are better for the addition of a little white sugar ; Resins and Gum-Resins should be pow- dered in a cold place, and if they are intended to be dissolved, a little fine well-washed white sand mixed with them assists the process of powdering. Tough roots, like Gentian and Ca- lumba, should be cut into thin slices ; and fibrous roots, like Ginger, cut slanting, otherwise the powder will be full of small fibres. Vegetable matters require to be dried before they are powdered.

BE CAREFUL NOT TO POUND TOO HARD in a glass, porcelain, or Wedge- wood-ware mortar; they are intended only for substances that pulverize easily, and for the purpose of mixing or incorporating medicines. Never use acids in a marble mortar, and be sure that you do not powder galls or any other astringent substances in any but a brass mortar.

SIFTING is frequently required for powdered substances, and this is usually done by employing a fine sieve, or tying the powder up in a piece of muslin, and striking it against the left hand over a piece of paper.

FILTERING is frequently required for the purpose of obtaining clear fluids, such as infusions, eye-washes, and other medicines; and it is, therefore, highly important to know how to perform this simple operation. We must first of all make the filter-paper; this is done by taking a square sheet of white blotting-paper, and doubling it over so as to form an angular cup. We next procure a piece of wire, and twist it into a form to place the funnel in, to prevent it passing too far into the neck of the bottle. Open out the filter-paper very carefully, and having placed it in the funnel, moisten it with a little water. Then place the wire in the space between the funnel and the bottle, and pour the liquid gently down the side of the paper, otherwise the fluid is apt to burst the paper.

MACERATION is another process that is frequently required to be performed in making up medicines, and consists simply in immersing the medicines in *cold water* or spirits for a certain time.

DIGESTION resembles maceration, except that the process is assisted by a gentle heat. The ingredients are placed in a flask, such as salad oil is sold in, which should be fitted with a plug of tow or wood, and have a piece of wire twisted round the neck. The flask is held, by means of the wire, over the flame of a spirit-lamp, or else placed in some sand warmed in an old iron saucepan over the fire, care being taken not to place more of the flask below the sand than the portion occupied by the ingredients.

INFUSION is one of the most frequent operations required in making up medicines, its object being to extract the aromatic and volatile principles of substances, that would be lost by

decoction or digestion; and to extract the soluble from the insoluble parts of bodies. Infusions may be made with cold water, in which case they are weaker, but more pleasant. The general method employed consists in slicing, bruising, or rasping the ingredients first, then placing them in a common pitcher (which should be as globular as possible), and pouring boiling water over them; cover the pitcher with a cloth folded six or eight times, but if there be a lid to the vessel so much the better; when the infusion has stood the time directed, hold a piece of *very coarse* linen over the spout, and pour the liquid through it into another vessel.

DECOCTION, or boiling, is employed to extract the mucilaginous or gummy parts of substances, their bitter, astringent, or other qualities, and is nothing more than boiling the ingredients in a saucepan with the lid slightly raised. Be sure never to use an iron saucepan for astringent decoctions, such as oak-bark, galls, etc., as they will turn the saucepan black, and spoil the decoction. The enamelled saucepans are very useful for decoctions, but an excellent plan is to put the ingredients into a jar and boil the jar, thus preparing it by a water bath, as it is technically termed; or by using a common pipkin, which answers still better. No decoction should be allowed to boil for more than ten minutes.

EXTRACTS are made by evaporating the liquors obtained by infusion or decoction, but these can be bought much cheaper and better of apothecaries, and so can tinctures, confections, cerates and plasters, and syrups; but as every one is not always in the neighborhood of apothecaries, we shall give recipes for those most generally useful, and the method of making them.

Precautions to be Observed in Giving Medicines. — SEX. — Medicines for females should not be so strong as those for males, therefore it is advisable to reduce the doses about one-third.

TEMPERAMENT.—Persons of a phleg

matic temperament bear stimulants and purgatives better than those of a sanguine temperament, therefore the latter require smaller doses.

HABITS. — Purgatives never act so well upon persons accustomed to take them as upon those who are not, therefore it is better to change the form of purgative from pill to potion, powder to draught, or aromatic to saline. Purgatives should never be given when there is an irritable state of the bowels.

STIMULANTS AND NARCOTICS never act so quickly upon persons accustomed to use spirits freely as upon those who live abstemiously.

CLIMATE. — The action of medicines is modified by climate and seasons. In summer, certain medicines act more powerfully than in winter, and the same person cannot bear the dose in July that he could in December.

GENERAL HEALTH. — Persons whose general health is good, bear stronger doses than the debilitated and those who have suffered for a long time.

IDIOSYNCRASY. — Walker's Dictionary will inform you that "idiosyncrasy" means a peculiar temperament or disposition not common to people generally. For example, some persons cannot take Calomel in the smallest dose without being salivated, or Rhubarb without having convulsions; others cannot take Squills, Opium, Senna, etc., and this peculiarity is called the patient's idiosyncrasy, therefore it is wrong to *insist* upon their taking these medicines.

FORMS BEST SUITED FOR ADMINISTRATION. — Fluids act quicker than solids, and powders sooner than pills.

BEST METHOD OF PREVENTING THE NAUSEOUS TASTE OF MEDICINES. — Castor Oil may be taken in milk, coffee, or spirit, such as brandy; but the best method of covering the nauseous flavor is to put a tablespoonful of strained orange juice in a wineglass, pour the Castor Oil into the centre of the juice, and then squeeze a few drops of lemon juice upon the top of the oil. Cod Liver Oil may be taken, like Castor Oil, in orange juice. Peppermint

water almost neutralizes the nauseous taste of Epsom Salts; a strong solution of Extract of Liquorice, that of Aloes; milk, that of Cinchona Bark; and cloves, of Senna.

AN EXCELLENT WAY TO PREVENT THE TASTE OF MEDICINES is to have the medicine in a glass, as usual, and a tumbler of water by the side of it; take the medicine, and retain it in the mouth, which should be kept closed, and if you then commence drinking the water, the taste of the medicine is washed away. Even the bitterness of Quinine and Aloes may be prevented by this means. If the nostrils are firmly compressed by the thumb and finger of the left hand, while taking a nauseous draught, and so retained till the mouth has been washed out with water, the disagreeable taste of the medicine will be quite unperceived.

GIVING MEDICINES TO PERSONS. — Medicines should be given in such a manner that the effect of the first dose shall not have ceased when the next dose is given, therefore the intervals between the doses should be regulated accordingly.

DOSES OF MEDICINE FOR DIFFERENT AGES. — It must be plain to every one that children do not require such powerful medicine as adults or old people, and therefore it is desirable to have some fixed method of determining or regulating the administration of doses of medicine. Now we will suppose that the dose for a full grown person is 1 dram, then the following proportions will be suitabe for the various ages given; keeping in view other circumstances, such as sex, temperament, habits, climate, state of *general health*, and idiosyncrasy.

Age.	Proportion.	Proportionate Dose.
7 weeks..............	one-fifteenth......	or grains 4
7 months............	one-twelfth........	or grains 5
Under 2 years...	one-eighth.........	or grains 7½
" 3 "	...one-sixth.........	or grains 10
" 4 "	...one-fourth........	or grains 15
" 7 "	...one-third	or scruple 1
" 14 "	...one-half	or dram ½
" 20 "	...two-fifths..........	or scruples 2
above 21 "	...the full dose......	or dram 1
" 65 "	...the inverse	gradation.

Drugs, with their Properties and Doses. — We have arranged the various drugs according to their properties, and have given the doses of each; but in compiling this we have necessarily omitted many from each class, because they cannot be employed except by a medical man. The *doses* are meant for adults.

MEDICINES HAVE BEEN DIVIDED into four grand classes — 1. General stimulants; 2. Local stimulants; 3. Chemical remedies; 4. Mechanical remedies.

General Stimulants. — General stimulants are subdivided into two classes, diffusible and permanent stimulants: the first comprising narcotics and anti-spasmodics, and the second tonics and astringents.

Narcotics are medicines which stupefy and diminish the activity of the nervous system. Given in small doses, they generally act as stimulants, but an increased dose produces a sedative effect. Under this head we include Alcohol, Camphor, Ether, the Hop, and Opium.

ALCOHOL, or rectified spirit, is a very powerful stimulant, and is never used as a remedy without being diluted to the degree called proof spirit; and even then it is seldom used internally. It is *used externally* in restraining bleeding, when there is not any vessel of importance wounded. It is also used as a lotion to burns, and is applied by dipping a piece of lint into the spirit, and laying it over the part. Freely diluted (one part to eighteen) with water, it forms a useful eye-wash in the last stage of ophthalmia. *Used internally*, it acts as a very useful stimulant when diluted and taken moderately, increasing the general excitement, and giving energy to the muscular fibres; hence it becomes very useful in certain cases of debility, especially in habits disposed to create acidity, and in the low stage of typhus fevers. *Dose.* — It is impossible to fix anything like a dose for this remedy, as much will depend upon the individual; but diluted with water

and sweetened with sugar, from ½ an ounce to 2 ounces may be given three or four times a day. In cases of extreme debility, however, much will depend upon the disease. *Caution.* — Remember that Alcohol is an irritant *poison*, and that the indulgence in its use daily originates dyspepsia, or indigestion, and many other serious complaints. Of all kinds of spirits, the best as a tonic and stomachic is *brandy.*

CAMPHOR is not a very steady stimulant, as its effect is transitory; but in large doses it acts as a narcotic, abating pain and inducing sleep. In moderate doses it operates as a diaphoretic, diuretic, and anti-spasmodic, increasing the heat of the body, allaying irritation and spasm. It is *used externally* as a liniment when dissolved in Oil, Alcohol, or Acetic Acid, being employed to allay rheumatic pains; and it is also useful as an embrocation in sprains, bruises, chilblains, and, when combined with Opium, it has been advantageously employed in flatulent colic and severe diarrhœa, being rubbed over the bowels. *When reduced to a fine powder*, by the addition of a little Spirit of Wine and friction, it is very useful as a local stimulant to indolent ulcers, especially when they discharge a foul kind of matter. A pinch is taken between the finger and thumb, and sprinkled into the ulcer, which is then dressed as usual. *When dissolved in Oil of Turpentine*, and a few drops are placed in a hollow tooth, and covered with jeweller's wool, or scraped lint, it gives almost instant relief to toothache. *Used internally*, it is apt to excite nausea, and even vomiting, especially when given in the solid form. *As a stimulant*, it is of great service in all low fevers, malignant measles, malignant sore throat, and confluent small-pox; and when combined with Opium and Bark, it is extremely useful in checking the progress of malignant ulcers and gangrene. *As a narcotic*, it is very useful, because it allays pain and irritation, without increasing the pulse very much. *When powdered and sprinkled* upon the surface of a blister, it prevents the cantharides acting in a peculiar and painful manner upon the bladder. *Combined with Senna*, it increases its purgative properties; and it is also used to correct the nausea produced by Squills, and the irritating effects of drastic purgatives and mezereon. *Dose*, from 4 grains to half a scruple, repeated at short intervals when used in small doses, and long intervals when employed in large doses. *Doses of the various preparations.* — Camphor mixture, from half an ounce to 3 ounces; Compound Tincture of Camphor (*Paregoric elixir*) from 15 minims to 2 drams. *Caution.* — When given in an overdose, it acts as a poison, producing vomiting, giddiness, delirium, convulsions, and sometimes death. Opium is the best antidote for Camphor, whether in excess or taken as a poison. *Mode of exhibition.* — It may be rubbed up with almond emulsion, or mucilage, or the yolk of eggs, and by this means suspended in water, or combined with chloroform as a mixture, in which form it is a valuable stimulant in cholera and other diseases.

ETHER is a diffusible stimulant, narcotic, and anti-spasmodic. *Sulphuric Ether is used externally* both as a stimulant and a refrigerant. In the former case, its evaporation is prevented by covering a rag moistened with it with oiled silk, in order to relieve headache; and in the latter case it is allowed to evaporate, and thus produce coldness; hence it is applied over scalded surfaces by means of rags dipped in it. *As a local application*, it has been found to afford almost instant relief in earache, when combined with Almond Oil, and dropped into the ear. *Internally*, it is used as a stimulant and narcotic in low fevers and cases of great exhaustion. *Dose*, from 15 minims to ½ a dram, repeated at short intervals, as its effects soon pass off. It is usually given in a little Camphor Julep, or Water.

NITRIC ETHER is a refrigerant, diuretic, and anti-spasmodic, and is well known as "*Sweet Spirit of Nitre*." *Used externally*, its evaporation relieves headache, and it is sometimes applied to burns. *Internally*, it is used to relieve nausea, flatulence, and thirst in fevers, also as a diuretic. *Dose*, from 10 minims to 1 dram.

COMPOUND SPIRIT OF SULPHURIC ETHER is a very useful stimulant, narcotic, and anti-spasmodic. *Used internally* in cases of great exhaustion, attended with irritability. *Dose*, from ½ a dram to 2 drams, in Camphor Julep. When combined with Laudanum, it prevents the nauseating effects of the opium, and acts more beneficially as a narcotic.

THE HOP is a narcotic, tonic, and diuretic. It reduces the frequency of the pulse, and does not affect the head, like most anodynes. *Used externally*, it acts as an anodyne and discutient, and is useful as a fomentation for painful tumors, rheumatic pains in the joints, and severe contusions. A pillow stuffed with Hops acts as a narcotic. When the powder is mixed with lard, it acts as an anodyne dressing in painful ulcers. *Dose*, of the *extract*, from 5 grains to 1 scruple; of the *tincture*, from ½ a dram to 2 drams; of the *powder*, from 3 grains to 1 scruple; of the *infusion*, ½ ounce to 1½ ounces.

OPIUM is a stimulant, narcotic, and anodyne. *Used externally* it acts almost as well as when taken into the stomach, and without affecting the head or causing nausea. Applied to irritable ulcers in the form of tincture, it promotes their cure, and allays pain. Cloths dipped in a strong solution, and applied over painful bruises, tumors, or inflamed joints, allay pain. A small piece of solid Opium stuffed into a hollow tooth relieves toothache. A weak solution of Opium forms a valuable collyrium in ophthalmia; 2 drops of the Wine of Opium dropped into the eye, acts as an excellent stimulant in bloodshot eye; or after long-continued inflammation, it is useful in strengthening the eye. Applied as a liniment, in combination with Ammo nia and Oil, or with Camphorated Spirit, it relieves muscular pain. When combined with Oil of Turpentine, it is useful as a liniment in spasmodic colic. *Used internally*, it acts as a very powerful stimulant, then as a sedative, and finally as an anodyne and narcotic, allaying pain in the most extraordinary manner, by acting directly upon the nervous system. In acute rheumatism, it is a most excellent medicine when combined with Calomel and Tartrate of Antimony; but its exhibition requires the judicious care of a medical man. *Doses of the various preparations.* — *Confection of Opium*, from 5 grains to ½ a dram; *Extract of Opium*, from 1 to 5 grains (this is a valuable form, as it does not produce so much after-derangement of the nervous system as solid Opium); *pills of Soap and Opium*, from 5 to 10 grains; *Compound Ipecacuanha Powder* ("Dover's Powder"), from 10 to 15 grains; *Compound Kino Powder*, from 5 to 15 grains; *Wine of Opium*, from 10 minims to 1 dram. *Caution.*— Opium is a powerful *poison* when taken in too large a quantity, and therefore should be used with extreme caution. It is on this account that we have omitted some of its preparations. The best antidote for Opium is Camphor.

Anti-Spasmodics are medicines which possess the power of overcoming the spasms of the muscles, or allaying any severe pain which is not attended by inflammation. The class includes a great many, but the most safe and serviceable are Ammonia, Assafœtida, Galbanum, Valerian Bark, Ether, Camphor, Opium, and Chloroform, with the minerals, Oxide of Zinc and Calomel.

AMMONIA, or "VOLATILE SALT," is an anti-spasmodic, antacid, stimulant, and diaphoretic. *Used externally*, combined with Oil, it forms a cheap and useful liniment, but it should be dissolved in *proof* spirit before the Oil is added. One part of this Salt, and three parts of Extract of Belladonna, mixed and spread upon leather, makes an excellent plaster for relieving rheumatic pains. As a local stimulant it is well known, as regards its effects in hysterics, faintness, and lassitude, when applied to the nose, as common smelling salts. It is *used internally* as an adjunct to Infusion of Gentian in dyspepsia or indigestion, and in moderate doses in gout. *Dose*, from 5 to 15 grains. *Caution.*—Overdoses act as a narcotic and irritant poison.

BICARBONATE OF AMMONIA, used *internally* the same as the "volatile salt." *Dose*, from 6 to 12 grains. It is frequently combined with Epsom Salts.

SOLUTION OF SESQUICARBONATE OF AMMONIA, used the same as the "volatile salt." *Dose*, from ½ a dram to 1 dram, combined with some milky fluid, like Almond Emulsion.

ASSAFŒTIDA is an anti-spasmodic, expectorant, excitant, and anthelmintic. *Used internally*, it is extremely useful in dyspepsia, flatulent colic, hysteria, and nervous diseases; and where there are no inflammatory symptoms, it is an excellent remedy in whooping-cough and asthma. *Used locally* as an enema, it is useful in flatulent colic, and convulsions that come on through teething. *Doses of various preparations.*—Solid gum, from 5 to 10 grains as pills; *mixture*, from ½ an ounce to 1 ounce; *tincture*, from 15 minims to 1 dram; *ammoniated tincture*, from 20 minims to 1 dram. *Caution.* — Never give it when inflammation exists.

GALBANUM is stimulant, anti-spasmodic, expectorant, and deobstruent. *Used externally*, it assists in dispelling indolent tumors when spread upon leather as a plaster, and is useful in weakness of the legs from rickets, being applied as a plaster to the loins. *Employed internally*, it is useful in chronic or old standing rheumatism and hysteria. *Doses of preparations.* — Of the *gum*, from 10 to 15 grains as pills; *tincture*, from 15 minims to 1 dram. It may be made into an emulsion with mucilage and water.

VALERIAN is a powerful anti-spasmodic, tonic, and excitant, acting chiefly on the nervous centres. *Used internally*, it is employed in hysteria, nervous languors, and spasmodic complaints generally. It is useful in low fevers. *Doses of various preparations.* — *Powder*, from 10 grains to ½ a dram, three or four times a day; *tincture*, from 2 to 4 drams; *ammoniated tincture*, from 1 to 2 drams; *infusion*, from 2 to 3 ounces, or more.

BARK, or, as it is commonly called, "Peruvian Bark," is an anti-spasmodic, tonic, astringent, and stomachic. *Used externally*, it is an excellent detergent for foul ulcers, and those that heal slowly. *Used internally*, it is particularly valuable in intermittent fever or ague, malignant measles, dysentery, diarrhœa, intermittent rheumatism, St. Vitus' dance, indigestion, nervous affections, malignant sore throat, and erysipelas; its use being indicated in all cases of debility. *Doses of its preparations.* — *Powder*, from 5 grains to 2 drams, mixed in wine, water, milk, syrup, or solution of liquorice; *infusion*, from 1 to 3 ounces; *decoction*, from 1 to 3 ounces; *tincture* and *compound tincture*, each from 1 to 3 drams. *Caution.* — If it causes oppression at the stomach, combine it with an aromatic; if it causes vomiting, give it in wine or soda water; if it purges, give opium; and if it constipates, give rhubarb.

ETHER (SULPHURIC) is given internally as an anti-spasmodic in difficult breathing and spasmodic asthma; also in hysteria, cramp of the stomach, hiccough, locked jaw, and cholera. It is useful in checking sea-sickness. *Dose*, from 20 minims to 1 dram. *Caution* — An overdose produces apoplectic symptoms.

CAMPHOR is given internally as an anti-spasmodic in hysteria, cramp in the stomach, flatulent colic, and St. Vitus' dance. *Dose*, from 2 to 20 grains.

OPIUM is employed internally in spasmodic affections, such as cholera, spasmodic asthma, whooping-cough, flatulent colic, and St. Vitus' dance. *Dose*, from ⅛ of a grain to 2 grains of the solid opium, according to the disease.

OXIDE OF ZINC is an anti-spasmodic, astringent, and tonic. *Used externally*, as an ointment, it forms an excellent astringent in affections of the eyelids, arising from relaxation; or as a powder, it is an excellent detergent for unhealthy ulcers. *Used internally*, it has proved efficacious in St. Vitus' dance, and some other spasmodic affections. *Dose*, from 1 to 6 grains, twice a day.

CALOMEL is an anti-spasmodic, alterative, deobstruent, purgative, and errhine. *Used internally*, combined with Opium, it acts as an anti-spasmodic in locked jaw, cholera, and many other spasmodic affections. As an alterative and deobstruent, it has been found useful in leprosy and itch, when combined with antimonials and guaiacum, and in enlargement of the liver and glandular affections. It acts beneficially in dropsies, by producing watery motions. In typhus it is of great benefit when combined with antimonials; and it may be given as a purgative in almost any disease, provided there is not any inflammation of the bowels, irritability of the system, or great debility. *Dose*, as a deobstruent and alterative, from 1 to 5 grains, daily; as a cathartic, from 5 to 15 grains; to produce ptyalism, or salivation, from 1 to 2 grains, in a pill, with a quarter of a grain of Opium, night and morning. *Caution.* — When taking Calomel, exposure to cold or dampness should be guarded against, as such an imprudence would bring out an eruption of the skin, attended with fever. When this does occur, leave off the Calomel, and give bark, wine, and purgatives; take a warm bath twice a day, and powder the surface of the body with powdered starch.

TONICS are given to improve the tone of the system, and restore the natural energies and general strength of the body. They consist of Bark,

Quassia, Gentian, Camomile, Worm wood, and Angostura Bark.

QUASSIA is a simple tonic, and can be used with safety by any one, as it does not increase the animal heat, or quicken the circulation. *Used internally*, in the form of infusion, it has been found of great benefit in indigestion and nervous irritability, and is useful after bilious fevers and diarrhœa. *Dose of the infusion*, from 1½ to 2 ounces, three times a day.

GENTIAN is an excellent tonic and stomachic; but when given in large doses, it acts as an aperient. It is *used internally* in all cases of general debility, and when combined with Bark, is used in intermittent fevers. It has also been employed in indigestion, and it is sometimes used, combined with Volatile Salt, in that disease; but at other times alone, in the form of infusion. After diarrhœa, it proves a useful tonic. *Used externally*, its infusion is sometimes applied to foul ulcers. *Dose*, of the *infusion*, 1½ to 2 ounces ; of the *tincture*, 1 to 4 drams; of the *extract*, from 10 to 30 grains.

CAMOMILE. — The flowers of the Camomile are tonic, slightly anodyne, anti-spasmodic, and emetic. They are *used externally* as fomentations, in colic, faceache, and tumors, and to unhealthy ulcers. They are *used internally* in the form of infusion, with Carbonate of Soda, Ginger, and other stomachic remedies, in dyspepsia, flatulent colic, debility following dysentery and gout. Warm infusion of the flowers acts as an emetic; and the powdered flowers are sometimes combined with Opium or Kino, and given in intermittent fevers. *Dose*, of the *powdered* flowers, from 10 grains to 1 dram, twice or thrice a day; of the *infusion*, from 1 to 2 ounces, as a tonic, three times a day, and from 6 ounces to 1 pint, as an emetic ; of the *extract*, from 5 to 20 grains.

WORMWOOD is a tonic and anthelmintic. It is *used externally* as a discutient and antiseptic. It is *used internally* in long-standing cases of dyspepsia, in the form of infusion,

with or without aromatics. It has also been used in intermittents. *Dose*, of the *infusion*, from 1 to 2 ounces, three times a day ; of the *powder*, from 1 to 2 scruples.

ANGOSTURA BARK, or Cusparia, is a tonic and stimulant. It expels flatulence, increases the appetite, and produces a grateful warmth in the stomach. It is *used internally* in intermittent fevers, dyspepsia, hysteria, and all cases of debility where a stimulating tonic is desirable, particularly after bilious diarrhœa. *Dose*, of the *powder*, from 10 to 15 grains, combined with Cinnamon Powder, Magnesia, or Rhubarb ; of the *extract*, from 3 to 10 grains ; of the *infusion*, from 1 to 2 ounces. *Caution.*—It should never be given in inflammatory diseases or hectic fever.

ASTRINGENTS are medicines given for the purpose of diminishing excessive discharges, and to act indirectly as tonics. This class includes Catechu, Kino, Oak Bark, Logwood, Rose Leaves, Chalk, and White Vitriol.

CATECHU is a most valuable astringent. It is *used externally*, when powdered, to promote the contraction of flabby ulcers. As a local astringent is useful in relaxed uvula, a small piece being dissolved in the mouth; small, spotty ulcerations of the mouth and throat, and bleeding gums, and for these two affections it is used in the form of infusion to wash the parts. It is *given internally* in diarrhœa, dysentery, and hemorrhage from the bowels. *Dose*, of the *infusion*, from 1 to 3 ounces ; of the *tincture*, from 1 to 4 drams ; of the *powder*, from 10 to 30 grains. *Caution.*—It must not be given with Soda or any alkali, nor Metallic Salts, Albumen, or Gelatine, as its property is destroyed by this combination.

KINO is a powerful astringent. It is *used externally* to ulcers, to give tone to them when flabby, and discharging foul and thin matter. It is *used internally* in the same diseases as Catechu. *Dose*, of the *powder*, from 10 to 15 grains; of the *tincture*, from 1 to 2 drams; of the *compound powder*, from 10 to 20 grains; of the *infusion*, from ½ to 1½ ounces. *Caution.* — Kino is used in combination with Calomel, when salivation is intended, to prevent, by its astringency, the action of the Calomel on the bowels, and thereby insure its affecting the constitution.

OAK BARK is an astringent and tonic. It is *used externally*, in the form of decoction, to restrain bleeding from lacerated surfaces. As a local astringent, it is used in the form of decoction, as a gargle in sore throat and relaxed uvula. It is *used internally* in the same diseases as Catechu, and when combined with aromatics and bitters, in intermittent fevers. *Dose*, of the *powder*, from 15 to 30 grains; of the *decoction*, from 2 to 8 drams.

LOGWOOD is not a very satisfactory astringent. It is *used internally* in diarrhœa, the last stage of dysentery, and a lax state of the intestines. *Dose*, of the *extract*, from 10 grains to 1 dram; of the *decoction*, from 1 to 3 ounces, three or four times a day.

ROSE LEAVES are astringent and tonic. They are *used internally* in spitting of blood, hemorrhage from the stomach, intestines, etc., as a gargle for sore throat, and for the night sweats of consumption. The infusion is frequently used as a tonic with diluted Sulphuric Acid (Oil of Vitriol), after low fevers, or in combination with Epsom Salts and Sulphuric Acid in certain states of the bowels. *Dose*, of *infusion*, from 2 to 4 ounces.

CHALK, when prepared by washing, becomes an astringent as well as antacid. It is *used internally* in diarrhœa, in the form of mixture, and *externally* as an application to burns, scalds, and excoriations. *Dose*, of the *mixture*, from 1 to 2 ounces.

WHITE VITRIOL, or Sulphate of Zinc, is an astringent, tonic, and emetic. It is *used externally* as a collyrium for ophthalmia, and as a detergent for scrofulous ulcers, in the proportion of 3 grains of the salt to 1 ounce of water. It is *used internally* in indigestion, and many other dis-

eases; *but it should not be given unless ordered by a physician, as it is a poison.*

Local Stimulants. — Local stimulants comprise Emetics, Cathartics, Diuretics, Diaphoretics, Expectorants, Sialogogues, Errhines, and Epispastics.

Emetics are medicines given for the purpose of causing vomiting, as in cases of poisoning. They consist of Ipecacuanha, Camomile, Antimony, Copper, Zinc, and several others.

IPECACUANHA is an emetic, diaphoretic, and expectorant. It is *used internally* to excite vomiting, in doses of from 10 to 20 grains of the powder, or 1 to 1½ ounces of the infusion, every half hour until vomiting takes place. To make it act well and easily, the patient should drink a half pint of warm water after each dose of the infusion. As a diaphoretic, it should be given in doses of 3 grains, mixed with some soft substance, such as crumbs of bread, and repeated every four hours. *Dose* of the *wine*, from 20 minims to 1 dram as a diaphoretic, and from 1 dram to 1½ ounces as an emetic. *Caution.*—Do not give more than the doses named above, because, although a safe emetic, yet it is an acrid narcotic poison.

MUSTARD is too well known to require describing. It is an emetic, diuretic, stimulant, and rubefacient. It is *used externally* as a poultice (which is made of the powder, bread crumbs, and water; or of 1 part of Mustard to 2 of flour: Vinegar is not necessary), in all cases where a stimulant is required, such as sore throat, rheumatic pains in the joints, cholera, cramps in the extremities, diarrhœa, and many other diseases. When applied it should not be left on too long, as it is apt to cause ulceration of the part. From ten to thirty minutes is quite long enough. When *used internally* as an emetic, a large teaspoonful mixed with a tumbler of warm water generally operates quickly and safely, frequently when other emetics have failed. In dropsy it is sometimes given in the form of whey, which is made by boiling ½ an ounce of the bruised seeds in a pint of milk, and straining off the curd. From 3 to 4 ounces of this is to be taken for a dose three times a day.

CATHARTICS are divided into laxatives and purgatives. The former comprise Manna, Tamarinds, Castor Oil, Sulphur, and Magnesia; the latter, Senna, Rhubarb, Jalap, Colocynth, Buckthorn, Aloes, Cream of Tartar, Scammony, Calomel, Epsom Salts, Glauber's Salts, Sulphate of Potash, and Venice Turpentine.

MANNA is a very gentle laxative, and therefore used for children and delicate persons. *Dose* for *children*, from 1 to 2 drams; and for *adults*, from 1 to 2 ounces, combined with Rhubarb and Cinnamon Water.

TAMARINDS are generally laxative and refrigerant. As it is agreeable, this medicine will generally be eaten by children when they will not take other medicines. *Dose*, from ½ to 1 ounce. As a refrigerant beverage in fevers it is extremely grateful.

CASTOR OIL is a most valuable medicine, as it generally operates quickly and mildly. It is *used externally*, combined with Citron Ointment, as a topical application in common leprosy. It is *used internally* as an ordinary purgative for infants, as a laxative for adults, and in diarrhœa and dysentery. In colic it is very useful and safe; and also after delivery. *Dose*, for *infants*, from 40 drops to 2 drams; for *adults*, from ½ to 1½ ounces.

SULPHUR. — Sublimed Sulphur is laxative and diaphoretic. It is *used externally* in skin diseases, especially itch, both in the form of ointment and as a vapor bath. It is *used internally* in hæmorrhoids, combined with Magnesia, as a laxative for children, and as a diaphoretic in rheumatism. *Dose*, from 1 scruple to 2 drams, mixed in milk or with molasses. When combined with an equal proportion of Cream of Tartar, it acts as a purgative.

MAGNESIA.—*Calcined Magnesia* possesses the same properties as the Carbonate. *Dose*, from 10 to 30 grains, in milk or water. *Carbonate of Magnesia*

is an antacid and laxative, and is very useful for children when teething, and for heartburn in adults. *Dose*, from ½ to 2 drams, in water or milk.

SENNA is a purgative, but is apt to gripe when given alone; therefore it is combined with some aromatic such as Cloves or Ginger, and the infusion should be made with *cold* instead of hot water. It usually acts in about four hours, but its action should be assisted by drinking warm fluids. *Dose*, of the *confection*, commonly called "*lenitive electuary*," from 1 to 3 or 4 drams at bedtime; of the *infusion*, from 1 to 2 ounces; of the *tincture*, from 1 to 2 drams; of the *syrup* (used for children), from 1 dram to 1 ounce. *Caution*. — Do not give Senna, in any form except confections, in hæmorrhoids, and never in irritability of the intestines.

RHUBARB is a purgative, astringent, and stomachic. It is *used externally* in the form of powder to ulcers, to promote a healthy action. It is given *internally* in diarrhœa, dyspepsia, and a debilitated state of the bowels. Combined with a mild preparation of Calomel, it forms an excellent purgative for children. *Dose*, of the *infusion*, from 1 to 2 ounces; of the *powder*, from 1 scruple to ½ a dram as a purgative, and from 6 to 10 grains as a stomachic; of the *tincture* and *compound tincture*, from 1 to 4 drams; of the *compound pill*, from 10 to 20 grains.

JALAP is a powerful cathartic and hydrogogue, and is therefore apt to gripe. *Dose*, of the *powder*, from 10 to 30 grains, combined with a drop or two of Aromatic Oil; of the *compound powder*, from 15 to 40 grains; of the *tincture*, from 1 to 3 drams; of the *extract*, from 10 to 20 grains. The watery extract is better than the alcoholic.

. COLOCYNTH is a powerful drastic cathartic, and should never be given alone, unless ordered by a medical man, as its action is too violent for some constitutions. *Dose*, of the *extract*, from 5 to 15 grains; of the *compound extract*, from 5 to 15 grains;

of the *compound Colocynth pill*, the best of all its preparations, from 10 to 20 grains.

BUCKTHORN is a brisk purgative for children in the form of syrup. *Dose* of the *syrup*, from 1 to 6 drams.

ALOES is a purgative and cathartic in large, and tonic in smaller, doses. *Dose*, of *powder*, from 2 to 10 grains ; combined with Soap, bitter extracts, or other purgative medicines, and given in the form of pills ; of the *compound pill*, from 5 to 20 grains ; of the *pill of Aloes and Myrrh*, from 5 to 20 grains ; of the *tincture*, from 4 drams to 1 ounce ; of the *compound tincture*, from 1 to 4 drams ; of the *extract*, from 6 to 10 grains ; of the *compound decoction*, from 4 drams to 2 ounces.

CREAM OF TARTAR is a purgative and refrigerant. It is *used internally* in dropsy, especially of the belly, in doses of from 1 scruple to 1 dram. As a refrigerant drink, it is dissolved in hot water, and sweetened with sugar, and is used in febrile diseases, care being taken not to allow it to rest too much upon the bowels. *Dose*, as a *purgative*, from 2 to 4 drams ; as a *hydrogogue*, from 4 to 6 drams, mixed with honey or molasses. *Caution.* — Its use should be followed by tonics, especially Gentian and Angostura.

SCAMMONY is a drastic purgative, generally acting quickly and powerfully, sometimes producing nausea, and even vomiting, and being very apt to gripe. It is *used internally*, to produce watery evacuations in dropsy, to remove intestinal worms, and correct the slimy motions of children. *Dose*, of the *powder*, from 5 to 16 grains, given in Liquorice-water, Molasses, or Honey ; of the *confection*, from 20 to 30 grains. *Caution.* — Do not give it in an irritable or inflamed state of the bowels.

EPSOM SALTS is a purgative and diuretic. It generally operates quickly, and therefore is extremely useful in acute diseases. It is found to be beneficial in dyspepsia, when combined with infusion of Gentian and a little Ginger. It forms an excellent enema

9

with Olive Oil. *Dose*, from ¼ to 2 ounces, dissolved in warm tea or water. Infusion of Roses partially covers its taste and assists its action. It is a noted fact with regard to Epsom Salts, that the *larger* the amount of water in which they are taken, the *smaller* the dose of Salts required : thus ½ an ounce properly dissolved may be made a strong dose. The action and efficacy of Epsom Salts may be very greatly increased by the addition of 1 grain of Tartar Emetic with a dose of Salts.

GLAUBER'S SALT is a very good purgative. *Dose*, from a ½ to 2 ounces, dissolved in warm water.

SULPHATE OF POTASH is a cathartic and deobstruent. It is *used internally*, combined with Aloes or Rhubarb, in obstructions of the bowels, and an excellent saline purgative in dyspepsia and jaundice. *Dose*, of the *powdered salt*, from 10 grains to 1 dram.

VENICE TURPENTINE is cathartic, diuretic, stimulant, and anthelmintic. It is *used externally* as a rubefacient, and is given *internally* in flatulent colic, in tapeworm, rheumatism, and other diseases. *Dose*, as a *diuretic*, from 10 grains to 1 dram ; as a *cathartic*, from 10 to 12 drams ; as an *anthelmintic*, from 1 to 2 ounces every eight hours, till the worm be ejected.

DIURETICS are medicines which promote an increased secretion of urine. They consist of Nitre, Acetate of Potassa, Squills, Juniper, Oil of Turpentine, and many others, vegetable and mineral.

NITRE is a diuretic and refrigerant. It is *used externally* as a detergent when dissolved in water, and as a lotion to inflamed and painful rheumatic joints. It is given *internally* in doses of from 10 grains to ½ a dram, or even 1 dram. In spitting blood it is given in 1 dram doses with great benefit. As a topical application, it is beneficial in sore throat, a few grains being allowed to dissolve in the mouth.

ACETATE OF POTASSA is diuretic and cathartic. It is given *internally* in dropsy with great benefit, in doses of from 1 scruple to 1 dram, every three or four hours, to act as a diuretic in combination with Infusion of Quassia. *Dose,* as a *cathartic,* from 2 to 3 drams.

SQUILLS is diuretic and expectorant when given in small doses, and emetic and purgative when given in large doses. It is *used internally* in dropsies, in combination with Calomel and Opium; in asthma, with Ammoniacum; in catarrh, in the form of Oxymel. *Dose,* of the *dried bulb powdered,* from 1 to 2 grains every six hours; of the *compound pill,* from 10 to 15 grains; of the *tincture,* from 10 minims to ½ a dram; of the oxymel, from ½ to 2 drams; of the vinegar, from 20 minims to 2 drams.

JUNIPER is diuretic and stomachic. It is given *internally* in dropsies. *Dose,* of the *infusion,* from 2 to 3 ounces every four hours ; of the *oil,* from 1 to 5 minims.

OIL OF TURPENTINE is a diuretic, anthelmintic, and rubefacient. It is *used externally* in flatulent colic, sprinkled over flannels dipped in hot water and wrung out dry. It is *used internally* in the same diseases as Venice Turpentine. *Dose,* from 5 minims to 2 drams.

DIAPHORETICS are medicines given to increase the secretion from the skin by sweating. They comprise Acetate of Ammonia, Calomel, Antimony, Opium, Camphor, and Sarsaparilla.

SOLUTION OF ACETATE OF AMMONIA is a most useful diaphoretic. It is *used externally* as a discutient, as a lotion to inflamed milk breasts, as an eyewash, and a lotion in scald head. It is given *internally* to promote perspiration in febrile diseases, which it does most effectually, especially when combined with Camphor mixture. This is the article so frequently met with in prescriptions, and called Spirits of Mindererus (*liquor ammonia acetatis*). *Dose,* from a ½ to 1½ ounces every three or four hours.

ANTIMONY. — *Tartar emetic* is diaphoretic, emetic, expectorant, altera-

tive, and rubefacient. It is *used externally* as an irritant in white swellings and deep-seated inflammations, in the form of an ointment. It is given *internally* in pleurisy, bilious fevers, and many other diseases; but its exhibition requires the skill of a medical man to watch its effects. *Dose,* from ⅛ of a grain to 4 grains. *Caution.*— It is a *poison,* and therefore requires great care in its administration.

ANTIMONIAL POWDER is a diaphoretic, emetic, and alterative. It is given *internally,* in febrile diseases, to produce determination to the skin. In rheumatism, when combined with Opium or Calomel, it is of great benefit. *Dose,* from 3 to 10 grains every four hours, taking plenty of warm fluids between each dose.

SARSAPARILLA is diaphoretic, alterative, diuretic, and tonic. It is given *internally* in cutaneous diseases, old-standing rheumatism, scrofula, and debility. *Dose,* of the *decoction,* from 4 to 8 ounces; of the *compound decoction,* from 4 to 8 ounces; of the *extract,* from 5 grains to 1 dram.

Expectorants are medicines given to promote the secretion from the windpipe, etc. They consist of Antimony, Ipecacuanha, Squills, Ammoniacum, and Tolu.

AMMONIACUM is an expectorant, antispasmodic, diuretic, and deobstruent. It is *used externally* as a discutient, and is given *internally,* with great benefit, in asthma, hysteria, and chronic catarrh. *Dose,* from 10 to 20 grains.

TOLU is an excellent expectorant, when there are no inflammatory symptoms. It is given *internally* in asthma and chronic catarrh. *Dose,* of the *balsam,* from 5 to 30 grains, combined with mucilage and suspended in water; of the *tincture,* from a ½ to 1 dram ; of the *syrup,* from a ½ to 4 drams.

Sialagogues are given to increase the flow of saliva or spittle. They consist of Ginger and Calomel, Pelletory of Spain, Tobacco, the acids and some others.

GINGER is a sialagogue, carminative.

and stimulant. It is *used internally* in flatulent colic, dyspepsia, and to prevent the griping of medicines. When chewed, it acts as a sialagogue, and is therefore useful in relaxed uvula. *Dose*, from 10 to 20 grains of the *powder ;* of the *tincture*, from 10 minims to 1 dram.

Epispastics and Rubefacients are those remedies which are applied to blister and cause redness of the surface. They consist of Cantharides, Ammonia, Burgundy Pitch, and Mustard.

CANTHARIDES, or Spanish Flies, when used internally, are diuretic and stimulant; and epispastic and rubefacient, when applied externally. *Mode of application.* — A portion of the blistering plaster is spread with the thumb upon brown paper, linen, or leather to the size required ; its surface then *slightly* moistened with Olive Oil, and sprinkled with Camphor, and the plaster applied by a *light* bandage ; or it is spread on adhesive plaster, and attached to the skin by the adhesive margin of the plaster. *Caution.* — If a blister is to be applied to the head, shave it at least ten hours before it is put on ; and it is better to place a thin piece of gauze, wetted with vinegar, between the skin and the blister. If a distressing feeling be experienced about the bladder, give warm and copious draughts of Linseed Tea, milk, or decoction of Quince seeds, and apply warm fomentations of milk and water to the blistered surface. The *period required* for a *blister* to remain on, varies from eight to ten hours for adults, and from twenty minutes to two hours for children ; as soon as it is removed, if the blister is not raised, apply a " Spongio-Piline " poultice, and it will then rise properly. When it is required to act as a rubefacient, the blister should remain on from one to three hours for adults, and from fifteen to forty minutes for children. *To dress a blister.* — Cut the bag or cuticle containing the serum at the lowest part, by snipping it with the scissors, so as to form an opening like this — V ; and then apply a piece of calico, spread

with spermaceti, or some other dressing. Such is the ordinary method ; but a much better and more expeditious plan, and one that prevents all pain and inconvenience in the healing, is, after cutting the blister as directed above, to immediately cover it with a warm bread-and-water poultice for about an hour and a half, and on the removal of the poultice to dust the raw surface with violet powder ; apply a handkerchief to retain the powder, and lastly dust the part every two hours. It will be healed in twelve hours. *Caution.* — Never attempt to take Cantharides internally, except under the advice of a physician, as it is a poison, and requires extreme caution in its use.

BURGUNDY PITCH is warmed and spread upon linen or leather, and applied over the chest in cases of catarrh, difficult breathing, and whooping-cough ; over the loins in debility or lumbago ; and over any part that it is desirable to excite a mild degree of inflammation in.

Chemical Remedies. — The chemical remedies comprise refrigerants, antacids, antalkalies, and escharotics.

Refrigerants are medicines given for the purpose of suppressing an unnatural heat of the body. They are Seville Oranges, Lemons, Tamarinds, Nitre, and Cream of Tartar.

SEVILLE ORANGES and Sweet Oranges are formed into a refrigerant beverage, which is extremely grateful in febrile diseases. The *rind* is an agreeable mild tonic, carminative, and stomachic. *Dose*, of the *tincture*, from 1 to 4 drams ; of the *infusion*, from 1 to 2 ounces.

LEMONS are used to form a refrigerant beverage, which is given to quench thirst in febrile and inflammatory diseases. Lemon *juice* is given with Carbonate of Potash ($\frac{1}{2}$ an ounce of the juice to 20 grains of the salt), and taken while effervescing, allays vomiting. A tablespoonful, taken occasionally, allays hysterical palpitations of the heart. It is useful in scurvy, caused by eating too much salt food, but requires to be taken with sugar. The *rind* forms a nice mild tonic and stomachic in certain forms of dyspepsia. *Dose* of the *infusion* (made the same as Orange Peel), from 1 to 2 ounces.

ANTACIDS are given to correct acidity in the system. They are Soda, Ammonia, Chalk, and Magnesia.

SODA, CARBONATE OF, and *Sesqui-carbonate of Soda*, are antacids and de-obstruents. They are *used internally* in acidity of the stomach and dyspepsia. *Dose*, of both preparations, from 10 grains to ½ a dram.

ANTALKALIES are given to neutralize an alkaline state of the system. They are Citric Acid, Lemon Juice, and Tartaric Acid.

CITRIC ACID is used to check profuse sweating, and as a substitute for lemon juice when it cannot be procured. *Dose*, from 10 to 30 grains.

TARTARIC ACID, when largely diluted, forms an excellent refrigerant beverage and antalkali. It enters into the composition of extemporaneous Soda and Seidlitz Waters. *Dose*, from 10 to 30 grains.

ESCHAROTICS are remedies used to destroy the vitality of a part. They comprise Lunar Caustic, Bluestone, and Solution of Chloride of Zinc.

BLUESTONE, or Sulphate of Copper, is used in a solution of from 4 to 15 grains to the ounce of water, and applied to foul and indolent ulcers, by means of a rag dipped in it; and is rubbed in substance on fungous growths, warts, etc., to destroy them. *Caution.*—It is a poison.

LUNAR CAUSTIC, or *Nitrate of Silver*, is an excellent remedy in erysipelas, when applied in solution (1 dram of the salt to 1 ounce of water), which should be brushed all over the inflamed part, and for an inch beyond it. This blackens the skin, but it soon peels off. To destroy warts, proud flesh, and unhealthy edges of ulcers, etc., it is invaluable; and as an application to bed-sores, pencilled over with a solution of the same strength, and in the same manner, as for erysipelas. *Caution.*—It is a poison.

SOLUTION *of Chloride of Zinc*, more commonly known as Sir William Burnett's "Disinfecting Fluid," is a valuable escharotic in destroying the parts of poisoned wounds, such as the bite of a mad dog. It is also very useful in restoring the hair after the scalp has been attacked with ringworm; but its use requires extreme caution, as it is a powerful escharotic. In itch, diluted (one part to thirty-two) with water, it appears to answer very well. *Caution.* — It is a most powerful poison.

Mechanical Remedies.— The mechanical remedies comprise anthelmintics, demulcents, diluents, and emollients.

ANTHELMINTICS are medicines given for the purpose of expelling or destroying worms. They are Cowhage, Scammony, Male Fern Root, Calomel, Gamboge, Tin, and Turpentine.

COWHAGE is used to expel the round worm, which it does by wounding it with the fine prickles. *Dose* of the *confection*, for a child three or four years old, a teaspoonful early, for three mornings, followed by a dose of Castor Oil. The mechanical anthelmintics are strictly confined to those agents which kill the worm in the body by piercing its cuticle with the sharp darts or spiculæ of the cowhage hairs, or the fine metallic points of the powdered tin. When these drops are employed, they should be given in Honey or Molasses for ten or fifteen days, and an aperient powder every fourth morning, to expel the killed worms.

MALE FERN ROOT is a powerful anthelmintic, and an astringent. It is used to kill tapeworm. *Dose*, 3 drams of the powdered root mixed in a teacupful of water, to be taken in the morning while in bed, and followed by a brisk purgative two hours afterwards; or 30 drops of the ethereal tincture, to be taken early in the morning.

GAMBOGE is a powerful drastic and anthelmintic. It is *used internally*, in dropsies, and for the expulsion of tapeworm; but its use requires caution, as it is an irritant poison. *Dose*, from 2 to 6 grains, in the form of pills, combined with Colocynth, Soap, Rhubarb, or Bread-crumbs.

DEMULCENTS are used to diminish irritation, and soften parts by protecting them with a viscid matter. They are Tragacanth, Linseed, Marsh-Mallow, Mallow, Liquorice, Arrow-root, Isinglass, Suet, Wax, and Almonds.

TRAGACANTH is used to allay tickling cough, and lubricate abraded parts. It is usually given in the form of mucilage. *Dose*, from 10 grains to 1 dram, or more.

LINSEED is emollient and demulcent. It is *used externally*, when reduced to powder, as a poultice; and the Oil, combined with Lime-water, is applied to burns and scalds. It is *used internally* as an infusion in diarrhœa, dysentery, and irritation of the intestines after certain poisons, and in catarrh. *Dose* of the *infusion*, as much as the patient pleases.

MARSH-MALLOW is *used internally* in the same diseases as Linseed. The leaves are *used externally* as a fomentation, and the boiled roots are bruised and applied as an emollient poultice. *Dose*, the same as Linseed.

MALLOW is *used externally* as a fomentation and poultice in inflammation, and the infusion is *used internally* in dysentery, diseases of the kidneys, and the same diseases as Marsh-Mallow. It is also used as an enema. The *dose* is the same as for Linseed and Marsh-Mallow.

LIQUORICE is an agreeable demulcent, and is given in the form of decoction in catarrh, and some forms of dyspepsia; and the extract is used in catarrh. *Dose*, of the *extract*, from 10 grains to 1 dram; of the *decoction*, from 2 to 4 ounces.

ARROWROOT, Isinglass, Almonds, Suet, and Wax, are too well known to require descriptions.

DILUENTS are chiefly watery compounds such as weak tea, water, thin Broth, Gruel, weak infusions of Balm, Horehound, Pennyroyal, Ground Ivy, Mint, and Sage.

EMOLLIENTS consist of unctuous remedies, such as cerates and ointments, and any materials that combine heat with moisture — poultices of Bread, Bran, Linseed Meal, Carrots, and Turnips.

Terms used to Express the Properties of Medicines.— ABSORBENTS are medicines which destroy acidities in the stomach and bowels, such as Magnesia, Prepared Chalk, etc.

ALTERATIVES are medicines which restore health to the constitution, without producing any sensible effect, such as Sarsaparilla, Sulphur, etc.

ANALEPTICS are medicines that restore the strength which has been lost by sickness, such as Gentian, Bark, etc.

ANODYNES are medicines which relieve pain, and they are divided into three kinds, *Sedatives*, *Hypnotics*, and *Narcotics* (see these terms). Camphor is anodyne as well as narcotic.

ANTACIDS are medicines which destroy acidity, such as Lime, Magnesia, Soda, etc.

ANTALKALIES are medicines given to neutralize alkalies in the system, such as Citric, Nitric, or Sulphuric Acids, etc.

ANTHELMINTICS are medicines used to expel and destroy worms from the stomach and intestines, such as Turpentine, Cowhage, Male Fern, etc.

ANTIBILIOUS are medicines which are useful in bilious affections, such as Calomel, etc.

ANTIRHEUMATICS are medicines used for the cure of rheumatism, such as Colchicum, Iodide of Potash, etc.

ANTISCORBUTICS are medicines against scurvy, such as Citric Acid, etc.

ANTISEPTICS are substances used to correct putrefaction, such as Bark, Camphor, Charcoal, Vinegar, and Creosote.

ANTISPASMODICS are medicines which possess the power of overcoming spasms of the muscles, or allaying severe pain from any cause unconnected with inflammation, such as Valerian, Ammonia, Opium, and Camphor.

APERIENTS are medicines which move the bowels gently, such as Rhubarb, Manna, and Grey Powder.

AROMATICS are cordial, spicy, and agreeably-flavored medicines, such as Cardamoms, Cinnamon, etc.

ASTRINGENTS are medicines which contract the fibres of the body, diminish excessive discharges, and act indirectly as tonics, such as Oak Bark, Galls, etc.

ATTENUANTS are medicines which are supposed to thin the blood, such as Ammoniated Iron, etc.

BALSAMICS are medicines of a soothing kind, such as Tolu, Peruvian Balsam, etc.

CARMINATIVES are medicines which allay pain in the stomach and bowels, and expel flatulence, such as Aniseed Water, etc.

CATHARTICS are strong purgative medicines, such as Jalap, etc.

CORDIALS are exhilarating and warming medicines, such as Aromatic Confection, etc.

CORROBORANTS are medicines and food which increase the strength, such as Iron, Gentian, Meat, and Wine.

DEMULCENTS correct acrimony, diminish irritation, and soften parts by covering their surfaces with a mild and viscid matter, such as Linseed Tea, Gum, Mucilage, Honey, and Marsh-Mallow.

DEOBSTRUENTS are medicines which remove obstructions, such as Iodide of Potash, etc.

DETERGENTS clean the surfaces over which they pass, such as Soap, etc.

DIAPHORETICS produce perspiration, such as Tartrate of Antimony, James's Powder, and Camphor.

DIGESTIVES are remedies applied to ulcers or wounds to promote the formation of matter, such as Resin Ointments, Warm Poultices, etc.

DISCUTIENTS possess the power of repelling or resolving tumors, such as Galbanum, Mercury, and Iodine.

DIURETICS act upon the kidneys and bladder, and increase the flow of urine, such as Nitre, Squills, Cantharides, Camphor, Antimony, and Juniper.

DRASTICS are violent purgatives, such as Gamboge, etc.

EMETICS produce vomiting, or the discharge of the contents of the stomach, such as Mustard and hot water, Tartar Emetic, Ipecacuanha, Sulphate of Zinc, and Sulphate of Copper.

EMOLLIENTS are remedies used externally to soften the parts they are applied to, such as Spermaceti, Palm Oil, etc.

EPISPASTICS are medicines which blister or cause effusion of serum under the cuticle, such as Spanish Flies, Burgundy Pitch, Rosin, and Galbanum.

ERRHINES are medicines which produce sneezing, such as Tobacco, etc.

ESCHAROTICS are medicines which corrode or destroy the vitality of the part to which they are applied, such as Lunar Caustic, etc.

EXPECTORANTS are medicines which increase expectoration, or the discharge from the bronchial tubes, such as Ipecacuanha, Squills, Opium, Ammoniacum.

FEBRIFUGES are remedies used in fevers, such as all the Antimonials, Bark, Quinine, Mineral Acids, Arsenic.

HYDRAGOGUES are medicines which aave the effect of removing the fluid of dropsy, by producing watery evacuations, such as Gamboge, Calomel, etc.

HYPNOTICS are medicines that relieve pain by producing sleep, such as Hops, Henbane, Morphia, Poppy.

LAXATIVES are medicines which cause the bowels to act rather more than natural, such as Manna, etc.

NARCOTICS are medicines which cause sleep or stupor, and allay pain, such as Opium, etc.

NUTRIENTS are remedies that nourish the body, such as Sugar, Sago, etc.

PAREGORICS are medicines which actually assuage pain, such as Compound Tincture of Camphor, Henbane, Hops, Opium.

PROPHYLACTICS are remedies employed to prevent the attack of any particular disease, such as Quinine, etc.

PURGATIVES are medicines that promote the evacuation of the bowels, such as Senna, Aloes, Jalap, Salts.

REFRIGERANTS are medicines which suppress an unusual heat of the body, such as Wood Sorrel, Tamarind, etc.

RUBEFACIENTS are medicaments which cause redness of the skin, such as Mustard, etc.

SEDATIVES are medicines which depress the nervous energy, and destroy sensation, so as to compose, such as Foxglove. (See PAREGORICS.)

SIALAGOGUES are medicines which promote the flow of saliva or spittle, such as Salt, Calomel, etc.

SOPORIFICS are medicines which induce sleep, such as Hops, etc.

STIMULANTS are remedies which increase the action of the heart and arteries, or the energy of the part to which they are applied, such as Food, Wine, Spirits, Ether, Sassafras, which is an internal stimulant, and Savine, which is an external one.

STOMACHICS restore the tone of the stomach, such as Gentian, etc.

STYPTICS are medicines which constrict the surface of a part, and prevent the effusion of blood, such as Kino, Friar's Balsam, Extract of Lead, and Ice.

SUDORIFICS promote profuse perspiration or sweating, such as Ipecacuanha, Antimony, James's Powder, Ammonia.

TONICS give general strength to the constitution, restore the natural energies, and improve the tone of the system, such as all the vegetable Bitters, most of the minerals, also some kinds of food, Wine, and Beer.

VESICANTS are medicines which blister, such as strong Liquid Ammonia, etc.

EVERY ONE HIS OWN SURGEON.

Domestic Surgery. — This will comprise such hints and advice as will enable any one to act on an emergency, or in ordinary trivial accidents requiring simple treatment: and also to distinguish between serious and simple accidents, and the best means to adopt in all cases that are likely to fall under a person's notice. These hints will be of the utmost value to heads of families, to emigrants, and to persons who are frequently called upon to attend the sick. We strongly recommend the parent, emigrant, and nurse, *to read over these directions occasionally, — to regard it as a duty to do so at least three or four times a year*, — so as to be prepared for emergencies whenever they may arise. When accidents occur, people are too excited to acquire immediately a knowledge of what they should do ; and many lives have been lost for want of this knowledge. Study, therefore, at moderate intervals, the *Domestic Surgery, Treatment of Poisons, Rules for the Prevention of Accidents, How to Escape from Fires, the Domestic Pharmacopœia, etc.*, which will be found in various pages. And let it be impressed upon your mind that THE INDEX will enable you to refer to *anything* you may require IN A MOMENT.

DRESSINGS. — These are substances usually applied to parts for the purpose of soothing, promoting their re-union when divided, protecting them from external injuries, as a means of applying various medicines, to absorb discharges, protect the surrounding parts, and insure cleanliness.

CERTAIN INSTRUMENTS are required for the application of dressings in domestic surgery, viz., — scissors, a pair of tweezers or simple forceps, a knife, needles and thread, a razor, a lancet, a piece of lunar caustic in a quill, and a sponge.

THE MATERIALS REQUIRED for dressings consist of lint, scraped linen, carded cotton, tow, ointment spread on calico, adhesive plaster, compresses, pads, bandages, poultices, old rags of linen or calico, and water.

THE FOLLOWING RULES should be attended to in applying dressings : — 1. Always prepare the new dressing before removing the old one. 2. Always have hot and cold water at hand, and a vessel to place the foul dressings in. 3. Have one or more persons at hand ready to assist, and tell each person what they are to do before you commence—it prevents confusion; thus one is to wash out and hand the sponges, another to heat the adhesive plaster, or hand the bandages and dressings, and, if requisite, a third to support the limb, etc. 4. Always stand on the outside of a limb to dress it. 5. Place the patient in as easy a position as possible, so as not to fatigue him. 6. Arrange the bed *after* changing the dressings; but in some cases you will have to do so before the patient is placed on it. 7. Never be in a hurry when applying dressings — do it quietly. 8. When a patient requires moving from one bed to another, the best way is for one person to stand on each *side* of the patient, and each to place an arm behind his back, while he passes his arms over their necks, then let their other arms be passed under his thighs, and by holding each other's hands, the patient can be raised with ease, and removed to another bed. If the leg is injured, a third person should steady it; and if the arm, the same precaution should be adopted. Sometimes a stout sheet is passed under the patient, and by several people holding the sides, the patient is lifted without any fatigue or much disturbance.

LINT MAY BE MADE in a hurry by nailing the corners of a piece of old linen to a board, and scraping its surface with a knife. It is used either alone or spread with ointment. Scraped lint is the fine filaments from ordinary lint, and is used to stimulate ulcers and absorb discharges.

SCRAPED LINT IS MADE into various shapes for particular purposes. For example, when it is screwed up into a conical or wedge-like shape, it is called a *tent*, and is used to dilate fistulous openings, so as to allow the matter to escape freely; to plug wounds, so as to promote the formation of a clot of blood, and thus arrest bleeding. When it is rolled into little balls they are called *boulettes*, and are used for absorbing matter in cavities, or blood in wounds. Another useful form is made by rolling a mass of scraped lint into a long roll, and then tying it in the middle with a piece of thread; the middle is then doubled and pushed into a deep-seated wound, so as to press upon the bleeding vessel, while the ends remain loose and assist in forming a clot; or it is used in deep-seated ulcers to absorb the matter and keep the edges apart. This form is called the *bourdonnet*. Another form is called the *pelote*, which is merely a ball of scraped lint tied up in a piece of linen rag, commonly called a dabber. This is used in the treatment of protrusion of the naval in children.

CARDED COTTON is used as a dressing for superficial burns, and care should be taken to free it from specks, as flies are apt to lay their eggs there,

and generate maggots.

TOW IS CHIEFLY EMPLOYED as a padding for splints, as a compress, and also as an outer dressing where there is much discharge from a surface.

OINTMENTS ARE SPREAD on calicoes, lint, or even thin layers of tow, by means of a knife; they should not be spread too thick.

ADHESIVE PLASTER is cut into strips, ranging in width, according to the nature of the wound, etc., but the usual width is about three-quarters of an inch. Isinglass plaster is not so irritating as Diachylon, and is more easily removed.

COMPRESSES ARE MADE of pieces of linen, calico, lint, or tow, doubled or cut into various shapes. They are used to confine dressings in their places, and to apply an equal pressure on parts. They should be free from darns, hems, and knots. Ordinary compresses are square, oblong, and triangular. The *pierced compress* is made by folding up a square piece of linen five or six times on itself, and then nicking the surface with scissors, so as to cut out small pieces. It is then opened out, and spread with ointment. It is applied to discharging surfaces, for the purpose of allowing the matter to pass freely through the holes, and is frequently covered with a thin layer of tow. Compresses are also made in the shape of a Maltese cross, and half a cross, sometimes split singly, and at other times doubly, or they are graduated by placing square pieces of folded cloth on one another, so arranged that they decrease in size each time. They are used for keeping up pressure upon certain parts.

PADS ARE MADE by sewing tow inside pieces of linen, or folding linen and sewing the pieces together. They are used to keep off pressure from parts, such as that caused by splints in fractures.

POULTICES ARE USUALLY MADE of Linseed Meal, Oatmeal, or Bread, either combined with water or other fluids; sometimes they are made of Carrots, Charcoal, Potatoes, Yeast, and

Linseed Meal, Mustard, etc., but the best and most economical kind of Poultice is a fabric made of Sponge and Wool felted together, and backed by India rubber. It is called "Markwick's Patent Spongio-Piline." The method of using this Poultice is as follows :— A piece of the material of the required form and size is cut off, and the edges are pared or bevelled off, with a pair of scissors, so that the caoutchouc may come in contact with the surrounding skin, in order to prevent evaporation of the fluid used; for, as it only forms the vehicle, we can employ the various Poultices generally used with much less expenditure of time and money, and increased cleanliness. For example, — Vinegar Poultice is made by moistening the fabric with distilled vinegar; an Alum Poultice, by using a strong solution of alum ; a Charcoal Poultice, by sprinkling powdered charcoal on the moistened surface of the material ; a Yeast Poultice, by using warm yeast, and moistening the fabric with hot water, which is to be well squeezed out previous to the absorption of the yeast ; a Beer Poultice, by employing warm porter-dregs or strong beer as the fluid ; and a Carrot Poultice, by using the expressed and evaporated liquer of boiled carrots. (If the Spongio-Piline cannot be obtained at the apothecaries, cut a piece of sponge the size required, and ¾ inch thick, and with a few stitches sew it on a piece of oil silk, or rubber-cloth, and use as directed for the Spongio-Piline.) As a fomentation it is most invaluable, and by moistening the material with Compound Camphor Liniment or Hartshorn, it acts the same as a Mustard Poultice.

BANDAGES.—Bandages are strips of calico, linen, flannel, muslin, elastic webbing, bunting, or some other substance, of various lengths, such as three, four, eight, ten, or twelve yards, and one, one and a half, two, two and a half, three, four, and six inches wide, free from hems or darns, soft and unglazed. They are better after they

have been washed. Their uses are to retain dressing apparatus, or parts of the body in their proper positions, support the soft parts, and maintain equal pressure.

BANDAGES ARE SIMPLE AND COMPOUND ; the former are simple slips rolled up tightly like a roll of ribbon. There is also another simple kind, which is rolled from both ends—this is called a double-headed bandage. The compound bandages are formed of many pieces.

BANDAGES FOR THE HEAD should be two inches wide and five yards long ; for the neck, two inches wide and three yards long ; for the arm, two inches wide and seven yards long ; for the leg, two inches and a half wide and seven yards long ; for the thigh, three inches wide and eight yards long ; and for the body, four or six inches wide and ten or twelve yards long.

TO APPLY A SINGLE-HEADED BANDAGE, lay the outside of the end next to the part to be bandaged, and hold the roll between the little, ring, and middle fingers, and the palm of the left hand, using the thumb and forefinger of the same hand to guide it, and the right hand to keep it firm, and pass the bandage partly round the leg towards the left hand. It is sometimes necessary to reverse this order, and therefore it is well to be able to use both hands. Particular parts require a different method of applying bandages, and therefore we shall describe the most useful separately ; and there are different ways of putting on the same bandage, which consist in the manner the folds or turns are made. For example, the circular bandage is formed by horizontal turns, each of which overlaps the one made before it ; the spiral consists of spiral turns ; the oblique follows a course oblique or slanting to the centre of the limb ; and the recurrent folds back again to the part whence it started.

CIRCULAR BANDAGES are used for the neck, to retain dressings on any part of it, or for blisters, setons, etc.; for the head, to keep dressings on the forehead or any part contained within a circle passing round the head; for the *arm*, previous to bleeding; for the *leg*, above the knee; and for the *fingers*, etc.

To CONFINE THE ENDS OF BANDAGES some persons use pins, others slit the end for a short distance, and tie the two strips into a knot, and some use a strip of adhesive plaster. Always place the point of a pin in such a position that it cannot prick the patient, or the person dressing the limb, or be liable to draw out by using the limb; therefore, as a general rule, turn the head of the pin from the free end of the bandage, or toward the upper part of the limb. The best mode is to *sew* the bandage on. A few stitches will hold it more securely than pins can.

THE OBLIQUE BANDAGE is generally used for arms and legs, to retain dressings.

THE SPIRAL BANDAGE is generally applied to the trunk and extremities, but is apt to fall off even when very carefully applied; therefore we generally use another, called the Recurrent, which folds back again.

THE RECURRENT BANDAGE is the best kind of bandage that we can employ for general purposes. The method of putting it on is as follows: —Apply the end of the bandage that is free, with the outside of it next the skin, and hold this end with the finger and thumb of the left hand, while some one supports the heel of the patient; then, with the right hand, pass the bandage over the piece you are holding, and keep it crossed thus, until you can place your right forefinger upon the spot where it crosses the other bandage, where it must be kept firm. Now hold the roll of the bandage in your left hand, with the palm turned upwards, *taking care to keep that part of the bandage between your right forefinger and the roll in your left hand quite slack;* turn your left hand over, and bring the bandage down upon the leg; then pass the roll under the leg toward your right hand, and repeat this until the leg is bandaged

up to the knee, taking care *not to drag* the bandage at any time during the process of bandaging. When you arrive at the knee, pass the bandage round the leg in circles just below the knee, and pin it as usual. Bandaging is very easy, and if you once see any one apply a bandage properly, and attend to these rules, there will not be any difficulty; but bear one thing in mind, without which you will never put on a bandage even decently, and that is, *never to drag* or pull at a bandage, but make the turns while it is slack, and you have your right forefinger placed upon the point where it is to be folded down. When a limb is properly bandaged, the folds should run in a line corresponding to the shin-bone. *Use*, to retain dressings, and for varicose veins.

A BANDAGE FOR THE CHEST is always placed upon the patient in a sitting posture; and it may be put on in circles, or spirally. *Use*, in fractures of the ribs, to retain dressings, and after severe contusions.

A BANDAGE FOR THE BELLY is placed on the patient as directed in the last, carrying it spirally from above downwards. *Use*, to compress the belly after dropsy, or retain dressings.

THE HAND IS BANDAGED by crossing the bandage over the back of the hand. *Use*, to retain dressings.

FOR THE HEAD, a bandage may be circular or spiral, or both; in the latter case, commence by placing one circular turn just over the ears; then bring down from left to right, and round the head again, so as to alternate a spiral with a circular turn. *Use*, to retain dressings on the head or over the eye; but this form soon gets slack. The circular bandage is the best, crossing it over both eyes.

FOR THE FOOT.— Place the end just above the outer ankle, and make two circular turns, to prevent its slipping; then bring it down from the inside of the foot over the instep toward the outer part; pass it under the sole of the foot, and upward and inward over the instep toward the inner ankle, then round the ankle and repeat again. *Use,* to retain dressings to the instep, heel, or ankle.

FOR THE LEG AND FOOT, commence and proceed as directed in the preceding paragraph; then continue it up the leg as ordered in the *Recurrent Bandage.*

AS IT SOMETIMES HAPPENS that it is necessary to apply a bandage at once, and the materials are not at hand, it is desirable to know how to substitute something else *that any one may apply with ease.* This is found to be effected by handkerchiefs, and an experienced surgeon (Mr. Mayor) has paid great attention to this subject, and brought it to much perfection. It is to him, therefore, that we are indebted for most of these hints.

ANY ORDINARY HANDKERCHIEF will do; but a square piece of linen folded into various shapes answers better. The shapes generally required are as follows:—The triangle, the long square, the cravat, and the cord.

THE TRIANGULAR HANDKERCHIEF is made by folding it from corner to corner. *Use,* as a bandage for the head. *Application.*—Place the base round the head, and the short part hanging down behind; then tie the long ends over it.

THE LONG SQUARE is made by folding the handkerchief into three parts, by doubling it once upon itself. *Use,* as a bandage to the ribs, belly, etc. If one handkerchief is not long enough, sew two together.

THE CRAVAT is folded as usual with cravats. *Use,* as a bandage for the head, arms, legs, feet, neck, etc.

THE CORD is used to compress vessels, when a knot is made in it, and placed over the vessel to be compressed. It is merely a handkerchief twisted in its long diameter.

TWO OR MORE HANDKERCHIEFS must sometimes be applied, as in a broken collar-bone, or when it is necessary to keep dressings under the arm. The bandage is applied by knotting the two ends of one handkerchief together, and passing the left arm through it, then passing another

handkerchief under the right arm, and tying it. By this means we can brace the shoulders well back, and the handkerchief will press firmly over the broken collar-bone; besides, this form of bandage does not readily slip or get slack, but it requires to be combined with the sling, in order to keep the arm steady.

FOR AN INFLAMED BREAST that requires support, or dressings to be kept to it, tie two ends of the handkerchief round the neck, and bring the body of it over the breast, and pass it upwards and backwards under the arm of that side, and tie the ends around the neck.

AN EXCELLENT SLING is formed by placing one handkerchief around the neck, and knotting the two ends over the breast-bone, then placing the other in triangle under the arm, to be supported with the base near to the hand: tie the ends over the handkerchief, and pin the top to the other part, after passing it around the elbow.

APPARATUS. — When a person receives a severe contusion of the leg or foot, or breaks his leg, or has painful ulcers over the leg, or is unable from some cause to bear the pressure of the bedclothes, it is advisable to know how to keep them from hurting the leg. This may be done by bending up a fire-guard, or placing a chair, resting upon the edge of its back and front of the seat, over the leg, or putting a box on each side of it, and placing a board over them. But the best way is to make a *cradle,* as it is called. This is done by getting three pieces of wood, and three pieces of iron wire, and passing the wire or hoop through the wood. This can be placed to any height, and is very useful in all cases where pressure cannot be borne. Wooden hoops cut in halves answer better than the wire.

WHEN A PERSON BREAKS HIS LEG, and *splints* cannot be had directly, get bunches of straw or twigs, roll them up in handkerchiefs, and placing one on each side of the leg or arm, bind another handkerchief firmly around them; or make a long bag about three inches in diameter, or even more, of coarse linen duck, or carpet, and stuff this full of bran, sawdust, or sand, sew up the end, and use this the same as the twigs. It forms an excellent extemporaneous splint. Another good plan is to get a hat-box made of chip, and cut it into suitable lengths. Or for want of all these, some bones out of a pair of stays, and run them through a stout piece of rug, protecting the leg with a fold of rug, linen, etc. A still better splint, or set of splints, can be extemporized by cutting a sheet of thick pasteboard into proper-sized slips, then passing each piece through a basin of hot water to soften it. It is then applied to the fractured limb like an ordinary splint, when it hardens as it dries, taking the exact shape of the part to which it is applied.

WHEN DRY WARMTH IS REQUIRED to be applied to any part of the body, fry a flour pancake, and lay it over the part; or warm some sand, and place in the patient's socks, and lay it to the part; salt does as well, and may be put into a paper bag; or warm water put into ginger-beer bottles or stone jars, and rolled up in flannel.

Minor Operations. — BLEEDING is sometimes necessary at once in certain accidents, such as concussion, and therefore it is well to know how to do this. First of all, bind up the arm above the elbow with a piece of bandage, or a handkerchief, pretty firmly, then place your finger over one of the veins at the bend of the arm, and feel if there is any pulsation; if there is, try another vein, and if it does not pulsate or beat, choose that one. Now rub the arm from the wrist towards the elbow, place the left thumb upon the vein, and hold the lancet as you would a pen, and nearly at right angles to the vein, taking care to prevent its going in too far, by keeping the thumb near to the point, and resting the hand upon the little finger. Now place the point of the lancet on the vein, push it suddenly inwards, depress the elbow, and raise the hand upwards and out-

wards, so as to *cut obliquely across* the vein. When sufficient blood is drawn off, which is known by feeling the pulse at the wrist and near the thumb, bandage the arm. If the pulse feel like a piece of cord, more blood should be taken away; but if it is soft, and can be easily pressed, the bleeding should be stopped. When you bandage the arm, place a piece of lint over the opening made by the lancet, and pass a bandage lightly but firmly around the arm, so as to cross it over the bend of the elbow, in the form of a figure 8.

DRY CUPPING is performed by throwing a piece of paper dipped into spirit of wine, and ignited, into a wine-glass, and placing it over the part, such as the neck, temples, etc. It thus draws the flesh into the glass, and causes a determination of blood to the part, which is useful in headache, and many other complaints. This is an excellent method of extracting the poison from wounds made by adders, mad dogs, fish, etc.

ORDINARY CUPPING is performed the same as Dry Cupping, with this exception, that the part is scarified or scratched with a lancet, so as to cause the blood to flow, or by the application of a scarificator, which makes by one action from seven to twenty-one light superficial cuts. Then the glass is placed over it again with the lighted paper in it, and when sufficient blood has been taken away, then the parts are sponged, and a piece of sticking-plaster applied over them.

Leeches, and their Application. — The Leech used for medical purposes is called the *Hirudo medicinalis*, to distinguish it from other varieties, such as the Horse Leech and the Lisbon Leech. It varies from two to four inches in length, and is of a blackish-brown color, marked on the back with six yellow spots, and edged with a yellow line on each side.

WHEN LEECHES ARE APPLIED to a part, it should be thoroughly freed from down or hair by shaving, and all liniments, etc., carefully and effectually cleaned away by washing. If the Leech is hungry it will soon bite, but sometimes great difficulty is experienced in getting them to fasten. When this is the case, roll the Leech into a little porter, or moisten the surface with a little blood or milk, or sugar and water. Leeches may be applied by holding them over the part with a piece of linen cloth, or by means of an inverted glass, under which they must be placed.

WHEN APPLIED TO THE GUMS, care should be taken to use a Leech glass, as they are apt to creep down the patient's throat: a large swan's quill will answer the purpose of a Leech glass. When Leeches are gorged they will drop off themselves. Never *tear* them off from a person, but just dip the point of a moistened finger into some salt, and touch them with it.

LEECHES ARE SUPPOSED TO AB-STRACT about 2 drams of blood, or six leeches draw about an ounce; but this is independent of the bleeding after they have come off, and more blood generally flows then than during the time they are sucking. The total amount of blood drawn and subsequently lost by each Leech-bite, is nearly half an ounce.

AFTER LEECHES COME AWAY, encourage the bleeding by flannels dipped in hot water, and wrung out dry, and then apply a warm "Spongio-Piline" poultice. If the bleeding is not to be encouraged, cover the bites with a rag dipped in Olive Oil, or spread with Spermaceti Ointment, having previously sponged the parts clean.

WHEN BLEEDING CONTINUES from Leech-bites, and it is desirable to stop it, apply pressure with the fingers over the part, or dip a rag in a strong solution of Alum and lay over them, or use the tincture of Sesquichloride of Iron, or apply a leaf of Matico to them, placing the under surface of the leaf next to the skin, or touch

each bite with a finely-pointed piece of Lunar Caustic, or lay a piece of Lint soaked in the Extract of Lead over the bites; and if all these tried in succession fail, pass a fine needle through a fold of the skin so as to include the bite, and twist a piece of thread round it. Be sure never to allow any one to go to sleep with Leech-bites bleeding, without watching them carefully; and never apply too many to children; or place them where their bites can be compressed if necessary. In other words, *never apply Leeches to children except over a bone.*

AFTER LEECHES HAVE BEEN USED, they should be placed in water containing sixteen per cent. of Salt, which facilitates the removal of the blood they contain; and they should afterwards be placed one by one in warm water, and the blood forced out by *gentle* pressure. The Leeches should then be thrown into fresh water, which is to be renewed every twenty-four hours; and they may then be re-applied after an interval of eight or ten days: a second time they may be disgorged. The best plan, however, is to strip the Leech by drawing the thumb and forefinger of the right hand along its body from the tail to the mouth, the Leech being firmly held at the sucker extremity by the fingers of the left hand. By this means, with a few minutes' rest between each application, the same Leech may be used four or five times in succession.

IF A LEECH BE ACCIDENTALLY SWALLOWED, or by any means should get into the body, employ an emetic, or enema of Salt and Water.

SCARIFICATION IS USEFUL in severe contusions and inflammation of parts. It is performed by scratching or slightly cutting through the skin with a lancet, holding the lancet as you would a pen when you are ruling lines on paper.

HOW TO PRESERVE HEALTH.

OUNCES OF PREVENTION WORTH MANY POUNDS OF CURE—CLEANLINESS AND EXERCISE SHOULD BE SCRUPULOUSLY OBSERVED.

Rules for the Preservation of Health.—HEALTH is a word of Saxon origin, signifying, as our readers are aware, freedom from bodily pain or sickness. This is a blessing which few enjoy in an unimpaired state, in this highly artificial condition of things; and when we say that a person is healthy, we must be understood to mean comparatively rather than positively so. Latterly the term *normal* has been much used in scientific writings to signify a natural or good state of Health : but in this signification we might as well keep to the good old Saxon term, *helth*, which is but another form of *heal*, as it expresses the same thing equally well, indeed better.

"Though health may be enjoyed without gratitude, it cannot be sported with without loss, nor regained by courage," says a great writer ; and truly it were well if men kept this saying in mind, for there is scarcely any earthly blessing they hold so lightly, nor deplore so deeply the loss of. What, we may ask, is a state of perfect health ? If a man eat well, and sleep well, and perform his allotted duties with ease and comfort; if there is a proper performance of all his bodily functions, so that he is not affected by any unpleasant sensation or pain, we may conclude that his health is in the highest possible condition.

Wholesome diet, moderately enjoyed, personal cleanliness, regular exercise, pure air, and an avoidance of undue mental excitement and bodily excesses —these are the grand preservatives of health. Inherited diseases cannot be guarded against, nor can accidents, nor the contraction of contagious or infectious diseases — these are the bodily ills to which the flesh is certainly heir, but these form a very small proportion of the ills that do afflict humanity; and it is a reproach alike to the common sense and the religious character of this so-called enlightened age, that health should be squandered as it is. If we really wish, as we pray, to have "a sound mind in a sound body," let us strive to preserve the body sound when we have it so; for, without it, the mind is scarcely likely to be really healthful.

PURE ATMOSPHERIC AIR is composed of nitrogen, oxygen, and a *very* small proportion of carbonic acid gas. Air once breathed has lost the chief part of its oxygen, and acquired a proportionate increase of carbonic acid gas. *Therefore*, health requires that we breathe the same air once only.

THE SOLID PART OF OUR BODIES is continually wasting, and requires to be repaired by fresh substances. *Therefore*, food, which is to repair the loss, should be taken with due regard to the exercise and waste of the body.

THE FLUID PART OF OUR BODIES also wastes constantly ; there is but one fluid in animals, which is water. *Therefore*, water only is necessary, and no artifice can produce a better drink.

THE FLUID OF OUR BODIES is to the solid in proportion as nine to one. *Therefore*, a like proportion should prevail in the total amount of food taken.

LIGHT EXERCISES AN IMPORTANT INFLUENCE upon the growth and vigor of animals and plants. *Therefore*, our dwellings should freely admit the solar rays.

DECOMPOSING ANIMAL AND VEGE- TABLE SUBSTANCES yield various noxious gases, which enter the lungs and corrupt the blood. *Therefore*, all impurities should be kept away from our abodes, and every precaution be observed to secure a pure atmosphere.

WARMTH IS ESSENTIAL to all the bodily functions. *Therefore*, an equal bodily temperature should be main- tained by exercise, by clothing, or by fire.

EXERCISE WARMS, INVIGORATES, and purifies the body; clothing pre- serves the warmth the body generates; fire imparts warmth externally. *There- fore*, to obtain and preserve warmth, exercise and clothing are preferable to fire.

FIRE CONSUMES THE OXYGEN of the air, and produces noxious gases. *Therefore*, the air is less pure in the presence of candles, gas, or coal fire, than otherwise, and the deterioration should be repaired by increased ven- tilation.

THE SKIN IS A HIGHLY-ORGANIZED MEMBRANE, full of minute pores, cells, bloodvessels, and nerves. It imbibes moisture or throws it off, according to the state of the atmosphere and the temperature of the body. It also "breathes," as do the lungs (though less actively). All the internal organs sympathize with the skin. *Therefore*, it should be repeatedly cleansed.

LATE HOURS AND ANXIOUS PUR- SUITS exhaust the nervous system, and produce disease and premature death. *Therefore*, the hours of labor and study should be short.

MENTAL AND BODILY EXERCISE are equally essential to the general health and happiness. *Therefore*, labor and study should succeed each other.

MAN WILL LIVE MOST HEALTHILY upon simple solids and fluids, of which a sufficient but temperate quantity

should be taken. *Therefore*, over-in- dulgence in strong drinks, tobacco, snuff, opium, and all mere indulgences, should be avoided.

SUDDEN ALTERNATIONS OF HEAT AND COLD are dangerous (especially to the young and the aged). *Therefore*, clothing, in quantity and quality, should be adapted to the alternations of night and day, and of the seasons. *And therefore, also,* drinking cold water when the body is hot, and hot tea and soups when cold, are productive of many evils.

MODERATION IN EATING and drink- ing, short hours of labor and study, regularity in exercise, recreation, and rest, cleanliness, equanimity of temper and equality of temperature, — these are the great essentials to that which surpasses all wealth, — *health of mind and body.*

BATHING.—If to preserve health be to save medical expenses, without even reckoning upon time and comfort, there is no part of the household arrangement so important to the domestic economist as cheap conve- nience for personal ablution. For this purpose baths upon a large and expen- sive scale are by no means necessary; but though temporary or tin baths may be extremely useful upon press- ing occasions, it will be found to be finally as cheap, and much more readily convenient, to have a perma- nent bath constructed, which may be done in any dwelling-house of moder- ate size, without interfering with other general purposes. As the object of these remarks is not to present essays, but merely useful economic hints, it is unnecessary to expatiate upon the architectural arrangement of the bath, or, more properly speaking, the bath- ing-place, which may be fitted up for the most retired establishment, differ- ing in size or shape agreeably to the spare room that may be appropriated to it, and serving to exercise both the fancy and the judgment in its prepara- tion. Nor is it particularly necessary to notice the salubrious effects resulting from the bath, beyond the two points of its being so conducive to both health and cleanliness, in keeping up a free circulation of the blood, without any violent muscular exertion, thereby really affording a saving of strength, and producing its effects without any expense either to the body or to the purse.

WHOEVER FITS UP A BATH in a house already built must be guided by circumstances; but it will always be proper to place it as near the kitchen fireplace as possible, because from thence it may be heated, or at least have its temperature preserved, by means of hot air through tubes, or by steam prepared by the culinary fireplace, without interfering with its ordinary uses.

TEMPERATURE OF BATHS. — From 50° to 75° of Fahrenheit is called a cold bath; from 75° to 85° a temperate bath; from 85° to 95° a tepid bath; from 95° to 98° (which is the heat of the surface of the body) is called a warm bath; from 98° to 105° is a hot bath.

CLEANLINESS.—The want of cleanliness is a fault which admits of no excuse. Where water can be had for nothing, it is surely in the power of every person to be clean.

THE DISCHARGE FROM OUR BODIES by perspiration renders frequent changes of apparel necessary.

CHANGE OF APPAREL greatly promotes the secretion from the skin, so necessary to health.

WHEN THAT MATTER which ought to be carried off by perspiration is either retained in the body or reabsorbed in dirty clothes, it is apt to occasion fevers and other diseases.

MOST DISEASES OF THE SKIN proceed from want of cleanliness. These indeed may be caught by infection, but they will seldom continue long where cleanliness prevails.

TO THE SAME CAUSE must we impute the various kinds of vermin that infest the human body, houses, etc. These may generally be banished by cleanliness alone.

PERHAPS the intention of nature, in permitting such vermin to annoy mankind, is to induce them to the practice of this virtue.

ONE COMMON CAUSE of putrid and malignant fevers is the want of cleanliness.

THESE FEVERS commonly begin among the inhabitants of close, dirty houses, who breathe bad air, take little exercise, eat unwholesome food, and wear dirty clothes. There the infection is generally hatched, which spreads far and wide, to the destruction of many. Hence cleanliness may be considered as an object of public attention. It is not sufficient that I be clean myself, while the want of it in my neighbor affects my health as well as his own.

IF DIRTY PEOPLE CANNOT BE REMOVED as a common nuisance, they ought at least to be avoided as infectious. All who regard their health should keep at a distance, even from their habitations. In places where great numbers of people are collected, cleanliness becomes of the utmost importance.

IT IS WELL KNOWN that infectious diseases are caused by tainted air. Everything, therefore, which tends to pollute the air, or spread the infection, ought, with the utmost care, to be avoided.

FOR THIS REASON, in great towns, no filth of any kind should be permitted to lie upon the streets. We are sorry to say that the importance of general cleanliness in this respect does by no means seem to be sufficiently understood.

INFLUENCE OF CLEANLINESS. — We have more than once expressed our conviction that the humanizing influence of habits of cleanliness, and of those decent observations which imply self-respect — the best, indeed the only foundation of respect for others — has never been sufficiently acted on. A clean, fresh, and well-ordered house exercises over its inmates a moral no less than a physical influence, and has a direct tendency to make the members of a family sober, peaceable, and considerate of the feelings and happiness of each other; nor is it difficult to trace a connection be-

10

tween habitual feelings of this sort and the formation of habits of respect for property, for the laws in general, and even for those higher duties and obligations the observance of which no laws can enforce.

EXERCISE.—Exercise in the open air is of the utmost importance to the human frame, yet how many are in a manner deprived of it by their own want of management of their time. Females with slender means are, for the most part, destined to indoor occupations, and have but little time allotted them for taking the air, and that little time is generally sadly encroached upon by the ceremony of dressing to go out. It may appear a simple suggestion, but experience only will show how much time might be redeemed by habits of regularity : such as putting the shawls, cloaks, gloves, shoes, rubbers, etc., etc., or whatever is intended to be worn, in readiness, instead of having to search one drawer, then another, for possibly a glove or collar — wait for shoes being cleaned, etc. — and this when (probably) the outgoing persons have to return to their employment at a given time. Whereas, if all were in readiness, the preparations might be accomplished in a few minutes, the walk not being curtailed by unnecessary delays.

THREE PRINCIPAL POINTS in the manner of taking exercise are necessary to be attended to : — 1. The kind of exercise. 2. The proper time for exercise. 3. The duration of it. With respect to the kinds of exercise, the various species of it may be divided into active and passive. Among the first, which admit of being considerably diversified, may be enumerated walking, running, leaping, swimming, riding, fencing, the military exercise, different sorts of athletic games, etc. Among the latter, or passive kinds of exercise, may be comprised riding in a carriage, sailing, friction, swinging, etc.

ACTIVE EXERCISES are more beneficial to youth, to the middle-aged, to the robust in general, and particularly

to the corpulent and the plethoric. PASSIVE KINDS of exercise, on the contrary, are better calculated for children ; old, dry, and emaciated persons of a delicate and debilitated constitution ; and particularly for the asthmatic and consumptive.

THE TIME at which exercise is most proper, depends on such a variety of concurrent circumstances, that it does not admit of being regulated by any general rules, and must therefore be collected from the observations made on the effects of air, food, drink, etc.

WITH RESPECT TO THE DURATION OF EXERCISE, there are other particulars, relative to a greater or less degree of fatigue attending the different species, and utility of it in certain states of the mind and body, which must determine this consideration as well as the preceding.

THAT EXERCISE IS TO BE PREFERRED which, with a view to brace and strengthen the body, we are most accustomed to. Any unusual one may be attended with a contrary effect.

EXERCISE SHOULD BE BEGUN and finished gradually, never abruptly.

EXERCISE IN THE OPEN AIR has many advantages over that used within doors.

TO CONTINUE EXERCISE until a profuse perspiration or a great degree of weariness takes place, is far from being wholesome.

IN THE FORENOON, when the stomach is not too much distended, muscular motion is both agreeable and healthful ; it strengthens digestion, and heats the body less than with a full stomach ; and a good appetite after it is a proof that it has not been carried to excess.

BUT at the same time it should be understood, that it is not advisable to take violent exercise immediately before a meal, as digestion might thereby be retarded.

NEITHER should we sit down to a substantial dinner or supper immediately on returning from a fatiguing walk, at a time when the blood is heated, and the body in a state of perspiration from previous exertion, as the worst consequences may arise, especially where cooling dishes, salad, or a glass of cold drink is begun with.

EXERCISE IS ALWAYS HURTFUL AFTER MEALS, from its impeding digestion, by propelling those fluids too much towards the surface of the body which are designed for the solution of the food in the stomach.

WALKING. — To walk gracefully, the body must be erect, but not stiff, and the head held up in such a posture that the eyes are directed forward. The tendency of untaught walkers is to look toward the ground near the feet; and some persons appear always as if admiring their shoe-ties. The eyes should not tnus be cast downward, neither should the chest bend forward to throw out the back, making what are termed round shoulders; on the contrary, the whole person must hold itself up, as if not afraid to look the world in the face, and the chest by all means be allowed to expand. At the same time, everything like strutting or pomposity must be carefully avoided. An easy, firm, and erect posture is alone desirable. In walking, it is necessary to bear in mind that the locomotion is to be performed entirely by the legs. Awkward persons rock from side to side, helping forward each leg alternately by advancing the haunches. This is not only ungraceful, but fatiguing. Let the legs alone advance, bearing up the body.

Utility of Singing. — It is asserted, and we believe with some truth, that singing is a corrective of the too common tendency to pulmonic complaints. Dr. Rush, an eminent physician, observes on this subject: "The Germans are seldom afflicted with consumption; and this, I believe, is in part occasioned by the strength which their lungs acquire by exercising them in vocal music—for this constitutes an essential branch of their education. The music-master of an academy has furnished me with a remark still more in favor of this opinion. He informed me that he had known several instances of persons who were strongly disposed to consumption, who were restored to health by the exercise of their lungs in singing."

The Weather and 'the Blood. — In dry, sultry weather, the heat ought to be counteracted by means of a cooling diet. To this purpose, cucumbers, melons, and juicy fruits are subservient. We ought to give the preference to such alimentary substances as lead to contract the juices which are too much expanded by the heat, and this property is possessed by all acid food and drink. To this class belong all sorts of salad, lemons, oranges, pomegranates, sliced and sprinkled with sugar, for the acid of this fruit is not so apt to derange the stomach as that of lemons; also cherries and strawberries, curds turned with lemon acid or cream of tartar; cream of tartar dissolved in water; lemonade, and Rhenish or Moselle wine mixed with water.

How to Get Sleep. — How to get sleep is to many persons a matter of high importance. Nervous persons, who are troubled with wakefulness and excitability, usually have a strong tendency of blood on the brain, with cold extremities. The pressure of the blood on the brain keeps it in a stimulated or wakeful state, and the pulsations in the head are often painful. Let such rise and chafe the body and extremities with a brush or towel, or rub smartly with the hands, to promote circulation, and withdraw the excessive amount of blood from the brain, and they will fall asleep in a few moments. A cold bath, or a sponge bath and rubbing, or a good run, or a rapid walk in the open air, or going up and down stairs a few times just before retiring, will aid in equalizing circulation and promoting sleep. These rules are simple, and easy of application in castle or cabin, and may minister to the comfort of thousands who would freely expend money for an anodyne to promote " Nature's sweet restorer, balmy sleep ! "

Early Rising. — Dr. Wilson Philip, in his "Treatise on Indigestion," says: "Although it is of consequence to the debilitated to go early to bed, there are few things more hurtful to them than remaining in it too long. Getting up an hour or two earlier often gives a degree of vigor which nothing else can procure. For those who are not much debilitated, and sleep well, the best rule is to get out of bed soon after waking in the morning. This at first may appear too early, for the debilitated require more sleep than the healthy; but rising early will gradually prolong the sleep on the succeeding night, till the quantity the patient enjoys is equal to his demand for it. Lying late is not only hurtful, by the relaxation it occasions, but also by occupying that part of the day at which exercise is most beneficial."

APPETITE. — Appetite is frequently lost through excessive use of stimulants, food taken too hot, sedentary occupation, costiveness, liver disorder, and want of change of air. The first endeavor should be to ascertain and remove the cause. Change of diet and change of air will frequently be found more beneficial than medicines.

TEMPERANCE. — "If," observes a writer, "men lived uniformly in a healthy climate, were possessed of strong and vigorous frames, were descended from healthy parents, were educated in a hardy and active manner, were possessed of excellent natural dispositions, were placed in comfortable situations in life, were engaged only in healthy occupations, were happily connected in marriage, and kept their passions in due subjection, there would be little occasion for medical rules." All this is very excellent and desirable; but, unfortunately for mankind, unattainable.

MAN MUST BE SOMETHING MORE THAN MAN to be able to connect the different links of this harmonious chain — to consolidate this *summum bonum* of earthly felicity into one uninterrupted whole; for, independent of all regularity or irregularity of diet, passions, and other sublunary circumstances, contingencies, and connections, relative or absolute, thousands are visited by diseases and precipitated into the grave, independent of accident, to whom no particular vice could attach, and with whom the appetite never overstepped the boundaries of temperance. Do we not hear almost daily of instances of men living near to and even upwards of a century? We cannot account for this either; because of such men we know but few who have lived otherwise than the world around them; and we have known many who have lived in habitual intemperance for forty or fifty years, without interruption, and with little apparent inconvenience.

THE ASSERTION HAS BEEN MADE by those who have attained a great age (Parr, and Henry Jenkins, for instance), that they adopted no particular arts for the preservation of their health; consequently, it might be inferred that the duration of life has no dependence on manners or customs, or the qualities of particular food. This, however, is an error of no common magnitude.

PEASANTS, LABORERS, AND OTHER HARD-WORKING PEOPLE, more especially those whose occupations require them to be much in the open air, may be considered as following a regular system of moderation; and hence the higher degree of health which prevails among them and their families. They also observe rules; and those which it is said were recommended by old Parr are remarkable for good sense; namely, "Keep your head cool by temperance, your feet warm by exercise; rise early, and go soon to bed; and if you are inclined to get fat, keep your eyes open and your mouth shut," — in other words, sleep moderately, and be abstemious in diet; — excellent admonitions, more especially to those inclined to corpulency.

THE ADVANTAGES TO BE DERIVED FROM A REGULAR MODE OF LIVING, with a view to the preservation of health and life, are nowhere better exemplified than in the precepts and practice of Plutarch, whose rules for this purpose are excellent; and by observing them himself, he maintained his bodily strength and mental faculties unimpaired to a very advanced age. Galen is a still stronger proof of the advantages of a regular plan, by means of which he reached the great age of one hundred and forty years, without having ever experienced disease. His advice to the readers of his "Treatise on Health" is as follows:—"I beseech all persons who shall read this work not to degrade themselves to a level with the brutes, or the rabble, by gratifying their sloth, or by eating and drinking promiscuously whatever pleases their palates, or by indulging their appetites of every kind. But whether they understand physic or not, let them consult their reason, and observe what agrees, and what does not agree with them, that, like wise men, they may adhere to the use of such things as conduce to their health, and forbear everything which, by their own experience, they find to do them hurt: and let them be assured that, by a diligent observation and practice of this rule, they may enjoy a good share of health, and seldom stand in need of physic or physicians."

Health in Youth.—Late hours, irregular habits, and want of attention to diet, are common errors with most young men, and these gradually, but at first imperceptibly, undermine the health, and lay the foundation for various forms of disease in after life. It is a very difficult thing to make young persons comprehend this. They frequently sit up as late as twelve, one, or two o'clock, without experiencing any ill effects; they go without a meal to-day, and to-morrow eat to repletion, with only temporary inconvenience. One night they will sleep three or four hours, and the next nine or ten; or one night, in their eagerness to get away into some agreeable company, they will take no food at all, and the next, perhaps, will eat a hearty sup-

per, and go to bed upon it. These, with various other irregularities, are common to the majority of young men, and are, as just stated, the cause of much bad health in mature life. Indeed, nearly all the shattered constitutions with which too many are cursed, are the result of a disregard to the plainest precepts of health in early life.

Sleeping Together.—The laws of life, says: More quarrels arise between brothers, between sisters, between hired girls, between school girls, between clerks in stores, between apprentices in mechanic shops, between hired men, between husbands and wives, owing to electrical changes through which their nervous systems go by lodging together night after night under the same bedclothes, than by any other disturbing cause. There is nothing that will so derange the nervous system of a person who is eliminative in nervous force. The absorber will go to sleep and rest all night, while the eliminator will be tumbling and tossing, restless and nervous, and wake in the morning, fretful, peevish, fault-finding, and discouraged. No two persons, no matter who they are, should habitually sleep together. One will thrive and the other will lose. This is the law, and in married life it is defied almost universally.

Disinfecting Liquid.—In a wine bottle of cold water, dissolve two ounces acetate of lead (sugar of lead), and then add two (fluid) ounces of strong nitric acid (aquafortis). Shake the mixture, and it will be ready for use. A very small quantity of the liquid, in its strongest form, should be used for cleansing all kinds of chamber utensils. For removing offensive odors, clean cloths thoroughly moistened with the liquid, diluted with eight or ten parts of water, should be suspended at various parts of the room. In this case the offensive and deleterious gases are neutralized by chemical action. Fumigation in the usual way is only the substitution of one odor for another. In using the above, or any other disinfectant, let it never be forgotten that *fresh air*, and plenty of it, is cheaper and more effective than any other material.

Disinfecting Fumigation. — Common salt, three ounces; black manganese, oil of vitriol, of each one ounce; water, two ounces; carried in a cup through the apartments of the sick; or the apartments intended to be fumigated, where sickness has been, may be shut up for an hour or two, and then opened.

Coffee a Disinfectant. — Numerous experiments with roasted coffee prove that it is the most powerful means, not only of rendering animal and vegetable effluvia innocuous, but of actually destroying them. A room in which meat in an advanced degree of decomposition had been kept for some time, was instantly deprived of all smell on an open coffee-roaster being carried through it, containing a pound of coffee newly roasted. In another room, exposed to the effluvium occasioned by the clearing out of the manure-pit, so that sulphuretted hydrogen and ammonia in great quantities could be chemically detected, the stench was completely removed in half a minute, on the employment of three ounces of fresh-roasted coffee, while the other parts of the house were permanently cleared of the same smell by being simply traversed with the coffee-roaster, although the cleansing of the pit continued for several hours after. The best mode of using the coffee as a disinfectant is to dry the raw bean, pound it in a mortar, and then roast the powder on a moderately heated iron plate, until it assumes a dark brown tint, when it is fit for use. Then sprinkle it in sinks or cesspools, or lay it on a plate in the room which you wish to have purified. Coffee acid or coffee oil acts more readily in minute quantities.

Charcoal as a Disinfectant. — The great efficacy of wood and animal charcoal in absorbing effluvia, and the greater number of gases and vapors, has long been known.

Charcoal powder has also, during many centuries, been advantageously employed as a filter for putrid water, the object in view being to deprive the water of numerous organic impurities diffused through it, which exert injurious effects on the animal economy.

It is somewhat remarkable that the very obvious application of a perfectly similar operation to the still rarer fluid in which we live — namely, the air, which not unfrequently contains even more noxious organic impurities floating in it than those present in water — should have for so long a period been so unaccountably overlooked.

Charcoal not only absorbs effluvia and gaseous bodies, but especially, when in contact with atmospheric air, oxidizes and destroys many of the easily alterable ones, by resolving them into the simplest combinations they are capable of forming, which are chiefly water and carbonic acid.

It is on this oxidizing property of charcoal, as well as on its absorbent power, that its efficacy as a deodorizing and disinfecting agent chiefly depends.

Effluvia and miasmata are usually regarded as highly organized, nitrogenous, easily alterable bodies. When these are absorbed by charcoal, they come in contact with highly condensed oxygen gas, which exists within the pores of all charcoal which has been exposed to the air, even for a few minutes; in this way they are oxidized and destroyed.

Drinking and Head Protection in Warm Weather. — Green leaves placed in the hat is very beneficial, but still more necessary is it to protect the eyes from the rays or reflection of the rays of the sun. It is very probable that the affection of the brain called "sunstroke" is caused by the sun reaching the brain through the eyes rather than from the top of the head.

Those who have a strong desire to drink cold water in great quantities in summer should take the twig of a birch, or elm, or other tree having a pleasant taste, cut it in short pieces, and place one in the mouth, changing it occasionally; this will to a great extent prevent the desire to drink. Another plan is to frequently wet the pulse (the wrists) with cold water; this will not only prevent thirst, but will be found very refreshing when wilting in the dog-days.

Ground ginger or Cayenne pepper, a little of it put into ice water, will prevent much of its injurious effects.

The Turn of Life. — Between the years of forty and sixty, a man who has properly regulated himself may be considered in the prime of life. His matured strength of constitution renders him almost impervious to the attacks of disease, and experience has given soundness to his judgment. His mind is resolute, firm, and equal; all his functions are in the highest order. He assumes mastery over business, builds up a competence on the foundation he has formed in early manhood, and passes through a period of life attended by many gratifications. Having gone a year or two past sixty, he arrives at a standstill. But athwart this is a viaduct, called the "Turn of Life," which is a turn either into a prolonged walk or into the grave. The system and powers, having reached their utmost expansion, now begin to either close in like flowers at sunset, or break down at once. One injudicious stimulant, a single excitement, may force it beyond its strength; while a careful supply of props, and the withdrawal of all that tends to force a plant, will sustain it in beauty and vigor until night has entirely set in.

To Keep Cool in Hot Weather. — Keep a clean conscience as well as clean body and clean clothing, and don't get excited. If uncomfortably warm at any time, immerse the hands, or feet, or both, in cold water for a short time, or let a stream of cold water run upon the wrists and ankles. This will cool the whole body in a short time.

VENTILATION. — The great importance of ventilation in our sitting and sleeping rooms, in our schools and public halls, is not sufficiently appreciated. It was well set forth in a lecture by a Cleveland professor. It is startling to learn the amount of carbonic acid emitted from the lungs of one person, or from a single gas-burner — enough to poison the whole atmosphere of a good-sized room in a very brief period of time. How many persons think that winter temperature demands the exclusion of fresh air to make their apartments warm and comfortable, when the fact that in the cold season we consume more oxygen, and consequently exhale a greater quantity of the poisonous carbonic acid gas, should lead to a directly opposite course. A bed-room in winter requires more ventilation than in summer, and the non-observance of this fact will readily account for the awful diseases to which frail humanity is subject.

We wonder if many of our readers are aware of the poisonous exhalations incident to a congregation of their "fellow citizens," in ball-rooms, churches, and lecture-halls. If they have not fully considered the vast importance of thorough ventilation, let them take these undeniable facts home to their serious thoughts. A person in health has eighteen breathings per minute, and thirty-five hogsheads of air pass through the lungs in twenty-four hours. Of this, from three to five per cent., or about two and a half hogsheads, is exhaled as carbonic acid gas; and thus one person would render two or three hogsheads of air unfit for breathing again. Let every person anxious for the preservation of his health take care that the windows of the dormitories are dropped a little, even during the winter nights. There is far less danger of taking cold than there is of inhaling the noxious atmosphere, which saps the health, undermines the constitution, and embitters life with suffering and disease that might have been avoided.

The Power of Hearty Laughter. — The *New Haven Palladium* is responsible for the following:—"The following incident comes to us thoroughly authenticated, although we are not at liberty to publish any names : A short time since, two individuals in this city were lying in one room very sick, one with brain fever, the other with an aggravated case of mumps. They were so low that watchers were needed every night, and it was thought doubtful if the one sick of fever recovered. A gentleman was engaged to watch one night, his duty being to wake the nurse whenever it became necessary to take the medicine. In the course of the night both watcher and nurse fell asleep. The man with the mumps lay watching the clock, and saw that it was time to give the fever patient his potion. He was unable to speak aloud, or to move any portion of his body except his arms; but, seizing a pillow, he managed to strike the watcher in the face with it. Thus suddenly awakened, the watcher sprang from his seat, falling to the floor and awakening both the nurse and fever patient. The incident struck both the sick men as very ludicrous, and they laughed most heartily at it for fifteen or twenty minutes. When the doctor came in the morning, he found his patients vastly improved—said he had never known so sudden a turn for the better ; and they are now both out and well. Who says laughter is not the best of medicine?"

The Effects of Marriage with Blood Relations.

The consequences of intermarriage have been the subject of much declamation and but little sober inquiry. Evils of every kind have been depicted by some and totally denied by others. Those who denounce and those who favor within limits the practice of intermarriage are both devoid of any large series of observation, or of any perfectly conclusive chain of argument. But it must be said that the balance of facts is in favor of the former.

Although marriage with a relation may not, and often does not, show any evil results, yet it is a question if some evil may not arise to their descendants after two or three generations. (In the same way that children are afflicted with scrofula, whose parents had no taint of the disease, but whose ancestors two or three generations back had been troubled with syphilis.) It is generally admitted that if intermarriage is frequent among relations the offspring of such marriages are less healthy and robust, more liable to weakness of sight and blindness, and a much larger proportion than the average are idiots. Dr. Liebreich, in citing a case, says the afflicted person's father had married a cousin of his, by whom he had thirteen children ; two of these died early, two became blind owing to pigmentary retinitis, and a fifth was both blind and afflicted with idiocy. One of his sisters married a cousin, and she had an idiot among her children.

Teeth Set on Edge.

All acid foods, drinks, medicines, and tooth washes and powders are very injurious to the teeth. If a tooth is put in cider, vinegar, lemon-juice, or tartaric acid, in a few hours the enamel will be completely destroyed, so that it can be removed by the finger nail as if it were chalk. Most people have experienced what is commonly called teeth set on edge. The explanation of it is, the acid of the fruit that has been eaten has so far softened the enamel of the tooth that the least pressure is felt by the exceedingly small nerves which pervade the thin membrane which connects the enamel and the bony part of the tooth. Such an effect cannot be produced without injuring the enamel. True, it will become hard again, when the acid has been removed by the fluids of the mouth, just as an egg-shell that has been softened in this way becomes hard again by being put in the water. When the effect of sour fruit on the teeth subsides, they feel as well as ever, but they are not as well. And the oftener it is repeated, the sooner the disastrous consequences will be manifested.

Effect of Tobacco upon Pulsation.

Dr. A. Smith states that tobacco-smoking increases the rate of pulsation in some persons and decreases it in others, hence there is a diversity in the action of tobacco upon different constitutions. He experimented with tobacco upon Dr. Dale, at Scarborough, and found that the effect of tobacco upon him was as follows: — During the first six minutes of smoking there was only an increase in the beat of his pulse of four beats per second, but after that there was a steady increase, and after smoking twenty-one minutes the beats increased to thirty-seven and a half per minute. After smoking had ceased, the pulsations rapidly decreased. Dr. Smith states that tobacco-smoking acts as a stimulant like alcohol upon those persons whose pulse is excited. When the body is of full habit, the use of tobacco, he believes, leads to disturbed sleep, and in some cases may end in apoplexy.

Special Rules for the Prevention of Cholera. — 1. We urge the necessity, in all cases of Cholera, of an instant recourse to medical aid, and also under every form and variety of indisposition; for all disorders are found to merge in the dominant disease.

2. LET IMMEDIATE RELIEF be sought under disorder of the bowels especially, however slight. The invasion of Cholera may thus be readily prevented.

3. LET EVERY IMPURITY, animal and vegetable, be quickly removed to a distance from the habitation, such as slaughter-houses, pig-sties, cesspools, necessaries, and all other domestic nuisances.

4. LET ALL UNCOVERED DRAINS be carefully and frequently cleansed.

5. LET THE GROUNDS in and around the habitation be drained, so as effectually to carry off moisture of every kind.

6. LET ALL PARTITIONS be removed from within and without habitations, which unnecessarily impede ventilation.

7. LET EVERY ROOM be daily thrown open for the admission of fresh air. This should be done about noon, when the atmosphere is most likely to be dry.

8. LET DRY SCRUBBING be used in domestic cleansing in place of water cleansing.

9. LET EXCESSIVE FATIGUE, and exposure to damp and cold, especially during the night, be avoided.

10. LET THE USE of cold drinks and acid liquors, especially under fatigue, be avoided, or when the body is heated.

11. LET THE USE of cold acid fruits and vegetables be avoided.

12. LET EXCESS in the use of ardent and fermented liquors and tobacco be avoided.

13. LET A POOR DIET, and the use of impure water in cooking, or for drinking, be avoided.

14. LET THE WEARING of wet and insufficient clothes be avoided.

15. LET A FLANNEL or woollen belt be worn round the belly.

16. LET PERSONAL CLEANLINESS be carefully observed.

17. LET EVERY CAUSE tending to depress the moral and physical energies be carefully avoided. Let exposure to extremes of heat and cold be avoided.

18. LET CROWDING of persons within houses and apartments be avoided.

19. LET SLEEPING in low or damp rooms be avoided.

20. LET FIRES be kept up during the night in sleeping or adjoining apartments, the night being the period of most danger from attack, especially under exposure to cold or damp.

21. LET ALL BEDDING and clothing be daily exposed during winter and spring to the fire, and in summer to the heat of the sun.

22. LET THE DEAD be buried in places remote from the habitations of the living. By the timely adoption of simple means such as these, Cholera, or other epidemic, will be made to lose its venom.

Cautions for the Prevention of Accidents. — The following regulations should be engraved on the memory of all:

As many sudden deaths come by water, particular caution is therefore necessary in its vicinity.

Stand not near a tree, or any leaden spout, iron gate, or palisade, in times of lightning.

Keep loaded guns in safe places, and never imitate firing a gun in jest.

Never sleep near charcoal; if drowsy at any work where charcoal fires are used, take the fresh air.

Carefully rope trees before they are cut down, that when they fall they may do no injury.

When benumbed by cold beware of sleeping out of doors; rub yourself, if you have it in your power, with snow, and do not hastily approach the fire.

Beware of damps.

Air vaults, by letting them remain open some time before you enter, or scattering powdered lime in them. Where a lighted candle will not burn, animal life cannot exist; it will be an excellent caution, therefore, before entering damp and confined places, to try this simple experiment.

Never leave saddle or draught horses, while in use, by themselves; nor go immediately behind a led horse, as he is apt to kick.

Do not ride on footways.

Be wary of children, whether they are up or in bed; and particularly when they are near the fire, an element with which they are very apt to amuse themselves.

Leave nothing poisonous open or accessible; and never omit to write the word "Poison" in large letters upon it, wherever it may be placed.

In walking the streets keep out of the line of the cellars, and never look one way and walk another.

Never throw pieces of orange-peel, or broken glass bottles, into the streets.

Never meddle with gunpowder by candle-light.

In trimming a lamp with naphtha, never fill it. Leave space for the spirit to expand with warmth.

Never quit a room leaving the poker in the fire.

When the brass rod of the stair-carpet becomes loose, fasten it immediately.

In opening effervescing drinks, such as soda water, hold the cork in your hand.

Quit your house with care on a frosty morning.

Have your horses shoes roughed directly there are indications of frost.

Keep lucifer matches in their cases, and never let them be strewed about.

Accidents in Carriages.— It is safer, as a general rule, to keep your place than to jump out. Getting out over the back, provided you can hold on a little while, and run, is safer than springing from the side. But it is best to keep your place, and hold fast. In accidents people act not so much from reason as from excitement: but good rules, firmly impressed upon the mind, generally rise uppermost, even in the midst of fear.

Life Belts.—An excellent and cheap life belt, for persons proceeding to sea, bathing in dangerous places, or learning to swim, may be thus made:— Take a yard and three-quarters of strong jean, double, and divide it into nine compartments. Let there be a space of two inches after each third compartment. Fill the compartments with very fine cuttings of cork, which may be made by cutting up old corks, or (still better) purchased at the corkcutter's. Work eyelet holes at the bottom of each compartment, to let the water drain out. Attach a neck-band and waist-strings of stout boot-web, and sew them on strongly.

ANOTHER.—Cut open an old boa, or victorine, and line it with fine cork-cuttings instead of wool. For ladies going to sea these are excellent, as they may be worn in stormy weather, without giving appearance of alarm in danger. They may be fastened to the body by ribbons or tapes, of the color of the fur. Gentlemen's waistcoats may be lined the same way.

Charcoal Fumes.— The usual remedies for persons overcome with the fumes of charcoal in a close apartment are, to throw cold water on the head, and to bleed immediately; also apply mustard or hartshorn to the soles of the feet.

Cautions in Visiting the Sick. — Do not visit the sick when you are fatigued, or when in a state of perspiration, or with the stomach empty — for in such conditions you are liable to take the infection. When the disease is very contagious, place yourself at the side of the patient which is nearest to the window. Do not enter the room the first thing in the morning, before it has been aired; and when you come away, take some food, change your clothing immediately, and expose the latter to the air for some days. Tobacco smoke is a preventive of malaria.

Children and Cutlery. — Serious accidents having occurred to babies through their catching hold of the blades of sharp instruments, the following hint will be useful:—If a child lay hold of a knife or razor, do not try to pull it away, or to force open the hand; but, holding the child's hand that is empty, offer to its other hand anything nice or pretty, and it will immediately open the hand, and let the dangerous instrument fall.

Prevention of Fires. — The following simple suggestions are worthy of observation: Add one ounce of alum to the last water used to rinse children's dresses, and they will be rendered uninflammable, or so slightly combustible that they would take fire very slowly, if at all, and would not flame. This is a simple precaution, which may be adopted in families of children. Bed curtains, and linen in general, may also be treated in the same way. Since the occurrence of many lamentable deaths by fire, arising partly from the fashion of wearing crinoline, the tungstate of soda has been recommended for the purpose of rendering any article of female dress incombustible. A patent starch is also sold, with which the tungstate of soda is incorporated. The starch should be used whenever it can be procured; and

any chemist will intimate to the purchaser the manner in which the tungstate of soda should be employed.

Precautions in Case of Fire.—The following precautions should be impressed upon the memory of all our readers:

SHOULD a fire break out, send off to the nearest engine or police station.

FILL BUCKETS WITH WATER, carry them as near the fire as possible, dip a mop into the water, and throw it in showers on the fire, until assistance arrives.

IF A FIRE IS VIOLENT, wet a blanket, and throw it on the part which is in flames.

SHOULD A FIRE BREAK OUT IN THE KITCHEN CHIMNEY, or any other, a wetted blanket should be nailed to the upper ends of the mantlepiece, so as to cover the opening entirely; the fire will then go out of itself: for this purpose two knobs should be permanently fixed in the upper ends of the mantlepiece, on which the blanket may be hitched.

SHOULD the bed or window curtains be on fire, lay hold of any woollen garment, and beat it on the flames until extinguished.

AVOID LEAVING THE WINDOW OR DOOR OPEN in the room where the fire has broken out, as the current of air increases the force of the fire.

SHOULD THE STAIRCASE BE BURNING, so as to cut off all communication, endeavor to escape by means of a trapdoor in the roof, a ladder leading to which should always be at hand.

AVOID HURRY AND CONFUSION; no person except a fireman, friend, or neighbor should be admitted.

IF A LADY'S DRESS TAKES FIRE, she should endeavor to roll herself in a rug, carpet, or the first woollen garment she meets with.

IT IS A GOOD PRECAUTION to have always at hand a large piece of baize, to throw over a female whose dress is burning, or to be wetted and thrown over a fire that has recently broken out.

A SOLUTION OF PEARLASH IN WATER, thrown upon a fire, extinguishes it instantly. The proportion is a quarter of a pound, dissolved in some hot water, and then poured into a bucket of common water.

IT IS RECOMMENDED TO HOUSE-HOLDERS to have two or three fire-buckets and a carriage-mop with a long handle near at hand; they will be found essentially useful in case of fire.

ALL HOUSEHOLDERS, but particularly hotel, tavern, and inn-keepers, should exercise a wise precaution by directing that the last person up should perambulate the premises previous to going to rest, to ascertain that all fires are safe and lights extinguished.

TO EXTINGUISH A FIRE in the chimney, besides any water at hand, throw on it salt, or a handful of flour of sulphur, as soon as you can obtain it; keep all the doors and windows tightly shut, and hold before the fireplace a blanket, or some woollen article, to exclude the air.

IN ESCAPING FROM A FIRE, creep or crawl along the room with your face close to the ground. Children should be early taught how to press out a spark when it happens to reach any part of their dress, and also that running into the air will cause it to blaze immediately.

READING IN BED at night should be avoided, as, besides the danger of an accident, it never fails to injure the eyes.

To Heat a Bed at a moment's notice, throw a little salt into the warming-pan, and suffer it to burn for a minute previous to use.

FLOWERS and shrubs should be excluded from a bed-chamber.

SWIMMING. — Every person should endeavor to acquire the power of swimming. The fact that the exercise is a healthful accompaniment of bathing, and that lives may be saved by it, even when least expected, is a sufficient argument for the recommendation. The art of swimming is, in reality, very easy. The first consideration is not to attempt to learn to swim too hastily; that is to say, you must not expect to succeed in your efforts to swim until you have become accustomed to the water, and have overcome your repugnance to the coldness and novelty of bathing. Every attempt will fail until you have acquired a certain confidence in the water, and then the difficulty will soon vanish.

Dr. Franklin's Advice to Swimmers.

The only obstacle to improvement in this necessary and life-preserving art is fear; and it is only by overcoming this timidity that you can expect to become a master of the following acquirements. It is very common for novices in the art of swimming to make use of corks or bladders to assist in keeping the body above water; some have utterly condemned the use of them; however, they may be of service for supporting the body while one is learning what is called the stroke, or that manner of drawing in and striking out the hands and feet that is necessary to produce progressive motion. But you will be no swimmer till you can place confidence in the power of the water to support you. I would, therefore, advise the acquiring that confidence in the first place, especially as I have known several who, by a little practice, necessary for that purpose, have insensibly acquired the stroke, taught, as it were, by nature. The practice I mean is this: choosing a place where the water deepens gradually, walk coolly into it till it is up to your breast; then turn round your face to the shore, and throw an egg into the water between you and the shore. It will sink to the bottom, and be easily seen there if the water be clear. It must lie in the water so deep that you cannot reach to take it up but by diving for it. To encourage yourself in order to do this, reflect that your progress will be from deep to shallow water, and that at any time you may, by bringing your legs under you, and standing on the bottom, raise your head far above the water; then plunge under it with your eyes open, which must be kept open on going under, as you cannot open the eyelids for the weight of water above you; throwing yourself towards the egg, and endeavoring by the action of your hands and feet against the water to get forward, till within reach of it. In this attempt you will find that the water buoys you up against your inclination; that it is not so easy to sink as you imagine, and that you cannot, but by active force, get down to the egg. Thus you feel the power of water to support you, and learn to confide in that power, while your endeavors to overcome it, and reach the egg, teach you the manner of acting on the water with your feet and hands, which action is afterwards used in swimming to support your head higher above the water, or to go forward through it.

I would the more earnestly press you to the trial of this method, because I think I shall satisfy you that your body is lighter than water, and that you might float in it a long time with your mouth free for breathing, if you would put yourself into a proper posture, and would be still, and forbear struggling; yet, till you have obtained this experimental conviction in the water, I cannot depend upon your having the necessary presence of mind to recollect the posture, and the directions I gave you relating to it. The surprise may put all out of your mind.

THOUGH THE LEGS, ARMS, AND HEAD of a human body, being solid parts, are specifically somewhat heavier than fresh water, as the trunk, particularly the upper part, from its hollowness, is so much lighter than water, so the whole of the body, taken altogether, is too light to sink wholly under water, but some part will remain above until the lungs become filled with water, which happens from drawing water to them instead of air, when a person, in the fright, attempts breathing while the mouth and nostrils are under water.

THE LEGS AND ARMS ARE SPECIFICALLY LIGHTER than salt water, and will be supported by it, so that a human body cannot sink in salt water, though the lungs were filled as above, but from the greater specific gravity of the head. Therefore a person throwing himself on his back in salt water, and extending his arms, may easily lie so as to keep his mouth and nostrils free for breathing: and, by a slight motion of his hand, may prevent turning, if he should perceive any tendency to it.

IN FRESH WATER, IF A MAN THROW HIMSELF ON HIS BACK near the surface, he cannot long continue in that situation but by proper action of his hands on the water; if he use no such action, the legs and lower part of the body will gradually sink till he come into an upright position, in which he will continue suspended, the hollow of his breast keeping the head uppermost.

BUT IF IN THIS ERECT POSITION the head be kept upright above the shoulders, as when we stand on the ground, the immersion will, by the weight of that part of the head that is out of the water, reach above the mouth and nostrils, perhaps a little above the eyes, so that a man cannot long remain suspended in water with his head in that position.

THE BODY CONTINUING SUSPENDED as before, and upright, if the head be leaned quite back, so that the face look upward, all the back part of the head being under water, and its weight consequently, in a great measure, supported by it, the face will remain above water quite free for breathing, will rise an inch higher every inspiration, and sink as much every expiration, but never so low as that the water may come over the mouth.

IF, THEREFORE, A PERSON UNACQUAINTED WITH SWIMMING, and falling accidentally into the water, could have presence of mind sufficient to avoid struggling and plunging, and to let the body take this natural position, he might continue long safe from drowning, till, perhaps, help should come; for, as to the clothes, their additional weight when immersed is very inconsiderable, the water supporting it; though, when he comes out of the water, he will find them very heavy indeed.

BUT I WOULD NOT ADVISE ANY ONE TO DEPEND ON HAVING THIS PRESENCE OF MIND on such an occasion, but learn fairly to swim, as I wish all men were taught to do in their youth; they would, on many occasions, be the safer for having that skill: and, on many more, the happier, as free from painful apprehensions of danger, to say nothing of the enjoyment in so delightful and wholesome an exercise. Soldiers particularly should, methinks, all be taught to swim; it might be of frequent use, either in surprising an enemy or saving themselves; and if I had now boys to educate, I should prefer those schools (other things being equal) where an opportunity was afforded for acquiring so advantageous an art, which, once learned, is never forgotten.

I KNOW BY EXPERIENCE, that it is a great comfort to a swimmer who has a considerable distance to go, to turn himself sometimes on his back, and to vary, in other respects, the means of procuring a progressive motion.

WHEN HE IS SEIZED WITH THE CRAMP in the leg, the method of driving it away is to give the parts effected a sudden, vigorous, and violent shock; which he may do in the air as he swims on his back.

DURING THE GREAT HEATS IN SUMMER, there is no danger in bathing, however warm he may be, in rivers which have been thoroughly warmed by the sun. But to throw one's self into cold spring water, when the body has been heated by exercise in the sun, is an imprudence which may prove fatal. I once knew an instance of four young men who, having worked at harvest in the heat of the day, with a view of refreshing themselves, plunged into a spring of cold water; two died upon the spot, a third next morning, and the fourth recovered with great difficulty. A copious draught of cold water, in similar circumstances, is frequently attended with the same effect in North America.

THE EXERCISE OF SWIMMING IS ONE OF THE MOST HEALTHY and agreeable in the world. After having swum for an hour or two in the evening, one sleeps coolly the whole night, even during the most ardent heat of summer. Perhaps the pores bein cleansed, the insensible perspiration increases, and occasions this coolness. It is certain that much swimming is the means of stopping diarrhœa, and even of producing a constipation. With respect to those who do not know how to swim, or who are affected with diarrhœa at a season which does not permit them to use that exercise, a warm bath, by cleansing and purifying the skin, is found very salutary, and often affects a radical cure. I speak from my own experience, frequently repeated, and that of others, to whom I have recommended this.

WHEN I WAS A BOY, I amused myself one day with flying a paper kite; and approaching the banks of a lake, which was nearly a mile broad, I tied the string to a stake, and the kite ascended to a very considerable height above the pond, while I was swimming. In a little time, being desirous of amusing myself with my kite, and enjoying at the same time the pleasure of swimming, I returned, and loosening from the stake the string, with the little stick which was fastened to it, went again into the water, where I found that, lying on my back, and holding the stick in my hand, I was drawn along the surface of the water in a very agreeable manner. Having then engaged another boy to carry my clothes round the pond, to a place which I pointed out to him on the other side, I began to cross the pond with my kite, which carried me quite over without the least fatigue, and with the greatest pleasure imaginable. I was only obliged occasionally to halt a little in my course, and resist its progress, when it appeared that by following too quickly, I lowered the kite too much; by doing which occasionally I made it rise again. I have never since that time practised this singular mode of swimming, and I think it not impossible to cross, in this manner, from Dover to Calais.

THOSE WHO PREFER THE AID OF BELTS will find it very easy and safe to make belts upon the plan explained; and by gradually reducing the floating power of the belts from day to day, they will gain confidence, and speedily acquire the art of swimming.

Strength of Men.

With a drawing-knife a man exerts a force of,..................100 lbs.

With an auger, both hands......100 lbs.
With a screw-driver, one hand.. 84 "
With a bench-vice handle...... 72 "
With a chisel, vertical pressure 72 "
With a windlass..................... 60 "
With pincers, compression...... 60 "
With a hand-plane................ 50 "
With a hand-saw.................... 36 "
With a thumb-vice................. 45 "

With a brace-bit, revolving...... 16 lbs.
Twisting by the thumb and }
    fingers only with a small } 14 "
    screw-driver................... }

The strength of 5 men is equivalent
to 1 animal horse.

The strength of 7½ men is equivalent
to 1 machinery horse-power.

EVERY ONE HIS OWN COOK.

THE CHOICE OF WHOLESOME FOOD—ECONOMY IN ITS SELECTION—THEORY AND PRACTICE OF GOOD COOKING.

Choice of Articles of Food.— Nothing is more important in the affairs of housekeeping than the choice of wholesome food. We have been amused by a conundrum, which is as follows : — " A man went to market and bought *two* fish. When he reached home he found they were the same as when he had bought them; yet there were *three!* How was this?" The answer is — " He bought two mackerel, and one *smelt!*" Those who envy him his bargain need not care about the following rules; but to others they will be valuable :

MACKEREL must be perfectly fresh, or it is a very indifferent fish ; it will neither bear carriage, nor being kept many hours out of the water. The firmness of the flesh, and the clearness of the eyes, must be the criterion of fresh mackerel, as they are of all other fish.

COD is known to be fresh by the rigidity of the muscles (or flesh); the redness of the gills, and clearness of the eyes. Crimping much improves this fish.

SALMON. — The flavor and excellence of this fish depends upon its freshness, and the shortness of time since it was caught; for no method can completely preserve the delicate flavor it has when just taken out of the water. A great deal of what is brought to market has been packed in ice.

HERRINGS should be eaten when very fresh ; and, like mackerel, will not remain good many hours after they are caught. But they are very excellent, especially for breakfast relishes, either salted, split, dried, and peppered, or pickled.

FRESH-WATER FISH. — The remarks as to firmness and clear fresh eyes, apply to this variety of fish.

LOBSTERS, recently caught, have always some remains of muscular action in the claws, which may be excited by pressing the eyes with the finger; when this cannot be produced, the lobster must have been too long kept. When boiled, the tail preserves its elasticity if fresh, but loses it as soon as it becomes stale. The heaviest lobsters are the best; when light, they are watery and poor. Hen lobsters may generally be known by the spawn, or by the breadth of the "flap."

CRAB AND CRAYFISH must be chosen by observations similar to those given above in the choice of lobsters. Crabs have an agreeable smell when fresh.

PRAWNS AND SHRIMPS, when fresh, are firm and crisp.

OYSTERS.—If fresh, the shell is firmly closed; when the shells of Oysters are open, they are dead, and unfit for food. The small-shelled Oysters are the finest in flavor. Larger kinds, called Rock Oysters, are generally considered only fit for stewing and sauces, though some persons prefer them.

BEEF.—The grain of ox beef, when good, is loose, the meat red, and the fat inclining to yellow. Cow beef, on the contrary, has a closer grain, a whiter fat, but meat scarcely as red as that of ox beef. Inferior beef, which is meat obtained from ill-fed animals, or from those which had become too old for food, may be known by a hard, skinny fat, a dark red lean, and, in old animals, a line of horny texture running through the meat of the ribs. When meat pressed by the finger rises up quickly, it may be considered as that of an animal which was in its prime; when the dent made by pressure returns slowly, or remains visible, the animal had probably passed its prime, and the meat consequently must be of inferior quality.

VEAL should be delicately white, though it is often juicy and well-flavored when rather dark in color. Butchers, it is said, bleed calves purposely before killing them, with a view to make the flesh white, but this also makes it dry and flavorless. On examining the loin, if the fat enveloping the kidney be white and firm looking, the meat will probably be prime and recently killed. Veal will not keep so long as an older meat, especially in hot or damp weather. When going, the fat becomes soft and moist, the meat flabby and spotted, and somewhat porous like sponge. Large, overgrown veal is inferior to a small, delicate, yet fat veal. The fillet of a cow-calf is known by the udder attached to it, and by the softness of the skin. It is preferable to the veal of a bull-calf.

MUTTON. — The meat should be firm and close in grain, and red in color, the fat white and firm. Mutton is in its prime when the sheep is about five years old, though it is often killed much younger. If too young, the flesh feels tender when pinched; if too old, on being pinched it wrinkles up, and so remains. In young mutton, the fat readily separates. In old, it is held together by strings of skin. In sheep diseased of the rot, the flesh is very pale-colored, the fat inclining to yellow. The meat appears loose from the bone, and if squeezed, drops of water ooze out from the grains; after cooking, the meat drops clean away from the bones. Wether Mutton is

preferred to that of the ewe. It may be known by the lump of fat on the inside of the thigh.

LAMB. — This meat will not keep long after it is killed. The large vein in the neck is bluish in color when the fore-quarter is fresh, green when becoming stale. In the hind-quarter, if not recently killed, the fat of the kidney will have a slight smell, and the knuckle will have lost its firmness.

PORK. — When good, the rind is thin, smooth, and cool to the touch; when changing, from being too long killed, it becomes flaccid and clammy. Enlarged glands, called kernels, in the fat, are marks of an ill-fed or diseased pig.

BACON should have a thin rind, and the fat should be firm, and tinged red by the curing; the flesh should be of a clear red, without intermixture of yellow, and it should firmly adhere to the bone. To judge the state of a ham, plunge a knife into it to the bone; on drawing it back, if particles of meat adhere to it, or if the smell is disagreeable, the curing has not been effectual, and the ham is not good; it should, in such a state, be immediately cooked. In buying a ham, a short thick one is to be preferred to one long and thin.

VENISON. — When good, the fat is clear, bright, and of considerable thickness. To know when it is necessary to cook it, a knife must be plunged into the haunch; and from the smell the cook must determine on dressing or keeping it.

TURKEY.—In choosing poultry, the age of the bird is the chief point to be attended to. An old turkey has rough and reddish legs; a young one smooth and black. Fresh killed, the eyes are full and clear, and the feet moist. When it has been kept too long, the parts about the vent have a greenish appearance.

COMMON DOMESTIC FOWLS, when young, have the legs and combs smooth; when old they are rough, and on the breast long hairs are found instead of feathers. Fowls and chickens should be plump on the breast, fat on the back, and white-legged.

GEESE. — The bills and feet are red when old, yellow when young. Fresh killed, the feet are pliable; stiff, when too long kept. Geese are called green while they are only two or three months old.

DUCKS. — Choose those with supple feet and hard plump breasts. Tame ducks have yellow feet, wild ones, red.

PIGEONS are very indifferent food when they are too long kept. Suppleness of the feet shows them to be young ; the state of the flesh is flaccid when they are getting bad from keeping. Tame pigeons are larger than the wild.

HARES AND RABBITS, when old, have the haunches thick, the ears dry and tough, and the claws blunt and ragged. A young hare has claws smooth and sharp, ears that easily tear, and a narrow cleft in the lip.

PARTRIDGES, when young, have yellowish legs and dark colored bills. Old partridges are very indifferent eating.

WOODCOCKS AND SNIPES, when old, have the feet thick and hard ; when these are soft and tender, they are both young and fresh killed. When their bills become moist, and their throats muddy, they have been too long killed.

Names and Situations of the Various Joints.— MEATS.— In different places the method of cutting up carcases varies. That which we describe below is the most general, and is known as the English method.

1. BEEF. — *Fore-quarter.* — Fore rib (five ribs) ; middle rib (four ribs) ; chuck (three ribs). Shoulder piece (top of fore leg) ; brisket (lower or belly part of the ribs) ; clod (fore shoulder blade) ; neck ; shin (below the shoulder) ; cheek. *Hind-quarter.*—Sirloin ; rump ; aitchbone—these are the three divisions of the upper part of the quarter ; buttock and mouse-buttock, which divide the thigh ; veiny piece, joining the buttock ; thick flank and thin flank (belly pieces) and leg. The

sirloin and rump of both sides form a baron. *Beef is in season all the year ; best in the winter.*

2. MUTTON.—Shoulder ; breast (the belly) ; over which are the loin (chump, or tail end) ; loin (best end) ; and neck (best end) ; neck (scrag end). A chine is two necks ; a saddle, two loins ; then there are the leg and head. *Mutton is the best in winter, spring, and autumn.*

3. LAMB is cut into fore-quarter and hind-quarter ; a saddle, or loin ; neck, breast, leg, and shoulder. *Grass Lamb is in season from Easter to Michaelmas ; House Lamb from Christmas to end of March.*

4. PORK is cut into leg, hand, or shoulder ; hind-loin ; fore-loin ; belly-part ; spare-rib (or neck) ; and head. *Pork is in season nearly all the year.*

5. VEAL is cut into neck (scrag end) ; neck (best end) ; loin (best end) ; loin (chump or tail end) ; fillet (upper part of hind leg) ; hind knuckle, which joins the fillet ; knuckle of fore leg ; blade (bone of shoulder) ; breast (best end) ; breast (brisket end), and hand. *Veal is always in season, but dear in the winter and spring.*

VENISON is cut into haunch (or back) ; neck ; shoulder ; and breast. *Doe venison is best in January, October, November, and December, and Buck venison in June, July, August, and September.*

SCOTTISH MODE OF DIVISION. — According to the English method the carcass of beef is disposed of more economically than upon the Scotch plan. The English plan affords better steaks and better joints for roasting ; but the Scotch plan gives a greater variety of pieces for boiling. The names of pieces in the Scotch plan, not found in the English, are the hough, or hind leg ; the nineholes, or English buttock ; the large and small runner, taken from the rib and chuck pieces of the English plan ; the shoulder-lyer, the English shoulder, but cut differently ; the spare-rib or fore-sye, the sticking piece, etc. The Scotch also cut mutton differently.

OX-TAIL is much esteemed for purposes of soup; so also is the CHEEK. The TONGUE is highly esteemed.

CALVES' HEADS are very useful for various dishes; so also are their KNUCKLES, FEET, HEART, etc.

The' city reader is fortunate who resides near a good market. A little system applied to the task of marketing will save much annoyance, time and labor. Be regular about the days and hour of going to market. Read the newspapers and keep posted about seasonable food and its cost.

Relative Economy of the Joints. —THE ROUND is, in large families, one of the most profitable parts: it is usually boiled, and, like most of the boiling parts of beef, is generally sold at a less price than roasting joints.

THE BRISKET is also less in price than the roasting parts. It is not so economical a part as the round, having more bone to be weighed with it, and more fat. Where there are children, very fat joints are not desirable, being often disagreeable to them, and sometimes prejudicial, especially if they have a dislike to fat. This joint also requires more cooking than many others; that is to say, it requires a double allowance of time to be given for boiling it; it will, when served, be hard and scarcely digestible if no more time be allowed to boil it than that which is sufficient for other joints and meats. When stewed it is excellent; and when cooked fresh (i. e., unsalted), an excellent stock for soup may be extracted from it, and yet the meat will serve as well for dinner.

THE EDGEBONE, or AITCHBONE, is not considered to be a very economical joint, the bone being large in proportion to the meat; but the greater part of it, at least, is as good as that of any prime part. It sells for less than roasting joints.

THE RUMP is the part of which the butcher makes great profit, by selling it in the form of steaks. In the country, as there is not an equal demand for steaks, the whole of it may be purchased as a joint, and at the price of other prime parts. It may be turned

to good account in producing many excellent dishes. If salted, it is simply boiled; if used unsalted, it is generally stewed.

THE VEINY PIECE is sold at a low price per pound; but, if hung for a day or two, it is very good and very profitable. Where there are a number of servants and children to have an early dinner, this part of beef will be found desirable.

THE LEG AND SHIN afford excellent stock for soup; and, if not reduced too much, the meat taken from the bones may be served as a stew with vegetables; or it may be seasoned, pounded with butter, and potted; or, chopped very fine, and seasoned with herbs, and bound together by egg and bread crumbs, it may be fried in balls, or in the form of large eggs, and served with a gravy made with a few spoonfuls of the soup.

OX CHEEK makes excellent soup. The meat, when taken from the bones, may be served as a stew.

THE SIRLOIN AND THE RIBS are the roasting parts of beef, and these bear, in all places, the highest price. The most profitable of these two joints at a family table is the ribs. The bones, if removed from the beef before it is roasted, will assist in forming the basis of a soup. When boned, the meat of the ribs is often rolled up, tied with strings, and roasted; and this is the best way of using it, as it enables the carver to distribute equally the upper part of the meat with the fatter and more skinny parts, at the lower end of the bones.

Indications of Wholesome Mushrooms. — Whenever a fungus is pleasant in flavor and odor, it may be considered wholesome; if, on the contrary, it have an offensive smell, a bitter, astringent, or styptic taste, or even if it leave an unpleasant flavor in the mouth, it should not be considered fit for food. The color, figure, and texture of these vegetables do not afford any characters on which we can safely rely; yet it may be remarked that in color the pure yellow, gold color, bluish pale, dark or lustre brown, wine red, or the violet, belong to many that are eatable; while the pale or sulphur-yellow, bright or blood-red, and the greenish, belong to few but the poisonous. The safe kinds have, most frequently, a compact, brittle texture; the flesh is white; they grow more readily in open places, such as dry pastures and waste lands, than in places humid or shaded by wood. In general, those should be suspected which grow in caverns and subterranean passages, on animal matter undergoing putrefaction, as well as those whose flesh is soft or watery.

To Distinguish Mushrooms from Poisonous Fungi. — Sprinkle a little salt on the spongy part or gills of the sample to be tried. If they turn yellow, they are poisonous, — if black, they are wholesome. Allow the salt to act before you decide on the question.

False mushrooms have a warty cap, or else fragments of membrane, adhering to the upper surface, are heavy, and emerge from a vulva or bag; they grow in tufts or clusters in woods, on the stumps of trees, etc., whereas the true mushrooms grow in pastures.

False mushrooms have an astringent, styptic, and disagreeable taste.

When cut they turn blue.

They are moist on the surface, and generally

Of a rose or orange color.

The gills of the true mushroom are of a pinky red, changing to a liver color.

The flesh is white.

The stem is white, solid, and cylindrical.

Drying Herbs. — Fresh herbs are preferable to dried ones, but as they cannot always be obtained, it is most important to dry herbs at the proper seasons : — *Basil* is in a fit state for drying about the middle of August. *Burret* in June, July, and August. *Chervil* in May, June, and July. *Elder Flowers*, in May, June, and July. *Fennel* in May, June, and July. *Knotted Marjoram* during July. *Lemon Thyme*, end of July and through August. *Mint*, end of June and July.

Orange Flowers, May, June, and July. *Orange Thyme* (a delicious herb), June and July. *Parsley*, May, June, and July. *Sage*, August and September. *Summer Savory*, end of July and August. *Thyme*, end of July and August. *Winter Savory*, end of July and August.

These herbs, always at hand, will be a great aid to the cook. Herbs should be gathered on a dry day; they should be immediately well cleansed, and dried by the heat of a stove. The leaves should then be picked off, pounded and sifted, put into stoppered bottles, labelled, and put away for use.

Rules for Marketing. — The best rule for marketing is to pay ready money for everything, *and to deal with the most respectable tradesmen* in your neighborhood. If you leave it to their integrity to supply you with a good article at the fair market price, you will be supplied with better provisions, and at as reasonable rates as those *bargain-hunters* who trot " *around, around, around about* " a market till they are trapped to buy some *unchewable* old poultry, *tough* mutton, *stringy* cowbeef, or *stale* fish, at a very little less than the price of prime and proper food. With *savings* like these, they toddle home in triumph, cackling all the way, like a goose that has got ankle-deep into good luck. All the skill of the most accomplished cook will avail nothing, unless she is furnished with prime provisions. The best way to procure these is to deal at stores of established character. You may appear to pay, perhaps, ten *per cent.* more than you would were you to deal with those who pretend to sell cheap, but you would be much more than in that proportion better served. Every trade has its tricks and deceptions. Those who follow them can deceive you if they please, and they are too apt to do so if you provoke the exercise of their over-reaching talent. Challenge them to a game at " *Catch who can,*" by entirely relying on your own judgment, and you will soon find nothing but very long experience can make you equal to the combat of marketing to the utmost advantage. If you think a tradesman has imposed upon you, never use a second word, if the first will not do, nor drop the least hint of an imposition; the only method to induce him to make an abatement is the hope of future favors. Pay the demand, and deal with the gentleman no more; but do not let him see that you are displeased, or as soon as you are out of sight your reputation will suffer as much as your pocket has. Before you go to market, look over your larder, and consider well what things are wanting — especially on a Saturday. No well-regulated family can suffer a disorderly caterer to be jumping in and out to make purchases on a Sunday morning. You will be enabled to manage much better if you will make out a bill of fare for the week on the Saturday before; for example, for a family of half-a-dozen : —

Sunday — Roast beef and pudding.
Monday — Fowl, what was left of pudding fried, or warmed in the oven.
Tuesday — Calf's head, apple pie.
Wednesday — Leg of mutton.
Thursday — Ditto broiled or hashed, and pancakes.
Friday — Fish, pudding.
Saturday — Fish, or eggs and bacon.

It is an excellent plan to have certain things on certain days. When your butcher or poulterer knows what you will want, he has a better chance of doing his best for you; and never think of ordering beef for roasting except for Sunday. When you order meat, poultry, or fish, tell the tradesman when you intend to dress it : he will then have it in his power to serve you with provision that will do him credit, which the finest meat, etc., in the world will never do, unless it has been kept a proper time to be ripe and tender.

We would here remark, what will soon be seen by a careful housewife, that we have tried to meet her wants, and have avoided the extravagances of the modern cook-book. Our aim is to give such directions as will enable her to keep a good table at a reasonable cost, and to dress it in such a manner that will banish the monster Dyspepsia from the household.

Amount of Food. — As a general rule, it may be set down that a healthy man, taking ordinary exercise, should consume daily—of Meat, about ¾ of a pound; of Bread, the same; of Potatoes and other Vegetables, 1½ pounds; of Cheese, 2 ounces; Butter, 1 ounce; Sugar, the same; Tea, ½ an ounce; or Coffee, 1 ounce. The Meat may, and should, be sometimes changed for its equivalent in Fish; and if Pudding or Pie be taken, so much Vegetables will not be required. A larger amount of solid food than the above cannot be conducive to health, and is very likely, if persisted in, to produce actual disease, the more especially if the food be of a rich and stimulating character. Females, whose habits generally are less active than those of males, cannot, as a rule, take, with advantage, above three-fourths, or perhaps half this quantity; nor can any person whose digestive powers are at all weak. It is of consequence that, by such, the kind of food which contains the most nourishment in a small compass should be taken. We would, therefore, advise the reduction in the above scale to be made in the Vegetables, and the Cheese must be dispensed with, as indeed it may well be in all cases. We should, perhaps, have included Milk in the scale, for, although in a liquid form, it contains a considerable proportion of solid matter; from 2 to 4 ounces daily may be taken with advantage by a healthy, active person. Those who require nourishment in a concentrated form may take at least double the quantity, and an Egg or two daily, if they find that they can digest it. Light farinaceous Puddings are also good for such, and when these are obtainable, Vegetables may be altogether discarded.

Various Processes of Cooking. — 1. "In the hands of an expert cook," says Majendie, "alimentary substances are made almost entirely to change their nature, their form, consistence, odor, savor, color, chemical composition, etc.; everything is so modified, that it is often impossible for the most exquisite sense of taste to recognize the substance which makes up the basis of certain dishes. The greatest utility of the kitchen consists in making the food agreeable to the senses, and rendering it easy of digestion."

2. To some extent the claims of either process of cooking depend upon the taste of the individual. Some persons may esteem the peculiar flavor of fried meats, while others will prefer broils or stews. It is important, however, to understand the theory of each method of cooking, so that whichever may be adopted, may be done well. Bad cooking, though by a good method, is far inferior to good cooking by a bad method.

ROASTING.— BEEF.— The noble sirloin of about fifteen pounds (if much thicker the outside will be done too much before the inner side is sufficiently roasted), will require to be before the fire about three and a half or four hours. Take care to spit it evenly, that it may not be heavier on one side than the other. Put a little clean dripping into the dripping-pan (tie a sheet of paper over it to preserve the fat), baste it well as soon as it is put down, and every quarter of an hour all the time it is roasting, till the last half-hour. Then take off the paper, and make some gravy for it, stir the fire and make it clear. To brown and froth it, sprinkle a little salt over it, baste it with butter, and dredge it with flour; let it go a few minutes longer, till the froth rises, take it up, put it on the dish, etc. Garnish it with hillocks of horse-radish, scraped as fine as possible with a very sharp knife.

A YORKSHIRE PUDDING is an excellent accompaniment.

RIBS OF BEEF.— The three first ribs, of fifteen or twenty pounds, will take three hours, or three and a half; the fourth and fifth ribs will take as long, managed in the same way, as the sir-

loin. Paper the fat and thin part, or it will be done too much, before the thick part is done enough.

RIBS OF BEEF BONED AND ROLLED. — When you have kept two or three ribs of beef till quite tender, take out the bones, and skewer it as round as possible (like a fillet of veal): before they roll it, some cooks egg it, and sprinkle it with veal stuffing. As the meat is in a solid mass, it will require more time at the fire than in the preceding recipe: a piece of ten or twelve pounds weight will not be well and thoroughly roasted in less than four and a half or five hours. For the first half-hour it should not be less than twelve inches from the fire, that it may get gradually warm to the centre; the last half-hour before it is finished, sprinkle a little salt over it, and if you so wish, froth it, flour it, etc.

MUTTON. — As beef requires a large sound fire, mutton must have a brisk and sharp one: if you wish to have mutton tender, it should be hung as long as it will keep, and then good eight-tooth, i. e. four years' old mutton, is as good eating as venison.

THE LEG, HAUNCH, AND SADDLE, will be the better for being hung up in a cool airy place for four or five days at least; in temperate weather, a week; in cold weather, ten days. A leg of eight pounds will take about two hours; let it be well basted.

A CHINE OR SADDLE—i. e., the two loins, of ten or eleven pounds—two hours and a half. It is the business of the butcher to take off the skin and skewer it on again, to defend the meat from extreme heat, and preserve its succulence. If this is neglected, tie a sheet of paper over it; baste the strings you tie it on with directly, or they will burn. About a quarter of an hour before you think it will be done, take off the skin or paper, that it may get a pale-brown color, and then baste it, and flour it lightly to froth it.

A SHOULDER of seven pounds, an hour and a half. Put the spit in close to the shank-bone, and run it along the blade-bone.

A LOIN OF MUTTON, from an hour and a half to an hour and three-quarters. The most elegant way of carving this, is to cut it lengthwise, as you do a saddle. A neck, about the same time as a loin. It must be carefully jointed, or it is very difficult to carve.

THE NECK AND BREAST are, in small families, commonly roasted together. The cook will then crack the bones across the middle before they are put down to roast. If this is not done carefully, they are very troublesome to carve. A breast, an hour and a quarter.

A HAUNCH — i. e., the leg and part of the loin of mutton. Send up two sauce-boats with it; one of rich-drawn mutton gravy, made without spice or herbs, and the other of sweet sauce. It generally weighs about fifteen pounds, and requires about three hours and a half to roast it.

MUTTON (Venison fashion). — Take a neck of good four or five-year old Southdown wether mutton, cut long in the bones; let it hang, in temperate weather, at least a week. Two days before you dress it, take allspice and black pepper, ground and pounded fine, a quarter of an ounce of each, rub them together, and then rub your mutton well with this mixture twice a day. When you dress it, wash off the spice with warm water, and roast it in paste.

VEAL requires particular care to roast it a nice brown. Let the fire be the same as for beef—a sound large fire for a large joint, and a brisker for a smaller: put it at some distance from the fire to soak thoroughly, and then draw it nearer to finish it brown. When first laid down it is to be basted; baste it again occasionally. When the veal is on the dish, pour over it half a pint of melted butter: if you have a little brown gravy by you, add that to the butter. With those joints which are not stuffed, send up forcemeat in balls, or rolled into sausages, as garnish to the dish, or fried pork sausages: bacon and greens are always expected with veal.

FILLET OF VEAL, of from twelve to sixteen pounds, will require from four to five hours at a good fire; make some stuffing or forcemeat, and put it under the flap, that there may be some left to eat cold, or to season a hash: brown it, and pour good melted butter over it. Garnish with thin slices of lemon, and cakes or balls of stuffing, or duck stuffing, or fried pork sausages, curry sauce, bacon and greens, etc.

A LOIN is the best part of the calf, and will take about three hours roasting. Paper the kidney fat, and the back: some cooks send up on a toast, which is eaten with the kidney and the fat of this part, which is more delicate than any marrow, etc. If there is more of it than you think will be eaten with the veal, before you roast it cut it out, it will make an excellent suet pudding: take care to have your fire long enough to brown the ends.

A SHOULDER OF VEAL, from three hours to three hours and a half: stuff it with the forcemeat ordered for the fillet of veal, in the under side.

NECK, the best end, will take two hours. The scrag part is best made into a pie or broth. Breast, from an hour and a half to two hours. Let the caul remain till it is almost done, then take it off, to brown it; baste, flour, and froth it.

VEAL SWEETBREAD. — Trim a fine sweetbread — it cannot be too fresh; parboil it for five minutes, and throw into a basin of cold water; roast it plain, or beat up the yolk of an egg, and prepare some fine bread crumbs. When the sweetbread is cold, dry it thoroughly in a cloth, run a lark spit or a skewer through it, and tie it on the ordinary spit; egg it with a paste brush, powder it well with bread-crumbs, and roast it. For sauce, fried bread-crumbs round it, and melted butter with a little mushroom ketchup and lemon juice, or serve on buttered toast, garnish with egg sauce, or with gravy.

LAMB is a delicate and commonly considered tender meat; but those who talk of tender lamb, while they are thinking of the age of the animal, forget that even a chicken must be kept a proper time after it has been killed, or it will be tough picking. Woeful experience has warned us to beware of accepting an invitation to dinner on Easter Sunday; and unless commanded by a thoroughbred gourmand, our incisors, molars, and principal viscera, have protested against the imprudence of encountering young, tough, stringy mutton under the misnomer of Grass-Lamb. To the usual accompaniments of roasted meat, green mint sauce or a salad is commonly added; and some cooks, about five minutes before it is done, sprinkle it with a little minced parsley.

WHEN GREEN MINT cannot be got, Mint Vinegar is an acceptable substitute for it.

HIND-QUARTER of eight pounds will take from an hour and three-quarters to two hours; baste, and froth it.

FORE-QUARTER of ten pounds, about two hours.

IT IS A PRETTY GENERAL CUSTOM, when you take off the shoulder from the ribs, to squeeze a Seville orange over them, and sprinkle them with a little pepper and salt.

LEG of five pounds, from an hour to an hour and a half.

SHOULDER, with a quick fire, an hour.

RIBS, about an hour to an hour and a quarter. Joint it nicely, crack the ribs across, and bend them up to make it easy to carve.

LOIN, an hour and a quarter. Neck, an hour. Breast, three quarters of an hour.

Poultry, Game, etc.

	H. M.
A small capon, fowl, or chicken, requires	0 20
A large fowl	0 45
A capon, full size	0 35
A goose	1 0
Wild ducks, and grouse	0 15
Pheasants, and turkey poults	0 20
A moderate sized turkey, stuffed	1 15
Partridges	0 25
Quail	0 10
A hare or rabbit	about 1 0
Leg of pork, ¼ hour for each pound, and above that allowance	0 20
A chine of pork	0 20
A neck of mutton	1 30
A hauuch of venison	about 3 30

ROASTING, BY CAUSING THE CONTRACTION of the cellular substance which contains the fat, expels more fat than boiling. The free escape of watery particles in the form of vapor, so necessary to produce flavor, must be regulated by frequent basting with the fat which has exuded from the meat, combined with a little salt and water, otherwise the meat would burn, and become hard and tasteless. A brisk fire at first will, by charring the outside, prevent the heat from penetrating, and therefore should only be employed when the meat is half roasted.

THE LOSS BY ROASTING varies, according to Professor Donovan, from 14⅜ths to nearly double that rate per cent. The average loss on roasting butcher's meat is 22 per cent.; and on domestic poultry is 20½.

THE LOSS PER CENT. ON ROASTING BEEF, viz., on sirloins and ribs together, is 19½th; on mutton, viz., legs and shoulders together, 24⅛ths; on fore-quarters of lamb, 22½d; on ducks, 27¼th; on turkeys, 20½; on geese, 19½; on chickens, 14⅜ths. So that it will be seen by comparison with the percentage given of the loss by boiling, that roasting is not so economical; especially when we take into account that the loss of weight by boiling is not actual loss of economic materials, for we then possess the principal ingredients for soups; whereas, after roasting, the fat only remains. The average loss in boiling and roasting together is 18 per cent. according to Donovan, and 28 per cent. according to Wallace—a difference that may be accounted for by supposing a difference in the fatness of the meat, duration and degree of heat, etc., employed.

BOILING.—This most simple of culinary processes is not often performed in perfection; it does not require quite so much nicety and attendance as roasting; to skim your pot well, and keep it really boiling (the slower the better) all the while—to know how long is required for doing the joint, etc., and to take it up at the critical moment when it is done enough—comprehends almost the whole art and mystery. This, however, demands a patient and perpetual vigilance, of which few persons are, unhappily, capable. The cook must take especial care that the water really boils all the while she is cooking, or she will be decieved in the time; and make up a sufficient fire (a frugal cook will manage with much less fire for boiling than she uses for roasting) at first to last all the time, without much mending or stirring, and thereby save much trouble. When the pot is coming to a boil, there will always, from the cleanest meat and clearest water, rise a scum to the top of it, proceeding partly from the foulness of the meat and partly from the water; this must be carefully taken off, as soon as it rises. On this depends the good appearance of all boiled things — an essential matter. When you have scummed well, put in some cold water, which will throw up the rest of the scum. The oftener it is scummed, and the clearer the surface of the water is kept, the cleaner will be the meat. If let alone, it soon boils down and sticks to the meat, which, instead of looking delicately white and nice, will have that coarse appearance we have too often to complain of, and the butcher and poulterer will be blamed for the carelessness of the cook, in not scumming her pot with due diligence. Many put in milk to make what they boil look white, but this does more harm than good; others wrap it up in a cloth; but these are needless precautions; if the scum be attentively removed, meat will have a much more delicate color and finer flavor than it has when muffled up. This may give rather more trouble — but those who wish to excel in their art must only consider how the processes of it can be most perfectly performed. A cook who has a proper pride and pleasure in her business will make this her maxim and rule on all occasions. Put your meat into cold water, in the proportion of about a quart of water to a pound of meat; it should be covered with water

during the whole of the process of boiling, but not drowned in it; the less water, provided the meat be covered with it, the more savory will be the meat, and the better will be the broth in every respect. The water should be heated gradually, according to the thickness, etc., of the article boiled; for instance, a leg of mutton of ten pounds weight should be placed over a moderate fire, which will gradually make the water hot, without causing it to boil for about forty minutes; if the water boils much sooner, the meat will be hardened, and shrink up as if it was scorched: by keeping the water a certain time heating without boiling, its fibres are dilated, and it yields a quantity of scum, which must be taken off as soon as it rises, for the reasons already mentioned. "If a vessel containing water be placed over a steady fire, the water will grow continually hotter, till it reaches the limit of boiling; after which the regular accessions of heat are wholly spent in converting it into steam; the water remains at the same pitch of temperature, however fiercely it boils. The only difference is, that with a strong fire it sooner comes to a boil, and more quickly boils away, and is converted into steam." Such are the opinions stated by Buchanan in his "Economy of Fuel." There was placed a thermometer in water in that state which cooks call gentle simmering — the heat was 212°, i. e., the same degree as the strongest boiling. Two mutton chops were covered with cold water, and one boiled fiercely, and the other simmered gently, for three-quarters of an hour; the flavor of the chop which was simmered was decidedly superior to that which was boiled; the liquor which boiled fast was in like proportion more savory, and, when cold, had much more fat on its surface; this explains why quick boiling renders meat hard, etc.,—because its juices are extracted in a greater degree.

RECKON THE TIME from the meat first coming to a boil. The old rule of fifteen minutes to a pound of meat, we think rather too little; the slower it boils, the tenderer, the plumper, and whiter it will be. For those who choose their food thoroughly cooked (which all will who have any regard for their stomachs), twenty minutes to a pound will not be found too much for gentle simmering by the side of the fire; allowing more or less time, according to the thickness of the joint and the coldness of the weather; always remembering, the slower it boils the better. Without some practice it is difficult to teach any art; and cooks seem to suppose they must be right, if they put meat into a pot, and set it over the fire for a certain time — making no allowance whether it simmers without a bubble, or boils at a gallop.

FRESH KILLED MEAT will take much longer time boiling than that which has been kept till it is what the butchers call ripe, and longer in cold than warm weather; if it be frozen, it must be thawed before boiling as before roasting; if it be fresh killed, it will be tough and hard, if you stew it ever so long, and ever so gently. In cold weather, the night before you dress it, bring it into a place of which the temperature is not less than 45° of Fahrenheit's thermometer. The size of the boiling-pots should be adapted to what they are to contain; the larger the saucepan the more room it takes upon the fire; and a larger quantity of water requires a proportionate increase of fire to boil it. In small families, we recommend block-tin saucepans, etc., as lightest and safest; if proper care is taken of them, and they are well dried after they are cleansed, they are by far the cheapest; the purchase of a new tin saucepan being little more than the expense of tinning a copper one. Take care that the covers of your boiling-pots fit close, not only to prevent unnecessary evaporation of the water, but that the smoke may not insinuate itself under the edge of the lid, and give the meat a bad taste.

THE FOLLOWING TABLE will be useful as an average of the time required to boil the various articles:

	H.	M.
A ham, 20 lbs. weight, requires	6	30
A tongue (if dry), after soaking	4	0
A tongue out of pickle	2½ to 3	0
A neck of mutton	1	30
A chicken	0	20
A large fowl	0	45
A capon	0	35
A pidgeon	0	15

IF YOU LET MEAT OR POULTRY REMAIN IN THE WATER after it is done enough, it will become sodden and lose its flavor.

BEEF AND MUTTON a little underdone (especially very large joints, which will make the better hash or broil) is preferred by some people. Lamb, pork, and veal are uneatable if not thoroughly boiled — but do not overdo them. A trivet, or fish-drainer, put on the bottom of the boiling-pot, raising the contents about an inch and a half from the bottom, will prevent that side of the meat which comes next the bottom being done too much, and the lower part will be as delicately done as the upper; and this will enable you to take out the meat without inserting a fork, etc., into it. If you have not a trivet, use four skewers, or a soup-plate laid the wrong side upwards.

TAKE CARE OF THE LIQUOR you have boiled poultry or meat in; in five minutes you may make it into soup.

THE GOOD HOUSEWIFE never boils a joint without converting the broth into some sort of soup.

IF THE LIQUOR BE TOO SALT, use only half the quantity, and the rest water; wash salted meat well with cold water before you put it into the boiler.

BOILING EXTRACTS A PORTION OF THE JUICE of meat, which mixes with the water, and also dissolves some of its solids; the more fusible parts of the fat melt out, combine with the water, and form soup or broth. The meat loses its red color, becomes more savory in taste and smell, and more firm and digestible. If the process is continued *too long*, the meat becomes indigestible, less succulent, and tough.

THE LOSS BY BOILING varies, according to Professor Donovan, from 6¼ to

16 per cent. The average loss on boiling butcher's meat, pork, hams, and bacon, is 12 per cent.; and on domestic poultry, 14¾.

THE LOSS PER CENT. on boiling salt beef is 15; on legs of mutton, 10; hams, 12½; salt pork, 13½; knuckles of veal, 8½; bacon, 6¼; turkeys, 16; chickens, 13¼.

Economy of Fat. — In most families many members are not fond of fat — servants seldom like it; consequently there is frequently much wasted; to avoid which, take off bits of suet fat from beefsteaks, etc., previous to cooking. They can be used for puddings. With good management there need be no waste in any shape or form.

BROILING requires a brisk, rapid heat, which, by producing a greater degree of change in the affinities of the raw meat than roasting, generates a higher flavor, so that broiled meat is more savory than roast. The surface becoming charred, a dark-colored crust is formed, which retards the evaporation of the juices; and, therefore, if properly done, broiled may be as tender and juicy as roasted meat.

BAKING does not admit of the evaporation of the vapors so rapidly as by the processes of broiling and roasting. The fat is also retained more, and becomes converted, by the agency of the heat, into an empyreumatic oil, so as to render the meat less fitted for delicate stomachs, and more difficult to digest. The meat is, in fact, partly boiled in its own confined water, and partly roasted by the dry, hot air of the oven. The loss by baking has not been estimated; and as the time required to cook many articles must vary with their size, nature, etc., we have considered it better to leave that until giving the recipes for them.

FRYING is, of all methods, the most objectionable, from the foods being less digestible when thus prepared, as the fat employed undergoes chemical changes. Olive-oil in this respect is preferable to lard or butter. The crackling noise which accompanies the process of frying meat in a pan is occasioned by the explosions of steam formed in fat, the temperature of which is much above 212°. If the meat is very juicy, it will not fry well, because it becomes sodden before the water is evaporated; and it will not brown, because the temperature is too low to scorch it. To fry fish well the fat should be boiling hot (600°), and the fish *well dried* in a cloth; otherwise, owing to the generation of steam, the temperature will fall so low that it will be boiled in its own steam, and not be browned. Meat, or indeed any article, should be frequently turned and agitated during frying, to promote the evaporation of the watery particles. To make fried things look well, they should be done over *twice* with egg and stale bread-crumbs.

BASTINGS. — 1, Fresh butter; 2, clarified suet; 3, minced sweet herbs, butter, and claret, especially for mutton and lamb; 4, water and salt; 5, cream and melted butter, especially for a flayed pig; 6, yolks of eggs, grated biscuit, and juice of oranges.

DREDGINGS. — 1, Flour mixed with grated bread; 2, sweet herbs dried and powdered, and mixed with grated bread; 3, lemon-peel dried and pounded, or orange-peel, mixed with flour; 4, sugar finely powdered, and mixed with pounded cinnamon, and flour or grated bread; 5, fennel seeds, corianders, cinnamon, and sugar, finely beaten, and mixed with grated bread or flour; 6, for young pigs, grated bread or flour, mixed with beaten nutmeg, ginger, pepper, sugar, and yolks of eggs; 7, sugar, bread, and salt mixed.

The **Housewife** who is anxious to dress no more meat than will suffice for the meal should know that beef loses about one pound in four in boiling, but in roasting, loses in the proportion of one pound five ounces, and in baking, about two ounces less, or one pound three ounces; mutton loses in boiling about fourteen ounces in four pounds; in roasting, one pound six ounces.

COOKS should be cautioned against

the use of charcoal in any quantity, except where there is a free current of air; for charcoal is highly prejudicial in a state of ignition, although it may be rendered even actively beneficial when boiled, as a small quantity of it, if boiled with meat on the turn, will effectually cure the unpleasant taint.

Baking, Boiling, Broiling, Frying, Roasting, Stewing, and Spoiling. — A DIALOGUE between the DUTCH OVEN, the SAUCEPAN, the SPIT, the GRIDIRON, and the FRYING-PAN, with reflections thereupon, in which all housekeepers and cooks are invited to take an interest.

We were once standing by our scullery, when all of a sudden we heard a tremendous clash and jingle — the Saucepan had tumbled into the Frying-pan; the Frying-pan had shot its handle through the ribs of the Gridiron; the Gridiron had bestowed a terrible thump upon the hollow head of the Dutch Oven; and the Spit had dealt a very skilful stroke, which shook the sides of all the combatants, and made them ring out the noises by which we were startled. Musing upon this incident, we fancied that we overheard the following dialogue:

FRYING-PAN. — Hollo, Saucepan! what are you doing here, with your dropsical corporation? Quite time that you were superannuated; you are a mere meat-spoiler. You adulterate the juices of the best joint, and give to the stomach of our master little else than watery compounds to digest.

SAUCEPAN. — Well! I like your conceit! You — who harden the fibre of flesh so much, that there is no telling whether a steak came from a bullock, a horse, or a bear! — who can't fry a slice of potato, or a miserable smelt, but you must be flooded with oil or fat, to keep your spiteful nature from burning or biting the morsel our master should enjoy. Not only that — you open your mouth so wide, that the soot of the chimney drops in, and frequently spoils our master's dinner; or you throw the fat over your sides, and set the chimney in a blaze!

SPIT. — Go on! go on! six of one and half-a-dozen of the other!

DUTCH OVEN. — Well, Mr. Spit, you needn't try to foment the quarrel. You require more attention than any of us; for if you are not continually watched, and helped by that useful little attendant of yours they call a Jack, your lazy, lanky figure would stand still, and you would expose the most delicious joint to the ravages of the fire. In fact, you need not only a Jack to keep you going, but a cook to constantly baste the joint confided to your care, without which our master would have but a dry bone to pick. Not only so, but you thrust your spear-like length through the best meat and make an unsightly gash in a joint which otherwise might be an ornament to the table.

SPIT. — What, Dutch Oven, is that you? venerable old sobersides, with a hood like a monk! Why, you are a mere dummy — as you are placed so you remain; there you stand in one place, gaping wide and catching the coals as they fall; if you were not well watched, you would burn the one half, and sodden the other, of whatever you were required to prepare. Bad luck to *your* impertinence!

GRIDIRON.— Peace! peace! We all have our merits and our demerits.— At this remark of the Gridiron, there was a general shout of laughter.

SAUCEPAN.— Well, I declare! I never thought that I should have *my* merits classed with those of the miserable skeleton called a Gridiron. That is a joke! A thing with six ribs and a tail to compare with so useful a member of the *cuisine* community as myself! Why you, Gridiron, waste one-half of the goodness of the meat in the fire, and the other half you send to the table tainted with smoke, and burnt to cinders! — A loud rattle of approbation went round, as the poor Gridiron fell under this torrent of derision from the Saucepan.

Coming away from the scene of confusion, we ordered the sullerymaid to go instantly and place each of the

utensils that lay in disorder upon the
ground into its proper place, charging
her to cleanse each carefully, until it
should be required for use.

Returning to our library, we thought
it would form no mean occupation
were we to spend a few hours in reflection upon the relative claims of the
disputants. We did so, and the following is the result:

THE GRIDIRON.—The Gridiron,
though the simplest of cooking instruments, is by no means to be despised.
The Gridiron, and indeed all cooking
utensils, should be kept scrupulously
clean; and when it is used, the bars
should be allowed to get warm before
the meat is placed upon it, otherwise the parts crossed by the bars
will be insufficiently dressed. The fire
should be sharp, clear, and free from
smoke. The heat soon forms a film
upon the surface of the meat, by which
the juices are retained. Chops and
steaks should not be too thick nor too
thin. From a half to three-quarters
of an inch is the proper thickness.
Avoid thrusting the fork into the
meat, by which you release the juice.
There is a description of Gridiron, in
which the bars are grooved to catch
the juice of the meat; but a much
better invention is the upright Gridiron, which is attached to the front of
the grate, and has a pan at the bottom
to catch the gravy. Kidneys, rashers,
etc., dressed in this manner will be
found delicious. There are some,
however, who think that the dressing
of meat over the fire secures a flavor
which cannot otherwise be obtained.
Remember that the Gridiron is devoted to the cooking of small dishes,
or snacks, for breakfast, supper, and
luncheon, and is therefore a most useful servant, ready at a moment's
notice. Remember, also, that every
moment which is lost, after the Gridiron has delivered up his charge, is a
delay to the prejudice of the Gridiron.
From the Gridiron to the table without loss of time should be the rule.

THE FRYING-PAN is less a favorite,
in our estimation, than the Gridiron;

but not to be despised, nevertheless.
He is a noisy and a greasy servant, requiring much watchfulness. Like the
Gridiron, the Frying-pan requires a
clear but not a large fire, and the pan
should be allowed to get thoroughly
hot, and be well covered with fat, before meat is put into it. The excellence of frying very much depends
upon the sweetness of the oil, butter,
lard, or fat that may be employed.
The Frying-pan is very useful in the
warming of cold vegetables and other
kinds of food, and in this respect may
be considered a real friend of economy.
All know the relish afforded by a pancake—a treat which the Gridiron
would be unable to afford us—to say
nothing of eggs and bacon, and various
kinds of fish, to which both the Saucepan and the Gridiron are quite unsuit-
ed, because they require that which is
the essence of frying, *boiling and browning in fat.*

THE SPIT is a very noble and very
useful implement of cookery; as ancient, we presume, as he is straightforward at his work. Perhaps the process of roasting stands only second in
the rank of excellence in cookery. The
process is perfectly sound in its chemical effects upon the food, while the
joint is kept so immediately under the
eye of the cook, that it must be the
fault of that functionary if it does not
go to the table in the highest state of
perfection. The process of roasting
may be commenced very slowly, by the
meat being kept a good distance from
the fire, and gradually brought forward, until it is thoroughly soaked
within and browned without. The
Spit has this advantage over the Oven,
and especially over the common oven,
that the meat retains its own flavor,
not having to encounter the evaporation from fifty different dishes, and
that the steam from its own substance
passes entirely away, leaving the
essence of the meat in its primest condition.

THE DUTCH OVEN, though not so
royal an instrument as the Spit, is,
nevertheless, of great utility for small

dishes of various kinds, which the Spit would spoil by the magnitude of its operations, or the Oven destroy by the severity of its heat. It combines, in fact, the advantages of roasting and baking, and may be adopted for compound dishes, and for warming cold scraps : it is easily heated, and causes no material expenditure of fuel.

THE SAUCEPAN.—When we come to speak of the Saucepan, we have to consider the claims of a very large, ancient, and useful family; and, perhaps, looking at the generic orders of the Saucepan, all other cooking implements must yield to its claims. There are large Saucepans, which we dignify with the name of Boilers, and small Saucepans, which come under the denomination of Stewpans. There are few kinds of meat or fish which it will not receive, and dispose of in a satisfactory manner; and few vegetables for which it is not adapted. The Saucepan, rightly used, is a very economical servant, allowing nothing to be lost — that which escapes from the meat while in its charge forms broth, or may be made the basis of soups. Fat rises upon the surface of the water, and may be skimmed off; while in various stews it combines, in an eminent degree, what we may term the *fragrance* of cookery, and the *piquancy* of taste. The French are perfect masters of the use of the Stewpan. And we shall find that, as all cookery is but an aid to digestion, the operations of the Stewpan resemble the action of the stomach very closely. The stomach is a close sac, in which solids and fluids are mixed together, macerated in the gastric juice, and dissolved by the aid of heat and motion, occasioned by the continual contractions and relaxations of the coats of the stomach during the action of digestion. This is more closely resembled by the process of stewing than by any other of our culinary methods.

In this rapid review of the claims of various cooking utensils, we think that we have done justice to each. They all have their respective advantages; besides which, they contribute to the VARIETY presented by our tables, without which the routine of eating would be very monotonous and unsatisfactory.

There is one process to which we must yet allude—the process of SPOIL-ING. Many cooks know how to *produce* a good dish, but too many of them know how to spoil it. They leave fifty things to be done just at the critical moment when the chief dish should be watched with an eye of keenness, and attended by a hand thoroughly expert. Having spent three hours in making a joint hot and rich, they forget that a quarter of an hour, after it is taken from the fire, may impair or spoil all their labors.

Baked or Roast Meat.—Meat is better roasted than baked; but in these days of cooking stoves, the latter mode of cooking is generally the most convenient; and if basted frequently, it can be rendered nearly as good as if roasted. Rub salt on the meat; have at least a pint of water in the dripping-pan, adding more as it cooks away; turn it over the meat while cooking, four or five times in the course of an hour; if not basted often, it will be dry and hard. Heat it gradually through, then increase the fire so that it will cook quick.

To Roast a Sirloin of Beef.—As a joint cannot be properly roasted without a good fire, see that it is well made up about ¾ hour before it is required, so that when the joint is put down, it is clear and bright. Choose a nice sirloin, the weight of which should not exceed 16 pounds, as the outside would be too much done, while the inside would not be done enough. Spit it or hook it on to the jack firmly, dredge it slightly with flour, and place it near the fire at first, as directed in the preceding recipe. Then draw it to a distance, and keep continually basting until the meat is done. Sprinkle a small quantity of salt over it, empty the dripping-pan of all the dripping, pour in some boiling water slightly salted, stir it about, and *strain* over the meat. Garnish with tufts of horse-radish, and send horseradish sauce and Yorkshire pudding to table with it.

Time, a sirloin of 10 lbs., 2½ hours; 14 to 16 lbs., about 4 or 4½ hours.

Sufficient, a joint of 10 lbs., for eight or nine persons. *Seasonable* at any time.

The rump, round, and other pieces of beef are roasted in the same manner, allowing for solid joints quarter of an hour to every pound.

Broiled Beef-steaks or Rump-steaks.

— INGREDIENTS. — *Steaks, a piece of butter the size of a walnut, salt to taste, 1 tablespoonful of good mush-room ketchup or Harvey's sauce.*

Mode. — As the success of a good broil so much depends on the state of the fire, see that it is bright and clear, and perfectly free from smoke; and do not add any fresh fuel *just before the gridiron is to be used.* Sprinkle a little salt over the fire, put on the gridiron for a few minutes, to get thoroughly hot through; rub it with a piece of fresh suet, to prevent the meat from sticking, and lay on the steaks, which should be cut of an equal thick-ness, about ¾ of an inch, or rather thinner, and level them by beating them (as *little* as possible) with a roll-ing-pin. Turn them frequently with steak-tongs (if these are not at hand, stick a fork in the edge of the fat, that no gravy escapes), and in from eight to ten minutes the steaks will be done. Have ready a very hot dish, into which put the ketchup, and, when liked, a little minced shalot; dish up the steaks, rub them over with butter, and season with pepper and salt. The exact time for broiling stakes must be determined by taste, whether they are liked under-done or well-done: more than from eight to ten minutes for a steak ¾ inch in thickness, we think, would spoil and dry up the juices of the meat. Great expedition is necessary in sending broiled steaks to table; and, to have them in perfection, they should not be cooked till everything else prepared for dinner has been dished up, as their ex-cellence entirely depends on their being served up hot. They may be garnished with scraped horseradish, or slices of cucumber. Oyster, tomato, onion, and many other sauces, are fre-quent accompaniments to rump-steak, but true lovers of this dish generally reject all additions but pepper, salt, and a tiny piece of butter.

Time, 8 to 10 minutes. *Sufficient.* — Allow ½ lb. to each person; if the party consist entirely of gentlemen, ¾ lb. will not be too much. *Seasonable* all the year, but not so good in the height of summer, as the meat cannot hang long enough to be tender.

To Dress a Bullock's Heart.

— Put the heart into warm water to soak for two hours; then wipe it well with a cloth, and, after cutting off the lobes, stuff the inside with a highly-seasoned forcemeat. Fasten it in, by means of a needle and coarse thread; tie the heart up in paper, and set it before a good fire, being very particular to keep it well basted, or it will eat dry, there being but very little of its own fat. Two or three minutes before serving, remove the paper, baste well, and serve with good gravy and red-currant jelly or melted butter. If the heart is very large, it will require two hours, and, covered with a caul, may be baked as well as roasted.

Time, large heart, two hours. *Suffi-cient* for six or eight persons. *Season-able*, all the year.

Note. — This is an excellent family dish, is very savory, and, though not seen at many good tables, may be recommended for its cheapness and economy.

Fried Rump - Steak.

— Although broiling is a far superior method of cooking steaks to frying them, yet, when the cook is not very expert, the latter mode may be adopted; and, when properly done, the dish may really look very inviting, and the flavor be good. The steaks should be cut rather thinner than for broiling, and with a small quantity of fat to each. Put some butter or clarified dripping into a frying-pan; let it get quite hot, then lay in the steaks. Turn them frequently until done, which will be in about eight minutes, or rather more, should the steaks be very thick. Serve on a very hot dish, in which put a small piece of butter, and a tablespoonful of ketchup, and season with pepper and salt. They should be sent to table quickly, as, when cold, the steaks are entirely spoiled.

Time, eight minutes for a medium-sized steak, rather longer for a very thick one. *Seasonable* all the year, but not good in summer, as the meat cannot hang to get tender.

Note.—Where much gravy is liked, make it in the following manner :—As soon as the steaks are done, dish them, pour a little boiling water into the frying-pan, add a seasoning of pepper and salt, a small piece of butter, and a tablespoonful of Harvey's sauce, or mushroom ketchup. Hold the pan over the fire for a minute or two, just let the gravy simmer, then pour on the steak, and serve.

Stewed Beef, or Rump-Steak (an Entree).

— INGREDIENTS. — *About* 2 *pounds of beef, or rump-steak, 3 onions, 2 turnips, 3 carrots, 2 or 3 ounces of butter, ½ pint of water, 1 teaspoonful of salt, ½ do. of pepper, 1 tablespoonful of ketchup, 1 tablespoonful of flour.*

Mode.— Have the steaks cut tolerably thick, and rather lean. Divide them into convenient-sized pieces, and fry them in the butter a nice brown on both sides. Cleanse and pare the vegetables, cut the onions and carrots into thin slices, and the turnips into dice, and fry these in the same fat that the steaks were done in. Put all into a saucepan, add ½ pint of water, or rather more should it be necessary, and simmer very gently for 2½ or 3 hours; when nearly done, skim well, add salt, pepper, and ketchup ·in the above proportions, and thicken with a tablespoonful of flour mixed with two of cold water. Let it boil up for a minute or two after the thickening is added, and serve. When a vegetable scoop is at hand, use it to cut the vegetables in fanciful shapes, and tomato, Harvey's sauce, or walnut-liquor, may be used to flavor the gravy. It is less rich if stewed the previous day, so that the fat may be taken off when cold. When wanted for table, it will merely require warming through.

Time, three hours. *Sufficient* for four or five persons. *Seasonable* at any time.

Baked Beef (Cold Meat Cookery).

I. INGREDIENTS.—*About* 2 *pounds of cold roast beef, 2 small onions, 1 large carrot or 2 small ones, 1 turnip, a small bunch of savory herbs, salt and pepper to taste, 12 tablespoonfuls of gravy, 3 tablespoonfuls of ale, crushed or mashed potatoes.*

Mode. — Cut the beef in slices, allowing a small amount of fat to each slice. Place a layer of this in the bottom of a pie-dish, with a portion of the onions, carrots, and turnips, which must be sliced. Mince the herbs, strew them over the meat, and season with pepper and salt. Then put another layer of meat, vegetables, and seasoning; and proceed in this manner until all the ingredients are used. Pour in the gravy and ale (water may be substituted for the former, but it is not so nice), cover with a crust or mashed potatoes, and bake for half an hour, or rather longer.

Time, rather more than half an hour. *Sufficient* for five or six persons. *Seasonable* at any time.

Note.—It is as well to parboil the carrots and turnips before adding them to the meat, and to use some of the liquor in which they were boiled as a substitute for gravy ; that is to say, when there is no gravy at hand. Be particular to cut the onions in very *thin* slices.

II. INGREDIENTS. — *Slices of cold roast beef, salt and pepper to taste, 1 sliced onion, 1 teaspoonful of minced savory herbs, about* 12 *tablespoonfuls of gravy or sauce of any kind, mashed potatoes.*

Mode.— Butter the sides of a deep dish, and spread mashed potatoes over the bottom of it. On this place layers of beef in thin slices (this may be minced if there is not sufficient beef to cut into slices), well seasoned with pepper and salt, and a very little onion and herbs, which should be previously fried of a nice brown ; then put another layer of mashed potatoes and beef, and other ingredients, as before. Pour in the gravy or sauce, cover the whole with another layer of potatoes, and bake for half an hour. This may be served in the dish, or turned out.

Time, half hour. *Sufficient*, a large pie-dish full for five or six persons. *Seasonable* at any time.

Broiled Beef and Mushroom Sauce.—Cold Meat Cookery.—IN-

GREDIENTS.— *2 or 3 dozen small button mushrooms*, 1 *ounce of butter, salt and Cayenne to taste,* 1 *tablespoonful of mushroom ketchup, mashed potatoes, slices of cold roast beef.*

Mode.—Wipe the mushrooms free from grit with a piece of flannel, and salt. Put them in a stewpan with the butter, seasoning, and ketchup; shake the pan over the fire until the mushrooms are quite done, then pour them in the middle of mashed potatoes, browned; then place round the potatoes slices of cold roast beef, nicely broiled, over a clear fire. In making the mushroom sauce, the ketchup may be dispensed with, if there is sufficient gravy.

Time, quarter hour. *Seasonable* from August to October.

Hashed Beef (Cold Meat Cookery). —INGREDIENTS.— *The remains of ribs or sirloin of beef,* 2 *onions,* 1 *carrot,* 1 *bunch of savory herbs, pepper and salt to taste,* ½ *blade of pounded mace, thickening of flour, rather more than* 1 *pint of water.*

Mode.— Take off all the meat from the bones of ribs or sirloin of beef. Remove the outside brown and gristle. Place the meat on one side, and well stew the bones and pieces, with the above ingredients, for about two hours, till it becomes a strong gravy, and is reduced to rather more than a half pint. Strain this, thicken with a teaspoonful of flour, and let the gravy cool. Skim off all the fat. Lay in the meat, let it get hot through, but do not allow it to boil, and garnish with sippets of toasted bread. The gravy may be flavored as in the preceding recipe.

Time, rather more than two hours. *Seasonable* at any time.

Note.— May be served in walls of mashed pota-

toes, brown, in which case the sippets should be omitted. Be careful that hashed meat does not boil, or it will become tough.

Potted Beef (Cold Meat Cookery.) —INGREDIENTS.— *The remains of cold roast or boiled beef,* ¼ *lb. of butter, Cayenne to taste,* 2 *blades of pounded mace.*

Mode. — The outside slices of boiled beef may, with a little trouble, be converted into a very nice addition to the breakfast table. Cut up the meat into small pieces, and pound it well, with a little butter, in a mortar; add a seasoning of Cayenne and mace, and be very particular that the latter ingredient is reduced to the finest powder. When all the ingredients are thoroughly mixed, put into glass or earthen potting-pots, and pour on the top a coating of clarified butter.

Seasonable at any time.

*Note.—*If cold roast beef is used, remove all pieces of gristle and dry outside pieces, as these do not pound well.

Stewed Beef with Oysters (Cold Meat Cookery). —INGREDIENTS. — *A few thick steaks of cold ribs or sirloin of beef,* 2 *ounces of butter,* 1 *onion sliced, pepper and salt to taste,* ¼ *glass of port wine, a little flour to thicken,* 1 *or* 2 *dozen oysters, rather more than* ½ *pint of water.*

Mode. — Cut the steaks rather thick, from cold sirloin or ribs of beef. Brown them lightly in a stewpan, with the butter and a little water. Add half a pint of water, the onion, pepper, and salt. Cover the stewpan closely, and let it simmer very gently for half an hour. Then mix about a teaspoonful of flour smoothly with a little of the liquor. Add the port wine and oysters, their liquor having been previously strained and put into the stewpan. Stir till the oysters plump, and serve. It should not boil after the oysters are added, or they will harden.

Boiled Aitch-bone of Beef.—After this joint has been in salt five or six days, it will be ready for use, and will not take so long boiling as a round, for it is not so solid. Wash the meat, and, if too salt, soak it for a few hours, changing the water once or twice, till

the required freshness is obtained. Put into a saucepan, or boiling pot, sufficient water to cover the meat; set it over the fire, and when it boils, plunge in the joint and let it boil up quickly. *Now draw the pot to the side of the fire,* and there let it remain until the water is sufficiently cooled that the finger may be borne in it. Then draw the pot nearer the fire, and keep the water *gently simmering* until the meat is done, or it will be hard and tough if *rapidly* boiled. Carefully remove the scum from the surface of the water, and continue doing this for a few minutes after it first boils. Carrots and turnips are served with this dish, and sometimes suet dumplings, all of which may be boiled with the beef. Garnish with a few of the carrots and turnips, and serve the remainder in a vegetable-dish.

Time, an aitch-bone of 10 pounds, 2½ hours after the water boils; one of 20 pounds, 4 hours. *Sufficient,* 10 pounds for seven or eight persons. *Seasonable* all the year, but best from September to March.

Note. — The liquor in which the meat has been boiled may be easily converted into a very excellent pea-soup. It will require but few vegetables, as it will be impregnated with the flavor of those boiled with the meat.

If the beef is not to be eaten until it is cold, do not take it out when it is sufficiently boiled, but remove the pot from the fire, and let it remain until nearly cold, then take out the beef. This is the secret of having cold corned beef juicy and full flavored, instead of dry as a chip.

Beef Minced.—Cut into small dice remains of cold beef: the gravy reserved from it on the first day of it being served should be put in the stewpan, with the addition of warm water, some mace, sliced shalot, salt, and black pepper. Let the whole simmer gently for an hour. A few minutes before it is served, take out the meat and dish it; add to the gravy some walnut ketchup, and a little lemon juice or walnut pickle. Boil up the gravy once more, and, when hot, pour it over the meat. Serve it with bread sippets.

Rump-Steak Pie.—Cut 3 pounds of rump-steak (that has been kept till tender) into pieces half as big as your hand, trim off all the skin, sinews, and every part which has not indisputable pretensions to be eaten, and beat them with a chopper. Chop very fine half a dozen shalots, and add to them half an ounce of pepper and salt mixed. Strew some of the mixture at the bottom of the dish, then a layer of steak, then some more of the mixture, and so on till the dish is full, and half a gill of mushroom ketchup, and the same quantity of gravy, or red wine. Cover it as in the preceding recipe, and bake it two hours. Large oysters, parboiled, bearded, and laid alternately with the steaks, their liquor reduced and substituted instead of the ketchup and wine, will be a variety.

Plain Beefsteak Pie. — INGREDIENTS.— *2½ pounds of beefsteak, a little pepper, salt, and Cayenne, a little water, or gravy if you have it, 1 tablespoonful of Worcestershire sauce, the yolk of 1 egg, ½ a pound of paste.*

Cut the steak into small pieces with a very little fat; dip each piece into flour, place them in a pie-dish, seasoning each layer with pepper, salt, and a very little Cayenne pepper. Fill the dish sufficiently with slices of steak to raise the crust in the middle; half fill the dish with water or any gravy left from roast beef, and a spoonful of Worcestershire sauce. Put a border of paste round the wet edge of the pie-dish, moisten it and lay the crust over it. Cut the paste even with the edge of the pie-dish all round, ornament it with leaves of paste, and brush it over with the beaten yolk of an egg. Make a hole with a knife in the top, and bake it in a hot oven one and a half hours.

A Beef Stew.—*Time, two hours and twenty minutes.*

INGREDIENTS. — *2 or 3 pounds of the rump of beef, 1 quart of broth, pepper and salt, the peel of 1 lemon, and the juice, 2 tablespoonfuls of Harvey sauce, 1 spoonful of flour, a little ketchup.*

Cut away all the skin and fat from

12

two or three pounds of the rump of beef, and divide it into pieces about two or three inches square. Put into a stewpan, and pour on it a quart of broth ; then let it boil, and sprinkle in pepper and salt to taste. When it has boiled very gently, or simmered two hours, shred finely the peel of a large lemon, and add it to the gravy. In twenty minutes pour in a flavoring, composed of two spoonfuls of Harvey sauce, the juice of the lemon, the flour, and a little ketchup. Add at pleasure a glass of sherry, a quarter of an hour after flavoring it, and serve.

Beefsteak Pudding. — *Time*, to boil, two hours, or a little longer.

INGREDIENTS.—1¼ *pounds of flour, ¼ a pound of chopped suet, 1 teaspoonful of salt, 2 pounds of steak, salt and black pepper to taste, 1 gill of water.*

Put a pound, or a little more, of flour in a basin, and mix it thoroughly with some very finely chopped suet ; put in a good heaped saltspoonful of salt. Mix it to a paste with water ; flour the paste board, the roller, and your hands. Take out the lump of paste, and roll it out about half an inch thick.

Butter a round-bottomed pudding-basin, line it with paste, turning a little over the edge. Cut up the steak into small pieces, with a little fat, flour them slightly, season highly with pepper and salt, then lay them in a basin, pour over them a gill of water. Roll out the rest of the paste, cover it over the top of the basin, pressing it down with the thumb.

Tie the basin in a floured pudding-cloth, and put it into a saucepan in a gallon of boiling water, keep it continually boiling for three hours, occasionally adding a little more water.

Take it up, untie the cloth, turn the pudding over on the dish, and take the basin carefully from it. Serve.

Some persons, of delicate digestion, like this pudding boiled without a basin, on account of the superior lightness the crust thus acquires, but it does not look nearly as well when served.

Stewed Shin of Beef. — A Family Dish.— *Time*, four hours and a quarter.

INGREDIENTS.—*A shin of beef, 1 bunch of sweet herbs, 1 large onion, 1 head of celery, 12 black pepper corns, 12 allspice, 3 carrots, 2 turnips, 12 small button onions.*

Saw the bone into three or four pieces ; put them into a stewpan, and just cover them with cold water. When the pot simmers, skim it clean ; and then add the sweet herbs, onions, celery, peppers, and allspice. Stew it very gently over a slow fire till the meat is tender. Then peel the carrots and turnips and cut them into shapes ; boil them with the button onions till tender. The turnips and onions will take a quarter of an hour to boil, the carrots *half* an hour. Drain them carefully. Put the meat when done on a dish, and keep it warm while you prepare some gravy thus :

Take a teacupful of the liquor in which the meat has been stewed, and mix with it three tablespoonfuls of flour ; add more liquor till you have ʔ pint and a half of gravy. Season with pepper, salt, and a wineglass of mushroom ketchup. Boil it up, skim off the fat, and strain it through a sieve. Pour it over the meat, and lay the vegetables around it.

Roast Leg of Mutton.—As mutton, when freshly killed, is never tender, hang it almost as long as it will keep ; flour it, and put it in a cool airy place for a few days, if the weather will permit. Wash off the flour, wipe it very dry, and cut off the shankbone ; put it down to a brisk clear fire, dredge with flour, and keep continually basting the whole time it is cooking. About twenty minutes before serving, draw it near the fire to get nicely brown ; sprinkle over it a little salt, dish the meat, pour off the dripping, add some boiling water slightly salted, strain it over the joint, and serve.

Time, a leg of mutton weighing ten pounds, about two and a quarter or two and a half hours ; one of seven pounds, about two hours, or rather less. *Sufficient.*—A moderate-sized leg of mutton sufficient for six or eight persons. *Seasonable*, at any time, but not so good in June, July, and August.

Roast Loin of Mutton.—Cut and trim off the superfluous fat, and see that the butcher joints the meat properly, as thereby much annoyance is saved to the carver when it comes to table. Have ready a nice clear fire (it need not be a very wide large one), put down the meat, dredge with flour, and baste well until it is done. Make the gravy as for roast leg of mutton, and serve very hot.

Time, a loin of mutton weighing six pounds, one hour and a half, or rather longer. *Sufficient* for four or five persons. *Seasonable*, at any time.

Broiled Mutton Chops.—Cut the chops from a well-hung tender loin of mutton, remove a portion of the fat, and trim them into a nice shape; slightly beat and level them; place the gridiron over a bright clear fire, rub the bars with a little fat, and lay on the chops. Whilst broiling, frequently turn them, and in about eight minutes they will be done. Season with pepper and salt, dish them on a very hot dish, rub a small piece of butter on each chop, and serve very hot and expeditiously.

Hashed Mutton.—INGREDIENTS.—*The remains of cold roast shoulder or leg of mutton, 6 whole peppers, 6 whole allspice, a faggot of savory herbs, ½ head of celery, 1 onion, 2 ounces of butter, flour.*
Mode.—Cut the meat in nice even slices from the bones, trimming off all superfluous fat and gristle; chop the bones and fragments of the joint; put them into a stewpan with the pepper, spice, herbs, and celery; cover with water, and simmer for one hour. Slice and fry the onion of a nice pale-brown color in the butter; dredge in a little flour to make it thick, and add this to the bones, etc. Stew for a quarter of an hour, strain the gravy, and let it cool; then skim off every particle of fat, and put it, with the meat, into a stewpan. Flavor with ketchup, Harvey's sauce, tomato sauce, or any flavoring that may be preferred, and let the meat gradually warm through, but not boil, or it will harden. To hash meat properly, it should be laid in cold gravy, and only left on the fire just long enough to warm through.

Time, one hour and a half to simmer the gravy. *Seasonable*, at any time. Or,

Make a gravy, and thicken it; then place some nice slices of mutton in the *cold* gravy, allow the meat to get thoroughly hot, but on no account let it boil.

Boiled Leg of Mutton.—A leg of mutton for boiling should not hang too long, as it will not look a good color when dressed. Cut off the shank-bone, trim the knuckle, and wash and wipe it very clean; plunge it into sufficient boiling water to cover it; let it boil up, then draw the saucepan to the side of the fire, where it should remain till the finger can be borne in the water. Then place it sufficiently near the fire, that the water may gently simmer, and be very careful that it does not boil fast, or the meat will be hard. Skim well, add a little salt, and in about 2¼ hours after the water begins to simmer, a moderate-sized leg of mutton will be done. Serve with carrots and mashed turnips, which may be boiled with the meat, and send caper sauce to table with it in a tureen.

Time, a moderate-sized leg of mutton of 9 pounds, 2¼ hours after the water boils; one of 12 pounds, 3 hours. *Sufficient.*—A moderate-sized leg of mutton for six or eight persons. *Seasonable* nearly all the year, but not so good in June, July, and August.

Note.—When meat is liked very *thoroughly* cooked, allow more time than stated above. The liquor this joint was boiled in should be converted into soup.

An excellent way to Cook a Breast of Mutton.—INGREDIENTS.—*Breast of mutton, 2 onions, salt and pepper to taste, flour, a bunch of savory herbs, green peas.*
Mode.—Cut the mutton into pieces about two inches square, and let it be tolerably lean; put it into a stewpan, with a little fat or butter, and fry it of

a nice brown; then dredge it in a little flour, slice the onions, and put it with the herbs in a stewpan; pour in sufficient water *just* to cover the meat, and simmer the whole gently until the mutton is tender. Take out the meat, strain, skim off all the fat from the gravy, and put both the meat and gravy back into the stewpan; add about a quart of young green peas, and let them boil gently until done. Two or three slices of bacon added and stewed with the mutton give additional flavor; and to insure the peas being a beautiful green color, *they may be boiled in water separately,* and added to the stew at the moment of serving.

Time, 2½ hours. *Sufficient* for four or five persons. *Seasonable* from June to August.

Roast Shoulder of Mutton. — Put the joint down to a bright, clear fire; flour it well, and keep continually basting. About ¼ hour before serving, draw it near the fire, that the outside may acquire a nice brown color, but not sufficiently near to blacken the fat. Sprinkle a little fine salt over the meat, empty the dripping-pan of its contents, pour in a little boiling water slightly salted, and strain this over the joint. Onion sauce, or stewed Spanish onions, are usually sent to table with this dish, and sometimes baked potatoes.

Time.—A shoulder of mutton weighing six or seven pounds, 1½ hours. *Sufficient* for five or six persons. *Seasonable* at any time.

Note. — Shoulder of mutton may be dressed in a variety of ways; boiled, and served with onion sauce; boned, and stuffed with a good veal forcemeat; or baked, with sliced potatoes, in the dripping-pan.

Roast Leg of Lamb. — Place the joint at a good distance from the fire at first, and baste well the whole time it is cooking. When nearly done, draw it nearer the fire to acquire a nice brown color. Sprinkle a little fine salt over the meat, empty the dripping-pan of its contents; pour in a little boiling water, and strain this over the meat. Serve with mint sauce and a fresh salad, and for vegetables send

peas, spinach, or cauliflowers to table with it.

Time. — A leg of lamb weighing five pounds, 1½ hours. *Sufficient* for four or five persons. *Seasonable* from Easter to Michaelmas.

Note. — A shoulder of lamb requires rather more than 1 hour to roast it. A small saddle, 1½ hours; a larger saddle, 2 hours, or longer. Loin of lamb, 1¼ to 1½ hours. Ribs of lamb, as they are thinner than the loin, from 1 to 1¼ hours.

Lamb Chops.—Trim off the flap from a fine loin of lamb, and cut into chops about three-quarters of an inch in thickness. Have ready a bright, clear fire; lay the chops on a gridiron, and broil them of a nice pale brown, turning them when required. Season them with pepper and salt, and serve very hot and quickly, and garnish with crisp parsley, or place them on mashed potatoes. Asparagus, spinach, or peas, are the favorite accompaniments to lamb chops.

Time, about eight or ten minutes. *Sufficient*—allow two chops to each person. *Seasonable* from Easter to Michaelmas.

Boiled Leg of Lamb.—Do not choose a very large joint, but one weighing about five pounds. Have ready a saucepan of boiling water, into which plunge the lamb, and when it boils up again, draw it to the side of the fire, and let the water cool a little. Then stew it very gently for about one and a quarter hours, reckoning from the time that the water begins to simmer. Make some white sauce; dish the lamb, pour the sauce over it, and garnish it with tufts of boiled cauliflower or carrots. When liked, melted butter may be substituted for the white sauce: this is a more simple method, but not nearly so nice. Send to table with it some of the sauce in a tureen, and boiled cauliflowers or spinach, with whichever vegetable the dish is garnished.

Time, one and a quarter hours after the water simmers. *Sufficient* for four or five persons. *Seasonable* from Easter to Michaelmas.

Broiled Mutton and Tomato Sauce

(**Cold Meat Cookery**).—Cut some nice slices from a cold leg or shoulder of mutton ; season them with pepper and salt, and broil over a clear fire. Make some tomato sauce, pour it over the mutton, and serve. This makes an excellent dish, and must be served very hot.

Time, about five minutes to broil the mutton. *Seasonable* in September and October, when tomatoes are plentiful and seasonable.

Baked Minced Mutton (Cold Meat Cookery). — INGREDIENTS. — *The remains of any joint of cold roast mutton, 1 or 2 onions, 1 bunch of savory herbs, pepper and salt to taste, 2 blades of pounded mace or nutmeg, 2 tablespoonfuls of gravy, mashed potatoes.*

Mode. — Mince an onion rather fine, and fry it a light-brown color ; add the herbs and mutton, both of which should be also finely minced and well mixed ; season with pepper and salt, and a little pounded mace or nutmeg, and moisten with the above proportion of gravy. Put a layer of mashed potatoes at the bottom of a dish, then the mutton and another layer of potatoes, and bake for about half an hour.

Time, half an hour. *Seasonable* at any time.

Note.—If there should be a large quantity of meat, use two onions instead of one.

Roast Leg of Pork. — Choose a small leg of pork, and score the skin across in narrow strips, about a quarter of an inch apart. Cut a slit in the knuckle, loosen the skin, and fill it with a sage-and-onion stuffing. Brush the joint over with a little salad-oil (this makes the crackling crisper, and a better color), and put it down to a bright, clear fire, not too near, as that would cause the skin to blister. Baste it well, and serve with a little gravy made in the dripping-pan, and do not omit to send to the table with it a tureen of well-made apple sauce.

Time.—A leg of pork weighing eight pounds, about three hours. *Sufficient* for six or seven persons. *Seasonable* from September to March.

Pork, Spare-rib. — Joint it nicely before roasting, and crack the ribs across. Take care not to have the fire too fierce. The joint should be basted with very little butter and flour, and may be sprinkled with fine dried sage. It takes from two to three hours. Apple sauce, mashed potatoes, and greens, are the proper accompaniments, also good mustard, fresh made.

Pork Cutlets or Chops.—INGREDIENTS.—*Loin, or fore-loin, of pork, egg and bread crumbs, salt and pepper to taste ; to every tablespoonful of bread-crumbs allow ½ teaspoonful of minced sage ; clarified butter.*

Mode. — Cut the cutlets from a loin, or fore-loin, of pork ; trim them the same as mutton cutlets, and scrape the top part of the bone. Brush them over with egg, sprinkled with bread crumbs, with which have been mixed minced sage and a seasoning of pepper and salt ; drop a little clarified butter on them, and press the crumbs well down. Put the frying-pan on the first with some lard in it ; when this is hot, lay in the cutlets, and fry them a light - brown on both sides. Take them out, put them before the fire to dry the greasy moisture from them, and dish them on mashed potatoes. Serve with them any sauce that may be preferred ; such as tomato sauce, sauce piquante, sauce Robert, or pickled gherkins.

Time, from fifteen to twenty minutes. *Sufficient*, allow six cutlets for four persons. *Seasonable* from October to March.

Note.—The remains of roast loin of pork may be dressed in the same manner.

To Bake a Ham.—As a ham for baking should be well soaked, let it remain in water for at least twelve hours. Wipe it dry, trim away any rusty places underneath, and cover it with a common crust, taking care that this is of sufficient thickness all over to keep in the gravy. Place it in a moderately-heated oven, and bake for nearly four hours. Take off the crust and skin, and cover with raspings, the same as for boiled ham, and garnish the knuckle with a paper frill. This method of cooking a ham is, by many persons, considered far superior to boiling it, as it cuts fuller of gravy and has a finer flavor, besides keeping a much longer time good.

Time, a medium-sized ham, four hours. *Seasonable,* all the year.

To Boil a Ham.—In choosing a ham, ascertain that it is perfectly sweet, by running a sharp knife into it, close to the bone; and if, when the knife is withdrawn, it has an agreeable smell, the ham is good; if, on the contrary, the blade has a greasy appearance and offensive smell, the ham is bad. If it has been long hung, and is very dry and salt, let it remain in soak from eight to twelve hours. Wash it thoroughly clean, and trim away from the underside all the rusty and smoked parts, which would spoil the appearance. Put it into a boiling-pot, with sufficient cold water to cover it; bring it gradually to a boil, and as the scum rises, carefully remove it. Keep it simmering very gently until tender, and be careful that it does not stop boiling, nor boil too quickly. When done, take it out of the pot, strip off the skin, and sprinkle over it a few fine bread-raspings, put a frill of cut paper round the knuckle, and serve. If to be eaten cold, let the ham remain in the water until nearly cold: by this method the juices are kept in, and it will be found infinitely superior to one taken out of the water hot; it should, however, be borne in mind that the ham must *not* remain in the saucepan all night. When the skin is removed, sprinkle over bread-raspings, or, if wanted particularly nice, glaze it. Place a paper frill round the knuckle, and garnish with parsley, or cut vegetable flowers.

Time, a ham weighing ten pounds, four hours to *simmer gently;* fifteen pounds, five hours; a very large one, about six hours. *Seasonable* all the year.

Boiled Leg of Pork.—For boiling, choose a small, compact, well-filled leg, and rub it well with salt; let it remain

in pickle for a week or ten days, turning and rubbing it every day. An hour before dressing it, put it into cold water for an hour, which improves the color. If the pork is purchased ready salted, ascertain how long the meat has been in pickle, and soak it accordingly. Put it into a boiling-pot, with sufficient cold water to cover it; let it gradually come to a boil, and remove the scum as it rises. Simmer it very gently until tender, and do not allow it to boil fast or the knuckle will fall to pieces before the middle of the leg is done. Carrots, turnips, or parsnips may be boiled with the pork, some of which should be laid round the dish as a garnish, and a well-made pease-pudding is an indispensable accompaniment.

Time.—A leg of pork weighing eight pounds, three hours after the water boils, and to be simmered very gently. *Sufficient* for seven or eight persons. *Seasonable* from September to March.

Note.—The liquor in which a leg of pork has been boiled makes excellent pea-soup.

Pig's Liver (a Savory and Economical Dish).— INGREDIENTS.—*The liver and lights of a pig, 6 or 7 slices of bacon, potatoes, 1 large bunch of parsley, 2 onions, 2 sage-leaves, pepper and salt to taste, a little broth or water.*

Mode.—Slice the liver and lights, wash these perfectly clean, and parboil the potatoes; mince the parsley and sage, and chop the onion rather small. Put the meat, potatoes, and bacon into a deep tin dish, in alternate layers, with a sprinkling of the herbs, and a seasoning of pepper and salt between each; pour on a little water or broth, and bake in a moderately-heated oven for two hours.

Time, two hours. *Sufficient* for six or seven persons. *Seasonable* from September to March.

To Boil Pickled Pork.—Should the pork be very salt, let it remain in water about two hours before it is dressed; put it into a saucepan with sufficient cold water to cover it, let it gradually come to a boil, then gently simmer until quite tender. Allow ample time for it to cook, as nothing is more disagreeable than underdone pork, and when boiled fast the meat becomes hard. This is sometimes served with boiled poultry and roast veal, instead of bacon; when tender, and not over salt, it will be found equally good.

Time, a piece of pickled pork weighing two pounds, one hour and a quarter; four pounds rather more than two hours. *Seasonable* at any time.

To Boil Bacon (*English Breakfast*).—As bacon is frequently excessively salt, let it be soaked in warm water for an hour or two previous to dressing it; then pare off the rusty parts, and scrape the under-side and rind as clean as possible. Put it into a saucepan of cold water, let it come gradually to a boil, and as fast as the scum rises to the surface of the water, remove it. Let it simmer very gently until it is *thoroughly* done; then take it up, strip off the skin, sprinkle over the bacon a few bread-raspings, and garnish with tufts of cauliflower or Brussels sprouts. When served alone, young and tender broad beans or green peas are the usual accompaniments.

Time, one pound of bacon, three-quarters of an hour; two pounds, one hour and a half. *Sufficient*, two pounds for eight persons, when served with poultry or veal. *Seasonable* at any time.

A Fillet of Veal.—A fillet is good baked. Take out the bone, and fill the vacancy with a dressing made of bread soaked soft, then squeezed out of the water and mixed with chopped raw pork and two eggs. Season it with salt and pepper, and add, if you like, sweet herbs. Close up the meat after putting in the dressing, put it in the baking-pan with about a quart of water, cover the top with the dressing, and bake it from two to three hours, according to the size of the piece of veal. Thicken the gravy, after taking up the meat, with some of the dressing, add a little butter, and if liked quite rich, put in a small quantity of wine, or ketchup.

Veal Cutlets. — INGREDIENTS. —

About 3 pounds of the prime part of the leg of veal, egg and bread crumbs, 3 tablespoonfuls of minced savory herbs, salt and pepper to taste, a small piece of butter.

Mode. — Have the veal cut into slices about three-fourths of an inch in thickness, and, if not divided evenly, level the meat with a cutlet-bat or rolling-pin. Shape and trim the cutlets, and brush them over with egg. Sprinkle with bread crumbs, with which have been mixed minced herbs and a seasoning of pepper and salt, and press the crumbs down. Fry them of a delicate brown in fresh lard or butter, and be careful not to burn them. They should be very thoroughly done, but not dry. If the cutlets be thick, keep the pan covered for a few minutes at a good distance from the fire, after they have acquired a good color. By this means the meat will be done through. Lay the cutlets in a dish, keep them hot, and make a gravy in the pan as follows: Dredge in a little flour, add a piece of butter the size of a walnut, brown it, then pour as much boiling water as is required over it, season with pepper and salt, add a little lemon-juice, give one boil, and pour it over the cutlets. They should be garnished with slices of broiled bacon, and a few forcemeat balls will be found a very excellent addition to this dish.

Time, for cutlets of a moderate thickness, about twelve minutes; if very thick, allow more time. *Sufficient* for six persons. *Seasonable* from March to October.

Note. — Veal cutlets may be merely floured and fried of a nice brown; the gravy and garnishing should be the same as in the preceding recipe. They may also be cut from the loin or neck.

Veal and Ham Pie. — INGREDIENTS. — *2 pounds of veal cutlets, ½ a pound of boiled ham, 2 tablespoonfuls of minced savory herbs, ¼ teaspoonful of grated nutmeg, 2 blades of pounded mace, pepper and salt to taste, a strip of lemon-peel finely minced, the yolks of 2 hard-boiled eggs, ½ pint of water, nearly ½ pint of good strong gravy, puff crust.*

Mode.—Cut the veal into nice square

pieces, and put a layer of them at the bottom of a pie-dish; sprinkle over these a portion of the herbs, spices, seasoning, lemon-peel, and the yolks of the eggs cut in slices. Cut the ham very thin, and put a layer of this in. Proceed in this manner until the dish is full, so arranging it that the ham comes at the top. Lay a puff-paste on the edge of the dish, and pour in about a half pint of water. Cover with crust, ornament it with leaves, brush it over with the yolk of an egg, and bake in a well-heated oven for one to one and a half hours, or longer should the pie be very large. When it is taken out of the oven, pour in at the top, through a funnel, nearly half a pint of strong gravy. This should be made sufficiently good that, when cold, it may cut in a firm jelly. This pie may be very much enriched by adding a few mushrooms, oysters, or sweetbreads; but it will be found very good without any of the last-named additions.

Time, one and a half hours, or longer should the pie be very large. *Sufficient* for five or six persons. *Seasonable* from March to October.

Stewed Knuckle of Veal and Rice. — INGREDIENTS. — *Knuckle of veal, 1 onion, 2 blades of mace, 1 teaspoonful of salt, ½ pound of rice.*

Mode. — Choose a small knuckle, or cut some cutlets from it, that it may be just large enough to be eaten the same day it is dressed, as cold boiled veal is not a particularly tempting dish. Break the shank-bone, wash it clean, and put the meat into a stewpan with sufficient water to cover it. Let it gradually come to a boil, put in the salt, and remove the scum as fast as it rises. When it has simmered gently for about three-quarters of an hour, add the remaining ingredients, and stew the whole gently for two and a quarter hours. Put the meat into a deep dish, pour over it the rice, etc., and send boiled bacon and a tureen of parsley and butter to table with it.

Time. — A knuckle of veal weighing **six** pounds, three hours' gentle stewing.

Sufficient for five or six persons. *Seasonable* from March to October.

Note. — Macaroni, instead of rice, boiled with the veal, will be found good; or the rice and macaroni may be omitted, and the veal sent to table smothered in parsley and butter.

Calf's Liver and Bacon. — INGREDIENTS. — *2 or 3 pounds of liver, bacon, pepper and salt to taste, a small piece of butter, flour, 2 tablespoonfuls of lemon juice, ½ pint of water.*

Mode. — Divide the liver into thin slices, and cut nearly as many slices of bacon as there are of liver. Fry the bacon first, and put that on a hot dish before the fire; fry the liver in the fat which comes from the bacon, after seasoning it with pepper and salt, and dredging over it a very little flour. Turn the liver occasionally to prevent its burning, and when done, lay it round the dish with a piece of bacon between each. Pour away the bacon fat, put in a small piece of butter, dredge in a little flour, add the lemon-juice and water, give one boil, and pour it in the *middle* of the dish. It may be garnished with slices of cut lemon or forcemeat balls.

Time, according to the thickness of the slices, from five to ten minutes. *Sufficient* for six or seven persons. *Seasonable* from March to October.

Calf's Head Boiled. — *Time*, to soak, one hour and a half; to simmer, one hour and a half.

INGREDIENTS. — *½ a calf's head, ½ pint of melted butter, with parsley, 1 lemon, a pinch of pepper and salt.*

Soak the half calf's head in cold water for an hour and a half, then for ten minutes in hot water before it is dressed. Put it into a saucepan with plenty of cold water (enough for the head to swim), and let it boil gently. When the scum rises, skim it *very* carefully. After the head boils, let it simmer gently an hour and a half. Serve it with melted butter and parsley over it, and garnish with slices of lemon and tiny heaps of fried parsley. Ham should be served with calf's head, or slices of bacon.

Stewed Breast of Veal and Peas.

— INGREDIENTS. — *Breast of veal, 2 ounces of butter, a bunch of savory herbs, including parsley, 2 blades of pounded mace, 2 cloves, 5 or 6 young onions, 1 strip of lemon-peel, 6 allspice, ¼ teaspoonful of pepper, 1 teaspoonful of salt, thickening of butter and flour, 2 tablespoonfuls of sherry, 2 tablespoonfuls of tomato sauce, 1 tablespoonful of lemon-juice, 2 tablespoonfuls of mushroom ketchup, green peas.*

Mode. — Cut the breast in half, after removing the bone underneath, and divide the meat into convenient-sized pieces. Put the butter into a frying-pan, lay in the pieces of veal, and fry until of a nice brown color. Now place these in a stewpan with the herbs, mace, cloves, onions, lemon-peel, allspice, and seasoning. Pour over them just sufficient boiling water to cover the meat. Well close the lid, and let the whole simmer very gently for about two hours. Strain off as much gravy as is required, thicken it with butter and flour, add the remaining ingredients, skim well, let it simmer for about ten minutes, then pour it over the meat. Have ready some green peas, boiled separately; sprinkle these over the veal and serve. It may be garnished with forcemeat balls, or rashers of bacon curled and fried. Instead of cutting up the meat, many persons prefer it dressed whole. In that case it should be half roasted before the water, etc., are put to it.

Time, two and a quarter hours. *Sufficient* for five or six persons.

Minced Veal. — INGREDIENTS. — *The remains of cold roast fillet or loin of veal, rather more than 1 pint of water, 1 onion, ½ teaspoonful of minced lemon-peel, salt and white pepper to taste, 1 blade of pounded mace, 2 or 3 young carrots, a faggot of sweet herbs, thickening of butter and flour, 1 tablespoonful of lemon-juice, 3 tablespoonfuls of cream or milk.*

Mode.—Take about one pound of veal, and should there be any bones, dredge them with flour, and put them into a stewpan with the brown outside, and a few meat trimmings ; add rather more than a pint of water, the onion cut in

slices, lemon-peel, seasoning, mace, carrots, and herbs ; simmer these well for rather more than one hour, and strain the liquor. Rub a little flour into some butter ; add this to the gravy, set it on the fire, and, when it boils, skim well. Mince the veal finely by *cutting,* and not chopping it ; put it in the gravy ; let it get warmed through gradually ; add the lemon-juice and cream, and, when it is on the point of boiling, serve. Garnish the dish with sippets of toasted bread and slices of bacon rolled and toasted. Forcemeat balls may also be added. If more lemon-peel is liked than is stated above, put a little very finely minced to the veal, after it is warmed in the gravy.

Time, one hour to make the gravy. *Seasonable* from March to October.

Ragout of Cold Veal. — Either a neck, loin, or fillet of veal will furnish this excellent ragout with a very little expense or trouble. Cut the veal into handsome cutlets ; put a piece of butter, or clean dripping, into a frying-pan ; as soon as it is hot, flour and fry the veal of a light brown ; take it out, and if you have no gravy ready, put a pint of boiling water into the frying-pan, give it a boil-up for a minute, and strain it in a basin while you make some thickening in the following manner : — Put an ounce of butter into a stewpan ; as soon as it melts, mix as much flour as will dry it up ; stir it over the fire for a few minutes, and gradually add the gravy you made in the frying-pan ; let them simmer together for ten minutes ; season with pepper, salt, a little mace, and a wineglassful of mushroom ketchup or wine ; strain it through a panis to the meat, and stew very gently till the meat is thoroughly warmed. If you have any ready-boiled bacon, cut it in slices, and put it to warm with the meat.

Veal Pie. — Take some of the middle or scrag of a small neck ; season it with pepper and salt, and put to it a few pieces of lean bacon or ham. If it be wanted of a high relish, add mace, Cayenne, and nutmeg to the salt and pepper, and also forcemeat and egg balls, and if you choose add truffles, morels, mushrooms, sweetbreads cut into small bits, and cocks' combs blanched, if liked Have a rich gravy to pour in after baking. It will be very good without any of the latter additions.

Roast Turkey. — *Choosing and Trussing.* — Choose cock turkeys by their short spurs and black legs, in which case they are young; if the spurs are long, and the legs pale and rough, they are old. If the bird has been long killed, the eyes will appear sunk, and the feet very dry; but if fresh, the contrary will be the case. Middling-sized fleshy turkeys are by many persons considered superior to those of an immense growth, as they are, generally speaking, much more tender. They should never be dressed the same day they are killed, but, in cold weather, should hang at least eight days; if the weather is mild, four or five days will be found sufficient. Carefully pluck the bird, singe it with white paper, and wipe it thoroughly with a cloth; draw it, preserve the liver and gizzard, and be particular not to break the gall-bag, as no washing will remove the bitter taste it imparts where it once touches. Wash it *inside* well, and wipe it thoroughly dry with a cloth; the *outside* merely requires nicely wiping, as we have just stated. Cut off the neck close to the back, but leave enough of the crop-skin to turn over; break the leg-bone close below the knee, draw out the strings from the thighs, and flatten the breast-bone to make it look plump. Have ready a forcemeat; fill the breast with this, and, if a trussing-needle is used, sew the neck over to the back; if a needle is not at hand, a skewer will answer the purpose. Run a skewer through the pinion and thigh into the body to the pinion and thigh on the other side, and press the legs as much as possible between the breast and the side bones, and put the liver under one pinion, and the gizzard under the other. Pass a string across the back of the bird, catch it over the

points of the skewer, tie it in the centre of the back, and be particular that the turkey is very firmly trussed. This may be more easily accomplished with a needle and twine than with skewers.

Mode. — Fasten a sheet of buttered paper on to the breast of the bird, put it down to a bright fire, at some little distance *at first* (afterwards draw it nearer), and keep it well basted the whole of the time it is cooking. About a quarter of an hour before serving, remove the paper, dredge the turkey lightly with flour, and put a piece of butter into the basting-ladle; as the butter melts, baste the bird with it. When of a nice brown, and well frothed, serve with a tureen of good brown gravy and one of bread sauce. Fried sausages are a favorite addition to roast turkey; they make a pretty garnish, besides adding very much to the flavor. When these are not at hand, a few forcemeat balls should be placed round the dish as a garnish. Turkey may also be stuffed with sausage meat, and a chestnut forcemeat with the same sauce is, by many persons, much esteemed as an accompaniment to this favorite dish.

Time, small turkey, one and a half hours; moderate-sized one, about ten pounds, two hours; large turkey, two and a half hours or longer. *Sufficient,* a moderate-sized turkey, for seven or eight persons. *Seasonable* from December to February.

Boiled Turkey. — A turkey for boiling should be prepared in the same manner as for roasting. Tie it up in a cloth in order to have it look white, unless rice is boiled with it. It will require about two-thirds of a cup of rice, if a soup is to be made of the water in which it is boiled. A pound of salt pork boiled with the turkey improves the flavor of it. Use drawn butter for a sauce, without you have oyster sauce. If a soup is to be made of the liquor, it should remain till the next day to have the fat skimmed off, unless liked very rich.

Hashed Turkey.—INGREDIENTS.—

The remains of cold roast turkey, 1 *onion, pepper and salt to taste, rather more than* 1 *pint of water*, 1 *carrot*, 1 *turnip*, 1 *blade of mace, a bunch of savory herbs*, 1 *tablespoonful of mushroom ketchup*, 1 *tablespoonful of port wine, thickening of butter and flour.*

Mode. — Cut the turkey into neat joints; the best pieces reserve for the hash, the inferior joints and trimmings put into a stewpan with an onion cut in slices, pepper and salt, a carrot, turnip, mace, herbs, and water in the above proportion; simmer these for an hour, then strain the gravy, thicken it with butter and flour, flavor with ketchup and port wine, and lay in the pieces of turkey to warm through. If there is any stuffing left, put that in also, as it so much improves the flavor of the gravy. When it boils, serve and garnish the dish with sippets of toasted bread.

Time, one hour to make the gravy. *Seasonable* from December to February.

To Broil the Legs of a Turkey. — *Time*, a quarter of an hour.

INGREDIENTS.— *The legs of a turkey, a little pepper, salt, Cayenne, and a squeeze of a lemon.*

Take the legs from a cold roast turkey, make some incisions across them with a sharp knife, and season them with a little pepper, salt, and a pinch of Cayenne. Squeeze over them a little lemon-juice, and place them on a gridiron well buttered, over a clear fire. When done a nice brown, put them on a hot dish, with a piece of butter on the top of each, and serve them up very hot.

Roast Goose. — When a goose is well picked, singed, and cleaned, make the stuffing, with about two ounces of onion (if you think the flavor of raw onions too strong, cut them in slices, and lay them in cold water for a couple of hours, add as much apple or potato as you have of onion), and half as much green sage, chop them very fine, adding four ounces, *i. e.*, about a large breakfast cupful, of stale bread-crumbs, a bit of butter about as big as a walnut, and a very little pepper and salt

(to this some cooks add half the liver, parboiling it first), the yolk of an egg or two, and incorporating the whole well together, stuff the goose; do not quite fill it, but leave a little room for the stuffing to swell. Spit it, tie it on the spit at both ends, to prevent it swinging round, and to prevent the stuffing from coming out. From an hour and a half to an hour and three-quarters will roast a fine full-grown goose. Send up gravy and apple-sauce with it.

Hashed Goose. — INGREDIENTS. — *The remains of cold roast goose*, 2 *onions*, 2 *ounces of butter*, 1 *pint of boiling water*, 1 *dessertspoonful of flour, pepper and salt to taste*, 1 *tablespoonful of port wine*, 2 *tablespoonfuls of mushroom ketchup.*

Mode. — Cut up the goose into pieces of the size required; the inferior joints, trimmings, etc., put into a stewpan to make the gravy; slice and fry the onions in the butter of a very pale brown; add these to the trimmings, and pour over about a pint of boiling water; stew these gently for three-quarters of an hour, then skim and strain the liquor. Thicken it with flour, and flavor with port wine and ketchup in the above proportion; add a seasoning of pepper and salt, and put in the pieces of goose; let these get thoroughly hot through, but do not allow them to boil, and serve with sippets of toasted bread.

Time, altogether, rather more than one hour. *Seasonable*, from September to March.

Roast Fowls. — Fowls to be tender should be killed a couple of days before they are dressed; when the feathers come out easily, then let them be picked and cooked. In drawing them, be careful not to break the gall-bag, as, wherever it touches, it would impart a very bitter taste; the liver and gizzard should also be preserved. Truss them in the following manner: — After having carefully picked them, cut off the head, and skewer the skin of the neck down over the back. Cut off the claws; dip the legs in boiling water, and scrape them; turn the pinions under; run a skewer through them and the middle of the legs, which should be passed through the body to the pinion and leg on the other side, one skewer securing the limbs on both sides. The liver and gizzard should be placed in the wings, the liver on one side and the gizzard on the other. Tie the legs together by passing a trussing-needle, threaded with twine, through the backbone, and secure it on the other side. If trussed like a capon, the legs are placed more apart. When firmly trussed, singe them all over; put them down to a bright clear fire, paper the breasts with a sheet of buttered paper, and keep the fowls well basted. Roast them for three-quarters of an hour, more or less, according to the size, and ten minutes before serving, remove the paper, dredge the fowls with a little fine flour, put a piece of butter into the basting-ladle, and as it melts, baste the fowls with it; when nicely frothed and of a rich color, serve with good brown gravy, a little of which should be poured over the fowls, and a tureen of well-made bread sauce. Mushroom, oyster, or egg sauce are very suitable accompaniments to roast fowl. Chicken is roasted in the same manner.

Time. — A very large fowl, quite one hour; medium-sized one, three-quarters of an hour; chicken, half an hour, or rather longer. *Seasonable* all the year, but scarce in early spring.

Boiled Fowls or Chickens.—*Time,* one hour for a large fowl; three-quarters of an hour for a medium size; half an hour for a chicken.

After the fowls or chickens are trussed for boiling, fold them in a nice white floured cloth and put them into a stewpan; cover them well with hot water, bring it gradually to a boil, and skim it very carefully as the scum rises, then let them simmer as *slowly as possible,* which will improve their appearance more than fast boiling, causing them to be whiter and plumper. When done, put them on a hot dish, remove the skewers, and pour over

them a little parsley and butter, oyster, lemon, celery, or white sauce, serving the sauce also separately in a tureen. Boiled tongue, ham, or bacon is usually served to eat with them.

Grilled Fowl.—Take the remains of cold fowls, and skin them or not, at choice; pepper and salt them, and sprinkle over them a little lemon-juice, and let them stand an hour; wipe them dry, dip them into clarified butter, and then into fine bread-crumbs, and broil gently over a clear fire. A little finely minced lean of ham or grated lemon-peel, with a seasoning of Cayenne, salt and mace, mixed with the crumbs, will vary this dish agreeably. When fried instead of broiled, the fowls may be dipped into yolk of egg instead of butter.

Fricasseed Fowl (Cold Poultry Cookery). — INGREDIENTS. — *The remains of cold roast fowl,* 1 *strip of lemon-peel,* 1 *blade of pounded mace,* 1 *bunch of savory herbs,* 1 *onion, pepper and salt to taste,* 1 *pint of water,* 1 *teaspoonful of flour,* ¼ *pint of cream, the yolks of* 2 *eggs.*

Mode.—Carve the fowls into nice joints; make gravy of the trimmings and legs, by stewing them with the lemon-peel, mace, herbs, onion, seasoning, and water, until reduced to half a pint; then strain, and put in the fowl. Warm it through, and thicken with a teaspoonful of flour; stir the yolks of the eggs into the cream; add these to the sauce; let it get thoroughly hot, but do not allow it to boil, or it will curdle.

Time, one hour to make the gravy, quarter of an hour to warm the fowl. *Seasonable* at any time.

Ragout of Fowl. — INGREDIENTS. — *The remains of cold roast fowl,* 3 *shallots,* 2 *blades of mace, a faggot of savory herbs,* 2 *or* 3 *slices of lean ham,* 1 *pint of stock or water, pepper and salt to taste,* 1 *onion,* 1 *dessertspoonful of flour,* 1 *tablespoonful of lemon-juice,* ½ *teaspoonful of pounded sugar,* 1 *ounce of butter.*

Mode. — Cut the fowls up into neat pieces, the same as for a fricassee;

put the trimmings into a stewpan with the shallots, mace, herbs, ham, onion, and stock (water may be substituted for this). Boil it slowly for one hour, strain the liquor, and put a small piece of butter into a stewpan; when melted, dredge in sufficient flour to dry up the butter, and stir it over the fire. Put in the strained liquor, boil for a few minutes, and strain it again over the pieces of fowl. Squeeze in the lemon-juice, add the sugar and a seasoning of pepper and salt, make it hot, but do not allow it to boil; lay the fowl neatly on the dish, and garnish with croûtous.

Time, altogether, one hour and a half. *Seasonable* at any time.

Chicken Pie.—*Time,* to bake, one hour and a quarter.

INGREDIENTS. — *Two small chickens, some forcemeat, a sweetbread, a few fresh mushrooms, a cupful of good gravy, a little flour and butter, 4 eggs, some puff paste.*

Cover the bottom of a pie-dish with a puff paste, upon that round the side lay a thin layer of forcemeat; cut two small chickens into pieces, season them highly with pepper and salt; put some of the pieces into the dish, then some sweetbread cut into pieces and well seasoned, a few fresh mushrooms, and the yolks of four or five hard-boiled eggs cut into four pieces, and strewed over the tops. Put in a little water, and cover the pie with a piece of puff paste, glaze it, ornament the edge, and bake it. When done, pour in through the hole in the top a cupful of good gravy, thickened with a little flour and butter.

Chicken and Veal Pot-pie. — Boil the meat until about half done. Chickens should be jointed before boiling, and veal cut into small pieces after it is boiled. Put it into a pot with a layer of crust to each layer of meat, having a layer of crust on top. A few slices of salt pork improves it. The meat should be well seasoned with salt and pepper before putting it in the pot. Cover the whole with the

liquor in which the meat was stewed; it should be hot when added, and keep a teakettle of boiling water, to turn in as the water boils away. Cold water will make the crust heavy. Let the whole stew just long enough to have the crust cooked; if overcooked, it will be clammy. The crust may be made like that for fruit pies, with less shortening, or like that for cream of tartar biscuit, but a raised pie-crust is the lightest and best. If you have unbaked wheat dough, add to it a little melted butter, and use it for the pie, if not, prepare the crust as follows: Mix together three pints of flour, half a teacup of melted butter, a teaspoonful of salt, a third of a teacup of yeast, and lukewarm milk or water just sufficient to enable you to roll it out. Set it in a warm place to rise, which will take five or six hours, unless brewers' or distillery yeast is used. The butter may be omitted, and seven or eight potatoes, boiled soft and mashed fine, substituted. When quite light, so as to be of a spongy appearance, roll it out half an inch thick, cut into small cakes, let them remain a few minutes, then put them with the meat.

Curried Fowl.—INGREDIENTS. —1 *fowl, 2 ounces of butter, 3 onions sliced, 1 pint of white veal gravy, 1 tablespoonful of curry-powder, 1 tablespoonful of flour, 1 apple, 4 tablespoonfuls of cream, 1 tablespoonful of lemon-juice.*

Mode. — Put the butter into a stewpan, with the onions sliced, the fowl cut into small joints, and the apple peeled, cored, and minced. Fry to a pale brown, add the stock, and stew gently for twenty minutes; rub down the curry powder and flour with a little of the gravy, quite smoothly, and stir this to the other ingredients; simmer for rather more than half an hour, and just before serving, add the above proportion of hot cream and lemon-juice. Serve with boiled rice, which may either be heaped lightly on a dish by itself, or put round the curry as a border.

Time, fifty minutes. *Sufficient for*

three or four persons. *Seasonable* in the winter.

Note.—This curry may be made of cold chicken, but undressed meat will be found far superior.

Roast Ducks.—*Choosing and Trussing.*—Choose plump ducks, with thick and yellowish feet. They should be trussed with the feet on, which should be scalded, and the skin peeled off, and then turned up close to the legs. Run a skewer through the middle of each leg, after having drawn them as close as possible to the body, to plump up the breast, passing the same quite through the body. Cut off the heads and necks, and the pinions at the first joint; bring these close to the sides, twist the feet round, and truss them at the back of the bird. After the duck is stuffed, both ends should be secured with strings, so as to keep in the seasoning.

Mode.—To insure ducks being tender, never dress them the same day they are killed; and if the weather permits, let them hang a day or two. Make a stuffing of sage or onion sufficient for one duck, and leave the other unseasoned, as the flavor is not liked by everybody. Put them down to a brisk clear fire, and keep them well basted the whole of the time they are cooking. A few minutes before serving, dredge them lightly with flour, to make them froth and look plump, and when the steam draws towards the fire, send them to table hot and quickly, with a good brown gravy poured *round*, but not *over* the ducks, and a little of the same in a tureen. When in season, green peas should invariably accompany this dish.

Time, full-grown ducks from three-quarters of an hour to one hour; ducklings, from twenty-five to thirty-five minutes. *Sufficient*, a couple of ducks for six or seven persons. *Seasonable*, ducklings from April to August; ducks from November to February.

Note.—Ducklings are trussed and roasted in the same manner, and served with the same sauces and accompaniments. When in season, apple sauce must not be omitted.

Stewed Duck and Peas (Cold Poultry Cookery).—INGREDIENTS.—The remains of cold roast duck, 2 ounces of butter, 3 or 4 slices of lean ham or bacon, 1 tablespoonful of flour, 2 pints of thin gravy, 1 large onion, or a small bunch of green onions, 3 sprigs of parsley, 3 cloves, 1 pint of young green peas, Cayenne and salt to taste, 1 teaspoonful of pounded sugar.

Mode.—Put the butter into a stewpan; cut up the duck into joints; lay them in with the slices of lean ham or bacon; make it brown, then dredge in a tablespoonful of flour, and stir this well in before adding the gravy. Put in the onion, parsley, cloves, and gravy, and when it has simmered for a quarter of an hour, add a pint of young green peas, and stew gently for about half an hour. Season with Cayenne, salt, and sugar; take out the duck, place it round the dish, and the peas in the middle. To insure the peas being of a good color, they should be boiled separately.

Time, three-quarters of an hour. *Seasonable* from June to August.

Hashed Duck (Cold Poultry Cookery).—INGREDIENTS. — The remains of cold roast duck, rather more than 1 pint of weak stock or water, 1 onion, 1 ounce of butter, thickening of butter and flour, salt and Cayenne to taste, ½ teaspoonful of minced lemon-peel, 1 dessertspoonful of lemon-juice, ½ glass of port wine.

Mode. — Cut the duck into nice joints, and put the trimmings into a stewpan; slice and fry the onion in a little butter; add these to the trimmings, pour in the above proportion of weak stock or water, and stew gently for one hour. Strain the liquor, thicken it with butter and flour, season with salt and Cayenne, and add the remaining ingredients; boil it up and skim well; lay in the pieces of duck, and let them get thoroughly hot through by the side of the fire, but do not allow them to boil: they should soak in the gravy for about half an hour. Garnish with sippets of toasted bread. The hash may be made richer by using a stronger and more highly-flavored gravy; a little spice or pounded mace may also be added, when their flavor is liked. *Time*, one hour and a half. *Seasonable* from November to February; ducklings, from May to August.

To Stew Giblets. -- *Time*, one hour and a half.

INGREDIENTS. — *One set of giblets, a bunch of parsley and thyme, a few sage leaves, pepper and salt, 1 onion, a quart of gravy, a wineglass of white wine.*

Mode. — Thoroughly clean and wash the giblets, cut them into pieces, and stew them for an hour and a half in a quart of gravy, adding a bunch of thyme and parsley, an onion, a few sage leaves, and a seasoning of pepper and salt. When done, put them into water, and trim them ready for serving. Strain the gravy through a fine hair sieve, add a glass of white wine and a piece of butter the size of a walnut, rolled in flour. Boil the giblets up in the gravy, and serve them quickly.

Giblet Pie. — INGREDIENTS. — *A set of duck or goose giblets, 1 pound of rump-steak, 1 onion, ½ teaspoonful of whole black pepper, a bunch of savory herbs, plain crust.*

Mode. — Clean, and put the giblets into a stewpan with an onion, whole pepper, and a bunch of savory herbs. Add rather more than a pint of water, and simmer gently for about one hour and a half. Take them out, let them cool, and cut them into pieces. Line the bottom of a pie-dish with a few pieces of rump-steak. Add a layer of giblets, and a few more pieces of steak. Season with pepper and salt, and pour in the gravy (which should be strained) that the giblets were stewed in. Cover with a plain crust, and bake for rather more than one and a half hours in a brisk oven. Place a piece of paper over the pie, to prevent the crust taking too much color.

Time, one hour and a half to stew the giblets, about one hour to bake the pie. *Sufficient* for five or six persons.

To Roast Pigeons. — *Time*, twenty minutes to half an hour.

INGREDIENTS. — *Some pigeons, ¼ pound of butter, pepper and salt.*

Mode. — Well wash and thoroughly clean the pigeons. Wipe them dry, season them inside with pepper and salt, and put a good-sized piece of butter into the body of each bird. Roast them before a clear bright fire, basting them well the whole of the time. Serve them with gravy and bread sauce. Or send up a tureen of parsley and butter, in which case the birds must be garnished with fried parsley; but for very plain cooking, they can have a little water added to the butter in the dripping-pan, and poured round them, adding a spoonful or two of gravy.

Jugged Pigeons. — *Time*, three hours.

INGREDIENTS. — *Some pigeons, 2 hard-boiled eggs, a sprig of parsley, the peel of ½ a lemon, the weight of the livers in beef suet, the same of bread-crumbs, pepper, salt, and nutmeg, 1 egg, 1½ ounces of butter, 1 head of celery, a glass of white wine, a bunch of sweet herbs, 4 cloves.*

Mode. — Pick and draw four or six pigeons, wipe them very dry, boil the livers a minute or two, then mince them fine, and bruise them with a spoon, or beat them in a mortar. Mix them with the yolks of two hard-boiled eggs, a sprig of parsley, and the peel of half a lemon, all shred fine, the weight of the livers in beef suet chopped as fine as possible, the same weight of bread crumbs, and a little pepper, salt, and grated nutmeg. Mix it well together with a well-beaten egg, and a little fresh butter. Stuff the pigeons and the crops with this forcemeat, sew up the vents, and dip the pigeons into warm water. Dredge over them some pepper and salt, and put them into a jar with the celery, sweet herbs, cloves, and beaten mace, with a glass of white wine. *Cover the jar closely*, and set it in a stewpan of boiling water for three hours, taking care the water does not get to the top of the jar. When done, strain the gravy into a stewpan, stir in a little butter rolled in flour, boil it up till it is thick, and pour it over the pigeons. Garnish with lemon.

Roast Grouse.—Let the birds hang as long as possible; pluck and draw them; wipe, but do not wash them, inside and out, and truss them without the head, the same as for a roast fowl. Many persons still continue to truss them with the head under the wing, but the former is now considered the most approved method. Put them down to a sharp, clear fire; keep them well basted the whole time they are cooking, and serve them on a buttered toast, soaked in the dripping-pan, with a little melted butter poured over them, or with bread sauce and gravy.

Time, half hour; if liked very thoroughly done, thirty-five minutes. *Sufficient*, two for a dish. *Seasonable* from the 12th of August to the beginning of December.

Roast Partridge. — *Choosing and Trussing.* — Choose young birds with dark-colored bills and yellowish legs, and let them hang a few days, or there will be no flavor to the flesh, nor will it be tender. The time they should be kept entirely depends on the taste of those for whom they are intended, as what some persons would consider delicious would be to others disgusting and offensive. They may be trussed with or without the head, the latter mode being now considered the most fashionable. Pluck, draw, and wipe the partridge carefully, inside and out; cut off the head, leaving sufficient skin on the neck to skewer back; bring the legs close to the breast, between it and the side-bones, and pass a skewer through the pinions and the thick part of the thighs. When the head is left on, it should be brought round and fixed on to the point of the skewer.

Mode. — When the bird is firmly and plumply trussed, roast it before a nice bright fire; keep it well basted, and a few minutes before serving, flour and froth it well. Dish it, and serve with gravy and bread sauce, and send to table hot and quickly. A little of the gravy should be poured over the bird.

Time, twenty-five to thirty-five minutes. *Sufficient*, two for a dish. *Seasonable* from the 1st of September to the beginning of February.

Roast Wild Duck.—Carefully pluck and draw them; cut off the heads close to the necks, leaving sufficient skin to turn over, and do not cut off the feet; some twist each leg at the knuckle, and rest the claws on each side of the breast. Roast the birds before a quick fire, and, when they are first put down, let them remain for five minutes without basting (this will keep the gravy in); afterwards baste plentifully with butter, and a few minutes before serving dredge them lightly with flour; baste well, and send them to table nicely frothed, and full of gravy. If overdone, the birds will lose their flavor. Serve with a good gravy in the dish, and send to table with them a cut lemon. To take off the fishy taste which wild fowl sometimes have, baste them for a few minutes with hot water, to which have been added an onion and a little salt; then take away the pan, and baste with butter.

Time, when liked underdressed, twenty to twenty-five minutes; well done, twenty-five to thirty-five minutes. *Sufficient*, two for a dish. *Seasonable* from November to February.

Roast Pheasant, or Guinea Fowl. — *Choosing and Trussing.* — Old pheasants may be known by the length and sharpness of their spurs; in young ones they are short and blunt. The cock bird is generally reckoned the best, ex cept when the hen is with egg. They should hang some time before they are dressed, as, if they are cooked fresh, the flesh will be exceedingly dry and tasteless. After the bird is plucked and drawn, wipe the inside with a damp cloth, and truss it in the same manner as partridge. If the head is left on, bring it round under the wing, and fix it on to the point of the skewer.

Mode. — Roast it before a brisk fire,

keep it well basted, and flour and froth it nicely. Serve with brown gravy (a little of which should be poured round the bird), and a tureen of bread sauce. Two or three of the pheasant's best tail-feathers are sometimes stuck in the tail as an ornament, and these give a very handsome appearance to the dish.

Time, half to one hour, according to size. *Sufficient*, one for a dish. *Seasonable* from the 1st of October to the beginning of February.

Roast Woodcock. — Woodcocks should not be drawn, as the trails are, by epicures, considered a great delicacy. Pluck, and wipe them well outside; truss them with the legs close to the body, and the feet pressing upon the thighs; skin the neck and head, and bring the beak round under the wing. Place some slices of toast in the dripping-pan to catch the trails, allowing a piece of toast for each bird. Roast before a clear fire from fifteen to twenty-five minutes; keep them well basted, and flour. and froth them nicely. When done, dish the pieces of toast with the birds upon them, pour round a very little gravy, and send some more to table in a tureen. These are most delicious birds when well cooked, but they should not be kept too long: when the feathers drop, or easily come out, they are fit for table.

Time. — When liked underdone, fifteen to twenty minutes; if liked well done, allow an extra five minutes. *Sufficient*, two for a dish. *Seasonable* from November to February.

Roast Rabbit. — *Time*, three-quarters of an hour.

INGREDIENTS. — 1 *large rabbit, pepper, salt, nutmeg, ½ a pound of butter, 4 dessertspoonfuls of milk, 1 tablespoonful of flour, yolks of 2 eggs, brown gravy, the peel of ½ a lemon grated.*

Procure a fine large rabbit, and truss it in the same manner as a hare; fill the paunch with veal stuffing, and roast it before a bright clear fire for three-quarters of an hour, if a large one, basting it well with butter. Before

serving mix a spoonful of flour with four of milk; stir into it the yolks of two well-beaten eggs, and season with a little grated nutmeg, pepper, and salt; baste the rabbit thickly with this, to form a light coating over it. When dry, baste it with butter, to froth it up; and when done, place it carefully in a dish, and pour round it some brown gravy, boiled up with the liver minced, and a little grated nutmeg. Serve with gravy in a tureen, and red jelly. A rabbit can be baked instead of roasted, and will require the same time in a good oven.

Boiled Rabbit. — *Time*, a very small rabbit, half an hour; medium size, three-quarters of an hour; a large rabbit, one hour.

When the rabbit is trussed for boiling, put it into a stewpan, and cover it with hot water, and let it boil very gently until tender. When done, place it on a dish, and smother it with onions, or with parsley and butter, or liver sauce, should the flavor of onion not be liked. If liver sauce is to be served, the liver must be boiled for ten minutes, minced very fine, and added to the butter sauce. An old rabbit will require quite an hour to boil it thoroughly.

To Truss Boiled Rabbits. — After well cleaning and skinning a rabbit, wash it in cold water, and then put it into warm water for about twenty minutes, to soak out the blood. Draw the head round to the side, and secure it with a thin skewer run through that and the body.

To Blanch Rabbits, Fowls, etc. — To blanch or whiten a rabbit or fowl it must be placed on the fire in a small quantity of water, and let it boil. As soon as it boils it must be taken out, and plunged into *cold water* for a few minutes.

To Fricassee Rabbits Brown. — *Time*, three-quarters of an hour.

Mode. — Take two young rabbits, cut them in small pieces, slit the head in two, season them with pepper and salt, dredge them with flour, and fry them a nice brown in fresh butter. Pour

13

out the fat from the stewpan, and put in a pint of gravy, a bunch of sweet herbs, half a pint of fresh mushrooms, if you have them, and three shallots chopped fine, season with pepper and salt, cover them close, and let them stew for half an hour. Then skim the gravy clean, add a spoonful of ketchup, and the juice of half a lemon. Take out the herbs, and stir in a piece of butter rolled in flour, boil it up till thick.

An Economical Way to Dress a Rabbit. — *Time*, one hour.

INGREDIENTS. — *A rabbit, ½ a pound of pickled pork, 1½ ounces of butter, a little flour, and some forcemeat balls.*

Mode. — Divide and cut the rabbit and pork into slices, shred the onion fine, and fry the whole a nice brown. Then put them into a stewpan with just sufficient water to cover them. Season it highly with pepper and salt, and let it simmer for a quarter of an hour or twenty minutes. Then thicken the gravy with a piece of butter rolled in flour. Add a few forcemeat balls, and let it again simmer until the gravy is the consistency of thick cream.

A Plain Rabbit Pie. — *Time*, to bake, one hour and a quarter.

INGREDIENTS. — *A large rabbit, ¾ of a pound of rather fat bacon, a sprig of parsley, pepper, salt, and 1 shallot, puff paste.*

Mode. — Skim and wash a fine large rabbit, cut it into joints, and divide the head. Then place it in warm water to soak until thoroughly clean. Drain it on a sieve, or wipe it with a clean cloth. Season it with pepper and salt, a sprig of parsley chopped fine, and one shallot if the flavor is liked (but it is equally good without it). Cut the bacon into small pieces, dredge the rabbit with flour, and place it with the bacon in a pie-dish, commencing with the inferior parts of the rabbit. Pour in a small cupful of water, or stock if you have it. Put a paste border round the edges of the dish, and cover it with puff paste

about half an inch thick. Ornament and glaze the top, make a hole in the centre, and bake it.

Rabbit Pudding. — *Time*, two hours to boil.

Mode. — Cut a small rabbit into small neat pieces, and have ready a few slices of bacon or ham. Line a basin with a good suet crust. Lay in the pieces of rabbit with the bacon or ham intermixed, season to your taste with pepper and salt, and pour in a cupful of water. Cover the crust over the top, press it securely with the thumb and finger, and boil it.

VENISON.—Haunch of Venison. —*Time*, three to four hours.

Haunch from 20 to 25 pounds.

This joint is trimmed by cutting off part of the knuckle and sawing off the chine bone, then the flap is folded over, and it is covered with a paste made of flour and water. This paste should be about an inch thick. Tie it up in strong and very thick paper, and place it in a cradle spit very close to the fire till the paste is well hardened or crusted, pouring a few ladlefuls of hot drippings over it occasionally to prevent the paper from catching fire. Then move it further from the fire, taking care that your fire is a *very* good one, clear and strong. When the venison has roasted for about four hours, take it up, remove the paper and paste, and run a thin skewer in to see if it is done enough. If the skewer goes in easily, it is dressed, if not, put it down again, as it depends greatly on the strength of the fire for so large a joint. When it is dressed glaze the top and salamander it. Put a frill round the knuckle, and serve very hot with strong gravy. Red currant jelly in a glass dish or a tureen. Vegetables: French beans.

Neck of Venison.—*Time*, a quarter of an hour for a pound.

Cover it with paste and paper as for the haunch, fix it on a spit, and roast.

To Hash Venison.—*Time*, one hour and a half.

INGREDIENTS.—*Some cold roast venison, 3 tablespoonfuls of port wine, a little mutton broth, ½ of a shallot, a pinch of Cayenne, 1½ ounces of butter, a spoonful of flour, and salt to taste.*

Mode.—Cut some cold roast venison into nice slices, and season them lightly with salt. Put the bones, trimmings, any cold gravy from the venison, and as much broth as you may require, into a stewpan, and let it simmer slowly for quite an hour, then strain it off. Stir the butter and flour over the fire until sufficiently brown to color the gravy, taking care it does not burn. Pour the gravy from the bones, add the port wine, and let it simmer until it boils. Then draw the stewpan to the side of the fire, put in the slices of venison, and when thoroughly *hot* serve it up, with red currant jelly in a glass dish. Garnish with forcemeat balls about the size of a marble.

Venison Pasty. — *Time,* to stew, three hours and a half; three hours to bake.

INGREDIENTS. — *A neck, or shoulder of venison, a quarter of a pint of port wine, 3 shallots, 3 blades of mace, pepper and salt, 9 allspice, a little veal stock or broth, raised pie-crust.*

For the Gravy.—A glass of port wine, juice of a small lemon, a piece of butter, and flour, some stock from the stewed venison.

Mode.—Take either of the above parts of venison, remove the bones and skin, and cut it into small square pieces. Put them into a stewpan with three shallots, pepper, salt, mace, and allspice. Add a quarter of a pint of port wine, and sufficient veal broth or stock to cover it, put it on a gentle fire, and let it stew until three parts done. Then take out the neatest pieces of venison for the pasty, and put them into a deep dish, in a cold place, with a little of the gravy poured over them. Pour the remainder of the gravy over the bones, etc., and boil for a quarter of an hour. Cover the pasty with some raised pie-crust, ornament the top in any way you please, and bake it

in a slow oven. When done, have ready the gravy left from the bones, strain and skim it clean, add a glass of port wine, the juice of a small lemon, and a piece of butter rolled in flour. Pour it into the pasty, and serve.

Pie of Larks or Sparrows.—*Time,* to bake, one hour and a half.

INGREDIENTS.—*A dozen small birds, a rumpsteak, a small bunch of savory herbs, the peel of ½ a lemon, a slice of stale bread, ½ a cupful of milk, 6 eggs, pepper and salt, 2 ounces of butter, puff paste.*

Mode. — Make a forcemeat with the slice of bread soaked in milk and beaten up, a small bunch of savory herbs chopped fine, the peel of half a lemon minced, a seasoning of pepper and salt, a piece of butter, and the yolks of six eggs; mix all together, put it into a stewpan and stir it over the fire for a few minutes until it becomes very stiff, and then fill the inside of each bird. Line a pie-dish with the rumpsteak, seasoned with pepper and salt, and fried lightly; place the birds on it, cover them with the yolks of the hard-boiled eggs cut into slices, and pour in a sufficient quantity of gravy. Put a paste round the edge of the dish and cover it over with the same, glaze it with the yolk of an egg brushed over it, make a hole in the top, and bake it.

To Boil Eggs for Breakfast, Salads, etc.—Eggs for boiling cannot be too fresh, or boiled too soon after they are laid; but rather a longer time should be allowed for boiling a new-laid egg than for one that is three or four days old. Have ready a saucepan of boiling water; put the eggs into it gently with a spoon, letting the spoon touch the bottom of the saucepan before it is withdrawn, that the egg may not fall, and consequently crack. For those who like eggs lightly boiled, three minutes will be found sufficient; three minutes and a half will be ample time to set the white nicely. Should the eggs be unusually large, as those of black Spanish fowls sometimes are, allow an extra half minute for them. Eggs for salads should be boiled ten minutes, and should be placed in a basin of cold water for a few minutes; they should then be rolled on the table with the hand, and the shell will peel off easily.

Time. — To boil eggs lightly, for invalids or children, two minutes and a half; to boil eggs to suit the generality of tastes, three to four minutes; to boil eggs hard, five minutes; for salads, ten minutes.

Poached Eggs. — INGREDIENTS. — *Eggs, water. To every pint of water allow 1 tablespoonful of vinegar.*

Mode. — Eggs for poaching should be perfectly fresh, but not quite new-laid; those that are about thirty-six hours old are the best for the purpose. If quite new-laid, the white is so milky it is almost impossible to set it; and, on the other hand, if the egg be at all stale, it is equally difficult to poach it nicely. Strain some boiling water into a deep, clean frying-pan; break the egg into a cup without damaging the yolk, and, when the water boils, remove the pan to the side of the fire, and gently slip the egg into it. Place the pan over a gentle fire, and keep the water simmering until the white looks nicely set, when the egg is ready. Take it up gently with a slice, cut away the ragged edges of the white, and serve either on toasted bread or on slices of ham or bacon, or on spinach, etc. A poached egg should not be overdone, as its appearance and taste will be quite spoiled if the yolk be allowed to harden. When the egg is slipped into the water, the white should be gathered together, to keep it a little in form, or the cup should be turned over it for half a minute. To poach an egg to perfection is rather a difficult operation; so, for inexperienced cooks, a tin egg-poacher may be purchased, which greatly facilitates this manner of dressing eggs. It consists of a tin plate with a handle, with a space for three perforated cups. An egg should be broken into each cup, and the machine then placed in

a stewpan of boiling water, which has been previously strained. When the whites of the eggs appear set, they are done, and should then be carefully slipped on to the toast or spinach, or with whatever they are served. In poaching eggs in a frying-pan, never do more than four at a time; and, when a little vinegar is liked mixed with the water in which the eggs are done, use the above proportion.

Time, two and a half to three and a half minutes, according to the size of the egg. *Seasonable,* at any time, but less plentiful in winter.

Eggs and Bacon. — *Time,* three to four minutes.

INGREDIENTS. — 6 *eggs,* ¼ *of a pound of dripping or butter, some slices of ham or bacon.*

Break five or six fresh eggs into cups, and slip them into a delicately clean frying-pan of boiling dripping or butter. When the whites are set, take them up with a slice, trim off the rough edges, and drain them from the grease. Then place them in the centre of the dish, and the slices of fried bacon round the edge, or the eggs may be served on the bacon, whichever you prefer.

Friar's Omelet. — INGREDIENTS. — 8 *or* 9 *large apples,* 2 *ounces of fresh butter, sugar to taste, bread-crumbs.*

Boil eight or nine large apples to a pulp, stir in two ounces of butter, and add pounded sugar to taste. When cold, add an egg well beaten up. Then butter the bottom of a deep baking dish, and the sides also. *Thickly* strew crumbs of bread, so as to stick all over the bottom and sides. Put in the mixture, and strew bread-crumbs plentifully over the top. Put it into a moderate oven, and when baked turn it out, and put powdered sugar over.

The Way to Make an Omelet. — It is surprising that a dish so easily prepared, and so delicious, as omelet, has come into use to so small an extent in this country. There are extensive districts where it has never been heard of, and many housekeepers who meet with it in their travels never have it upon their own tables, because their cooks do not know how to prepare it.

Omelet is simply egg beaten and fried in butter. Break three fresh eggs into a bowl, add a little pinch of salt and a teaspoonful of water, and beat the eggs thoroughly. Then put a tablespoonful of good butter into a flat frying-pan, and hold the pan over the fire with the handle a little elevated so as to incline the bottom at a small angle. As soon as the pan is warm pour in the eggs, and as the mass begins to cook run a case-knife under it to keep it from burning to the pan. As soon as the surface is about dry fold one half of the omelet over the other, and it is ready to serve. It can be made in five minutes, and is an exceedingly delicate and delicious morsel.

Ordinary Omelet. — Take four eggs, beat the yolks and whites together, with a tablespoonful of milk, a little salt and pepper; put two ounces of butter into a frying-pan to boil, and let it remain until it begins to brown; pour the batter into it, and let it remain quiet for a minute; turn up the edges of the omelet gently from the bottom of the pan with a fork; shake it, to keep it from burning at the bottom, and fry it till of a bright brown. It will not take more than five minutes frying.

How to Tell Good Eggs. — Place the large end of the egg against the tongue; if it becomes immediately warm to the tongue, the egg is very fresh; if it becomes warm slowly, it is stale; if no heat is felt, the egg is bad. The degree of freshness of eggs is thus easily ascertained.

Oxford Sausages. — INGREDIENTS. — 1 *pound of lean veal, 1 pound of young pork, 1 pound of beef suet, ½ a pound of grated bread, peel of ½ a lemon, 1 nutmeg grated, 6 sage leaves, 1 teaspoonful of pepper, 2 of salt, a sprig of thyme, savory, and marjoram.*

Take a pound of lean veal, and the same quantity of young pork, fat and lean together, free from skin and gristle, and a pound of beef suet; chop all separately as fine as possible, and then mix together; add the grated bread, the peel of half a lemon shred fine, a nutmeg grated, a teaspoonful of pepper, two of salt, and the sage leaves, thyme, savory, and marjoram, all chopped as fine as you can; mix all thoroughly together, and press it down into a prepared skin. When you use them, fry them in fresh butter a fine brown. Serve as hot as possible.

Bologna Sausages. — Take equal quantities of bacon (fat and lean), beef, veal, pork, and beef suet; chop them small, season with pepper, salt, etc., sweet herbs, and sage rubbed fine. Have a well-washed intestine, fill, and prick it; boil gently for an hour, and lay on straw to dry. They may be smoked the same as hams.

Mutton Sausages. — The lean of the leg is the best. Add half as much of beef suet; that is, a pound of lean and half a pound of suet (this proportion is good for all sausages). Add oysters, anchovies chopped very fine, and flavor with seasoning. No herbs. These will require a little fat in the pan to fry.

Veal Sausages are made exactly as Oxford sausages, except that you add ham fat or fat bacon; and, instead of sage, use marjoram, thyme, and parsley.

Preparing Sausage Skins. — Turn them inside out, and stretch them on a stick; wash and scrape them in several waters. When thoroughly cleansed, take them off the sticks, and soak in salt and water two or three hours before filling.

Sausages should be well cooked; let them remain in the frying-pan long enough to be well cooked all through. As soon as they are done, remove them from the pan, and take two or three slices of bread, dip them quickly in cold water, then put them in the pan while the fat is boiling hot, place the frying-pan on the fire, and let the bread be well browned on both sides; then place the bread on a dish, and the sausages on top of it. This bread will be found a great addition to the sausages.

SWEETBREAD. — Trim a fine sweetbread (it cannot be too *fresh*), parboil it for five minutes, and throw it into a basin of cold water. Then roast it plain, or beat up the yolk of an egg, and prepare some fine bread-crumbs; or when the sweetbread is cold, dry it thoroughly in a cloth; run a lark-spit or a skewer through it, and tie it on the ordinary spit; egg it with a paste-brush; powder it well with bread-crumbs, and roast it. For sauce, fried bread-crumbs, melted butter, with a little mushroom ketchup, and lemon-juice, or serve on buttered toast, garnished with egg sauce, or with gravy. Instead of spitting the sweetbread, you may put it into an oven, or fry it.

Sweetbreads Plain. — Parboil and slice them as before, dry them in a clean cloth, flour them, and fry them a delicate brown; take care to drain the fat well, and garnish with slices of lemon, and sprigs of chervil or parsley, or crisp parsley. Serve with sauce, and slices of ham or bacon, or force-meat balls.

KIDNEYS.—Cut them through the long way, score them, sprinkle a little pepper and salt on them, and run a wire skewer through to keep them from curling on the gridiron, so that they may be evenly broiled. Broil over a clear fire, taking care not to prick them with the fork, turning them often till they are done; they will take about ten or twelve minutes, if the fire is brisk: or fry them in butter, and make gravy for them in the pan (after you have taken out the kidneys), by putting in a teaspoonful of flour. As soon as it looks brown, put in as much water as will make gravy; they will take five minutes more to fry than to broil.

DEVIL. — The gizzard and rump, or legs, etc., of a dressed turkey, capon, or goose, or mutton or veal kidney, scored, peppered, salted, and broiled, sent up for a relish, being made very hot, has obtained the name of a "Devil."

BACON. — The boiling of bacon is a very simple subject to comment upon; but our main object is to teach common cooks the art of dressing common food in the best manner. Cover a pound of nice streaked bacon with cold water; let it boil gently for three-quarters of an hour; take it up, scrape the under-side well, and cut off the rind. Grate a crust of bread, not only on the top but all over it, as you would ham; put it before the fire for a few minutes, not too long, or it will dry and spoil it. Bacon is sometimes as salt as salt can make it; therefore, before it is boiled, it must be soaked in warm water for an hour or two, changing the water once. Then pare off the rusty and smoked part, trim it nicely on the under-side, and scrape the rind as clean as possible.

Ham or Bacon Slices should not be more than one-eighth of an inch thick, and, for delicate persons, should be soaked in hot water for a quarter of an hour, and then well wiped and dried before broiling. If you wish to curl it, roll it up, and put a wooden skewer through it; then it may be dressed in a cheese-toaster or a Dutch oven.

SOUPS.— General Directions for Making Soups.—LEAN, JUICY BEEF, MUTTON, AND VEAL, form the basis of all good soups; therefore it is advisable to procure those pieces which afford the richest succulence, and such as are fresh-killed. Stale meat renders soups bad, and fat is not well adapted for making them. The principal art in composing good rich soup is so to proportion the several ingredients that the flavor of one shall not predominate over another, and that all the articles of which it is composed shall form an agreeable whole. Care must be taken that the roots and herbs are perfectly well cleaned, and that the water is proportioned to the quantity of meat and other ingredients, allowing a quart of water to a pound of meat for soups, and half that quantity for gravies. In making soups or gravies, gentle stewing or simmering is absolutely necessary. It may be remarked, moreover, that a really good soup can never be made but in a well-closed vessel, although, perhaps, greater wholesomeness is obtained by an occasional exposure to the air. Soups will, in general, take from four to six hours doing, and *are much better prepared the day before they are wanted.* When the soup is cold, the fat may be easily and completely removed; and in pouring it off, care must be taken not to disturb the settlings at the bottom of the vessel, which are so fine that they will escape through a sieve. A very fine hair sieve or cloth is the best strainer, and if the soup is strained while it is hot, let the tamis or cloth be previously soaked in cold water. Clear soups must be perfectly transparent, and thickened soups about the consistency of cream. To obtain a really clear and transparent soup, it is requisite to continue skimming the liquor until there is not a particle of scum remaining, this being commenced immediately after the water is added to the meat. To thicken and give body to soups and gravies, potato mucilage, arrowroot, bread-raspings, isinglass, flour and butter, barley, rice, or oatmeal, are used. A piece of boiled beef pounded to a pulp, with a bit of butter and flour, and rubbed through a sieve, and gradually incorporated with the soup, will be found an excellent addition. When soups and gravies are kept from day to day in hot weather, they should be warmed up every day, put into fresh-scalded pans or tureens, and placed in a cool larder. In temperate weather, every other day may be sufficient. Stock made from meat only, keeps good longer than that boiled with vegetables, the latter being liable to turn the mixture sour, particularly in very warm weather.

Clear Stock for Soups.—*Time,* six hours and a half.

INGREDIENTS.—*6 or 7 pounds of knuckle of veal or beef, ½ pound of lean ham or bacon, ¼ pound of butter, salt, 2 onions, 1 carrot, 1 turnip, ⅓ a head of celery, 2 gallons of water.*

Mode.—Cut fresh meat and ham into very small pieces, and put them into a stewpan which has been rubbed over with a quarter of a pound of butter; add half a pint of water, the salt, onions, turnip, carrot, and celery cut into slices; cover the stewpan, and place it over a very quick fire until the bottom of the pan is glazed, but stirring it round frequently to prevent its burning; then pour in the two gallons of water, and when on the point of boiling, draw it to the side of the fire to simmer for six and a half or seven hours, if the stock is made of beef; skim it thoroughly, and when done pass it through a very fine sieve for use. A little browning or gravy must be used to color it.

General Stock-Pot.—Stock, in its composition, is not confined to the above proportions; any meat or bones are useful; pieces of beef, from any part of which gravy can be extracted; bones, skin, brisket, or tops of ribs, ox-cheek, pieces of mutton, bacon, ham, and trimmings of turkeys, fowls, veal, etc.; and also of hare, chicken, etc.; they are old and fit for no other purpose — in fact anything that will become a jelly — will assist in making stock; to this medley of ingredients add carrots cut into slices, herbs, onions, pepper, salt, spice, etc., and when all have stewed until the stock is of a rich consistency, take it from the fire and pour it out to cool. When cold, all the fat must be taken off, and it must be poured clear from the sediment. When the soup is required to be very rich, the jelly from a cow-heel, or a lump of butter rolled in flour, must be added to the stock.

The stock-pot should never be suffered to be empty, as almost any meats (save salt meats) or fowls make stock; the remains should never be thrown anywhere but into the stock-pot, and should too much stock be already in your possession, boil it down to a glaze; waste is thus avoided.

Economical Stock.—INGREDIENTS.

The liquor in which a joint of meat has been boiled, say 4 quarts, trimmings of fresh meat or poultry, shank-bones, etc., roast-beef bones, any pieces the larder may furnish, vegetables, spices, and seasoning.

Mode.—Let all the ingredients simmer gently for five hours, taking care to skim carefully at first. Strain the stock off, and put it by for use.

Time, five hours.

White Stock—*To be used in the preparation of white soups.*—INGREDIENTS. —*4 pounds of knuckle of veal, any poultry trimmings, 4 slices of lean ham, 1 carrot, 2 onions, 1 head of celery, 12 white peppercorns, 1 ounce of salt, 1 blade of mace, 1 ounce of butter, 4 quarts of water.*

Mode.—Cut up the veal, and put it, with the bones and trimmings of poultry and the ham, into the stewpan, which has been rubbed with the butter. Moisten with half a pint of water, and simmer till the gravy begins to flow. Then add the four quarts of water with the remainder of the ingredients, and simmer for five hours. After skimming and straining it carefully through a very fine hair sieve, it will be ready for use.

Time, five and a half hours.

Note.—When stronger stock is desired, double the quantity of veal, or put in an old fowl. The liquor in which a young turkey has been boiled is an excellent addition to all white stock or soups.

Browning for Stock.—INGREDIENTS.—*2 ounces of powdered sugar, and ½ a pint of water.*

Mode.—Place the sugar in a stewpan over a slow fire until it begins to melt, keeping it stirred with a wooden spoon until it becomes black, then add the water, and let it dissolve. Cork closely, and use a few drops when required.

Note.—In France, burnt onions are made use of for the purpose of browning. As a general rule, the process of browning is to be discouraged, as apt to impart a slightly unpleasant flavor to the stock, and, consequently, all soups made from it.

To Clarify Stock.—INGREDIENTS. —*The whites of two eggs, ½ pint of water, 2 quarts of stock.*

Mode.—Supposing that by some accident the soup is not quite clear, and that its quantity is two quarts, take the whites of two eggs, carefully separated from their yolks, whisk them well together with the water, and add gradually the two quarts of boiling stock, still whisking. Place the soup on the fire, and when boiling and well skimmed, whisk the eggs with it till nearly boiling again; then draw it from the fire, and let it settle, until the whites of the eggs become separated. Pass through a fine cloth, and the soup should be clear.

Note.—The rule is, that all clear soup should be of a light-straw color, and should not savor too strongly of the meat; and that all white or brown thick soups should have no more consistency than will enable them to adhere slightly to the spoon when hot.

A good Family Soup.—INGREDIENTS.—*Remains of a cold tongue, 2 pounds of shin of beef, any cold pieces of meat or beef-bones, 2 turnips, 2 carrots, 2 onions, 1 parsnip, 1 head of celery, 4 quarts of water, ½ teacupful of rice ; salt and pepper to taste.*

Mode.—Put all the ingredients in a stewpan, and simmer gently for four hours, or until all the goodness is drawn from the meat. Strain off the soup, and let it stand to get cold. The kernels and soft parts of the tongue must be saved. When the soup is wanted for use, skim off all the fat, put in the kernels and soft parts of the tongue, slice in a small quantity of fresh carrot, turnip, and onion ; stew till the vegetables are tender, and serve with toasted bread.

Time, five hours. *Seasonable* at any time.

Gravy Soup.—INGREDIENTS.—*4 pounds of shin of beef, a piece of the knuckle of veal weighing 3 pounds, a few pieces or trimmings of meat or poultry, 3 slices of nicely flavored lean ham, ½ pound of butter, 2 onions, 4 carrots, 1 turnip, nearly a head of celery, 1 blade of mace, 6 cloves, a bunch of savory herbs, seasonings of salt and pepper to taste, 3 lumps of sugar, 5 quarts of boiling soft water. It can be flavored with* ketchup, or *Harvey's sauce, and a little soy.*

Mode.—Slightly brown the meat and ham in the butter, but do not let them burn. When this is done, pour to it the water, put in the salt, and as the scum rises take it off; when no more appears, add all the other ingredients, and let the soup simmer slowly by the fire for six hours without stirring it any more from the bottom; take it off, and pass it through a sieve. When perfectly cold and settled, all the fat should be removed, leaving the sediment untouched, which serves very nicely for thick gravies, hashes, etc. The flavoring should be added when the soup is heated for table.

Time, seven hours. *Seasonable* all the year.

Mock Turtle.—INGREDIENTS.—½ a calf's head, ¼ pound of butter, ¼ pound of lean ham, 2 tablespoonfuls of minced parsley, a little minced lemon, thyme, sweet marjoram, basil, 2 onions, a few chopped mushrooms (when obtainable), 2 shallots, 2 tablespoonfuls of flour, 2 glasses of Madeira or sherry, forcemeat balls, Cayenne, salt and mace to taste, the juice of 1 lemon and 1 Seville orange, 1 dessertspoonful of powdered sugar, 3 quarts of best strong stock.

Mode.—Scald the head with the skin on, remove the brain, tie the head up in a cloth, and let it boil for one hour. Then take the meat from the bones, cut it into small square pieces, and throw them into cold water. Now take the meat, put it into a stewpan, and cover with stock; let it boil gently for an hour, or rather more, if not quite tender, and set it on one side. Melt the butter in another stewpan, and add the ham, cut small, with the herbs, parsley, onions, shallot, mushrooms, and nearly a pint of stock; let these simmer slowly for two hours, and then dredge in as much flour as will dry up the butter. Fill up with the remainder of the stock, add the wine, let it stew gently for ten minutes, rub it through a sieve, and put it to the calf's head; season with Cayenne, and, if required, a little salt; add the

juice of the orange and lemon; and when liked, quarter teaspoonful of pounded mace, and sugar. Put in the forcemeat balls, simmer five minutes, and serve very hot. The wine may be omitted if preferred.

Time, four hours and a half. *Seasonable* in winter.

Note.—The bones of the head should be well stewed in the liquor it was first boiled in, and will make good white stock, flavored with vegetables, etc.

Mock Turtle, or Calf's Head Soup (*Economical*).—Boil the head till very tender, then take it up, strain the liquor, and set it away until the next day. Then skim off the fat, cut up the meat, together with the lights, and put them into the liquor, and stew the whole gently for half an hour. Season the soup with salt, pepper, and sweet herbs. Add cloves, or curry powder, if you want it seasoned highly, and, just as you take it up, stir in half a pint of white wine. If you wish for forcemeat balls in the soup, they should be prepared and added to the soup when put on to boil.

Clear Gravy Soup.—This may be made from shin of beef, which should not be large or coarse. The meat will be found serviceable for the table. From ten pounds of the meat let the butcher cut off five or six from the thick fleshy part, and again divide the knuckle, that the whole may lie compactly in the vessel in which it is to be stewed. Pour in three quarts of cold water, and when it has been brought slowly to boil, and been well skimmed, throw in an ounce and a half of salt, half a large teaspoonful of peppercorns, eight cloves, two blades of mace, a faggot of savory herbs, a couple of small carrots, and the heart of a root of celery; to these add a mild onion or not, at choice. When the whole has stewed very softly for four hours, probe the large bit of beef and, if quite tender, lift it out for table. Let the soup be simmered from two to three hours longer, and then strain it through a fine sieve, into a clean pan. When it is perfectly cold, clear off every particle of fat. Heat a couple of quarts; stir in, when it boils, half an ounce of sugar, a small tablespoonful of good soy, and twice as much of Harvey's sauce, or, instead of this, of clear and fine mushroom ketchup. If carefully made, the soup will be perfectly transparent, and of good color and flavor. A thick slice of ham will improve it, and a pound or so of the neck of beef, with an additional pint of water, will likewise enrich its quality. A small quantity of good broth may be made of the fragments of the whole, boiled down with a few fresh vegetables.

Ox Tail Soup. — INGREDIENTS. — *2 ox-tails, 2 slices of ham, 1 ounce of butter, 3 carrots, 2 turnips, 3 onions, 1 leek, 1 head of celery, 1 bunch of savory herbs, 1 bay-leaf, 12 whole peppercorns, 4 cloves, a tablespoonful of salt, 3 small lumps of sugar, 2 tablespoonfuls of ketchup, ½ glass of port wine, 3 quarts of water.*

Mode. — Cut up the tails, separating them at the joints. Wash them, and put them in a stewpan, with the butter. Put in half a pint of water, and stir them over a sharp fire till the juices are drawn. Fill up the stewpan with the water, and, when boiling, add the salt. Skim well. Cut the vegetables in slices, add them, with the peppercorns and herbs, and simmer very gently for four hours, or until the tails are tender. Take them out, skim and strain the soup, thicken with flour, and flavor with the ketchup and port wine. Put back the tails, simmer for five minutes, and serve.

Time, four and a half hours. *Seasonable* in winter.

Tomato Soup. — Take the remains of any roast meat you may happen to have, or beefsteak; boil it with more than sufficient water to cover it. When quite tender, take it out of the liquor, cut off all the fat, cut up the lean into small pieces, put it into the liquor, together with skinned ripe tomatoes, in the proportion of a dozen to three quarts of the liquor. Boil the whole

together for three-quarters of an hour, season it while boiling with a large spoonful of sugar, pepper, and salt, and add cloves if you like.

Oyster Soup. — Separate the oysters from the liquor; rinse the oysters in cold water, in order to get off the bits of shell which adhere to them; strain the liquor, and to each quart of it put a pint of milk, or water. Set it where it will boil, and thicken it when it boils with a little flour and water mixed smoothly together; season it with pepper, add a little vinegar, if you like, then put in the oysters, and let them be in just long enough to get scalded through; otherwise they will be hard. Add salt after taking up the soup; if added before it will shrink the oysters. Serve up the soup with crackers.

Pea Soup (Green).—INGREDIENTS. — *3 pints of green peas, ¼ pound of butter, 2 or 3 thin slices of ham, 4 onions sliced, 4 shredded lettuces, the crumbs of 2 French rolls, 2 handfuls of spinach, 1 lump of sugar, 2 quarts of stock.*

Mode. — Put the butter, ham, one quart of the peas, onions, and lettuces, to a pint of stock, and simmer for an hour; then add the remainder of the stock, with the crumbs of the French rolls, and boil for another hour. Now boil the spinach, squeeze it very dry, and rub it, *with the soup*, through a sieve, to give the preparation a good color. Have ready a pint of *young* peas boiled; add them to the soup, put in the sugar, give one boil, and serve. If necessary, add salt.

Time, two hours and a half. *Seasonable* from June to the end of August.

Note. — It will be well to add, if the peas are not quite young, a little more sugar. Where economy is essential, water may be used instead of stock for this soup, boiling in it likewise the peashells, and using rather a larger quantity of vegetables.

Winter Pea Soup (Yellow). — INGREDIENTS. — *1 quart of split peas, 2 pounds of shin of beef, trimmings of meat or poultry, a slice of bacon, 2 large carrots, 2 turnips, 5 large onions, 1 head of celery, seasoning to taste, 2 quarts of soft water, any bones left from roast meat, 2* quarts of common stock, or liquor in which a joint of meat has been boiled.

Mode. — Put the peas to soak over night in soft water, and float off such as rise to the top. Boil them in water till tender euough to pulp; then add the ingredients mentioned above, and simmer for two hours, stirring the soup occasionally, to prevent it from burning to the bottom of the saucepan. Press the whole through a sieve, skim well, season, and serve with toasted bread cut in dice.

Time, four hours. May be made all the year round, but is more suitable for cold weather.

Macaroni Soup. — *Time,* three-quarters of an hour.

INGREDIENTS. — 4 *ounces of macaroni,* 1 *large onion,* 5 *cloves,* 1 *ounce of butter, and* 2 *quarts of clear gravy soup.*

Put into a stewpan of boiling water four ounces of macaroni, one ounce of butter, and an onion stuck with five cloves. When the macaroni has become quite tender, drain it very dry, and pour on it two quarts of clear gravy soup. Let it simmer for ten minutes, taking care that the macaroni does not burst or become a pulp. It will then be ready to serve. It should be sent to table with grated Parmesan cheese.

Macaroni is a great improvement to white soup, or to clear gravy soup, but it must be previously boiled for twenty minutes in water.

Vegetable Soups. — The vegetables should be nicely prepared. Cut carrots in thin rounds, with the edges notched; grated, they give an amber color to soup; wash parsley carefully, and cut it small; cut turnips into thin slices, and then divide the round into four; cut leeks in slices; cut celery in half inch lengths, the delicate green leaves impart a fine flavor to the soup. Take the skins from tomatoes and squeeze out some of the seeds. Add a lump of sugar to soups of vegetables or roots, to soften them and improve the flavor.

Pepperpot. — *Time,* three hours and a half.

INGREDIENTS. — 4 *pounds of gravy beef,* 6 *quarts of water, a bouquet of savory herbs,* 2 *small crabs or lobsters, a large bunch of spinach,* ½ *a pound of cold bacon, a few suet dumplings (made of flour, beef-suet, and yolk of one egg),* 1 *pound of asparagus tops, Cayenne pepper, pepper and salt to taste, juice of a lemon.*

Put four pounds of gravy beef into six quarts of water, with the bouquet of savory herbs; let it simmer well till all the goodness is extracted, skimming it well. Let it stand till cold, that all the fat may be taken off it. Put it into a stewpan and heat it. When hot, add the flesh of two middling-sized crabs or lobsters, nicely cut up, spinach well boiled and chopped fine, half a pound of cold bacon or pickled pork, dressed previously and cut into small pieces, a few small dumplings, made very light with flour, beef-suet, yolk of egg, and a little water. Add one pound of asparagus tops, season to your taste with Cayenne, salt, pepper, and juice of a lemon; stew for about half an hour, stirring it constantly.

Beef Extract (AS RECOMMENDED BY BARON LIEBIG). — Take a pound of good juicy beef from which all the skin and fat has been cut away, chop it up like sausage meat; mix it thoroughly with a pint of cold water, place it on the side of the stove to heat *very slowly,* and give an occasional stir. It may stand two or three hours before it is allowed to simmer, and will then require but fifteen minutes of gentle boiling. Salt should be added when the boiling commences, and this, for invalids in general, is the only seasoning required. When the extract is thus far prepared, it may be poured from the meat into a basin, and allowed to stand until any particles of fat on the surface can be skimmed off, and the sediment has subsided and left the soup quite clear, when it may be poured off gently, heated in a clean saucepan, and served. The scum should be well cleared as it accumulates.

Beef Glaze, or Portable Soup, is simply the essence of beef condensed by evaporation. It may be put into pots, like potted meats, or into skins, as sausages, and will keep for many months. If further dried in cakes or lozenges, by being laid on pans or dishes, and frequently turned, it will keep for years, and supply soup at any moment.

Four Excellent Sandwiches. —

Cheese: Take two-thirds of good cheese, grated, and one-third of butter, add a little cream; pound all together in a mortar; then spread it on slices of brown bread; lay another slice over each; press them gently together, and cut in small square pieces. — *Egg:* Boil fresh eggs for five minutes; put them in cold water, and when quite cold, peel them, and after taking a little of the white off each one of the eggs, cut the remainder in four slices; lay them between bread and butter. — *Fried Egg:* Beat some eggs well; fry them in butter as a pancake; when cold, cut them in small squares, and lay them between slices of brown bread and butter. — *Omelet:* Take four eggs, two tablespoonfuls of bread crumbs, and half an ounce of chopped parsley. After beating the eggs well, add the bread crumbs, then the parsley, and two tablespoonfuls of water; season, and fry in small fritters, and when cold, put them between slices of brown bread and butter.

FISH. — GENERAL RULE IN CHOOSING FISH. —

A proof of freshness and goodness in most fishes is their being covered with scales; for, if deficient in this respect, it is a sign of their being stale, or having been ill-used.

Cod's Head and Shoulders. —

INGREDIENTS. — *Sufficient water to cover the fish; 5 ounces of salt to each gallon of water.*

Mode. — Cleanse the fish thoroughly, and rub a very little salt over the thick part and inside of the fish, one or two hours before dressing it, as this very much improves the flavor. Lay it in the fish-kettle, with sufficient cold water to cover it. Be very particular not to pour the water on the fish, as it is liable to break it, and only keep it just simmering. If the water should

boil away, add a little by pouring it in at the side of the kettle, and not on the fish. Add salt in the above proportion, and bring it gradually to a boil. Skim very carefully, draw it to the side of the fire, and let it gently simmer till done. Take it out and drain it; serve on a hot napkin, and garnish with cut lemon, horseradish, and the liver.

Time, according to size, half an hour, more or less. *Seasonable* from November to March.

Note. — Oyster sauce and plain melted butter should be served with this.

To Choose Cod. —

The cod should be chosen for the table when it is plump and round near the tail, when the hollow behind the head is deep, and when the sides are undulated as if they were ribbed. The glutinous parts about the head lose their delicate flavor after the fish has been twenty-four hours out of the water. The great point by which the cod should be judged is the firmness of its flesh; and although the cod is not firm when it is alive, its quality may be arrived at by pressing the finger into the flesh. If this rises immediately, the fish is good; if not, it is stale. Another sign of its goodness is, if the fish, when it is cut, exhibits a bronze appearance, like the silver side of a round of beef. When this is the case, the flesh will be firm when cooked. Stiffness in a cod, or in any other fish, is a sure sign of freshness, though not always of quality. Sometimes codfish, though exhibiting signs of rough usage, will eat much better than those with red gills, so strongly recommended by many cookery-books. This appearance is generally caused by the fish having been knocked about at sea, in the well-boats, in which they are conveyed from the fishing-grounds to market.

Salt Cod, commonly called "Salt Fish." —

Wash the fish, and lay it all night in water, with a quarter pint of vinegar. When thoroughly soaked, take it out, see that it is perfectly clean, and put it in the fish-kettle, with sufficient cold water to cover it. Heat it gradually, and do not let it boil fast, or the fish will be hard. Skim well, and when done, drain the fish, and put it on a napkin garnished with hard-boiled eggs, cut in rings.

Time, about one hour. *Seasonable* in the spring.

Note.—Serve with egg sauce and parsnips. This is an especial dish on Ash Wednesday.

Cod Pie (*Economical*). — INGREDIENTS. — *Any remains of cold cod,* 12 *oysters, sufficient melted butter to moisten it, mashed potatoes enough to fill up the dish.*

Mode. — Flake the fish from the bone, and carefully take away all the skin. Lay it in a pie-dish, pour over the melted butter and oysters (or oyster sauce, if there is any left), and cover with mashed potatoes. Bake for half an hour, and send to table of a nice brown color.

Time, half an hour. *Seasonable* from November to March.

Fried Eels. — INGREDIENTS. — 1 *pound of eels,* 1 *egg, a few bread crumbs, hot lard.*

Mode. — Wash the eels, cut them into pieces three inches long, trim, and wipe them very dry. Dredge with flour, rub them over with egg, and cover with bread crumbs. Fry of a nice brown in hot lard. If the eels are small, curl them round, instead of cutting them up. Garnish with fried parsley.

Time, twenty minutes or rather less. *Seasonable* from June to March.

Eel Pie. — INGREDIENTS. — 1 *pound of eels, a little chopped parsley,* 1 *shallot, grated nutmeg, pepper and salt to taste, the juice of* ½ *a lemon, small quantity of forcemeat,* ¼ *pint of good gravy, puff paste.*

Mode. — Skin and wash the eels, cut them into pieces two inches long, and line the bottom of the pie-dish with forcemeat. Put in the eels and sprinkle them with the parsley, shallots, nutmeg, seasoning, and lemon-juice, and cover with puff paste. Bake for one hour, or rather more. Make the gravy hot, pour it into the pie, and serve.

Time, rather more than one hour. *Seasonable* from June to March.

Fish and Oyster Pie. — INGREDIENTS. — *Any remains of cold fish, such as cod or haddock,* 2 *dozen oysters, pepper and salt to taste, bread crumbs sufficient for the quantity of fish,* ¼ *teaspoonful of grated nutmeg,* 1 *teaspoonful of finely chopped parsley, some made melted butter.*

Mode. — Clear the fish from the bones, and put a layer of it in a pie-dish, which sprinkle with pepper and salt; then a layer of bread crumbs, oysters, nutmeg, and chopped parsley. Repeat this till the dish is quite full. A covering may be formed either of bread crumbs, which should be browned, or puff paste. The latter should be cut into long strips, and laid in cross-bars over the fish, with a line of the paste first laid round the edge. Before putting on the top, pour in some made melted butter, or a little thin white sauce, and the oyster liquor, and bake.

Time, if made of cooked fish, quarter to half an hour. If made of fresh fish and puff paste, three-quarters of an hour. *Seasonable* from September to April.

Note.— A nice little dish may be made by flaking any cold fish, adding a few oysters, seasoning with pepper and salt, and covering with mashed potatoes. A quarter to half an hour will bake it.

Baked Haddock.—Fill the interior of the fish with veal stuffing. Sew it up with packthread, and truss it with the tail in its mouth. Rub a piece of butter over the back, or egg, and bread crumb it over. Set it on a baking-dish, which put into a moderate oven to bake. A common haddock would require but half an hour. The better plan is to run the point of a knife down to the backbone, from which if the flesh parts easily, it is done. Dress it upon a dish without a napkin, and serve a sauce round.

Boiled Haddock. — INGREDIENTS. — *Sufficient water to cover the fish,* ¼ *pound of salt to each gallon of water.*

Mode. — Scrape the fish, take out the inside, wash it thoroughly, and lay it in a kettle, with enough water to cover it, adding salt in the above proportion. Simmer gently from fifteen to twenty minutes, or rather more, should the fish be very large. For small haddocks, fasten the tails in their mouth, and put them into boiling water; ten to fifteen minutes will cook them. Serve with plain melted butter, or anchovy sauce.

Time, large haddock, half an hour; small, a quarter of an hour, or rather less. *Seasonable* from August to February.

Lobster Salad. — INGREDIENTS. — 1 *hen lobster, lettuces, endive, small salad (whatever is in season), a little chopped beetroot, 2 hard-boiled eggs, a few slices of cucumber. For dressing, equal quantities of oil and vinegar, 1 teaspoonful of made mustard, the yolks of 2 eggs, Cayenne and salt to taste, ¼ teaspoonful of anchovy sauce. These ingredients should be mixed perfectly smooth, and form a creamy-looking sauce.*

Mode. — Wash the salad, and thoroughly dry it by shaking it in a cloth. Cut up the lettuces and endive, pour the dressing on them, and lightly throw in the small salad. Mix all well together with the pickings from the body of the lobster; pick the meat from the shell, cut it up into nice square pieces; put half in the salad, the other half reserve for garnishing.

To Boil a Lobster. — *Time,* half an hour.

Boiling a lobster may be made a horrible operation if the advice we are about to give is not attended to; and its cries in dying are said to be most painful. Happily, it is possible to kill it immediately. It is done thus:

Put into a large kettle water enough to cover the lobster, with a quarter of a pound of salt to every gallon of water. When it boils fast put in the lobster, *head first;* this is a little difficult to achieve, as the lobster is not easy to hold thus over the hot steam, but we are sure any humane cook will do it. If the head goes in first it is killed instantly. Boil it briskly for an hour, then take it from the hot water with the tongs, and lay it to drain. Wipe off all the scum from it; tie a little piece of butter in a cloth and rub it over with it.

A lobster weighing a pound takes one hour to boil, others in like proportion, more or less.

To Dress Lobsters. — When sent to the table, separate the body from the tail, remove the large claws, and crack them at each joint carefully, and split the tail down the middle with a sharp knife; place the body upright in the centre of a dish on a napkin, and arrange the tail and claws on each side. Garnish it with double parsley.

To Make Anchovies. — Procure a quantity of sprats, as fresh as possible; do not wash or wipe them, but just take them as caught, and for every peck of the fish, take two pounds of common salt, a quarter of a pound of bay salt, four pounds of saltpetre, two ounces of sal-prunella, and two-pennyworth of cochineal. Pound all these ingredients in a mortar, mixing them well together. Then take stone jars or small kegs, according to your quantity of sprats, and place a layer of the fish and a layer of the mixed ingredients alternately, until the pot is full; then press hard down, and cover close for six months; they will then be fit for use. We can vouch for the excellence and cheapness of the anchovies made in this manner. In fact, most of the *fine Gorgona* anchovies sold in the oil and pickle shops are made in this or a similar manner, from British sprats.

Boiled Mackerel. — INGREDIENTS. — ¼ *pound of salt to each gallon of water.*

Mode. — Cleanse the inside of the fish thoroughly, and lay them in the kettle with sufficient water to cover them, with salt as above; bring them gradually to boil, skim well, and simmer gently till done; dish them on a hot napkin, heads and tails alternately, and garnish with fennel. Fennel sauce and plain melted butter are the usual accompaniments to boiled mackerel; but caper or anchovy sauce is sometimes served with it.

Time, after the water boils, ten minutes; for large mackerel, allow more time. *Seasonable* from April to July.

Note. — When variety is desired, fillet the mackerel, boil it, and pour over parsley and butter; send some of this, besides, in a tureen.

To Choose Mackerel. — In choosing this fish, purchasers should, to a great extent, be regulated by the brightness of its appearance. If it have a transparent, silvery hue, the flesh is good; but if it be red about the head, it is stale.

Broiled Mackerel. — INGREDIENTS. — *Pepper and salt to taste; a small quantity of oil.*
Mode. — Mackerel should never be washed when intended to be broiled, but merely wipe very clean and dry, after taking out the gills and insides. Open the back, and put in a little pepper, salt, and oil; broil it over a clear fire, turn it over on both sides, and also on the back. When sufficiently cooked, the flesh can be detached from the bone, which will be in about ten minutes for a small mackerel. Chop a little parsley, work it up in the butter, with pepper and salt to taste, and a squeeze of lemon-juice, and put it in the back. Serve before the butter is quite melted, with anchovy sauce in a tureen.
Time, small mackerel ten minutes. *Seasonable* from April to July.

Baked Mackerel. — INGREDIENTS. — *4 middling-sized mackerel, a nice delicate forcemeat, 3 ounces of butter, pepper and salt to taste.*
Mode. — Clean the fish, take out the roes, fill up with forcemeat, and sew up the slit. Flour, and put them in a dish, heads and tails alternately, with the roes; and between each layer put some little pieces of butter, and pepper and salt. Bake for half an hour, and either serve with plain melted butter or anchovy sauce.
Time, half an hour. *Seasonable* from April to July.

Note. — Baked mackerel may be dressed in the same way as baked herrings, and may also be stewed in wine.

Pickled Mackerel. — INGREDIENTS. — *12 peppercorns, 2 bay-leaves, ¼ pint of vinegar, 4 mackerel.*
Mode. — Boil the mackerel as in the recipe, and lay them in a dish; take half the liquor they were boiled in; add as much vinegar, and the above proportion of peppercorns and bay-leaves; boil this mixture for ten minutes, and when cold, pour it over the fish.

Boiled Salmon. — INGREDIENTS. — *6 ounces of salt to each gallon of water, sufficient water to cover the fish.*
Mode. — Scale and clean the fish, and be particular that no blood is left inside; lay it in the fish-kettle with sufficient cold water to cover it, adding salt in the above proportion. Bring it quickly to a boil, take off all the scum, and let it simmer gently till the fish is done, which will be when the meat separates easily from the bone. Experience alone can teach the cook to fix the time for boiling fish; but it is especially to be remembered, that it should never be underdressed, as then nothing is more unwholesome. Neither let it remain in the kettle after it is sufficiently cooked, as that would render it insipid, watery, and colorless. Drain it; and if not wanted for a few minutes, keep it warm by means of warm cloths laid over it. Serve on a hot napkin, garnish with cut lemon and parsley, and send lobster or shrimp sauce and plain melted butter to table with it. A dish of dressed cucumber usually accompanies this fish.
Time, eight minutes to each pound for large thick salmon; six minutes for thin fish. *Seasonable* from April to August.

Note. — Cut lemon should be put on the table with this fish; and a little of the juice squeezed over it is considered by many persons a most agreeable addition. Boiled peas are also, by some connoisseurs, considered especially adapted to be served with salmon.

To Choose Salmon. — To be good the belly should be firm and thick, which may readily be ascertained by feeling it with the thumb and finger.

The circumstance of this fish having red gills, though given as a standing rule in most cookery-books, as a sign of its goodness, is not at all to be relied on, as this quality can be easily given them by art.

Salmon Cutlets.—Cut the slices one inch thick, and season them with pepper and salt; butter a sheet of white paper, lay each slice on a separate piece, with their ends twisted: broil gently over a clear fire, and serve with anchovy or caper sauce. When higher seasoning is required, add a few chopped herbs and a little spice.

Time, five to ten minutes.

Pickled Salmon.—INGREDIENTS. —*Salmon,* ½ *ounce of whole pepper,* ½ *ounce of whole allspice,* 1 *teaspoonful of salt,* 2 *bay-leaves, equal quantities of vinegar and the liquor in which the fish was boiled.*

Mode.—After the fish comes from table, lay it in a nice dish with a cover to it, as it should be excluded from the air, and take away the bone; boil the liquor and vinegar with the other ingredients for ten minutes, and let it stand to get cold; pour it over the salmon, and in twelve hours it will be fit for the table.

Time, ten minutes.

SHAD.—Fresh shad are good baked or broiled, but much the best broiled. For broiling, sprinkle on salt and pepper in the inside when cleaned, and let them remain a number of hours. If fresh, they may be kept eight or ten hours in a cool place. The spawn and liver are good fried or boiled. Salt shad for broiling should be soaked ten or twelve hours in cold water; for boiling they need not be soaked only long enough to enable the scales to be removed easily, unless liked quite fresh; if so, soak them in lukewarm water for an hour.

Fried Fish.—After cleaning and washing the fish, lay them on a towel to absorb all the moisture. When thoroughly dried, rub over them flour or Indian meal; use no salt to them, as it will prevent their browning well. If you have salt pork, fry a few slices;

take them up, and put in the fish, and fry them till quite brown on both sides. The fat should be quite hot when they are put in. If you have not pork, use lard or beef drippings for frying; but do not use butter, as it gives them a bad taste and dingy color. When you have taken up the fish, mix a little flour and water smoothly together, and stir it into the fat in which the fish was fried. Season the gravy with pepper and salt, and if you wish a very rich gravy, add a little butter, wine, and ketchup, or spices; turn it, when it boils up, on the fish.

To Bake Smelts.—INGREDIENTS.— 12 *smelts, bread crumbs,* ¼ *pound of fresh butter,* 2 *blades of pounded mace, salt and Cayenne to taste.*

Mode.—Wash, and dry the fish thoroughly in a cloth, and arrange them nicely in a flat baking dish. Cover them with fine bread crumbs, and place little pieces of butter all over them. Season and bake for fifteen minutes. Just before serving, add a squeeze of lemon-juice, and garnish with fried parsley and cut lemon.

Time, quarter of an hour. *Seasonable* from October to May.

To Choose Smelts.—When good, this fish is of a fine silvery appearance, and when alive, their backs are of a dark brown shade, which, after death, fades to a light fawn. They ought to have a refreshing fragrance, resembling that of a cucumber.

To Fry Smelts.—INGREDIENTS.— *Egg and bread crumbs, a little flour, boiling lard.*

Mode.—Smelts should be very fresh, and not washed more than is necessary to clean them. Dry them in a cloth, lightly flour, dip them in egg, sprinkle over with very fine bread crumbs, and put them into boiling lard. Fry of a nice pale brown, and be careful not to take off the light roughness of the crumbs, or their beauty will be spoiled. Dry them before the fire on a drainer, and serve with plain melted butter. This fish is often used as a garnish.

Time, five minutes. *Seasonable* from October to May.

CHOWDER. — Clean the fish, and cut it up into a number of slices. Fry six, or more, slices of pork, if the chowder is to be a large one ; take them up, and put in the pork-fat, a layer of the fish, several bits of the fried pork, crackers that have been soaked tender in cold water, season with salt and pepper, and add onions and spices to it, if you like. This process repeat till you get in all the fish required for the chowder ; then turn in sufficient cold water to cover the whole, and stew the fish from twenty-five to thirty minutes. When you have taken the fish out of the pot, thicken the gravy with mixed flour and water, add a little butter, and if you want it rich, stir in half a pint of white wine, or a large spoonful of ketchup. Bass and cod are the best fish for chowder. Black fish and clams make tolerably good ones ; the hard part of the clams should be thrown away.

Cod Sounds and Tongues. — Soak them in lukewarm water three or four hours, then scrape off the skin, cut them in two, and stew them in milk. Just before taking them up, stir in a little butter and flour.

HALIBUT. — Is nice cut in slices, salted, and peppered, then broiled or fried. The fins and thick part are good boiled.

Black Fish. — They are best boiled or fried. They will do to broil, but are not so good as when cooked in any other way.

Fish Forcemeat Balls. — Chop a little uncooked fresh fish with salt pork, mix with them two raw eggs, a few fine bread crumbs, and season with pepper and spices, if you like. Do the mixture up into small balls, and fry them until brown.

Fish Cakes. — Chop cold fresh fish that has been previously cooked with raw salt pork, mix with bread crumbs two or three raw eggs, season the mixture with salt and pepper, and mould it up into small cakes, and fry till brown in lard. Cold salt codfish may be chopped with potatoes, moistened with a little water, a little melted butter added, and moulded into small cakes.

14

Flour the hands, to prevent them sticking. Have pork-fat in your frying-pan quite hot, then put them in, and fry till brown on both sides. This is an easy way of making them, when you have cooked potatoes; but they are the best to have the potatoes fresh boiled, and mashed, instead of being chopped ; mix them with the fish and add butter and water to moisten the whole ; then take up a portion of the fish in a tablespoon, mash it down compactly with a knife, and scrape it out with the knife into the frying-pan, so as to form a small cake. This repeat until you get the pan full. The fat for them, as well as for all other kinds of fish, should be quite hot when they are put in, or they will soak up the fat and be greasy, and not brown.

SCOLLOPS. — Boil them, and take them out of the shells ; when boiled, pick out the hearts and throw the rest away, as the heart is the only part that is fit to eat. They are good pickled like oysters after boiling, or fried. Dip them in flour, and fry them brown. They are also good stewed, with a little water, salt, and pepper ; add butter when you remove from the fire.

TROUT. — These, as well as all other kinds of fresh fish, are apt to have an earthy taste. It can be removed by soaking them in salt and water for a few minutes after cleaning. They may be boiled, broiled, or fried ; the small ones are the best fried. They are also good stewed, with a little water and bits of salt pork.

CLAMS. — Wash and put them in a pot, with enough water to prevent their burning at the bottom of the pot. Heat them till the shells open, then take them out and warm them up, with a little of the clam broth ; season with salt and pepper, add butter when you take them up, have a couple of slices of buttered toast in the dish with the clams, putting in enough of the broth to soak the toast. Long clams, if large, are nice taken out of the shells and broiled.

Clam Pancakes. — Mix flour and milk together, so as to form a thick batter; to each pint of the milk put a couple of eggs and a few clams. If they are quite small, stew them and put them in whole; if large, take them out of the shells, without stewing, and chop them; season the batter with salt and pepper, and drop it, by the large spoonful, into hot fat. Some cooks use the clam liquor, instead of milk, for pancakes, but it does not make them as light as the milk.

EELS. — If small, are the best fried; If large, split them open, salt, and pepper, and cut them into pieces of about a finger's length. Let them remain several hours before broiling.

Stewed Oysters. — Strain the liquor, and rinse off the bits of shell that adhere to the oyster. Heat the liquor with the oysters. If there is not much of it, a little water may be added. As soon as scalding hot, turn them on to buttered toast, and season with salt and pepper. They should not be allowed to boil, and no salt added to them till cooked; if so, they will shrink and be hard. Oysters should be eaten as soon as cooked.

Fried Oysters. — Take those that are large, dip them in beaten eggs, then in flour, or fine bread crumbs, and fry them in lard. They are also good dipped into a batter like that for oyster pancakes, and then fried. They are a nice garnish for fish. They can be kept for several months, if fried when first caught, seasoned well with salt and pepper, then corked up tight in a bottle. Whenever they are to be eaten, warm them in a little water.

Oyster Pancakes. — Mix equal quantities of oyster juice and milk, and to a pint of the mixed liquor put a pint of wheat flour, a couple of beaten eggs, a little salt, and a few of the oysters. Drop by the large spoonful into hot lard.

Oyster Pie. — Line a deep pie-plate with pie-crust, fill it with dry pieces of bread, cover it with nice pastry, and bake it in a quick oven till of a light brown. Have the oysters stewed, and seasoned just as the pastry is baked. Take off the upper crust, remove the bread, and put in the oysters. Cover with the crust, and serve up while hot.

Scolloped Oysters. — Pound crackers or rusked bread fine. Then butter scolloped shell or small tinpans, put in alternate layers of the crumbs and oysters, having a layer of the crumbs on the top. Season them with salt and pepper, and add a little butter, and enough oyster juice to moisten the whole. Bake them till brown.

Apple Sauce for Geese, Pork, etc. — INGREDIENTS. — 6 good-sized apples, sifted sugar to taste, a piece of butter the size of a walnut, water.

Mode.—Pare, core, and quarter the apples, and throw them into cold water to preserve their whiteness. Put them in a saucepan, with sufficient water to moisten them, and boil till soft enough to pulp. Beat them up, adding sugar to taste, and a small piece of butter. This quantity is sufficient for a good-sized tureen.

Time, according to the apples, about three-quarters of an hour. This quantity is sufficient for a goose or couple of ducks. *Seasonable* from August to March.

Bread Sauce, to serve with Roast Turkey, Fowl, Game, etc.

INGREDIENTS. — 1 *pint of milk, ¾ of a pound of the crumbs of a stale loaf, 1 onion, pounded mace, Cayenne, and salt to taste, 1 ounce of butter.*

Mode. — Peel and quarter the onion, and simmer it in the milk till perfectly tender. Break the bread, which should be stale, into small pieces, carefully picking out any hard outside pieces; put it in a very clean saucepan, strain the milk over it, cover it up, and let it remain for an hour to soak. Now beat it up with a fork very smoothly, add a seasoning of pounded mace, Cayenne, and salt, with one ounce of butter; give the whole one boil, and serve. To enrich this sauce, a small quantity of cream may be added just before sending it to table.

Time, altogether, one hour and three-quarters. *Sufficient* to serve with a turkey, pair of fowls, or brace of partridges.

Caper Sauce for Boiled Mutton.—

INGREDIENTS.— ½ pint of melted butter, 3 tablespoonfuls of capers or nasturtiums, 1 tablespoonful of their liquor.

Mode.— Chop the capers twice or thrice, and add them, with their liquor, to half a pint of melted butter, made very smoothly; keep stirring well; let the sauce just simmer, and serve in a tureen. Pickled nasturtium pods are fine.

Melted Butter. — INGREDIENTS. —

½ pound of butter, a dessertspoonful of flour, a teacupful of water, salt to taste.

Mode. — Cut the butter up into small pieces, put it into a saucepan, dredge over the flour, and add the water and a seasoning of salt; stir it one way constantly till the whole of the ingredients are melted and thoroughly blended. Let it just boil, when it is ready to serve. If the butter is to be melted with cream, use the same quantity as of water, but omit the flour; keep stirring it, but do not allow it to boil.

Time, one minute to simmer.

Melted Butter made with Milk.—

INGREDIENTS. — 1 teaspoonful of flour, 2 ounces of butter, ½ pint of milk, a few grains of salt.

Mode. — Mix the butter and flour smoothly together on a plate; put it into a lined saucepan, and pour in the milk. Keep stirring it one way over a sharp fire; let it boil quickly for a minute or two, and it is ready to serve. This is a very good foundation for onion, lobster, or oyster sauce, and is the melted butter we recommend in preference to either of the preceding: using milk instead of water makes the preparation look so much whiter and more delicate.

Time, altogether, ten minutes.

Egg Sauce for Salt Fish.—

INGREDIENTS. — 4 eggs, ½ pint of melted butter, when liked a very little lemon-juice.

Mode. — Boil the eggs until quite hard, which will be in about twenty minutes, and put them into cold water for half an hour. Strip off the shells, chop the eggs into small pieces, not, however, too fine. Make the melted butter very smoothly; when boiling, stir in the eggs, and serve very hot. Lemon-juice may be added at pleasure.

Time, twenty minutes to boil the eggs. Sufficient for three or four pounds of fish.

Note.— When a thicker sauce is required, use one or two more eggs to the same quantity of melted butter.

Mint Sauce, to serve with Roast Lamb. — INGREDIENTS. — 4 dessert-spoonfuls of chopped mint, 2 dessert-spoonfuls of pounded white sugar, ¼ pint of vinegar.

Mode.—Wash the mint, which should be young and fresh-gathered, free from grit; pick the leaves from the stalks, mince them very fine, and put them into a tureen; add the sugar and vinegar, and stir till the former is dissolved. This sauce is better by being made two or three hours before wanted for table, as the vinegar then becomes impregnated with the flavor of the mint. By many persons, the above proportion of sugar would not be considered sufficient; but as tastes vary, we have given the quantity which we have found to suit the general palate. Sufficient to serve with a middling-sized joint of lamb.

Note.— Where green mint is scarce and not obtainable, mint vinegar may be substituted for it, and will be found very acceptable in early spring.

Oyster Sauce, to serve with Fish, Boiled Poultry, etc. — INGREDIENTS. — 3 dozen oysters, ½ pint of melted butter, made with milk.

Mode. — Open the oysters carefully, and save their liquor; strain it into a clean saucepan (a lined one is best), put in the oysters, and let them just come to the boiling-point, when they should look plump. Take them off the fire immediately, and put the whole into a basin. Strain the liquor from them, mix with it sufficient milk to make half a pint altogether. When the melted butter is ready and very smooth, put in the oysters. Set it by the side of the fire to get thoroughly hot, but do not allow it to boil, or the oysters will immediately harden. Using cream instead of milk makes this sauce extremely delicious. When liked, add a seasoning of Cayenne, or anchovy sauce; but, as we have before stated, a plain sauce *should* be plain, and not be overpowered by highly-flavored essences; therefore we recommend that the above directions be implicitly followed, and no seasoning added. *Sufficient* for six persons. Never allow fewer than six oysters to one person, unless the party is very large. *Seasonable* from September to April.

Parsley and Butter, to serve with Calf's Head, Boiled Fowls, etc.— INGREDIENTS. — *2 tablespoonfuls of minced parsley, ½ pint of melted butter.*

Mode. — Put into a saucepan a small quantity of water, slightly salted, and when it boils, throw in a good bunch of parsley which has been previously washed and tied together in a bunch; let it boil for five minutes, drain it, mince the leaves *very fine*, and put the above quantity in a tureen; pour over it half pint of smoothly made melted butter; stir once, that the ingredients may be thoroughly mixed, and serve.

Time, five minutes to boil the parsley. *Sufficient* for one large fowl; allow rather more for a pair. *Seasonable* at any time.

White Onion Sauce for Boiled Rabbits, Roast Shoulder of Mutton, etc.— INGREDIENTS. — *9 large onions or 12 middle-sized ones, 1 pint melted butter made with milk, ½ teaspoonful of salt.*

Mode. — Peel the onions and put them into water, to which a little salt has been added, to preserve their whiteness, and let them remain for a quarter of an hour, then put them in a stewpan, cover them with water, and let them boil one hour, or until tender, and if the onions should be very strong, change the water after they have been boiling a quarter of an hour. Train them thoroughly, chop them, and rub them through a sieve. Make one pint of melted butter, and when that boils, put in the onions, with a seasoning of salt; stir it till it simmers, when it will be ready to serve.

Sauce for Cold Meat, Fish, or Salad. — Boil a couple of eggs three minutes, mix them with half a teacup of salad oil, or melted butter, half a cup of vinegar, a teaspoonful of made mustard, a little salt and pepper. Add, if you like, a large spoonful of ketchup.

Wine Sauce for Venison or Mutton. — Warm half a pint of the drippings, and mix together a couple of teaspoonfuls of flour, with a little water, so that it will be free from lumps, and stir into it the drippings, when boiling. Season the gravy with salt, pepper, and cloves, and stir in, just before removing from the fire, a gill of white wine.

Rice Sauce. — Boil half a teacup of rice with an onion, and a blade of mace, till the rice is quite soft; if it has not then absorbed the water, turn it off, stir in two-thirds of a pint of milk, a teaspoonful of salt, and strain the sauce. This is a nice accompaniment to game.

Cranberry Sauce. — Stew the cranberries till soft, with a little water; when tender, add sugar sufficient to sweeten; let it scald in well. Strain it, if you like; it is good without straining.

Tomato Sauce. — *Time*, one hour and five minutes.

INGREDIENTS. — *6 tomatoes, ½ an ounce of celery, 1 ounce of butter, 1 ounce of bacon, ½ an onion, a bay-leaf, a bunch of thyme, a little salt, pepper, Cayenne, ½ a pint of broth, and a little flour.*

Mode. — Take out the seeds and remove the stalks from six tomatoes, put them into a stewpan with half an ounce of celery, one ounce of butter, one ounce of bacon, half an onion cut into slices, a bay-leaf, a bunch of thyme, pepper, salt, and Cayenne. Stew it gently until tender, then stir in the flour, moisten with half a pint of broth, boil it up for five or six minutes, strain it through a sieve, and then put it back into the stewpan to simmer until rather thick. Serve it with meat or poultry.

Tomato Ketchup. — To each gallon

of ripe tomatoes, pour four table-spoonfuls of salt, five of black pepper, three of ground mustard, half a large spoonful of allspice, the same of cloves, simmer the whole slowly together, with a little water at the bottom of the stewpan to prevent their burning. Let them stew slowly for three hours, then strain through a sieve. When cold, bottle, and cork, and seal them; keep them in a cool cellar. The ketchup should be made in tin, and as late in the season as practicable, in order to have it keep well.

Stewed Tomatoes.—They should be fully ripe; and to make them skin easily, turn on boiling water, and let them remain in it four or five minutes. When peeled, put them in a stewpan. If not quite ripe and juicy, put in a very little water to prevent their burning. When they have stewed a few minutes, they are improved by turning off part of the juice. Season them with salt, pepper, and sugar, in the proportion of a couple of teaspoonfuls of sugar to half a peck of tomatoes. Stew them half an hour, then turn them on to buttered toast. They are considered very nice by epicures cooked as follows: Skin and lay them in a deep dish, with alternate layers of bread crumbs; season each layer with salt, pepper, a little sugar, a small bit of butter, and add cloves if you like. Have a layer of bread crumbs on top, and bake three-quarters of an hour.

Tomato Ketchup.—Take good solid tomatoes, wash clean and drain all the water off them, cut up and mash into a kettle, boil till they are in rags, then rub them through a cullender, crushing them through till nothing but the skin remains, then strain through a wire sieve, leaving nothing but the seeds, then put 3 half pints salt, 4 ounces mustard, 3 ounces pepper, ½ ounce red pepper, 4 nutmegs grated, ground cinnamon and ginger each 2 ounces, whole cloves and allspice each 2 ounces, put in a muslin bag with ½ ounce mace, put in the spices cold and stir till it thickens; boil 4 hours, then

add 3 pints (or 4 if very thick) of the very best cider vinegar, boil 4 hours more on a moderate fire, clean the bottles well before putting in the ketchup.

Mushroom Ketchup.—Put a layer of fresh mushrooms in a deep dish, sprinkle a little salt over them, add successive layers of mushrooms and salt till you get them all into the dish. Let them remain a number of days, then mash them fine, and to each quart put a tablespoonful of vinegar, half a teaspoonful of black pepper, and a quarter of a teaspoonful of cloves. Turn the whole into a stone jar, set it into a pot of hot water, and boil it a couple of hours. Strain without squeezing the mushrooms. Boil the juice a quarter of an hour, and strain it well. When cold, bottle, cork, and seal up tight, and keep it in a cool place.

Essence of Mushroom.—This delicate relish is made by sprinkling a little salt over either flap or button mushrooms; three hours after, mash them, next day strain off the liquor that will flow from them, put it into a stewpan, and boil it till it is reduced one half. I⁺ will not keep long, but is preferable to any of the ketchups containing spices, etc., to preserve them, which overpowers the flavor of the mushrooms. An artificial mushroom bed will supply these all the year round.

Hot Sauce, resembling Worcestershire Sauce. — *Time*, ten days.

INGREDIENTS. — *¾ of an ounce of Cayenne pepper, 1 quart of vinegar, 2 tablespoonfuls of soy, 3 cloves of garlic, 5 anchovies, 3 cloves of shallots.*

Mode. — Mix well and rub through a sieve three-quarters of an ounce of Cayenne pepper, two tablespoonfuls of soy, three cloves of garlic pounded, five anchovies, bruised fine, and three cloves of shallots pounded, add one quart of vinegar. Strain, and keep it corked up for ten days, then bottle it up for use. It can be strained or not, as preferred.

Gooseberry Sauce.—Take fruit,

just ripe, pick off the tops and stems, and weigh an equal quantity of sugar to the fruit, dividing the sugar into two equal portions. Make a syrup of one portion, and put the gooseberries into it, over the fire; let them remain till they are transparent, then remove them, and make a syrup of the reserved sugar, adding to it the syrup of the gooseberries, gently dipping it off. Let it boil till thick and rich, and then pour it over the fruit. The fruit, by this process, will be less tough, and keep its flavor better than if cooked longer.

Bread Sauce for Roast Turkey, or Game. — *Time,* one hour and a half.

INGREDIENTS. — 1 *pint of milk, breakfastcupful of stale bread,* 1 *onion, a little mace, Cayenne, and salt,* 1 *ounce of butter.*

Mode. — Peel and slice an onion, and simmer it in a pint of new milk until tender, break the bread into pieces, and put it into a stewpan. Strain the hot milk over it, cover it close, and let it soak for an hour. Then beat it up smooth with a fork, add the pounded mace, Cayenne, salt, and an ounce of butter. Boil it up, serve it in a tureen. The onion must be taken out before the milk is poured over the bread.

Chestnut Sauce for Turkey or Fowls. — *Time,* one hour and thirty-five minutes.

INGREDIENTS. — ½ *a pint of veal stock,* ½ *a pound of chestnuts, peel of* ½ *a lemon, a cupful of cream or milk, a very little Cayenne and salt.*

Mode. — Remove the dark shell of the chestnuts, and scald them until the inner skin can be easily taken off. Then put them into a stewpan with the stock, the lemon-peel cut very thin, and a very little Cayenne pepper and salt. Let it simmer until the chestnuts are quite soft. Rub or press it through a sieve, add the seasoning and cream, and let it simmer for a few minutes, stirring it constantly, but taking care it does not boil.

Oyster Ketchup. — Take fine, fresh oysters; wash them in their own liquor, strain it, pound them in a marble mortar; to a pint of oysters add a pint of sherry; boil them up, and add an ounce of salt, two drams of pounded mace, and one of Cayenne; let it just boil up again, skim it, and rub it through a sieve; and when cold, bottle it, cork well, and seal it down.

Horseradish Vinegar. — Pour a quart of best vinegar on three ounces of scraped horseradish, an ounce of minced shallot, and one dram of Cayenne; let it stand a week, and you will have an excellent relish for cold beef, salads, etc., costing scarcely anything. Horseradish is in the highest perfection about November.

Mint Vinegar. — Put into a wide-mouthed bottle fresh nice clean mint leaves enough to fill it loosely; then fill up the bottle with good vinegar, and after it has been corked close for two or three weeks, it is to be poured off clear into another bottle, and kept well corked for use. Serve with lamb when mint cannot be obtained.

Cress Vinegar. — Dry and pound half an ounce of *cress seed* (such as is sown in the garden with mustard), pour upon it a quart of the best vinegar, let it steep for ten days, shaking it up every day. This is very strongly flavored with cress, and for salads, and cold meats, etc., it is a great favorite with many; the quart of sauce costs only a penny more than the vinegar. Celery vinegar may be made in the same manner.

Cheap and Good Vinegar. — To eight gallons of clear rain water, add three quarts of molasses; turn the mixture into a clean tight cask, shake it well two or three times, and add three spoonfuls of good yeast, or two yeast cakes; place the cask in a warm place, and in ten or fifteen days add a sheet of common wrapping paper, smeared with molasses, and torn into narrow strips, and you will have good vinegar. The paper is necessary to form the "mother," or life of the vinegar.

Good Cider Vinegar. — Take ten

gallons of apple juice fresh from the press, and suffer it to ferment fully, which may be in about two weeks, or sooner if the weather is warm; and then add eight gallons of like juice, new, for producing a second fermentation; in two weeks more add another like new quantity, for producing a third fermentation. This third fermentation is material. Now stop the bunghole with an empty bottle, with the neck downward, and expose it to the sun for some time. When the vinegar is come, draw off one half into a vinegar cask, and set it in a cool place above ground, for use when clear. With the other half in the first cask, proceed to make more vinegar in the same way. Thus one cask is to make in, the other to use from. When making the vinegar, let there be a moderate degree of heat, and free access of external air.

Oyster Powder. — Open the oysters carefully, so as not to cut them, except in dividing the gristle which adheres to the shells. Put them into a mortar, and when you have got as many as you can conveniently pound at once, add about two drams of salt to a dozen oysters; pound them, and rub them ·hrough the back of a hair sieve, and put them into a mortar again (previously thoroughly dried) with as much flour as will convert them into a paste; roll this paste out several times, and lastly, flour it, and roll it out the thickness of half a crown, and cut it into pieces about one inch square; lay them in a Dutch oven, where they will dry so gently as not to get burned; turn them every half hour, and when they begin to dry, crumble them. They will take about four hours to dry. Pound them, sift them, and put them into dry bottles; cork and seal them. Three dozen of oysters require seven ounces and a half of flour to make them into a paste weighing eleven ounces, and when dried, six and a half ounces. To make half a pint of sauce, put one ounce of butter into a stewpan with three drams of oyster powder, and six tablespoonfuls of milk; set it on a

slow fire, stir it till it boils, and season it with salt. As a sauce, it is excellent for fish, fowls, or rump steaks. Sprinkled on bread and butter, it makes a good sandwich.

Apple Sauce. — Pare and core three good-sized baking apples, put them into a well-tinned pint saucepan, with two tablespoonfuls of cold water; cover the saucepan close, and set it on a trivet over a slow fire a couple of hours before dinner, — some apples will take a long time stewing, others will be ready in a quarter of an hour. When the apples are done enough, pour off the water, let them stand a few minutes to get dry; then beat them up with a fork, with a bit of butter about as big as a nutmeg, and a teaspoonful of powdered sugar: some persons add lemon-peel, grated or minced fine, or boil a small piece with the apples. Many persons are fond of apple sauce with cold pork.

Horseradish Powder. — The time to make this is during November and December. Slice the horseradish the thickness of a shilling, and lay it to dry very gradually in a slow oven (a strong heat soon evaporates its flavor); when dry enough, pound it and bottle it.

Curry Powder (*a genuine Indian recipe*). — Turmeric, coriander, black pepper, four ounces each; fenugreek, three ounces; ginger, two ounces; cummin seed, ground rice, one ounce each; Cayenne pepper, cardamums, half an ounce each.

Sage and Onion, or Goose Stuffing Sauce. — Chop very fine an ounce of onion and half an ounce of green sage leaves, put them into a stewpan with four spoonfuls of water, simmer gently for ten minutes, then put in a teaspoonful of pepper and salt, and one ounce of fine bread crumbs; mix well together; then pour to it a quarter of a pint of broth, or gravy, or melted butter; stir well together, and simmer it a few minutes longer. This is a very relishing sauce for roast pork, poultry, geese, or ducks, or green peas.

Beef Gravy Sauce (*or Brown Sauce for Ragout, Game, Poultry, Fish,*

&c.)—If you want gravy, furnish a thick and well-tinned stewpan with a thin slice of fat ham or bacon, or an ounce of butter, and a middling-sized onion; on this lay a pound of nice juicy gravy beef (as the object in making gravy is to extract the nutritious qualities of the meat, it must be beaten so as to reduce the containing vessels, and scored to render the surface more susceptible to the action of the water); cover the stewpan, set it on a slow fire; when the meat begins to brown, turn it about, and let it get slightly browned (but *take care it is not at all burnt*); then pour in a pint and a half of boiling water, set the pan on the fire; when it boils, carefully catch the scum, and then put in a crust of bread toasted brown (don't jurn it), a sprig of winter savory, or lemon, thyme, and parsley, a roll of thin-cut lemon-peel, a dozen berries of allspice, and a dozen of black pepper; cover the stewpan close, let it *stew very gently* for about two hours, then strain it through a sieve into a basin. If you wish to thicken it, set a clean stewpan over a slow fire, with about an ounce of butter in it; when it is melted, dredge into it (by degrees) as much flour as will dry it up, stirring them intimately; when thoroughly mixed, pour in a little of the gravy, stir it well together, and add the remainder by degrees; set it over the fire, let it simmer gently for fifteen or twenty minutes longer, and skim off the fat, etc., as it rises; when it is about as thick as cream, squeeze it through a tamis or fine sieve, and you will have a fine rich brown sauce, at a very moderate expense, and without much trouble. *Observe*— If you wish *to make it still more relishing,* — for *poultry,* you may pound the liver with a piece of butter, rub it through a sieve, and stir it into the sauce when you put in the thickening.

Chutney Sauce. — One pound of salt, one pound of mustard seed, one pound of stoned raisins, one pound of brown sugar, twelve ounces of garlic, six ounces of Cayenne pepper, two quarts of unripe gooseberries, two quarts of best vinegar. The mustard seed gently dried and bruised; the sugar made into a syrup with a pint of the vinegar; the gooseberries dried and boiled in a quart of the vinegar; the garlic to be well bruised in a mortar. When cold, gradually mix the whole in a large mortar, and with the remaining vinegar thoroughly amalgamate them. To be tied down close. The longer it is kept the better it will become.

Wow Wow Sauce. — Chop parsley leaves fine; take two or three pickled cucumbers, or walnuts, and divide into small squares, and set them by in readiness; put into a saucepan butter as big as an egg; when it is melted, stir into it a tablespoonful of fine flour, and half a pint of the broth of the beef; add a tablespoonful of vinegar, one of mushroom ketchup, or port wine, or both, and a teaspoonful of made mustard; simmer together till it is as thick as you wish, put in the parsley and pickles to get warm, and pour it over the beef, or send it up in a sauce-tureen. This is excellent for stewed or boiled beef.

GARNISHES.—Parsley is the most universal garnish for all kinds of cold meat, poultry, fish, butter, cheese, and so forth. Horseradish is the garnish for roast beef, and for fish in general; for the latter, slices of lemon are sometimes laid alternately with the horseradish.

Slices of lemon for boiled fowl, turkey, and fish, and for roast veal and calf's head.

Carrot in slices for boiled beef, hot or cold.

Barberries, fresh or preserved, for game.

Red beet-root sliced for cold meat, boiled beef, and salt fish.

Fried smelts as garnish for turbot.

Fried sausages or forcemeat balls are placed round turkey, capon, or fowl.

Lobster coral and parsley round boiled fish.

Fennel for mackerel and salmon, either fresh or pickled.   •

Currant jelly for game, also for custard or bread pudding.

Seville orange in slices for wild
ducks, widgeons, teal, and so forth.

Mint, either with or without parsley,
for roast lamb, either hot or cold.

Pickled gherkins, capers, or onions,
for some kinds of boiled meat and stews.

Relish for Chops, etc. — Pound fine
an ounce of black pepper, and half an
ounce of allspice, with an ounce of
salt, and half an ounce of scraped
horseradish, and the same of shallots,
peeled and quartered; put these into a
pint of mushroom ketchup, or walnut
pickle, and let them steep for a fortnight, and then strain it. *Observe.*—A
teaspoonful or two of this is generally
an acceptable addition, mixed with the
gravy usually sent up for chops and
steaks ; or added to thick melted butter.

**Forcemeat for Veal, Turkeys,
Fowls, Hare, etc.** — INGREDIENTS. —
*2 ounces of ham or lean bacon, ¼ pound
of suet, the rind of ½ a lemon, 1 teaspoonful of minced parsley, 1 teaspoonful
of minced sweet herbs, salt, Cayenne, and*
*pounded mace to taste, 6 ounces of bread
crumbs, 2 eggs.*

Mode. — Shred the ham or bacon,
chop the suet, lemon-peel, and herbs,
taking particular care that all be very
finely minced ; add a seasoning to
taste, of salt, Cayenne, and mace, and
blend all thoroughly together with the
bread crumbs, before wetting. Now
beat and strain the eggs ; work these
up with the other ingredients, and the
forcemeat will be ready for use. When
it is made into balls, fry of a nice
brown, in boiling lard, or put them on
a tin and bake for half an hour in a
moderate oven. As we have stated
before, no one flavor should predominate greatly, and the forcemeat should
be of sufficient body to cut with a
knife, and yet not dry and heavy. For
very delicate forcemeat, it is advisable
to pound the ingredients together before binding with the egg ; but for
ordinary cooking, mincing very finely
answers the purpose.

Sufficient for a turkey, a moderate-
sized fillet of veal, or a hare.

THE ART OF CARVING.

How to Perform an Embarrassing Task Gracefully—Instructions which will be found Profitable to the Man of the House.

The Art of Carving.—CEREMONIES OF THE TABLE, ETC.—A dinner-table should be well laid, well lighted, and always afford a little spare room. It is better to invite one friend less in number, than to destroy the comfort of the whole party.

THE LAYING OUT OF A TABLE must greatly depend upon the nature of the dinner or supper, the taste of the host, the description of the company, and the appliances possessed. It would be useless, therefore, to lay down specific rules. The whiteness of the table-cloth, the clearness of glass, the polish of plate, and the judicious distribution of ornamental groups of fruits and flowers, are matters deserving the utmost attention.

A SIDEBOARD will greatly relieve a crowded table, upon which may be placed many things incidental to the successive courses, until they are required.

A BILL OF FARE at large dinner parties, where there are several courses, should be provided, neatly inscribed upon small tablets, and distributed about the table, that the diners may know what there is to come.

NAPKINS should be folded neatly. The French method, which is very easy, of folding the napkin like a fan, placing it in a glass, and spreading out the upper part, is very pleasing. But the English method of folding it like a slipper, and placing the bread inside of it, is convenient as well as neat.

BREAD should be cut the last thing after the table is laid. If cut too early

it becomes dry. A tray should be provided, in which there should be a further supply of bread, new, stale, and brown.

CARVING-KNIVES should be " put in edge " before the dinner commences, for nothing irritates a good carver, or perplexes a bad one, more than a knife which refuses to perform its office; and there is nothing more annoying to the company than to see the carving-knife dancing to and fro over the steel while the dinner is getting cold, and their appetites are being exhausted by delay.

JOINTS THAT REQUIRE CARVING should be set upon dishes sufficiently large. The space of the table may be economized by setting upon small dishes those things that do not require carving.

THE CARVER SHOULD HAVE PLENTY OF ROOM, however closely the diners are compelled to sit together.

THE VEGETABLES, if the table is very crowded, may be placed upon the sideboard, and handed round by the waiters.

GEESE, TURKEYS, POULTRY, SUCKING-PIGS, etc., may be CARVED BEFORE BEING SENT TO TABLE ; especially in those cases where the whole or the principal part of such dishes is likely to be consumed.

THE CARVER should supply the plates, and the waiter hand them round, instead of putting the question to each guest as to which part he prefers, and then striving to serve him with it, to the prejudice of others present.

LADIES should be assisted before gentlemen.

NOTHING detracts from the dignity of a host so much as inefficient carving; and there are few things that make a guest appear so small as being unable to offer to assist the hostess in manipulating a joint.

THERE are some people who should never attempt to carve; for instance, those who are weak in their wrists, or those who are short-sighted. In the one case, failure is inevitable; in the other, nothing looks worse than to see a man peering in a purblind manner into a dish.

CARVING requires a large amount of constant practice, in order to arrive at proficiency; and the earlier the practice is commenced, the easier will the tyro find it to be. Boys on leaving school, though of course not expected to take the head of the table, should always be requested to help some dish — beginning with some easy dish, such as a ham or tongue, and proceeding by degrees to the dismemberment of a fowl or turkey.

There are two departments in presiding at table — namely, carving and helping. The former is the result of skilful manipulation; the other of careful discrimination. The proficient in the first-named art will be able to carefully anatomize any joint that is placed before him; whilst the adept in the second will be able to select the tit-bits in a proper proportion of each concomitant of the dish for the gratification of his guest.

With regard to carving, we may state, in a few words, that there are only two ways — namely, a right and a wrong way. No treatise ever written on the subject could prove that there were more ways than one of cutting a round of beef or dissecting a partridge.

Our object in this work is to make everything as plain as possible. The great drawback in the majority of manuals on carving is the elaboration and intricacy of the diagrams illustrating the subject, which naturally tend to mystify and mislead the would-be pupil. Our drawings are, therefore, quite simple. For this reason, we have left out the dishes usually placed in such drawings, and have confined our "dotted lines" to within the barest limits necessary for the elucidation of the text.

We must merely promise, that in all cases, the drawings of joints, etc., are placed before the reader in exactly the same position as if he were about to commence to carve them.

SOUPS. — The first course at all dinners is invariably the soup, and from that circumstance, as well as from the fact of its being the easiest dish to preside over, we place it first in our remarks and directions concerning carving. It should be ladled into the plate in about two dips. It is better to have the trouble of lading twice or thrice rather than run the risk of spilling the soup on the cloth, on account of the ladle being too full.

With regard to Julienne soups, or any kind of soups wherein there are vegetables, pieces of meat, or forcemeat balls, care should be taken to give the composition a stir round before serving, in order that each guest may have a just proportion of liquid and solid.

SALMON. — Serve a slice of the thick with a smaller slice of the thin part. Keep the flakes of the thick part as firm as possible.

COD'S HEAD AND SHOULDERS. — The thick part of the back is best. It should be carved in unbroken slices, and each solid slice should be accompanied by a bit of the sound, from under the back-bone, or from the cheek, jaws, tongue, etc., of the head.

MACKEREL should be served in pieces cut through the side when they are large. If small, they may be divided through the back-bone, and served in halves. The shoulder part is considered the best.

EELS are usually cut into several pieces, either for stewing or frying. The thick parts are considered best.

THE SIRLOIN OF BEEF. — The sirloin may be carved in two ways, either in long slices from 1 to 2, by which means a due proportion of fat and lean is served, or cut across the middle as at 3. The latter method is apt to spoil

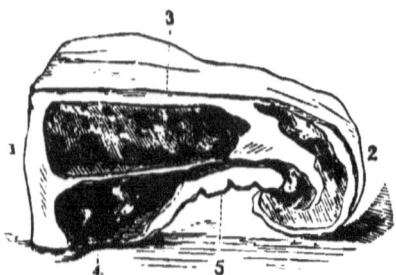

the appearance of the noble joint. Should the "under-side" be required, the joint should be turned over, and slices cut across at 4. Do not forget to serve with each slice some of the prime soft fat at 5.

RIBS OF BEEF. — Ribs of beef are carved in the same manner as the second method mentioned above — viz., across the joint. Occasionally the bones are removed; then it is customary to carve it in the same way as a round of beef.

THE EDGE-BONE, OR AITCH-BONE. — The edge-bone or aitch-bone of beef should be carved in the following manner: —

ner: — Cut a thick slice off the outside from 1 to 2, then cut thin slices, gradually getting the joint to a level at the line 2 to 5. It should be remembered that just at this point is the prime cut of the joint. In serving each slice, do not forget to add to each plate some of the marrowy and solid fats, which may be found respectively at 3

and 4.

THE ROUND OF BEEF. — This may be carved in a similar way to the above, care being taken to cut the slices as thin as possible. Indeed, in carving all joints, it would be well to recollect the saying of a certain noble old *bon vivant*, "You can always tell a man's breeding by his cutting beef *thin* and mutton *thick*."

SADDLE OF MUTTON. — The saddle of mutton is always a popular joint. Carve in the following way: — Slice across from 1 to 2, serving moderately

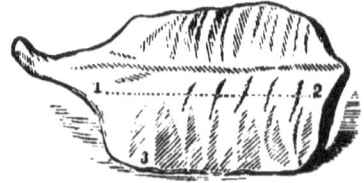

thick slices, with a portion of fat from 3. Finish one side always before commencing the other.

HAUNCH OF MUTTON, OR VENISON. — In cutting a haunch of mutton, first make an incision at 2, 4, say about three inches long. Then cut thin

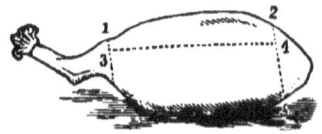

slices from 3 to the cross-line 2, 4, 5. The gravy will be found in copious supply in the cavity at 4. In carving this joint, always cut the slices towards yourself.

ROAST LEG OF MUTTON. — In carving a roast leg of mutton, always have the shank to the left hand, as depicted in the drawing. Place the fork in at about 7, to hold it steady, and cut right down to the bone in the direction 1, 2; the knife will thus pass through the kernel of fat denominated the "pope's eye," of which some people are particularly fond. The most juicy slices are to be obtained from

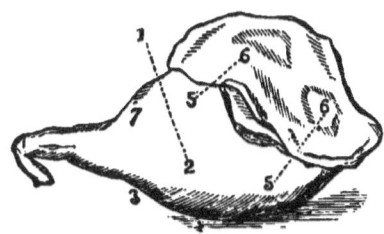

the line 1, 2, upwards towards 5, though some people prefer the shank or knuckle. Fat may be found on the ridges 5, 5, and should be cut in the direction 5, 6.

Should you desire to cut out what is called the "cramp-bone," take hold of the shank-bone with your left hand, then cut down to the thigh-bone at the point 4, and after passing the knife under the cramp-bone in the direction 4, 3, it can easily be extricated.

BOILED LEG OF MUTTON. — A boiled leg of mutton may be carved in the like manner to the roast; but in helping, care should be taken to give a due proportion of caper sauce with each slice.

SHOULDER OF MUTTON. — A shoulder of mutton, though perhaps one of the most repulsive joints ever brought to table, is, nevertheless, greatly admired by some persons, who think the flavor of it superior to that of the leg, and it requires some skill in carving. When first cut it should be

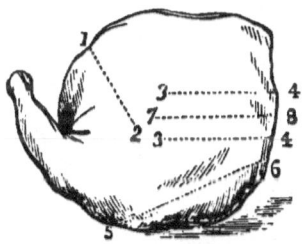

in the direction of 1, 2, cutting right down to the bone, causing the gravy to run into the dish. The prime fat may be found on the outer edge, and may be sliced off in the direction 5, 6. If there is a large company, after the bottom part in the line 1, 2, is finished,

there are some very delicate slices on each side of the ridge of the blade-bone in the lines 3, 4. The 7, 8 marks the direction of the edge of the blade-bone, and cannot be cut across.

Some persons prefer the under side of the shoulder, as being more full of gravy.

LOIN OF MUTTON. — This joint requires but little skill in carving, but it should always be properly jointed by the butcher before being brought to table: there is nothing to do but to separate the meat into chops, and help one of each all round.

A FORE-QUARTER OF LAMB. — The carving a fore-quarter of lamb must be commenced by passing the knife under in the direction of 3, 7, 4, 5, in order to

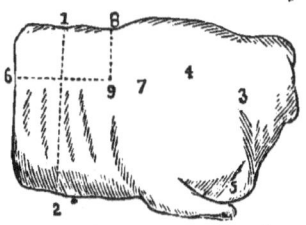

separate the shoulder from the breast and ribs. When this is accomplished, the juice of a lemon, together with a little salt, should be squeezed upon the part from which it was taken.

The gristly part may be separated from the ribs at the line 6, 7. The ribs are generally the most esteemed, and can easily be separated one from the other by cutting in the direction of the line 1, 2. If any one prefers the gristly part, a piece may be cut off in line 8, 9.

Should the fore-quarter run very large, the shoulder must be placed in another dish, and carved in the same manner as a shoulder of mutton.

LEG OF LAMB is carved in the same manner as a leg of mutton.

LOIN OF LAMB is carved in the same manner as loin of mutton, except that in lamb the fat is more delicate, consequently a larger proportion may be given to each guest.

LEG OF PORK. — A leg of pork,

whether roasted or boiled, should be carved across the middle, exactly like the ordinary way of cutting a ham. If it is roasted, be sure to take care to give a due proportion of stuffing and crackling to each plate.

ROAST PIG. — A pig is very rarely sent to table whole: the cook generally cuts it up, takes off the head, splits the body down the back, and garnishes the dish with the chaps and ears, etc.

Before any one is helped, the legs and shoulders should be separated from the carcass. The choice part of a pig is about the neck. The next best parts may be cut from the ribs.

LOIN OF PORK must be carved like a loin of mutton.

HAND OF PORK may be treated in a similar manner to a shoulder of mutton.

CALF'S HEAD.—Commence by cutting right along the cheek in the line 3, 2, and several handsome slices may be taken from this part. At the end of the jaw-bone may be found the

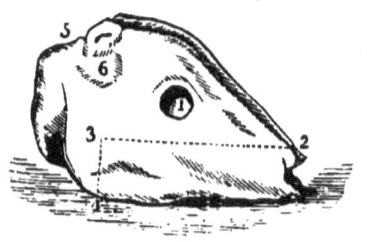

throat-sweetbread, which is esteemed a great delicacy: this may be found by cutting in deeply at the line 3, 4. There is some choice gristly fat to be discovered about the ear, 6. The eye, too, is greatly relished, and may be obtained by cutting round its socket at 1: the palate also is one of the tit-bits.

Tongue and brains are usually served in a separate dish: the best part of the tongue is a slice close to the root.

FILLET OF VEAL.—A fillet of veal is cut in the same manner as a round of beef. Recollect that some people

prefer the brown outside, and do not forget to serve a portion of stuffing to each plate.

LOIN OF VEAL is usually carved in the same way as a loin of mutton: it should be borne in mind, however, that the choice portions are the fat and kidney underneath.

A GIGOT OF VEAL is generally carved after the manner of a leg of mutton.

A SHOULDER OF VEAL is served like a shoulder of mutton.

KNUCKLE OF VEAL.—A knuckle of veal is certainly not one of the easiest joints to carve, though, at first glance, it appears to be so. It should be cut

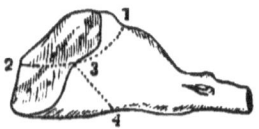

with a sort of semicircular sweep from 1 to 2. The bones should be cut from 3 to 4. The fat, which is to be found at 4, is greatly esteemed.

ROAST FOWL. — Perhaps the most difficult thing to carve is a roast fowl; indeed, he who can accomplish this properly, can soon make himself a proficient in every other branch of the art.

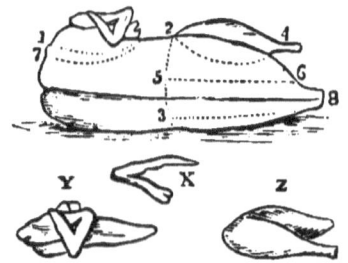

The cut which we give here shows the fowl on its side, with a leg, a wing, and a neck-bone taken off. It is often more convenient to take the bird on a plate, and as you detach the joints in the line 1, 2, 4, place them in the dish. The next thing is to cut off the neck-bones. This is accomplished by inserting the knife at 7, running it under the broad part of the bone in the line 7, 2, then lifting it, and breaking off the end of the shortest part of the bone. Then divide the breast from back by cutting through the ribs on each side from the neck to the tail. Turn the back upwards, fix the fork under the rump, and lay the edge of the knife in the line 2, 5, 3, press it down, raise the tail, and you will find it will easily divide in the line 2, 5, 3.

Lastly, put the lower part of the back upwards with the head toward you, and cut off the side-bones by forcing the knife through in the line 5, 6.

X, Y, and Z represent respectively a neck-bone, wing, and leg, in the forms they ought to be when skilfully carved.

BOILED FOWL. — Boiled fowl is carved in a similar manner to the above. The prime parts are usually considered to be the wings and breast. In a boiled fowl the legs are more tender than those of the roasted fowl.

THE GOOSE. — The goose should be

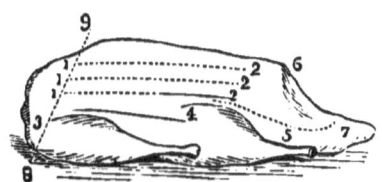

placed with the neck end before you. Cut three long gashes in lines 1, 1, 1, to 2, 2, 2, quite to the bone; detach these slices from the bone, and proceed to take off the leg by turning the bird on one side, putting the fork through the small end of the leg-bone, and pressing it close to the body. By this means, when the knife has entered at 4, the joint can easily be raised. Pass the knife under the leg in the direction of 4, 5. If the leg still hangs at 5, turn it back with the fork, and it will easily separate.

The leg being removed, the next matter is to take off the wing. This is done by passing the fork through the pinion, pressing it close to the body, and inserting the knife at the notch 3,

and passing it beneath the wing in the line 3, 4. It requires a good deal of practice to be able to do this nicely. You may now proceed to take off the leg and wing on the other side.

Having done this, you may proceed to cut off the apron in the line 6, 5, 7; and the merrythought in the line 9, 8. The other parts are taken off in a similar manner to those of the fowl.

The best parts of a goose are slices from the breast and the fleshy part of the wing. The stuffing of sage and onions is generally to be found just above the spot marked 7. This should be obtained by means of a spoon inserted into the interior of the bird, and a small portion served to each plate.

A GREEN GOOSE. — A green goose may be cut up like a duck. Only about a couple of slices should be taken from the breast, and then the separated joints cut off in the ordinary manner. In this case, as with a fowl or duck, the bird should be entirely cut up before any of the guests are served.

A DUCK. — A duck is served in a similar way to the preceding. The wings and breast are considered the most delicious morsels.

DUCKLINGS. — Ducklings are usually cut down the middle lengthways. It is not considered too much to give half a duckling to each guest.

PIGEONS are served in a similar manner to the foregoing.

ROASTED TURKEY. — Roasted turkey may be served in the same manner as a fowl, excepting the breast. This is the prime part, and many good slices, which should be cut lengthways, may be obtained therefrom. These should be served with small portions of the stuffing, and also sausages and forcemeat balls. It should be borne in mind that the turkey has no merrythought.

BOILED TURKEY. — A boiled turkey should be carved in a similar manner.

A HAM. — There are three ways of cutting a ham. One method is to begin at the knuckle, on the line 4, 5, and cut thin slices, gradually working up to the prime part of the joint: this is the most

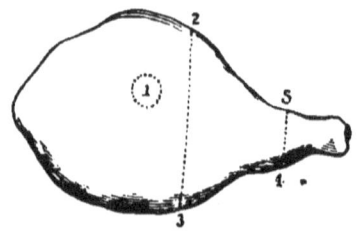

economical way of carving it. Another plan is to cut in at 2, 3, and serve slices from either side; whilst a third method is to take out a small piece at 1, and cut thin circular slices, thus enlarging the cavity by degrees. The advantage of this method is that it preserves the gravy and keeps the joint moist; it is, of course, only practised when the ham is served *hot*.

THE TONGUE.—The tongue should be cut nearly through at the line 1, 2, and slices served from right or left.

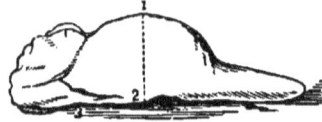

Some people are particularly partial to the fat and roots, which should be cut from 3 and 2.

THE PARTRIDGE.—The partridge is cut up almost in the same manner as a fowl. The wings must be taken off at

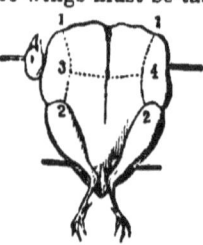

the lines 1, 2, and the merrythought in the line 3, 4. The wings and breast are usually regarded as the prime parts; but the tip of the wing is generally considered the most delicate portion in the whole bird.

At hunting-breakfasts and bachelors'-parties, where the birds are frequently served cold, it is not unusual to cut the bird in half, and give half a partridge to each guest.

GROUSE are carved in a similar manner to the above, while woodcocks, snipes, quails, and other smaller birds, are generally cut in half. Larks are usually served on skewers of four to each guest.

GOOD THINGS TO EAT.

Pickling.—There are three methods of pickling; the most simple is merely to put the article into cold vinegar. The strongest pickling vinegar of white wine should always be used for pickles; and for white pickles use distilled vinegar. This method we recommend for all such vegetables as, being hot themselves, do not require the addition of spice, and such as do not require to be softened by heat, as capsicums, chili, nasturtiums, button onions, radish-pods, horseradish, garlic, and shallots. Half fill the jars with best vinegar, fill them up with the vegetables, and tie down immediately with bladder and leather. One advantage of this plan is, that those who grow nasturtiums, radish-pods, and so forth, in their own gardens, may gather them from day to day, when they are exactly of the proper growth. They are very much better if pickled quite fresh, and all of a size, which can scarcely be obtained if they be pickled all at the same time. The onions should be dropped in the vinegar as fast as peeled; this secures their color. The horcradish should be scraped a little outside, and cut up in rounds half an inch deep. Gather barberries before they are quite ripe; pick away all bits of stalk and leaf, and injured berries, and drop them in cold vinegar; they may be kept in salt and water, changing the brine whenever it begins to ferment; but the vinegar is best.

THE SECOND METHOD OF PICKLING is that of heating vinegar and spice, and pouring them hot over the vege-

tables to be pickled, which are previously prepared by sprinkling with salt, or immersing in brine. Do not boil the vinegar, for if so its strength will evaporate. Put the vinegar and spice into a jar, bung it down tightly, tie a bladder over, and let it stand on the hob or on a trivet by the side of the fire for three or four days; shake it well three or four times a day. This method may be applied to gherkins, French beans, cabbage, brocoli, cauliflowers, onions, and so forth.

THE THIRD METHOD OF PICKLING is when the vegetables are in a greater or less degree done over the fire. Walnuts, artichokes, artichoke bottoms, and beetroots are done thus, and sometimes onions and cauliflowers.

Onions. — Onions should be chosen about the size of marbles: the silver-skinned sort are the best. Prepare a brine, and put them into it hot; let them remain one or two days, then drain them, and when quite dry, put them into clean, dry jars, and cover them with hot pickle, in every quart of which has been steeped one ounce each of horseradish, sliced, black pepper, allspice, and salt, with or without mustard seed. In all pickles the vinegar should always be two inches or more above the vegetables, as it is sure to shrink, and if the vegetables are not thoroughly immersed in pickle they will not keep.

WALNUTS. — Be particular in obtaining them exactly at the proper season. Then make a pickle of vinegar, adding to every quart, black pepper one ounce, ginger, shallots, salt,

15

and mustard-seed, one ounce each. Most pickle vinegar, when the vegetables are used, may be turned to use, walnut pickle in particular. Boil it up, allowing to each quart four or six anchovies chopped small, and a large tablespoonful of shallots, also chopped. Let it stand a few days, till it is quite clear, then pour off and bottle. It is an excellent store sauce for hashes, fish, and various other purposes.

Beet Roots. — Boil or bake gently until they are nearly done. According to the size of the root, they will require from an hour and a half to two hours. Drain them, and when they begin to cool, peel and cut in slices half an inch thick, then put them into a pickle composed of black pepper and allspice, of each one ounce; ginger, pounded, horseradish sliced, and salt, of each half an ounce to every quart of vinegar, steeped. Two capsicums may be added to a quart, or one dram of Cayenne.

ARTICHOKES. — Gather young artichokes as soon as formed. Throw them into boiling brine, and let them boil two minutes. Drain them. When cold and dry, put them in jars, and cover with vinegar, prepared in method the third, but the only spices employed should be ginger, mace, and nutmeg.

Artichoke Bottoms. — Select full-grown artichokes and boil them, not so much as for eating, but just until the leaves can be pulled. Remove them and the choke. In taking off the stalk, be careful not to break it off, so as to bring away any of the bottom. It would be better to pare them with a silver knife, and leave half an inch of tender stalk coming to a point. When cold, add vinegar and spice, the same as for artichokes.

MUSHROOMS. — Choose small white mushrooms. They should be but one night's growth. Cut off the roots, and rub the mushrooms clean with a bit of flannel and salt. Put them in a jar, allowing to every quart of mushrooms one ounce each of salt and ginger, half an ounce of whole pepper, eight blades of mace, a bay-leaf, a strip of lemon-rind, and a wine-glassful of sherry. Cover the jar close, and let it stand on the hob or on a stove, so as to be thoroughly heated, and on the point of boiling; so let it remain a day or two, till the liquor is absorbed by the mushrooms and spices. Then cover them with hot vinegar, close them again, and stand till it just comes to a boil, then take them away from the fire. When they are quite cold, divide the mushrooms and spice into wide-mouthed bottles. Fill them up with the vinegar, and tie them over. In a week's time, if the vinegar has shrunk so as not entirely to cover the mushrooms, add cold vinegar. At the top of each bottle put a teaspoonful of salad or almond oil. Cork close, and dip in bottle resin.

SAMPHIRE. — On the seacoast this is merely preserved in water, or equal parts of sea-water and vinegar; but as it is sometimes sent fresh as a present to inland parts, the best way of managing it under such circumstances is to steep it two days in brine, then drain and put it in a stone jar covered with vinegar, and having a lid, over which put thick paste of flour and water, and set in a very cool oven all night, or in a warmer oven till it nearly but not quite boils. Then let it stand on a warm hob for half an hour, and allow it to become quite cold before the paste is removed; then add cold vinegar, if any more is required, and secure as other pickles.

Indian Pickle. — The vegetables to be employed for this favorite pickle are small hard knots of white cabbage, sliced; cauliflowers or brocoli in flakes; long carrots, not larger than a finger, or large carrots sliced (the former are far preferable); gherkins, French beans, small button onions, white turnip radishes half grown, radish-pods, shallots, young hard apples, green peaches, before the stones begin to form, vegetable marrow, not larger than a hen's egg, small green melons, celery, shoots of green elder, horseradish, nasturtiums, capsicums, and garlic. As all these vegetables do not come in season together, the best method is to prepare a large jar of pickle at such time of the year as most of the things may be obtained, and add the others as they come in season. Thus the pickle will be nearly a year in making, and ought to stand another year before using, when, if properly managed, it will be excellent, but will keep and continue to improve for years. For preparing the several vegetables, the same directions may be observed as for pickling them separately, only take this general rule — that, if possible, boiling is to be avoided, and soaking in brine to be preferred; be very particular that every ingredient is perfectly dry before putting into the jar, and that the jar is very closely tied down every time that it is opened for the addition of fresh vegetables. Neither mushrooms, walnuts, nor red cabbage are to be admitted. For the pickle:—To a gallon of the best white wine vinegar add salt three ounces, flour mustard half a pound, turmeric two ounces, white ginger sliced three ounces, cloves one ounce, mace, black pepper, long pepper, white pepper, half an ounce each, Cayenne two drams, shallots peeled four ounces, garlic peeled two ounces; steep the spice in vinegar on the hob or trivet for two or three days. The mustard and turmeric must be rubbed smooth with a little cold vinegar, and stirred into the rest when as near boiling as possible. Such vegetables as are ready may be put in; when Cayenne, nasturtiums, or any other vegetables mentioned in the first method of pickling come in season, put them in the pickle as they are; any in the second method, a small quantity of hot vinegar without spice; when cold, pour it off, and put the vegetables into the general jar. If the vegetables are greened in vinegar, as French beans and gherkins, this will not be so necessary, but will be an improvement to all. Onions had better not be wet at all; but if it be desired not to have the full flavor, both

onions, shallots, and garlic may be sprinkled with salt in a cullender, to draw off all the strong juice; let them lie two or three hours. The elder, apples, peaches, and so forth, to be greened as gherkins. The roots, radishes, carrots, celery, are only soaked in brine and dried. Half a pint of salad oil, or of mustard oil, is sometimes added. It should be rubbed with the flour of mustard and turmeric. — It is not essential to Indian pickle to have every variety of vegetable here mentioned; but all these are admissible, and the greater variety the more it is approved.

To Pickle Gherkins. — Put about two hundred and fifty in a pickle of two pounds, and let them remain in it three hours. Put them in a sieve to drain, wipe them and place them in a jar. For a pickle, best vinegar, 1 gallon; common salt, 6 ounces; allspice, 1 ounce; mustard seed, 1 ounce; cloves, ½ an ounce; mace, ½ an ounce; 1 nutmeg sliced; 1 stick of horseradish sliced; boil fifteen minutes; skim it well. When cold, pour it over them, and let stand twenty-four hours, covered up; put them into a pan over the fire, and let them simmer only until they attain a green color. Tie the jars down closely with bladder and leather.

Pickled Eggs.—If the following pickle were generally known it would be more generally used. It is an excellent pickle to be eaten with cold meat, etc. The eggs should be boiled hard (say ten minutes), and then divested of their shells; when *quite cold* put them in jars, and pour over them vinegar (sufficient to quite *cover* them), in which has been previously boiled the usual spices for pickling; tie the jars down tight with bladder, and keep them until they begin to change color.

PICKLING. — Do not keep pickles in common earthenware, as the glazing contains lead, and combines with vinegar. Vinegar for pickling should be sharp, though not the sharpest kind, as that injures the pickles. If you use copper, bell-metal, or brass vessels for pickling, never allow the vinegar to cool in them, as it then is poisonous. Add a teaspoonful of alum and a tea-cupful of salt to each three gallons of vinegar, and tie up a bag, with pepper, ginger root, spices of all the different sorts in it, and you have vinegar prepared for any kind of pickling. Keep pickles only in wood or stoneware. Anything that has held grease will spoil pickles. Stir pickles occasionally, and if there are soft ones take them out, and scald the vinegar, and pour it hot over the pickles. Keep enough vinegar to cover them well. If it is weak, take fresh vinegar and pour on hot. Do not boil vinegar or spice above five minutes.

PICCALILLI.—Piccalilli is a mixture of all kinds of pickles. Select pickles, from the salt brine, of a uniform size and of various colors; as small cucumbers, button onions, small bunches of cauliflowers, carrots cut in fanciful shape, radishes, radish-pods, bean pods, Cayenne pods, mace, ginger, olives, limes, grapes, strips of horse-radish, etc.

Arrange your selection tastefully in glass jars, and pour over them a liquid prepared in the following manner: To 1 gallon of white wine vinegar add 8 tablespoonfuls of salt, 8 of mustard-flour, 4 of ground ginger, 2 of pepper, 2 of allspice, 2 of turmeric, and boil all together one minute; the mustard and turmeric must be mixed together by vinegar before they are put into the liquor; when the liquor has boiled, pour it into a pan, cover it closely, and when it has become cold, pour it into the jars containing the pickles; cover the jars with cork and bladder and let them stand six months, when they will contain good pickles.

CHOW-CHOW.—Take a quarter of a peck of green tomatoes, the same quantity each of pickling beans and white onions, one dozen each of cucumbers and green peppers, one head of cabbage. Season to the taste with mustard, celery-seed, and salt. Pour over these the best cider vinegar, sufficient to cover. Boil slowly for two hours, continually stirring, and add while hot two tablespoonfuls of the finest salad oil.

Pickled Nasturtiums (a very good substitute for Capers). — INGREDIENTS. — *To each pint of vinegar 1 ounce of salt, 6 peppercorns, nasturtiums.*

Mode.—Gather the nasturtium-pods on a dry day, and wipe them clean with a cloth, put them in a dry glass bottle, with vinegar, salt, and pepper in the above proportion. If you cannot find enough ripe to fill a bottle, cork up what you have got until you have some more fit; they may be added from day to day. Bung up the bottles and seal or rosin the tops. They will be fit for use in ten or twelve months, and the best way is to make them one season for the next.

Seasonable. — Look for nasturtium-pods from the end of July to the end of August.

English Mixed Pickle. — INGREDIENTS. — *To each gallon of vinegar allow ¼ pound of bruised ginger, ¼ pound of mustard, ¼ pound of salt, 2 ounces of mustard-seed, 1½ ounces of turmeric, 1 ounce of ground black pepper, ¼ ounce of Cayenne, cauliflowers, onions, celery, sliced cucumbers, gherkins, French beans, nasturtiums, capsicums.*

Mode. — Have a large jar, with a tightly-fitting lid, in which put as much vinegar as is required, reserving a little to mix the various powders to a smooth paste. Put into a basin the mustard, turmeric, pepper, and Cayenne; mix them with vinegar, and stir well until no lumps remain; add all the ingredients to the vinegar, and mix well. Keep this liquor in a warm place, and thoroughly stir every morning for a month with a wooden spoon, when it will be ready for the different vegetables to be added to it. As these come into season, have them gathered on a dry day, and, after merely wiping them with a cloth, to free them from moisture, put them into the pickle. The cauliflowers, it may be said, must be divided into small bunches. Put all these into the pickle raw, and as the end of the season, when there have been added as many of the vegetables as could be procured, store it away in jars, and tie over with bladder. As none of the ingredients are boiled, this pickle will not be fit to eat till twelve months have elapsed. While the pickle is being made, keep a wooden spoon tied to the jar; and its contents, it may be repeated, must be stirred every morning.

Seasonable. — Make the pickle-liquor in May or June, to be ready as the season arrives for the various vegetables to be picked.

Potting Herrings and similar Small Fish. — The following is the mode practised in the Isle of Man for potting herrings, the fame of which is current in Europe: — Take fifty herrings, wash and clean them well, cut off the heads, tails, and fins. Put them into a stewpan with three ounces of ground allspice, a tablespoonful of coarse salt, and a little Cayenne pepper. The fish must be laid in layers, and the spice, etc., sprinkled upon them equally. A few bay-leaves and anchovies are then interspersed among the fish — the latter improve the flavor greatly. Pour upon the whole a pint of vinegar mixed with a little water. Tie over them a clean bladder and bake in a slow oven. Skim off the oil; boil half a pint of port or claret wine with a small quantity of the liquor and add it to the fish. If required to be sent any distance it is better to cover the whole with some clarified butter.

SALAD. — The mixing of salad is an art which is easy to attain with care. The main point is to incorporate the several articles required for the salad, and to serve up at table as fresh as possible. The herbs should be " morning gathered," and they will be much refreshed by laying an hour or two in spring water. Careful picking, and washing, and drying in a cloth, in the kitchen, are also very important, and the due proportion of each herb requires attention. The sauce may be thus prepared: — Boil

two eggs for ten or twelve minutes, and then put them in cold water for a few minutes, so that the yolks may become quite cold and hard. Rub them through a coarse sieve with a wooden spoon, and mix them with a tablespoonful of water or cream, and then add two tablespoonfuls of fine flask oil, or melted butter. Mix and add by degrees a teaspoonful of salt, and the same quantity of mustard. Mix till smooth, when incorporate with the other ingredients about three tablespoonfuls of vinegar. Then pour this sauce down the side of the salad bowl, but do not stir up the salad till wanted to be eaten. Garnish the top of the salad with the white of the eggs, cut in slices; or these may be arranged in such manner as to be ornamental on the table. Some persons may fancy they are able to prepare a salad without previous instruction, but, like everything else, a little knowledge in this case is not thrown away.

A Winter Salad.

Two large potatoes, passed through kitchen sieve,
Unwonted softness to the salad give;
Of mordant mustard add a single spoon —
Distrust the condiment which bites so soon;
But deem it not, thou man of herbs, a fault
To add a double quantity of salt;
Three times the spoon with oil of Lucca crown,
And once with vinegar procured from town.
True flavor needs it, and your poet begs
The pounded yellow of two well-boiled eggs;
Let onion atoms lurk within the bowl,
And, scarce suspected, animate the whole;
And lastly, on the favored compound toss
A magic teaspoon of anchovy sauce;
Then, though green turtle fail, though venison's tough,
And ham and turkey be not boiled enough,
Serenely full, the epicure may say, —
" Fate cannot harm me — I have dined to-day."

Summer Salad. — INGREDIENTS. — 3 *lettuces, a good quantity of mustard and cress, some young radishes, boiled beetroot, hard-boiled eggs.*

Mode. — Wash and carefully remove the decayed leaves from the lettuce and mustard and cress, drain them well from the water, and cut them and the radishes into small pieces. Arrange them on the dish lightly with the mustard and cress mixed with them, and any of the salad mixtures you prefer poured *under*, not over them. Garnish with boiled beetroot, cucumbers, and hard-boiled eggs cut into slices, and some vegetable flowers. Slices of cold poultry, or flaked fish, may be added to a summer salad, and are extremely good.

Preparation of Vegetables.—There is nothing in which the difference between an elegant and an ordinary table is more seen, than in the dressing of vegetables, more especially of greens; they may be equally as fine at first at one place as at another, but their look and taste are afterwards very different, entirely from the careless way in which they have been cooked. They are in greatest perfection when in greatest plenty, *i. e.* when in full season. By season, we do not mean those early days when luxury in the buyers and avarice in the sellers force the various vegetables, but the time of the year in which, by nature and common culture, and the mere operation of the sun and climate, they are most plenteous and in perfection.

POTATOES and peas are seldom worth eating before midsummer.

UNRIPE VEGETABLES are as insipid and unwholesome as unripe fruits.

AS TO THE QUALITY OF VEGETABLES, the middle size are preferred to the largest or the smallest; they are more tender, juicy, and full of flavor, just before they are quite full-grown; freshness is their chief value and excellence, and I should as soon think of roasting an animal alive, as of boiling vegetables after they are dead. The eye easily discovers if they have been kept too long; they soon lose their beauty in all respects.

ROOTS, GREENS, SALADS, etc., and the various productions of the garden, when first gathered, are plump and firm, and have a fragrant freshness no art can give them again; though it will refresh them a little to put them into cold spring water for some time before they are dressed.

To Boil Vegetables. — Soft water will preserve the color best of such as are green; if you have only hard water,

put to it a teaspoonful of carbonate of potash.

TAKE CARE TO WASH AND CLEANSE THEM thoroughly from dust, dirt, and insects — this requires great attention. Pick off all the outside leaves, trim the vegetables nicely, and if they are not quite fresh-gathered and have become flaccid, it is absolutely necessary to restore their crispness before cooking them, or they will be tough and unpleasant; lay them in a pan of clean water, with a handful of salt in it, for an hour before you dress them. Most vegetables being more or less succulent, their full proportion of fluids is necessary for their retaining that state of crispness and plumpness which they have when growing.

ON BEING CUT OR GATHERED, the exhalation from their surface continues, while from the open vessels of the cut surface there is often great exudation or evaporation, and thus their natural moisture is diminished; the tender leaves become flaccid, and the thicker masses or roots lose their plumpness. This is not only less pleasant to the eye, but is a serious injury to the nutritious powers of the vegetable; for in this flaccid and shrivelled state its fibres are less easily divided in chewing, and the water, which exists in the form of their respective natural juices, is less directly nutritious.

THE FIRST CARE IN THE PRESERVATION OF SUCCULENT VEGETABLES, therefore, is to prevent them from losing their natural moisture. They should always be boiled in a saucepan by themselves, and have plenty of water: if meat is boiled with them in the same pot, they will spoil the look and taste of each other.

TO HAVE VEGETABLES DELICATELY CLEAN, put on your pot, make it boil, put a little salt in, and skim it perfectly clean before you put in the greens, etc., which should not be put in till the water boils briskly; the quicker they boil the greener they will be.

WHEN THE VEGETABLES SINK, they are generally done enough, if the water has been kept constantly boiling. Take them up immediately, or they will lose their color and goodness. Drain the water from them thoroughly before you send them to table. This branch of cookery requires the most vigilant attention.

IF VEGETABLES are a minute or two too long over the fire, they lose all their beauty and flavor.

IF NOT THOROUGHLY BOILED TENDER, they are tremendously indigestible, and much more troublesome during their residence in the stomach than underdone meats.

TAKE CARE YOUR VEGETABLES ARE FRESH.—To preserve or give color in cookery many good dishes are spoiled; but the rational epicure, who makes nourishment the main end of eating, will be content to sacrifice the shadow to enjoy the substance. As the fishmonger often suffers for the sins of the cook, so the cook often gets undeservedly blamed instead of the green grocer.

TO CLEANSE VEGETABLES OF INSECTS.—Make a strong brine of one pound and a half of salt to one gallon of water; into this place the vegetables, with the stalk ends uppermost, for two or three hours: this will destroy all the insects which cluster in the leaves, and they will fall out and sink to the bottom of the water.

POTATOES.—We are all potato eaters (for ourselves, we esteem potatoes beyond any other vegetable), yet few persons know how to cook them. Shall we be bold enough to commence our hints by presuming to inform our "grandmothers" how

TO BOIL POTATOES.—Put them into a saucepan with scarcely sufficient water to cover them. Directly the skins begin to break, lift them from the fire, and as rapidly as possible pour off *every drop* of the water. Then place a coarse (we need not say clean) towel over them, and return them to the fire again until they are thoroughly done, and quite dry. A little salt, to flavor, should be added to the water before boiling.

POTATOES FRIED WITH FISH.—Take cold fish and cold potatoes. Pick all the bones from the former, and mash the fish and the potatoes together; form into rolls, and fry with lard until the outsides are brown and crisp. For this purpose, the drier kinds of fish, such as cod, hake, etc., are preferable; turbot, soles, eels, etc., are not so good. This is an economical and excellent relish.

POTATOES MASHED WITH ONIONS.—Prepare some boiled onions, by putting them through a sieve, and mix them with potatoes. Regulate the portions according to taste.

POTATO CHEESECAKES.—One pound of mashed potatoes, quarter of a pound of currants, quarter of a pound of sugar and butter, and four eggs, to be well mixed together; bake them in patty-pans, having first lined them with puff-paste.

POTATO COLCANON.—Boil potatoes and greens and spinach, separately; mash the potatoes; squeeze the greens dry; chop them quite fine, and mix them with the potatoes, with a little butter, pepper, and salt. Put into a mould, buttering it well first: let it stand in a hot oven for ten minutes.

POTATOES ROASTED UNDER MEAT.—Half boil large potatoes; drain the water; put them into an earthen dish, or small tin pan, under meat roasting before the fire; baste them with the dripping. Turn them to brown on all sides; send up in a separate dish.

MASHED POTATOES. — INGREDIENTS. — *Potatoes ; to every pound of mashed potatoes allow 1 ounce of butter, 2 tablespoonfuls of milk, salt to taste.*

Mode.—Boil the potatoes in their skins; when done, drain them, and let them get thoroughly dry by the side of the fire; then peel them, and, as they are peeled, put them into a clean saucepan, and with a *large fork* beat them to a light paste; add butter, milk, and salt in the above proportion, and stir all the ingredients well over the fire. When thoroughly hot, dish them lightly, and draw the fork backwards over the potatoes to make the surface rough, and serve. When dressed in this manner, they may be browned at the top with a salamander, or before the fire. Some cooks press the potatoes into moulds, then turn them out, and brown them in the oven; this is a pretty mode of serving, but it makes them heavy. In whatever way they are sent to the table, care must be taken to have them quite free from lumps.

Time, from half an hour to three-quarters of an hour to boil the potatoes.

POTATOES FRIED IN SLICES. — Peel large potatoes, slice them about a quarter of an inch thick, or cut them into shavings, as you would peel a lemon; dry them well in a clean cloth, and fry them in lard or dripping. Take care that the fat and frying-pan are quite clean; put it on a quick fire, and as soon as the lard boils, and is still, put in the slices of potato, and keep moving them until they are crisp; take them up, and lay them to drain on a sieve. Send to table with a little salt sprinkled over them.

POTATOES ESCALLOPED. — Mash potatoes in the usual way; then butter some nice clean scollop-shells, patty-pans, or teacups or saucers; put in your potatoes; make them smooth at the top; cross a knife over them; strew a few fine bread crumbs on them; sprinkle them with a paste-brush with a few drops of melted butter, and set them in a Dutch oven. When nicely browned on the top, take them carefully out of the shells, and brown on the other side. Cold potatoes may be warmed up this way.

POTATO SCONES. — Mash boiled potatoes till they are quite smooth, adding a little salt; then knead out the flour, or barley-meal, to the thickness required; toast on the girdle, pricking them with a fork to prevent them blistering. When eaten with fresh or salt butter they are equal to crumpets — even superior, and very nutritious.

POTATO PIE. — Peel and slice your potatoes very thinly into a pie-dish. Between each layer of potatoes put a little chopped onion, and sprinkle a little pepper and salt. Put in a little water, and cut about two ounces of fresh butter into bits, and lay them on the top. Cover it close with paste. The yolks of four eggs may be added, and when baked, a tablespoonful of good mushroom ketchup poured in through a funnel. Another method is to put between the layers small bits of mutton, beef, or pork. In Cornwall, turnips are added. This constitutes (on the Cornish method) a cheap and satisfactory dish for families.

COLD POTATOES. — There are few articles in families more subject to waste, whether in paring, boiling, or being actually wasted, than potatoes. And there are few cooks who do not boil twice as many potatoes every day as are wanted, and fewer still who do not throw the residue away as being totally unfit in any shape for the next day's meal; yet, if they would take the trouble to beat up the despised cold potatoes with an equal quantity of flour, they would find them produce a much lighter dumpling or pudding than they can make with flour alone; and by the aid of a few spoonfuls of good gravy, they will provide a cheap and agreeable appendage to the dinner table.

BAKED POTATOES. — Choose large potatoes, as much of a size as possible; wash them in lukewarm water, and scrub them well, for the browned skin of a baked potato is by many persons considered the better part of it. Put them into a moderate oven, and bake them for two hours, turning them three or four times while they are cooking. Serve them in a napkin immediately they are done, as, if kept a long time in the oven, they have a shrivelled appearance. Potatoes may also be roasted before the fire, in an American oven; but when thus cooked, they must be done very slowly. Do not forget to send to table with them a piece of cold butter.

Time, large potatoes, in a hot oven, one and a half to two hours; in a cool oven, two to two and a half hours.

French or String Beans. — Cut away the stalk end, and strip off the strings, then cut them into shreds. If not quite fresh, have a basin of spring water, with a little salt dissolved in it, and as the beans are cleaned and stringed throw them in. Put them on the fire in boiling water, with some salt in it; after they have boiled fifteen or twenty minutes, take one out and taste it. As soon as they are tender, take them up, throw them into a cullender or sieve to drain. Send up the beans whole when they are very young. When they are very large, they look pretty cut into lozenges.

Boiled Turnip Radishes. — Boil in plenty of salted water, and in about twenty-five minutes they will be tender. Drain well, and send them to table with melted butter. Common radishes, when young, tied in bunches, boiled for twenty minutes, and served on a toast, are excellent.

ASPARAGUS — (often miscalled " *Asparagrass* "). — Scrape the stalks till they are clean, throw them into a pan of cold water, tie them up in bundles of about a quarter of a hundred each, cut off the stalks at the bottom to a uniform length, leaving enough to serve as a handle for the green part; put them into a stewpan of boiling water, with a handful of salt in it. Let it boil, and skim it. When they are tender at the stalk, which will be in from twenty to thirty minutes, they are done enough. Watch the exact time of their becoming tender, take them up that instant. While the asparagus is boiling, toast a round of a large loaf, about half an inch thick, brown it delicately on both sides, dip it lightly in the liquor the asparagus was boiled in, and lay it in the middle of a dish, melt some butter, but do not put it over them. Serve butter in a butter-boat.

ARTICHOKES. — Soak them in cold water, wash them well, put them into plenty of boiling water, with a handful of salt, and let them boil gently for an hour and a half or two hours, trim them and drain on a sieve,

send up melted butter with them, which some put into small cups, one for each guest.

Stewed Water-Cress. — The following recipe may be new, and will be found an agreeable and wholesome dish : — Lay the cress in strong salt and water, to clear it from insects. Pick and wash nicely, and stew it in water for about ten minutes; drain and chop, season with pepper and salt, add a little butter, and return it to the stewpan until well heated. Add a little vinegar previously to serving; put around it sippets of toast or fried bread. The above, made thin, as a substitute for parsley and butter, will be found an excellent sauce for a boiled fowl. There should be more of the cress considerably than of the parsley, as the flavor is much milder.

Stewed Mushrooms. — Cut off the ends of the stalks, and pare neatly some middle-sized or button mushrooms, and put them into a basin of water with the juice of a lemon as they are done. When all are prepared, take them from the water with the hands to avoid the sediment, and put them into a stewpan with a little fresh butter, white pepper, salt, and a little lemon-juice; cover the pan close, and let them stew gently for twenty minutes or half an hour; then thicken the butter with a spoonful of flour, and add gradually sufficient cream, or cream and milk, to make the same about the thickness of good cream. Season the sauce to palate, adding a little pounded mace or grated nutmeg. Let the whole stew gently until the mushrooms are tender. Remove every particle of butter which may be floating on the top before serving.

Boiled Brussels Sprouts. — *To each gallon allow 2 teaspoonfuls of salt, and a small piece of soda.*

Clean the sprouts from insects, nicely wash them, and pick off any dead leaves from the outsides; put them into a saucepan of boiling water, with salt and soda in the above proportion. Keep the pan uncovered, and let them boil quickly over a brisk fire until tender; drain, dish, and serve with a tureen of melted butter, or with a maître-d'hôtel sauce poured over them. Another mode of serving is, when they are dished, to stir in about one ounce and a half of butter, and a seasoning of pepper and salt. They must, however, be sent to table very quickly, as, being so small, this vegetable soon cools. Where the cook is expeditious, this vegetable, when cooked, may be arranged on the dish in the form of a pineapple, and, so served, has a very pretty appearance.

Time, from nine to twelve minutes after the water boils.

Boiled Cabbage. — *To each ½ gallon of water allow 1 heaped tablespoonful of salt ; a very small piece of soda.*

Pick off all the dead outside leaves, cut off as much of the stalk as possible, and cut the cabbage across twice, at the stalk end; if they should be very large, quarter them. Wash them well in cold water, place them in a cullender and drain; then put them into *plenty* of *fast-boiling* water, to which have been added salt and soda in the above proportions. Stir the cabbages down once or twice in the water, keep the pan uncovered, and let them boil quickly until tender. The instant they are done, take them up in a cullender, place a plate over them, let them thoroughly drain, dish, and serve.

Time, large cabbages, or savoys, one half to three-quarters of an hour; young summer cabbage, ten to twelve minutes, after the water boils.

Boiled Carrots. — *To each ½ gallon of water allow 1 heaped tablespoonful of salt.*

Cut off the green tops, wash and scrape the carrots, and should there be any black specks, remove them. If very large, cut them in halves, divide them lengthwise into four pieces, and put them into boiling water, salted in the above proportion; let them boil until tender, which may be ascertained by thrusting a fork into them; dish, and serve very hot. This vegetable is an indispensable accompaniment to boiled beef. When thus served, it is

usually boiled with the beef; a few carrots are placed round the dish as a garnish, and the remainder sent to table in a vegetable-dish. Young carrots do not require nearly so much boiling, nor should they be divided: these make a nice addition to stewed veal, etc.

Time, large carrots, one and three-quarters to two and a quarter hours ; young ones, about half an hour.

Boiled Cauliflowers. — *To each ½ gallon of water allow 1 heaped tablespoonful of salt.*

Choose cauliflowers that are close and white; trim off the decayed outside leaves, and cut the stalk off flat at the bottom. Open the flower a little in places to remove the insects, which generally are found about the stalk, and let the cauliflowers lie in salt and water for an hour previous to dressing them, with their heads downwards: this will effectually draw out all the vermin. Then put them into fast-boiling water, with the addition of salt in the above proportion, and let them boil briskly over a good fire, keeping the saucepan uncovered. The water should be well skimmed; and when the cauliflowers are tender, take them up with a slice; let them drain, and, if large enough, place them upright in the dish. Serve with plain melted butter, a little of which may be poured over the flower.

Time, small cauliflower, twelve to fifteen minutes ; large one, twenty to twenty-five minutes, after the water boils.

CELERY. — This vegetable is usually served with the cheese, and is then eaten in its raw state. Let the roots be washed free from dirt, all the decayed and outside leaves being cut off, preserving as much of the stalk as possible, and all specks or blemishes being carefully removed. Should the celery be large, divide it lengthwise into quarters, and place it, root downwards, in a celery-glass, which should be rather more than half filled with water. The top leaves may be curled, by shredding them in narrow strips with the point of a clean skewer, at a distance of about four inches from the top.

Note. — This vegetable is exceedingly useful for flavoring soups, sauces, etc., and makes a very nice addition to winter salad.

To Dress Cucumbers. — INGREDIENTS. — *3 tablespoonfuls of salad-oil, 3 tablespoonfuls of vinegar, salt and pepper to taste ; cucumber.*

Mode. — Pare the cucumber, cut it equally into *very thin* slices, and commence cutting from the *thick end;* if commenced at the stalk, the cucumber will most likely have an exceedingly bitter taste, far from agreeable. Put the slices into a dish, sprinkle over salt and pepper, and pour over oil and vinegar in the above proportion; turn the cucumber about, and it is ready to serve. This is a favorite accompaniment to boiled salmon, is a nice addition to all descriptions of salads, and makes a pretty garnish to lobster salad.

Baked Spanish Onions. — Put the onions, with their skins on, into a saucepan of boiling water slightly salted, and let them boil quickly for an hour. Then take them out, wipe them thoroughly, wrap each one in a piece of paper separately, and bake them in a moderate oven for two hours, or longer, should the onions be very large. They may be served in their skins, and eaten with a piece of cold butter and a seasoning of pepper and salt; or they may be peeled, and a good brown gravy poured over them.

Stewed Spanish Onions. — INGREDIENTS. — *5 or 6 Spanish onions, 1 pint of good broth or gravy.*

Mode. — Peel the onions, taking care not to cut away too much of the tops or tails, or they would then fall to pieces; put them into a stewpan capable of holding them at the bottom without piling them one on the top of another ; add the broth or gravy, and simmer *very gently* until the onions are perfectly tender. Dish them, pour the gravy round, and serve. Instead of using broth, Spanish onions may be stewed with a large piece of butter : they must be done very gradually over a slow fire or hot plate, and will produce plenty of gravy.

Time, to stew in gravy, two hours, or longer if very large.

Note. — Stewed Spanish onions are a favorite accompaniment to roast shoulder of mutton.

Boiled Parsnips. — *To each ½ gallon of water allow 1 heaped tablespoonful of salt.*

Wash the parsnips, scrape them thoroughly, and, with the point of the knife, remove any black specks about them, and, should they be very large, cut the thick part into quarters. Put them into a saucepan of boiling water salted in the above proportion, boil them rapidly until tender, which may be ascertained by thrusting a fork in them ; take them up, drain them, and serve in a vegetable-dish. This vegetable is usually served with salt fish, boiled pork, or boiled beef; when sent to table with the latter, a few should be placed alternately with carrots round the dish, as a garnish.

Time, large parsnips, one hour to one hour and a half; small ones, one-half to one hour.

Boiled Green Peas. — *To each ½ gallon of water allow 1 small teaspoonful of moist sugar, 1 heaped tablespoonful of salt.*

This delicious vegetable, to be eaten in perfection, should be young, and not *gathered* or *shelled* long before it is dressed. Shell the peas, wash them well in cold water, and drain them ; then put them into a saucepan with plenty of *fast-boiling* water, to which salt and *moist sugar* have been added in the above proportion ; let them boil quickly over a brisk fire with the lid of the saucepan uncovered, and be careful that the smoke does not draw in. When tender, pour them into a cullender; put them into a hot vegetable-dish, and quite in the centre of the peas place a piece of butter, the size of a walnut. Many cooks boil a small bunch of mint *with* the *peas,* or garnish them with it, by boiling a few sprigs in a saucepan by themselves. Should the peas be very old, and difficult to boil a good color, a very tiny piece of soda may be thrown in the water previous to putting them in; but this must be very sparingly used, as it causes the peas, when boiled, to have a smashed and broken appearance. With young peas, there is not the slightest occasion to use it.

Time, young peas, ten to fifteen minutes; the large sorts, such as marrow-fats, etc., eighteen to twenty-four minutes; old peas, half an hour.

To Boil Brocoli. — *Time*, ten to fifteen minutes if small; twenty to twenty-five minutes if large.

2 or 3 heads of brocoli, 2 quarts of water, and a little fine salt.

Strip off the dead outside leaves, and cut the inside ones even with the flower; cut off the stalk close, and put them into cold salt and water for an hour before they are dressed, to cleanse them from all insects; put them into a large saucepan of boiling salt and water, and boil them quickly for about twelve or fifteen minutes with the pan uncovered. When tender, take them carefully out, drain them dry, and serve them with a little melted butter poured over them, and some in a separate tureen.

Mashed Turnips. — INGREDIENTS. —10 *or* 12 *large turnips, to each* ½ *gallon of water allow* 1 *heaped tablespoonful of salt,* 2 *ounces of butter, Cayenne or white pepper to taste.*

Mode. — Pare the turnips, quarter them, and put them into boiling water, salted in the above proportion; boil them until tender; then drain them in a cullender, and squeeze them as dry as possible by pressing them with the back of a large plate. When quite free from water, rub the turnips with a wooden spoon through the cullender, and put them into a very clean saucepan; add the butter, white pepper, or Cayenne, and, if necessary, a little salt. Keep stirring them over the fire until the butter is well mixed with them, and the turnips are thoroughly hot; dish, and serve. A little cream or milk added after the turnips are pressed through the cullender, is an improvement to both the color and flavor of this vegetable.

Time, from half an hour to three-quarters to boil the turnips; ten minutes to warm them through.

Summer Squashes. — If young and tender, they may be boiled whole; if not, pare, quarter, and take out the seeds. When boiled tender, take them out of the water, put them in a strong cloth, and press out all the water. Mash them. Salt and butter to your taste.

Winter Squash. — The neck is the best part. Cut it in narrow strips, take off the rind, and boil till tender, with salt. Then drain off the water, and let the squash steam over a moderate fire a few minutes. It is good not mashed. If mashed, add a small bit of butter. The winter squash makes a much better pie than pumpkins.

Sweet Corn. — Corn is much the sweetest when boiled on the cob. It requires boiling from twenty to thirty minutes, varying with age. For succotash, cut it from the cob, and boil it with Lima beans and a piece of salt pork. The beans and pork should be boiled half an hour before putting in the corn.

Succotash. — Take one can of shelled beans, and two cans of corn, mix well together, and put in a saucepan with half a pound of butter, and thoroughly warm. Season to taste. A little cream or broth may be added if desired. Some people prefer salt pork in place of the butter.

Hominy. — Rinse it thoroughly in cold water. If large ground, boil it about five hours, with a quart of water to a pint of the hominy. Turn off all the water, and add a little salt and butter. The small ground will cook in less time. Hominy is nice when cold, cut in slices and fried.

Baked Beans. — This dish, so celebrated in New England, is very economical and nutritious. Take one quart of small white beans, wash them and pick out the small colored ones, then put the beans in a kettle with half a pound of corned pork and three quarts of water. Boil slowly one hour. Just before taking them up, put in half a teaspoonful of salaratus. Strain the beans, and put them in an earthenware jar with three tablespoonfuls of molasses, and two teaspoonfuls of salt. Place the pork in the middle of the beans, leaving the rind even with the top. Put in just enough water to cover them, and bake them five or six hours in a slow oven, adding a little more water if required. When cooked, put away the few beans that are dried on top. Serve a little of the pork with the beans.

Baked and Boiled Pudding. — For boiled puddings you will require either a mould, a basin, or a pudding-cloth; the former should have a close-fitting cover, and be rubbed over the inside with butter before putting the pudding in it, that it may not stick to the side; the cloth should be dipped in boiling water, and then well floured on the inside. A pudding-cloth must be kept very clean, and in a dry place. Bread-puddings should be tied very loosely, as they swell very much in boiling.

The water must be boiling when the pudding is put in, and continue to boil until it is done. If a pudding is boiled in a cloth it must be moved frequently whilst boiling, otherwise it will stick to the saucepan.

There must always be enough water to cover the pudding if it is boiled in a cloth; but if boiled in a tin mould, do not let the water quite reach the top.

To boil pudding in a basin, dip a cloth in hot water, dredge it with flour, and tie it closely over the basin. When the pudding is done, take it from the water, plunge whatever it is boiling in, whether cloth or basin, suddenly into cold water, then turn it out immediately; this will prevent its sticking. If there is any delay in serving the pudding, cover it with a napkin, or the cloth in which it was boiled; but it is better to serve it as soon as removed from the cloth, basin, or mould.

Always leave a little space in the pudding basin for the pudding to swell; or tie the pudding cloth loosely for the same reason.

Boiled Apple Puddings. — One pound of flour, six ounces of very finely minced beef suet; roll thin, and fill with one pound and a quarter of boiling apples; add the grated rind and strained juice of a small lemon, tie it in a cloth; boil for one hour and twenty minutes, or longer. A small slice of fresh butter stirred into it when it is sweetened will be an acceptable addition; grated nutmeg, or cinnamon in fine powder, may be substituted for lemon rind. For a richer pudding use half a pound of butter for the crust, and add to the apples a spoonful or two of orange or quince marmalade.

Boston Apple Pudding. — Peel and core one dozen and a half of good apples; cut them small; put them into a stewpan with a little water, cinnamon, two cloves, and the peel of a lemon; stew over a slow fire till soft; sweeten with moist sugar, and pass it through a hair sieve; add the yolks of four eggs and one white, a quarter of a pound of good butter, half a nutmeg, the peel of a lemon grated, and the juice of one lemon; beat well together; line the inside of a pie-dish with good puff paste; put in the pudding, and bake half an hour.

Bread Pudding. — Unfermented brown bread, two ounces; milk, half a pint; one egg; sugar, quarter of an ounce. Cut the bread into slices, and pour the milk over it boiling hot; let it stand till well soaked, and stir in the egg and sugar, well beaten, with a little grated nutmeg; and bake or steam for one hour.

Elegant Bread Pudding. — Take light white bread, and cut it in thin slices. Put into a pudding shape a layer of any sort of preserve, then a slice of bread, and repeat until the mould is almost full. Pour over all a pint of warm milk, in which four beaten eggs have been mixed; cover the mould with a piece of linen, place it in a saucepan with a little boiling water, let it boil twenty minutes, and serve with pudding sauce.

Plain Suet Pudding. — *Time*, two hours and a half to three hours.

1 *pound of flour, ¼ ounces of beef suet, a pinch or two of salt, ½ a pint of water.*

Chop the suet very fine, and mix it with the flour, and a pinch or two of salt, and work the whole into a smooth paste with about half a pint of water. Tie the pudding in a cloth, the shape of a bolster, and when done cut it in slices and put butter between each slice. Or boil it in a buttered basin, turn it out when done, and serve it whole and without butter.

One or two beaten eggs added to the above, with a less quantity of water, may be used.

Baked Batter Pudding, with Dried or Fresh Fruit. — INGREDI-ENTS. — *1½ pints of milk, 4 tablespoonfuls of flour, 3 eggs, 2 ounces of finely-shreaded suet, ¼ pound of currants, a pinch of salt.*

Mode.—Mix the milk, flour, and eggs to a smooth batter; add a little salt, the suet, and the currants, which should be well washed, picked, and dried; put the mixture into a buttered pie-dish, and bake in a moderate oven for one hour and a quarter. When fresh fruits are in season, this pudding is exceedingly nice, with damsons, plums, red currants, gooseberries, or apples; when made with these, the pudding must be thickly sprinkled over with sifted sugar. Boiled batter pudding, with fruit, is made in the same manner, by putting the fruit into a buttered basin, and filling it up with batter made in the above proportion, but omitting the suet. It must be sent quickly to table, and covered plentifully with sifted sugar.

Time, baked batter pudding, one hour and a quarter to one hour and a half; boiled ditto, one hour and a half to one hour and three-quarters, allowing that both are made with the above proportion of batter. Smaller puddings will be done enough in three-quarters of an hour or one hour.

Boiled Batter Pudding. — INGRE-DIENTS.—*3 eggs, 1 ounce of butter, 1 pint of milk, 3 tablespoonfuls of flour, a little salt.*

Mode.—Put the flour into a basin, and add sufficient milk to moisten it; carefully rub down all the lumps with a spoon, then pour in the remainder of the milk, and stir in the butter, which should be previously melted; keep beating the mixture, add the eggs and a pinch of salt, and when the batter is quite smooth, put it into a well-buttered basin, tie it down very tightly, and put it into boiling water; move the basin about for a few minutes after it is put into the water, to prevent the flour settling in any part, and boil for one hour and a quarter. This pudding may also be boiled in a floured cloth that has been wetted in hot water; it will then take a few minutes less than when boiled in a basin. Send these puddings very quickly to table, and serve with sweet sauce, wine sauce, stewed fruit, or jam of any kind; when the latter is used, a little of it may be placed round the dish in small quantities as a garnish.

Boiled Rhubarb Pudding. — IN-GREDIENTS. — *4 or 5 sticks of fine rhubarb, ¼ pound of moistened sugar, ¾ pound of suet-crust.*

Mode. — Make a suet-crust with three-quarters of a pound of flour (see Suet Pudding), and line a buttered basin with it. Wash and wipe the rhubarb, and, if old, string it—that is to say, pare off the outside skin. Cut it into inch lengths, fill the basin with it, put in the sugar, and cover with crust. Pinch the edges of the pudding together, tie over it a floured cloth, put it into boiling water, and boil from two to two hours and a half. Turn it out of the basin, and serve with a pitcher of cream and sifted sugar.

Yorkshire Pudding. — *Time*, one hour and a half.

1½ pints of milk, 7 tablespoonfuls of flour, 3 eggs, and a little salt.

Put the flour into a basin with a little salt and sufficient milk to make it into a stiff, smooth batter, add the remainder of the milk and the eggs well beaten. Beat all well together, and pour it into a shallow tin which has been previously rubbed with butter. Bake it for half an hour, then place it under the meat for half an hour to catch a little of the gravy that flows from it, cut the pudding into small square pieces, and serve them with hot roast beef.

Note.—When eggs are dear, they may be omitted, and a little ale used instead.

The English Plum Pudding.—

Take one pound each of flour, raisins, suet, sugar, and grated bread crumbs, the whites of six and yolks of eight eggs, one ounce of citron, one nutmeg grated, and the juice of one lemon. Cut the raisins just sufficient to remove the seeds, then close them up, wash and rub the currants dry with a cloth, cut the suet and citron very fine, beat the eggs well into a froth, then mix the whole well together with one and a half pints of milk,—pour into bowls. Wet a cloth and dredge a little flour on, and tie it over the bowl, turning up the loose ends and pinning them over the top; boil them seven or eight hours; they will keep three weeks. The day you wish to eat one, place it in a slow oven one hour, or boil it for an hour (or they may be eaten when first boiled); serve it with brandy or wine sauce.

Christmas Plum Pudding.—IN-
GREDIENTS. — 1½ *pounds of raisins, ½ pound of currants, ½ pound of mixed peel, ¾ of a pound of bread crumbs, ¾ of a pound of suet, 8 eggs, 1 wineglassful of brandy.*

Mode.—Stone and cut the raisins in halves, but do not chop them ; wash, pick, and dry the currants, and mince the suet finely ; cut the candied peel into thin slices, and grate down the bread into fine crumbs. When all these dry ingredients are prepared, mix them well together, then moisten the mixture with the eggs, which should be well beaten, and the brandy ; stir well, that everything may be very thoroughly blended, and press the pudding into a buttered mould, tie it down tightly

with a floured cloth, and boil for five or six hours. It may be boiled in a cloth without a mould, and will require the same time allowed for cooking. As Christmas puddings are usually made a few days before they are required for table, when the pudding is taken out of the pot hang it up immediately, and put a plate or saucer underneath to catch the water that may drain from it. The day it is to be eaten, plunge it into boiling water, and keep it boiling for at least two hours, then turn it out of the mould, and serve with brandy-sauce. On Christmas day a sprig of holly is usually placed in the middle of the pudding, and about a wineglassful of brandy poured round it, which, at the moment of serving, is lighted, and the pudding thus brought to the table encircled in flame.

Time, five or six hours the first time of boiling, two hours the day it is to be served. *Seasonable* on the twenty-fifth of December and on various festive occasions till March.

Huckleberry Pudding.— Make a
paste with one quart of flour and half a pound of butter ; rub one half the butter into the flour, mix this with cold water, roll it out and put on the remainder of the butter in little pieces ; roll it out half an inch thick, spread the cloth previously dipped in water and well floured over the cullender, lay the paste on it, fill it with berries, tie the cloth tight, put it into boiling water and boil two hours. Serve with sweetened cream, flavored.

To Make Hasty Puddings.—*Time,*
twenty minutes.

½ a pint of milk, 1 egg, 1 heaped tablespoonful of flour, and a little salt, ½ a teacupful of cold milk.

Put half a pint of fresh milk into a saucepan to boil; beat an egg, yolk and white together, *well,* add to it a good tablespoonful of flour and a little salt, beat the egg and flour together with a little cold milk to make a batter. Pour it to the boiling milk, and keep stirring it until it is well boiled together.

Oatmeal Hasty Pudding. — *Time,* twenty minutes.

¼ *a pint of boiling milk,* ⅓ *a teacupful of cold milk,* 1 *dessertspoonful of flour,* 1 *of oatmeal, a little salt.*

Boil half a pint of milk, beat the flour and oatmeal into a paste with cold milk, add to it the boiling milk, and keep stirring it always in the same direction till it is done.

Jam Roly-poly Pudding. — *Time,* two hours.

½ *a pound of suet-crust,* ½ *a pound of jam.*

Make a light suet-crust and roll it out rather thin, spread any jam over it, leaving a small margin of paste where the pudding joins. Roll it round and tie it in a floured cloth, put it into boiling water, and in two hours it will be ready to serve.

Potato Pudding. — Boil mealy potatoes in their skins, according to the rule laid down, skin and mash them with a little milk, pepper, and salt: this will make a good pudding to bake under roast meat. With the addition of a bit of butter, an egg, milk, pepper, and salt, it makes an excellent batter for a meat pudding baked. Grease a baking dish; put a layer of potatoes, then a layer of meat cut in bits, and seasoned with pepper, salt, a little allspice, either with or without chopped onions; a little gravy of roast meat is a great improvement: then put another layer of potatoes, then meat, and cover with potatoes. Put a buttered paper over the top, to prevent it from being burnt, and bake it an hour or an hour and a half.

Peas Pudding. — Dry a pint or quart of split peas thoroughly before the fire; then tie them up loosely in a cloth, put them into warm water, boil them a couple of hours or more, until quite tender; take them up, beat them well in a dish with a little salt (some add the yolk of an egg), and a bit of butter. Make it quite smooth, tie it up again in a cloth, and boil it an hour longer. This is highly nourishing.

Baked Bread-and-Butter Pudding.

—INGREDIENTS.—9 *thin slices of bread and butter,* 1½ *pints of milk,* 4 *eggs, sugar to taste,* ¼ *pound of currants, flavoring of vanilla, grated lemon-peel or nutmeg.*

Mode.— Cut nine slices of bread and butter, not very thick, and put them into a pie-dish, with currants between each layer and on the top. Sweeten and flavor the milk, either by infusing a little lemon-peel in it, or by adding a few drops of essence of vanilla; well whisk the eggs, and stir these to the milk. *Strain* this over the bread and butter, and bake in a moderate oven for one hour, or rather longer. This pudding may be very much enriched by adding cream, candied peel, or more eggs than stated above. It should not be turned out, but sent to table in the pie-dish, and is better for being made about two hours before it is baked.

Boiled Bread Pudding. — INGREDIENTS. —1½ *pints of milk,* ¾ *pint of bread crumbs, sugar to taste,* 4 *eggs,* 1 *ounce of butter,* 3 *ounces of currants,* ¼ *teaspoonful of grated nutmeg.*

Mode. — Make the milk boiling, and pour it on the bread crumbs; let these remain till cold; then add the other ingredients, taking care that the eggs are well beaten, and the currants well washed, picked, and dried. Beat the pudding well, and put it into a buttered basin; tie it down tightly with a cloth, plunge it into boiling water, and boil for one hour and a quarter; turn it out of the basin, and serve with sifted sugar. Any odd pieces or scraps of bread answer for this pudding; but they should be soaked over night, and, when wanted for use, should have the water well squeezed from them.

Black or Red Currant Pudding. — INGREDIENTS. — 1 *quart of red or black currants, measured with the stalks,* ¼ *pound of moist sugar, suet-crust or butter-crust.*

Mode. — Make, with three-quarters of a pound of flour, either a suet-crust or butter-crust (the former is usually made); butter a basin, and line it with part of the crust; put in the currants, which should be stripped from the stalks, and sprinkle the sugar over them ; put the cover of the pudding on ; make the edges very secure, that the juice does not escape ; tie it down with a floured cloth, put it into boiling water, and boil from two and a half to three hours. Boiled without a basin, allow half an hour less. We have given rather a large proportion of sugar ; but we find fruit puddings are so much more juicy and palatable when *well sweetened* before they are boiled, besides being more economical. A few raspberries added to red-currant pudding are a very nice addition : about half a pint would be sufficient for the above quantity of fruit. Fruit puddings are very delicious if, when they are turned out of the basin, the crust is browned with a salamander, or put into a very hot oven for a few minutes to color it ; this makes it crisp on the surface.

Time, two and a half to three hours ; without a basin, two to two and a half hours.

Baked Custard Pudding.—INGRE-DIENTS.— 1½ *pints of milk, the rind of ¼ lemon, ¼ pound of moist sugar, 4 eggs.*

Mode. — Put the milk into a saucepan with the sugar and lemon-rind, and let this infuse for about half an hour, or until the milk is well flavored ; whisk the eggs, yolks and whites ; pour the milk to them, stirring all the while; then have ready a pie-dish, lined at the edge with paste ready baked ; strain the custard into the dish, grate a little nutmeg over the top, and bake in a *very slow* oven for about half an hour, or rather longer. The flavor of this pudding may be varied by substituting bitter almonds for the lemon-rind ; and it may be very much enriched by using half cream and half milk, and doubling the quantity of eggs.

Note. — This pudding is usually served cold with fruit tarts.

Damson Pudding.— INGREDIENTS. — 1½ *pints of damsons*, 1 *pound of moist sugar, ¾ pound of suet or butter-crust.*

Mode. — Make a suet - crust with three-quarters of a pound of flour; line a
16

buttered pudding-basin with a portion of it ; fill the basin with the damsons, sweeten them, and put on the lid ; pinch the edges of the crust together, that the juice does not escape ; tie over a floured cloth, put the pudding into boiling water, and boil from two and a half to three hours.

Boiled Lemon Pudding. — INGRE-DIENTS. — ½ *pound of chopped suet, ¾ pound of bread crumbs, 2 small lemons, 6 ounces of moist sugar, ¼ pound of flour, 2 eggs, milk.*

Mode. — Mix the suet, bread crumbs, sugar, and flour well together, adding the lemon-peel, which should be very finely minced, and the juice, which should be strained. When these ingredients are well mixed, moisten with the eggs and sufficient milk to make the pudding of the consistency of thick batter ; put it into a well-buttered mould, and boil for three and a half hours ; turn it out, strew sifted sugar over, and serve with wine sauce, or not, at pleasure.

Note. — This pudding may also be baked, and will be found very good. It will take about two hours.

Suet Pudding (to serve with Roast Meat). — INGREDIENTS. — 1 *pound of flour, 6 ounces of finely-chopped suet, ½ saltspoonful of salt, ¼ saltspoonful of pepper, ½ pint of milk or water.*

Mode. — Chop the suet very fine, after freeing it from skin, and mix it well with the flour ; add the salt and pepper (this latter ingredient may be omitted if the flavor is not liked), and make the whole into a smooth paste with the above proportion of milk or water. Tie the pudding in a floured cloth, or put it into a buttered basin, and boil from two and a half to three hours. To enrich it, substitute three beaten eggs for some of the milk or water, and increase the proportion of suet.

Note.—When there is a joint roasting or baking, this pudding may be boiled in a long shape, and then cut into slices a few minutes before dinner is served ; these slices should be laid in the dripping-pan for a minute or two, and then browned before the fire. Most children like this accompaniment to roast meat. Where there is a large family of children, and the meats of keeping them are limited, it is a most economical plan to serve up the pudding before the meat; as, in this case, the consumption of the latter article will be much smaller than it otherwise would be.

Custard (Baked).— Boil in a pint of milk a few coriander seeds, a little cinnamon and lemon-peel; sweeten with four ounces of loaf sugar, mix with it a pint of cold milk; beat eight eggs for ten minutes; add the other ingredients; pour it from one pan into another six or eight times, strain through a sieve; let it stand; skim the froth from the top, fill it in earthen cups, and bake immediately in a hot oven; give them a good color; ten minutes will do them.

Rice and Tapioca Pudding.— *Time*, four hours.

1 teacupful of rice and tapioca, half the quantity of loaf sugar, a little ground cinnamon.

Put into a deep dish a teacupful of rice and tapioca mixed — rather more of the rice than the tapioca (do not wash or crack it) — half the quantity of loaf sugar, and three pints of cold milk; sprinkle a little ground cinnamon over the top, and bake in a slow oven.

Rice and Apple Pudding.--*Time*, ten minutes for rice; pudding one hour.

1 cupful of rice, 6 apples, 2 cloves, a little lemon-peel, 2 teaspoonfuls of sugar.

Boil the rice for ten minutes, drain it through a hair sieve until it is perfectly dry. Put a cloth into a pudding basin, lay the rice all round it like a crust. Quarter some apples as you would do for a tart, and lay them in the middle of the rice, add a little chopped lemon-peel and two cloves, and two teaspoonfuls (or to your taste) of sugar, cover the apples with rice. Boil the pudding for an hour. Serve it with melted butter poured over it.

Note.—Tapioca may be used instead of rice; it makes an excellent pudding.

Plain Boiled Rice for Children.— *Time*, two hours.

¾ *of a pound of rice, jam, or melted butter and sugar.*

Wash the rice in water, tie it in a cloth rather loosely, to give it room to swell, and put it into a saucepan of cold water. When done, turn it out on a dish, and serve with sweet sauce or jam.

Baked Apple Dumplings. — *Time*, three-quarters of an hour.

Some baking apples, white of an egg, some pounded sugar, puff-paste.

Make some puff-paste, roll it thin, and cut it into square pieces; roll one apple into each piece, put them into a baking dish, brush them with the white of an egg beaten stiff, and sift pounded sugar over them. Put them in a gentle oven to bake.

Boiled Apple Dumplings. — *Time*, to boil, one hour.

Eight apples and some suet-crust.

Pare and core eight fine apples, and cut them into quarters. Roll a nice suet-crust half an inch thick, cut it into round pieces, and lay in the centre of each piece as many pieces of apple as it will contain. Gather the edges up, and pinch them together over the apple. When all the dumplings are made, drop them into a saucepan of boiling water, and let them boil gently for nearly or quite an hour, then take each one carefully out with a skimmer, place them all on a dish, and serve them quickly with butter, sugar, and nutmeg. To be eaten cut open, and the butter and sugar put into them.

Lemon Sauce for Sweet Puddings. — INGREDIENTS. — *The rind and juice of 1 lemon, 1 tablespoonful of flour, 1 ounce of butter, 1 large wineglassful of sherry, 1 wineglassful of water, sugar to taste, the yolks of 4 eggs.*

Mode. — Rub the rind of the lemon on to some lumps of sugar; squeeze out the juice and strain it. Put the butter and flour into a saucepan, stir them over the fire, and when of a pale-brown, add the wine, water, and strained lemon-juice. Crush the lumps of sugar that were rubbed on the lemon. Stir these into the sauce, which should be very sweet. When these ingredients are well mixed, and the sugar is melted, put in the beaten yolks of four eggs, keep stirring the sauce until it thickens, when serve. Do not, on any account, allow it to boil, or it will curdle, and be entirely spoiled.

Time, altogether, fifteen minutes.

Sweet Sauce for Puddings. — IN-GREDIENTS. — ½ *pint of melted butter made with milk, 3 heaped teaspoonfuls of pounded sugar, flavoring of grated lemon-rind, or nutmeg, or cinnamon.*

Mode. — Make half pint of melted butter, omitting the salt. Stir in the sugar, add a little grated lemon-rind, nutmeg, or powdered cinnamon, and serve. Previously to making the melted butter, the milk can be flavored with bitter almonds, by infusing about half a dozen of them in it for about half an hour. The milk should then be strained before it is added to the other ingredients. This simple sauce may be served for children with rice, batter, or bread puddings.

Time, altogether, fifteen minutes.

Wine Sauce for Puddings. — INGREDIENTS. — ½ *pint of sherry, ¼ pint of water, the yolks of 5 eggs, 2 ounces of pounded sugar, ½ teaspoonful of minced lemon-peel, a few pieces of candied citron cut thin.*

Mode. — Separate the yolks from the whites of five eggs. Beat them, and put them into a very clean saucepan (if at hand, a lined one is best). Add all the other ingredients, place them over a sharp fire, and keep stirring until the sauce begins to thicken; then take it off and serve. If it is allowed to boil, it will be spoiled, as it will immediately curdle.

Time, to be stirred over the fire, three or four minutes, but it must not boil. *Sufficient* for a large pudding. Allow half this quantity for a moderate-sized one.

Wine or Brandy Sauce for Puddings. — INGREDIENTS. — ½ *pint of melted butter, 3 heaped teaspoonfuls of pounded sugar, 1 large wineglassful of port or sherry, or ¾ of a small glassful of brandy.*

Mode. — Make half a pint of melted butter by recipe, omitting the salt, then stir in the sugar and wine or spirit in the above proportion, and bring the sauce to the point of boiling. Serve in a boat or tureen separately, and, if liked, pour a little of it over the pudding. To convert this into punch sauce, add to the sherry and brandy a small wineglassful of rum and the juice, and grated rind of half a lemon. Liqueurs, such as Maraschino or Curaçoa, substituted for the brandy, make excellent sauces.

Time, altogether, fifteen minutes.

Boil your Molasses. —When molasses is used in cooking, it is a very great improvement to boil and skim it before you use it. It takes out the unpleasant raw taste, and makes it almost as good as sugar. Where molasses is used much for cooking, it is well to prepare two or three gallons in this way at a time.

Very Good Puff-Paste. — INGREDIENTS.—*To every pound of flour allow 1 pound of butter, and not quite ½ pint of water.*

Mode. — Carefully weigh the flour and butter, and have the exact proportion; squeeze the butter well, to extract the water from it, and afterwards wring it in a clean cloth, that no moisture may remain. Sift the flour; see that it is perfectly dry, and proceed in the following manner to make the paste, using a very *clean* pasteboard and rolling-pin :—Supposing the quantity to be one pound of flour, work the whole into a smooth paste, with not quite half a pint of water, using a knife to mix it with : the proportion of this latter ingredient must be regulated by the discretion of the cook ; if too much be added, the paste when baked will be tough. Roll it out until it is of an equal thickness of about an inch ; break four ounces of the butter into small pieces ; place these on the paste, sift over it a little flour, fold it over, roll out again, and put another four ounces of butter. Repeat the rolling and buttering until the paste has been rolled out four times, or equal quantities of flour and butter have been used. Do not omit, every time the paste is rolled out, to dredge a little flour over that and the rolling-pin, to prevent both from sticking. Handle the paste as lightly as possible, and do not press heavily upon it with the rolling-pin. The next thing to be considered is the oven, as the baking of pastry requires particular attention. Do not put it into the oven until it is sufficiently hot to raise the paste; for the best prepared paste, if not properly baked, will be good for nothing. Brushing the paste as often as rolled out, and the pieces of butter placed thereon, with the white of an egg, assists it to rise in *leaves* or *flakes*. As this is the great beauty of puff-paste, it is well to try this method.

Common Paste, for Family Pies. —INGREDIENTS.—1½ pounds of flour, ½ pound of butter, rather more than ½ pint of water.

Mode. — Rub the butter lightly into the flour, and mix it to a smooth paste with the water; roll it out two or three times, and it will be ready for use. This paste may be converted into an excellent short crust for sweet tarts, by adding to the flour, after the butter is rubbed in, two tablespoonfuls of fine-sifted sugar.

Suet-Crust, for Pies or Puddings. — INGREDIENTS.— To every pound of flour allow 5 or 6 ounces of beef suet, ½ pint of water.

Mode.—Free the suet from skin and shreds; chop it extremely fine, and rub it well into the flour; work the whole to a smooth paste with the above proportion of water; roll it out, and it is ready for use. This crust is quite rich enough for ordinary purposes, but when a better one is desired, use from half to three-quarters of a pound of suet to every pound of flour. Some cooks, for rich crusts, pound the suet in a mortar, with a small quantity of butter. It should then be laid on the paste in small pieces, the same as for puff-crust, and will be found exceedingly nice for hot tarts. Five ounces of suet to every pound of flour will make a very good crust; and

even a quarter of a pound will answer very well for children, or where the crust is wanted very plain.

Dripping Crust, for Kitchen Puddings, Pies, etc.—INGREDIENTS.—To every pound of flour allow 6 ounces of clarified beef dripping, ½ pint of water.

Mode.— After having clarified the dripping, weigh it, and to every pound of flour allow the above proportion of dripping. With a knife, work the flour into a smooth paste with the water, rolling it out three times, each time placing on the crust two ounces of the dripping, broken into small pieces. If this paste is lightly made, if good dripping is used, and *not too much* of it, it will be found good; and by the addition of two tablespoonfuls of fine moist sugar, it may be converted into a common short crust for fruit pies.

MINCEMEAT, No. 1. — INGREDIENTS. — 2 pounds of raisins, 3 pounds of currants, 1½ pounds of lean beef, 3 pounds of beef suet, 2 pounds of moist sugar, 2 ounces of citron, 2 ounces of candied lemon-peel, 2 ounces of candied orange-peel, 1 small nutmeg, 2 quarts of apples, the rind of 2 lemons, the juice of 1, ½ pint of brandy.

Mode. — Stone and *cut* the raisins once or twice across, but do not chop them; wash, dry, and pick the currants free from stalks and grit, and mince the beef and suet, taking care that the latter is chopped very fine; slice the citron and candied peel, grate the nutmeg, and pare, core, and mince the apples; mince the lemon-peel, strain the juice, and when all the ingredients are thus prepared, mix them well together, adding the brandy when the other things are well blended; press the whole into a jar, carefully exclude the air, and the mincemeat will be ready for use in a fortnight.

MINCEMEAT, No. 2.—Take seven pounds of currants, well picked and cleaned; of finely chopped beef suet, the lean of a sirloin of beef minced raw, and finely chopped apples (Kentish or golden pippins), each three and a half pounds; citron, lemon-peel, and orange-peel cut small, each half a pound; fine moist sugar, two pounds; mixed spice, an ounce; the rind of four lemons and four Seville oranges. Mix well, and put into a deep pan. Mix a bottle of brandy and white wine, the juice of the lemons and oranges that have been grated, together in a basin. Pour half over and press down tight with the hand, then add the other half and cover closely. Some families make this one year so as to use the next.

Mince Pies. —*Mode.* — Make some good puff-paste by either of the above recipes. Roll it out to the thickness of about a quarter of an inch, and line some good-sized pattypans with it. Fill them with mincemeat, cover with paste, and cut it off all round close to the edge of the tin. Put the pies into a brisk oven, to draw the paste up, and bake for twenty-five minutes, or longer, should the pies be very large. Brush them over with the white of an egg, beaten with the blade of a knife to a stiff froth; sprinkle over pounded sugar, and put them into the oven for a minute or two, to dry the egg. Dish the pies on a white doyley, and serve hot. They may be merely sprinkled with pounded sugar instead of being glazed, when that mode is preferred. To rewarm them, put the pies on the pattypans, and let them remain in the oven for ten minutes or a quarter of an hour, and they will be almost as good as if freshly made.

Time, twenty-five to thirty minutes; ten minutes to rewarm them.

Apple Pie. — INGREDIENTS. —*Puff-paste apples; to every pound of unpared apples, allow 2 ounces of moist sugar, ½ teaspoonful of finely-minced lemon-peel, 1 tablespoonful of lemon-juice.*

Mode. — Make half a pound of puff-paste by either of the above-named recipes, place a border of it round the edge of a pie-dish, and fill it with apples pared, cored, and cut into slices. Sweeten with moist sugar, add the lemon-peel and juice, and two or three tablespoonfuls of water. Cover with crust, cut it evenly round close to the edge of the pie-dish, and bake in a hot oven from half to three-quarters of an hour, or rather longer, should the pie be very large. When it is three parts done, take it out of the oven, put the white of an egg on a plate, and with the blade of a knife whisk it to a froth. Brush the pie over with this, then sprinkle upon it some sifted sugar, and then a few drops of water. Put the pie back into the oven, and finish baking, and be particularly careful that it does not catch or burn, which it is very liable to do after the crust is iced. If made with a plain crust, the icing may be omitted.

Time, half an hour before the crust is iced; ten to fifteen minutes afterwards.

Note. — Many things are suggested for the flavoring of apple pie. Some say two or three tablespoonfuls of beer, others the same quantity of sherry, which very much improves the taste; while the old fashioned addition of a few cloves is, by many persons, preferred to anything else, as also a few slices of quince.

Creamed Apple Tart. — INGREDIENTS. —*Puff-crust apples; to every pound of pared and cored apples, allow 2 ounces of moist sugar, ½ teaspoonful of minced lemon-peel, 1 tablespoonful of lemon-juice, ½ pint of boiled custard.*

Mode. — Make an apple tart by the preceding recipe, with the exception of omitting the icing. When the tart is baked, cut out the middle of the lid or crust, leaving a border all round the dish. Fill up with a nicely-made boiled custard, grate a little nutmeg over the top, and the pie is ready for table. This tart is usually eaten cold, is rather an old fashioned dish, but, at the same time, extremely nice.

Time, half to three-quarters of an hour.

Plain Apple Pie. — Pare, core, and quarter the apples; boil the cores and parings in sugar and water; strain off the liquor, adding more sugar ; grate the rind of a lemon over the apples, and squeeze the juice into the syrup ; mix half a dozen cloves with the fruit, put in a piece of butter the size of a walnut. Cover with puff-paste.

Cup in a Pie-Dish.—The custom of placing an inverted cup in a fruit pie, the cook will inform us, is to retain the juice while the pie is baking in the oven, and prevent its boiling over; and she is the more convinced in her theory, because, when the pie is withdrawn from the oven, the cup will be found full of juice. When the cup is first put into the dish it is full of cold air, and when the pie is placed in the oven, this air will expand by the heat and fill the cup, and drive out all the juice and a portion of the present air it contains, in which state it will remain until removed from the oven, when the air in the cup will condense, and occupy a very small space, leaving the remainder to be filled with juice; but this does not take place till the danger of the juice boiling over is passed. If a small glass tumbler is inverted in the pie, its contents can be examined into while it is in the oven, and it will be found what has been advanced is correct.

Cherry Tart. — INGREDIENTS.— 1½ *pounds of cherries, 2 small tablespoonfuls of moist sugar, ½ pound of short crust.*
Mode. — Pick the stalks from the cherries, put them, with the sugar, into a *deep* pie-dish just capable of holding them, with a small cup placed upside down in the midst of them. Make a short crust with half a pound of flour, as before given. Lay a border round the edge of the dish; put on the cover, and ornament the edges; bake in a brisk oven from half an hour to forty minutes. Strew finely-sifted sugar over, and serve hot or cold, although the latter is the more usual mode. It is more economical to make two or three tarts at one time, as the trimmings from one tart answer for lining the edges of the dish for another, and so much paste is not required as when they are made singly. Unless for family use, never make fruit pies in very *large* dishes; select them, however, as *deep* as possible.

Note.—A few currants added to the cherries will be found to impart a nice piquant taste to them.

Rhubarb Tart.—INGREDIENTS. — ½ *pound of puff-paste, about 5 sticks of large rhubarb, ¼ pound of moist sugar.*
Mode.—Make a puff-crust, as given; line the edges of a deep pie-dish with it, and wash, wipe, and cut the rhubarb into pieces about one inch long. Should it be old and tough, string it— that is to say, pare off the outside skin. Pile the fruit high in the dish, as it shrinks very much in the cooking; put in the sugar, cover with crust, ornament the edges, and bake the tart in a well-heated oven from one-half to three-quarters of an hour. If wanted very nice, brush it over with the white of an egg beaten to a stiff froth, then sprinkle on it some sifted sugar, and put it in the oven just to set the glaze. This should be done when the tart is nearly baked. A small quantity of lemon-juice, and a little of the peel minced, are by many persons considered an improvement to the flavor of rhubarb tart.

Open Apple Tart. — *Time,* to bake in a quick oven, until the paste loosens from the dish.

1 *quart of sliced apples,* 1 *teacupful of water,* 1 *of fine moist sugar,* ½ *a nutmeg, yolk of* 1 *egg, a little loaf sugar and milk, puff-paste.*

Peel and slice some cooking apples and stew them, putting a small cupful of water and the same of moist sugar to a quart of sliced apples, and half a nutmeg and the peel of a lemon grated; when they are tender, set them to cool. Line a shallow tin pie-dish with rich pie-paste or light puff-paste, put in the stewed apples half an inch deep, roll out some of the paste, wet it slightly over with the yolk of an egg beaten with a little milk, and a tablespoonful of powdered sugar, cut it in very narrow strips and lay them in crossbars or diamonds across the tart, lay another strip round the edge, trim off the outside neatly with a sharp knife, and bake in a quick oven until the paste loosens from the dish.

Gooseberry Tart. — *Time,* to bake about three-quarters of an hour.

1 *quart of gooseberries, rather more*

than ⅓ *a pound of short crust*, 5 *or* 6 *ounces of moist sugar.*

Cut off the tops and tails from a quart of gooseberries, put them into a deep pie-dish with five or six ounces of good moist sugar, line the edge of the dish with short crust, put on the cover, ornament the edges and top in the usual manner, and bake in a brisk oven. Serve with boiled custard or a jug of good cream.

Cocoanut Pie.—Cut off the brown part of the cocoanut, grate the rest and put it with a quart of milk, using the milk of the nut. Simmer the meat of the nut and the milk for a quarter of an hour, then mix three tablespoonfuls of white sugar, two of melted butter, a small cracker pounded fine, and half a nutmeg grated; when cool add a small glass of wine and five eggs beaten to a froth; turn into deep plates, on which a puff-crust has been placed. Bake directly in a quick oven. Eat when cold.

CHEESECAKES. — *Time,* fifteen to twenty minutes.

½ a pint of good curd, 4 eggs, 3 spoonfuls of rich cream, a ¼ of a nutmeg, 1 spoonful of ratafia, a ¼ of a pound of currants, puff-paste.

Beat half a pint of good curd with four eggs, three spoonfuls of rich cream, a quarter of a nutmeg grated, a spoonful of ratafia, and a quarter of a pound of currants washed and dried. Mix all well together, and bake in patty-pans lined with a good puff-paste.

Baked Custard.—Allow six eggs to a quart of milk, for a rich custard; for a plain one, four eggs is sufficient. Beat the eggs to a froth, with two heaping tablespoonfuls of fine sugar, then stir them into the milk. Flavor the custard with extract of peach, or nutmeg, bake it in cups or a deep dish. It will be less likely to whey, if the cups are set into a pan of water while baking; the water should be warm when they are put in, and nearly to the top of the cups. If the oven is hot, the custard will bake in cups in the course of twenty minutes, if in a large dish, a longer time will be required.

A Nice Plum Cake for Children. — INGREDIENTS. — 4 *pounds of dough,* ⅓ *of a pound of moist sugar,* ¼ *of a pound of butter or good beef dripping,* ¼ *of a pint of warm milk,* ½ *grated nutmeg, or* ½ *ounce of caraway seeds.*

Mode. — If you are not in the habit of making bread at home, procure the dough from the baker's, and, as soon as it comes in, put it into a basin near the fire; cover the basin with a thick cloth, and let the dough remain a little while to rise. In the meantime, beat the butter to a cream, and make the milk warm; and when the dough has risen, mix with it thoroughly all the above ingredients, and knead the cake well for a few minutes. Butter some cake-tins, half fill them, and stand them in a warm place, to allow the dough to rise again. When the tins are three parts full, put the cakes into a good oven, and bake them from one and three-quarters to two hours. A few currants might be substituted for the caraway seeds when the flavor of the latter is disliked.

A Nice Plum Cake. — INGREDIENTS.—1 *pound of flour,* ¼ *pound of butter,* ½ *pound of sugar,* ½ *pound of currants,* 2 *ounces of candied lemon-peel,* ½ *pint of milk,* 1 *teaspoonful of ammonia or carbonate of soda.*

Mode. — Put the flour into a basin with the sugar, currants, and sliced candied peel; beat the butter to a cream, and mix all these ingredients together with the milk. Stir the ammonia into two tablespoonfuls of milk, add it to the dough, and beat the whole well, until everything is thoroughly mixed. Put the dough into a buttered tin, and bake the cake from one and a half to two hours.

Pound Cake. — INGREDIENTS. — 1 *pound of butter,* 1¼ *pounds of flour,* 1 *pound of pounded loaf sugar,* 1 *pound of currants,* 9 *eggs,* 2 *ounces of candied peel,* ½ *ounce of citron,* ½ *ounce of sweet almonds; when liked, a little pounded mace.*

Mode.—Work the butter to a cream, dredge in the flour, add the sugar, currants, candied peel, which should be cut into neat slices, and the almonds, which should be blanched and chopped, and mix all these well together, whisk the eggs, and let them be thoroughly blended with the dry ingredients. Beat the cake well for twenty minutes, and put it into a round tin, lined at the bottom and sides with a strip of white buttered paper. Bake it from one and a half to two hours, and let the oven be well heated when the cake is first put in, as, if this is not the case, the currants will all sink to the bottom of it. To make this preparation light, the yolks and whites of the eggs should be beaten separately and added separately to the other ingredients. A glass of wine is sometimes added to the mixture, but this is scarcely necessary, as the cake will be found to be quite rich enough without it.

Common Seed-Cake. — INGREDI-ENTS.—*2 pounds of dough, ¼ pound of good dripping, 6 ounces of moist sugar, ½ ounce of caraway seeds, 1 egg.*

Mode.—If the dough is sent in from the baker's, put it into a basin, covered with a cloth, and set it in a warm place to rise. Then with a wooden spoon beat the dripping to a liquid, add it, with the other ingredients, to the dough, and beat it until everything is very thoroughly mixed. Put it into a buttered tin, and bake the cake for rather more than two hours.

Soda-Cake. — INGREDIENTS. — *¼ pound of butter, 1 pound of flour, ½ pound of currants, ¼ pound of moist sugar, 1 teacupful of milk, 3 eggs, 1 teaspoonful of carbonate of soda.*

Mode. — Rub the butter into the flour, add the currants and sugar, and mix these ingredients well together. Whisk the eggs well, stir them to the flour, etc., with the milk, in which the soda should be previously dissolved, and beat the whole up together with a wooden spoon or beater. Divide the dough into two pieces, put them into buttered moulds or cake-tins, and bake in a moderate oven for nearly an hour. The mixture must be extremely well beaten up, and not allowed to stand after the soda is added to it, but must be placed in the oven immediately.

Great care must also be taken that the cakes are quite done through, which may be ascertained by thrusting a knife into the middle of them: if the blade looks bright when withdrawn, they are done. If the tops acquire too much color before the inside is sufficiently baked, cover them over with a piece of clean white paper, to prevent them from burning.

Icing for Cakes.—*White of 3 eggs, 1 pound of sugar, flavoring of vanilla or lemon.*

Beat the whites of the eggs to a high froth, then add to them a quarter of a pound of white sugar pounded and sifted, flavor it with vanilla or lemon, and beat it with a large spoon in each hand until it is light and very white, but not quite so stiff as meringue mixture. The longer it is beaten the more firm it will become. Beat it until it may be spread smoothly on the cake.

How to "Ornament" with Icing. — If you wish to "ornament" your cake after the fashion of the confectioners, when the coating has become "hard dry," form a sheet of writing paper into a cone, fill with icing, and doubling over the top to secure the contents, press the paper gently with one hand, while guiding the point with the other, so that the icing will flow readily from the point. The exercise of a little artistic talent, with dexterous handling, — *trimming* and *slitting* the *point* of the cone occasionally — will enable you to form some of the very pleasing objects you see in the show-windows, such as cross-lines, initials, names, pierced hearts, Cupids, birds, flowers, vines, leaves, etc.

A Rich Plum Cake. — *Time,* two hours or more.

1 pound of fresh butter, 12 eggs, 1 quart of flour, 1 pound of moist sugar, ½ a pound of mixed spice, 3 pounds of currants, 1 pound of raisins, ¼ a pound of almonds, ¼ a pound of candied peel.

Beat the butter to a cream with your hand, and stir into it the yolks of the twelve eggs well beaten with the sugar; then add the spice and the almonds chopped very fine. Stir in the flour;

add the currants, washed and dried, the raisins chopped up, and the candied peel cut into pieces. As each ingredient is added, three teaspoonfuls of German yeast, a little milk, and nutmeg.

Put the flour, sugar, and nutmeg into a bowl, and mix it thoroughly with three teaspoonfuls of German yeast. Set it to rise, and *just* before setting it in the oven mix it up with the butter, warmed in a little milk, as stiff as you can, and bake it one hour. Add a few caraway seeds or citron, if you please.

Plain Short Bread. —*Time*, twenty-five to thirty minutes for three cakes.

1 pound of flour, ½ a pound of butter, 3 ounces of brown sugar.

Mix these ingredients and roll them out thick, and bake.

Molasses Cake.—Take one cup of molasses, one cup of sugar, one cup of water, one small tablespoonful of baking soda, one teaspoonful of cream of tartar, four cups of flour, half cup of lard (or quarter cup of butter), dissolve the soda and cream of tartar in the water, mix the lard (or butter) into the flour, then work the whole together; put in the tin and bake in a moderately hot oven.

Fruit Cake. — One cup of butter, two cups of sugar, one cup of molasses, one cup of coffee, one pound of chopped raisins, three eggs, a dessertspoonful of each kind of spice, one nutmeg, teaspoonful of saleratus. Add flour enough to make it a little stiffer than pound cake. This cake will keep a long time. A little citron in very thin slices through the cake improves it, and currants may be substituted for part of the raisins.

Pork Cake. — Two cups of sugar, one cup of molasses, one cup of sour milk, one pound of pork minced fine, one pound of raisins, four eggs, one nutmeg, one teaspoonful of soda, one tablespoonful of cinnamon, stir as fruit cake. Warranted to keep for six months.

Butter Cake. — Take half a pound of butter, beaten to a cream, half a pound of coffee sugar, half a pound of corn starch. Take one spoonful of sugar and one of starch. Stir it into the butter. Do so with all, till both starch and sugar are all stirred into the butter. Take four eggs, beat one yolk in at a time, one half cup of milk, put whites of eggs in fast. One cup of flour, half a teaspoonful of soda, and one teaspoonful of cream of tartar, should be dissolved in the milk.

Tea Cakes. — Take of flour one pound; sugar, one ounce; butter, one ounce; muriatic acid, two drams; bicarbonate of soda, two drams; milk six ounces; water, six ounces. Rub the butter into the flour; dissolve sugar and soda in the milk, and the acid in the water. First add the milk, etc., to the flour, and partially mix; then the water and acid, and mix well together; divide into three portions, and bake twenty-five minutes. Flat round tins or earthen pans are the best to bake them in. If the above be made with baking powder, a teaspoonful may be substituted for the acid and soda in the foregoing recipe, and all the other directions carried out as before stated. If buttermilk is used, the acid, milk, and water must be left out.

Gingerbread Snaps. — One pound of flour, half a pound of molasses, half a pound of sugar, quarter of a pound of butter, half an ounce of best prepared ginger, sixteen drops of essence of lemon, potash the size of a nut dissolved in a tablespoonful of hot water.

Drop Cakes. — One pint of flour, half a pound of butter, quarter of a pound of pounded lump sugar, half a nutmeg grated, a handful of currants, two eggs, and a large pinch of carbonate of soda, or volatile salts. To be baked in a slack oven for ten minutes or a quarter of an hour. The above quantity will make about thirty excellent cakes.

Cake of Mixed Fruits. — Extract the juice from red currants by simmering them very gently for a few minutes over a slow fire; strain it through folded muslin, and to one pound of the juice add a pound and a half of nonsuches, or of freshly-gathered apples, pared, and rather deeply cored, that the fibrous part may be avoided. Boil these quite slowly until the mixture is perfectly smooth; then, to evaporate part of the moisture, let the boiling be quickened. In from twenty-five to thirty minutes, draw the pan from the fire, and throw in gradually a pound and a quarter of sugar in fine powder; mix it well with the fruit, and when it is dissolved, continue the boiling rapidly for twenty minutes longer, keeping the mixture constantly stirred; put it into a mould, and store it, when cold, for winter use, or serve it for dessert, or for the second course; in the latter case, decorate it with spikes of almonds, blanched, and a heap solid whipped cream round it, or pour a custard into the dish. For dessert, it may be garnished with dice of the palest apple jelly. Juice of red currants, one pound; apples (pared and cored), one pound and a half. Twenty-five to thirty minutes. Sugar, one pound and a half, — twenty minutes.

Banbury Cakes.—Roll out the paste about half an inch thick, and cut it into pieces; then roll again till each piece becomes twice the size. Put some Banbury meat in the middle of one side, fold the other over it, and pinch it up into a somewhat oval shape; flatten it with your hand at the top, letting the seam be quite at the bottom; rub the tops over with the white of an egg, laid on with a brush, and dust loaf sugar over them; bake in a moderate oven. The meat for this cake is made thus :—Beat up a quarter of a pound of butter until it becomes in the state of cream; then mix with it half a pound of candied orange and lemon-peel, cut fine; one pound of currants, a quarter of an ounce of ground cinnamon, and a quarter of an ounce of all-spice : mix all well together, and keep in a jar till wanted for use.

Bath Buns. — A quarter of a pound of flour, four yolks and three whites of eggs, with four spoonfuls of solid fresh yeast. Beat in a bowl, and set before

the fire to rise; then rub into one pound of flour ten ounces of butter. Put in half a pound of sugar, and caraway-comfits. When the eggs and yeast are pretty light, mix by degrees all together; throw a cloth over it, and set before the fire to rise. Make the buns, and, when on the tins, brush over with the yolk of egg and milk; strew them with caraway-comfits; bake in a quick oven.

Pic-Nic Biscuits.—Take two ounces of fresh butter, and well work it with a pound of flour. Mix thoroughly with it half a saltspoonful of pure carbonate of soda, two ounces of sugar. Mingle thoroughly with the flour, make up the paste with spoonfuls of milk— it will require scarcely a quarter of a pint. Knead smooth, roll a quarter of an inch thick, cut in rounds about the size of the top of a small wineglass. Roll these out thin, prick them well, lay them on lightly floured tins, and bake in a gentle oven until crisp. When cold put into dry canisters. Thin cream used instead of milk in the paste will enrich the biscuits. Caraway seeds or ginger can be added, to vary these, at pleasure.

Ginger Biscuits and Cakes.—Work into small crumbs three ounces of butter, two pounds of flour, and three ounces of powdered sugar and two of ginger, in fine powder. Knead into a stiff paste, with new milk; roll thin, cut out with a cutter; bake in a slow oven until crisp through. Keep of a pale color. Additional sugar may be used when a sweeter biscuit is desired. For good ginger cakes,—butter, six ounces, sugar eight, for each pound of flour; wet the ingredients into a paste with eggs. A little lemon-peel grated will give an agreeable flavor.

Sugar Biscuits. — Cut the butter into the flour. Add the sugar and caraway seeds. Pour in the brandy, and then the milk; lastly, put in the pearl-ash. Stir all well with a knife, and mix it thoroughly till it becomes a lump of dough. Flour your paste-board, and lay the dough on it. Knead it very well. Divide it into eight or ten pieces, and knead each piece separately. Then put them all together, and knead them very well into one lump. Cut the dough in half, and roll it out into sheets about half an inch thick. Beat the sheets of dough very hard on both sides with the rolling-pin. Cut them out into round cakes with the edge of a tumbler. Butter iron pans, and lay the cakes in them. Bake them of a very pale - brown. If done too much, they will lose their taste. Let the oven be hotter at the top than at the bottom. These cakes kept in a stone jar, closely covered from the air, will continue perfectly good for several months.

Ginger Snaps. — *Time*, twenty minutes to bake.

½ pound of molasses, ¼ pound of brown sugar, 1 pound of flour, 1 tablespoonful of ground ginger, 1 of caraway seeds.

Work a quarter of a pound of butter into a pound of fine flour, then mix it with the molasses, brown sugar, ginger, and caraway seeds. Work it all well together, and form it into cakes not larger than a crown piece; place them on a baking tin in a moderate oven, when they will be dry and crisp.

To Make Good Plain Buns. — INGREDIENTS. — *1 pound of flour, 6 ounces of good butter, ¼ pound of sugar, 1 egg, nearly ¼ pint of milk, 2 small teaspoonfuls of baking-powder, a few drops of essence of lemon.*

Mode. — Warm the butter, without oiling it; beat it with a wooden spoon; stir the flour in gradually with the sugar, and mix these ingredients well together. Make the milk lukewarm, beat up with it the yolk of the egg and the essence of lemon, and stir these to the flour, etc. Add the baking-powder, beat the dough well for about ten minutes, divide it into twenty-four pieces, put them into buttered tins or cups, and bake in a brisk oven from twenty to thirty minutes.

Snow Cake (a genuine Scotch recipe). — INGREDIENTS.—*1 pound of arrowroot, ½ pound of pounded white sugar, ½ pound of butter, the whites of*

6 eggs, flavoring to taste, of essence of almonds, or vanilla, or lemon.

Mode. — Beat the butter to a cream; stir in the sugar and arrowroot gradually, at the same time beating the mixture. Whisk the whites of the eggs to a stiff froth, add them to the other ingredients, and beat well for twenty minutes. Put in whichever of the above flavorings may be preferred; pour the cake into a buttered mould or tin, and bake it in a moderate oven from one to one hour and a half.

Baker's Gingerbread. — Two cups of molasses (New Orleans best), four tablespoonfuls of butter stirred together without melting; add one cup of flour, two tablespoonfuls of soda dissolved in one cup of milk, one teaspoonful of alum dissolved in one-third of a cup of boiling water, and one tablespoonful of ginger. Stir all well together, adding flour gradually. Roll thin, cut in slices, and bake quickly.

RELISHES. — **Toasted Cheese,** or **Welsh Rare-bit.** — INGREDIENTS. — *Slices of bread, butter, rich cheese, mustard, and pepper.*

Mode. — Cut the bread into slices about half an inch in thickness; pare off the crust, toast the bread slightly without hardening or burning it, and spread it with butter. Cut some slices, not quite so large as the bread, from a good rich fat cheese; lay them on the toasted bread in a cheese-toaster; be careful that the cheese does not burn, and let it be equally melted. Spread over the top a little made mustard and a seasoning of pepper, and serve very hot, with very hot plates. To facilitate the melting of the cheese, it may be cut into thin flakes or toasted on one side before it is laid on the bread. As it is so essential to send this dish hot to table, it is a good plan to melt the cheese in small round silver or metal pans, and to send these pans to table, allowing one for each guest. Slices of dry or buttered toast should always accompany them, with mustard, pepper, and salt.

Time, about five minutes to melt the cheese.

Mock Crab—Sailor Fashion.—

Cut a slice of rich cheese rather thin, but of good size round. Mash it up with a fork to a paste, mix it with vinegar, mustard, and pepper. It has a great flavor of crab.

Toasted Cheese.—*Time,* ten minutes.

Cut equal quantities of rich cheese, and having pared into *extremely* small pieces, place it in a pan with a little milk, and a small slice of butter. Stir it over a slow fire until melted and quite smooth. Take it off the fire quickly, mix the yolk of an egg with it, and brown it in a toaster before the fire.

To Make Hot Buttered Toast.—

A loaf of household bread about two days old answers for making toast better than cottage bread, the latter not being a good shape, and too crusty for the purpose. Cut as many nice even slices as may be required, rather more than one-fourth of an inch in thickness, and toast them before a very bright fire, without allowing the bread to blacken, which spoils the appearance and flavor of all toast. When of a nice color on both sides, put it on a hot plate, divide some good butter into small pieces, place them on the toast, set this before the fire, and when the butter is just beginning to melt, spread it lightly over the toast. Trim off the crust and ragged edges, divide each round into four pieces, and send the toast quickly to table. Some persons cut the slices of toast across from corner to corner, so making the pieces of a three-cornered shape. Soyer recommends that each slice should be cut into pieces as soon as it is buttered, and when all are ready, that they should be piled lightly on the dish they are intended to be served on. He says that by cutting through four or five slices at a time, all the butter is squeezed out of the upper ones, while the bottom one is swimming in fat liquid. It is highly essential to use good butter for making this dish.

Anchovy Toast

is made by spreading anchovy paste upon buttered toast made as above, or if preferred, dry toast may be used. It is a delicious relish.

To Make Pancakes.—INGREDIENTS.—*Eggs, flour, milk; to every egg allow 1 ounce of flour, about 1 gill of milk, ⅛ saltspoonful of salt.*

Mode.—Ascertain that the eggs are fresh, break each one separately in a cup, whisk them well in a basin, add the flour, salt, and a few drops of milk, and beat the whole to a perfectly smooth batter, then pour in by degrees the remainder of the milk. The proportion of this latter ingredient must be regulated by the size of the eggs, etc., etc.; but the batter, when ready for frying, should be of the consistency of thick cream. Place a small frying-pan on the fire to get hot; let it be delicately clean, or the pancakes will stick, and when quite hot, put into it a small piece of butter, allowing about half an ounce to each pancake. When it is melted, pour in the batter, about half a teacupful to a pan five inches in diameter, and fry it for about four minutes, or until it is nicely brown on one side. By only pouring in a small quantity of batter, and so making the pancakes thin, the necessity of turning them (an operation rather difficult to unskilful cooks) is obviated. When the pancake is done, sprinkle over it some pounded sugar, roll it up in the pan, and take it out with a large slice, and place it on a dish before the fire. Proceed in this manner until sufficient are cooked for a dish, then send them quickly to table, and continue to send in a further quantity, as pancakes are never good unless eaten almost immediately they come from the frying-pan. The batter may be flavored with a little grated lemon-rind, or the pancakes may have preserves rolled in them instead of sugar. Send sifted sugar and a cut lemon to table with them. To render the pancakes very light, the yolks and whites of the eggs should be beaten separately, and the whites added the last thing to the batter before frying.

Time, from four to five minutes for

a pancake that does not require turning; from six to eight minutes for a thicker one.

Savory Omelet.—Make batter as for a pancake, chop a little parsley and green onions, and pepper and salt, stir in, and fry in plenty of lard. It may be served either dry or with gravy.

Preserving Fruit. — The grand secret of preserving is to deprive the fruit of its water of vegetation in the shortest time possible; for which purpose the fruit ought to be gathered just at the point of proper maturity. An ingenious French writer considers fruit of all kinds as having four distinct periods of maturity — the maturity of vegetation, of honeyfication, of expectation, and of coction.

THE FIRST PERIOD he considers to be that when, having gone through the vegetable processes up to the ripening, it appears ready to drop spontaneously. This, however, is a period which arrives sooner in warm climates than in cold ones, but its absolute presence may be ascertained by the general filling out of the rind, by the bloom, by the smell, and by the facility with which it may be plucked from the branch.

THE SECOND PERIOD, or that of Honeyfication, consists in the ripeness and flavor which fruits of all kinds acquire if plucked a few days before arriving at their first maturity, and preserved under a proper degree of temperature. Apples may acquire or arrive at this second degree of maturity upon the tree, but it too often happens that the flavor of the fruit is thus lost, for fruit over-ripe is always found to have parted with a portion of its flavor.

THE THIRD STAGE, or of Expectation, as the theorist quaintly terms it, is that which is acquired by pulpy fruits, which, though sufficiently ripe to drop off the tree, are even then hard and sour. This is the case with several kinds both of apples and pears, not to mention other fruits, which always improve after keeping in the confectionery, — but with respect to the medlar and the quince, this maturity of expectation is absolutely necessary.

THE FOURTH DEGREE of maturity, or of Coction, is completely artificial, and is nothing more nor less than the change produced upon fruit by the aid of culinary heat.

Hints about Making Preserves.— It is not generally known that boiling fruit a long time, and *skimming it well*, *without sugar*, and *without a cover* to the preserving-pan, is a very economical and excellent way — economical, because the bulk of the scum rises from the *fruit*, and not from the *sugar;* but the latter should be good. Boiling it without a *cover* allows the evaporation of all the watery particles therefrom, and renders the preserves firm and well flavored. The proportions are, three-quarters of a pound of sugar to a pound of fruit. Jam made in this way of currants, strawberries, raspberries, or gooseberries, is excellent. The sugar should be added after the skimming is completed.

To Make a Syrup. — Dissolve one pound of sugar in about a gill of water, boil for a few minutes, skimming it till quite clear. To every two pounds of sugar add the white of one egg well beaten. Boil very quickly, and skim carefully while boiling. In the season for "preserves" our readers may be glad of the above instructions, which have been adopted with great success.

Covering for Preserves. — White paper cut to a suitable size, dipped in brandy, and put over the preserves when cold, and then a double paper tied over the top. All preserves should stand a night before they are covered. Instead of brandy, the white of eggs may be used to glaze the paper covering, and the paper may be pasted round the edge of the pot instead of tied — it will exclude the air better.

To Bottle Fruits.—Burn a match in a bottle to exhaust all air, then place in the fruit to be preserved, quite dry, and without blemish; sprinkle sugar between each layer, put in the bung, and tie bladder over, setting the bottles, bung downwards, in a large stewpan of cold water, with hay between to prevent breaking. When the skin is just cracking, take them out. All preserves require exclusion from the air. Place a piece of paper dipped in sweet oil over the top of the fruit; prepare thin paper, immersed in gum-water, and, while wet, press it over and around the top of the jar; as it dries, it will become quite firm and tight.

APPLES for keeping should be laid out on a *dry* floor for three weeks. They may then be packed away in layers, with dry straw between them. Each apple should be rubbed with a dry cloth as it is put away. They should be kept in a cool place, but should be sufficiently covered with straw to protect them from frost. They should be plucked on a dry day.

Dried Apples are produced by taking fine apples of good quality, and placing them in a very slow oven for several hours. Take them out occasionally, rub and press them flat. Continue until they are done. If they look dry, rub over them a little clarified sugar.

Preserved Rhubarb. — Peel one pound of the finest rhubarb, and cut it into pieces of two inches in length; add three-quarters of a pound of white sugar, and the rind and juice of one lemon—the rind to be cut into narrow strips. Put all into a preserving kettle, and simmer gently until the rhubarb s quite soft; take it out carefully with a silver spoon, and put it into jars; then boil the syrup a sufficient time to make it keep well (say one hour), and pour it over the fruit. When cold, put a paper soaked in brandy over it, and tie the jars down with a bladder to exclude the air. This is a very good recipe, and should be taken advantage of in the spring.

Dry Apricots.— Gather before ripe, scald in a jar put into boiling water; pare and stone them; put into a syrup of half their weight of sugar, in the proportion of half a pint of water to

two pounds of sugar. Scald, and then boil until they are clear. Stand for two days in the syrup, then put into a thin candy, and scald them in it. Keep two days longer in the candy, heating them each day, and then lay them on glasses to dry.

Preserved Peaches. — Wipe and pick the fruit, and have ready a quarter of the weight of fine sugar in powder. Put the fruit into an ice-pot that shuts very close; throw the sugar over it, and then cover the fruit with brandy. Between the top and cover of the pot put a double piece of gray paper. Set the pot in a saucepan of water till the brandy is as hot as you can bear to put your finger into, but do not let it boil. Put the fruit into a jar, and pour on the brandy. Cover in same manner as preserves.

To Preserve Peaches. — Procure glass jars with any simple and effective stopper, select good solid peaches, pare and take out the stones, take one pound of the parings, one pint of water, half a pound of white sugar, boil well together for forty minutes in a brass kettle, then strain through a cloth, let the syrup cool, fill the jars with the pared peaches, pour in the syrup until the jars are full. Take a convenient vessel, put a cloth in the bottom, set in the jars, then fill the vessel or the space around the jars with cold water, to come within three inches of the top of the jars, set on the stove, bring gradually to a boil, boil well for thirty minutes, take the jars out of the vessel, put on the stoppers, screw tight while hot. Peaches put up in this way will stay solid, and keep the natural color and flavor for any length of time.

Brandy Peaches.— Drop them into a weak boiling lye, until the skin can be wiped off. Make a thin syrup to cover them, boil until they are soft to the finger-nail; make a rich syrup, and add, after they come from the fire, and while hot, the same quantity of brandy as syrup. The fruit must be covered.

Preserved Plums.—Cut your plums in half (they must not be quite ripe), and take out the stones. Weigh the plums, and allow a pound of loaf sugar to a pound of fruit. Crack the stones, take out the kernels, and break them in pieces. Boil the plums and kernels very slowly for about fifteen minutes, in as little water as possible. Then spread them on a large dish to cool, and strain the liquor. Next day add your syrup, and boil for fifteen minutes. Put into jars, pour the juice over when warm, and tie them up, when cold, with brandy paper. — Plums for common use are very good done in molasses. Put your plums into an earthen vessel that holds a gallon, having first slit each plum with a knife. To three quarts of plums put a pint of molasses. Cover them over, and set them on hot coals in the chimney corner. Let them stew for twelve hours or more, occasionally stirring, and next day put them up in jars. Done in this manner, they will keep till the next spring.

Red-Currant Jam.—INGREDIENTS. — To every pound of fruit allow ¾ pound of loaf sugar.

Mode.—Let the fruit be gathered on a fine day; weigh it, and then strip the currants from the stalks; put them into a preserving-pan with sugar in the above proportion; stir them, and boil them for about three-quarters of an hour. Carefully remove the scum as it rises. Put the jam into pots, and, when cold, cover with oiled papers; over these put a piece of tissue-paper brushed over on both sides with the white of an egg; press the paper round the top of the pot, and, when dry, the covering will be quite hard and air-tight. Black-currant jam should be made in the same manner as the above.

Time, half to three-quarters of an hour, reckoning from the time the jam boils all over. *Sufficient*, allow from six to seven quarts of currants to make twelve one-pound pots of jam. Make this in July.

Red-Currant Jelly.—INGREDIENTS. — Red currants, to every pint of juice allow ¾ pound of loaf sugar.

Mode. — Have the fruit gathered in fine weather; pick it from the stalks,

put it into a jar, and place this jar in a saucepan of boiling water over the fire, and let it simmer gently until the juice is well drawn from the currants; then strain them through a jelly-bag or fine cloth, and, if the jelly is wished very clear, do not squeeze them *too much*, as the skin and pulp from the fruit will be pressed through with the juice, and so make the jelly muddy. Measure the juice, and to each pint allow three-quarters of a pound of loaf sugar; put these into a preserving-pan, set it over the fire, and keep stirring the jelly until it is done, carefully removing every particle of scum as it rises, using a wooden or silver spoon for the purpose, as metal or iron ones would spoil the color of the jelly. When it has boiled from twenty minutes to half an hour, put a little of the jelly on a plate, and if firm when cool, it is done. Take it off the fire, pour it into small gallipots, cover each of the pots with an oiled paper, and then with a piece of tissue paper, brushed over on both sides with the white of an egg. Label the pots, adding the year when the jelly was made, and store away in a dry place. A jam may be made with the currants if they are not squeezed too dry, by adding a few fresh raspberries, and boiling all together, with sufficient sugar to sweeten it nicely. As this preserve is not worth storing away, but is only for immediate eating, a smaller proportion of sugar than usual will be found enough; it answers very well for children's puddings, or for a nursery preserve. Black-currant jelly can also be made from the above recipe.

Time, from three-quarters to one hour to extract the juice; twenty minutes to half hour to boil to a jelly. *Sufficient*, eight quarts of fruit will make from ten to twelve pots of jelly. Make this in July.

Note.—Should the above proportion of sugar not be found sufficient for some tastes, add an extra quarter pound to every pint of juice, making altogether one pound.

Baked Damsons for Winter use.— INGREDIENTS.— *To every pound of fruit allow 6 ounces of pounded sugar.*

Mode.—Choose sound fruit, not too ripe; pick off the stalks, weigh it, and to every pound allow the above proportion of pounded sugar. Put the fruit into large dry stone jars, sprinkle the sugar among it; cover the jars with saucers, place them in a rather cool oven, and bake the fruit until it is quite tender. When cold, cover the top of the fruit with a piece of white paper cut to the size of the jar; pour over this melted mutton suet about an inch thick, and cover the tops of the jars with thick brown paper, well tied down. Keep the jars in a cool dry place, and the fruit will remain good till the following Christmas, but not much longer.

Time, from five to six hours to bake the damsons, in a very cool oven. Make in September and October.

Raspberry or Blackberry Jam. —

INGREDIENTS. — *To every pound of raspberries allow* 1 *pound of sugar,* ¼ *pint of red-currant juice.*

Mode. — Let the fruit for this preserve be gathered in fine weather, and used as soon after it is picked as possible. Take off the stalks, put the raspberries into the preserving-pan, break them well with a wooden spoon, and let them boil for a quarter of an hour, keeping them well stirred. Then add the currant juice and sugar, and boil again for half an hour. Skim the jam well after the sugar is added, or the preserve will not be clear. The addition of the currant juice is a very great improvement to this preserve, as it gives it a piquant taste, which the flavor of the raspberries seems to require.

Time, quarter of an hour to simmer the fruit without the sugar; half an hour after it is added. *Sufficient,* — allow about one pint of fruit to fill a one-pound pot. *Seasonable* in July and August.

To Preserve Cherries. — Take

cherries that are not very ripe, and allow a pound of white sugar to each pound of them. Make syrup of the sugar, and just sufficient water to cover the cherries; boil them with the stems on till transparent. If you wish to preserve them without the pits, remove them carefully, saving the juice; make a syrup of it with white sugar, add very little water; put in the cherries and boil them till of a thick consistency. They should be very ripe, if preserved in this way. Put them in small jars when cold, cork and seal them tight; put the jars in boxes filled with dry sand, and keep in a cool place. If a little brandy is turned over them when put in the jars, they will be less liable to ferment. It is very difficult to keep any acid fruit well which is preserved early in the summer.

Bottling Cherries.—To every pound

of fruit add six ounces of powdered lump sugar. Fill the jars with fruit; shake in the sugar over, and tie each jar down with two bladders, as there is danger of one bursting during the boiling. Place the jars in a boiler of cold water, and after the water has boiled, let them remain three hours; take them out, and when cool, put them in a dry place, where they will keep over a year.

Tomato Jam.—Take ripe tomatoes,

peel them and take out the seeds; put them into a preserving kettle, with half a pound of sugar to each pound of tomatoes; boil one or two lemons soft, then pound them fine, take out the pits, add the lemon to the tomato, and boil slowly; mash to a smooth mass; continue to stir until smooth and thick; then put into jars or tumblers.

To Can Tomatoes Whole. — Scald

and remove the skin; place in the jars until full. Boil twenty minutes, and at the same time boil some tomatoes in a dish or pan; when ready to seal, fill up the jars or cans with tomatoes and juice from this dish, and seal boiling hot. Tomatoes should be cooked and canned in nothing but their own juice.

Orange Marmalade. — Cut the

oranges in half, then take out the pulp and juice, separating all the skins and pips. Put the rinds into salt and water for a night; the next morning put them into a stewpan with fresh water. Let them stew until soft, so that a straw can be run through them easily; cut the peels into thin strips. To every pound of fruit add one pound and a half of coarse white sugar. Put the juice, pulp, and peel, with the sugar, into the stewpan and let it boil twenty minutes. Seville oranges must be used, and the marmalade is better if kept six months. The juice and grated rind of two lemons to every dozen oranges is a great improvement.

How to Keep Grapes. — It is reported that a vineyardist in California keeps his grapes any desirable length of time by packing them, when perfectly free from external moisture, in nail casks, the interstices filled with perfectly dry sawdust, and then burying them in the ground, under a shed.

To Remove Burnt Fruit or other Burnt Victuals from a Kettle. — Put a shovelful of ashes from the stove-hearth into the kettle, a quart of water, and boil. In a few minutes all the burnt crust may be easily washed off of the kettle.

Strawberry Jam. — *Time,* one hour. *To 6 pounds of strawberries allow 3 pounds of sugar.*

Procure some fine scarlet strawberries, strip off the stalks, and put them into a preserving pan over a moderate fire; boil them for half an hour, keeping them constantly stirred. Break the sugar into small pieces, and mix them with the strawberries after they have been removed from the fire. Then place it again over the fire, and boil it for another half hour very quickly. Put it into pots, and when cold, cover it over with brandy papers and a piece of paper moistened with the white of an egg over the tops.

Black Currant Jam. — *Time,* three-quarters of an hour to an hour. *To every pound of currants allow ¾ of a pound of sugar.*

Gather the currants when they are thoroughly ripe and dry, and pick them from the stalks. Bruise them lightly in a large bowl, and to every pound of fruit put three-quarters of a pound of finely-beaten loaf sugar. Put sugar and fruit into a preserving pan, and boil

17

them from three-quarters to one hour, skimming as the scum rises, and stirring constantly; then put the jam into pots, cover them with brandy paper, and tie them closely over.

Black Currant Jelly. — *Time,* two hours.

To every 5 quarts of currants allow rather more than ½ a pint of water; to every pint of juice 1 pound of loaf sugar.

Gather the currants when ripe on a dry day; strip them from the stalks, and put them into an earthen pan, or jar, and to every five quarts allow the above proportion of water. Tie the pan over, and set it in the oven for an hour and a quarter; then squeeze out the juice through a coarse cloth, and to every pint of juice put a pound of loaf sugar, broken into pieces, boil it for three-quarters of an hour, skimming it well; then pour it into small pots, and when cold, put brandy papers over them, and tie them closely over.

CONFECTIONERY.—Thick Apple Jelly or Marmalade (for Entremets or Dessert Dishes). — INGREDIENTS.—*Apples; to every pound of pulp allow ¾ pound of sugar, ¼ teaspoonful of minced lemon-peel.*

Mode. — Peel, core, and boil the apples with only sufficient water to prevent them from burning; beat them to a pulp, and to every pound of pulp allow the above proportion of sugar in lumps. Dip the lumps into water, put these into a saucepan, and boil till the syrup is thick and can be well skimmed, then add this syrup to the apple pulp, with the minced lemon-peel, and stir it over a quick fire for about twenty minutes, or until the apples cease to stick to the bottom of the pan. The jelly is then done, and may be poured into moulds which have been previously dipped in water, when it will turn out nicely for dessert or a side-dish; for the latter a little custard should be poured round, and it should be garnished with strips of citron or stuck with blanched almonds.

Time, from a half to three-quarters of an hour to reduce the apples to a pulp; twenty minutes to boil after the sugar is added.

Stewed Apples and Custard—(a pretty dish for a Juvenile Supper).— INGREDIENTS.—7 good sized apples, the rind of ½ lemon or 4 cloves, ½ pound of sugar, ¾ pint of water, ½ pint of custard.

Mode.—Pare and take out the cores of the apples without dividing them, and, if possible, leave the stalks on; boil the sugar and water together for ten minutes, then put in the apples with the lemon-rind or cloves, whichever flavor may be preferred, and simmer gently until they are tender, taking care not to let them break. Dish them neatly on a glass dish, reduce the syrup by boiling it quickly for a few minutes; let it cool a little, then pour it over the apples. Have ready quite half a pint of custard, pour it round, but not over, the apples when they are quite cold, and the dish is ready for table. A few almonds blanched and cut into strips, and stuck in the apples, would improve their appearance.

Time, from twenty to thirty minutes to stew the apples.

Arrowroot Blanc - Mange — (an inexpensive Supper Dish). — INGRE- DIENTS.—4 heaped tablespoonfuls of ar- rowroot, 1½ pints of milk, 3 laurel leaves or the rind of ½ a lemon, sugar to taste.

Mode.—Mix to a smooth batter the arrowroot with a half pint of milk; put the other pint on the fire, with laurel leaves or lemon-peel, whichever may be preferred, and let the milk steep until it is well flavored. Then strain the milk, and add it, boiling, to the mixed arrowroot; sweeten it with sifted sugar, and let it boil, stirring it all the time, till it thickens sufficiently to come from the saucepan. Grease a mould with pure salad-oil, pour in the blanc-mange, and when quite set, turn it out on a dish, and pour round it a compôte of any kind of fruit, or garnish it with jam. A tablespoonful of brandy stirred in just before the blanc-mange is moulded, very much improves the flavor of this sweet dish.

Time, altogether, half an hour.

Boiled Custards. — INGREDIENTS.

— 1 pint of milk, 5 eggs, 3 ounces of loaf sugar, 3 laurel leaves, or the rind of ½ a lemon, or a few drops of essence of vanilla, 1 tablespoonful of brandy.

Mode. — Put the milk into a lined saucepan, with the sugar, and which- ever of the above flavorings may be preferred (the lemon-rind flavors cus tards most deliciously), and let the milk steep by the side of the fire until it is well flavored. Bring it to the point of boiling, then strain it into a basin; whisk the eggs well, and, when the milk has cooled a little, stir in the eggs, and *strain* this mixture into a jug. Place this jug in a saucepan of boiling water over the fire. Keep stirring the custard *one way* until it thickens; but on no account allow it to reach the boiling point, as it will instantly curdle and be full of lumps. Take it off the fire, stir in the brandy, and, when this is well-mixed with the custard, pour it into glasses, which should be rather more than three parts full. Grate a little nutmeg over the top, and the dish is ready for table. To make custards look and eat better, ducks' eggs should be used, when ob- tainable; they add very much to the flavor and richness, and so many are not required as of the ordinary eggs— four ducks' eggs to the pint of milk making a delicious custard. When desired extremely rich and good, cream should be substituted for the milk, and double the quantity of eggs used, to those mentioned, omitting the whites.

Time, half an hour to infuse the lemon-rind, about ten minutes to stir the custard.

Lemon Blanc-Mange. — INGREDI- ENTS. — 1 *quart of milk, the yolks of 4 eggs, 3 ounces of ground rice, 6 ounces of pounded sugar, 1½ ounces of fresh butter, the rind of 1 lemon, the juice of 2, ½ ounce of gelatine.*

Mode. — Make a custard with the yolks of the eggs and half a pint of the milk, and, when done, put it into a basin; put half the remainder of the milk into a saucepan with the ground rice, fresh butter, lemon-rind, and three ounces of the sugar, and let these ingredients boil until the mixture is stiff, stirring them continually; when done, pour it into the bowl where the custard is, mixing both well together. Put the gelatine with the rest of the milk into a saucepan, and let it stand by the side of the fire to dissolve. Boil for a minute or two, stir carefully into the basin, adding three ounces more of pounded sugar. When cold, stir in the lemon-juice, which should be carefully strained, and pour the mixture into a well-oiled mould, leaving out the lemon-peel, and set the mould in a pan of cold water until wanted for table. Use eggs that have rich-looking yolks; and, should the weather be very warm, rather a larger proportion of gelatine must be allowed.

Time, altogether, half an hour.

How to Mould Bottled Jellies. — Uncork the bottle. Place it in a saucepan of hot water until the jelly is reduced to a liquid state. Taste it, to ascertain whether it is sufficiently flavored, and if not, add a little wine. Pour the jelly into moulds which have been soaked in water. Let it set, and turn it out by placing the mould in hot water for a minute; then wipe the outside, put a dish on the top, and turn it over quickly. The jelly should then slip easily away from the mould, and be quite firm. It may be garnished as taste dictates.

CANDIES.— Plain Taffy. — Boil a quart of molasses over a slow fire for half an hour, keep stirring it, do not let it boil over; add half teaspoonful of powdered carbonate of soda; when it thickens, drop a little in cold water; if it becomes brittle it is done; flavor it with vanilla, lemon, or any of the essences, to taste, then pour it into a shallow dish that has been buttered; set away to cool.

Everton Taffy. — Melt three ounces of fresh butter and one pound of brown sugar; boil over a clear fire until the syrup becomes brittle, when drop into cold water: this will require about a quarter of an hour; (if desired it may be flavored when first put over the fire

with essence of lemon or ground ginger;) pour into a shallow dish buttered, and set away to cool.

Molasses Candy.—One pound granulated sugar, two pints best New Orleans molasses, boil slowly ten minutes, then add three tablespoonfuls of vinegar, and boil until it becomes brittle, when a little is dropped into cold water, then stir in a little carbonate of soda, pour it into a dish, and work with the hand; the more it is pulled out the whiter it will become.

Note. — Some persons prefer three pints of molasses, instead of sugar and molasses; before pouring it out of the kettle it may be flavored to the taste with any kind of extract.

Ginger Candy.—One pound refined crushed sugar, one-third pint of water, boil it to a thin syrup, then take out a little of the syrup, and mix it smoothly with a teaspoonful of ground ginger, then stir it altogether in the kettle, boil it slowly a minute, then add the grated rind of a lemon, and keep stirring it until it will fall in a mass from the spoon. Should it accidentally be boiled too much, so as to fall into a powder, add a little water, and boil again; when done, drop it on buttered plates in small cakes.

Cream Candy. — Boil three pounds of loaf sugar and half pint of water over a slow fire for half an hour, then add a teaspoonful of carbonate of soda and a tablespoonful of vinegar; keep it stirring, and boil it until it becomes brittle; flavor it to taste with a little lemon, vanilla, or other extract, as preferred; rub some butter on the hands, and pull it about until it becomes white, then twist it, or cut it into the shape required.

Cocoanut Candy. — Pare and grate a cocoanut, or cut into small pieces, for each half pound; boil half pound loaf sugar, and two tablespoonfuls of water; when it comes to a boil, stir in the cocoanut, keep stirring until it is boiled brittle, then flavor it with lemon, or any other essence required; immediately pour it into a buttered dish, and cut it any form desired.

Candy Drops. — May be made

almost any flavor and color. Pound refined sugar, and sift it through a fine
sieve, put it into an earthen vessel,
with a little water, and a little of the
flavoring extract required. (If too
liquid the syrup will be too thin, and
the drops will run together; if too
thick, it cannot be poured out easily.)
When well mixed into a stiff paste,
put it into a small saucepan and set it
over the fire; when it begins to bubble,
stir it a little, and take it from the fire,
and drop it in small lumps on sheets
of buttered tin; after standing two
hours, place them inside the oven to
finish drying; as soon as hard and transparent, take them away from the fire.

Note. — Strawberry, raspberry, orange, clove,
jessamine, or any other kind may be made by
adding those extracts before taking the saucepan
off the fire. The syrup may be colored before
taking it off the fire, as follows: — For red, use
carmine lakes or cochineal; for violet, use blue
and carmine lakes; for orange, use yellow lakes
or saffron.

Peppermint Lozenges.—INGREDI-
ENTS.—*1 ounce picked gum tragacanth,
soaked six hours, with 2 ounces tepid
water, in a gallipot, and then prepared
by squeezing or wringing it through a
cloth, 1½ pounds fine icing sugar, and a
teaspoonful essence of peppermint.*
Work the prepared gum with the
flattened fist, on a very clean dish,
until it becomes perfectly white and
elastic, then gradually work in the
sugar, adding the peppermint when
the paste has acquired a compact,
smooth, elastic substance: a few drops
of thick wet cobalt blue should be
added while working the mass, to give
it a brilliant whiteness. This paste is
now to be rolled out, with fine sugar
dredged over the slab, to the thickness
of two-penny pieces; it may now be
cut out with a circular cutter the size
of a dime, and place them on a sugar-
powdered paper to dry; when quite
dry, keep them in well-stoppered bottles in a dry place.

Note. — Instead of using a circular cutter, they
may be cut in squares with a buttered knife.

Ginger Lozenges are made same
as Peppermint, except one ounce of
ground ginger to flavor, and a few
drops thick wet gamboge to color.

Hoarhound Lozenges. — INGREDI-
ENTS. — *1 ounce of gum dragon, soaked
in a ¼ of a pint of strong extract of hoar-
hound, and 1½ pounds of fine icing sugar.*
Proceed the same as for Peppermint
Lozenges.

Cinnamon Lozenges.—The same as
Peppermint, except a dessertspoonful
of essence of cinnamon for flavoring,
and a few drops of thick wet burnt
umber, with a pinch of carmine to color.

Clove Lozenges.—The same as Peppermint, except essence of cloves to
flavor and a few drops of wet burnt
umber to color.

Orange Lozenges.— INGREDIENTS.
—*1 ounce prepared gum, 1½ pounds fine
sugar, 2 ounces orange; sugar the gum
to be soaked in 2 ounces of orange-flower
water.* Proceed same as for Peppermint
Lozenges.

Cough Lozenges. — INGREDIENTS.
— *1 ounce prepared gum soaked in 2
ounces of orange-flower water, 2 pounds
fine sugar, 50 drops of paregoric, 20
drops ipecacuanha, 1½ ounces syrup of
squills.* Work the gum on the slab with
one-third of the sugar, gradually work
in the syrup of squills, then the remainder of the sugar, and the ipecacuanha. Finish this excellent lozenge
the same as directed for Peppermint.

Coltsfoot Lozenges.—INGREDIENTS.
—*1 ounce gum dragon, soaked in 2 ounces
of orange-flower water, 1½ pounds of fine
sugar, and ½ ounce of essence of Coltsfoot.*
Proceed as for Peppermint Lozenges.

Cayenne and Catechu Lozenges.—
INGREDIENTS. — *1 ounce gum dragon,
soaked in 2 ounces of water, 2 pounds
fine sugar, ½ ounce essence Cayenne, and
½ ounce prepared catechu.* Proceed as
for Peppermint Lozenges.

Brown's Bronchial Troches. — IN-
GREDIENTS. — *4 ounces gum Arabic,
soaked in 4 ounces of water, 1½ pounds
fine sugar, 4 ounces pulverized cubebs, 1
ounce pulverized extract of conium, and
1 pound of pulverized extract of liquorice.* Proceed as for Peppermint Lozenges. Excellent for coughs and throat
affections.

Ice Cream. —FREEZING WITH ICE. — The use of ice in cooling depends upon the fact of its requiring a vast quantity of heat to convert it from a solid into a liquid state, or in other words, to melt it; and the heat so required is obtained from those objects with which it may be in contact. A pound of ice requires nearly as much heat to melt it as would be sufficient to make a pound of cold water boiling hot: hence its cooling power is extremely great. But ice does not begin to melt until the temperature is above the freezing-point, and therefore it cannot be employed in freezing liquids, etc., but only in cooling them. If, however, any substance is mixed with ice which is capable of causing it to melt more rapidly, and at a lower temperature, a still more intense cooling effect is the result; such a substance is common salt (though *rock salt* is invariably used by professional manufacturers), and the degree of cold produced by the mixture of one part of salt with two parts of snow or pounded ice, is greater than thirty degrees below freezing. In making ice cream and dessert ices, the following articles are required: — Pewter ice-pots with tightly-fitting lids, furnished with handles; wooden ice-pails, to hold the rough ice and salt, which should be stoutly made, about the same depth as the ice-pots, and nine or ten inches more in diameter, — each should have a hole in the side, fitted with a good cork, in order that the water from the melted ice may be drawn off as required. In addition, a broad spatula, about four inches long, rounded at the end, and furnished with a long wooden handle, is necessary to scrape the frozen cream from the sides of the ice-pot, and for mixing the whole smoothly together; or a long knife, having a straight blade, will answer the purpose. When making ices, place the mixture of cream and fruit to be frozen in the ice-pot, cover it with the lid, and put the pot in the ice-pail, which proceed to fill up with coarsely-pounded ice and salt, in the proportion of about one part of salt to three of ice. Let the whole remain a few minutes (if covered by a blanket, so much the better), then whirl the pot briskly by the handle for a few minutes, take off the lid, and with a spatula, or knife, scrape the iced cream from the sides, mixing the whole smoothly. Put on the lid, and whirl again, repeating all the operations every few minutes until the whole of the cream is well frozen. Great care and considerable labor are required in stirring, so that the whole cream may be smoothly frozen, and not in hard lumps. When finished, if it is required to be kept any time, the melted ice and salt should be allowed to escape, by removing the cork, and the pail filled up with fresh materials. It is scarcely necessary to add, that if any of the melted ice and salt is allowed to mix with the cream, the latter is spoiled.

Note. — Amateur ice cream makers are not generally aware that the operation of "*beating*," by which the *quality* of the cream is vastly *improved*, and the *quantity* turned out *nearly doubled*; as, for instance, *five quarts* of the mixed liquid cream will, when "*beaten up*" after freezing, turn out, by measurement, from *eight* to *ten quarts* of the luscious delicacy.

FREEZING WITHOUT ICE. — From the difficulty of obtaining ice in places distant from large towns, and in hot countries, and from the impracticability of keeping it any length of time, or, in fact, of keeping small quantities more than a few hours, its use is much limited, and many have been the attempts to obtain an efficient substitute. For this purpose various salts have been employed, which, when dissolved in water, or in acids, absorb a sufficient amount of heat to freeze substances with which they may be placed in contact.

Many of the freezing mixtures which are to be found described in books are incorrectly so named, for although they themselves are below the freezing point, yet they are not sufficiently powerful to freeze any quantity of water, or other substances, when placed in a vessel within them.

The following is the composition of

the new freezing preparation, which is now exported so largely to India, and the composition of which *has hitherto never been made public:* Actual quantities — one pound of muriate of ammonia, or sal ammoniac, finely powdered, is to be *intimately* mixed with two pounds of nitrate of potash or saltpetre, also in powder; this mixture we may call No. 1. No. 2 is formed by crushing three pounds of the best soda. In use, an equal bulk of both No. 1 and No. 2 is to be taken, stirred together, placed in the ice-pail surrounding the ice-pot, and rather less cold water poured on than will dissolve the whole; if one quart of No. 1, and the same bulk of No. 2 are taken, it will require about one quart of water to dissolve them, and the temperature will fall, if the materials used are cool, to nearly thirty degrees below freezing. Those who fail, may trace their want of success to one or other of the following points:—the use of too small a quantity of the preparation,—the employment of a few ounces; whereas, in freezing ices, the ice-pot must be entirely surrounded with the freezing material: no one would attempt to freeze with four ounces of ice and salt. Again, too large a quantity of water may be used to dissolve the preparation, when all the excess of water has to be cooled down instead of the substance it is wished to freeze. All the materials used should be pure, and as cool as can be obtained. The ice-pail in which the mixture is made must be of some non-conducting material, as wood, which will prevent the access of warmth from the air; and the ice-pot, in which the liquor to be frozen is placed, should be of pewter, and surrounded nearly to its top by the freezing mixture. Bear in mind that the making of ice cream, under any circumstances, is an operation requiring considerable dexterity and practice.

Strawberry Ice Cream. — Take one pint of strawberries, one pint of cream, nearly half a pound of powdered white sugar, the juice of a lemon; mash the fruit through a sieve, and take out the seeds; mix with the other articles, and freeze. A little new milk added makes the whole freeze more quickly.

Raspberry Ice Cream. — The same as strawberry. These ices are often colored by cochineal, but the addition is not advantageous to the flavor. Strawberry or raspberry jam may be used instead of the fresh fruit, or equal quantities of jam and fruit employed. Of course the quantity of sugar must be proportionately diminished.

Chocolate Ice Cream. — Boil one quart of milk, grate half pound best chocolate, and stir into the milk; let it boil until it becomes thick, then add a quarter of a pound of fine sugar; when cool add one quart of cream, stir well and pour into the freezer.

Cherry Ice Cream. — Pound half a pound unstoned preserved cherries, put them into a basin with a pint of cream, the juice of a lemon, and a quarter of a pint of syrup; pass it through a sieve and freeze it.

Currant Ice Cream. — Put three large spoonfuls of currant jelly in a basin, with a quarter of a pint of syrup, the juice of three lemons, add one quart of cream and a little cochineal; mix it well together, pass it through a sieve, then freeze it.

Lemon Ice Cream. — Mix the juice of four lemons, the peel of one grated, and half a pint of syrup, with one pint of cream; work it well together, pass it through a sieve, then freeze it.

Pineapple Ice Cream. — Pound or grate the inside of a pineapple, rub one pound of this pulp through a strainer, then put it in a stewpan with three-quarters of a pound of fine sugar, the yolks of three eggs, and one and a half pints of cream; mix well together, then place it over the fire to thicken, but do not let it boil, then pass it through a sieve, and freeze it.

Coffee Ice Cream. — Mix one large cupful of made coffee, quite strong, with half a pound of fine sugar, and the yolks of two eggs well beaten, into a stewpan; place it over the fire to thicken, stir it well, but do not let it boil; pass it through a sieve, add one quart of cream, and then freeze it.

Note.—Fresh fruits or jam, or the essence or extracts of those fruits, may be used to flavor ice cream, but when fresh fruits are used it should *always* be well mixed with the sugar or syrup *before adding the cream*, and should be almost cold before mixing, or it is liable to curdle. In all cases where fine sugar is mentioned, finely powdered loaf sugar of the best quality is intended, and where syrup is mentioned, plain syrup is intended, and is made as follows:—PLAIN SYRUP.— Take two and a half pounds of best loaf sugar, and a pint of water; dissolve the sugar in the water by heat, remove any scum that may arise, and strain while hot.

Strawberry - Water Ice. — One
large pottle of scarlet strawberries, the juice of a lemon, a pound of sugar, or one pint of strong syrup, half a pint of water. Mix, — first rubbing the fruit through a sieve,—and freeze.

Raspberry-Water Ice, and Currant-Water Ice,
are made in the same manner as given above for Strawberry Ice.

Lemon-Water Ice. — Lemon juice
and water, each half a pint; strong syrup, one pint; the rind of the lemons should be rasped off, before squeezing, with lump sugar, which is to be added to the juice; mix the whole; strain after standing an hour, and freeze. Beat up with a little sugar the whites of two or three eggs, and as the ice is beginning to set, work this in with the spatula, which will much improve the consistency and taste.

Orange-Water Ice in the same
way.

Any kind of water ices may be made of the juice of the fruit (such as currants, raspberry, strawberry, plum, damson, gooseberry, etc.,) mixed raw with fine sugar.

Wine-Making. — The whole art of
wine-making consists in the proper management of the fermenting process; the same quantity of fruit, whether it be rhubarb, currants, gooseberries, grapes (unripe), leaves, tops and tendrils, water, and sugar, will produce two different kinds of wine, by varying the process of fermentation only — that is, a dry wine like sherry, or a brisk beverage like champagne; but

neither rhubarb, currants, nor gooseberries will produce a wine with the true champagne flavor; it is to be obtained only from the fruit of the grape, ripe or unripe, its leaves, tops, and tendrils. The recipe here given will do for rhubarb, or any of the above-mentioned fruits.

To MAKE TEN GALLONS OF ENGLISH CHAMPAGNE, IMPERIAL MEASURE. — Take fifty pounds of rhubarb and thirty-seven pounds of fine moist sugar. Provide a tub that will hold from fifteen to twenty gallons, taking care that it has a hole for a tap near the bottom. In this tub bruise the rhubarb; when done, add four gallons of water; let the whole be well stirred together; cover the tub with a cloth or blanket, and let the materials stand for twenty-four hours; then draw off the liquor through the tap; add one or two more gallons of water to the pulp, let it be well stirred, and then allowed to remain an hour or two to settle, then draw off; mix the two liquors together, and in it dissolve the sugar. Let the tub be made clean, and return the liquor to it, cover it with a blanket, and place it in a room the temperature of which is not below 60° Fahr.; here it is to remain for twenty-four, forty-eight, or more hours, until there is an appearance of fermentation having begun, when it should be drawn off into a ten-gallon cask, as fine as possible, which cask must be filled up to the bung-hole with water, if there is not liquor enough; let it lean to one side a little, that it may discharge itself; if there is any liquor left in the tub not quite fine, pass it through flannel, and fill up with that instead of water. As the fermentation proceeds and the liquor diminishes, it must be filled up daily, to encourage the fermentation, for ten or twelve days; it then becomes more moderate, when the bung should be put in, and a gimlet hole made at the side of it, fitted with a spile; this spile should be taken out every two or three days, according to the state of the fermentation, for eight or ten days, to allow some of the carbonic acid gas to escape. When this state is passed, the cask may be kept full by pouring a little liquor in at the vent-hole once a week or ten days, for three or four weeks. This operation is performed at long intervals, of a month or more, till the end of December, when on a fine frosty day it should be drawn off from the lees as fine as possible ; the turbid part passed through flannel. Make the cask clean, return the liquor to it, with one dram of isinglass (pure) dissolved in a little water; stir the whole together, and put the bung in firmly. Choose a clear dry day in March for bottling. They should be champagne bottles — common wine bottles are not strong enough ; secure the corks in a proper manner with wire, etc. The liquor is generally made up to two or three pints over the ten gallons, which is bottled for the purpose of filling the cask as it is wanted. For several years past wine has been made with ripe and unripe grapes, according to the season, equally as good as any foreign produce. It has always spirit enough without the addition of brandy, which Dr. Maculloch says, in his treatise on wines, spoils all wines ; a proper fermentation produces spirit enough. The way to obtain a dry wine from these materials is to keep the cask constantly filled up to the bung-hole, daily or every other day, as long as any fermentation is perceptible by applying the ear near to the hole ; the bung may then be put in lightly for a time, before finally fixing it ; it may be racked off on a fine day in December, and fined with isinglass as above directed, and bottled in March.

Parsnip Wine. — Take fifteen pounds of sliced parsnips, and boil until quite soft in five gallons of water ; squeeze the liquor well out of them, run it through a sieve, and add three pounds of coarse lump sugar to every gallon of liquor. Boil the whole for three-quarters of an hour. When it is nearly cold, add a little yeast on toast. Let it remain in a tub for ten days, stirring it from the bottom every

day ; then put it into a cask for a year. As it works over, fill it up every day.

Turnip Wine. — Take a large number of turnips, pare and slice them ; then place in a cider-press, and obtain all the juice you can. To every gallon of juice add three pounds of lump sugar and half a pint of brandy. Pour into a cask, but do not bung until it has done working ; then bung it close for three months, and draw off into another cask ; when it is fine, bottle, and cork well.

Blackberry Wine. — Gather the fruit when ripe, on a dry day. Put into a vessel, with the head out, and a tap fitted near the bottom ; pour on boiling water to cover it. Mash the berries with your hands, and let them stand covered till the pulp rises to the top and forms a crust, in three or four days. Then draw off the fluid into another vessel, and to every gallon add one pound of sugar ; mix well, and put it into a cask, to work for a week or ten days, and throw off any remaining lees, keeping the cask well filled, particularly at the commencement. When the working has ceased, bung it down ; after six to twelve months it may be bottled.

Another very excellent method, and which will produce a wine equal in value to Port: Take ripe blackberries or dewberries, press the juice from them ; let it stand thirty-six hours to ferment, lightly covered ; skim off whatever rises to the top ; then to every gallon of the juice add one quart of water and three pounds of sugar (brown will do), let it stand in an open vessel for twenty-four hours ; skim and strain it, then barrel it ; let it stand eight or nine months, when it should be racked off and bottled and corked close — age improves it.

Blackberry Cordial. — To three pounds of ripe blackberries add one pound of white sugar ; let them stand twelve hours, then press out the juice and strain it ; add one-third of good spirits ; to every quart add one teaspoonful of finely-powdered allspice.

It is at once fit for use. Our native grapes produce the best of wine, which is easily made.

Common Grape Wine. — Take any quantity of sound, ripe grapes; with a common cider-press press out the juice, put it into barrels, cover the bung lightly; after fermentation has ceased cork it; place it in a cellar or house. In twelve months you will have good wine, which improves by age; let it stand on its lees.

Elderberry Wine. — Gather the berries ripe and dry, pick them, bruise them with your hands, and strain them. Set the liquor by in glazed earthen vessels for twelve hours, to settle; put to every pint of juice a pint and a half of water, and to every gallon of this liquor three pounds of good moist sugar; set in a kettle over the fire, and when it is ready to boil, clarify it with the whites of four or five eggs; let it boil one hour, and when it is almost cold, work it with strong ale yeast, and tun it, filling up the vessel from time to time with the same liquor, saved on purpose, as it sinks by working. In a month's time, if the vessel holds about eight gallons, it will be fine and fit to bottle, and after bottling, will be fit to drink in twelve months

Raspberry Wine. — Bruise the finest ripe raspberries with the back of a spoon; strain them through a flannel bag into a stone jar; allow one pound of fine powdered loaf-sugar to one quart of juice; stir these well together, and cover the jar closely; let it stand three days, stirring the mixture up every day; then pour off the clear liquid, and put two quarts of sherry to each quart of juice, or liquid. Bottle it off, and it will be fit for use in a fortnight. By adding Cognac brandy instead of sherry, the mixture will be raspberry brandy.

Red Currant Wine. — To eight quarts of currants put one quart of water, press and strain, and put three pounds and three-quarters of sugar to one gallon of juice. Let it set twenty-four hours. Skim and fill the demi-

johns. Do not boil it at all. It can be used in a month. Wine made from this recipe took the premium at Lynchburg Fair.

Currant Wine. — Dissolve eight pounds of honey in fifteen gallons of boiling water, to which, when clarified, add the juice of eight pounds of red or white currants; then ferment for twenty-four hours; to every two gallons add two pounds of sugar, and clarify with whites of eggs.

Ginger Wine. — Put three pounds of sugar and the shell and white of one egg into one gallon of spring water, boil it one hour, removing the scum that rises; when the liquor is cold, squeeze in the juice of one lemon and one orange, then boil the peels of one lemon and one orange, with two ounces of ginger, in two pints of water, for an hour; when cold, put it altogether in a barrel, leaving the bung out, with a teaspoonful of yeast, a quarter of an ounce of isinglass, and half pound of raisins, (if required to fill an eight-gallon barrel, use eight times the amount of each ingredient,) stir it well once a day, at the same time fill up the barrel with some of the surplus; after nine days put the bung in the barrel; in two months it will be ready for use.

Madeira Wine. — Boil three quarts of water, the rind of one lemon and three oranges, and three pounds of sugar, with the white and shell of one egg, for one hour; remove the scum that rises on top; when cold, add one quart of new ale (from the brewery) that has not done working, and the juices of one lemon and one sweet and two Seville oranges, one pound of raisins cut in half, color with a little burnt sugar. (The above is for one gallon of wine; if eight gallons are required, take eight times the quantity of each ingredient.) Put it into a barrel and stir once a day, keeping it full at the bung; after nine days, add a little brandy and a little isinglass put the bung in the barrel, and at the end of three months bottle it; if kept a year it will be excellent.

Family Wine. — The following recipe is given by Dr. Ure (no mean authority). Take black, red, and white currants, ripe cherries (black hearts are the best), and raspberries, of each an equal quantity. To four pounds of the mixed fruit, well bruised, put one gallon of clear soft water, steep three days and nights, in open vessels, frequently stirring it up, then strain through a hair sieve; press the residuary pulp to dryness, and add its juice to the former. In each gallon of the mixed liquors, dissolve three pounds of good yellow muscovado sugar; let the solution stand other three days and nights, frequently skimming and stirring it up; then turn it into casks, which should remain full, and purging at the bung-hole about two weeks. Lastly, to every nine gallons put one quart of good Cognac brandy (but not the drugged imitations made with grain whiskey), and bung down. If it does not soon become fine, a steeping of isinglass may be stirred into the liquid, in the proportion of half an ounce to nine gallons. I have found the addition of one ounce of cream of tartar to each gallon of the fermentable liquor improves the quality of the wine, and makes i resemble more nearly the product of the grape.

Mock Champagne. — *Time*, to work, three weeks; to stand, six months.

To every quart of grapes, 1 quart of water; to every gallon of juice, allow 3 pounds of loaf sugar, ½ an ounce of isinglass to every 10 gallons of wine, and a quart of brandy to every 5 gallons.

Pick the grapes when full-grown and just beginning to change color, bruise them in a tub, pour in the water, and let them stand for three days, stirring once each day; then press the fruit through a cloth, let the juice stand for three or four hours, pour it carefully from any sediment, and add to it the sugar. Barrel it, and put the bung slightly in. At the end of three weeks, or when it has

done working, put in the isinglass, previously dissolved in some of the liquor. Stir it once a day for three days, and at the last stirring add the brandy. In three or four days, bung it down close, and in six months it should be bottled, and the corks tied down, or wired.

Rhine Wine. — Take one gallon of Delaware grapes, crush them, and add one gallon of water. Let it stand eight days, then draw it off, and add three pounds of sugar to each gallon of wine, well stirring it in. Let it stand twelve hours, then it may be put in barrels or bottles. The longer it is kept, the better it is, and soon becomes equal to the imported wine.

Ginger Beer for Immediate Use. — The following is a very good way to make it: Take of ginger, bruised or sliced, one and a half ounces; cream of tartar, one ounce; loaf sugar, one pound; one lemon sliced; put them into a pan, and pour six quarts of boiling water upon them. When nearly cold, put in a little yeast, and stir it for about a minute. Let it stand till next day, then strain and bottle it. It is fit to drink in three days, but will not keep good longer than a fortnight. The corks should be tied down, and the bottles placed upright in a cool place.

Ginger Beer.—White sugar, twenty pounds; lemon or lime-juice, eighteen (fluid) ounces; honey, one pound; bruised ginger, twenty-two ounces; water, eighteen gallons. Boil the ginger in three gallons of water for half an hour, then add the sugar, the juice, and the honey, with the remainder of the water, and strain through a cloth. When *cold*, add the white of one egg, and half an ounce (fluid) of essence of lemon. After standing four days, bottle. This yields a very superior beverage, and one which will keep for many months.

Ginger Beer Powders.—*Blue paper.* — Carbonate of soda, thirty grains; powdered ginger, five grains; ground white sugar, one dram to one dram and a half; essence of lemon, one drop. Add the essence to the sugar, then the other ingredients. A quantity should be mixed and divided, as recommended for Seidlitz powders. *White paper.* — Tartaric acid, thirty grains. *Directions.*—Dissolve the contents of the blue paper in water; stir in the contents of the white paper, and drink during effervescence. Ginger-beer powders do not meet with such general acceptation as lemon and kali, the powdered ginger rendering the liquid slightly turbid.

LEMONADE. — Powdered sugar, four pounds; citric or tartaric acid, one ounce; essence of lemon, two drams. Mix well. Two or three teaspoonfuls make a very sweet and agreeable glass of extemporaneous lemonade.

Milk Lemonade. — Dissolve three-quarters of a pound of loaf sugar in one pint of boiling water, and mix with them one gill of lemon-juice, and one gill of sherry; then add three gills of cold milk. Stir the whole well together, and strain it.

Summer Champagne. — To four parts of seltzer water add one of Moselle wine (or hock), and put a teaspoonful of powdered sugar into a wineglassful of this mixture. An ebullition takes place, and you have a sort of champagne which is more wholesome in hot weather than the genuine wine known by that name.

Lemon and Kali, or Sherbet.— Large quantities of this wholesome and refreshing preparation are manufactured and consumed every summer. It is sold in bottles, and also as a beverage, made by dissolving a large teaspoonful in a tumbler two-thirds filled with water. Ground white sugar, half a pound; tartaric acid, carbonate of soda, of each a quarter of a pound; essence of lemon, forty drops. All the powders should be well dried. Add the essence to the sugar, then the other powders; stir all together, and mix by passing twice through a hair sieve. Must be kept in tightly-corked bottles, into which a damp spoon must not be inserted. All the materials may be

obtained at a wholesale druggist's. The sugar must be ground, as, if merely powdered, the coarser parts remain un-dissolved.

Soda Water Powders. — One pound of carbonate of soda, and thirteen and a half ounces of tartaric acid, supply the materials for two hundred and fifty-six powders of each sort. Put into blue papers thirty grains of carbonate of soda, and into white papers twenty-five grains of tartaric acid. *Directions.* — Dissolve the contents of the blue paper in half a tumbler of water, stir in the other powder, and drink during effervescence. Soda powders furnish a saline beverage which is very slightly laxative, and well calculated to allay the thirst in hot weather.

Seidlitz Powders. — Seidlitz powders are usually put up in two papers. The larger blue paper contains tartarized soda (also called Rochelle salt) two drams, and carbonate of soda two scruples. In practice it will be found more convenient to mix the two materials in larger quantity by passing them twice through a sieve, and then divide the mixture either by weight or measure, than to make each powder separately. One pound of tartarized soda, and five ounces and a half of carbonate of soda, will make sixty powders. The smaller powder, usually put up in white paper, consists of tartaric acid, half a dram. — *Directions for Use.* — Dissolve the contents of blue paper in half a tumbler of cold water, stir in the other powder, and drink during effervescence.

Wine Whey. — *Time*, five minutes. ½ *pint of milk, sugar to taste,* 1 *wine glass of white wine.*
Put half a pint of milk over the fire, sweeten it to taste, and when boiling, throw in a wineglass of sherry. As soon as the curd forms, strain the whey through muslin into a tumbler.

Egg Flip. — 3 *eggs, a quarter of a pound of good moist sugar, a pint and a half of beer.*
Beat three whole eggs with a quarter of a pound of good moist sugar; make a pint and a half of beer **very**

hot, but do not let it boil; then mix it gradually with the beaten eggs and sugar, toss it to and fro from the saucepan into a jug two or three times, grate a little nutmeg on the top and serve. A wineglassful of spirits may be added if liked.

To Keep Cider Sweet. — In thirty gallons of cider, put two quarts of malt, or, instead of malt, put in two pounds of raisins, and quarter of a pound of mustard seeds. Instead of driving the bung in, paste a piece of brown paper over the hole.

Cider Wine. — To ten gallons of good new cider, put twenty pounds of sugar, two pounds of raisins, cut in half, and five ounces of isinglass. Put it into a ten-gallon cask, let it stand, filling it up at the bung daily. After nine days, put the bung in the barrel; in four months bottle it for use. It will be so good, you will wish you had made more of it.

Raspberry Vinegar.—Put a pound of very fine ripe raspberries in a bowl, *bruise them well*, and pour upon them a quart of the best white wine vinegar; next day strain the liquor on a pound of fresh ripe raspberries; bruise *them* also, and the following day do the same, *but do not squeeze the fruit, or it will make it ferment;* only drain the liquor as dry as you can from it. Finally, pass it through a canvas bag, previously wet with the vinegar, to prevent waste. Put the juice into a stone jar, with a *pound of sugar*, broken into lumps, to *every pint of juice;* stir, and when melted, put the jar into a pan of water; let it simmer, and skim it; let it cool, then bottle it; when cold it will be fine and thick, like strained honey, newly prepared.

Scotch Punch, or Whiskey Toddy — (*The Duke of Athol's Recipe*). — Pour about a wineglassful of *boiling* water into a half-pint tumbler, and sweeten according to taste. Stir well up, then put in a wineglassful of whiskey, and add a wineglassful and a half more boiling water. *Be sure the water is boiling.* Never put lemon into toddy. The two in combination, in almost every instance, produce acidity in the stomach. If possible, store your whiskey *in the wood*, not in bottles, as keeping it in the cask mellows it, and dissipates the coarser particles.

Mulled Wine. — INGREDIENTS. — ½ *pint of wine,* ¼ *pint of water,* 1 *egg, sugar, nutmeg.*

Mix the wine and water together, and let it boil; beat the eggs in a pan, pour them into the wine, then quickly pour the whole from one vessel into another five or six times; add sugar and nutmeg to taste.

Mulled Cider. — INGREDIENTS. — 1 *pint of cider,* 2 *eggs, sugar and nutmeg.* Boil the cider, have the eggs well beaten, pour them into the cider, then quickly pour the whole from one vessel to another five or six times; add sugar and nutmeg to taste.

Economy of Tea. — A given quantity of tea is similar to malt — only imparting strength to a given quantity of water, therefore any additional quantity is waste. Two small teaspoonfuls of good black tea, and one three parts full of green, is sufficient to make three teacupfuls agreeable, the water being put in, in a boiling state, at once; a second addition of water gives a vapid flavor to tea.

In Preparing Tea a good economist will be careful to have the best water, that is, the softest and least impregnated with foreign mixture; for if tea be infused in hard and in soft water, the latter will always yield the greatest quantity of the tannin matter, and will strike the deepest black with sulphate of iron in solution.

Tea-Making. — Dr. Kitchiner recommends that all the water necessary should be poured in at once, as the second drawing is bad. When much tea is wanted, it is better to have two teapots instead of two drawings.

Another Method. — The water should be fresh boiled (not exhausted by long boiling). Scald the teapot and empty it; then put in as much water as necessary for the first cups; put the tea on it as in brewing, and close the lid as quickly as possible. Let it stand three minutes and a half, or, if the quantity be large, four minutes, then fill the cups. This is greatly superior to the ordinary method, the aroma being preserved instead of escaping with the steam, as it does when the water is poured on the tea.

Substitute for Cream in Tea or Coffee. — Beat the white of an egg to a froth, put to it a very small lump of butter, and mix well. Then stir it in gradually, so that it may not curdle. If perfectly mixed, it will be an excellent substitute for cream.

A French chemist asserts that if tea be ground like coffee before hot water is poured upon it, it will yield nearly double the amount of its exhilarating qualities.

Another writer says: "If you put a piece of lump sugar the size of a walnut into a teapot, you will make the tea infuse in half the time." Persons who have tried this last experiment say that the result is satisfactory.

In Making Coffee, observe that the broader the bottom and the smaller the top of the vessel, the better the coffee will be.

Turkish Mode of Making Coffee. — The Turkish way of making coffee produces a very different result from that to which we are accustomed. A small conical saucepan, with a long handle, and calculated to hold about two tablespoonfuls of water, is the vessel used. The fresh roasted berry is pounded, not ground, and about a dessertspoonful is put into the minute boiler; it is then nearly filled with water, and thrust among the embers. A few seconds suffice to make it boil, and the decoction, grounds and all, is poured out into a small cup, which fits into a brass socket, much like the cup of an acorn, and holding the china cup as that does the acorn itself. The Turks seem to drink this decoction boiling, and swallow the grounds with the liquid. We allow it to remain a minute, in order to leave the sediment at the bottom. It is always taken plain; sugar or cream would be thought

to spoil it; and Europeans, after a little practice (longer, however, than we had), are said to prefer it to the clear infusion drunk in France. In every hut these coffee boilers may be seen suspended, and the means for pounding the roasted berry are always ready at hand.

For a long time we used the coffee ground as coarsely as it is usually sold in the stores. Although procuring the best berries possible, we did not uniformly succeed in obtaining at the breakfast table a first rate beverage. We consulted many wiseacres, some of whom said that the water used should be hotter, others that the coffee should be first soaked in cold water, etc., etc. By accident, one day we happened to have the coffee reground to the fineness of snuff. Herein lay the mystery. We have never since failed to obtain a strong full-flavored beverage, and that too without using so large a quantity of coffee. If not convenient to grind it so fine, use it as sold at the stores, but let the quantity required for breakfast be put in cold water overnight, in the morning just boil a minute, and you will have a much better cup of coffee than usual. (Try this once.)

In Sweden, they make excellent coffee. On inquiring at the little hotel how they made it, the following method was given: Take any kind of coffee-pot or urn, and suspend a bag of felt or very heavy flannel, so long that it reaches the bottom, bound on a wire just fitting the top; put in the fresh ground pure coffee, and pour on freshly boiled water. The fluid filters through the bag and may be used at once; needs no settling and retains all the aroma. The advantage of this over the ordinary filter is its economy, as the coffee stands and soaks out the strength, instead of merely letting the water pass through it.

Beet-Root Coffee. — A very good coffee can be made of beet-root in the following manner: Cut dry beet-root into very small pieces, then gradually heat it in a close pan over the fire for about fifteen minutes. Now introduce a little sweet fresh butter, and bring it up to the roasting heat. The butter prevents the evaporation of the sweetness and aroma of the beet-root, and when fully roasted it is taken out, ground, and used like coffee. A beverage made of it is cheap, and as good for the human system as coffee or chicory.

Chicory.—This is the dried and roasted root of a plant allied to the dandelion, and it is found by almost unanimous testimony to be an agreeable flavorer of coffee. It is "diuretic and aperient"—qualities in its favor, for it is the prevailing defect of our food that it is too astringent and heating, and the fact that chicory finds such general approbation we believe rests in these qualities. We know a respectable grocer who, from conscientious motives, ceased to mix chicory with coffee; the immediate effect was the falling off of his coffee trade, his customers declaring that his coffee was not so good as previously; and he was compelled again to mix chicory with it, to meet their taste. Chicory is found to be "adulterated" with carrots, parsnips, and mangold-wurzel. But as these roots are all of them highly nutritious and agreeable, instead of detracting from the claims of chicory, the facts stated rather elevate "chicory" in our estimation, and point to the probability *that the roots mentioned possess qualities hitherto imperfectly ascertained, and worthy of further examination and development.* Our remarks are not merely of conjecture, they are founded upon observation and analysis.

To Clear Coffee.—When the coffee has boiled sufficiently remove it from the fire, and immediately dash in half a teacupful of quite cold water; let it stand a minute, then pour out, and you will have clear coffee. This plan may be too simple for some, and they may prefer to throw an egg-shell in the coffee to settle it. (We propose to remove the mystery from this.) It is not the shell of the egg that clears the liquid, but the albumen in the shape of the white of the egg adhering to the shell, so that a little of the white of an egg poured into the coffee will clear it just as well as the egg-shells.

When eggs are scarce, it is extravagant to use a whole one for clearing coffee at one time. Take an egg, make a hole in the end, and let a teaspoonful run out, then put a bit of paper over the hole in the egg and it will not dry up, but will clear coffee a number of times, and a little is just as good as a whole one.

CHOCOLATE.—Boil one tablespoonful of scraped chocolate in one quart of water for twenty minutes, then add a pint of new milk, and sugar to taste; boil it up for a minute, remove it from the fire, and let it settle, and it is ready for use.

COCOA may be made the same as chocolate.

Coffee Milk.—(FOR THE SICK-ROOM.)—Boil a dessertspoonful of ground coffee, in nearly a pint of milk, a quarter of an hour, then put into it a shaving or two of isinglass, and clear it; let it boil a few minutes, and set it by the side of the fire to clarify. This is a very fine breakfast; but it should be sweetened with sugar of a good quality.

Iceland Moss Chocolate.—(FOR THE SICK-ROOM.)—Iceland moss has been in the highest repute on the Continent as a most efficacious remedy in incipient pulmonary complaints: combined with chocolate, it will be found a nutritious article of diet, and may be taken as a morning and evening beverage. *Directions.*—Mix a teaspoonful of the chocolate with a teaspoonful of boiling water or milk, stirring it constantly until it is completely dissolved.

Alum Whey.—A pint of cow's milk boiled with two drams of alum, until a curd is formed. Then strain off the liquor, and add spirit of nutmeg, two ounces, syrup of cloves, an ounce. It is used in diabetes, and in uterine fluxes, etc.

Barley Water.—Pearl barley, two

ounces; wash till freed from dust in cold water. Boil in a quart of water a few minutes, strain off the liquor, and throw it away. Then boil the barley in four pints and a half of water, until it is reduced one half.

Agreeable Effervescent Drink for Heart-Burn, etc. — Orange-juice (of one orange), water, and lump sugar to flavor, and in proportion to acidity of orange, bicarbonate of soda, about half a teaspoonful. Mix orange-juice, water, and sugar together in a tumbler, then put in the soda, stir, and the effervescence ensues.

Apple Water. — A tart apple well baked and mashed; on which pour a pint of boiling water. Beat up, cool, and strain. Add sugar, if desired. Cooling drink for sick persons.

Tincture of Lemon-Peel. — A very easy and economical way of obtaining and preserving the flavor of lemon-peel, is to fill a wide-mouthed pint bottle half full of brandy, or proof-spirit; and when you use a lemon, pare the rind off very thin, and put it into the brandy, etc.; in a fortnight it will impregnate the spirit with the flavor very strongly.

Camomile Tea. — One ounce of the flowers to a quart of water boiling. Simmer for fifteen minutes and strain. Emetic when taken warm; tonic when cold. _Dose_, from a wineglassful to a breakfast-cup.

Yeast. — Boil, say on Monday morning, two ounces of the best hops in four quarts of water for half an hour; strain it, and let the liquor cool to new-milk warmth; then put in a small handful of salt and half a pound of sugar; beat up one pound of the best flour with some of the liquor, and then mix well all together. On Wednesday add three pounds of potatoes, boiled, and then mashed, to stand till Thursday; then strain it and put it into bottles, and it is ready for use. _It must be stirred frequently while it is making, and kept near the fire._ Before using, shake the bottle up well. It will keep in a cool place for two months, and is best at the latter part of the time. The

beauty of this yeast is that it ferments spontaneously, not requiring the aid of other yeast; and if care be taken to let it ferment well in the earthen bowl in which it is made, you may cork it up tight when bottled. The quantity above given will fill four seltzer-water bottles.

Domestic Yeast. — Ladies who are in the habit (and a most laudable and comfortable habit it is) of making domestic bread cake, etc., are informed that they can easily manufacture their own yeast by attending to the following directions: — Boil one pound of good flour, a quarter of a pound of brown sugar, and a little salt, in two gallons of water, for one hour. When milk-warm, bottle it, and cork it close. It will be fit for use in twenty-four hours. One pint of this yeast will make eighteen pounds of bread.

Potato Yeast, that will Keep in the Hottest Weather. — Grate seven medium-size potatoes into a teacupful of brown sugar, then boil a handful of hops, and two large tablespoonfuls of salt, in two quarts of water. Strain out the hops, and pour the liquor over the potatoes and sugar, then put all back into the pot, and boil for fifteen minutes.

What is Saleratus? — Wood is burnt to ashes, these are lixivated, and lye is the result. Lye is evaporated by boiling, black salt is the residuum. The salt undergoes purification by fire, and the potash of commerce is obtained. By another process we change potash into pearlash. Now put these in sacks and place them over a distillery mash - tub, where the fermentation evolves carbonic acid gas, and the pearlash absorbs it and is rendered solid; the product being heavier, whiter, and drier than the pearlash. It is now saleratus. How much such salts of lye and carbonic acid gas one can bear and remain healthy, is a question for a saleratus eater.

Hot Biscuit. — There are some families that must, and will, have warm biscuit every morning and evening; all that is necessary is to keep a jar of "bread sponge," made as thick as stiff batter; a quart of this and one tea-spoonful of baking soda stirred stiff with flour so as to be moulded, makes excellent biscuit for breakfast or tea. To renew the sponge every day, take one cupful of hop water or hop tea, three cupfuls of flour, three cupfuls of boiling water, one teaspoonful of salt, two teaspoonfuls of sugar, and three teaspoonfuls of butter or lard, and after stirring all together pour into the jar to replenish it. The jar should hold at least twice or thrice times the quantity that is daily used out of it.

Home-made Bread. — To seven pounds of flour, add two dessertspoonfuls of salt, and mix them well; mix four tablespoonfuls of good fresh yeast with one pint of warm, but not hot water; make a hole with your hand in the middle of the flour, but not quite touching the bottom of the pan; pour the water and yeast into this hole, and stir it with a spoon till you have made a thin batter; sprinkle this over with flour, cover the pan over with a dry cloth, and let it stand in a warm room for an hour; not near the fire, except in cold weather, and then not too close; then add a pint of water a little warm, and knead the whole well together, till the dough comes clean through the hand (some flour will require a little more water; but in this, experience must be your guide), let it stand again for about a quarter of an hour, and then bake at pleasure.

Indian Corn Flour and Wheaten Bread.—The peculiarity of this bread consists in its being composed in part of Indian corn flour, which is richer in gluten and fatty matter than the flour of wheat, to which circumstance it owes its highly nutritive character:

Take seven pounds of Indian corn *flour*, pour upon it four quarts of boiling water, stirring it all the time; let it stand till about new - milk warm, then mix it with fourteen pounds of fine wheaten flour, to which a quarter of a pound of salt has been previously

added. Make a depression on the surface of this mixture, and pour into it two quarts of yeast, which should be thickened to the consistence of cream with some of the flour; let it stand all night. On the following morning the whole should be well kneaded, and allowed to stand for three hours; then divide it into loaves, which are better baked in tins, in which they should stand for half an hour, then bake. Thirty-two pounds of wholesome, nutritive, and very agreeable bread will be the result. It is of importance that the flour of Indian corn should be procured, as Indian corn meal is that which is commonly met with at the shops, and the coarseness of the husk in the meal might to some persons be prejudicial.

Unfermented Bread.—Three pounds wheat meal, half an ounce, avoirdupois, muriatic acid, half an ounce, avoirdupois, carbonate soda, water enough to make it of a proper consistence. For white flour, four pounds of flour, half an ounce, avoirdupois, muriatic acid, half an ounce, avoirdupois, carbonate soda, water, about a quart. The way of making is as follows: — First mix the soda and flour well together by rubbing in a pan; then pour the acid into the water, and mix well by stirring. Mix all together to the required consistence, and bake in a hot oven immediately. The gain from this method of baking is as follows:—Four pounds of wheat meal made seven pounds nine ounces of excellent light bread; and four pounds of seconds flour made six pounds of excellent light bread. It keeps moist longer than bread made with yeast, and is far more sweet and digestible. This is especially recommended to persons who suffer from indigestion, who will find the brown bread invaluable.

A great increase on Home-made Bread, even equal to one-fifth, may be produced by using bran water for kneading the dough. The proportion is three pounds of bran for every twenty-eight pounds of flour, to be boiled for an hour, and then strained through a hair sieve.

There are two advantages in making bread with bran water instead of plain water; the one being that there is considerable nourishment in bran, which is thus extracted and added to the bread; the other, that flour imbibes much more of bran water than it does of plain water; so much more, as to give in the bread produced almost a fifth in weight more than the quantity of flour made up with plain water would have done. These are important considerations to the poor. Fifty-six pounds of flour, made with plain water, would produce sixty-nine and a half pounds of bread; made with bran water, it will produce eighty-three and a half pounds.

Use of Lime-water in making Bread. — It has lately been found that water saturated with lime produces in bread the same whiteness, softness, and capacity of retaining moisture, as results from the use of alum; while the former removes all acidity from the dough, and supplies an ingredient needed in the structure of the bones, but which is deficient in the *cerealia*. The best proportion to use is, five pounds of water saturated with lime to every nineteen pounds of flour. No change is required in the process of baking. The lime most effectually coagulates the gluten, and the bread weighs well; bakers must therefore approve of its introduction, which is not injurious to the system, like alum, etc. A large quantity of this kind of bread is now made in Munich, and is highly esteemed.

Tea Cakes or Loaves. — *Time,* half or three-quarters of an hour.

1 *egg,* 2 *ounces of butter,* ½ *a pound of flour,* 2 *or* 3 *knobs of sugar.*

Rub the butter into the flour, add the sugar pounded, and mix it with one beaten egg.

It will make two small loaves for tea or breakfast.

Breakfast or Tea Rolls. — *Time,* fifteen to twenty minutes.

1 *pound of flour, a* ¼ *of a pound of* butter, 1 *tablespoonful of good yeast,* 1 *egg, a little warm milk.*

Rub the butter into the flour, then add the yeast, breaking in one egg, both yolk and white. Mix it with a little warm milk poured into the middle of the flour; stir all well together, and set it by the fire to rise, then make it into light dough, and again set it by the fire. Make up the rolls, lay them on a tin, and set them in front of the fire for ten minutes before you put them into the oven, brushing them over with egg. This paste may be used for fancy bread.

Breakfast or Tea Cakes Hot. — *Time,* half an hour.

6 *handfuls of flour,* ½ *a pint of milk, a small piece of butter,* 2 *ounces of German yeast,* 1 *egg.*

Put the flour in a basin, with half a pint of milk, and a small piece of butter; warm the milk — in the winter increase its temperature. Mix two ounces of German yeast in a little cold water; add it to the milk and butter. Make a hole in the flour, and pour the mixed milk and yeast into it, stirring it round until it is a thick batter; add to it one beaten egg; cover it over, and set it before the fire, keeping it warm. When it has risen a little, mix it into a dough, knead it well, put it again before the fire, and, when it has risen a great deal, form your rolls. They will take nearly half an hour to bake, or according to the size you make them. Rub them once while hot with a paste-brush dipped in milk.

Graham, or Dyspepsia Bread. — Persons often fail to make this bread good because the so-called Graham, or unbolted flour, is made from inferior wheat. We avoid this by using the best flour, and mixing the bran with it ourselves; that is, we buy our flour and our bran separately, and mix it ourselves. In this way we get our Graham bread good and cheap. Wet up the flour with lukewarm water, salt and yeast in the proportion as for wheat bread. Knead in sufficient flour to make it stiff: add a very little best

18

molasses. Let it rise, then bake. It will take about two hours.

French Bread and Rolls.—Take a pint and a half of milk; make it quite warm; half a pint of small-beer yeast; add sufficient flour to make it as thick as batter. Put it into a pan, cover it over, and keep it warm. When it has risen as high as it will, add a quarter of a pint of warm water, and half an ounce of salt. Mix them well together, rub into a little flour two ounces of butter; then make your dough, not quite so stiff as for your bread. Let it stand for three-quarters of an hour, and it will be ready to make into rolls, etc. Let them stand till they have risen, and bake them in a quick oven.

Wholesome Bread. — This bread contains no other ingredients than simple wheat meal and water, and is used as a standard article of diet at a number of the leading hygienic institutions in this country, as well as in very many private families.

It is made as follows:—Stir together wheat meal and cold water (nothing else, not even salt) to the consistency of a thick batter. Bake in small circular pans, from three to three and a half inches in diameter (ordinary tin "patty pans" do very well), in a quick, hot oven. It is quite essential that it is baked in this sized cake, as it is upon this that the raising depends. A better pan for the purpose may be had at most any of the house-furnishing stores, being a number of circular iron pans, cast together in one large form. If this is used, it is best to heat it before filling with the batter.

Rye Bread. — 1 *quart rye flour*, 1 *quart flour*, 2 *teaspoons salt*, ⅔ *of a cup molasses*, 1 *quart milk and water*, *half and half*, 1 *yeast cake in a cup of water*.

Boston Brown Bread.—½ *cup flour*, 1 *cup Indian meal*, 2 *cups rye*, ⅔ *cup molasses*, 2 *teaspoons cream of tartar*, 1 *teaspoon soda ; mix soft with cold water or milk ; tablespoon of salt*.

Put in a deep tin, and bake slowly three or four hours ; or, what is better, put it in an earthen pan, and stand in a slow oven all night.

Note.—Cooked in a steamer for three hours, it is a good pudding.

MAKING HOME COMFORTABLE.

SELECTING AND FURNISHING A HOUSE—WAYS TO LESSEN THE PERPLEXI-
TIES OF EVERY-DAY DOMESTIC LIFE.

Taking a House. — Before taking a house, be careful to calculate that the rent is not too high in proportion to your means; for remember that the rent is a claim that must be paid with but little delay.

HAVING DETERMINED THE AMOUNT OF RENT which you can afford to pay, be careful to select the best house which can be obtained for that sum. And in making that selection, let the following matters be carefully considered:

FIRST — CAREFULLY REGARD THE HEALTHFULNESS OF THE SITUATION. Avoid the neighborhood of graveyards, and of factories giving forth unhealthy vapors. Avoid low and damp districts, the course of canals, and localities of reservoirs of water, gas-works, etc. Make inquiries as to the drainage of the neighborhood, and inspect the drainage and water supply of the premises. A house standing on an incline is likely to be better drained than one standing upon the summit of a hill, or on a level below a hill. Endeavor to obtain a position where the direct sunlight falls upon the house, for this is absolutely essential to health; and give preference to a house the openings of which are sheltered from the north and east winds.

SECOND — CONSIDER THE DISTANCE OF THE HOUSE from your place of occupation; and also its relation to provision markets, and shops in the neighborhood.

HAVING CONSIDERED THESE MATERIAL AND LEADING FEATURES, examine the house in detail, carefully looking into its state of repair; notice the windows that are broken; whether the chimneys smoke; whether they have been recently swept; whether the paper on the walls is damaged, especially in the lower parts, and the corners, by the skirtings; whether the locks, bolts, handles of doors, and window-fastenings are in proper condition; make a list of the fixtures; ascertain whether all rent and taxes have been paid by the previous tenant, and whether the person from whom you take the house is the original landlord, or his agent or tenant. And do not commit yourself by the signing of any agreement until you are satisfied upon all these points, *and see that all has been done which the landlord had undertaken.*

If you are about to Furnish a House, do not spend all your money, be it much or little. Do not let the beauty of this thing, and the cheapness of that, tempt you to buy unnecessary articles. Dr. Franklin's maxim was a wise one — "Nothing is cheap that we do not want." Buy merely enough to get along with at first. It is only by experience that you can tell what will be the wants of your family. If you spend all your money, you will find you have purchased many things you do not want, and have no means left to get many things which you do want. If you have enough, and more than enough, to get everything suitable to your situation, do not think you must spend it all, merely because you happen to have it. Begin humbly. As riches increase, it is easy and pleasant to increase in comforts; but it is always painful and inconvenient to decrease. After all, these things are viewed in their proper light by the truly judicious and respectable. Neatness, tastefulness, and good sense may be shown in the management of a small household, and the arrangement of a little furniture, as well as upon a larger scale; and these qualities are always praised, and always treated with respect and attention. The consideration which many purchase by living beyond their income, and, of course, living upon others, is not worth the trouble it costs. The glare there is about this false and wicked parade is deceptive; it does not, in fact, procure a man valuable friends, or extensive influence.

How to Beautify your Rooms. —

The first condition of success in furnishing either a large or a small room is that there must be no overcrowding. — This is absolute. When outline is lost, beauty, as a matter of fact, is lost also. We must all know many drawing-rooms in which, perhaps, the worth and beauty of each individual thing is indisputable, on entering which the first thing that strikes one is a sense of incongruity. — What might have been an art collection is degraded to the level of an old curiosity shop. Most women are born with a love of beauty. But generally, unless this love is cultivated and trained, it runs to waste, and fritters itself away upon small things. Women go into a shop and hover a counter for an hour, engrossed in the purchase of fifty minute things, each one of which is pretty enough in itself if taken up in the hand and inspected; but not one of which can be clearly defined at a distance of two yards, and not one of which repays the trouble of the minute inspection. These are packed away in shiny cabinets that are blazing with ormolu scroll-work, on spindle-legged what-nots that seem to be designed for no other earthly purpose than to be knocked down at

brief intervals, and on mantlepieces that confuse one's brain during the long periods when the need of being near the fire forces one to face them. It is a better and higher system of economy to buy two or three good bronzes or marbles, on which the eye can always rest with pleasure, than to spend ten times that sum on a heterogeneous mass of the parti-colored rubbish which may accumulate, "In order," they call it, "to take off the naked look of their room." Better the naked look ten thousand times than the false decorations.

CARPETS. — In buying carpets, as in everything else, those of the best quality are cheapest in the end. As it is extremely desirable that they should look as clean as possible, avoid buying carpet that has any white in it. Even a very small portion of white interspersed through the pattern will in a short time give a dirty appearance to the whole; and certainly no carpet can be worse for use than one with a white ground.

A CARPET IN WHICH ALL THE COLORS ARE LIGHT never has a clean, bright effect, from the want of dark tints to contrast and set off the light ones.

FOR A SIMILAR REASON, carpets whose colors are all of what artists call middle tint (neither dark nor light), cannot fail to look dull and dingy, even when quite new.

THE CAPRICES OF FASHION at times bring these ill-colored carpets into vogue; but, in apartments where elegance is desirable, they always have a bad effect.

FOR A CARPET TO BE REALLY BEAUTIFUL, and in good taste, there should be, as in a picture, a judicious disposal of light and shadow, with a gradation of very bright and of very dark tints; some almost white, and others almost or quite black.

THE MOST TRULY CHASTE, rich, and elegant carpets are those where the pattern is formed by one color only, but arranged in every variety of shade. For instance, we have seen a Brussels carpet entirely red; the pattern formed by shades or tints varying from the deepest crimson (almost a black), to the palest pink (almost a white). Also one of green only, shaded from the darkest bottle-green, in some parts of the figure, to the lightest pea-green in others. Another, in which there was no color but brown, in all its various gradations, some of the shades being nearly black, others of a light buff. All these carpets had much the look of rich cut velvet.

THE CURTAINS, SOFAS, ETC., must be of corresponding colors, that the effect of the whole may be noble and elegant.

CARPETS of many gaudy colors are much less in demand than formerly. Two colors only, with the dark and light shades of each, will make a very handsome carpet.

A VERY LIGHT BLUE GROUND, with the figure of shaded crimson or purple, looks extremely well; so does a salmon color or buff ground, with a deep green figure; or a light yellow ground, with a shaded blue figure.

IF YOU CANNOT OBTAIN A HEARTH-RUG that exactly corresponds with the carpet, get one entirely different; for a decided contrast looks better than a bad match.

WE HAVE SEEN VERY HANDSOME HEARTH-RUGS with a rich, black velvet-looking ground, and the figure of shaded blue, or of various tints of yellow and orange.

NO CARPET decidedly light colored throughout looks effective on the floor, or continues long clean.

IN CHOOSING PAPER FOR A ROOM, avoid that which has a variety of colors, or a large showy figure, as no furniture can appear to advantage with such. Large figured papering makes a small room look smaller.

THE BEST COVERING FOR A KITCHEN FLOOR is a thick unfigured oil-cloth, of one color.

Hints for Home Comfort. — Eat
slowly and you will not over-eat.

Keeping the feet warm will prevent headaches.

Late at breakfast — hurried for dinner — cross at tea.

A short needle makes the most expedition in plain sewing.

Between husband and wife little attentions beget much love.

Always lay your table neatly, whether you have company or not.

Put your balls or reels of cotton into little bags, leaving the ends out.

Whatever you may choose to give away, always be sure to *keep your temper*.

Dirty windows speak to the passer-by of the negligence of the inmates.

In cold weather a leg of mutton improves by being hung three, four, or five weeks.

When meat is hanging, change its position frequently, to equally distribute the juices.

There is much more injury done by admitting visitors to invalids than is generally supposed.

Matches, out of the reach of children, should be kept in every bedroom. They are cheap enough.

Apple and suet dumplings are lighter when boiled in a net than in a cloth. Scum the pot well.

When chamber towels get thin in the middle, cut them in two, sew the selvages together, and hem the sides.

When you are particular in wishing to have precisely what you want from a butcher's, go and purchase it yourself.

One flannel petticoat will wear nearly as long as two, if turned behind part before, when the front begins to wear thin.

People in general are not aware how very essential to the health of the inmates is the free admission of light into their houses.

When you dry salt for the table, do not place it in the salt-cells until it is cold, otherwise it will harden into a lump.

Never put away plate, knives and forks, etc., uncleaned, or great inconvenience will arise when the articles are wanted.

Feather beds should be opened every third year, the ticking well dusted, soaped, and waxed, the feathers dressed and returned.

Persons of defective sight, when threading a needle, should hold it over something white, by which the sight will be assisted.

In mending sheets and shirts, put the pieces sufficiently large, or in the first washing the thin parts give way, and the work is all undone.

Reading by candle-light, place the candle behind you, that the rays may pass over your shoulder on to the book. This will relieve the eyes.

A wire fire-guard, for each fireplace in a house, costs little, and greatly diminishes the risk to life and property. Fix them before going to bed.

In winter, get the work forward by daylight, to prevent running about at night with candles. Thus you escape grease spots, and risks of fire.

Be at much pains to keep your children's feet dry and warm. Don't bury their bodies in heavy flannels and wools, and leave their knees and legs naked.

Apples and pears, cut into quarters and stripped of the rind, baked with a little water and sugar, and eaten with boiled rice, are capital food for children.

A leather strap, with a buckle to fasten, is much more commodious than a cord for a box in general use for short distances. Cording and uncording is a tedious job.

After washing, overlook linen, and stitch on buttons, hooks, and eyes, etc.; for this purpose keep a "housewife's friend," full of miscellaneous threads, cottons, buttons, hooks, etc.

For ventilation open your windows both at top and bottom. The fresh air rushes in one way, while the foul makes its exit the other. This is letting in your friend and expelling your enemy.

There is not any real economy in purchasing cheap calico for gentlemen's night-shirts. Cheap calico soon wears into holes, and becomes discolored in washing.

Persons very commonly complain of indigestion. How can it be won-

dered at, when they seem, by their habit of swallowing their food wholesale, to forget for what purpose they are provided with teeth?

Never allow your servants to put wiped knives on your table, for, generally speaking, you may see that they have been wiped with a dirty cloth. If a knife is brightly cleaned, they are compelled to use a clean cloth.

There is not anything gained in economy by having very young and inexperienced servants at low wages; they break, waste, and destroy more than an equivalent for higher wages setting aside comfort and respectability.

No article in dress tarnishes so readily as black crape trimmings, and few things injure it more than damp; therefore, to preserve its beauty on bonnets, a lady in nice mourning should, in her evening walks, at all seasons of the year, take as her companion an old parasol to shade her crape.

Family Tool Chests. — Much inconvenience and considerable expense might be saved, if it were the general custom to keep in every house certain tools for the purpose of performing at home what are called small jobs, instead of being always obliged to send for a mechanic and pay him for executing little things that, in most cases, could be sufficiently well done by a man or boy belonging to the family, if the proper instruments were at hand.

THE COST OF THESE ARTICLES is very trifling, and the advantages of having them always in the house are far beyond the expense.

FOR INSTANCE, there should be an axe, a hatchet, a saw (a large wood-saw also, with a buck or stand, if wood is burned), a claw-hammer, a mallet, two gimlets of different sizes, two screw-drivers, a chisel, a small plane, one or two jack-knives, a pair of large scissors or shears, and a carpet-fork or stretcher.

ALSO AN ASSORTMENT OF NAILS of various sizes, from large spikes down to small tacks, not forgetting brass-headed nails, some larger and some smaller.

THE NAILS and screws should be kept in a wooden box, made with divisions to separate the various sorts, for it is very troublesome to have them mixed.

PRINTED PAPERS ARE UNFIT FOR WRAPPING anything, as the printing-ink rubs off on the articles enclosed in them, and also soils the gloves of the person that carries the parcel.

WHEN SHOPPING, if the person at the counter proceeds to wrap up your purchase in a newspaper (a thing rarely attempted in a genteel shop), refuse to take it in such a cover. It is the business of every respectable shopkeeper to provide proper paper for this purpose, and printed paper is not proper.

Beds for the Poor. — Maple or beech-tree leaves are recommended for filling the beds of poor persons. They should be gathered on a dry day in the autumn, and perfectly dried. It is said that they smell grateful, and will not harbor vermin. They are also very springy.

To Preserve Tables. — A piece of oil-cloth (about twenty inches long) is a useful appendage to a common sitting-room. Kept in the closet, it can be available at any time to place jars upon, etc., etc., which are likely to soil your table during the process of dispensing their contents: a wing and duster are harmonious accompaniments to the oil-cloth.

Gilt Frames may be protected from flies and dust by oiled tarlatan pinned over them. Tarlatan, already prepared, may be purchased at the upholsterer's. If it cannot be procured, it is easily made by brushing boiled oil over cheap tarlatan. It is an excellent material for keeping dust from books, vases, wool work, and every description of household ornament.

Damp Walls. — The following method is recommended to prevent the effect of damp walls on paper in rooms: — Line the damp part of the wall with sheet lead, rolled very thin, and fastened up with small copper nails. It may be immediately covered with paper. The lead is not to be thicker than that which lines tea-chests.

BEDROOMS should not be scoured in the winter time, as colds and sickness may be produced thereby. Dry scouring, upon the French plan, which consists of scrubbing the floors with dry brushes, may be resorted to, and will be found more effective than can at first be imagined. If a bedroom is wet scoured, a dry day should be chosen — the windows should be opened, the linen removed, and a fire should be lit when the operation is finished.

To get Rid of a Bad Smell in a Room newly Painted. — Place a vessel full of lighted charcoal in the middle of the room, and throw on it two or three handfuls of juniper berries, shut the windows, the chimney, and the door close; twenty-four hours afterwards, the room may be opened, when it will be found that the sickly, unwholesome smell will be entirely gone. The smoke of the juniper berry possesses this advantage, that should anything be left in the room, such as tapestry, etc., none of it will be spoiled.

PAINT. — To get rid of the smell of oil-paint plunge a handful of hay into a pailful of water, and let it stand in the room newly painted.

If a Larder, by its position, will not admit of opposite windows, then a current of air must be admitted by means of a flue from the outside.

For Keeping a Door Open, place a brick, covered neatly with a piece of carpet, against the door.

To Ascertain whether a Bed be Aired. — Introduce a glass goblet between the sheets for a minute or two, just when the warming-pan is taken out; if the bed be dry, there will only be a slight cloudy appearance on the glass, but if not, the damp of the bed will assume the more formidable appearance of drops, the warning of danger.

To Prevent the Smoking of a Lamp. — Soak the wick in strong vinegar, and dry it well before you use it; it will then burn clear and bright, and give much satisfaction for the trifling trouble in preparing it.

WATER of every kind, except rain-water, will speedily cover the inside of a tea-kettle with an unpleasant crust. This may easily be guarded against by placing a clean oyster-shell in the tea-kettle, which will always keep it in good order, by attracting the particles of earth or of stone.

To Soften Hard Water, or purify river water, simply boil it, and then leave it exposed to the atmosphere.

Cabbage Water should be thrown away immediately it is done with, and the vessel rinsed with clean water, or it will cause unpleasant smells.

A little Charcoal mixed with clear water thrown into a sink will disinfect and deodorize it.

Where a Chimney Smokes only when a fire is first lighted, it may be guarded against by allowing the fire to kindle gradually.

Ground Glass.—The frosted appearance of ground glass may be very nearly imitated by gently dabbing the glass over with a piece of glazier's putty, stuck on the ends of the fingers. When applied with a light and even touch, the resemblance is considerable.

Family Clocks ought only to be oiled with the very purest oil, purified by a quart of lime-water to a gallon of oil, in which it has been well shaken, and suffered to stand for three or four days, when it may be drawn off.

Neat Mode of Soldering.—Cut out a piece of tinfoil the size of the surfaces to be soldered. Then dip a feather in a solution of sal-ammoniac, and wet over the surfaces of the metal; then place them in their proper position, with the tinfoil between. Put it so arranged on a piece of iron hot enough to melt the foil. When cold, the surfaces will be found firmly soldered together.

Maps and Charts. — Maps, charts, or engravings may be effectually varnished by brushing a very delicate coating of gutta-percha solution over their surface. It is perfectly transparent, and is said to improve the appearance of pictures. By coating both sides of important documents they can be kept waterproof and preserved perfectly.

FURNITURE made in the winter, and brought from a cold warehouse into a warm apartment, is very liable to crack.

Paper Fire-Screens should be coated with transparent varnish, otherwise they will soon become soiled and discolored.

Pastils for Burning. —' Cascarilla bark, eight drams; gum benzoin, four drams; yellow sanders, two drams; styrax, two drams; olibanum, two drams; charcoal, six ounces; nitre, one and a half drams; mucilage of tragacanth, sufficient quantity. Reduce the substances to a powder, and form into a paste with the mucilage, and divide into small cones. Then put them into an oven until quite dry.

Easy Method of Breaking Glass to any required Figure.—Make a small notch by means of a file on the edge of a piece of glass, then make the end of a tobacco-pipe, or of a rod of iron of the same size, red hot in the fire; apply the hot iron to the notch, and draw it slowly along the surface of the glass in any direction you please; a crack will follow the direction of the iron.

Bottling and Fining. — Corks should be sound, clean, and sweet. Beer and porter should be allowed to stand in the bottles a day or two before being corked. If for speedy use, wiring is not necessary. Laying the bottles on their sides will assist the ripening for use. Those that are to be kept should be wired, and put to stand upright in sawdust. Wines should be bottled in spring. If not fine enough, draw off a pitcherful and dissolve isinglass in it, in the proportion of half an ounce to ten gallons, and then pour back through the bung-hole. Let it stand a few weeks longer. Tap the cask above the lees. When the isinglass is put into the cask, stir it round with a stick, taking great care not to touch the lees at the bottom. For white wine only, mix with the isinglass a quarter of a pint of milk to each gallon of wine, some whites of eggs, beaten with some of the wine. One white of an egg to four gallons makes a good fining.

To Sweeten Casks. — Mix half a pint of vitriol with a quart of water, pour it into the barrel, and roll it about; next day add one pound of chalk, and roll again. Bung down for three or four days, then rinse well with hot water.

Oil Paintings hung over the mantlepiece are liable to wrinkle with the heat.

To Loosen Glass Stoppers of Bottles. — With a feather rub a drop or two of salad oil round the stopper, close to the mouth of the bottle or decanter, which must then be placed before the fire, at the distance of about eighteen inches; the heat will cause the oil to insinuate itself between the stopper and the neck. When the bottle or decanter has grown warm, gently strike the stopper on one side, and then on the other, with any light wooden instrument; then try it with the hand; if it will not yet move, place it again before the fire, adding another drop of oil. After a while strike again as before; and, by persevering in this process, however tightly it may be fastened in, you will at length succeed in loosening it. This is decidedly the best plan.

Lamp Wicks. — Old cotton stockings may be made into lamp wicks, and will answer very well.

The Best Lamp Oil is that which is clear and nearly colorless, like water.

China Teapots are the safest, and, in many respects, the most pleasant. Wedgewood-ware is very apt, after a time, to acquire a disagreeable taste.

Care of Linen. — When linen is well dried and laid by for use, nothing more is necessary than to secure it from damp and insects; the latter may be agreeably performed by a judicious mixture of aromatic shrubs and flowers, cut up and sewed in silken bags, to be interspersed among the drawers and shelves. These ingredients may consist of lavender, thyme, roses, cedar shavings, powdered sassafras, cassia lignea, etc., into which a few drops of otto of roses, or other strong-scented perfume, may be thrown. In all cases it will be found more consistent with economy to examine and repair all washable articles, more especially linen, that may stand in need of it, previous to sending them to the laundry. It will also be prudent to have every article carefully numbered, and so arranged, after washing, as to have their regular turn and term in domestic use.

MENDING. — When you make a new article, always save the pieces until "mending - day," which may come sooner than expected. It will be well even to buy a little extra quantity for repairs.

Cleansing of Furniture. — The cleaning of furniture forms an important part of domestic economy, not only in regard to neatness, but also in point of expense.

THE READIEST MODE indeed consists in good manual rubbing, or the essence of elbows, as it is whimsically termed; but our finest cabinet-work requires something more, where brilliancy of polish is of importance.

THE ITALIAN CABINET-WORK in this respect excels that of any other country. The workmen first saturate the surface with olive-oil, and then apply a solution of gum arabic in boiling alcohol. This mode of varnishing is equally brilliant, if not superior, to that employed by the French in their most elaborate works.

BUT ANOTHER MODE may be substituted, which has less the appearance of a hard varnish, and may always be applied so as to restore the pristine beauty of the furniture by a little manual labor. Heat a gallon of water, in which dissolve one pound and a half of potash; add a pound of virgin wax, boiling the whole for half an hour, then suffer it to cool, when the wax will float on the surface. Put the wax into a mortar, and triturate it with a marble pestle, adding soft water to it until it forms a soft paste, which, laid neatly on furniture, or even on paintings, and carefully rubbed, when dry, with a woollen rag, gives a polish of great brilliancy, without the harshness of the drier varnishes.

CARPETS. — If the corner of a carpet becomes loose, and prevents the door opening, or trips every one up that enters the room, nail it down at once. A dog's-eared carpet marks the sloven as well as the dog's-eared book. A gentleman, travelling some years ago, took a hammer and tacks with him, because he found dog's-eared carpets at all the inns where he rested. At one of these inns he tacked down the carpet, which, as usual, was loose near the door, and soon afterwards rang for his dinner. While the carpet was loose, the door could not be opened without a hard push ; so when the waiter came up, he just unlatched the door, and then going back a couple of yards, he rushed against it, as his habit was, with a sudden spring to force it open. But the wrinkles of the carpet were no longer there to stop it, and not meeting with the expected resistance, the unfortunate waiter fell full length into the room. It had never entered his head that so much trouble might be saved by means of a hammer and half a dozen tacks, until his fall taught him that makeshift is a very unprofitable kind of shift. There are a good many houses where a similar practical lesson might be of service.

Cleaning Carpets. — Take a pail of cold water, and add to it three gills of ox-gall. Rub it into the carpet with a soft brush. It will raise a lather, which must be washed off with clear cold water. Rub dry with a clean cloth. In nailing down a carpet after the floor has been washed, be certain that the floor is quite dry, or the nails will rust and injure the carpet. Fuller's earth is used for cleaning carpets, and weak solutions of alum or soda are used for reviving the colors. The crumb of a hot wheaten loaf rubbed over a carpet has been found effective.

Beat a Carpet on the wrong side first, and then more gently on the right side. Beware of using sticks with sharp points, which may tear the carpet.

Sweeping Carpets. — Persons who are accustomed to use tea-leaves for sweeping their carpets, and find that they leave stains, will do well to employ fresh-cut grass instead. It is better than tea-leaves for preventing dust, and gives the carpets a very bright, fresh look. Or, clean paper may be torn into small pieces, and, after being wet, scattered over the floor.

A Half-worn Carpet may be made to last longer by ripping it apart, and transposing the breadths.

A Stair Carpet should never be swept down with a long broom, but always with a short-handled brush, and a dust-pan held closely under each step of the stairs.

Oil Cloth should never be scrubbed with a brush, but, after being first swept, it should be cleansed by washing with a large soft cloth and lukewarm or cold water. On no account use soap or hot water, as either will bring off the paint.

Straw Matting may be cleaned with a large coarse cloth dipped in salt and water, and then wiped dry : the salt prevents the matting from turning yellow.

Method of Cleaning Paper-Hangings. — Take an average size square loaf two days old, and cut it into four pieces. With one of these pieces, after having blown off all the dust from the paper to be cleaned, by the means of a good pair of bellows, begin at the top of the room, holding the crust in the hand, and wiping lightly downward with the crumb, about half a yard at each stroke, till the upper part of the hangings is completely cleaned all round. Then go round again, with the like sweeping stroke downwards, always commencing each successive course a little higher than the upper stroke had extended, till the bottom be finished. This operation, if carefully performed, will frequently make very old paper look almost equal to new. Great caution must be used not by any means to rub the paper hard, nor to attempt cleaning it the cross or horizontal way. The dirty part of the bread, too, must be each time cut away, and the pieces renewed as soon as it may become necessary.

Rosewood Furniture should be rubbed gently every day with a clean soft cloth to keep it in order.

Ottomans and Sofas, whether covered with cloth, damask, or chintz, will look much the better for being cleaned occasionally with bran and flannel.

Dining Tables may be polished by rubbing them for some time with a soft cloth and a little cold drawn linseed oil.

A Mahogany Frame should be first well dusted, and then cleaned with a flannel dipped in sweet oil.

To Clean Cane-bottom Chairs. — Turn up the chair bottom, etc., and with hot water and a sponge wash the canework well, so that it may become completely soaked. Should it be very dirty, you must add soap. Let it dry in the open air, if possible, or in a place where there is a thorough draught, and it will become as tight and firm as when new, provided it has not been broken.

ALABASTER. — For cleaning it there is nothing better than soap and water. Stains may be removed by washing with soap and water, then whitewashing the stained part, letting it stand some hours, then washing off the whitewash, and rubbing the stained part.

To Clean Marble. — Take two parts of common soda, one part of pumicestone, and one part of finely-powdered chalk; sift it through a fine sieve, and mix it with water; then rub it well all over the marble, and the stains

will be removed; then wash the marble over with soap and water, and it will be as clean as it was at first.

To Clean Silver Plate. — Fill a large saucepan with water; put into it one ounce of carbonate of potash and a quarter of a pound of whiting. Now put in all the spoons, forks, and small plate, and boil them for twenty minutes; after which take the saucepan off the fire and allow the liquor to become cold; then take each piece out and polish with soft leather. A soft brush must be used to clean the embossed and engraved parts.

GLASS should be washed in cold water, which gives it a brighter and clearer look than when cleaned with warm water.

Glass Vessels, and other utensils, may be purified and cleaned by rinsing them out with powdered charcoal.

BOTTLES. — There is no easier method of cleaning glass bottles than putting into them fine coals, and well shaking, either with water or not, hot or cold, according to the substance that fouls the bottle. Charcoal left in a bottle or jar for a little time will take away disagreeable smells.

To Clean Paint. — There is a very simple method to clean paint that has become dirty, and if our housewives should adopt it, it would save them a great deal of trouble. Provide a plate with some of the best whiting to be had, and have ready some clean warm water and a piece of flannel, which dip into the water and squeeze nearly dry; then take as much whiting as will adhere to it, apply it to the painted surface, when a little rubbing will instantly remove any dirt or grease. After which wash the part well with clean water, rubbing it dry with a soft chamois. Paint thus cleaned looks as well as when first laid on, without any injury to the most delicate colors. It is far better than using soap, and does not require more than half the time and labor.

To Restore Scratched Furniture. — Scrape one pound of beeswax into shavings in a pan; add half a gallon of spirits of turpentine, and one pint of linseed oil. Let it remain twelve hours, then stir it well with a stick into a liquid; while stirring add one-quarter pound shellac varnish and one ounce alkanet root. Put this mixture into a gallon jar, and stand it before the fire or in an oven for a week (to keep it just warm); shake it up three or four times a day; then strain it through a hair sieve and bottle it. Pour about a teaspoonful on a wad of baize; go lightly over the face and other parts of mahogany furniture; then rub briskly with a similar dry wad, and in three minutes it will produce a dark brilliant polish unequalled.

Boards, to Scour.—Lime, one part; sand, three parts; soft soap, two parts. Lay a little on the boards with the scrubbing-brush, and rub thoroughly. Rinse with clean water, and rub dry. This will keep the boards of a good color, and will also keep away vermin.

CHARCOAL. — All sorts of glass vessels and other utensils may be purified from long retained smells of every kind, in the easiest and most perfect manner, by rinsing them out well with charcoal powder, after the grosser impurities have been scoured off with sand and potash. Rubbing the teeth and washing out the mouth with fine charcoal powder, will render the teeth beautifully white, and the breath perfectly sweet, where an offensive breath has been owing to a scorbutic disposition of the gums. Putrid water is immediately deprived of its bad smell by charcoal. When meat, fish, etc., from intense heat, or long keeping, are likely to pass into a state of corruption, a simple and pure mode of keeping them sound and healthful is by putting a few pieces of charcoal, each about the size of an egg, into the pot or saucepan wherein the fish or flesh is to be boiled. Among others, an experiment of this kind was tried upon a turbot, which appeared to be too far gone to be eatable; the cook, as advised, put three or four pieces of charcoal, each the size of an egg, under the strainer, in the fish kettle; after boil-ing the proper time, the turbot came to the table sweet and firm.

To Take out Stains from Mahogany Furniture. — Stains and spots may be taken out of mahogany furniture with a little aquafortis or oxalic acid and water, rubbing the part by means of a cork, till the color is restored, observing afterwards to wash the wood well with water, and to dry and polish as usual.

To Take Ink-Stains out of Mahogany. — Put a few drops of spirits of nitre in a teaspoonful of water. Touch the spot with a feather dipped in the mixture, and on the ink disappearing, rub it over immediately with a rag wetted in cold water, or there will be a white mark, which will not be easily effaced.

To Remove Ink-Stains from Silver. —The tops and other portions of silver inkstands frequently become deeply discolored with ink, which is difficult to remove by ordinary means. It may, however, be completely eradicated by making a little chloride of lime into a paste with water, and rubbing it upon the stains. Chloride of lime has been misnamed "The general bleacher," but it is a foul enemy to all metallic surfaces.

To Take Ink-Stains out of a Colored Table-Cover.— Dissolve a teaspoonful of oxalic acid in a teacup of hot water; rub the stained part well with the solution.

To Take Ink out of Boards. — Strong muriatic acid, or spirits of salts, applied with a piece of cloth; afterwards well washed with water.

Oil Grease may be removed from a hearth by covering it immediately with thick hot ashes, or with burning coals.

Marble may be Cleaned by mixing up a quantity of the strongest soap-lees with quicklime, to the consistence of milk, and laying it on the marble for twenty-four hours; clean it afterwards with soap and water.

Silver and Plated Ware should be washed with a sponge and warm soap-suds every day after using, and wiped dry with a clean soft towel.

Cleaning Mirrors.—Mix some fine whitening in a little diluted alcohol, and smear it upon the glass with a soft rag, after which rub off with chamois leather. Looking-glasses may thus be cleaned, and fly specks, etc., removed.

If the frames are not varnished, the greatest care is necessary to keep them quite dry, so as not to touch them with the sponge, as this will discolor or take off the gilding. To clean the frames, take a little raw cotton in the state of wool, and rub the frames with it; this will take off all the dust and dirt without injuring the gilding. If the frames are well varnished, rub them with spirit of wine, which will take out all spots, and give them a fine polish. Varnished doors may be done in the same manner. Never use any cloth to *frames* or *drawings*, or unvarnished oil paintings, when cleaning and dusting them.

SPIRITS OF HARTSHORN (Ammonia) is also an excellent cleaner. A few drops added to water will instantly remove all dirt from your mirrors and window-panes.

To Anneal Glass or Crockery Ware.—When new, before using these articles, place them in a large boiler, and cover them with cold water. Place the boiler over the fire, and let it come slowly to a boil. Continue to boil for half an hour, then remove the boiler from the fire, and let it cool slowly; then take out the articles, which will not be so liable to crack when hot water is put in them.

Lamp Chimneys annealed in this way will outlast three not so treated.

To Temper New Ovens and Iron Ware.—New ovens, previous to being used, should have a fire kept in them for half a day. When the fire is removed, the mouth of the oven should be closed. It should not be baked in till heated the second time. If not treated in this manner, it will not retain its heat well. New flat-irons, previous to using them, should be heated for half a day, in order to have them retain their heat well. Iron

cooking utensils will be less liable to crack if heated previous to using them, five or six hours. They should be heated gradually, and cooled in the same manner. Cold water should not be turned into empty iron pots that are hot, as it will crack them by cooling the surface too suddenly.

To Temper Stoves or Heaters.—All stoves, grates, or furnaces, when new, should have the fire kindled in them slowly, letting it burn up gradually until the heat is as great as it will be required. Keep up the fire to this heat for an hour, then let the fire gradually burn out. Stoves and furnaces so treated will not only keep in better repair and last longer, but will work better, and retain and give a more uniform heat.

ASHES, when left in the grate or on the hearth, absorb a great deal of heat; and it will be found that a small fire in a clear grate and a clean hearth, will give out more heat than a large fire cumbered with ashes.

A Large Stove is much more economical, and requires much less coal to give as much heat as a small one, and requires much less care.

By using a small stove it has to be put on a good draught, and thus a good portion of heat is drawn up the chimney, and clinkers form in the stove, and the lining burns out. By using a large stove, large coal (which gives a stronger heat) can be used, and the draught may be nearly shut off, thus giving a larger body of fire with a steady heat, and preventing its escape through the chimney, and insuring a perfect combustion of the coal. A stove should never be allowed to become red hot, for in this state the iron becomes very porous, and admits of the escape (through these pores) of the deleterious gases from the burning coals into the room; this, together with the air in the room, being burnt or deprived of its oxygen by coming in contact with the red-hot stove, renders it unfit for breathing.

It is a good plan to place a vessel containing clear water on top of stoves or heaters, to prevent the air from becoming too dry for healthy respiration.

To Remove Clinkers from Stoves.
—Some kinds of coal are liable to form clinkers, which adhere to the fire-brick lining of stoves, grates, and furnaces, and become the source of great annoyance, as they cannot be removed by usual means without breaking the fire-brick. Persons who are thus annoyed will be glad to know that by putting a few oyster-shells in the fire close to the clinkers, the latter will become so loose as to be readily removed without breaking the lining.

Filling Lamps.
— This should always be done by daylight — it can then be done without coming near fire; to fill one lamp while another one is burning near it, is very dangerous. If it should be forgotten to fill the lamps by daylight, insist on having candles used until daylight comes again. The lamps will generally be ready after this.

To Extinguish a Lamp,
turn it half way down, and then blow sideways at the *bottom* of the chimney. *Never blow down the chimney!* Many fatal accidents have resulted lately through this practice. And never attempt to kindle a fire by pouring coal oil, benzine, or turpentine upon your wood or shavings. Scores of deaths result from this latter course. Domestics, through ignorance of the terribly destructive properties of these agents, are very apt to employ them in the manner referred to. A strict caution, therefore, should be given them in every instance.

To Remove Iron Rust from White Goods.
— A remedy which I have tried and found effectual, is this: One ounce of oxalic acid dissolved in one quart of water. Wet the iron rust spots in this solution and lay in the hot sun; the rust will disappear in from three to twenty minutes, according to its depth. I have just experimented by holding a rusted cloth, wet in this solution, over the steam of a boiling tea-kettle, and the rust disappeared almost instantly. In either

case, the cloth should be well rinsed in water as soon as the rust disappears, to prevent injury from the acid. Many use this acid to remove fruit and ink stains from white fabrics. When diluted still more, it may be used to remove fruit or ink stains from the hands.

To Remove Stains from a Mattress.
— Make a thick paste by wetting starch with cold water. Spread this over the stain, first placing the mattress in the sun. Rub off in a couple of hours, and if the ticking is not perfectly clean, repeat the process.

To remove the stains on spoons
caused by using them for boiled eggs, take a little common salt moist between the thumb and finger, and briskly rub the stain, which will soon disappear.

To Take Marking-Ink out of Linen.
— Use a saturated solution of cyanuret of potassium applied with a camel-hair brush. After the marking-ink disappears, the linen should be well washed in cold water.

To Remove Ink from Paper, etc.
— The process of thoroughly extracting all traces of writing-ink, whether accidentally spilt or written in error, is to alternately wash the paper with a camel-hair brush dipped in a solution of cyanuret of potassium and oxalic acid; then when the ink has disappeared, wash the paper with pure water. By this process checks have been altered when written on "patent check paper," from which it was supposed by a recent inventor to be impossible to remove writing.

To Take Stains of Wine out of Linen.
— Hold the articles in milk while it is boiling on the fire, and the stains will soon disappear.

Fruit Stains in Linen.
— To remove them, rub the part on each side with yellow soap, then tie up a piece of pearlash in the cloth, etc., and soak well in hot water, or boil; afterwards expose the stained part to the sun and air until removed.

Mildewed Linen
may be restored by soaping the spots while wet, covering them with fine chalk scraped to powder, and rubbing it well in.

To keep Moths, Beetles, etc., from Clothes. — Put a piece of camphor in a linen bag, or some aromatic herbs in the drawers, among linen or woollen clothes, and neither moth nor worm will come near them.

Clothes Closets that have become infested with moths should be well rubbed with a strong decoction of tobacco, and repeatedly sprinkled with spirits of camphor.

Iron Stains may be removed from marble by wetting the spots with oil of vitriol, or with lemon-juice, or with oxalic acid diluted in spirit of wine, and, after a quarter of an hour, rubbing them dry with a soft linen cloth.

Scouring Drops, for removing grease:—Mix three ounces of camphor and one ounce essence of lemon. Pour it over the part that is greasy, rub it until quite dry with a piece of clean flannel. If the grease is not quite removed, repeat the application. When done, brush the part well, and hang it in the open air to take away the smell.

To Extract Grease Spots from Books or Paper. — Gently warm the greased or spotted part of the book or paper, and then press upon it pieces of blotting-paper, one after another, so as to absorb as much of the grease as possible. Have ready some fine clear essential oil of turpentine heated almost to a boiling state, warm the greased leaf a little, and then, with a soft clean brush, apply the heated turpentine to both sides of the spotted part. By repeating this application, the grease will be extracted. Lastly, with another brush dipped in rectified spirits of wine, go over the place, and the grease will no longer appear, neither will the paper be discolored.

Stains and Marks from Books.— A solution of oxalic acid, citric acid, or tartaric acid, is attended with the least risk, and may be applied upon the paper and prints without fear of damage. These acids, taking out writing-ink, and not touching the printing, can be used for restoring books where the margins have been written upon, without injuring the text.

To Wash Flannel. — Never rub soap upon it. Make a suds by dissolving the soap in warm water. Rinse in warm water. Very cold or hot water will shrink flannel. Shake it out several minutes before hanging to dry.

Cleaning Old Clothes. — Grease spots should first be taken out with liquid ammonia, and then you apply the remedy of some of the Chatham street dealers in old clothes, namely, one or two ounces of common tobacco boiled in half a gallon of water. In the hot decoction you dip a stiff brush, and rub the clothes thoroughly in all directions, no matter what color of cloth. When the liquid is well penetrated, rub in one direction and suspend the cloth to dry; by this treatment it becomes clean and lustrous, and singularly enough, no tobacco smell will remain.

Washing Woollen Bed Clothing. — It is said by some, wash in warm water; by others in cold water. We know that warm water will cause shrinking. A large, fine rose blanket washed six to seven inches each washing. In the centre it pulled up and made a shapeless thing. We were told to wash in warm water and rinse in water of the same temperature. It was done, and with perfect success. The blanket is even longer and more even. The shrinking seems to take place on the sudden change of the temperature from warm water to cold. The gradual cooling and drying afterward does not seem to affect it any; so the slow change in the temperature of frozen fruit leaves the fruit unhurt.

To Wash Calico without Fading. — Infuse three gills of salt in four quarts of water; put the calico in while hot, and leave it till cold, and in this way the colors are rendered permanent, and will not fade by subsequent washing. So says a lady who has frequently made the experiment.

Washing Silk. — No person should

ever wring or crush a piece of silk when it is wet, because the creases thus made will remain forever, if the silk is thick and hard. The way to wash silk is to spread it smoothly upon a clean board, rub white soap upon it and brush it with a clean hard brush. The silk must be rubbed until all the grease is extracted, then the soap should be brushed off with clean cold water, applied to both sides. The cleansing of silk is a very nice operation. Most of the colors are liable to be extracted with washing in hot suds, especially blue and green colors. A little alum dissolved in the last water that is brushed on the silk, tends to prevent the colors from running. Alcohol and camphene mixed together is used for removing grease from silk.

Cleaning Silks, Satins, Colored Woollen Dresses, etc. — Four ounces of soft soap, four ounces of honey, the white of an egg, and a wineglassful of gin ; mix well together, and scour the article with a rather hard brush thoroughly ; afterwards rinse it in cold water, leave to drain, and iron while quite damp. — A friend informs us that she believes this recipe has never been made public ; she finds it an excellent one, having used it for a length of time with perfect success.

Grease Spots from Silk. — Upon a deal table lay a piece of woollen cloth or baize, upon which lay smoothly the part stained, with the right side downwards. Having spread a piece of brown paper on the top, apply a flat iron just hot enough to scorch the paper. About five or eight seconds is usually sufficient. Then rub the stained part briskly with a piece of tap-paper.

To Keep Silk.—Silk articles should not be kept folded in white paper, as the chloride of lime used in bleaching the paper will probably impair the color of the silk. Brown or blue paper is better ; the yellowish smooth Indian paper is best of all. Silk intended for dress should not be kept long in the house before it is made up, as lying in the folds will have a ten-

dency to impair its durability by causing it to cut or split, particularly if the silk has been thickened by gum. Thread lace veils are very easily cut ; satin and velvet being soft are not easily cut, but dresses of velvet should not be laid by with any weight above them. If the nap of thin velvet is laid down, it is not possible to raise it up again. Hard silk should never be wrinkled, because the thread is easily broken in the crease, and it never can be rectified. The way to take the wrinkles out of silk scarfs or handkerchiefs is to moisten the surface evenly with a sponge and some weak glue, and then pin the silk with toilet pins around the selvages on a mattress or feather bed, taking pains to draw out the silk as tight as possible. When dry the wrinkles will have disappeared. The reason of this is obvious to every person. It is a nice job to dress light colored silk, and few should try it. Some silk articles may be moistened with weak glue or gum water, and the wrinkles ironed out on the wrong side by a hot flat-iron.

How to Smooth Ribbons. — Take a moderately hot flat-iron on the ironing board, then place the ribbon on the left side of the iron, and pull it carefully through underneath the iron. If the ribbon is not pulled too fast, and the iron is the right warmth, this will be found to be a much better way than simply rubbing the iron over the ribbon.

To make Silk which has been wrinkled and "tumbled" appear exactly like new, sponge it on the surface with a weak solution of gum arabic or white glue, and iron it on the wrong side.

To Renovate Silks.—Sponge faded silks with warm water and soap, then rub them with a dry cloth on a flat board ; afterwards iron them on the *inside* with a smoothing iron. Old black silks may be improved by sponging with spirits ; in this case, the ironing may be done on the right side, thin paper being spread over to prevent glazing.

Black Silk Reviver.—Boil logwood in water for half an hour; then simmer the silk half an hour; take it out, and put into the dye a little blue vitriol, or green copperas; cool it, and simmer the silk for half an hour. Or, boil a handful of fig-leaves in two quarts of water until it is reduced to one pint; squeeze the leaves, and bottle the liquor for use. When wanted, sponge the silk with this preparation.

Restoring Color to Silk.—When the color has been taken from silk by acids, it may be restored by applying to the spot a little hartshorn, or sal volatile.

Preserving the Color of Dresses. —The colors of merinos, mousseline-de-laines, ginghams, chintzes, printed lawns, etc., may be preserved by using water that is only milk-warm; making a lather with white soap, *before* you put in the dress, instead of rubbing it on the material; and stirring into a first and second tub of water a large tablespoonful of ox-gall. The gall can be obtained from the butcher, and a bottle of it should always be kept in every house. No colored articles should be allowed to remain long in the water. They must be washed fast, and then rinsed through two cold waters. Into each rinsing water stir a teaspoonful of vinegar, which will help to brighten the colors; and after rinsing, hang them out immediately. When *ironing dry* (or still a little damp), bring them in; have irons ready heated, and iron them at once, as it injures the colors to allow them to remain damp too long, or to sprinkle and roll them up in a cover for ironing next day. If they cannot be conveniently ironed immediately, let them hang till they are *quite* dry, and then damp and fold them on the *following day*, a quarter of an hour before ironing. The best way is not to do colored dresses on the day of the general wash, but to give them a morning by themselves. They should only be undertaken in clear bright weather. If allowed to freeze, the colors will be irreparably injured. We need scarcely say that no colored articles should ever be boiled or scalded. If you get from a shop a slip for testing the durability of colors, give it a fair trial by washing it as above; afterwards pinning it to the edge of a towel, and hanging it to dry. Some colors (especially pinks and light greens), though they may stand perfectly well in washing, will change as soon as a warm iron is applied to them; the pink turning purplish, and the green bluish. No colored article should be smoothed with a *hot* iron.

To Remove Water Stains from Black Crape.—When a drop of water falls on a black crape veil or collar, it leaves a conspicuous white mark. To obliterate this, spread the crape on a table (laying on it a large book or a paper-weight to keep it steady), and place underneath the stain a piece of old black silk; with a large camel-hair brush dipped in common ink go over the stain, and then wipe off the ink with a small piece of old soft silk. It will dry immediately, and the white mark will be seen no more.

To Remove Stains from Mourning Dresses. — Boil a handful of fig-leaves in two quarts of water until reduced to a pint. Bombazines, crape, cloth, etc., need only be rubbed with a sponge dipped in this liquor, and the effect will be instantly produced.

WAX may be taken out of cloth by holding a red-hot iron within an inch or two of the marks, and afterwards rubbing them with a soft clean rag.

When Velvet gets Plushed from pressure, hold the parts over a basin of *hot* water, with the lining of the article next to the water; the pile will soon raise, and assume its original beauty.

Worsted and Lambs'-wool Stockings should never be mended with worsted or lambs'-wool, because the latter being new, it shrinks more than the stockings, and draws them up till the toes become short and narrow, and the heels have no shape left.

All Flannels should be soaked before they are made up, first in cold,

19

then in hot water, in order to shrink them.

To Clean Black Cloth Clothes.—

Clean the garments well, then boil four ounces of logwood in a boiler or copper containing two or three gallons of water for half an hour; dip the clothes in warm water, and squeeze dry, then put them into the copper and boil for half an hour. Take them out, and add three drams of sulphate of iron; boil for half an hour, then take them out, and hang them up for an hour or two; take them down, rinse them thrice in cold water, dry well, and rub with a soft brush which has had a few drops of olive oil applied to its surface. If the clothes are threadbare about the elbows, cuffs, etc., raise the nap with a teasel or half-worn hatters' card, filled with flocks, and when sufficiently raised, lay the nap the right way with a hard brush. We have seen old coats come out with a wonderful dash of respectability after this operation.

Liquid for Preserving Furs from Moths.—

Warm water, one pint; corrosive sublimate, twelve grains. If washed with this, and afterwards dried, furs are safe from moth. Care should be taken to label the liquid—*Poison*.

To Clean Furs. —

Strip the fur articles of their stuffing and binding, and lay them as nearly as possible in a flat position. They must then be subjected to a very brisk brushing with a stiff clothes-brush; after this, any moth-eaten parts must be cut out, and neatly replaced by new bits of fur to match. Sable, chinchilla, squirrel, fitch, etc., should be treated as follows:— Warm a quantity of new bran in a pan, taking care that it does not burn, to prevent which it must be actively stirred. When well warmed, rub it thoroughly into the fur with the hand. Repeat this two or three times: then shake the fur, and give it another sharp brushing until free from dust. White furs, ermine, etc., may be cleaned as follows: — Lay the fur on a table, and rub it well with bran made moist with warm water; rub until quite dry, and afterwards with dry bran. The wet bran should be put on with flannel, and the dry with a piece of book muslin. The light furs, in addition to the above, should be well rubbed with magnesia, or a piece of book muslin, after the bran process. Furs are usually much improved by stretching, which may be managed as follows : To a pint of soft water add three ounces of salt, dissolve ; with this solution, sponge the inside of the skin (taking care not to wet the fur) until it becomes thoroughly saturated ; then lay it carefully on a board with the fur side downwards, in its natural position ; then stretch as much as it will bear, and to the required shape, and fasten with small tacks. The drying may be accelerated by placing the skin a little distance from the fire or stove.

Cleansing Feathers of their Animal Oil.—

The following recipe gained a premium from the Society of Arts :— Take for every gallon of clean water one pound of quicklime, mix them well together, and when the undissolved lime is precipitated in fine powder, pour off the clean lime-water for use. Put the feathers to be cleaned in another tub, and add to them a quantity of the clean lime-water, sufficient to cover them about three inches when well immersed and stirred about therein. The feathers, when thoroughly moistened, will sink, and should remain in the lime-water three or four days ; after which the foul liquor should be separated from them, by laying them in a sieve. The feathers should be afterwards well washed in clean water, and dried upon nets, the meshes of which may be about the fineness of cabbage nets. The feathers must be from time to time shaken on the nets, and as they get dry, will fall through the meshes, and are to be collected for use. The admission of air will be serviceable in drying. The process will be completed in three weeks ; and when thus prepared, the feathers will only require to be beaten to get rid of the dust.

To Clean White Ostrich Feathers.

— Four ounces of white soap, cut small, dissolved in four pints of water, rather hot, in a large basin; make the solution into a lather by beating it with birch rods, or wires. Introduce the feathers, and rub well with the hands for five or six minutes. After this soaping, wash in clean water, as hot as the hand can bear. Shake until dry.

Cleaning Straw Bonnets. — They may be washed with soap and water, rinsed in clear water, and dried in the air. Then wash them over with white of egg well beaten. Remove the wire before washing. Old straw bonnets may be picked to pieces, and put together for children, the head parts being cut out.

To Bleach a Faded Dress. —Wash it well in hot suds, and boil it until the color seems to be gone, then wash, and rinse, and dry it in the sun; if still not quite white, repeat the boiling.

Bleaching Straw Bonnets, etc. — Wash them in pure water, scrubbing them with a brush. Then put them into a box in which has been set a saucer of burning sulphur. Cover them up, so that the fumes may bleach them.

To Wash China Crape Scarfs, etc. — If the fabric be good, these articles of dress can be washed as frequently as may be required, and no diminution of their beauty will be discoverable, even when the various shades of green have been employed among other colors in the patterns. In cleaning them, make a strong lather of boiling water. Suffer it to cool; when cold, or nearly so, wash the scarf quickly and thoroughly, dip it immediately in cold hard water in which a little salt has been thrown (to preserve the colors), rinse, squeeze, and hang it out to dry in the open air. Pin it at its extreme edge to the line, so that it may not in any part be folded together. The more rapidly it dries, the clearer it will be.

To Wash a White Lace Veil. — Put the veil into a strong lather of white soap and very clear water, and let it simmer slowly for a quarter of an hour. Take it out and squeeze it well, but be sure not to rub it. Rinse it twice in cold water, the second time with a drop or two of liquid blue. Have ready some very clear weak gum arabic water, or some thin starch, or rice water. Pass the veil through it, and clear it by clapping; then stretch it out evenly, and pin it to dry on a linen cloth, making the edge as straight as possible, opening out all the scallops, and fastening each with pins. When dry, lay a piece of thin muslin smoothly over it, and iron it on the wrong side.

Blond Lace may be revived by breathing upon it, and shaking and flapping it. The use of the iron turns the lace yellow.

WASHING. — To save your linen and your labor, pour on half a pound of soda two quarts of boiling water, in an earthenware pan. Take half a pound of soap, shred fine. Put it into a saucepan with two quarts of cold water. Stand it on a fire till it boils, and when perfectly dissolved and boiling, add it to the former. Mix it well, and let it stand till cold, when it will have the appearance of a strong jelly. Let your linen be soaked in water, the seams and any other soiled part rubbed in the usual way, and remain till the following morning. Get your copper ready, and add to the water about a pint-basin full; when *lukewarm* put in your linen, and allow it to boil for twenty minutes. Rinse it in the usual way, and that is all which is necessary to get it clean, and to keep it in good color. The above recipe is invaluable to housekeepers. If you have not tried it, do so without delay.

WHEN WATER IS HARD, and will not readily unite with soap, it will always be proper to boil it before use, which will be found sufficiently efficacious, if the hardness depends solely upon the impregnation of lime. Even exposure to the atmosphere will produce this effect in a great degree upon spring water so impregnated, leaving it much fitter for lavatory purposes. In both cases the water ought to be

carefully poured off from the sediment, as the neutralized lime, when
freed from its extra quantity of carbonic acid, falls to the bottom by its
own gravity. To economize the use
of soap, put any quantity of pearlash
into a large jar, covered from the
dust; in a few days the alkali will become liquid, which must be diluted in
double its quantity of soft water, with
an equal quantity of new slacked lime.
Boil it half an hour, frequently stirring it, adding as much more hot
water, and drawing off the liquor,
when the residuum may be boiled
afresh, and drained, until it ceases to
feel acrid to the tongue.

SOAP AND LABOR MAY BE SAVED
by dissolving alum and chalk in bran
water, in which the linen ought to be
boiled, then well rinsed out, and exposed to the usual process of bleaching.

SOAP MAY BE DISPENSED WITH, or
nearly so, in the getting up of muslins
and chintzes, which should always be
treated agreeably to the Oriental manner; that is, to wash them in plain
water, and then boil them in congee,
or rice water: after which they ought
not to be submitted to the operation
of the smoothing iron, but rubbed
smooth with a polished stone.

THE ECONOMY which must result
from these processes renders their consideration important to every family,
in addition to which, we must state
that the improvements in philosophy
extend to the laundry as well as to the
wash-house.

Gum Arabic Starch.— Procure two
ounces of fine white gum arabic, and
pound it to powder. Next put it into
a pitcher, and pour on it a pint or
more of boiling water, according to the
degree of strength you desire, and then,
having covered it, let it set all night.
In the morning, pour it carefully from
the dregs into a clean bottle, cork it,
and keep it for use. A tablespoonful
of gum water stirred into a pint of
starch that has been made in the usual
manner will give to lawns (either white
or printed) a look of newness to which
nothing else can restore them after

washing. It is also good (much diluted) for thin white muslin and bob-
binet.

Mildew out of Linen.— Rub the
linen well with soap; then scrape some
fine chalk, and rub it also on the linen.
Lay it on the grass. As it dries, wet
it a little, and the mildew will come
out with a second application.

**To render Linen, etc., Incombusti-
ble.**— All linen, cotton, muslins, etc.,
etc., when dipped in a solution of
tungstate of soda or common alum,
will become incombustible.

Sweet Bags for Linen.—These may
be composed of any mixtures of the
following articles:—Flowers, dried and
pounded; powdered cloves, mace, nutmeg, cinnamon; leaves — dried and
pounded — of mint, palm, dragon-
wort, southernwood, ground-ivy, laurel, hyssop, sweet marjoram, origanum,
rosemary; woods, such as cassia, juniper, rhodium, sandal-wood, and rosewood; roots of angelica, zedoary, orris:
all the fragrant balsams — ambergris,
musk, and civet. These latter should
be carefully used on linen.

Laundry Gloss. — The beautiful
finish of linen got up for sale is imparted by pressure and friction upon
curved surfaces of hard pasteboard.
Try a true cylinder, or convex table,
veneered with the best quality of press-
board, such as printers use, instead of
the usual domestic "ironing sheet."

Gall Soap, for the washing of fine
silken cloths and ribbons, is prepared
in the following manner: In a vessel
of copper one pound of cocoa-nut oil is
heated to 60° Fahr., whereupon half a
pound of caustic soda is added with
constant stirring. In another vessel,
half a pound of white Venetian turpentine is heated, and when quite hot,
stirred into the copper kettle. This
kettle is then covered and left for four
hours, being gently heated, after
which the fire is increased until the
contents are perfectly clear, whereupon
one pound of ox-gall is added. After
this, enough good, perfectly dry castile
soap is stirred into the mixture to
cause the whole to yield but little

under the pressure of the finger; for which purpose, from one to two pounds of soap are required for the above quantity. After cooling, the soap is cut into pieces. It is excellent, and will not injure the finest colors.

The Best Soap to clean very dirty clothes, paint, or in fact almost anything, and to save labor, is made as follows : — Cut two pounds of bar-soap into strips, put it into a wash-boiler with five gallons of water, five pounds of sal soda, quarter of a pound of carbonate of ammonia, one ounce of sal ammoniac, and a quarter of an ounce of camphor ; let it soak in the cold water two or three hours, then set it on the fire and heat it slowly, let it boil until dissolved, stirring it well : be careful it does not boil over ; it will require about two hours after putting on the fire. *If you once make this soap you will never be without it. The inventor of it, from whom we bought the recipe, realized a large amount from its sale.*

Ironing Without Heat. — Much time and trouble may be saved by "ironing" without heat and flat-irons. When rinsing the clothes, fold coarse sheets, towels, and tablecloths in the shape they are wanted, and pass them through the wringer as tight as possible. Unfold and hang to dry where the wind does not blow very hard. They will need little or no ironing. The tablecloths should be dipped in old, sweet, skimmed milk; this gives them a lustre, and they need no starch.

To Keep Meat. — Meat is much better for family use when at least one week old in cold weather. The English method for keeping meat for some time has great merit. Experts say, hang up quarter of meat with the cut end up, being the reverse of the usual way, by the leg, and the juice will remain in the meat, and not run to the cut and dry up by evaporation. It may be kept several days in the height of summer, sweet and good, by lightly covering it with bran, and hanging it in some high or windy room, or in a passage where there is a current of air.

Dry Salting. — This is the English

way of curing meat instead of pickling it. All kinds of meat are cured in this way, and may be eaten green or undried, or may be dried or smoked. Trim the hams from all loose flesh and fat, and make them shapely. Remove the ribs from the sides, and cut them into pieces of about twenty pounds each. Procure a solid bench of oak plank on which to pack the meat. Take coarse salt, and mix with each pound of it a tablespoonful of pulverized saltpetre. With this rub the meat on both sides, leaving considerable of the mixture loose on the flesh side. Pile the meat in heaps, as the pieces are rubbed, on the bench, with the flesh side upward. Allow the moisture to drain away. Every second day rub the meat with fresh salt, and place that which was previously at the top of the pile at the bottom. This should be continued for two weeks, when the meat is to be removed to the smoke-house, or hung up to dry if it is not to be smoked. It should be smoked with corn-cobs or hickory brush for a few days, when, after being well dried, it may be packed in bran in boxes or barrels, or in perfectly dry wood ashes, in which flies cannot injure it; or it may be sewn up in cotton cloth and covered with two coats of thick lime-wash.

Curing of Hams and Bacon. — It is simply to use the same quantity of common soda as saltpetre — one ounce and a half of each to the fourteen pounds of ham or bacon, using the usual quantity of salt. The soda prevents that harshness in the lean of the bacon which is so often found, and keeps it quite mellow all through, besides being a preventative of rust This recipe has been very extensively tried among my acquaintance for the last fifteen years, and *invariably* approved.

To Pickle Meat. — *To 1 gallon of water, take 1½ pounds of salt, ½ pound of sugar, ¼ ounce of saltpetre, ¼ ounce of potash, and ¼ of a pint of molasses.* In this ratio the pickle can be increased to any quantity desired. Let these be boiled together until all the dirt from the sugar rises to the top and is skimmed off. Then throw it into a tub to cool, and when *cold*, pour it over your beef or pork, to remain the usual time, say two to three weeks. The meat must be well covered with pickle, and should not be put down for at least two days after killing, during which time it should be slightly sprinkled with powdered saltpetre, which removes all the surface-blood, etc., leaving the meat fresh and clean. Some omit boiling the pickle, and find it to answer well, though the operation of boiling purifies the pickle by throwing off the dirt always to be found in salt and sugar.

Beef Extra.—The pickle for this is made of the same ingredients as the last, but used as below:—When the water is ready to receive the rest of the material, pour in the saltpetre *only*, and when dissolved and the water boiling, dip your beef, piece by piece, into the boiling saltpetre water, holding it for a few seconds only in the hot bath. When the beef has all been thus immersed and becomes quite cool, pack it in the cask where it is to remain. Then proceed with your pickle as at first directed, and when perfectly cold, pour it upon the meat, which should be kept down by a cover and stone.

The immersing of the beef in hot saltpetre water contracts the surface by closing the pores, and prevents the juices of the meat from going out into the pickle. The saltpetre absorbed by the contracted or cooked surfaces will modify the salt that passes through it, the whole producing the most perfect result.

Beef cured in this manner will preserve its color, and cut almost as juicy and inviting as a fresh roast. It is as unlike the hard, blue, briny, knotted substance sold at markets, and frequently cured at home, miscalled "corned beef," as a sirloin differs from a steak cut three inches back of the horns.

For Curing Meats in the Hottest Climate, and which has been practised in most of the Southern States not less than fifteen or twenty years at any rate. The plan is to dig a hole in the earth, from four to six feet deep, and large enough for the amount of meat you have to cure; lay boards on the bottom, and on this pack your meat in salt—the usual quantity—and then cover the hole with boards and earth, keeping it in this condition till the meat is sufficiently salted. By this mode of preserving, no person need lose a pound of meat in the warmest climate.

To Prevent Skippers in Hams.—It is simply to keep your smoke-house dark, and the moth that deposits the egg will never enter it. There are other ways of doing the same thing, but they injure the flavor of the meat. Green hickory wood is the best to use. This is important, as the flavor of bacon is often utterly destroyed by smoking it with improper wood.

How to Cut Hard Dried Beef.—Take a sharp plane, not too rankly set, invert it, and, taking the beef firmly in the hand, push it across the plane, and the beef, very nicely shaven, will drop through the opening in the plane on to a towel below. It must be very dry to cut thus, but when dry, it is much more expeditiously and nicely done than with a knife.

Keeping Eggs for Winter.—A lady says:—"In August I generally commence saving eggs, and am very careful to save only good and fresh ones. I take boxes which hold about one thousand two hundred, put on the bottom a layer of oats, and set my eggs all point downwards, so that not one touches the other, until the layer is full; then cover with oats, and make another layer, and so on until the box is full, and then cover and set in a cool, dry place, where it does not freeze, until used. I have followed this way for the last twenty years, and cannot say that I ever lost more than one or two out of fifty, and then generally found that it was knocked or put down unsound. I use small boxes, so that I can use first the eggs which I put down first. I have never thought of changing my way, although I have read so many ways to do it, — for instance, in ashes, in fat, in lime, in lime-water, and even varnishing them, — because my way seemed to me the simplest and cleanest; and I am just as sure to have good eggs next February and March, which I lay in now, as I can have good eggs now. There is no danger of having any musty taste to the eggs if you keep them in a dry place, and are careful to use dry oats."

To Preserve Eggs. — It has been long known to housewives, that the great secret of preserving eggs fresh is to place the small end downwards, and keep it in that position — other requisites not being neglected, such as to have the eggs perfectly fresh when deposited for keeping, not allowing them to become wet, keeping them cool in warm weather, and avoiding freezing in winter. Take an inch board of convenient size, say a foot wide, and two and a half feet long, and bore it full of holes, each about an inch and a half in diameter. A board of this size may have five dozen holes bored in it, for as many eggs. Then nail strips of thin board, two inches wide, round the edges to serve as a ledge. Boards such as this may now be made to constitute the shelves of a cupboard in a cool cellar. The only precaution necessary is to place the eggs as fast as they are laid in these holes, with the small end downwards, and they will keep for months perfectly fresh. The great advantage of this plan is the perfect ease with which the fresh eggs are packed away, and again obtained when wanted. A carpenter would make such a board for a trifling charge.

It should be borne in mind, that violent shaking destroys the vitality of eggs. If eggs are subjected to the vibration or shaking of a railway car for a considerable distance, the vitality will be destroyed to the extent that at least half of them would not produce a chicken if placed under a good hen. Or if eggs are subjected to a railway journey, or other shaking process, before preserving, one-half of them will be worthless. This will explain to some of our friends why they get no chickens from eggs of a fancy breed procured from a distance.

To Keep Milk Sweet. — A teaspoonful of fine salt or of horse-radish, in a pan of milk, will keep it sweet for several days. Milk can be kept a year or more as sweet as when taken from the cow by the following method : — Procure bottles, which must be perfectly clean, sweet, and dry. Draw the milk from the cow into the bottles, and, as they are filled, immediately cork them well, and fasten the cork with packed thread or wire. Then spread a little straw in the bottom of a boiler, on which place the bottles, with straw between them, until the boiler contains a sufficient quantity. Fill it up with cold water, heat the water, and as soon as it begins to boil, draw the fire, and let the whole gradually cool. When quite cold, take out the bottles and pack them in sawdust in hampers, and stow them away in the coolest part of the house.

To Keep Honey. — Heat the strained honey to the boiling-point, and stow it in covered jars, where it will keep without candying. To prevent danger of burning, set the vessel in which it is to be heated into another containing water.

Fresh Tomatoes till Winter. — If late in the season, just before frosts, the vigorous late-bearing tomato vine be pulled, and hung up in a moderately dry cellar, the fruit will gradually mature, and thus furnish the table with fine luscious tomatoes from time to time, even into the winter season. So say they who have tried it.

REV. SIDNEY SMITH, in hints on household management, inquires : — Have you ever observed what a dislike servants have to anything cheap? They hate saving their master's money. I tried this experiment with great success the other day. Finding we consumed a vast deal of soap, I sat down in my thinking chair, and took the soap question into consideration, and I found reason to suspect we were using a very expensive article where a much cheaper one would serve the purpose better. I ordered half a dozen pounds of both sorts, but took the precaution of changing the papers on which the prices were marked before giving them into the hands of Betty. " Well, Betty, which soap do you find washes best ? " " Oh, please sir, the dearest, in the blue paper; it makes a lather as well again as the other." " Well, Betty, you shall always have it then ; " and thus the unsuspecting Betty saved me some pounds a year, and washed the clothes better.

An ever-Dirty Hearth, and a grate always choked with cinders and ashes, are infallible evidences of bad housekeeping.

Economy. — If you have a strip of land, do not throw away soapsuds. Both ashes and soapsuds are good manure for bushes and young plants.

Do NOT let coffee and tea stand in tin.

SCALD your wooden-ware often, and keep your tin-ware dry.

PRESERVE the backs of old letters to write upon.

SEE THAT NOTHING IS THROWN AWAY which might have served to nourish your own family or a poorer one.

AS FAR AS POSSIBLE, have pieces of bread eaten up before they become hard ; spread those that are not eaten, and let them dry, to be pounded for puddings, or soaked for brewis.

BREWIS is made of crusts and dry pieces of bread, soaked a good while in hot milk, mashed up, and eaten with salt. Above all, do not let crusts accumulate in such quantities that they cannot be used. With proper care, there is no need of losing a particle of bread.

ALL THE MENDING in the house should be done once a week, if possible.

NEVER PUT OUT SEWING. If it be not possible to do it in your own family, hire some one into the house, and work with them.

A WARMING-PAN full of coals, or a shovel of coals, held over varnished furniture, will take out white spots. Care should be taken not to hold the clothes near enough to scorch : and the place should be rubbed with a flannel while warm.

SAL VOLATILE or hartshorn will restore colors taken out by acid. It may be dropped upon any garment without doing harm.

NEW IRON should be very gradually heated at first. After it has become inured to the heat, it is not so likely to crack.

CLEAN A BRASS KETTLE, before using it for cooking, with salt and vinegar.

THE OFTENER CARPETS are shaken the longer they wear; the dirt that collects under them grinds out the threads.

LINEN RAGS should be carefully saved, for they are extremely useful in sickness. If they have become dirty and worn by cleaning silver, etc., wash them and scrape them into lint.

IF YOU ARE TROUBLED TO GET SOFT WATER FOR WASHING, fill a tub or barrel half full of wood-ashes, and fill it up with water, so that you may have lye whenever you want it. A gallon of strong lye, put into a great kettle of hard water, will make it as soft as rain water. Some people use pearlash, or potash ; but this costs something, and is very apt to injure the texture of the cloth.

DO NOT LET KNIVES be dropped into hot dish-water. It is a good plan to have a large tinpot to wash them in, just high enough to wash the blades *without wetting* the handles.

IT IS BETTER to accomplish perfectly a very small amount of work, than to half do ten times as much.

CHARCOAL POWDER will be found a very good thing to give knives a first-rate polish.

A BONNET AND TRIMMINGS may be worn a much longer time, if the dust be brushed well off after walking.

MUCH KNOWLEDGE may be obtained by the good housewife observing how things are managed in well-regulated families.

THE SHANKS OF MUTTON make a good stock for nearly any kind of gravy, and they are very cheap — a dozen is enough to make a quart of delicious soup.

REGULARITY in the payment of accounts is essential to housekeeping. All tradesmen's bills should be paid weekly, for then any errors can be detected while the transactions are fresh in the memory.

"WILFUL WASTE MAKES WOFUL WANT." — Do not cook a fresh joint while any of the last remains uneaten — hash it up, and with gravy and a little management, eke out another day's dinner.

Signs of the Weather. — DEW. — If the dew lies plentifully on the grass after a fair day, it is a sign of another fair day. If not, and there is no wind, rain must follow. A red evening portends fine weather; but if it spread too far upward from the horizon in the evening, and especially morning, it foretells wind or rain, or both. When the sky, in rainy weather, is tinged with sea-green, the rain will increase; if with deep blue, it will be showery.

CLOUDS. — Previous to much rain falling, the clouds grow bigger, and increase very fast, especially before thunder. When the clouds are formed like fleeces, but dense in the middle and bright toward the edges, with the sky bright, they are signs of a frost, with hail, snow, or rain. If clouds form high in air, in thin white trains like locks of wool, they portend wind, and probably rain. When a general cloudiness covers the sky, and small black fragments of clouds fly underneath, they are a sure sign of rain, and probably it will be lasting. Two currents of clouds always portend rain, and, in summer, thunder.

HEAVENLY BODIES. — A haziness in the air, which fades the sun's light, and makes the orb appear whitish, or ill-defined — or at night, if the moon and stars grow dim, and a ring encircles the former, rain will follow. If the sun's rays appear like Moses' horns — if white at setting, or shorn of his rays, or if he goes down into a bank of clouds in the horizon, bad weather is to be expected. If the moon looks pale and dim, we expect rain; if red, wind; and if of her natural color, with a clear sky, fair weather. If the moon is rainy throughout, it will clear at the change, and, perhaps, the rain return a few days after. If fair throughout, and rain at the change, the fair weather will probably return on the fourth or fifth day.

Weather Precautions. — If the weather appears doubtful, always take the precaution of having an umbrella when you go out, particularly in going to church. You thereby avoid incurring one of three disagreeables : in the first place, the chance of getting wet — or encroaching under a friend's umbrella — or being under the necessity of borrowing one, consequently involving the trouble of returning it, and possibly (as is the case nine times out of ten) inconveniencing your friend by neglecting to do so. Those who disdain the use of umbrellas, generally appear with shabby hats, tumbled bonnet ribbons, wrinkled silk dresses, etc., etc., the consequence of frequent exposure to unexpected showers, to say nothing of colds taken, no one can tell how.

Leech Barometer. — Take an eight ounce phial, and put in it three gills of water, and place in it a healthy leech, changing the water in summer once a week, and in winter once in a fortnight, and it will most accurately prognosticate the weather. If the weather is to be fine, the leech lies motionless at the bottom of the glass, and coiled together in a spiral form; if rain may be expected, it will creep up to the top of its lodgings, and remain there till the weather is settled; if we are to have wind, it will move through its habitation with amazing swiftness, and seldom goes to rest till it begins to blow hard; if a remarkable storm of thunder and rain is to succeed, it will lodge for some days before almost continually out of the water, and discover great uneasiness in violent throes and convulsive-like motions; in frost, as in clear summer-like weather, it lies constantly at the bottom; and in snow, as in rainy weather, it pitches its dwelling in the very mouth of the phial. The top should be covered over with a piece of muslin.

The Chemical Barometer. — Take a long narrow bottle, such as an old-fashioned Eau-de-Cologne bottle, and put into it two and a half drams of camphor, and eleven drams of spirit of wine; when the camphor is dissolved, which it will readily do by slight agitation, add the following mixture: -- Take water, nine drams; nitrate of potash (saltpetre), thirty-eight grains; and muriate of ammonia (sal ammoniac), thirty-eight grains. Dissolve these salts in the water prior to mixing with the camphorated spirit; then shake the whole well together. Cork the bottle well, and wax the top, but afterwards make a very small aperture in the cork with a red-hot needle. The bottle may then be hung up, or placed in any stationary position. By observing the different appearances which the materials assume, as the weather changes, it becomes an excellent prognosticator of a coming storm, or of a sunny sky.

Cheap Ice Pitcher. — The following is a simple method of keeping ice water for a long time in a common pitcher or jug: — Place between two sheets of paper (newspaper will answer, thick brown is better), a layer of cotton batting about half an inch in thickness, fasten the ends of paper and batting together, forming a circle, then sew or paste a crown over one end, making a box the shape of a stove-pipe hat minus the rim. Place this over an ordinary pitcher filled with ice water, making it deep enough to rest on the table, so as to exclude the air, and the reader will be astonished at the length of time his ice will keep and the water remain cold after the ice is melted.

Hints for Husbands. — When once a man has established a home his most important duties have fairly begun. The errors of youth may be overlooked; want of purpose, and even of honor, in his earlier days may be forgotten. But from the moment of his marriage he begins to write his indelible history; not by pen and ink, but by actions—by which he must ever afterwards be reported and judged. His conduct at home; his solicitude for his family; the training of his children; his devotion to his wife; his regard for the great interests of eternity: these are the tests by which his worth will ever afterwards be estimated by all who think or care about him. These will determine his position while living, and influence his memory when dead. He uses well or ill the brief space allotted to him, out of all eternity, to build up a fame founded upon the most solid of all foundations—private worth.

Custom entitles you to be considered the "lord and master" over your household. But don't assume the *master* and sink the *lord*. Remember that noble generosity, forbearance, amiability, and integrity, are among the more lordly attributes of man. As a husband, therefore, exhibit the true nobility of man, and seek to govern your own household by the display of high moral excellence. A domineering spirit—a fault-finding petulance—impatience of trifling delays—and the exhibition of unworthy passions at the slightest provocation, can add no laurel to your own "lordly" brow, impart no sweetness to home, and call forth no respect from those by whom you may be surrounded. It is one thing to be a *master*—another thing to be a *man*. The latter should be the husband's aspiration; for he who cannot govern himself is ill-qualified to govern another.

If your wife complains that young ladies "now-a-days" are very forward, don't accuse her of jealousy. A little concern on her part only proves her love for you, and you may enjoy your triumph without saying a word. Don't evince your weakness either, by complaining of every trifling neglect. What though her chair is not set so close to yours as it used to be, or though her knitting and crochet seem to absorb too large a share of her attention; depend upon it, that as her eyes watch the intertwinings of the threads, and the manœuvres of the needles as they dance in compliance to her delicate fingers, she is thinking of courting days, love-letters, smiles, tears, suspicions, and reconciliations, by which your two hearts became entwined together in the network of love, whose meshes you can neither of you unravel nor escape.

You can hardly imagine how refreshing it is to occasionally call up the recollection of your courting days. How tediously the hours rolled away prior to the appointed time of meeting; how swiftly they seemed to fly when you had met; how fond was the first greeting; how tender the last embrace; how fervent were your vows; how vivid your dreams of future happiness, when, returning to your home, you felt yourself secure in the confessed love of the object of your warm affections! Is your dream realized? — are you as happy as you expected? Consider whether, as a husband, you are as fervent and constant as you were when a lover. Remember that the wife's claims to your unremitting regard, great before marriage, are now exalted to a much higher degree. She has left the world for you—the home of her childhood, the fireside of her parents, their watchful care and sweet intercourse have all been yielded up for you. Look, then, most jealously upon all that may tend to attract you from home, and to weaken that union upon which your temporal happiness mainly depends; and believe that in the solemn relationship of husband is to be found one of the best guarantees for man's honor and happiness.

Summer is the season of love! Happy birds mate, and sing among the trees; fishes dart athwart the running streams, and leap from their element in resistless ecstasy; cattle group in peaceful nooks, by cooling streams; even the flowers seem to love, as they twine their tender arms around each other, and throw their wild tresses about in beautiful profusion; the happy swain sits with his loved and loving mistress beneath the sheltering oak, whose arms spread out, as if to shield and sanctify their pure attachment. What shall the husband do now, when earth and heaven seem to meet in happy union? Must he still pore over the calculations of the counting-house, or ceaselessly pursue the toils of the work-room—sparing no moment to taste the joys which heaven measures out so liberally? No! "Come, dear wife, let us once more breathe the fresh air of heaven, and look upon the beauties of earth. The summers are few we may dwell together; we will not give them all to Mammon. Again let our hearts glow with emotions of renewed love — our feet shall again tread the green sward, and the music of the rustling trees shall mingle in our whisperings of love!"

If you meet losses, and times are hard, tell your wife just how you stand. Show her your balance-sheet. Let her look over the items. You think it will hurt her feelings. No, it won't do any such thing! She has been taught to believe that money was with you, just as little boys think it is with their fathers — terribly hard to be reached, yet inexhaustible. She has had her suspicions already. She has guessed you were not so prosperous as you talked. But you had so befogged your money affairs that she, poor thing, knows nothing about them. Tell it right out to her, that you are living beyond your income. Take her into partnership, and we'll warrant you'll never regret it.

A Wife's Power. —The power of a wife for good or evil is irresistible. Home must be the seat of happiness, or it must be forever unknown. A good wife is to a man wisdom, and courage, and strength, and endurance. A bad wife is confusion, weakness, discomfiture, and despair. No condition is hopeless where the wife possesses firmness, decision, and economy. There is no outward prosperity which can counteract indolence, extravagance, and folly at home. No spirit can long endure bad domestic influence. Man is strong, but his heart is not adamant. He delights in enterprise and action; but to sustain him he needs a tranquil mind and a whole heart. He needs his moral force in the conflicts of the world. To recover his equanimity and composure, home must be to him a place of repose, of peace, of cheerfulness, of comfort; and his soul renews its strength again, and goes forth with fresh vigor to encounter the labor and troubles of life. But if at home he find no rest, and is there met with bad temper, sullenness, or gloom, or is assailed by discontent or complaint, hope vanishes, and he sinks into despair.

Hints for Wives.—If your husband occasionally looks a little troubled when he comes home, do not say to him, with an alarmed countenance, "What ails you, my dear?" Don't bother him; he will tell you of his own accord, if need be. Don't rattle a hailstorm of fun about his ears either. Be observant and quiet. Don't suppose, whenever he is silent and thoughtful, that you are of course the cause. Let him alone until he is inclined to talk; take up your book or your needlework (pleasantly, cheerfully; no pouting—no sullenness) and wait until he is inclined to be sociable. Don't let him ever find a shirt-button missing — a shirt-button being off a collar or wristband has frequently produced the first hurricane in married life. Men's shirt-collars never fit exactly; see that your husband's are made as well as possible, and then, if he does fret a little about them, never mind it; men have a prescriptive right to fret about shirt-collars.

Never complain that your husband pores too much over the newspaper, to the exclusion of that pleasing converse which you formerly enjoyed with him. Don't hide the paper; don't give it to the children to tear; don't be sulky when the boy leaves it at the door, but take it in pleasantly, and lay it down before your spouse. Think what man would be without a newspaper. Treat it as if a great agent in the work of civilization, — which it assuredly is,— and think how much good newspapers have done by exposing bad husbands and bad wives, by giving their errors to the eye of the public. But manage you in this way: when your husband is absent, instead of gossiping with neighbors, or looking into store-windows, sit down quietly, and look over that paper; run your eye over its home and foreign news; glance rapidly at the accidents and casualties; carefully scan the leading articles; and at tea-time, when your husband again takes up the paper, say, "My dear, what an awful state of things there seems to be in Europe!" or, "What a terrible calamity at Santiago!" or "Trade appears to be flourishing in the north;" and depend upon it, down will go the paper. If he has not read the information, he will hear it all from your lips; and when you have done, he will ask, "Did you, my dear, read Banting's Letter on Corpulence?" And whether you did or not, you will gradually get into as cosy a chat as you ever enjoyed; and you will soon discover that, rightly used, the newspaper is the wife's real friend, for it keeps the husband at home, and supplies capital topics for everyday table-talk.

Don't imagine, when you have obtained a husband, that your attention to personal neatness and deportment may be relaxed. Then, in reality, is the time for you to exhibit superior taste and excellence in the cultivation of your dress, and the becoming elegance of your appearance. If it required some little care to foster the admiration of a lover, how much more is requisite to keep yourself lovely in the eyes of him to whom there is now no privacy or disguise — your hourly companion! And if it was due to your lover that you should always present to him, who *proposed* to wed and cherish you, a neat and lady - like aspect, how much more is he entitled to a similar mark of respect who has *kept his promise with honorable fidelity*, and linked all his hopes of future happiness with yours! If you can manage these matters without appearing to study them, so much the better. Some husbands are impatient of the routine of the toilette, and not unreasonably so — they possess active and energetic spirits, sorely disturbed by any waste of time. Some wives have discovered an admirable facility in dealing with this difficulty; and it is a secret which, having been discovered by some, may be known to all, and is well worth the finding out.

It is astonishing how much the cheerfulness of a wife contributes to the happiness of home. She is the sun — the centre of a domestic system, and her children are like planets around her, reflecting her rays. How merry the little ones look when the mother is joyous and good-tempered; and how easily and pleasantly her household labors are overcome! Her cheerfulness is reflected everywhere : it is seen in the neatness of her toilette, the order of her table, and even the seasoning of her dishes. We remember hearing a husband say that he could always gauge the temper of his wife by the quality of her cooking: good temper even influenced the seasoning of her soups, and the lightness and delicacy of her pastry. When ill-temper pervades, the pepper is dashed in as a cloud — perchance the top of the pepper-box is included, as a kind of a diminutive thunderbolt; the salt is all in lumps ; and the spices seem to betake themselves to one spot in a pudding, as if dreading the frowning face above them. If there be a husband who could abuse the smiles of a really good-tempered wife, we should like to look at him! No, no, such a phenomenon does not exist. Among elements

of domestic happiness, the amiability of the wife and mother is of the utmost importance — it is one of the best securities for the HAPPINESS OF HOME.

Perchance you think that your husband's disposition is much changed; that he is no longer the sweet-tempered, ardent lover he used to be. This may be a mistake. Consider his struggles with the world — his everlasting race with the busy competition of trade. What is it makes him so eager in the pursuit of gain — so energetic by day, so sleepless by night — but his love of home, wife, and children, and a dread that their respectability, according to the light in which he has conceived it, may be encroached upon by the strife of existence? This is the true secret of that silent care which preys upon the hearts of many men ; and true it is, that when love is least apparent, it is nevertheless the active principle which animates the heart, though fears and diappointments make up a cloud which obscures the warmer element. As above the clouds there is glorious sunshine, while below are showers and gloom, so with the conduct of man — behind the gloom of anxiety is a bright fountain of high and noble feeling. Think of this in those moments when clouds seem to lower upon your domestic peace, and, by tempering your conduct accordingly, the gloom will soon pass away, and warmth and brightness take its place.

Woman has always been described as clamoring for the last word : actors, authors, preachers, and philosophers, have agreed in attributing this trait to her, and in censuring her for it. Yet why they should condemn her, unless they wish the matter reversed, and thus committed themselves to the error imputed to her, it were difficult to discover. However, so it is ; — and it remains for some one of the sex, by an exhibition of noble example, to aid in sweeping away the unpleasant imputation. The wife who will establish the rule of allowing her husband to have the last word, will achieve for herself and her sex a great moral victory! Is he *right?* — it were a great error to oppose him. Is he *wrong?* — he will soon discover it, and applaud the self-command which bore unvexed his pertinacity. And gradually there will spring up such a happy fusion of feelings and ideas, that there will be no "last word" to contend about, but a steady and unruffled flow of generous sentiment.

Model Mothers. — Models are of the first importance in moulding the nature of a child; and if we would have fine characters, we must necessarily present before them fine models. Now the model most constantly before every child's eye is the mother. "One good mother," said George Herbert, "is worth a hundred schoolmasters. In the home she is loadstone to all hearts and loadstar to all eyes." Imitation of her is constant — imitation which Bacon likens to a "globe of precepts." It is instruction. It is teaching without words, often exemplifying more than tongue can teach. In the face of bad example the best precepts are of but little avail. The example is followed, not the precepts. Indeed, precept at variance with practice is worse than useless, inasmuch as it only serves to teach that most cowardly of vices — hypocrisy. Even children are judges of hypocrisy, and the lessons of the parent who says one thing and does the opposite are quickly seen through.

Tired Mothers.

A little elbow leans upon your knees, —
　Your tired knee, that has so much to bear;
A child's dear eyes are looking lovingly
　From underneath a thatch of tangled hair.
Perhaps you do not heed the velvet touch
　Of warm, moist fingers, folding yours so tight;
You do not prize this blessing over-much —
　You almost are too tired to pray to-night.

But it is blessedness! A year ago
　I did not see it as I do to-day —
We are so dull and thankless, and too slow
　To catch the sunshine till it slips away.
And now it seems surpassing strange to me,
　That, while I wore the badge of motherhood,
I did not kiss more oft and tenderly
　The little child that brought me only good.

And if, some night, when you sit down to rest,
　You miss this elbow from your tired knee,
This restless, curling head from off your breast,
　This lisping tongue that chatters constantly;
If from your own the dimpled hands have slipped,
　And ne'er would nestle in your palm again;
If the white feet into their grave had tripped —
　I could not blame you for your heartache then.

I wonder so that mothers ever fret
　At little children clinging to their gowns;
Or that the footprints, when the days are wet,
　Are ever black enough to make them frown.
If I could find a little muddy boot,
　Or cap, or jacket, on my chamber floor;
If I could kiss a rosy, restless foot,
　And hear its patter in my house once more;

If I could mend a broken cart to-day,
　To-morrow make a kite to reach the sky—
There is no woman in God's world could say
　She was more blissfully content than I.
But ah! the dainty pillow next my own
　Is never rumpled by a shining head;
My singing bird from its nest is flown;
　The little boy I used to kiss is dead!

WE LEARN FROM DAILY EXPERIENCE that children who have been the least indulged thrive much better, unfold all their faculties quicker, and acquire more muscular strength and vigor of mind, than those who have been constantly favored, and treated by their parents with the most solicitous attention; bodily weakness and mental imbecility are the usual attributes of the latter.

THE FIRST AND PRINCIPAL RULE of education ought never to be forgotten — that man is intended to be a free and independent agent; that his moral and physical powers ought to be *spontaneously* developed; that he should, as soon as possible, be made acquainted with the nature and uses of all his faculties, in order to attain that degree of perfection which is consistent with the structure of his organs; and that he was not originally designed for what we endeavor to make of him by artificial aid.

THE GREATEST ART in educating children consists in a continued vigilance over all their actions, without ever giving them an opportunity of discovering that they are guided and watched.

CHILDREN should not be allowed to ask for the same thing twice. This may be accomplished by parents, teacher, or whoever may happen to have the management of them, paying attention to their little wants, if proper, at once, when possible. Children should be instructed to understand that when they are not answered immediately, it is because it is not convenient. Let them learn patience by waiting.

To AWAKEN CHILDREN from their sleep with a noise, or in an impetuous manner, is extremely injudicious and hurtful; nor is it proper to carry them from a dark room immediately into a glaring light, or against a dazzling wall; for the sudden impression of light debilitates the organs of vision, and lays the foundation of weak eyes, from early infancy.

Biting the Nails. — This is a habit that should be immediately corrected in children, as, if persisted in for any length of time, it permanently deforms the nails. Dipping the finger-ends in some bitter tincture will generally prevent children from putting them in their mouth; but if this fails, as it sometimes will, each finger-end ought to be encased in a stall until the propensity is eradicated.

Counsels for the Young.—Never be cast down by trifles. If a spider break his thread twenty times, twenty times will he mend it again. Make up your mind to do a thing, and you will do it. Fear not if a trouble comes upon you; keep up your spirits, though the day be a dark one. If the sun is going down, look up to the stars. If the earth is dark, keep your eye on heaven. With God's promises, a man or a child may be cheerful. Mind what you run after. Never be content with a bubble that will burst, firewood that will end in smoke and darkness. Get that which you can keep, and which is worth keeping. Fight hard against a hasty temper. Anger will come, but resist it strongly. A fit of passion may give you cause to mourn all the days of your life. Never revenge an injury. If you have an enemy, act kindly to him and make him your friend. You may not win him over at once, but try again. Let one kindness be followed by another, till you have compassed your end. By little and little, great things are completed; and repeated kindness will soften the heart of stone. Whatever you do, do it willingly. A boy that is whipped to school never learns his lessons well. A man who is compelled to work cares not how badly it is performed. He that pulls off his coat cheerfully, strips up his sleeves in earnest, and sings while he works, is the man of action.

Advice to Young Ladies. — If you have blue eyes you need not languish.

If black eyes you need not stare.

If you have pretty feet there is no occasion to wear short petticoats.

If you are doubtful as to that point, there can be no harm in letting the petticoats be long.

If you have good teeth, do not laugh for the purpose of showing them.

If you have bad ones, do not laugh less than the occasion may justify.

If you have pretty hands and arms, there can be no objection to your playing on the harp, if you play well.

If they are disposed to be clumsy, work tapestry.

If you have a bad voice, rather speak in a low tone.

If you have the finest voice in the world, never speak in a high tone.

If you dance well, dance but seldom.

If you dance ill, never dance at all.

If you sing well, make no previous excuses.

If you sing indifferently, hesitate not a moment when you are asked, for few people are judges of singing, but every one is sensible of a desire to please.

If you would preserve beauty, rise early.

If you would preserve esteem, be gentle.

If you would obtain power, be condescending.

If you would live happily, endeavor to promote the happiness of others.

DAUGHTERS.—Mothers who wish not only to discharge well their own duties in the domestic circle, but to train up their daughters for a later day to make happy and comfortable firesides for their families, should watch well, and guard well, the notions which they imbibe and with which they grow up. There will be so many persons ready to fill their young heads with false and vain fancies, and there is so much always afloat in society opposed to duty and common sense, that if mothers do not watch well their children may contract ideas very fatal to their future happiness and usefulness, and hold them till they grow into habits of thought or feeling. A wise mother will have her eyes open, and be ready for every emergency. A few words of common, downright practical sense, timely uttered by her, may be enough to counteract some foolish idea or belief put into her daughter's head by others, while if it be left unchecked, it may take such possession of the mind that it cannot be corrected at a later time. One falsity abroad in this age is the notion that women, unless compelled to it by absolute poverty, are out of place when engaged in domestic affairs. Now mothers should have a care lest their daughters get hold of this conviction as regards themselves—there is danger of it; the fashion of the day engenders it, and the care that an affectionate family take to keep a girl, during the time of her education, free from other occupations than those of her tasks or her recreations, also endangers it. It is possible that affection may err in pushing this care too far; for as education means a fitting for life, and as a woman's life is much connected with domestic and family affairs—or ought to be so—if the indulgent consideration of parents abstain from all demands upon the young pupil of the school not connected with her books or her play, will she not naturally infer that the matters with which she is never asked to concern herself are, in fact, no concern to her, and that any attention she ever may bestow on them is not a matter of simple duty,

but of grace, or concession, or stooping, on her part? Let mothers avoid such danger. If they would do so, they must bring up their daughters from the *first* with the idea that in this world it is required to give as well as to receive, to minister as well as to enjoy; that every person is bound to be useful—practically, literally useful, —in his own sphere, and that a woman's first sphere is the house, and its concerns and demands. Once really imbued with this belief, and taught to see how much the comfort and happiness of woman herself, as well as of her family, depends on this part of her discharge of duty, a young girl will usually be anxious to learn all that her mother is disposed to teach, and will be proud and happy to aid in any domestic occupations assigned to her. These need never be made so heavy as to interfere with the peculiar duties or enjoyments of her age. If a mother wishes to see her daughter become a good, happy, and rational woman, never let there be contempt for domestic occupations, or suffer them to be deemed secondary.

BOYS. — What to do with boys is a question which sometimes troubles wise heads. We know some people consider them a sort of nuisance, capable of making any amount of noise, and always ready for mischief, whether it be pulling the cat's tail, teasing little sisters, or playing with powder and matches in the barn; but, with all their pranks and capers, we like them, and consider them a very much misused portion of society. Boys are very much what we make them by our treatment of them. Girls are nice little bodies, so we dress them nicely, make birthday parties for them — but a boy's birthday party, who ever heard of such a thing? and as to fixing them up, why that is altogether out of the question. But never mind, boys; while the girls are confined indoors to prevent their clothes from becoming soiled, you can climb trees, fish, build dams, and have more real fun than could be gotten out of the most splendid suit of clothes in town, besides building up a strong constitution in your already robust little body.

Boys must have amusement and recreation after their day's labor. If they cannot find it at home, they will be apt to seek it away from home; hence it becomes parents to provide entertainment at home. If fond of music, furnish them an instrument, if your means permit, whether it be violin, guitar, or piano; if games interest them, provide innocent ones; if fond of reading, by all means supply the best of literature, and endeavor to cultivate that taste where it is deficient, although plain clothes must be worn in order to incur the necessary expense of purchasing suitable books and papers. Amusements are not the only things necessary to make boys feel an interest in home affairs. If they can claim something as their own, it will be a stimulus to them. If they like bees, let them have a swarm all their own, the avails of which go into their own pockets; or let them manage some of the poultry, raise a calf or pig for their own — not theirs until killing or selling time comes, when it belongs to father.

Few boys have the right idea of courage. It is often possessed by quiet and gentle boys, who are looked upon by their mates as the least courageous. The boy who will not quarrel when he is abused; the boy who keeps himself pure in speech and act when others are rough and wicked; the boy who defends the weak against the strong; the boy who loves God, and is not afraid to show it — he is the brave boy, and makes the noble man. Don't forget, dear boy.

A lazy boy makes a lazy man, just as sure as a crooked sapling makes a crooked tree. Who ever yet saw a boy grow up in idleness, that did not make a shiftless vagabond when he became a man, unless he had a fortune left him to keep up appearances? The great mass of thieves, paupers, and criminals have come to what they are by being brought up in idleness. Those who

20

constitute the business part of the community — those who make our great and useful men — were taught to be industrious.

Boys, Learn Trades! — The annual report of Hon. J. P. Wickersham, State Superintendent of Common Schools for 1872, contains the following significant paragraph, pointing parents to the importance of having their children learn some useful mechanical trade. The statistics given are brief and startling. Mr. Wickersham says: "There are multitudes idly waiting for vacant clerkships and unfilled offices, while mechanical work, more honorable and more remunerative, invites on all sides the efforts of willing hands. It is a fact as startling as it is significant that of seventeen thousand criminals in the United States in 1868, ninety-seven per cent. of them had never learned a trade. Out of two hundred and forty convicts received at the Eastern Penitentiary (Pennsylvania) last year, only twelve had been apprenticed and served their time."

Wanted — an Honest, Industrious, Steady Boy. — We lately saw an advertisement headed as above. It conveys to every boy an impressive moral lesson. "An honest, industrious boy," is always *wanted*. He will be sought for; his services will be in demand; he will be respected and loved; he will be spoken of in terms of high commendation; he will always have a home; will grow up to be a man of known worth and established character. He will be wanted. The merchant will want him for a salesman or clerk; the master mechanic will want him for an apprentice or foreman; those with a job to let will want him for a contractor; clients will want him for a lawyer; patients for a physician; religious congregations for a pastor; parents for a teacher of their children; and the people for an officer. He will be wanted — townsmen will want him for a citizen; acquaintance as a neighbor; neighbors as a friend; families as a visitor; the world as an acquaintance; nay, girls will want him as a beau, and finally, for a husband! An honest, industrious boy! Just think of it, boys; will you answer this description? Can you apply for this situation? Are you sure that *you* will be wanted? You may be smart and active, but that does not fill the requisition — are you *honest?* You may be capable — are you *industrious?* You may be well dressed, and create a favorable impression at first sight, but are you honest, steady, and industrious? You may apply for a good situation — are you sure that your friends, teachers, and acquaintances can recommend you for these qualities? Nothing else will make up for a lack of them; no readiness or aptness for business will do it. *You must be honest, steady, and industrious!*

SERVANTS. — There are frequent complaints in these days, that servants are bad, and apprentices are bad, and dependants and aiding hands generally are bad. It may be so. But if it is so, what is the inference? In the working of the machine of society, class moves pretty much with class; that is, one class moves pretty much with its equals in the community (equals so far as social station is concerned), and apart from other classes, as much those below as those above itself; but there is one grand exception to this general rule, and that is, in the case of domestic servants. The same holds, though in less degree, with apprentices and assistant hands; and in less degree only, because in this last case, the difference of grade is slighter. Domestic servants, and assistants in business and trade, come most closely and continually into contact with their employers; they are about them from morning till night, and see them in every phase of character, in every style of humor, in every act of life. How powerful is the force of example! Rectitude is promoted, not only by precept but by example, and, so to speak, by contact it is increased more widely. Kindness is communicated in the same way. Virtue of every kind acts like an electric shock. Those

who come under its influence imbibe its principles. The same with qualities and tempers that do no honor to our nature. If servants come to you bad, you may at least improve them possibly almost change their nature. Here follows, then, a receipt to that effect: — *Receipt for obtaining good servants.* — Let them observe in your conduct to others just the qualities and virtues that you would desire they should possess and practice as respects you. Be uniformly kind and gentle. If you reprove, do so with reason and with temper. Be respectable, and you will be respected by them. Be kind, and you will meet kindness from them. Consider their interests, and they will consider yours. A friend in a servant is no contemptible thing. Be to every servant a friend; and heartless, indeed, will be the servant who does not warm in love to you.

READY MONEY will always command the best and cheapest of every article of consumption, if expended with judgment: and the dealer, who intends to act fairly, will always prefer it.

TRUST NOT him who seems more anxious to give credit than to receive cash.

THE FORMER hopes to secure custom by having a hold upon you in his books; and continues always to make up for his advance, either by an advanced price, or an inferior article; while the latter knows that your custom can only be secured by fair dealing.

THERE IS, LIKEWISE, ANOTHER CONSIDERATION, as far as economy is concerned, which is not only to buy with ready money, but to buy at proper seasons; for there is with every article a cheap season and a dear one; and with none more than coals: insomuch, that the master of a family who fills his coal-cellar in the middle of the summer, rather than the beginning of the winter, will find it filled at less expense than it would otherwise cost him, and will be enabled to see December's snows falling without feeling his enjoyment

THE USE OF LANGUAGE.

ERRORS TO BE AVOIDED IN CONVERSATION—RULES OF PRONUNCIATION—
HOW TO SPELL AND PUNCTUATE CORRECTLY.

CONVERSATION. — There are many talkers, but few who know how to converse agreeably. Speak distinctly, neither too rapidly nor too slowly. Accommodate the pitch of your voice to the hearing of the person with whom you are conversing. Never speak with your mouth full. Tell your jokes, and laugh afterwards. Dispense with superfluous words — such as, " Well, I should think."

THE WOMAN who wishes her conversation to be agreeable will avoid conceit or affectation, and laughter which is not natural and spontaneous. Her language will be easy and unstudied, marked by a graceful carelessness, which, at the same time, never oversteps the limits of propriety. Her lips will readily yield to a pleasant smile; she will not love to hear herself talk; her tones will bear the impress of sincerity, and her eyes kindle with animation as she speaks. The art of pleasing is, in truth, the very soul of good breeding; for the precise object of the latter is to render us agreeable to all with whom we associate — to make us, at the same time, esteemed and loved.

WE NEED SCARCELY ADVERT to the rudeness of interrupting any one who is speaking, or to the impropriety of pushing, to its full extent, a discussion which has become unpleasant.

SOME MEN HAVE A MANIA for Greek and Latin quotations: this is peculiarly to be avoided. It is like pulling up the stones from a tomb wherewith to kill the living. Nothing is more wearisome than pedantry.

IF YOU FEEL YOUR INTELLECTUAL SUPERIORITY to any one with whom you are conversing, do not seek to bear him down : it would be an inglorious triumph, and a breach of good manners. Beware, too, of speaking lightly of subjects which bear a sacred character. WITLINGS OCCASIONALLY GAIN A REPUTATION in society; but nothing is more insipid and in worse taste than their conceited harangues and self-sufficient air.

IT IS A COMMON IDEA that the art of writing and the art of conversation are one ; this is a great mistake. A man of genius may be a very dull talker.

THE TWO GRAND MODES of making your conversation interesting, are to enliven it by recitals calculated to affect and impress your hearers, and to intersperse it with anecdotes and smart things.

Errors in Speaking. — There are several kinds of errors in speaking. The most objectionable of them are those in which words are employed that are unsuitable to convey the meaning intended. Thus, a person wishing to express his intention of going to a given place, says, " I *propose* going," when, in fact, he *purposes* going. An amusing illustration of this class of error was overheard by ourselves. A venerable matron was speaking of her son, who, she said, was quite stage-struck. " In fact," remarked the old lady, " he is going to a *premature* performance this evening ! " Considering that most *amateur* performances are *premature*, we hesitate

307

to say that this word was misapplied; though, evidently, the maternal intention was to convey quite another meaning.

OTHER ERRORS ARISE from the substitution of sounds similar to the words which should be employed; that is, spurious words instead of genuine ones. Thus, some people say, "*renumerative*," when they mean "*remunerative.*" A nurse, recommending her mistress to have one of the newly-invented carriages for her child, advised her to purchase a *preamputator!*

OTHER ERRORS ARE OCCASIONED by imperfect knowledge of the English grammar. Thus, many people say, "Between you and I," instead of "Between you and *me.*" By the misuse of the adjective: "What *beautiful* butter! What a *nice* landscape!" They should say, "What a *beautiful landscape!* What *nice butter!*" And by numerous other departures from the rules of grammar, which will be pointed out hereafter.

BY THE MISPRONUNCIATION OF WORDS. Many persons say *pronunciation* instead of *pronunciation;* others say pro-nun-she-a-shun, instead of pro-nun-ce-a-shun.

BY THE MISDIVISION OF WORDS and syllables. This defect makes the words *an ambassador* sound like *a nambassador*, or *an adder* like *a nadder.*

BY IMPERFECT ENUNCIATION, as when a person says *hebben* for *heaven*, *ebber* for *ever*, *jocholate* for *chocolate*, etc.

BY THE USE OF PROVINCIALISMS, or words retained from various dialects.

Rules and Hints for Correct Speaking. — *Who* and *whom* are used in relation to persons, and *which* in relation to things. But it was once common to say, "the man *which.*" This should now be avoided. It is now usual to say, "Our Father *who* art in heaven," instead of "*which* art in heaven."

Whose is, however, sometimes applied to things as well as to persons.

We may therefore say, "The country *whose* inhabitants are free." [Grammarians differ in opinion upon this subject, but general usage justifies the rule.]

Thou is employed in solemn discourse, and *you* in common language. *Ye* (plural) is also used in serious addresses, and *you* in familiar language.

The uses of the word *It* are various, and very perplexing to the uneducated. It is not only used to imply persons, but things, and even ideas, and therefore, in speaking or writing, its assistance is constantly required. The perplexity respecting this word, arises from the fact that in using it in the construction of a long sentence, sufficient care is not taken to insure that when *it* is employed it really points out or refers to the object intended. For instance, "It was raining when John set out in his cart to go to the market, and he was delayed so long that it was over before he arrived." Now what is to be understood by this sentence? Was the rain over? or the market? Either or both might be inferred from the construction of the sentence, which, therefore, should be written thus: "It was raining when John set out in his cart to go to the market, and he was delayed so long that the market was over before he arrived."

Rule. — After writing a sentence, always look through it, and see that wherever the word *It* is employed, it refers to or carries the mind back to the object which it is intended to point out.

The general distinction between *This* and *That* is, *this* denotes an object present or near, in time or place, *that* something which is absent.

These refers, in the same manner, to present objects, while *those* refers to things that are remote.

Who changes, under certain conditions, into *whose* and *whom.* But *that* and *which* always remain the same.

That may be applied to nouns or subjects of all sorts; as, the *girl that* went to school, the *dog that* bit me, tho *ship that* went to London, the *opinion that* he entertained.

The misuse of these pronouns gives rise to more errors in speaking and writing than any other cause.

When you wish to distinguish between two or more persons, say, "*Which* is the happy man?" — not *who* — "*Which* of those ladies do you admire?"

Instead of "*Who* do you think him to be?" — Say, "*Whom* do you think him to be?"

Whom should I see?
To *whom* do you speak?
Who said so?
Who gave it to you?
Of *whom* did you procure them?
Who was *he?*
Who do men say that *I* am?
Whom do they represent me to be?

In many instances in which *who* is used as an interrogative, it does not become *whom;* as "*Who* do you speak to?" "*Who* do you expect?" "*Who* is she married to?" "*Who* is this reserved for?" "*Who* was it made by?" Such sentences are found in the writings of our best authors, and it would be presumptuous to consider them as ungrammatical. If the word *whom* should be preferred, then it would be best to say, "For *whom* is this reserved?" etc.

Instead of "After *which* hour," say, "After *that* hour."

Self should never be added to *his, their, mine,* or *thine.*

Each is used to denote every individual of a number.

Every denotes all the individuals of a number.

Either and *or* denote an alternative: "I will take *either* road, at your pleasure;" "I will take this *or* that."

Neither means *not either;* and *nor* means *not the other.*

Either is sometimes used for *each* — "Two thieves were crucified, on *either* side one."

"Let *each* esteem others as good as themselves," should be, "Let *each* esteem others as good as *himself.*"

"There are bodies *each* of which *are*

so small," should be, "each of which *is* so small."

Do not use double superlatives, such as *most straightest, most highest, most finest.*

The term *worser* has gone out of use; but *lesser* is still retained.

The use of such words as *chiefest, extremest,* etc., has become obsolete, because they do not give any superior forms to the meanings of the primary words, *chief, extreme,* etc.

Such expressions as *more impossible, more indispensable, more universal, more uncontrollable, more unlimited,* etc., are objectionable, as they really enfeeble the meaning which it is the object of the speaker or writer to strengthen. For instance, *impossible* gains no strength by rendering it *more* impossible. This class of error is common with persons who say, "A *great large* house," "A *great big* animal," "A *little small* foot," "A *tiny little* hand."

Here, there, and *where,* originally denoting place, may now, by common consent, be used to denote other meanings; such as "*There* I agree with you," "*Where* we differ," "We find pain *where* we expected pleasure," "*Here* you mistake me."

Hence, whence, and *thence* denoting departure, etc., may be used without the word *from.* The idea of *from* is included in the word *whence* — therefore it is unnecessary to say, "*From whence.*"

Hither, thither, and *whither,* denoting to a place, have generally been superseded by *here, there,* and *where.* But there is no good reason why they should not be employed. If, however, they are used, it is unnecessary to add the word *to,* because that is implied — "*Whither* are you going?" "*Where* are you going?" Each of these sentences is complete. To say, "Where are you going *to?*" is redundant.

Two *negatives* destroy each other, and produce an affirmative. "*Nor* did he *not* observe them," conveys the idea that he *did* observe them.

But negative assertions are allowable. "His manners are not unpolite," which implies that his manners are, in some degree, marked by politeness.

Instead of "I *had* rather walk," say "I would rather walk."

Instead of "I *had better* go," say "It were better that I should go."

Instead of "I doubt not *but* I shall be able to go," say "I doubt not that I shall be able to go."

Instead of "Let you and *I*," say "Let you and me."

Instead of "I am not so tall as *him*," say "I am not so tall as he."

When asked "Who is there?" do not answer "*Me*," but "I."

Instead of "For you and *I*," say "For you and me."

Instead of "*Says I*," say "I said."

Instead of "You are taller than *me*," say "You are taller than I."

Instead of "I *ain't*," or "I *arn't*," say "I am not."

Instead of "Whether I be present or *no*," say "Whether I be present or not."

For "Not that I know *on*," say "Not that I know."

Instead of "*Was* I to do so," say "Were I to do so."

Instead of "I would do the same if I *was him*," say "I would do the same if I were he."

Instead of "I had *as lief* go myself," say "I would as soon go myself," or "I would rather."

It is better to say "Bred and born," than "Born and bred."

It is better to say "Six weeks ago," than "Six weeks back."

It is better to say "Since which time," than "Since when."

It is better to say "I repeated it," than "I said so over again."

It is better to say "A physician," or "A surgeon" (according to his degree), than "A doctor."

Instead of "He was too young to *have* suffered much," say "He was too young to suffer much."

Instead of "*Less* friends," say "Fewer friends." Less refers to quantity.

Instead of "We *accuse him for*," say "We accuse him of."

Instead of "We *acquit* him *from*," say "We acquit him of."

Instead of "I am averse *from* that," say "I am averse to that."

Instead of "I confide *on* you," say "I confide in you."

Instead of "I differ *with* you," say "I differ from you."

Instead of "As soon *as ever*," say "As soon as."

Instead of "The *very best*," or "The *very worst*," say "The best or the worst."

Instead of "A *winter's morning*," say "A winter morning," or "A wintry morning."

Instead of "Fine morning, *this* morning," say "This is a fine morning."

Instead of "How *do* you *do?*" say "How are you?"

Instead of "Not so well as I could wish," say "Not quite well."

Avoid such phrases as "No great shakes," "Nothing to boast of," "Down in my boots," "Suffering from the blues." All such sentences indicate vulgarity.

Instead of "No one *cannot* prevail upon him," say "No one can prevail upon him."

Instead of "No one *hasn't* called," say "No one has called."

Avoid such phrases as "If I was you," or even "If I were you." Better say ". I advise you how to act."

Instead of "You have a *right* to pay me," say "It is right that you should pay me."

Instead of "I am going *on* a tour," say "I am about to take a tour," or "going."

Instead of "I am going *over* the bridge," say "I am going *across* the bridge."

Instead of "He is coming here," say "He is coming hither."

Instead of "He lives opposite the square," say "He lives opposite to the square."

Instead of "He *belongs* to the Reform Club," say "He is a member of the Reform Club."

Instead of "This villa *to let*," say "This villa to be let."

Instead of "I am slight in comparison *to you*," say "I am slight in comparison with you."

Instead of "I went *for* to see him," say "I went to see him."

Instead of "The cake is all *eat up*," say "The cake is all eaten."

Instead of "It is bad *at the best*," say "It is very bad."

Instead of "Handsome is *as* handsome does," say "Handsome is who handsome does."

Instead of "As I *take* it," say "As I see," or "As I understand it."

Iustead of "The book fell *on* the floor," say "The book fell to the floor."

Instead of "His opinions are *approved of* by all," say "His opinions are approved by all."

Instead of "I will add *one more* argument," say "I will add one argument more," or "another argument."

Instead of "Captain Reilly was killed *by* a bullet," say "Captain Reilly was killed with a bullet."

Instead of "A sad curse is war," say "War is a sad curse."

Instead of "He stands *six foot* high," say "He measures six feet," or "His height is six feet."

Instead of "I go *every now and then*," say "I go often, or frequently."

Instead of "Who finds him in clothes," say "Who provides him with clothes."

Say "The first two," and "the last two," instead of "The *two first*," "the two last;" leave out all expletives, such as "of all," "first of all," "last of all," "best of all," etc., etc.

Instead of "His health was *drank with enthusiasm*," say "His health was drunk enthusiastically."

Instead of "*Except* I am prevented," say "Unless I am prevented."

Instead of "In its *primary sense*," say "In its primitive sense."

Instead of "It grieves me to *see* you," say "I am grieved to see you."

Instead of "Give me *them* papers," say "Give me those papers."

Instead of "*Those* papers I hold in my hand," say "These papers I hold in my hand."

Instead of "I could scarcely imagine but *what*," say "I could scarcely imagine but that."

Instead of "He was a man *notorious* for his benevolence," say "He was noted for his benevolence."

Instead of "She was a woman *celebrated* for her crimes," say "She was notorious on account of her crimes."

Instead of "What may your name be?" say "What is your name?"

Instead of "Bills are requested not to be stuck here," say "Bill-stickers are requested not to stick bills here."

Instead of "By *smoking it often* becomes habitual," say "By smoking often it becomes habitual."

Instead of "I lifted it *up*," say "I lifted it."

Instead of "It is *equally of the same* value," say "It is of the same value," or "equal value."

Instead of "I knew it *previous* to your telling me," say "I knew it previously to your telling me."

Instead of "You *was* out when I called," say "You were out when I called."

Instead of "I thought I should *have won* this game," say "I thought I should win this game."

Instead of "*This* much is certain," say "Thus much is certain," or, "So much is certain."

Instead of "He went away *as it may be* yesterday week," say "He went away yesterday week."

Instead of "He came *the Saturday as it may be before the Monday*," specify the Monday on which he came.

Instead of "Put your watch *in* your pocket," say "Put your watch into your pocket."

Instead of "He has *got* riches," say "He has riches."

Instead of "Will you *set* down?" say "Will you sit down?"

Instead of "The hen is *setting*," say "The hen is sitting."

Instead of "It is raining *very hard*," say "It is raining very fast."

Instead of "A *quantity* of people," say "A number of people."

Instead of "*He and they* we know," say "Him and them."

Instead of "*As* far as I can see," say "So far as I can see."

Instead of "If I am *not mistaken,*" say "If I mistake not."

Instead of "You *are mistaken,*" say "You mistake."

Instead of "What *beautiful* tea!" say "What good tea!"

Instead of "What a *nice* prospect!" say "What a *beautiful* prospect!"

Instead of "A *new pair* of gloves," say "A pair of new gloves."

Instead of saying "*He* belongs to the *house,*" say "The house belongs to him."

Instead of saying "*Not no* such thing," say "Not any such thing."

Instead of "I hope you'll think nothing *on* it," say "I hope you'll think nothing of it."

Instead of "Restore it *back* to me," say "Restore it to me."

Instead of "I suspect the *veracity* of his story," say "I doubt the truth of his story."

Instead of "I seldom *or ever* see him," say "I seldom see him."

Instead of "*Rather warmish,*" or "A *little* warmish," say "Rather warm."

Instead of "I expected *to have* found him," say "I expected to find him."

Instead of "*Shay,*" say "Chaise."

Instead of "He is a very *rising* person," say "He is rising rapidly."

Instead of "Who *learns* you music?" say "Who teaches you music?"

Instead of "I *never* sing *whenever* I can help it," say "I never sing when I can help it."

Instead of "Before I do that I must *first* ask leave," say "Before I do that I must ask leave."

Instead of "To *get over* the difficulty," say "To overcome the difficulty."

The phrase "*get over*" is in many cases misapplied, as, to "get over a person," to "get over a week," to "get over an opposition."

Instead of saying "The *observation*

of the rule," say "The observance of the rule."

Instead of "A man *of* eighty years of age," say "A man eighty years old."

Instead of "Here *lays* his honored head," say "Here lies his honored head."

Instead of "He died from *negligence,*" say "He died through neglect," or "in consequence of neglect."

Instead of "Apples are plenty," say "Apples are plentiful."

Instead of "The *latter end* of the year," say "The end, or the close of the year."

Instead of "The *then* government," say "The government of that age, or century, or year, or time."

Instead of "For *ought* I know," say "For aught I know."

Instead of "A *couple* of chairs," say "Two chairs."

Instead of "*Two couples,*" say "Four persons."

But you may say "A married couple," or "A married pair," or "A couple of fowls," etc., in any case where one of each sex is to be understood.

Instead of "They are *united together* in the bonds of matrimony," say "They are united in matrimony," or "They are married."

Instead of "We travel *slow,*" say "We travel slowly."

Instead of "He plunged *down* into the river," say "He plunged into the river."

Instead of "He jumped *from off of* the scaffolding," say "He jumped off from the scaffolding."

Instead of "He came the last *of all,*" say "He came the last."

Instead of "*universal,*" with reference to things that have any limit, say "general;" "generally approved," instead of "universally approved;" "generally beloved," instead of "universally beloved."

Instead of "They ruined *one another,*" say "They ruined each other."

Instead of "If *in case* I succeed," say "If I succeed."

Instead of "A *large enough* room,' say "A room large enough."

Avoid such phrases as "I am up to you," "I'll be down upon you," "Cut," or "Mizzle."

Instead of "I *should just* think I could," say "I think I can."

Instead of "There has been a *good deal*," say "There has been much."

Instead of "*Following up* a principle," say "Guided by a principle."

Instead of "Your *obedient, humble servant*," say "Your obedient," or, "Your humble servant."

Instead of saying "The effort you are making *for* meeting the bill," say "The effort you are making to meet the bill."

Instead of saying "It *shall* be submitted to investigation and inquiry," say "It shall be submitted to investigation," or, "to inquiry."

Dispense with the phrase "*Conceal from themselves the fact ;*" it suggests a gross anomaly.

Never say "*Pure and unadulterated,*" because the phrase embodies a repetition.

Instead of saying "Adequate for," say "Adequate to."

Instead of saying "A *surplus over and above,*" say "A surplus."

Instead of saying "A *lasting and permanent* peace," say "A permanent peace."

Instead of saying "I left you *behind at Boston*," say "I left you behind me at Boston."

Instead of saying "*Has been* followed by immediate dismissal," say "Was followed by immediate dismissal."

Instead of saying "Charlotte was met *with* Thomas," say "Charlotte was met by Thomas." But if Charlotte and Thomas were walking together, "Charlotte and Thomas were met by," etc.

Instead of "It is strange that no author should *never* have written," say "It is strange that no author should ever have written."

Instead of "I won't never write," say "I will never write."

To say "Do *not* give him *no more* of your money," is equivalent to saying "Give him some of your money." Say

"Do not give him *any* of your money."

Instead of saying "They are not what nature *designed* them," say "They are not what nature designed them to be."

Instead of "By this *means*," say "By these means."

Instead of saying "A beautiful *seat and gardens*," say "A beautiful seat and its gardens."

Instead of "All that was *wanting*," say "All that was wanted."

Instead of saying "I had not the pleasure of hearing his sentiments when I wrote that letter," say "I had not the pleasure of having heard," etc.

Instead of "The quality of the apples *were* good," say "The quality of the apples was good."

Instead of "The want of learning, courage, and energy *are* more visible," say "is more visible."

Instead of "We are conversant *about* it," say "We are conversant with it."

Instead of "We called *at* William," say "We called on William."

Instead of "We die *for* want," say "We die of want."

Instead of "He died *by* fever," say "He died of fever."

Instead of "I *enjoy* bad health," say "My health is not good."

Instead of "*Either* of the three," say "Any one of the three."

Instead of "Better *nor* that," say "Better than that."

Instead of "We often think *on* you," say "We often think of you."

Instead of "Though he came, I did not see him," say "Though he came, yet I did not see him."

Instead of "Mine is *so* good as yours," say "Mine is as good as yours."

Instead of "He was remarkable handsome," say "He was remarkably handsome."

Instead of "Smoke ascends *up* the chimney," say "Smoke ascends the chimney."

Instead of "You will *some* day be convinced," say "You will one day be convinced."

Instead of saying "Because I don't

choose to," say "Because I would rather not."

Instead of "*Because* why?" say "Why?"

Instead of "That *there* boy," say "That boy."

Instead of "*Direct* your letter to me," say "Address your letter to me."

Instead of "The horse is not *much worth*," say "The horse is not worth much."

Instead of "The *subject-matter* of debate," say "The subject of debate."

Instead of saying "When he *was* come back," say "When he had come back."

Instead of saying "His health has been *shook*," say "His health has been shaken."

Instead of "It was *spoke* in my presence," say "It was spoken in my presence."

Instead of "*Very* right," or "*Very* wrong," say "Right," or "Wrong."

Instead of "The *mortgager* paid him the money," say "The mortgagee paid him the money." The mortgagee lends; the mortgager borrows.

Instead of "This town is not *as* large as we thought," say "This town is not so large as we thought."

Instead of "I *took you to be* another person," say "I mistook you for another person."

Instead of "On *either* side of the river," say "On each side of the river."

Instead of "*There's* fifty," say "There are fifty."

Instead of "The *best* of the two," say "The better of the two."

Instead of "My clothes have *become too small* for me," say "I have grown too stout for my clothes."

Instead of "Is Mr. Adams *in?*" say "Is Mr. Adams within?"

Instead of "Two *spoonsful* of physic," say "Two spoonfuls of physic."

Instead of "He *must* not do it," say "He needs not do it."

Instead of "She *said*, says she," say "She said."

Avoid such phrases as "I said, says I," "Thinks I to myself, thinks I," etc.

Instead of "I don't think so," say "I think not."

Instead of "He was in *eminent* danger," say "He was in *imminent* danger."

Instead of "The weather is *hot*," say "The weather is very warm."

Instead of "I *sweat*," say "I perspire."

Instead of "I *only* want two dollars," say "I want only two dollars."

Instead of "*Whatsomever*," say "Whatever," or "Whatsoever."

Avoid such exclamations as "God bless me!" "God deliver me!" "By God!" "By Gor'!" "My Lor'!" "Upon my soul!" etc.

"THOU SHALT NOT TAKE THE NAME OF THE LORD THY GOD IN VAIN."

PRONUNCIATION. — Accent is a particular stress or force of the voice upon certain syllables or words. This mark ´ in printing denotes the syllable upon which the stress or force of the voice should be placed.

A WORD MAY HAVE MORE THAN ONE ACCENT. Take as an instance *aspiration*. In uttering this word we give a marked emphasis of the voice upon the first and third syllables, and therefore those syllables are said to be accented. The first of these accents is less distinguishable than the second, upon which we dwell longer, therefore the second accent is called the primary, or chief accent of the word.

WHEN THE FULL ACCENT FALLS ON A VOWEL, that vowel should have a long sound, as in *vo'cal;* but when it falls on a consonant, the preceding vowel has a short sound, as in *hab'it.*

TO OBTAIN A GOOD KNOWLEDGE OF PRONUNCIATION, it is advisable for the reader to listen to the examples given by good speakers, and by educated persons. We learn the pronunciation of words, to a great extent, by *imitation*, just as birds acquire the notes of other birds which may be near them.

BUT IT WILL BE VERY IMPORTANT to bear in mind that there are many words having a double meaning or application, and that the difference of meaning is indicated by the difference of the accent. Among these words, *nouns* are distinguished from *verbs* by this means; *nouns* are mostly accented on the first syllable, and *verbs* on the last.

NOUN SIGNIFIES NAME; *nouns* are the names of persons and things, as well as of things not material and palpable, but of which we have a conception and knowledge, such as *courage, firmness, goodness, strength;* and *verbs* express *actions, movements,* etc. If the word used signifies that anything has been done, or is being done, or is, or is to be done, then that word is a *verb.*

THUS, WHEN WE SAY that anything is "an in'sult," that word is a *noun,* and is accented on the first syllable; but when we say he did it "to insult' another person," the word insult' implies *acting,* and becomes a *verb,* and should be accented on the last syllable. The effect is, that, in speaking, you should employ a different pronunciation in the use of the same word, when uttering such sentences as these: —"What an in'sult!" "Do you mean to insult' me?" In the first instance you would lay the stress of voice upon the *in',* and in the latter case upon the *sult'.*

WE WILL NOW GIVE A LIST of nearly all the words that are liable to this variation:

Ab'ject	To abject'
Ab'sent	To absent'
Ab'stract	To abstract'
Ac'cent	To accent'
Af'fix	To affix'
As'sign	To assign'
At'tribute	To attribute'
Aug'ment	To augment'
Bom'bard	To bombard'
Col'league	To colleague'
Col'lect	To collect'
Com'pact	To compact'
Com'plot	To complot'
Com'pound	To compound'
Com'press	To compress'
Con'cert	To concert'
Con'crete	To concrete'
Con'duct	To conduct'
Con'fect	To confect'
Con'fine	To confine'
Con'flict	To conflict'

Con'serve	To conserve'
Con'sort	To consort'
Con'test	To contest'
Con'text	To context'
Con'tract	To contract'
Con'trast	To contrast'
Con'verse	To converse'
Con'vert	To convert'
Con'vict	To convict'
Con'voy	To convoy'
Des'cant	To descant'
Des'ert	To desert'
De'tail	To detail'
Di'gest	To digest'
Dis'cord	To discord'
Dis'count	To discount'
Es'cort	To escort'
Es'say	To essay'
Ex'ile	To exile'
Ex'port	To export'
Ex'tract	To extract'
Fer'ment	To ferment'
Fore'taste	To foretaste'
Fre'quent	To frequent'
Im'part	To impart'
Im'port	To import'
Im'press	To impress'
In'cense	To incense'
In'crease	To increase'
In'lay	To inlay'
In'sult	To insult'
Ob'ject	To object'
Per'fume	To perfume'
Per'mit	To permit'
Pre'fix	To prefix'
Pre'mise	To premise'
Pre'sage	To presage'
Pres'ent	To present'
Prod'uce	To produce'
Proj'ect	To project'
Prot'est	To protest'
Reb'el	To rebel'
Rec'ord	To record'
Ref'use	To refuse'
Re'tail	To retail'
Sub'ject	To subject'
Sur'vey	To survey'
Tor'ment	To torment'
Tra'ject	To traject'
Trans'fer	To transfer'
Trans'port	To transport'

CEMENT' IS AN EXCEPTION to the above rule, and should always be ac cented on the last syllable. So also the word Consols'.

PROVINCIALISTS who desire to correct the defects of their utterance, cannot do better than to exercise themselves frequently upon those words respecting which they have been in error.

HINTS FOR THE CORRECTION OF THE IRISH BROGUE.—An Irishman wishing to throw off the brogue of his mother country should avoid hurling out his words with a superfluous quantity of breath. It is not *broadher* and *widher* that he should say, but the *d*, and every other consonant, should be neatly delivered by the tongue, with as little riot, clattering, or breathing as possible. Next, let him drop the roughness or rolling of the *r* in all places but the beginning of syllables; he must not say *stor-rum* and *far-rum*, but let the word be heard in one smooth syllable. He should exercise himself until he can convert *plaze* into *please*, *plinty* into *plenty*, *Jasus* into *Jesus*, and so on. He should modulate his sentences, so as to avoid directing his accent all in one manner — from the acute to the grave. Keeping his ear on the watch for good examples, and exercising himself frequently upon them, he may become master of a greatly improved utterance.

HINTS FOR CORRECTING THE SCOTCH BROGUE.—The same authority remarks, that as an Irishman uses the closing accent of the voice too much, so a Scotchman has the contrary habit, and is continually drawling his tones from the grave to the acute, with an effect which, to southern ears, is suspensive in character. The smooth guttural *r* is as little heard in Scotland as in Ireland, the trilled *r* taking its place. The substitution of the former instead of the latter must be a matter of practice. The peculiar sound of the *u*, which in the north so often borders on the French *u*, must be compared with the several sounds of the letter as they are heard in the south ; and the long quality which a Scotchman is apt to give to the vowels that ought to be

essentially short, must be clipped. In fact, oral observation and lingual exercise are the only sure means to the end ; so that a Scotchman going to a well for a bucket of water, and finding a countryman bathing therein, would exclaim, "Hey, Colin, dinna ye ken the watter's for drink, and nae for bathin'?"

OF PROVINCIAL BROGUES it is scarcely necessary to say much, as the foregoing advice applies to them.

Rules of Pronunciation.—C before *a*, *o*, and *u*, and in some other situations, is a close articulation, like *k*. Before *e*, *i*, and *y*, c is precisely equivalent to *s* in *same, this;* as in *cedar, civil, cypress, capacity.*

E final indicates that the preceding vowel is long ; as in hate, mete, sire, robe, lyre, abate, recede, invite, remote, intrude.

E final indicates that *c* preceding has the sound of *s ;* as in *lace, lance;* and that *g* preceding has the sound of *j*, as in *charge, page, challenge.*

E final, in proper English words, never forms a syllable, and in the most-used words, in the terminating unaccented syllable it is silent. Thus, *motive, genuine, examine, juvenile, reptile, granite,* are pronounced *motiv, genuin, examin, juvenil, reptil, granit.*

E final, in a few words of foreign origin, forms a syllable ; as *syncope, simile.*

E final is silent after *l* in the following terminations, — *ble, cle, dle, fle, gle, kle, ple, tle, zle ;* as in *able, manacle, cradle, ruffle, mangle, wrinkle, supple, rattle, puzzle,* which are pronounced *a'bl, man'acl, cra'dl, ruf'fl, man'gl, wrin'kl, sup'pl, puz'zl.*

E is usually silent in the termination *en ;* as in *token, broken;* pronounced *tokn, brokn.*

OUS, in the termination of adjectives and their derivations, is pronounced *us ;* as in *gracious, pious, pompously.*

CE, CI, TI, before a vowel, have the sound of *sh ;* as in *cetaceous, gracious, motion, partial, ingratiate;* pronounced *cetashus, grashus, moshon, ɣarshal, ingrashiate.*

TI, after a consonant, have the sound of *ch;* as in *Christian, bastion;* pronounced *Chrischan, baschan.*

SI, after an accented vowel, are pronounced like *zh;* as in *Ephesian, confusion;* pronounced *Ephezhan, confuzhan.*

When CI or TI precede similar combinations, as in pronun*cia*tion, negotia*tion,* they may be pronounced *ce* instead of *she,* to prevent a repetition of the latter syllable; as *pronunceashon* instead of *pronunsheashon.*

GH, both in the middle and at the end of words, are silent; as in *caught, bought, fright, nigh, sigh;* pronounced *caut, baut, frite, ni, si.* In the following exceptions, however, *gh* are pronounced as *f: cough, chough, clough, enough, laugh, rough, slough, tough, trough.*

When WH begin a word, the aspirate *h* precedes *w* in pronunciation; as in *what, whiff, whale;* pronounced *hwat, hwiff, hwale, w* having precisely the sound of *oo,* French *ou.* In the following words *w* is silent: *who, whom, whose, whoop, whole.*

H after *r* has no sound or use; as in *rheum, rhyme;* pronounced *reum, rime.*

H should be sounded in the middle of words; as in fore*h*ead, ab*h*or, be*h*old, ex*h*aust, in*h*abit, un*h*orse.

H should always be sounded except in the following words: heir, herb, honest, honor, hospital, hostler, hour, humor, and humble; and all their derivatives, such as humorously, derived from humor.

K and G are silent before *n,* as *k*now, *g*naw; pronounced *no, naw.*

W before *r* is silent; as in *w*ring, *w*reath; pronounced *ring, reath.*

B after *m* is silent; as in *dumb, numb;* pronounced *dum, num.*

L before *k* is silent; as in *balk, walk, talk;* pronounced *bauk, wauk, tauk.*

PH have the sound of *f;* as in *philosophy;* pronounced *filosophy.*

NG has two sounds; one as in *singer,* the other as in *fin-ger.*

N after *m,* and closing a syllable, is silent; as in *hymn, condemn.*

P before *s* and *t* is mute; as in *psalm, pseudo, ptarmigan;* pronounced *sam, sudo, tarmigan.*

R has two sounds, one strong and vibrating, as at the beginning of words and syllables, such as *robber, reckon, error;* the other as at the terminations of words, or when it is succeeded by a consonant, as *farmer, morn.*

Before the letter R there is a slight sound of *e* between the vowel and the consonant. Thus, *bare, parent, apparent, mere, mire, more, pure, pyre,* are pronounced nearly *baer, paerent, apparent, me-er, mier, moer, puer, pyer.* This pronunciation proceeds from the peculiar articulation *r,* and it occasions a slight change of the sound of *a,* which can only be learned by the ear.

There are other rules of pronunciation affecting the combinations of vowels, etc.; but as they are more difficult to describe, and as they do not relate to errors which are commonly prevalent, we shall content ourselves with giving examples of them in the following list of words.

Words with their Pronunciations

Again, a-*gen,* not as spelled.

Alien, ale-*yen,* not a-*lye*-n.

Antipodes, an-*tip*-o-dees.

Apostle, without the *t.*

Arch, *artch* in compounds of our own language, as in archbishop, archduke; but *ark* in words derived from the Greek, as archaic, ar-*ka*-ik; archæology, ar-ke-*ol*-o-gy; archangel, ark-*ain*-gel; archetype, *ar*-ke-type; archiepiscopal, ar-ke-e-*pis*-co-pal; archipelago, ar-ke-*pel*-a-go; archives, ar-kivz, etc.

Asia, asha.

Asparagus, not asparagrass.

Awkward, awk-*wurd,* not awk-*urd.*

Bade, bad.

Because, be-*cawz,* not be-*cos.*

Been, bin.

Beloved, as a verb, be-*luvd*; as an adjective, be-*luv*-ed. Blessed, cursed, etc., are subject to the same rule.

Beneath, with the *th* in breath, not with the *th* in breathe.

Biog'raphy, as spelled, not beography.
Buoy, bwoy, not boy.
By and my, in conversation, be, me. When emphatic, and in poetic reading, by and my.
Canal', as spelled, not ca-nel.
Caprice, capreece.
Catch, as spelled, not ketch.
Chaos, ka-oss.
Charlatan, sharlatan.
Chasm, kazm.
Chasten, chasn.
Chivalry, shivalry.
Chemistry, kim-is-trey.
Choir, kwire.
Clerk, klark.
Combat, kum-bat.
Conduit, kun-dit.
Corps, core; plural, cores.
Covetous, cuv-e-tus, not cuv-e-chus.
Courteous, curt-yus.
Courtesy (politeness), cur-te-sey.
Courtesy (a lowering of the body), curt-sey.
Cresses, as spelled, not creeses.
Cu'riosity, cu-re-os-e-ty, not curosity.
Cushion, coosh-un, not coosh-in.
Daunt, dänt, not dawnt.
Design and desist have the sound of s, not of z.
Desire should have the sound of z.
Despatch, de-spatch, not dis-patch.
Dew, due, not doo.
Diamond, as spelled, not di-mond.
Diploma, de-plo-ma, not dip-lo-ma.
Diplomacy, de-plo-macy, not dip-lo-ma-cy.
Direct, de-reckt, not di-rect.
Divers (several), di-verz; but diverse (different), di-verse.
Dome, as spelled, not doom.
Drought, drowt, not drawt.
Duke, as spelled, not dook.
Dynasty, dyn-as-te, not dy-nas-ty.
Edict, e-dickt, not ed-ickt.
E'en and e'er, een and air.
Egotism, eg-o-tizm, not e-go-tism.
Either, e-ther, not i-ther.
Engine, en-jin, not in-jin.
Ensign, en-sign; ensigncy, en-sin-cey.
Epistle, without the t.
Epitome, e-pit-o-me.
Epoch, ep-ock, not e-pock.
Equinox, eq-kwe-nox, not e-qui-nox.

Europe, U-rope, not U-rup. Euro-pe-an, not Eu-ro-pean.
Every, ev-er-ey, not ev-ry.
Executor, egz-ec-utor, not with the sound of x.
Extraordinary, ex-tror-de-nar-ey, not ex-tra-ordinary, nor extrornarey.
February, as spelled, not Febuary.
Finance, fe-nance, not fi-nance.
Foundling, as spelled, not fond-ling.
Garden, gar-dn, not gar-den, nor garding.
Gauntlet, gant-let, not gawnt-let.
Geography, as spelled, not jography, nor gehography.
Geometry, as spelled, not jom-etry.
Haunt, hant, not hawnt.
Height, hite, not highth.
Heinous, hay-nus, not hee-nus.
Highland, hi-land, not hee-land.
Horizon, ho-ri-zn, not hor-i-zon.
Housewife, huz-wif.
Hymeneal, hy-men-e-al, not hy-menal.
Instead, in-sted, not instid.
Isolate, iz-o-late, not i-zo-late, nor is-o-late.
Jalap, jal-ap, not jolup.
January, as spelled, not Jenuary, nor Janewary.
Leave, as spelled, not leaf.
Legend, led-gend, not le-gend.
Lieutenant, lev-ten-ant, not leu-ten-ant.
Many, men-ney, not man-ny.
Marchioness, mar-shun-ess, not as spelled.
Massacre, mas-sa-cur, not mas-sa-cre.
Mattress, as spelled, not mat-trass.
Matron, ma-trun, not mat-ron.
Medicine, med-e-cin, not med-cin.
Minute (sixty seconds), min-it.
Minute (small), mi-nute.
Miscellany, mis-cellany, not mis-cel-lany.
Mischievous, mis-chiv-us, not mis-cheev-us.
Ne'er, for never, nare.
Neighborhood, nay-bur-hood, not nay bur-wood.
Nephew, nev-u, not nef-u.
New, nū, not noo.
Notable (worthy of notice), no-ta-bl.
Notable (thrifty), not-a-bl.
Oblige, as spelled, not obleege.
Oblique, ob-leek, not o-blike.

Odorous, o-dur-us, not od-ur-us.
Of, ov, except when compounded with there, here, and where, which should be pronounced here-of, there-of, and where-of.
Off, of, not awf.
Organization, or-gan-e-za-shuu, not or-ga-ni-za-shun.
Ostrich, os-tritch, not os-tridge.
Pageant, pad-jant, not pa-jant.
Parent, pare-ent not par-ent
Partisan, par-te-zan, not par-te-zan, nor par-ti-zan.
Patent, pat-ent, not pa-tent.
Physiognomy, not physionnomy.
Pincers, pin-cerz, not pinch-erz.
Plaintiff, as spelled, not plan-tiff.
Pour, pore, not so as to rhyme with our.
Precedent (an example), press-e-dent; pre-ce-dent is the pronunciation of the adjective.
Prologue, prol-og, not pro-loge.
Quadrille, ka-dril, not quod-ril.
Quay, key, not as spelled.
Radish, as spelled, not red-ish.
Raillery, ral-ler-ey, not as spelled.
Rather, not raather.
Resort, rezort.
Resound, rezound.
Respite, res-pit not as spelled.
Rout (a party; and to rout) should be pronounced rowt. Route (a road),root.
Saunter, san-ter, not sawnter.
Sausage, saw-sage not sos-sidge, nor sas-sage.
Schedule, shed-ule, not shed-dle.
Seamstress, sem-stress.
Sewer, soor, not shore nor shure.
Shire, sheer, not as spelled.
Shone, shŏn, not shun, nor as spelled.
Soldier, sole-jer.
Solecism, sol-e-cizm, not so-le-cizm
Soot, as spelled, not sut.
Sovereign, sov-er-in, not suv-er-in.
Specious, spe-shus, not spesh-us.
Stomacher, stum-a-cher.
Stone (weight), as spelled, not stun.
Synod, syn-ud, not sy-nod.
Tenure, ten-ure, not te-nure.
Tenet, ten-et, not te-net.
Than, as spelled, not thun.
Tremor, trem-ur, not tre-mor.
Twelfth, should have the th sounded.
Umbrella, as spelled, not um-ber-el-la.

Vase, văze, not vawze.
Was, woz, not wuz.
Weary, weer-ey not wary.
Were, wer, not ware.
Wont, wunt, not as spelled.
Wrath, rawth, not rath; as an adjective it is spelled wroth, and pronounced with the vowel sound shorter, as wrăth-ful, etc.
Yacht, yot, not yat.
Yeast, as spelled, not yĕst.
Zenith, zen-ith, not ze-nith.
Zodiac, zo-de-ak.
Zoology should have both o's sounded, as zo-ol-o-gy, not zoo-lo-gy.
PRONOUNCE—
—ace, not iss, as furnace, not furniss.
—age, not idge, as cabbage, courage, postage, village.
—ain, aue, not in, as certain, certane, not certin.
—ate, not it, as moderate, not moderit.
—ct, not c, as aspect, not aspec; subject, not subjec.
—ed, not id, or ud, as wicked, not wickid, or wickud.
—el, not l, model, not modl; novel, not novl.
—en, not n, as sudden, not suddn.— Burden, burthen, garden, lengthen, seven, strengthen, often, and a few others, have the e silent.
—ence, not unce, as influence, not influ-unce.
—es, not is, as pleases, not pleasis.
—ile should be pronounced il, as fertil, not fertile, in all words except chamomile (cam), exile, gentile, infantile, reconcile, and senile, which should be pronounced ile.
—in, not n, as Latin, not Latn.
—nd, not n, as husband, not husban; thousand, not thousan.
—ness, not niss, as carefulness, not carefulniss.
—ng, not n, as singing, not singin; speaking, not speakin.
—ngth, not nth, as strength, not strenth.
—son, the o should be silent; as in treason, tre-zn, not tre-son.
—tal, not tle, as capital, not capitle: metal, not mettle; mortal, not mortle; periodical, not periodicle.
—xt, not x, as next, not nex.

H OR NO H? THAT IS THE QUES-
TION.—Few things point so directly to
the want of *cultivation* as the misuse of
the letter *h* by persons in conversation.
We hesitate to assert that this common
defect in speaking indicates the absence
of *education* — for, to our surprise, we
have heard even educated persons frequently commit this common and vulgar error.

Memorandum on the Use of the Letter H.

Pronounce—Herb,	'Erb.	
"	Heir,	'Eir.
"	Honesty,	'Onesty.
"	Honor,	'Onor.
"	Hospital,	'Ospital.
"	Hostler,	'Ostler.
"	Hour,	'Our.
"	Humor,	'Umor.
"	Humble,	'Umble.
"	Humility,	'Umility.

*In all other cases the H is to be sounded
when it begins a word.*

Mem. — Be careful to sound the *h*
slightly in such words as *where*, *when*,
what, *why*,—don't say were, wen, wat,
wy.

COMPOSITION. — If you would
write to any purpose, you must be perfectly free from without, in the first place,
and yet more free from within. Give
yourself the natural rein ; think on no
pattern, no patron, no paper, no press,
no public: think on nothing, but follow
your own impulses. Give yourself as
you are, what you are, and how you see
it. Every man sees with his own eyes,
or does not see at all. This is incontro-
vertibly true. Bring out what you
have. If you have nothing, be an
honest beggar rather than a respectable thief. Great care and attention
should be devoted to epistolary correspondence, as nothing exhibits want
of taste and judgment so much as a
slovenly letter. It is recognized as a
rule that all letters should be prepaid.
The following hints may be worthy of
attention :

ALWAYS PUT A STAMP on your envelope, at the top of the right-hand
corner.

LET THE DIRECTIONS be written
very plain ; this will save the postman
trouble, and facilitate business by preventing mistakes.

AT THE HEAD OF YOUR LETTER,
in the right-hand corner, put your
address in full, with the day of the
month underneath ; do not omit this,
though you may be writing to your
most intimate friend three or four
times a day.

WHAT YOU HAVE TO SAY IN YOUR
LETTER, say as plainly as possible, as
if you were speaking : this is the best
rule. Do not revert three or four times
to one circumstance, but finish as you
go on.

LET YOUR SIGNATURE be written
as plainly as possible (many mistakes
will be avoided, especially in writing to
strangers), and without any flourishes,
as these do not add in any way to the
harmony of your letter. We have seen
signatures that have been almost impossible to decipher, being a mere mass
of strokes, without any form to indicate
letters. This is done chiefly by the
ignorant, and would lead one to suppose that they were ashamed of signing what they had written.

DO NOT CROSS YOUR LETTERS:
surely paper is cheap enough now to
admit of your using an extra half-
sheet, in case of necessity. (This practice is chiefly prevalent among young
ladies.)

IF YOU WRITE TO A STRANGER for
information, or on your own business,
be sure to send a stamped envelope,
with your address plainly written ;
this will not fail to procure you an
answer.

IF YOU ARE NOT A GOOD WRITER
it is advisable to use the best ink, paper, and pens, as, though they may
not alter the character of your handwriting, yet they will assist to make
your writing look better.

PUNCTUATION. — Punctuation
teaches the method of placing *Points*,
in written or printed matter, in such a
manner as to indicate the pauses which
would be made by the author if he

were communicating his thoughts orally instead of by written signs. WRITING AND PRINTING are substitutes for oral communication ; and correct punctuation is essential to convey the meaning intended, and to give due force to such passages as the author may wish to impress upon the mind of the person to whom they are being communicated.

THE POINTS are as follows :

The Comma ,
The Semicolon ;
The Colon :
The Period, or Full Point.
The Apostrophe '
The Hyphen, or Conjoiner -
The Note of Interrogation ?
The Note of Exclamation !
The Parentheses ( )
The Asterisk, or Star *

As these are all the points required in simple epistolary composition, we will confine our explanations to the rules which should govern the use of them.

THE OTHER POINTS, however, are the paragraph ¶; the section §; the dagger †; the double dagger ‡; the dash —; the parallel ∥; the bracket [ ]; and some others. These, however, are quite unnecessary except for elaborate works, in which they are chiefly used for notes or marginal references.

THE COMMA , denotes the shortest pause; the semicolon ; a little longer pause than the comma; the colon : a little longer pause than the semicolon ; the period, or full point . the longest pause.

THE RELATIVE DURATION of these pauses is described as —

While you count

Comma...................One.
Semicolon...............Two.
Colon ....Three.
Period.......... ....Four.

This, however, is not an infallible rule, because the duration of the pauses should be regulated by the degree of rapidity with which the matter is being read. In slow reading, the duration of the pauses should be increased.

THE OTHER POINTS are rather in-
21

dications of expression, and of meaning and connection, than of pauses, and therefore we will notice them separately.

THE MISPLACING of even so slight a point, or pause, as the comma, will often alter the meaning of a sentence. The contract made for lighting the town of Liverpool, during the year 1819, was thrown void by the misplacing of a comma in the advertisements, thus :—" The lamps at present are about 4050, and have in general two spouts each, composed of not less than twenty threads of cotton." The contractor would have proceeded to furnish each lamp with the said twenty threads, but this being but half the usual quantity, the commissioners discovered that the difference arose from the comma following instead of preceding the word *each.* The parties agreed to annul the contract, and a new one was ordered.

THE FOLLOWING SENTENCE shows how difficult it is to read without the aid of the points used as pauses :

Death waits not for storm nor sunshine within a dwelling in one of the upper streets respectable in appearance and furnished with such conveniences as distinguish the habitations of those who rank among the higher classes of society a man of middle age lay on his last bed eiomently awaiting the final summons all that the most skilful medical attendance all that love warm as the glow that fires an angel's bosom could do had been done by day and night for many long weeks had ministering spirits such as a devoted wife and loving children are done all within their power to ward off the blow but there he lay his raven hair smoothed off from his noble brow his dark eyes lighted with unnatural brightness and contrasting strongly with the pallid hue which marked him as an expectant of the dreaded messenger.

THE SAME SENTENCE, properly pointed, and with capital letters placed after full points, according to the adopted rule, may be easily read and understood :

Death waits not for storm nor sunshine. Within a dwelling in one of the upper streets, respectable in appearance, and furnished with such conveniences as distinguish the habitations of those who rank among the higher classes of society, a man of middle age lay on his last bed, momently awaiting the final summons. All that the most skilful medical attendance—all that love, warm as the glow that fires an angel's bosom, could do, had been done; by day and night, for many long weeks, had ministering spirits, such as a devoted wife and loving children are, done all within their power to ward off the blow. But there he lay, his raven hair smoothed off from his noble brow, his dark eyes lighted with unnatural brightness, and contrasting strongly with the pallid hue which marked him as an expectant of the dread messenger.

THE APOSTROPHE ' is used to indicate the combining of two words in one, — as John's book, instead of John, his book; or to show the omission of parts of words, as *Glo'ster*, for Gloucester, *tho'* for though. These abbreviations should be avoided as much as possible. Cobbett says the apostrophe "ought to be called the mark of *laziness* and vulgarity." The first use, however, of which we give an example, is a necessary and proper one.

THE HYPHEN, or conjoiner -, is used to unite words which, though they are separate and distinct, have so close a connection as almost to become one word, as water-rat, wind-mill, etc. It is also used in writing and printing, at the end of a line, to show where a word is divided and continued in the next line. Look down the ends of the lines in this column, and you will notice the hyphen in several places.

THE NOTE OF INTERROGATION ? indicates that the sentence to which it is put asks a question; as, "What is the meaning of that assertion? What am I to do?"

THE NOTE OF EXCLAMATION or of admiration ! indicates surprise, pleasure, or sorrow; as, "Oh! Ah! Goodness! Beautiful! I am astonished! Woe is me!"

Sometimes, when an expression of strong surprise or pleasure is intended, two notes of this character are employed, thus ! !

THE PARENTHESIS ( ) are used to prevent confusion by the introduction to a sentence of a passage not necessary to the sense thereof. "I am going to meet Mr. Smith (though I am no admirer of him) on Wednesday next." It is better, however, as a rule, not to employ parenthetical sentences.

THE ASTERISK, OR STAR *, may be employed to refer from the text to a note of explanation at the foot of a column, or at the end of a letter. *₊* Three stars are sometimes used

to call particular attention to a paragraph.

Hints upon Spelling.— The following rules will be found of great assistance in writing, because they relate to a class of words about the spelling of which doubt and hesitation are frequently felt:

All words of one syllable ending in *l*, with a single vowel before it, have double *l* at the close; as, *mill, sell.*

All words of one syllable ending in *l*, with a double vowel before it, have one *l* only at the close; as *mail, sail.*

Words of one syllable ending in *l*, when compounded, retain but one *l* each; as, *fulfil, skilful.*

Words of more than one syllable ending in *l*, have one *l* only at the close; as, *delightful, faithful;* except *befall, downfall, recall, unwell,* etc.

All derivatives from words ending in *l* have one *l* only; as, *equality,* from *equal; fulness,* from *full;* except they end in *er* or *ly:* as, *mill, miller; full, fully.*

All participles in *ing* from verbs ending in *e* lose the *e* final: as, *have, having; amuse, amusing;* unless they come from verbs ending in double *e,* and then they retain both: as *see, seeing; agree, agreeing.*

All adverbs in *ly,* and nouns in *ment* retain the *e* final of the primitives: as, *brave, bravely; refine, refinement;* except *acknowledgment, judgment,* etc.

All derivatives from words ending in *er,* retain the *e* before the *r:* as, *refer, reference;* except *hindrance,* from *hin der; remembrance,* from *remember; dis astrous,* from *disaster; monstrous,* from *monster; wondrous,* from *wonder; cumbrous,* from *cumber,* etc.

Compound words, if both end not in *l,* retain their primitive parts entire: as, *millstone, changeable, raceless;* except *always, also, deplorable, although, almost, admirable,* etc.

All one-syllables ending in a consonant, with a single vowel before it, double that consonant in derivatives: as, *sin, sinner; ship, shipping; big, bigger; glad, gladder,* etc.

One-syllables ending in a consonant,

with a double vowel before it, do not double the consonant in derivatives: as, *sleep, sleepy; troop, trooper.*

All words of more than one syllable ending in a single consonant, preceded by a single vowel, and accented on the last syllable, double that consonant in derivatives: as, *commit, committee; compel, compelled; appal, appalling; distil, distiller.*

Nouns of one syllable ending in *y*, preceded by a consonant, change *y* into *ies* in the plural; and verbs ending in *y*, preceded by a consonant, change *y* into *ies* in the third person singular of the present tense, and into *ied* in the past tense and past participle: as, *fly, flies; I apply, he applies; we reply, we replied,* or *have replied.* If the *y* be preceded by a vowel, this rule is not applicable: as, *key, keys; I play, he plays;* we have *enjoyed* ourselves.

Compound words, whose primitives end in *y*, change *y* into *i:* as, *beauty, beautiful; lovely, loveliness.*

RULES OF POLITENESS.

Etiquette is the Unwritten Laws of Society.—Introduction to Society. — Avoid all extravagance and mannerism, and be not over - timid at the outset. Be discreet and sparing of your words. Awkwardness is a great misfortune, but it is not an unpardonable fault. To deserve the reputation of moving in good society, something more is requisite than the avoidance of blunt rudeness. Strictly keep to your engagements. Punctuality is the essence of politeness.

The Toilet. — Too much attention cannot be paid to the arrangements of the toilet. A man is often judged by his appearance, and seldom incorrectly. A neat exterior, equally free from extravagance and poverty, almost always proclaims a right-minded man. To dress appropriately, and with good taste, is to respect yourself and others. A gentleman walking, should always wear gloves, this being one of the characteristics of good breeding. Fine linen, and a good hat, gloves, and boots, are evidences of the highest taste in dress.

Visiting Dress. — A black coat and trousers are indispensable for a visit of ceremony, an entertainment, or a ball. The white or black waistcoat is equally proper in these cases.

Officers' Dress. — Upon public and state occasions officers should appear in uniform.

Ladies' Dress. — Ladies' dresses should be chosen so as to produce an agreeable harmony. Never put on a dark-colored bonnet with a light spring costume. Avoid uniting colors which

will suggest an epigram; such as a straw-colored dress with a green bonnet.

Excess of Lace and Flowers. — Whatever be your style of face, avoid an excess of lace, and let flowers be few and choice.

Appropriateness of Ornaments. —In a married women a richer style of ornament is admissible. Costly elegance for her—for the young girl, a style of modest simplicity.

Simplicity and Grace. — The most elegant dress loses its character if it is not worn with grace. Young girls have often an air of constraint, and their dress seems to partake of their want of ease. In speaking of her toilet, a woman should not convey the idea that her whole skill consists in adjusting tastefully some trifling ornaments. A simple style of dress is an indication of modesty.

Cleanliness.—The hands should receive especial attention. They are the outward signs of general cleanliness. The same may be said of the face, the neck, the ears, and the teeth. The cleanliness of the system generally, and of bodily apparel, pertains to health, and is treated of under this head.

The Handkerchief. — There is considerable art in using this accessory of dress and comfort. Avoid extreme patterns, styles, and colors. Never be without a handkerchief. Hold it freely in the hand, and do not roll it into a ball. Hold it by the centre, and let the corners form a fan-like expansion. Avoid using it too much. With some persons the habit becomes troublesome

324

Dinner Table. — It is taken for granted that every place at a friend's table is equally a place of honor, and equally agreeable. It is therefore becoming the custom for the guests to sit in the order they enter the room. Ladies sit on the right of gentlemen. When seated, take off your gloves, place your table napkin across your knees, and the bread it contains on the left side of your plate. While thus engaged, converse with the lady sitting beside you. Do not talk of the dinner appointments, and never discuss the merits of the food, or anything set before you.

Soup is served first — one ladle to each plate. Eat it from the side of your spoon. Pip's lesson in etiquette, from Dickens' "Great Expectations," is concise and amusing. We quote:

It is not the custom to put the knife in the mouth, for fear of accident; and while the fork is reserved for that use, it is not put further in than necessary. Also, the spoon is not generally used overhand, but under. This has two advantages — you get at your mouth better (which after all is the object), and you save a good deal of the attitude of opening oysters, on the part of the right elbow.

Do not make a noise with your mouth in eating soup; never scrape up the last drop, or tilt the plate to get at it, and do not send twice for either soup or fish.

VISITS AND PRESENTATIONS. — Friendly calls should be made in the forenoon, and require neatness, without costliness of dress.

Calls to give invitations to dinner-parties, or balls, should be very short, and should be paid in the afternoon.

Visits of condolence require a grave style of dress.

A formal visit should never be made before noon. If a second visitor is announced, it will be proper for you to retire, unless you are very intimate both with the host and the visitor announced; unless, indeed, the host express a wish for you to remain.

Visits after balls or parties should be made within a mouth.

In the latter, it is customary to enclose your card in an envelope, bearing the address outside. This may be sent by post, if you reside at a distance.

But, if living in the neighborhood, it is polite to send your servant, or to call. In the latter case a corner should be turned down.

Scrape your shoes and use the mat. Never appear in a drawing-room with mud on your boots.

When a new visitor enters a drawing-room, if it be a gentleman, the ladies bow slightly; if a lady, the guests rise.

Hold your hat in your hand, unless requested to place it down. Then lay it beside you.

The last arrival in a drawing-room takes a seat left vacant near the mistress of the house.

A lady is not required to rise to receive a gentleman, nor to accompany him to the door.

When your visitor retires, ring the bell for the servant. You may then accompany your guest as far towards the door as the circumstances of your friendship seem to demand.

Request the servant, during the visit of guests, to be ready to attend to the door the moment the bell rings.

When you introduce a person, pronounce the name distinctly, and say whatever you can to make the introduction agreeable. Such as "an old and valued friend," a "schoolfellow of mine," "an old acquaintance of our family."

Never stare about you in a room as if you were taking stock.

The gloves should not be removed during a visit.

Be hearty in your reception of guests; and where you see much diffidence, assist the stranger to throw it off.

A lady does not put her address on her visiting card.

Do not imagine that to be expensively or extravagantly dressed, is to be well dressed. Simplicity is always elegant, and good taste can lend a grace to dress which no outlay of money on its materials can purchase. The most perfect cleanliness is the first essential.

A lady's hair should be always well arranged in the style she chooses to wear it — which had better be one of those sanctioned by the fashion of the day. The teeth should be attended to carefully. The first things a lady ought to think about are her gloves and shoes; gloves should fit well and be unsoiled, and should harmonize in color with the dress, but soft neutral tints will suit any dress. Her boots should be well made, large enough for comfort, and always thick enough to keep the feet dry and warm.

Ladies are not obliged to consider their ball-partners as acquaintances, unless they please.

It is the lady's place to bow first to the gentleman.

To answer a letter promptly is a civility, and in some cases a kindness.

Invitations ought to receive an immediate reply.

At dinner, the gentleman sits at the right hand of the lady.

You should begin, or appear to begin, to eat as soon as it is put before you.

Never by any chance put a knife near your mouth.

Do not bite your bread; the rule about eating it is this:

Cut it at breakfast, when you generally take a thick piece, and butter it yourself.

Break it at dinner.

Bite it at tea, when it is in thin slices.

Eat your soup from the side of the spoon, not take it from the point; beware of tasting it while too hot, or of swallowing it fast enough to make you cough.

Conversation is supposed to belong especially to the dinner table. A delicate perception of what may wound the feelings of others is essential here — "Do unto others as you would have them do unto you." Do not say to a friend whose complexion is of too deep a red, "How flushed your face is!" or to a stout lady, "How warm you look!"

Never talk about yourself if you can help it, nor about your own affairs.

Never introduce religious arguments in society; if the subject is forced, avow your opinions, moderately, but decline anything like a defence of them; it is in better taste not to argue on any subject.

Do not sit stupidly silent; do your best to be agreeable. Talk as well as you can, and at least try to appear amused.

But silence is preferable to talking too much.

Always look at people when you speak to them.

It is rude to speak in whispers, and offensive to take a person aside to whisper to them.

Slang phrases (even those of the drawing-room) must be avoided.

Give your own opinion of people if you choose, but do not repeat the opinions of others.

Vary your toilet sufficiently that idlers and others may not make your dress the description of your person.

Dress plainly for walking in the street. To wear a bonnet fit for a carriage, when not in one, or to walk through the dust or mud clothed in satin or lace, is the extreme of bad taste.

WALKING. — Endeavor to acquire an elegant walk. Hold yourself erect without stiffness. Walk noiselessly in the house and lightly in the street. Do not turn your feet out too much, it is as bad a fault as to turn them inwards, and causes an unseemly shaking of the garments.

Never look behind you in the street, nor about you so as to attract attention. Do not talk or laugh loud on the street, but pursue a quiet manner, and a smooth, graceful walk.

A lady shakes hands with gentlemen who are friends or intimate acquaintances, but she must do so gently, without vehemence of action.

A young lady rather gives her own hand than shakes that of a gentleman.

Never allow a gentleman to pay for your admission into any theatre, or public exhibition, unless he is a *relative*, or *particular friend*.

In the present day, when the distinctions of rank are becoming constantly less marked, and the circles of good society are so constantly receiving into themselves the men who have risen from the cottage or the workshop, a knowledge of these social laws becomes important for his wife and daughters. Society has its "grammar," as language has; and the rules of that grammar *must* be learnt, either orally or from reading. To assist in this, the Hints on Etiquette have been introduced here, but the foundation of all good breeding lies in Christianity itself, for society requires "love, joy, peace, long suffering, gentleness, goodness," "and all things that be lovely."

If self be put out of sight, and kindness, courtesy, and thought for others take its place, a very slight training in mere etiquette is all that is required to make a well-bred lady.

A GENTLEMAN. — Moderation, decorum, and neatness distinguish the gentleman; he is at all times affable, diffident, and studious to please. Intelligent and polite, his behavior is pleasant and graceful. When he enters the dwelling of an inferior, he endeavors to hide, if possible, the difference between their ranks in life; ever willing to assist those around him, he is neither unkind, haughty, nor overbearing. In the mansions of the rich, the correctness of his mind induces him to bend to etiquette, but not to stoop to adulation; correct principle cautions him to avoid the gaming-table, inebriety, or any other foible that could occasion him self-reproach. Gratified with the pleasures of reflection, he rejoices to see the gaieties of society, and is fastidious upon no point of little import. Appear only to be a gentleman, and its shadow will bring upon you contempt; be a gentleman, and its honors will remain even after you are dead.

AVOID INTERMEDDLING with the affairs of others. This is a most common fault. A number of people seldom meet but they begin discussing the affairs of some one who is absent. This

is not only uncharitable, but positively unjust. It is equivalent to trying a *cause in the absence of the person implicated.* Even in the criminal code a prisoner is presumed to be innocent until he is found guilty. Society, however, is less just, and passes judgment without hearing the defence. Depend upon it, as a certain rule, *that the people who unite with you in discussing the affairs of others will proceed to scandalize you in your absence.*

BE CONSISTENT in the avowal of principles. Do not deny to-day that which you asserted yesterday. If you do, you will stultify yourself, and your opinions will soon be found to have no weight. You may fancy that you gain favor by subserviency; but so far from gaining favor, you lose respect.

AVOID FALSEHOOD. — There can be found no higher virtue than the love of truth. The man who deceives others must himself become the victim of morbid distrust. Knowing the deceit of his own heart, and the falsehood of his own tongue, his eyes must be always filled with suspicion, and he must lose the greatest of all happiness — confidence in those who surround him.

THE FOLLOWING ELEMENTS of manly character are worthy of frequent meditation:

To be wise in his disputes.
To be a lamb in his home.
To be brave in battle and great in moral courage.
To be discreet in public.
To be a bard in his chair.
To be a teacher in his household.
To be a council in his nation.
To be an arbitrator in his vicinity.
To be a hermit in his church.
To be a legislator in his country.
To be conscientious in his actions.
To be happy in his life.
To be diligent in his calling.
To be just in his dealing.
That whatever he doeth be to the will of God.

AVOID MANIFESTATIONS OF ILL-TEMPER. — Reason is given for man's guidance. Passion is the tempest by which reason is overthrown. Under the effects of passion, man's mind becomes disordered, his face disfigured, his body deformed. A moment's passion has frequently cut off a life's friendship, destroyed a life's hope, embittered a life's peace, and brought unending sorrow and disgrace. It is scarcely worth while to enter into a comparative analysis of ill-temper and passion; they are alike discreditable, alike injurious, and should stand equally condemned.

AVOID PRIDE. — If you are handsome, God made you so; if you are learned, some one instructed you; if you are rich, God gave you what you own. It is for others to perceive your goodness; but you should be blind to your own merits. There can be no comfort in deeming yourself better than you really are: that is self-deception. The best men throughout all history have been the most humble.

AFFECTATION IS A FORM OF PRIDE. It is, in fact, pride made ridiculous and contemptible. Some one writing upon affectation has remarked as follows:

If anything will sicken and disgust a man, it is the affected, mincing way in which some people choose to talk. It is perfectly nauseous. If those young jackanapes, who screw their words into all manner of diabolical shapes, could only fool how perfectly disgusting they were, it might induce them to drop it. With many, it soon becomes such a confirmed habit that they cannot again be taught to talk in a plain, straightforward, manly way. In the lower order of ladies' boarding-schools, and, indeed, too much overywhere, the same sickening, mincing tone is too often found. Do pray, good people, do talk in your natural tone, if you don't wish to be utterly ridiculous and contemptible.

WE HAVE ADOPTED THE FOREGOING PARAGRAPH because we approve of some of its sentiments, but chiefly because it shows that persons who object to affectation may go to the other extreme—vulgarity. It is vulgar, we think, to call even the most affected people "Jackanapes, who screw their words into all manner of diabolical shapes." Avoid vulgarity in manner, in speech, and in correspondence. To conduct yourself vulgarly is to offer offence to those who are around you;

to bring upon yourself the condemnation of persons of good taste; and to incur the penalty of exclusion from good society. Thus, cast among the vulgar, you become the victim of your own error.

AVOID SWEARING. An oath is but the wrath of a perturbed spirit. It is *mean.* A man of high moral standing would rather treat an offence with contempt than show his indignation by an oath. It is *vulgar:* altogether too low for a decent man. It is *cowardly:* implying a fear either of not being believed or obeyed. It is *ungentlemanly.* A gentleman, according to Webster, is a *genteel man* — wellbred, refined. It is *indecent:* offensive to delicacy, and extremely unfit for human ears. It is *foolish.* "Want of decency is want of sense." It is *abusive* — to the mind which conceives the oath, to the tongue which utters it, and to the person at whom it is aimed. It is *venomous:* showing a man's heart to be as a nest of vipers; and every time he swears, one of them starts out from his head. It is *contemptible:* forfeiting the respect of all the wise and good. It is *wicked:* violating the Divine law, and provoking the displeasure of Him who will not hold him guiltless who takes His name in vain.

BE HONEST. Not only because "honesty is the best policy," but because it is a duty to God and to man. The heart that can be gratified by dishonest gains; the ambition that can be satisfied by dishonest means; the mind that can be devoted to dishonest purposes, must be of the worst order.

HAVING LAID DOWN THESE GENERAL PRINCIPLES for the government of personal conduct, we will epitomize what we would still enforce:

AVOID IDLENESS — it is the parent of many evils. Can you pray, "Give us this day our daily bread," and not hear the reply, "Do thou this day thy daily duty"?

AVOID TELLING IDLE TALES, which is like firing arrows in the dark; you know not into whose heart they may fall.

AVOID TALKING ABOUT YOURSELF, praising your own works, and proclaiming your own deeds. If they are good they will proclaim themselves; if bad, the less you say of them the better.

AVOID ENVY, for it cannot benefit you, nor can it injure those against whom it is cherished.

AVOID DISPUTATION for the mere sake of argument. The man who disputes obstinately, and in a bigoted spirit, is like the man who would stop the fountain from which he should drink. Earnest discussion is commendable; but factious argument never yet produced a good result.

BE KIND IN LITTLE THINGS. The true generosity of the heart is more displayed by deeds of minor kindness than by acts which may partake of ostentation.

BE POLITE. Politeness is the poetry of conduct, and, like poetry, it has many qualities. Let not your politeness be too florid, but of that gentle kind which indicates a refined nature.

BE SOCIABLE—avoid reserve in society. Remember that the social elements, like the air we breathe, are purified by motion. Thought illumines thought, and smiles win smiles.

BE PUNCTUAL. One minute too late has lost many a golden opportunity. Besides which, the want of punctuality is an affront: offered to the person to whom your presence is due.

THE FOREGOING REMARKS may be said to apply to the moral conduct, rather than to the details of personal manners. Great principles, however, suggest minor ones; and hence, from the principles laid down, many hints upon personal behavior may be gathered.

PREFER TO LISTEN rather than to talk.

BEHAVE, EVEN IN THE PRESENCE of your relations, as though you felt respect to be due to them.

IN SOCIETY NEVER FORGET that you are but one of many.

WHEN YOU VISIT A FRIEND, conform to the rules of his household. Lean not upon his tables, nor rub your feet against his chairs.

PRY NOT INTO LETTERS that are not your own.

PAY UNMISTAKABLE RESPECT to ladies everywhere.

BEWARE OF FOPPERY, and of silly flirtation.

IN PUBLIC PLACES be not too pertinacious of your own rights, but find pleasure in making concessions.

SPEAK DISTINCTLY, look at the person to whom you speak, and when you have spoken, give him an opportunity to reply.

AVOID DRUNKENNESS as you would a curse; and modify all appetites, especially those that are acquired.

DRESS WELL, but not superfluously; be neither like a sloven nor like a stuffed model.

KEEP AWAY ALL UNCLEANLY APPEARANCES from the person. Let the nails, the teeth, and, in fact, the whole system receive *salutary* rather than *studied* care. But let these things receive attention at the toilet—not elsewhere.

AVOID DISPLAYING EXCESS OF JEWELRY. Nothing looks more effeminate upon a man.

EVERY ONE OF THESE SUGGESTIONS may be regarded as the centre of many others, which the earnest mind cannot fail to discover.

A GENTLEMAN has perfect control of his temper, and will avoid arguments or points likely to lead to the expression of strong feelings. If religious or political subjects are introduced, he will not discuss them with warmth. It is not to be inferred that he is therefore a coward or a fool; but simply that, while conscious what is due to himself, he does not forget what he owes to others.

PERSONAL APPEARANCE depends greatly on the careful toilet and scrupulous attention to dress.

THE FIRST POINT which marks the gentleman, is rigid cleanliness in the body, and everything which covers it.

There is no indication of a gentleman truer than a pure white hand—white in the sense of being clean—and perfect-kept nails. The hair and teeth should receive the utmost attention. The head should be, in respect of the skin, as white as the hand, the hair thoroughly brushed and kept. To curl it artificially is not in good taste.

A GENTLEMAN "follows the fashion" to an extent, because it is an affectation to outrage it; but he does not seize on every extravagance; he concedes only to the limits of good taste, and always with an eye to his age, position, and individual peculiarities.

ADAPT your conversation to your company. This is somewhat trite, but it is the golden rule on this subject. Do not speak in a loud voice, or assume a dictatorial manner. If any statement is made which you know to be incorrect or untrue, be very careful of the manner in which you correct the speaker.

BE VERY CAREFUL not to interrupt a person while speaking, and should he hesitate for a word, never supply it.

PUNS AND SLANG TERMS are to be avoided as much as possible, and remember there are various kinds of slang: there is the slang of the drawing-room as well as of the stable. Every expression has its own technical terms, and set of expressions, which should be avoided in general society.

IN SPEAKING of third persons, always use the prefix "Mr." or "Mrs." to their names. Do not refer to them by their initials, as Mr. or Mrs. B. Never allude to any one as a "party" or a gent (remember a gent is not always a gentleman).

CORRESPONDENCE is a point of special importance, for by it others form (perhaps unconsciously) an estimate of the writer's worth and pretensions. It is difficult to overcome the effect produced by a badly-written, indifferently spelt, and unsightly letter. Therefore observe these rules:

Let your stationery be of the best quality, your handwriting plain, your style simple, and always inclined to brevity. Never omit to put your address, and the date on which you write; and if it is a business, or very informal letter, add the name of the person addressed at the foot of the letter.

Always reply promptly to a letter, no matter of what nature. (If you are not a good penman, it is the more particular to observe these rules.)

Balls and Evening Parties. — An invitation to a ball should be given at least a week beforehand.

If the invitation comes from a host or hostess, never fail to answer at the earliest possible moment. The host naturally desires to invite as many of his friends as he may conveniently entertain, and you should inform him at once if you cannot attend that he may extend his hospitality to another. The host always wishes to know how many guests to prepare for, and an answer is desirable on this account.

If desirable, accept the engagement at once, and then you can readily make your duties and other appointments conform to it. The earlier you make the engagement the longer will you enjoy the pleasure of anticipating the enjoyment it will afford. It is always well to cultivate a habit of definite and positive action, and the observance of this rule in one's social life will be of aid in the discharge of business duties.

If the invitation is received by a lady from a gentleman, the obligation of giving a prompt answer is even stronger. After a gentleman has invited a lady he is always subject to a embarrassment until he obtains a reply. The fundamental principle of etiquette is consideration for others, and a considerate young woman will always observe this important rule.

Upon entering, first address the lady of the house; and after her, the nearest acquaintances you may recognize in the house.

If you introduce a friend, make him acquainted with the names of the chief persons present. But first present him to the lady of the house, and to the host.

Appear in full dress.

Always wear gloves.

Do not wear rings on the outside of your gloves.

Avoid an excess of jewelry.

Do not select the same partner frequently.

Distribute your attentions as much as possible.

Pay respectful attention to elderly persons.

Be cordial when serving refreshments, but not importunate.

If there are more dancers than the room will accommodate, do not join in every dance.

In leaving a large party it is unnecessary to bid farewell, and improper to do so before the guests.

A Paris card of invitation to an evening party usually implies that you are invited for the season.

In balls and large parties there should be a table for cards, and two packs of cards placed upon each table.

Chess and all unsociable games should be avoided.

Although many persons do not like to play at cards except for a stake, the stakes agreed to at parties should be very trifling, so as not to create excitement or discussion.

The host and hostess should look after their guests, and not confine their attentions. They should, in fact, assist those chiefly who are the least known in the room.

Avoid political and religious discussions. If you have a "hobby," keep it to yourself.

After dancing, conduct your partner to a seat.

Resign her as soon as her next partner advances.

Do not cross a room in an anxious manner, and force your way up to a lady merely to receive a bow. If you are desirous of being noticed by any one, put yourself in their way as if by accident, not appear to have singled them out.

Among the middle classes, evening dress is often considered an affectation, except on special occasions; it is well, therefore, to avoid it when it is not likely to be adopted.

Never wear but one ring at a time. Use no perfumes.

When making a call, do not be frightened at the presence of other morning callers, nor appear stiff, or embarrassed, though they may not be introduced to you. Join in the conversation, which the lady of the house is sure to try to promote, by any light remark of the small talk order. If you are *tête-à-tête* with the lady, and other visitors are announced, do not betray alarm, or embarrassment, but wait for a reasonable time after they are seated, then rise to take your leave; bowing to the other visitors, and politely resisting the formal invitation to remain, which you will probably receive, as a matter of courtesy, and nothing more.

Formal visits should never be protracted beyond twenty minutes; but do not look at your watch to see if it is time to go: wait for a lull in the conversation, and avail yourself of it.

However good the terms on which you may be with a lady, never stop her in the street to speak, and never offer your hand: she will stop, you raise your hat, and if it is agreeable to her, she will offer her hand. She, too, decides when the conversation is to end. If, while speaking, she moves onward, you should turn and accompany her: if she makes a slight inclination, as of dismissal, raise your hat, bow, and go on your way.

In walking with a lady, never permit her to encumber herself with a book, parcel, or anything of that kind, but always offer to carry it. Never break an appointment, but be punctual to the moment in keeping it.

Never permit a lady to pay for carriages, railway tickets, etc., when you accompany her to places of public resort.

If you are in a crowd, and you and your lady are obliged to proceed singly, you should lead the way.

In accompanying a lady, and the stairway is not wide enough for you to walk by her side, walk before her in ascending; and behind her in descending.

COURTSHIP. — The first real awakening of the heart to the influences of woman, is an epoch in a life never to be forgotten. It may have been preceded, and often is, by flashes of admiration and interest, such as the schoolboy calls love; but these are as nothing to that fast, true, deep, absorbing passion, which it is impossible to mistake. It is not necessary that the object of it should be either beautiful or worthy. She may be a plain woman, full of faults, whims, caprices, selfishness, unattractive in manner, and with a heart of marble — it matters not, he loves and is happy.

Equally strong and absorbing is the influence of love in its bright rosy dawn on the gentle nature of woman. The newly-awakened emotion fills her life, and lends a mystical beauty, both to earth and sky. What a proud, joyous, happy moment that is, when a young and innocent girl first says to herself: "I am beloved, and my lover is dearer to me than the whole world, — dearer to me than my life?" Poets and novelists never tire of depicting the charms of the springtide of love in woman. They show us how it adds beauty to the beautiful, and invests even those of ordinary attractions with a singular charm and fascination, the result of happiness and lightness of earth. These latter are the best cosmetics. In them lies the magic of perpetual youth, and they should at least accompany the dawn of love in woman's heart.

Out of love, naturally and properly, springs courtship.

He who loves, courts the object of that love. Cobbett assures us that "between fifteen and twenty-two, all people will fall in love." Shakspeare extends this season to the age of forty-five: while old Burton, writing on love-melancholy, gives us a still further extension of the case. What an idea this gives of the courtship that must be perpetually going on? And it must be borne in mind that in most cases the success of the love-suit depends on the manner in which the courtship is conducted. There is a happy arrangement prevailing in an East Indian tribe, by which the women enjoy the prerogative of courtship. The process adopted is very simple. If a lady is pleased with one of the opposite sex, she sends a friend to pin a handkerchief to his cap with a pin that she uses to fasten her hair. This is done in public, her name being mentioned at the time, and the favored one is then obliged to marry her, or, if not, to pay a substantial sum to her father. Unfortunately, perhaps, our customs are less primitive. The lover must make the advance, must disclose his passion, press his suit, and devote himself seriously to the business of that probationary routine which we call courtship.

Often a man's courting days are the happiest of his life. They should always be so, but it does not always follow that they are. It is so easy, so delicious to love—the heart learns *that* lesson so readily—but the expression that love in accordance with set forms and conventional rules, is often rather a trial than otherwise. The bashful man finds himself put to the blush. The man unaccustomed to society, and to ladies' society especially, is forever at fault. Both are nervous, anxious, and ill at ease. Both need the advice and suggestions of those who have already acquired their experience. That advice and those suggestions are not always readily obtained; in such cases these hints may be useful.

DISENGAGED. — Everything in life worth having must be paid for. It is not very gallant to say it, but it is very true that this applies even to the position of a lover.

He sacrifices something for the privileges he enjoys.

The halcyon days of love are preceded by a period of existence not altogether unenviable.

There is a delicious freedom about it. The disengaged man is wholly irresponsible. He goes where he will, and does what he likes. As some one has said, "Everything is forgiven him on account of his position. If he talks nonsense, it is his high spirits; if he dances incessantly the whole evening, it is that he may please those 'dear girls'; if he is marked in his attention to ladies, he is only on his probation; if he has a few fast, lounging habits, it is held all very well in a young fellow like that." Society has a perpetual welcome for him; the men like him for his social qualities, and the ladies receive him with rapture, if for no other reason than simply because he is disengaged.

Nor is the position of the disengaged lady without its charms. If she has beauty or wit, accomplishments or conversational powers, she goes into society only to be courted and admired. The restrictions of society weigh less heavily upon her than upon others. In her innocent gaiety of heart she breaks through them with impunity. It is her privilege to receive attentions from all, and to be compromised by none. In the ball-room she reigns supreme; she may give a smile to one, a passing word to another, and her motives will be misconstrued as little as her kindness will be presumed on. She will never be more happy, people tell her, and they may be right. But what then? Youth, and homage, and absolute sway are delightful, but they are not to be retained by remaining for life — disengaged. No! just as the young bachelor finds life change for him against his will—finds mammas grow frigid, and daughters shy of the man who never proposes— so the life of the careless, light-hearted girl assumes imperceptibly a fresh phase. She grows older, she loves, and then the life that was so glorious satisfies her no longer. A fresh ambition fills her mind; it is that of enjoying the whole and sole attention of the chosen one who is destined some day to make her his wife.

PROPOSING. — Much is said of love at first sight. Perhaps all love, deserving the name — that is, as distinguished from the mild glow of affection—is of that nature. But a proposal should always be the result of second thought. It is only a fool who suffers himself to be led into putting the rest of his life in jeopardy on the spur of the moment; and certainly no prudent woman would consent to accept an offer of marriage, at the hands of a man whom she had only known a few days or weeks, as the case might be. Yet this sort of thing is perpetually done. A modern essayist observes, with great truth— "The most common source of unsuitable marriages is plainly the sheer thoughtlessness with which many women marry. The process resembles nothing so much as raffling. Virtually the whole thing is an affair of accident or chance." It is sad that this should be literally true, because the marriage tie is so close and binding; the happiness of those united by it can only be secured by such thorough union and accord, that it is the grossest folly, not to say wickedness, for persons to incur the responsibility of matrimony in ignorance of each other's antecedents, principles, habits, tastes, inclinations, and modes of thinking. Avowals of love, or proposals, are made in various ways, the very worst of which is doing it by proxy.

Faint-hearted lovers—timid, nervous persons — sometimes adopt the expedient of proposing by letter. This is always objectionable where a personal interview is to be had, because a man can tell his love so much better than he can write about it. The passion of his breast glows in his eyes — the sincerity of those feelings to which he struggles to give utterance is gathered from the tone of his voice. Now, in a letter there are only words, and generally ill-chosen ones. There is nothing so difficult to write as a love-letter. Either it is too impassioned and savors of exaggeration, or it is too matter-of-fact and conveys an idea of coldness. However, there are circumstances — absence among others — which sometimes oblige a man to write.

Asking Papa. — In these days, the lover and the object of his choice generally come to an understanding without much being said about it on either side; a favorable opportunity brings an avowal from the lips of the gentleman, who entreats permission to pay his addresses, and receives an assurance that it would not be distasteful to the lady herself, but that he must "ask papa."

When the proposal is made by the gentleman in writing, he usually asks permission to obtain the consent of the lady's parents. This also is sometimes done in writing; but it is much better that, for each of the two great steps in the courtship — proposing to the lady, and asking the father's or mother's consent — a personal interview should be obtained.

If the lover is too diffident to approach the subject in his own proper person, or if circumstances compel him to write, he should bear in mind that his letter ought to treat of two points — first, his regard for the lady; and secondly, the circumstances which warrant him in seeking to make her his wife.

A letter of this kind should be brief and to the purpose; without having the formality of a purely business epistle, it should be free from romance or sentiment. It may be distasteful to the lover to have to speak calmly of his character and his means, instead of going into raptures over his passion, and the charms that have inspired it; but under the circumstances, it is incumbent on him to do so. A father who is called to part with his child to another, is called on to regard the step not from a lover's point of view, but from that of a man of the world.

The point has often been debated as to how far a parent's judgment, feelings, or prejudices, ought to be respected by a son or a daughter in a matter of such moment as that of the choice of a partner for life. On this point, some sound and sensible views have been expressed to the following effect:

"There are a great many nice questions with reference to the exact duty of parents in preventing matrimonial mistakes on the part of their daughters.

Of course, if a girl has set her heart on somebody whom they know to be an unprincipled scamp, her father and mother would be gravely to blame if they did not promptly take every possible step to prevent the marriage. But suppose the favored suitor is what they call 'a very deserving young man,' but needy, are they to prohibit the match in the face of the daughter's vehement inclination? Or a case may arise in which they know nothing against the character or the position of the suitor, but entertain a vague misgiving, an indistinct prejudice against him. May this be justly allowed to counterbalance the daughter's deliberate preference?

"There are a hundred shades of feeling between cordial approbation of a man for a son-in-law, and a repugnance which nothing can overcome; and it is impossible to draw the line at any one point, and say, 'Here the father is justified in withholding his consent.' In every case very much depends upon the character of the daughter herself. If she is naturally weak and wrong-headed, the exercise of parental authority can hardly be carried too far, in order to protect her. But if she has habitually displayed a sound judgment and a solid temper, the question how far a father will be wise in imposing his veto is one which there must be a good deal of practical difficulty in deciding."

ENGAGED.—"I am not sure that if you really love a person, and are quite confident about him, that having to look forward to being married is not the best part of all."

It is the friends who experience the inconvenience.

A closer intimacy is permitted to the engaged in this country than in most others. It is preceded by the introduction of the suitor to the lady's relatives, after which the lady is introduced to his family.

An "engaged" ring is generally given by the gentleman, and worn by the lady on the fourth finger, as it is called; that is, the finger next the little one on the *right* hand. After marriage it is transferred to the similar finger on the *left* hand, and becomes the guard or keeper of the wedding-ring.

There are many delicate ways in which the engaged lover may express his devotion besides giving costly presents. A few flowers, arranged to express attachment, or conveying a compliment, according to the language of flowers; the loan or gift of a volume of some favorite writer, with a page turned down at a suggestive passage, are attentions sure to be appreciated.

Speaking of both parties to the engagement, we may add that affected indifference is in bad taste; so is exclusiveness. Do not behave with too great freedom; and do not, on the other hand, sit apart, hand clasped in hand, or make displays of affection and fondness — either of which are out of place in society.

The lady may have money, in which case it is desirable that some legal control over it should be secured to her, that, in the event of trouble or difficulty, it cannot be touched by the husband, or his creditors, without the wife's consent. Among the middle and lower classes this kind of thing is not and cannot be insisted on. It is, however, becoming the custom for the betrothed to insure his life in favor of his intended, and this is a plan which cannot be too highly commended.

REFUSAL. — As a woman is not bound to accept an offer, so no sensible man will think the worse of her, or feel himself personally injured, by a refusal. That it will give him pain is most probable; if his heart does not suffer, his vanity will; but in time he will appreciate the fact that his feelings were not trifled with, but were met in an earnest, candid spirit.

Young ladies should remember that, charming and fascinating as they may be, the man who proposes pays them a high compliment — the highest in his power.

In refusing, the lady ought to convey her full sense of the honor intended

her, and to add, seriously, but not offensively, that it is not in accordance with her inclinations, or that circumstances compel her to give an unfavorable answer.

It is only a flirt who keeps an honorable man in suspense for the purpose of glorifying herself by his attentions in the eyes of friends. A lady will not boast of an offer received and rejected. Such an offer is a privileged communication. The secret of it should be held sacred.

The duty of the rejected suitor is clear. Etiquette demands that he shall accept the lady's decision, and retire from the field.

MARRIAGE. — June, July, and August are favorite months for weddings. Easter week is a very popular time. As a general rule, marriages are not celebrated during Lent. The approximate time is generally arranged by the young people, but the mother of the bride generally names the exact day.

WEDDING DRESS. — It is impossible to lay down specific rules for dress, as fashions change and tastes differ. The great art consists in selecting the style of dress most becoming to the person. A stout person should adopt a different style from a thin person; a tall one from a short one. Peculiarities of complexion, and form of face and figure, should be duly regarded; and in these matters there is no better course than to call in the aid of any respectable milliner and dressmaker, who will be found ready to give the best advice. The bridegroom should simply appear in full dress, and should avoid everything eccentric and broad in style. The bridesmaids should always be made aware of the bride's dress before they choose their own, which should be determined by a proper harmony with the former.

THE ORDER OF GOING TO CHURCH is as follows: — The BRIDE, accompanied by her *father*, not unfrequently her *mother*, and uniformly by a *bridesmaid*, occupies the *first carriage*. The father hands out the bride, and leads her to the church, the mother and the bridesmaid following. After them come the other bridesmaids, attended by the groomsmen, if there are more than one.

THE BRIDEGROOM occupies the *last* carriage with the principal groomsman — an intimate friend, or brother. He follows, and stands with *the bride at his left hand.* The father places himself behind, with the mother, if she attends.

THE CHIEF BRIDESMAID occupies a place on the *left* of the *bride,* to hold her gloves, and handkerchief, and flowers; her *companions* range themselves on *the left.*

FEES. — In determining the fee to be given to the officiating minister, no arbitrary rule can be given ; it ranges from five to one hundred dollars, perhaps ten dollars is the most usual fee. The standing of the minister and the circumstances of the bridegroom have a bearing on this point. Whatever the amount, it had better be given to a friend of the groom, who will present it in an envelope to the minister. This same friend should also pay the sexton for his preparation for and attendance at the ceremony. Although a gentleman should be liberal at this time, he ought not to tax himself above his means. In some rich families, where the officiating minister is an old friend, the marriage of a member of the family is made the occasion to make him a valuable present.

THE ORDER OF RETURN FROM CHURCH differs from the above only in the fact that the bride and bridegroom now ride together, the bride being on his left, and a bridesmaid and a groomsman, or the father of the bride, occupying the front seats of the carriage. On their return to the house a reception is generally held to give the friends of the families an opportunity to offer their congratulations. After this, when a wedding tour is intended, the happy pair generally take their departure.

CARDS. — A newly married couple send out cards immediately after the ceremony to their friends and acquain-

tances, who, on their part, return either notes or cards of congratulation on the event. As soon as the lady is settled in her new home, she may expect the calls of her acquaintance; for which it is not absolutely necessary to remain at home, although politeness requires that they should be returned as soon as possible. But, having performed this, any further intercourse may be avoided (where it is deemed necessary) by a polite refusal of invitations. Where cards are to be left, the number must be determined according to the various members of which the family called upon is composed. For instance, where there are the mother, aunt, and daughters (the latter having been introduced to society), three cards should be left. Recently, the custom of sending cards has been in a great measure discontinued, and instead of this, the words "No cards" are appended to the ordinary newspaper advertisement, and the announcement of the marriage, with this addition, is considered all-sufficient.

FUNERALS.—The management of funerals vary so much in different States and cities, that no general rule will apply. But it is safe to say that when death occurs, it is best at once to consult an undertaker. In the excited and troubled state of mind existing at that time, there is an unfitness, if not an inability, on the part of the relatives to attend to the many details, such as laying out, coffin, hearse, cemetery arrangements, minister, etc., etc. All these things just at that time are bewildering to those unused to them. But in the hands of the undertaker all goes well and orderly. It may be thought more expensive to place all in the care of an undertaker. Perhaps it *may* cost more, but who does not wish that these last sad rites should be performed in an orderly manner, and that the solemnities of the occasion may not be marred by confusion? But we are not sure that it *does* cost more. If your resources are limited, tell the undertaker so. He will be guided by what you tell him in this respect, and his experience will enable him to so arrange that there will be a uniform consistency in the whole.

We are glad to find that extravagance and show at funerals is fast giving way before the good sense of the people. Our best families everywhere are setting examples which it will be well to follow. The false pride and extravagance which runs a family into debt for a year, to pay for a showy funeral for one of its members, has received a check from the pulpits of many of our cities. Let us pay all the respect we can to our dead; but it must be in a manner proportionate to our means. For the poor man to half starve his living children to meet the needless expense of a fashionable funeral for the loved one who has died, is feeding the vanity of the living, rather than showing respect for the dead.

Terms used to Describe the Movements of Dances.

Balancez. — Set to partners.

Chaine Anglaise. — The top and bottom couples right and left.

Chaine Anglaise double. — The right and left double.

Chaine des Dames. — The ladies' chain.

Chaine des Dames double. — The ladies' chain double, which is performed by all the ladies commencing at the same time.

Chassez.—Move to the right and left.

Chassez croisez. — Gentlemen change places with partners, and back again.

Demie Chaine Anglaise. — The four opposite persons half right and left.

Demi Promenade. — All eight half promenade.

Dos-à-dos. — The two opposite persons pass round each other.

Demi Moulinet. — The ladies all advance to the centre, giving hands, and return to places.

La Grande Chaine. — All eight chassez quite round, giving alternately right and left hands to partners, beginning with the right.

Le Grande Rond. — All join hands and advance and retire twice.

Pas d'Allemande. — The gentlemen turn the partners under their arms.

Traversez. — The two opposite persons change places.

Vis-à-vis. — The opposite partner.

QUADRILLES. — THE FIRST SET. — *First Figure, Le Pantalon.* — Right and left. Balancez to partners; turn partners. Ladies' chain. Half promenade; half right and left. (Four times.) — *Second Figure, L'Eté.* Leading lady and opposite gentleman advance and retire; chassez to right and left; cross over to each other's places; chassez to right and left. Balancez and turn partners. (Four times.) *Or Double L'Eté.* — Both couples advance and retire at the same time; cross over; advance and retire again; cross to places. Balancez and turn partners. (Four times.) *Third Figure, La Poule.* — Leading lady and opposite gentleman cross over, giving right hands; recross, giving left hands, and fall in a line. Set four in a line; half promenade. Advance two, and retire (twice). Advance four, and retire; half right and left. (Four times.) *Fourth Figure, La Pastorale.* — The leading couple advance twice, leaving the lady opposite the second time. The three advance and retire twice. The leading gentleman advance and set. Hands four half round; half right and left. (Four times.) *Fifth Figure, Galop Finale.* — Top and bottom couples galopade quite round each other. Advance and retire; four advance again, and change the gentlemen. Ladies' chain. Advance and retire four, and regain your partners in your places. The fourth time all galopade for an unlimited period. (Four times.) *Or,* All galopade or promenade, eight bars. Advance four *en galop oblique,* and retire, then half promenade, eight bars. Advance four, retire, and return to places with the half promenade, eight bars. Ladies' chain, eight bars. Repeated by the side couples, then by the top and bot-

22

om, and lastly by the side couples, finishing with grand promenade. LANCERS.—1. *La Rose.*—First gentleman and opposite lady advance and set—turn with both hands, retiring to places—return, leading outside—set and turn at corners. 2. *La Lodoiska.*—First couple advance twice, leaving the lady in the centre—set in the centre—turn to places—all advance to two lines—all turn partners. 3. *La Dorset.*—First lady advance and stop, then the opposite gentleman—both retire, turning around—ladies' hands across half round, and turn the opposite gentlemen with left hands—repeat back to places, and turn partners with left hands. 4. *L'Etoile.*—First couple set to couple at right—set to couple at left—change places with partners, and set, and pirouette to places—right and left with opposite couple. 5. *Les Lanciers.*—The grand chain. The first couple advance and turn facing the top; then the couple at right advance behind the top couple; then the couple at left, and the opposite couple do the same, forming two lines. All change places with partners and back again. The ladies turn in a line on the right, the gentlemen in a line on the left. Each couple meet up the centre. Set in two lines, the ladies in one line, the gentlemen in the other. Turn partners to places. Finish with the grand chain.

THE CALEDONIANS. — *First Figure.* — The first and opposite couples hands across round the centre, and back to places—set and turn partners. Ladies chain. Half promenade—half right and left. Repeated by the side couples. *Second Figure.* — The first gentleman advance and retire twice. All set at corners, each lady passing into the next lady's place on the right. Promenade by all. Repeated by the other couples. *Third Figure.*—The first lady and opposite gentleman advance and retire, bending to each other. First lady and opposite gentleman pass round each other to places. First couple cross over, having hold of hands, while the opposite couple cross on the

outside of them—the same reversed. All set at corners, turn, and resume partners. All advance and retire twice, in a circle with hands joined—turn partners. *Fourth Figure.*—The first lady and opposite gentleman advance and stop; then their partners advance; turn partners to places. The four ladies move to right, each taking the next lady's place, and stop—the four gentlemen move to left, each taking the next gentleman's place, and stop—the ladies repeat the same to the right—then the gentlemen to the left. All join hands and promenade round to places, and turn partners. Repeated by the other couples. *Fifth Figure.*—The first couple promenade or waltz round inside the figure. The four ladies advance, join hands round, and retire—then the gentlemen perform the same—all set and turn partners. Chain figure of eight half round, and set. All promenade to places and turn partners. All change sides, join right hands at corners, and set—back again to places. Finish with grand promenade. — These three are the most admired of the quadrilles: the First Set invariably takes precedence of every other dance.

SPANISH DANCE. — Danced in a circle or a line by sixteen or twenty couples. The couples stand as for a Country Dance, except that the first gentleman must stand on the ladies' side, and the first lady on the gentlemen's side. First gentleman and second lady balancez to each other, while first lady and second gentleman do the same, and change places. First gentleman and partner balancez, while second gentleman and partner do the same, and change places. First gentleman and second lady balancez, while first lady and second gentleman do the same, and change places. First gentleman and second lady balancez to partners, and change places with them. All four join hands in the centre, and then change places, in the same order as the foregoing figure, four times. All four poussette, leaving the second lady and gentleman at the top, the same as in a Country Dance. The first lady and gentleman then go through the same figure with the third lady and gentleman, and so proceed to the end of the dance. This figure is sometimes danced in eight-bars time, which not only hurries and inconveniences the dancers, but also ill accords with the music.

WALTZ COTILLON. — Places the same as quadrille. First couple waltz round inside ; first and second ladies advance twice and cross over, turning twice ; first and second gentlemen do the same ; third and fourth couples the same ; first and second couples waltz to places, third and fourth do the same ; all waltz to partners, and turn half round with both hands, meeting the next lady ; perform this figure until in your places ; form two side lines, all advance twice and cross over, turning twice ; the same, returning ; all waltz round ; the whole repeated four times.

LA GALOPADE is an extremely graceful and spirited dance, in a continual chassez. An unlimited number may join. It is danced in couples, as waltzing.

THE GALOPADE QUADRILLES. — 1st, Galopade. 2d, Right and left, sides the same. 3d, Set and turn hands all eight. 4th, Galopade. 5th, Ladies' chain, sides the same. 6th, Set and turn partners all eight. 7th, Galopade. 8th, Tirois, sides the same. 9th, Set and turn partners all eight. 10th, Galopade. 11th, Top lady and bottom gentleman advance and retire, the other six do the same. 12th, Set and turn partners all eight. 13th, Galopade. 14th, Four ladies advance and retire, gentlemen the same. 15th, Double ladies' chain. 16th, Set and urn partners all eight. 17th, Galopade. :8th, Poussette, sides the same. 19th, Set and turn. 20th, Galopade waltz.

THE MAZURKA. — This dance is of Polish origin — first introduced into England by the Duke of Devonshire, on his return from Russia. It consists of twelve movements ; and the first eight bars are played (as in quadrilles) before the first movement commences.

THE REDOWA WALTZ is composed of three parts, distinct from each other

1st, The pursuit. 2d, The waltz called Redowa. 3d, The waltz à Deux Temps, executed to a peculiar measure, and which, by a change of the rhythm, assumes a new character. The middle of the floor must be reserved for the dancers who execute the promenade, called the pursuit, while those who dance the waltz turn in a circle about the room. The position of the gentleman is the same as for the waltz. The gentleman sets out with the left foot, and the lady with the right. In the pursuit the position is different, the gentleman and his partner face, and take each other by the hand. They advance or fall back at pleasure, and balance in advance and backwards. To advance, the step of the pursuit is made by a glissade forward, without springing, *coupé* with the hind foot, and *jeté* on it. You recommence with the other foot, and so on throughout. The retiring step is made by a sliding step of the foot backwards, without spring, *jeté* with the front foot, and *coupé* with the one behind. It is necessary to advance well upon the sliding step, and to spring lightly in the two others, *sur place*, balancing equally in the *pas de poursuite*, which is executed alternately by the left in advance, and the right backwards. The lady should follow all the movements of her partner, falling back when he advances, and advancing when he falls back. Bring the shoulders a little forward at each sliding step, for they should always follow the movement of the leg as it advances or retreats ; but this should not be too marked. When the gentleman is about to waltz, he should take the lady's waist, as in the ordinary waltz. The step of the Redowa, in turning, may be thus described : For the gentleman — *jeté* of the left foot, passing before the lady. *Glissade* of the right foot behind to the fourth position aside — the left foot is brought to the third position behind — then the *pas de basque* is executed by the right foot, bringing it forward, and you recommence with the left. The *pas de basque* should be made in three very equal beats, as in the Mazurka. The lady performs the same steps as the gentleman, beginning by the *pas de basque* with the right foot. To waltz à deux temps to the measure of the Redowa, we should make each step upon each beat of the bar, and find ourselves at every two bars, the gentleman with his left foot forwards, and the lady with her right, that is to say, we should make one whole and one half step to every bar. The music is rather slower than for the ordinary waltz.

VALSE CELLARIUS. — The gentleman takes the lady's left hand with his right, moving one bar to the left by *glissade*, and two hops on his left foot, while the lady does the same to the right, on her right foot; at the second bar they repeat the same with the other foot — this is repeated for sixteen bars; they then waltz sixteen bars, *glissade* and two hops, taking care to occupy the time of two bars to get quite round. The gentleman now takes both hands of the lady, and makes the grand square — moving three bars to his left — at the fourth bar making two beats while turning the angle ; his right foot is now moved forward to the other angle three bars — at the fourth, beat again while turning the angle ; the same repeated for sixteen bars — the lady having her right foot forward when the gentleman has his left foot forward ; the waltz is again repeated ; after which several other steps are introduced, but which must needs be seen to be understood.

CIRCULAR WALTZ. — The dancers form a circle, then promenade during the introduction — all waltz sixteen bars — set, holding partner's right hand, and turn—waltz thirty-two bars — rest, and turn partners slowly — face partner and chassez to the right and left — pirouette lady twice with the right hand, all waltz sixteen bars — set and turn — all form a circle, still retaining the lady by the right hand, and move round to the left, sixteen bars — waltz for finale.

POLKA WALTZES. — The couples take hold of hands as in the usual waltz. *First Waltz*. The gentleman hops the left foot well forward, then back, and *glissades* half round. He then hops the right foot forward, and back, and *glissades* the other half round. The lady performs the same steps, beginning with the right foot. *Second*. The gentleman, hopping, strikes the left heel three times against the right heel, and then jumps half round on the left foot ; he then strikes the right heel three times against the left, and jumps on the right foot, completing the circle. The lady does the same steps with reverse feet. *Third*. The gentleman raises up the left foot, steps it lightly on the ground forward, then strikes the left heel smartly twice, and *glissades* half round. The same is then done with the other foot. The lady begins with the right foot.

VALSE À DEUX TEMPS. — This waltz contains, like the common waltz, three times, but differently divided. The first time consists of a gliding step ; the second a chassez, including two times in one. A chassez is performed by bringing one leg near the other, then moving it forward, backward, right, left, and round. The gentleman begins by sliding to the left with his left foot, then performing a chassez towards the left with his right foot without turning at all during the first two times. He then slides backwards with his right leg, turning half round ; after which he puts his left leg behind to perform a chassez forward, turning then half round for the second time. The lady waltzes in the same manner, except that the first time she slides to the right with the right foot, and also performs the chassez on the right, and continues the same as the gentleman, except that she slides backwards with her right foot when the gentleman slides with his left foot to the left ; and when the gentleman slides with his right foot backwards, she slides with the left foot to the left. To perform this waltz gracefully, care must be taken to avoid jumping, but merely to slide, and keep the knees slightly bent.

CIRCASSIAN CIRCLE. — The company is arranged in couples round the room — the ladies being placed on the right of the gentlemen,— after which, the first and second couples lead off the dance. *Figure.* Right and left, set and turn partners — ladies chain, waltz. At the conclusion, the first couple with fourth, and the second with the third couple, recommence the figure,— and so on until they go completely round the circle, when the dance is concluded.

POLKA. — In the polka there are but two principal steps, all others belong to fancy dances, and much mischief and inconvenience is likely to arise from their improper introduction into the ball-room. *First step.* The gentleman raises the left foot slightly behind the right, the right foot is then jumped upon, and the left brought forward with a glissade. The lady commences with the right, jumps on the left, and glissades with the right. The gentleman during his step has hold of the lady's left hand with his right. *Second step.* The gentleman lightly hops the left foot forward on the heel, then hops on the toe, bringing the left foot slightly behind the right. He then glissades with the left foot forward ; the same is then done, commencing with the right foot. The lady dances the same step, only beginning with the right foot. There are a variety of other steps of a fancy character, but they can only be understood with the aid of a master, and even when well studied, must be introduced with care. The polka should be danced with grace and elegance, eschewing all *outré* and ungainly steps and gestures, taking care that the leg is not lifted too high, and that the dance is not commenced in too abrupt a manner. Any number of couples may stand up, and it is the privilege of the gentleman to form what figure he pleases, and vary it as often as his fancy and taste may dictate. *First figure.* Four or eight bars are devoted to setting forwards and backwards, turning from and towards your partner, making a slight hop at the commencement of each set, and holding your partner's left hand ; you then perform the same step (forwards) all round the room. *Second figure.* The gentleman faces his partner, and does the same step backwards all round the room, the lady following with the opposite foot, and doing the step forwards. *Third figure.* The same as the second figure, only reversed, the lady stepping backwards, and the gentleman forwards, always going the same way round the room. *Fourth figure.* The same step as figures two and three, but turning as in a waltz.

THE GORLITZA is similar to the polka, the figures being waltzed through.

THE SCHOTTISCHE.—The gentleman holds the lady precisely as in the polka. Beginning with the left foot, he slides it forward, then brings up the right foot to the place of the left, slides the left foot forward, and springs or hops on this foot. This movement is repeated to the right. He begins with the right foot, slides it forward, brings up the left foot to the place of the right foot, slides the right foot forward again, and hops upon it. The gentleman springs twice on the left foot, turning half round ; twice on the right foot ; twice *encore* on the left foot, turning half round ; and again twice on the right foot, turning half round. Beginning again, he proceeds as before. The lady begins with the right foot, and her step is the same in principle as the gentleman's. Vary, by a *reverse turn ;* or by going in a straight line round the room. Double, if you like, each part, by giving four bars to the first part, and four bars to the second part. The *time* may be stated as precisely the same as in the polka ; but let it not be forgotten that *La Schottische* ought to be danced *much slower.*

COUNTRY DANCES. — *Sir Roger de Coverley.* — First lady and bottom gentleman advance to centre, salute, and retire; first gentleman and bottom lady, same. First lady and bottom gentleman advance to centre, turn, and retire ; first gentleman and bottom lady the same. Ladies promenade, turning off to the right down the room, and back to places, while gentlemen do the same, turning to the left; top couple remain at bottom; repeat to the end of dance.

LA POLKA COUNTRY DANCES.—All form two lines, ladies on the right, gentlemen on the left. *Figure:* Top lady and second gentleman heel and toe (polka step) across to each other's place—second lady and top gentleman the same. Top lady and second gentleman retire back to places — second lady and top gentleman the same. Two couples polka step down the middle and back again — two first couples polka waltz. First couple repeat with the third couple, then with fourth, and so on to the end of dance.

THE HIGHLAND REEL.—This dance is performed by the company arranged in parties of three, along the room, in the following manner: a lady between two gentlemen, in double rows. All advance and retire — each lady then performs the reel with the gentleman on her right hand, and retires with the opposite gentleman to places — hands three round and back again — all six advance and retire—then lead through to the next trio, and continue the figure to the end of the room. Adopt the Highland step, and music of three-part tune.

Language of Flowers.

Flowers.	Sentiment.
Amaranth	Immortality.
Anemone	Frailty.
Aster	Beauty in retirement.
Acacia	Platonic love.
Apple-blossom	Fame speaks you great and good.
Ash	Grandeur.
Alyssum	Worth beyond Beauty.
Bachelor's Button	Hope in Misery.
Balm	Sweets of social intercourse.
Balm of Gilead	I am cured.
Balsam	Impatience.
Barbary	Petulance.
Bay Leaf	I change but in dying.
Birch	Gracefulness.
Bindweed	Humility.
Blue Bell	Constancy.
Box	Stoicism.
Broome	Neatness.
Burdock	Importunity
Calla	Feminine modesty.
Chamomile	Energy in adversity.
Candytuft	Indifference.
Cardinal Flower	Distinction.

Flowers.	Sentiment.
Carnation	Pride.
Catchfly	A snare.
Cedar Tree	Spiritual strength.
Cherry-blossom	Spiritual beauty.
China Aster	Your sentiments meet with a return.
Chrysanthemum	A heart left to desolation.
Cinquefoil	Love, constant but hopeless.
Clematis	Mental excellence.
Columbine	I cannot give thee up.
Corn	Riches.
Cowslip	Native grace.
Coreopsis	Always cheerful.
Coriander	Concealed merit.
Cypress	Disappointed hopes.
Dahlia	Elegance and dignity.
Daisy	Beauty and innocence.
Dandelion	Coquetry.
Dew-plant	Serenade.
Elder	Compassion.
Eglantine	Poetry.
Everlasting	Always remembered.
Evergreen	Poverty and worth.
Fir	Time.
Flowering Reed	Confidence in heaven.
Forget-me-not	True love.
Foxglove	I am not ambitious for myself but for you.
Fuchsia	Humble love.
Gentian	Virgin pride.
Geranium, Rose	Preference.
" Scarlet	Thou art changed.
" Oak	True friendship.
" Lemon	Tranquillity of mind.
" Silver-leaved	Recall.
Gilly Flower	Lasting beauty.
Golden Rod	Encouragement.
Grape	Charity.
Grass	Submission.
Hawthorn	Hope.
Hazel	Reconciliation.
Heliotrope	Devotion.
Hibiscus	Beauty is vain.
Hollyhock	Ambition.
Honeysuckle	Fidelity.
Hop	Injustice.
Houstonia	Quiet happiness.
Hydrangia	Heartlessness.
Ice Plant	Your looks freeze me.
Iris	A message.
Ivy	I have found one true heart
Jasmine	Amiability.
Jonquil	Affection returned.
King-cup	I wish I was rich.
Laburnum	Pensive beauty.
Lady's Slipper	Capricious beauty.
Larkspur	Inconstancy.
Laurel	Virtue is true beauty.
Lavender	Acknowledgment.
Lemon	Discretion.
Lettuce	Cold-hearted.
Lilac	First emotion of love.
Lily	Purity.
Lily of the Valley	Heart withering in secret.
Locust	Affection beyond the grave.
Lupine	Dejection.
London Pride	Frivolity.
Mallows	Sweet disposition.
Maple	Reserve.
Marygold	Contempt.
Mignonette	Moral beauty.
Mimosa	Sensitiveness.
Moss	Maternal love.
Myrtle	Love in absence.
Nasturtion	Patriotism.

Flowers.	Sentiment.
Nightshade	Dark thought.
Oak	Hospitality.
Oleander	Beware.
Orange Flowers	Woman's worth.
Pansy	Tender and pleasant thoughts.
Passion Flower	Religious fervor.
Pea, Everlasting	Wilt thou go?
Pea, Sweet	Departure.
Peach-blossom	I am your captive.
Petunia	Thou art less proud than they deem thee.
Peony	Ostentation.
Phlox	Our souls are united.
Pine	Time and faith.
Pink, White	Lovely and pure affection.
Pink, Red	Woman's love.
Polyanthus	Confidence.
Potato	Beneficence.
Poppy	Forgetfulness.
Primrose	Modest worth.
Primrose, Evening	I am more faithful than thou.
Rose-bud	Confession of love.
Rose, Bridal	Happy love.
Rose, Burgundy	Simplicity and beauty.
Rose, Damask	Bashful love.
Rose, Moss	Superior merit.
Rose, Multiflora	Grace.
Rose, White	Too young to love.
Rose, Red-leaved	Diffidence.
Sage	Domestic virtues.
Snapdragon	Dazzling, but dangerous.
Snowball	Thoughts of heaven.
Snowdrop	I am not a summer friend.
Star of Bethlehem	Let us follow Jesus.
Strawberry	Perfect excellence.
Sumach	Splendid misery.
Sunflower	Smile on me still.
Sweet William	Gallantry.
Syringa	Memory.
Thistle	Never forget.
Tulip	Beautiful eyes.
Verbena	Sensibility.
Violet	Faithfulness.
Vernal Grass	Poor, but happy.
Wallflower	Fidelity in misfortune.
Water Lily	Eloquence.
Willow	Forsaken.
Witch Hazel	A spell.
Woodbine	Fraternal love.
Yarrow	A cure for the heartache.
Zinnia	I mourn your absence.

To Soften the Skin and Improve the Complexion.

If flowers of sulphur be mixed in a little milk, and, after standing an hour or two, the milk (without disturbing the sulphur) be rubbed into the skin, it will keep it soft, and make the complexion clear. It is to be used before washing. A lady of our acquaintance, being exceedingly anxious about her complexion, adopted the above suggestion. In about a fortnight she wrote to us to say that the mixture became so disagreeable after it had been made a few days, that she could not use it. We should have wondered if she could — the milk became putrid! A little of the mixture should have been prepared over night with evening milk, and used the next morning, but not afterwards. About a wine-glassful made for each occasion would suffice.

EYELASHES.—The mode adopted by the beauties of the East to increase the length and strength of their eyelashes, is simply to clip the split ends with a pair of scissors about once a month. Mothers perform the operation on their children, both male and female, when they are mere infants, watching the opportunity while they sleep. The practice never fails to produce the desired effect. We recommend it to the attention of our fair readers, as a safe and innocent means of enhancing the charms which so many of them, no doubt, already possess.

The Teeth.—Dissolve two ounces of borax in three pints of water; before quite cold, add thereto one teaspoonful of tincture of myrrh, and one tablespoonful of spirits of camphor: bottle the mixture for use. One wine-glassful of the solution, added to half a pint of tepid water, is sufficient for each application. This solution, applied daily, preserves and beautifies the teeth, extirpates tartarous adhesion, produces a pearl-like whiteness, arrests decay, and induces a healthy action in the gums.

Our Teeth.—They decay. Hence unseemly mouths, bad breath, imperfect mastication. Everybody regrets it. What is the cause? I reply, want of cleanliness. A clean tooth never decays. The mouth is a warm place — 98°. Particles of meat between the teeth soon decompose. Gums and teeth must suffer. Perfect cleanliness will preserve the teeth to old age. How shall it be secured? Use a quill pick, and rinse the mouth after eating. Brush and castile soap every morning; the brush and simple water on going to bed. Bestow this trifling care upon your precious teeth, and you will keep them and ruin the dentists. Neglect, it, and you will be sorry all your lives. Children forget. Watch them. The first teeth determine the character of the second set. Give them equal care. Sugar, acids, saleratus, and hot things, are nothing when compared with food decomposing between the teeth. Mercurialization may loosen the teeth, long use may wear them out, but keep them clean and they will never decay. This advice is worth more than thousands of dollars to every boy and girl.

Camphorated Dentifrice. — Prepared chalk, one pound; camphor, one or two drams. The camphor must be finely powdered by moistening it with a little spirit of wine, and then intimately mixing it with chalk.

Myrrh Dentifrice. — Powdered cuttlefish, one pound; powdered myrrh, two ounces.

American Tooth Powder. — Coral, cuttlefish bone, dragon's blood, of each eight drams; burnt alum and red sanders, of each four drams; orris root, eight drams; cloves and cinnamon, of each half a dram; vanilla, eleven grains; rosewood, half a dram; rose pink, eight drams. All to be finely powdered and mixed.

Quinine Tooth Powder. — Rose pink, two drams; precipitated chalk, twelve drams; carbonate of magnesia, one dram; quinine (sulphate), six grains. All to be well mixed together.

THE chlorate of potash has now come into extensive use for the removal of fetid breath. It is chiefly used, diluted with water and alcohol, to rinse the mouth. It may be made by condensing chlorine gas in a solution of potash. A solution of soda will answer nearly as well.

Hair Dye, USUALLY STYLED COLOMBIAN, ARGENTINE, ETC., ETC. — Solution No. 1, Hydrosulphuret of ammonia, one ounce; solution of potash, three drams; distilled or rain water, one ounce (all by measure). Mix and put into small bottles, labelling it No. 1.—Solution No. 2. Nitrate of silver, one dram; distilled or rain

water, two ounces. Dissolved and labelled No. 2.

Directions How to Apply.—The solution No. 1 is first applied to the hair with a tooth-brush, and the application continued for fifteen or twenty minutes. The solution No. 2 is then brushed over, a comb being used to separate the hairs, and allow the liquid to come in contact with every part. Care must be taken that the liquid does not touch the skin, as the solution No. 2 produces a permanent dark stain on all substances with which it comes in contact. If the shade is not sufficiently deep, the operation may be repeated. The hair should be cleansed from grease before using the dye.

To TEST HAIR DYE. — To try the effect of hair dye upon hair of any color, cut off a lock and apply the dye thoroughly as directed above. This will be a guarantee of success, or will at least guard against failure.

THE PROPER APPLICATION OF HAIR DYES. — The efficacy of hair dyes depends as much upon their proper application as upon their chemical composition. If not evenly and patiently applied, they give rise to a mottled and dirty condition of the hair. A lady, for instance, attempted to use the lime and litharge dye, and was horrified on the following morning to find her hair spotted red and black, almost like the skin of a leopard. She wrote to us in great excitement and implored our aid. But what could we do? The mixture had not been properly applied. Our own hair is becoming gray, and we don't mind telling the reader what we intend to do: we have resolved to let it remain so, and bear " our gray hairs to the grave," deeming them to be no dishonor.

Compounds to Promote the Growth of Hair. — When the hair falls off, from diminished action of the scalp, preparations of cantharides often prove useful; they are sold under the names of Depuytren's Pomade, Cazenaze's Pomade, etc. The following directions are as good as any of the more complicated recipes:

POMADE AGAINST BALDNESS.—Beef marrow, soaked in several waters, melted and strained, half a pound; tincture of cantharides (made by soaking for a week one dram of powdered cantharides in one ounce of proof-spirit), one ounce; oil of bergamot, twelve drops.

ERASMUS WILSON'S LOTION AGAINST BALDNESS.—Eau-de-Cologne, two ounces; tincture of cantharides, two drams; oil of lavender or rosemary, of either ten drops. These applications must be used once or twice a day for a considerable time; but if the scalp become sore, they must be discontinued for a time, or used at longer intervals.

Glycerine Cream.—This superior cosmetic is the well-known cold cream, with glycerine substituted for rose water. Melt together three ounces spermaceti, and half an ounce white wax, in half a pint of sweet almond-oil. Then remove from the fire, and stir in two ounces of glycerine; and when congealing, perfume with ten drops of attar of roses, or other attar that may be chosen.

Pomade Rosat.—*For the lips.*—Melt together one ounce of white wax, two ounces oil of sweet almonds, and one and a half drams alkanet. Digest for several hours, strain, and add six drops attar of roses.

Macassar Oil.—One quart oil of ben, one pint oil of noisette, half pint strong alcohol, half dram attar of roses, six drams attar of bergamot, five drams attar of Portugal, and six drams tincture of musk. Mix together, digest, with alkanet root (for color), in a stoppered bottle for a week, then strain and bottle.

Marfit's Hair Tonic.—Scald one ounce of black tea with two quarts of boiling water; strain, and add one and a half ounces glycerine, quarter of an ounce tincture of cantharides, and one pint of bay rum. Mix well by shaking, and then perfume.

Shampoo Liquor.—This excellent wash for the hair is made by dissolving a quarter ounce carbonate of ammonia, and half an ounce of borax, in one pint of water, and adding thereto one ounce of glycerine, three pints New England rum, and one pint of bay rum. The hair having been moistened with this liquor, it is to be shampooed with the hands, until a slight lather is formed; and the latter, being washed out with clean water, leaves the head clean, and the hair moist and glossy.

Camphorated Chalk.— *Tooth Powder.*—A quarter pound prepared chalk, one pound powdered orris root, one ounce powered camphor. Reduce the camphor to fine powder by triturating it in a mortar with a little alcohol; then add the other ingredients, and when the mixture is complete, sift through the finest sifting cloth.

Violet Mouth-Wash.—Tincture of orris, essence of rose, and alcohol, each four ounces, attar of almonds, three drops; mix.

Violet Powder.—Three pounds wheat starch, half pound powdered orris; mix together, and add one dram attar of lemon, and half ounce each of attar of bergamot and cloves.

Pearl Powder.—Prepared chalk, finely bolted-and perfumed. The French add oxides of zinc and bismuth, each one ounce to the pound of chalk.

Carmine Rouge.—One ounce finely bolted talc (French chalk), half dram carmine; mix together with a little warm, thin solution of gum tragacanth. For lighter shades, the proportion of carmine must be increased. For commoner pastes, rose pink replaces the carmine as coloring matter. It may be made into a pomade.

Bloom of Roses.—Half a dram best carmine, digested with one ounce of strong ammonia, in a tightly-stoppered bottle, for two days, at the ordinary temperature of the atmosphere; then add a quarter pint of rose water, and one ounce essence of rose. After a week's repose, the upper stratum of clear liquid may be decanted and bottled.

Bandoline, or Fixature.—Several preparations are used; the following are the best:—1. Mucilage of clean picked Irish moss, made by boiling a quarter of an ounce of the moss in one quart of water until sufficiently thick, rectified spirit in the proportion of a teaspoonful to each bottle, to prevent its being mildewed. The quantity of spirit varies according to the time it requires to be kept.—2. Gum tragacanth, one dram and a half; water, half a pint; proof-spirit (made by mixing equal parts of rectified spirit and water), three ounces; attar of roses, ten drops; soak for twenty-four hours and strain.

Excellent Hair Wash.—Take one ounce of borax, half an ounce of camphor; powder these ingredients fine, and dissolve them in one quart of boiling water; when cool, the solution will be ready for use; damp the hair frequently. This wash effectually cleanses, beautifies, and strengthens the hair, preserves the color, and prevents early baldness. The camphor will form into lumps after being dissolved, but the water will be sufficiently impregnated.

Hair Oils.—ROSE OIL.—Olive oil, one pint; attar of roses, five to sixteen drops. Essence of bergamot, being much cheaper, is commonly used instead of the more expensive attar of roses.

RED ROSE OIL.—The same. The oil colored before scenting, by steeping in it one dram of alkanet root, with a gentle heat, until the desired tint is produced.

OIL OF ROSES.—Olive oil, two pints; attar of roses, one dram; oil of rosemary, one dram: mix. It may be colored red by steeping a little alkanet root in the oil (with heat) before scenting it.

POMATUMS.—For making pomatums, the lard, fat, suet, or marrow used must be carefully prepared by being melted with as gentle a heat as possible, skimmed, strained, and cleared from the dregs which are deposited on standing.

COMMON POMATUM.—Mutton suet, prepared as above, one pound; lard, three pounds; carefully melted together, and stirred constantly as it cools, two ounces of bergamot being added.

HARD POMATUM.—Lard and mutton suet carefully prepared, of each one pound; white wax, four ounces: essence of bergamot, one ounce.

Castor Oil Pomade.—Castor oil, four ounces; prepared lard, two ounces; white wax, two drams; bergamot, two drams; oil of lavender, twenty drops. Melt the fat together, and on cooling add the scents, and stir till cold.

Hair Curling Liquid.—Take borax, two ounces; gum arabic, one dram; add hot water (not boiling), one quart; stir, and as soon as the ingredients are dissolved, add three tablespoonfuls of strong spirits of camphor. On retiring to rest wet the hair with the above liquid, and roll it in twists of paper, as usual.

Superfluous Hair.—Any remedy is doubtful; many of those commonly used are dangerous. The safest plan is as follows: The hairs should be perseveringly plucked up by the roots, and the skin, having been washed twice a day with warm soft water, without soap, should be treated with the following wash, commonly called MILK OF ROSES: Beat four ounces of sweet almonds in a mortar, and add half an ounce of white sugar during the process; reduce the whole to a paste by pounding; then add, in small quantities at a time, eight ounces of rose water. The emulsion thus formed should be strained through a fine cloth, and the residue again pounded, while the strained fluid should be bottled in a large stoppered vial. To the pasty mass in the mortar add half an ounce of sugar, and eight ounces of rose water, and strain again. This process must be repeated three times. To the thirty-two ounces of fluid, add twenty grains of the bichloride of mercury, dissolved in two ounces of alcohol, and shake the mixture for five minutes. The fluid should be applied with a towel, immediately after washing, and the skin gently rubbed with a dry cloth till *perfectly* dry. Wilson, in his work on *Healthy Skin*, writes as follows: "Substances are sold by the perfumers called depilatories, which are represented as having the power of removing hair. But the hair is not destroyed by these means—the root and that part of the shaft implanted within the skin still remain, and are ready to shoot up with increased vigor as soon as the depilatory is withdrawn. The effect of the depilatory is the same, in this respect, as that of a razor, and the latter is, unquestionably, the better remedy. It must not, however, be imagined that depilatories are negative remedies, and that, if they do no permanent good, they are, at least, harmless; that is not the fact; they are violent irritants, and require to be used with the utmost caution. After all, the safest depilatory is a pair of tweezers, and patience."

To Clean Hair Brushes. —As hot water and soap very soon soften the hair, and rubbing completes its destruction, use soda, dissolved in cold water, instead; soda having an affinity for grease, it cleans the brush with little friction. Do not set them near the fire, nor in the sun, to dry, but after shaking them well, set them on the point of the handle in a shady place; or wash them in a mixture of one part hartshorn and two parts water; this will clean them well and stiffen the bristles.

How to Take Care of your Hat. — 1. Should you get caught in a shower, always remember to brush your hat well while wet. When dry, brush the glaze out, and gently iron it over with a smooth flat iron. 2. If your hat is VERY wet, or stained with *sea* water, get a basin of clean cold water, and a good stiff brush; wash it well all over, but be careful to keep the nap straight; brush it as dry as you can, then put it on a peg to dry. When dry, brush the glaze out, and gently iron it over as above. 3. Should you get a spot of grease on your hat, just drop one drop of benzine on the place, and then rub it briskly with a piece of cloth until out. 4. Should you be travelling, always tie your hat up in your handkerchief before putting it into your case; this will save it from get-

ting rubbed or damaged through the friction of the rail or steamboat. 5. Never put your hat flat on the brim, as it will spoil its shape; but always hang it up on a peg. 6. Never put your hat, wet or dry, in front of the fire, as it will soften it, and throw it all out of shape. 7. Before putting your hat down, be careful to see if the place is free from spots of grease, beer, sugar, etc., as these things often spoil a good hat more than a twelvemonths' wear, and are often very difficult to remove. These simple rules will save a good hat for a very long time.

The Management of the Finger-Nails. — The correct management of the nails is to cut them of an oval shape, corresponding with the shape of the fingers. Never allow them to grow too long, as it makes it difficult to keep them clean; nor too short, as it causes the tips of the fingers to become flattened, and enlarged, and turn upwards, which gives the hand an awkward appearance. The skin which grows in a semicircle on the top of the nail requires much attention, as it is often drawn on with its growth, dragging the skin below the nail so tight as to cause it to divide into what are termed agnails. This is to be prevented by separating the skin from the nail by a blunt half-circular instrument. Many persons cut this pellicle, which causes it to grow very thick and uneven, and sometimes damages the growth of the nail. It is also injurious to prick under the nail with a pin, or penknife, or point of the scissors. The nails should be scrubbed with a brush not too hard, and the semicircular flesh pressed back with the towel without touching the quick. This method, if pursued daily, will keep the nails in proper order. When the nails are badly formed or ill-shaped, the ridges or fibres should be scraped and rubbed with a lemon, and well dried afterwards; but if the nails are very thin, the above remedy will not do them any good, but might cause them to split.

The Hands. — Take a wineglassful

of eau-de-Cologne, and another of lemon-juice; then scrape two cakes of brown Windsor soap to a powder, and mix well in a mould. When hard, it will be an excellent soap for whitening the hands.

To Whiten the Nails.—Diluted sulphuric acid, two drams; tincture of myrrh, one dram; spring water, four ounces: mix. First cleanse with white soap, and then dip the fingers into the mixture. A delicate hand is one of the chief points of beauty; and these applications are really effective.

STAINS may be removed from the hands by washing them in a small quantity of oil of vitriol and cold water without soap.

To Preserve the Hands Dry for Delicate Work.—Take club moss (lycopodium) in fine powder and rub a little over the hands.

Feet Wash.—The feet of some persons naturally evolve a disagreeable odor. Wash them in warm water, to which a little hydrochloric acid or chloride of lime has been added.

GARTERS, by the pressure which they exert, retard the passage of the arterial blood to the feet and prevent its return, giving rise to cold feet and congestion of the head or some internal organ. They frequently occasion enlargement of the veins. Garters should be abolished. The stockings can be attached to the drawers, or kept in place by various other methods. Tight boots and shoes are another almost universal mode of applying pressure, resulting in deformed feet, corns, bunions, etc. It also prevents the circulation of the blood, and is another cause of cold feet. Shoes should be made to fit the feet, and not the feet made to fit the fashionable shape of the shoe, and should be large enough to allow the free circulation of the blood.

Woollen Wristlets.—A pair of warm wool wristlets is about equal to an additional garment for keeping the whole body warm. The blood which the heart pumps into the arteries with each beat comes very near the surface

wherever you can feel the pulse beating, as at the wrists. Keep these warm and the whole circulation is favorably affected.

Blistered Hands and Feet.—As a remedy against blistering of hands in rowing, or fishing, etc., or of feet in walking, the quickest is, lighting a tallow candle, and letting the tallow drop into cold water (to purify it, it is said, from salt), then rubbing the tallow to the hands or feet, mixed with brandy or any other strong spirits. For mere tenderness nothing is better than the above, or vinegar a little diluted with water.

Fitting Boots and Shoes to the Feet.—Whenever one procures a pair of new boots or shoes which do not fit the feet uniformly, let the part or parts of the upper leather which set uncomfortably tight be thoroughly saturated with hot water while the boots are on the feet; then let them be worn until the leather has become quite dry. If by wetting once the upper leather does not stretch so as to accommodate itself to the formation of the feet, let the process be repeated. In some instances it will be well to wet all the upper leather. But let it be remembered that if boots or shoes are allowed to dry when not on one's feet, the leather will shrink so that it will sometimes be impracticable to get them on the feet until the leather has been wetted and stretched.

When one has a pair of rather heavy boots, before the leather is oiled or blacked, let the upper part be soaked for a few minutes in warm water, then let the boots be worn until the leather has become quite dry, after which oil and black them, and they will fit the feet far more satisfactorily than they can ever be made to fit without wetting and drying while they are being worn. To prevent the soles from shrinking they should be well saturated with linseed oil before they are worn. If this is not done, they will sometimes shrink half an inch in length; this accounts for boots becoming too short for the feet.

The Science of Blacking You

Boots. — *By a Member of the Boot-black Brigade.* —Don't do it in the sunshine, for it won't shine your boots. The warmth dries the blacking rapidly and prevents a good polish. Boots, to retain their polish, should be taken off the feet and allowed to become dry before polishing, and when this process is completed, they ought not to be worn until the moisture in the polish has evaporated. If they are worn immediately the heat from the foot will force the moisture out through the polish, and cause it to assume a dull appearance.

Care for the Feet. — Many are careless in the keeping of the feet. If they wash them once a week they think they are doing well. They do not consider that the largest pores of the system are located in the bottom of the foot, and that the most offensive matter is discharged through the pores. They wear stockings from the beginning to the end of the week without change, which will become completely saturated with offensive matter. Ill health is generated by such treatment of the feet. The pores are not only repellants, but absorbents, and this fetid matter, to a greater or less extent, is taken back into the system. The feet should be washed every day with pure water only, as well as the arm-pits, from which an offensive odor is also emitted, unless daily ablution is practiced. Stockings should not be worn more than a day or two at a time. They may be worn for one day, and then aired and sunned and worn another day, if necessary. If you have cold feet, immerse them morning and evening in cold water, rub with a rough towel, and run about your room till they warm. In one month you will be entirely relieved. All these red pepper and mustard applications are like rum to the stomach, — relieve you to-day, but leave you colder to-morrow. But if cold feet proceed from moisture (perspiration), cotton stockings should be worn over woollen ones. The woollen stockings will absorb the moisture as it accumulates in the cot-

ton sock, and keep the latter comparatively dry.

Effect of Flannel on the Skin. — Dr. Fox remarks that under the use of flannel, local heat is intensified, and itching often increased and kept up. He gives us a practical rule: "Whenever you have a congestive state of the skin, or any disposition to neurosis, take off the flannel and place it, if necessary, outside the linen; this will prevent any catching cold."

Why Run up Stairs? — We do not run in the street, nor in the park or garden. Why then run up stairs, and then complain that the stairs are so high? It is difficult to answer this question; nevertheless, American people generally do run up stairs, while foreigners are well satisfied with walking up. Servants frequently complain of the height of the stairs, and leave their places in consequence. Houses of six and eight stories are now built in American cities as they are in Paris and Edinburgh. Now, there is really but little more difficulty in ascending several flights of stairs than there is in walking a straight line, provided we take sufficient time to do it, which should be about twice as long as we should be in walking the same distance in the street. Walk up stairs slowly, rest at each landing, again walk steadily, and you will reach the top flight without exhaustion or fatigue.

RAZORS. — Engineers, as a class, were the first to head the modern "beard movement" in this country; but many may like to read the following extract from a little work by Mr. Kingsbury, a practical razor-maker:— "The edge of a razor, a penknife, and every other very keen instrument, consists of a great number of minute points, commonly called teeth, which, if the instrument is in itself good, and in good condition, follow each other through its whole extent with great order and closeness, and constitute, by their unbroken regularity, its excessive keenness. The edge of such an instrument acts on the beard, the skin, or anything else, not so much by the direct application of weight or force, as being drawn, even slightly, along it; because by this operation the fine teeth of which it consists pass in quick succession, in the same direction, and over the same part of the substance. My readers will be convinced of this if they will make the following experiment on their glove or their hand, as they like best: — Let them hold the razor either perpendicularly or obliquely, and press on it with some considerable force in a direct line from right to left, and they will have no great reason to fear the consequences. But let them move it from that direction— let them draw it toward them, or push it from them, in the smallest degree, in the gentlest manner, and it will instantly make an incision. When they have made this experiment, they will be convinced of the truth of what I have asserted, namely, that in the operation of shaving, very little weight and even very little force are necessary." Hence it follows that the best razor will have the teeth of its edge set almost as regularly as a good saw, and that the best test in buying a razor is to examine the edge by means of a strong magnifying-glass. This also explains the good effect on the keenness of a razor caused by dipping it in hot water, which necessarily clears the edges of any small clogging substances.

Removing a Tight Finger Ring. — It is seldom necessary to file off a ring which is too tight to readily pass the joint of the finger. If the finger is swollen, apply cold water to reduce the inflammation, then wrap a small rag wet in hot water around the ring, to expand the metal, and soap the finger. A needle threaded with strong silk can then be passed between the ring and finger, and a person holding the two ends, and pulling the silk while slowly sliding it around the periphery of the ring, may readily remove the ring. If the ring is a plain hoop, this process is easy; if it has a setting or protuberance, more care will be required. Another method

is to pass a piece of sewing silk under the ring, and wind the thread, in pretty close spirals, and snugly, around the finger to the end. Then take the lower end— that below the ring — and begin unwinding. The ring is certain to be removed, unless the silk is very weak. The winding compresses the finger, and renders the operation less difficult.

How to Take Care of your Watch. — In the first place, see that the key is well fitted, and do not carry it in your pocket, but keep it in some place where dirt or dust will not reach it, or the dirt will soon find its way into the watch, and injure it. Wind it slowly, and at the same time every day — (a good plan is to keep the key hanging in the chamber, and wind the watch every night on going to bed). Do not let the watch lie on its back, but hang it up in the same position it is carried in the pocket. *Do not hang it against a wall, or other hard surface*, or the jar will soon spoil the watch. Heat expands and cold contracts all metals,— a watch should, therefore, be kept at an equal temperature. When carried in the pocket, it is in a moderately-warm place; it should therefore be hung up in a moderately warm place when not worn. Do not move the hands of a chronometer or duplex watch backward; in fact, it is best not to turn the hands of any watch backward, or forward either, to any extent; it had better be allowed to run down, and then wind it up at the time indicated on its face. If a watch runs too slow, take it into a warm, dry room, free from dust, open it carefully, and move the regulator a trifle toward the place where marked FAST. If it runs too fast, move it a little to where marked SLOW. Move it as gently as possible, and a little at a time, for it is better to have to re-move it three times in one direction, than to move it too far, and have to re-move it back. The less a watch is opened the better. In fact, a good rule with a watch is to "let it alone as much as possible." The above rules being attended to, and

EVERY-DAY RECEIPTS.

PRACTICAL HINTS ABOUT HOUSEHOLD AND FARM WORK—THINGS EVERY HOUSEWIFE AND FARMER SHOULD KNOW HOW TO DO.

STAINING.—GENERAL OBSERVATIONS. — When *alabaster, marble,* and other *stones* are colored, and the stain is required to be deep, it should be poured on boiling hot, and brushed equally over every part, if made with water ; if with spirit, it should be applied cold, otherwise the evaporation being too rapid, would leave the coloring matter on the surface, without any, or very little, being able to penetrate. In grayish or brownish stones, the stain will be wanting in brightness, because the natural color combines with the stain ; therefore, if the stone be a pure color, the result will be a combination of the color and stain. In staining *bone* or *ivory,* the colors will take better before than after polishing; and if any dark spots appear, they should be rubbed with chalk, and the article dyed again, to produce uniformity of shade. On removal from the boiling-hot dye-bath, the bone should be immediately plunged into cold water, to prevent cracks from the heat. If *paper* or *parchment* is stained, a broad varnish brush should be employed, to lay the coloring on evenly. When the stains for *wood* are required to be very strong, it is better to soak and *not* brush them ; therefore, if for inlaying or fine work, the wood should be previously split or sawed into proper thicknesses; and when directed to be brushed several times over with the stains, it should be allowed to dry between each coating. When it is wished to render any of the stains more durable and beautiful, the work should be well rubbed with Dutch or common rushes after it is colored, and then varnished with seed-lac varnish, or if a better appearance is desired, with three coats of the same, or shellac varnish. Common work only requires frequent rubbing with linseed oil and woollen rags. The remainder, with the exception of *glass,* will be treated of in this paper.

ALABASTER, MARBLE, AND STONE, may be stained of a yellow, red, green, blue, purple, black, or any of the compound colors, by the stains used for wood.

Bone and Ivory. — *Black.* — 1. Lay the article for several hours in a strong solution of nitrate of silver, and expose to the light. 2. Boil the article for some time in a stained decoction of logwood, and then steep it in a solution of persulphate or acetate of iron. 3. Immerse frequently in ink, until of sufficient depth of color.

BONE AND IVORY. *Blue.* — 1. Immerse for some time in a dilute solution of sulphate of indigo — partly saturated with potash — and it will be fully stained. 2. Steep in a strong solution of sulphate of copper.

BONE AND IVORY. *Green.* — 1. Dip blue-stained articles for a short time in nitro-hydrochlorate of tin, and then in a hot decoction of fustic. 2. Boil in a solution of verdigris in vinegar until the desired color is obtained.

BONE AND IVORY. *Red.* — 1. Dip the articles first in the tin mordant used in dyeing, and then plunge into a hot decoction of Brazil wood — half a pound to a gallon of water — or cochineal. 2. Steep in red ink until sufficiently stained.

BONE AND IVORY. *Scarlet.* — Use lac dye instead of the preceding.

BONE AND IVORY. *Violet.*— Dip in the tin mordant, and then immerse in a decoction of logwood.

BONE AND IVORY. *Yellow.*—1. Impregnate with nitro-hydrochlorate of tin, and then digest with heat in a strained decoction of fustic. 2. Steep for twenty-four hours in a strong solution of the neutral chromate of potash, and then plunge for some time in a boiling solution of acetate of lead. 3. Boil the articles in a solution of alum — a pound to half a gallon — and then immerse for half an hour in the following mixture : — Take half a pound of turmeric, and a quarter of a pound of pearlash ; boil in a gallon of water. When taken from this, the bone must be again dipped in the alum solution.

To Restore Faded Writing.— When writing by common ink has become faded by age, so as to be nearly or quite illegible, it may be restored to its original hue by moistening it with a camel's-hair pencil or feather dipped in tincture of galls, or a solution of ferrocyanide of potassium, slightly acidulated with hydrochloric acid. Either of these washes should be very carefully applied, so that the ink may not spread.

Sharpening Lead Pencils.—A narrow blade — a pen-blade — should be used for this purpose, as the back of a wide blade is almost certain to break the lead point just before the point is finished. A little thought will readily show the reason of this.

Removing Corks from Bottles. — Sometimes a cork is pushed down into the bottle or vial which it is desirable to remove. A very effectual way to do it is to insert a strong twine in a loop and engage the cork in any direction most convenient. It can then be withdrawn by a "strong pull," the cork generally yielding sufficiently to pass through the neck.

Loosening Ground Glass Stopples. —Sometimes the ground glass stopples of bottles become, from one cause or another, fixed in the neck, and cannot be removed by pulling or torsion. An effectual method is to wrap a rag wet with hot water around the neck, and let it remain a few seconds. The heat will expand the neck of the bottle, when the stopple can be removed before the heat penetrates the stopple itself.

SQUINTING.—Squinting frequently arises from the unequal strength of the eyes, the weaker eye being turned away from the object, to avoid the fatigue of exertion. Cases of squinting of long standing have often been cured by covering the stronger eye, and thereby compelling the weaker one to exertion.

Method of Ascertaining the State of the Lungs. — Persons desirous of ascertaining the true state of the lungs are directed to draw in as much breath as they conveniently can ; they are then to count as far as they are able, in a slow and audible voice, without drawing in more breath. The number of seconds they can continue counting must be carefully observed ; in a consumptive, the time does not exceed ten, and is frequently less than six seconds; in pleurisy and pneumonia, it ranges from nine to four seconds. When the lungs are in a sound condition, the time will range as high as from twenty to thirty-five seconds.

To Avoid Catching Cold. — Accustom yourself to the use of sponging with cold water every morning on first getting out of bed. It should be followed by a good deal of rubbing with a wet towel. It has considerable effect in giving tone to the skin, and maintaining a proper action in it, and thus proves a safeguard to the injurious influence of cold and sudden changes of temperature. Sir Astley Cooper said, "The methods by which I have preserved my own health are— temperance, early rising, and sponging the body every morning with cold water, immediately after getting out of bed, — a practice which I have adopted for thirty years

To Find the Age of a Horse.—The colt is born with twelve grinders. When four front teeth have made their appearance the colt is twelve days old, and when the next four appear it is four weeks old. When the corner teeth appear, it is eight months old; and when the latter have attained the height of the front teeth it is a year old. The two-year old colt has the kernel (the dark substance in the middle of the tooth's crown) ground or worn out of all the front teeth. In the third year the middle front teeth are being shifted, and when three years old, these are substituted for the horse teeth. In the fourth year, the next four are shifted; and in the fifth year the corner teeth are shifted. In the sixth year the kernel is worn out of the middle front teeth, and the bridle teeth have now attained their full growth. At seven years a hook has been formed on the corner teeth of the upper jaw; the kernel of the teeth next to the middle is worn out, and the bridle teeth begin to wear off. At eight years of age the kernel is worn out of all the lower front teeth, and begins to decrease in the middle upper fronts. In the ninth year the kernel has wholly disappeared from the upper middle front teeth; the hook on the corner teeth has increased in size, and the bridle teeth lose their point. In the tenth year the kernel has worn out of the teeth next to the middle fronts of the upper jaw; and in the eleventh year the kernel has entirely disappeared from the corner teeth of the same jaw. At twelve years the crowns of all the front teeth in the lower jaw have become triangular, and the bridle teeth are much worn down. As the horse advances in age, the gums shrink away from the teeth, which appear long and narrow, and the kernel becomes changed into darkish points. Gray hairs increase in the forehead, and the chin becomes angular.

To Ascertain the Age of Sheep.—The age of sheep may be known by the front teeth, which are eight in number, and appear the first year, all of a size. In the second year the two middle ones fall out, and are supplanted by two large ones. During the third year a small tooth appears on each side. In the fourth year the large teeth are six in number. In the fifth year all the front teeth are large, and in the sixth year the whole begin to get worn.

To Make a Sheep Own a Lamb.—Sometimes it is desirable to make one sheep own the lamb of another, but often it is a difficult task. The following experiment has been tried, was easily conducted, and proved a perfect success: — A sheep lost her lamb; in a few days a yearling dropped a lamb, which she did not own, and, in fact, had no milk for it. The lamb was taken, immediately after it was dropped, and sprinkled with fine salt, and then placed with the sheep that had lost her lamb. In a short time she was as fond of it as she had been of her own, and took the greatest care of her adopted charge.

Feeding Horses. — The London Omnibus Company have lately made a report on feeding horses, which discloses some interesting information, not only to farmers, but to every owner of a horse. As a great number of horses are now used in the army for cavalry, artillery, and draught purposes, the facts stated are of great value at the present time. The London Company uses no less than six thousand horses; three thousand of this number had for their feed bruised oats and cut hay and straw, and the other three thousand got whole oats and hay. The allowance accorded to the first was: bruised oats, 16 lbs.; cut hay, 7½ lbs.; cut straw, 2¼ lbs. The allowance accorded to the second: unbruised oats, 19 lbs.; uncut hay, 13 lbs. The bruised oats, cut hay and cut straw amounted to 26 lbs.; and the unbruised oats, etc., to 32 lbs. The horse which had bruised oats, with cut hay and straw, and consumed 26 lbs. per day, could do the same work as well, and was kept in as good con-

28

dition, as the horse which received 32 lbs. per day. Here was a saving of 6 lbs. per day on the feeding of each horse receiving bruised oats, cut hay and cut straw. The advantage of bruised oats and cut hay over unbruised oats and uncut hay is estimated at five cents per day on each horse, amounting to three hundred dollars per day for the Company's six thousand horses. It is by no means an unimportant result with which this experiment has supplied us. To the farmer who expends a large sum in the support of horse-power, there are two points this experiment clearly establishes, which, in practice, must be profitable: first, the saving of food to the amount of 6 lbs. per day; and second, no loss of horse-power arising from that saving.

To Prevent Flies from Teasing Horses.—Take two or three small handfuls of walnut leaves, upon which pour two or three quarts of soft cold water; let it infuse one night, and pour the whole next morning into a kettle, and let it boil for fifteen minutes. When cold, it will be fit for use. No more is required than to wet a sponge, and before the horse goes out of the stable, let those parts which are most irritated be smeared over with the liquor.

A Mere Stumble. — When a horse stumbles, never raise your voice — the creature dreads its master's chiding. Never jog the reins--the mouth of the horse is far more sensitive than the human lips. Never use the lash—the horse is so timid, that the slightest correction overpowers its reasoning faculties. Speak to the creature; reassure the palpitating frame; seek to restore those perceptions which will form the best guard against any repetition of the faulty action.

Power of a Horse's Scent. — There is one perception which a horse possesses that but little attention has been paid to, and that is the power of scent. With some horses it is as acute as with the dog, and for the benefit of those who have to drive nights, such as physicians and others, this knowl-

edge is invaluable. We never knew it to fail, and we have ridden hundreds of miles dark nights; and, in consideration of this power of scent, this is our simple advice—never check your horse at nights, but give him a free head, and you may rest assured that he will never get off the road, and will carry you expeditiously and safe.

OATS should always be bruised for an old horse, because through age and defective teeth, he cannot chew them properly.

WHEN your horse refuses food, after drinking, go no further that day, because the poor creature is thoroughly beaten.

Amount of Pork from a Bushel of Corn. — A friend of ours obtained a hundred pounds of pork from seven bushels of corn, or one pound of pork from four and a half pounds of corn; the grain was ground and moistened with water before feeding. Another, by wetting his meal with five times its weight of hot water, and letting it stand twelve to eighteen hours before feeding, obtained one pound of pork from two and a half pounds of corn. Doubtless different results would be obtained from different breeds of swine.

Raise More Ducks. — A farmer of considerable experience writes: — I could never understand why our farmers through the State did not keep ducks; as a matter of profit they are more profitable than hens. It may be the impression that in order to keep ducks, a person must have a pond or stream of water near by, has deterred many from keeping them, but there is no need of anything of the kind. It is true that it is better to have a pond or stream — but you can raise ducks just as well elsewhere. I know of parties that are very successful in raising them — they have only a shallow tub set in the ground and filled from the pump occasionally. In fact, the trouble of raising ducks, and about the only one, is letting the young go into the water too soon after they leave the nest. When I speak of the profits from ducks,

I do not have reference to the common duck that is seen every day. I mean a breed of ducks that will weigh twelve pounds to the pair, alive, such as the Rouen and Aylesbury, and both excellent layers, easily kept and reared, and being very large and excellent for the market, and it costs no more to rear them than the common ducks that will only weigh on the average about eight pounds to the pair. The Rouen is a very handsome duck in plumage; the drake has a glassy green head and neck down to a white ring on his neck, and the lower part of his body is a beautiful green brown gray, and shaded with brown on the back. The duck is of a beautiful brown, with about every feather shaded on the outer edge with black. They are acknowledged the best of the varieties, laying very early and continuing through the season, and late in winter. The Aylesbury is pure white, both the duck and drake, and about the same size as the Rouen. Both become very familiar, and being very large and heavy, do not care to roam as much as the common kind.

Care of Young Ducks.—Take three boards, about a foot wide, and make a yard, either square or triangular shaped, and put the hen and coop in one corner of it. Keep the hen cooped until the ducklings are about two weeks old, then give her her liberty. She will stay with the ducklings some time longer. No more than twelve or fourteen ducklings should be kept in one yard, as they are apt to pile upon one another at night, and smother each other. The ducklings should be confined in a yard until they are well feathered, for if they go through wet grass they almost invariably die. The yard should be moved every two weeks, and care should be taken to have a good shelter in one corner.

Raising Turkeys.—The turkey is the most tender when young, and most difficult to raise of all the domestic fowls; yet with proper care in setting the eggs under game hens and cooping the brood at night regularly, while the turkeys are young, they may be easily reared in great abundance. Never feed the young turkeys with boiled eggs or corn meal dough, or wheat bread crumbs. They need very little food of any kind under seven days of age, and should have nothing but sour milk set in pans. At about a week or ten days give them also wheat screenings or crumbs soaked in sour milk. Let this be their only feed till they begin to feather, and then give them grain of any kind. Tie the hen (which has the young turkeys) to a peg off to herself, with a coop near by her, so that she can enter at night to roost. At two weeks old let the hen loose to roam, and if she be a game hen she will do the work of rearing the brood.

To Make Hens Lay Perpetually.— Give to each hen half an ounce of fresh meat, chopped fine, once a day, while the ground is frozen that they cannot get worms or insects; allow no roosters to run with them. They will require plenty of grain, water, gravel, and lime. Treated in this way it is said they will lay perpetually.

BOILED OATS, fried in fat, are recommended for laying hens as the very best food for the production of eggs.

Choosing Hatching Eggs. — Eggs for hatching should be chosen of the fair average size usually laid by the hen they are from, any unusually large or small being rejected. Some hens lay immensely large eggs, and others small ones. A fat hen will always lay small eggs, which can only produce small and weakly chickens. Absolute size in eggs is, therefore, of but little importance. Round short eggs are usually the best to select; *very* long eggs, especially if much pointed at the small end, almost always breed birds with some awkwardness in style of carriage. Neither should rough-shelled eggs be chosen; they usually show some derangement of the organs, and are often sterile. Smooth-shelled eggs alone are proper for hatching. It is a farce to suppose that the sex of a bird can be determined by the shape of the egg.

How the English Fatten Fowls.

—Among the various modes of fattening fowls which are from time to time presented to the public, none is more highly commended than the following, which is the method largely practised in England, and, it is said, always with great economy and perfect success. In this method the custom is to put the fowls into coops as usual, but where they can get no gravel. Keep corn in their feed-boxes all the time, and also give them cornmeal dough, well cooked, once a day. For drink give them fresh skimmed milk, with a sprinkling of charcoal, well pulverized, in it. Fed in this way, it is said they will fatten nicely in from ten to twelve days. If kept beyond that time it is customary to furnish them with gravel, to prevent them from falling away. One extensive English fowl-breeder states that he has tried this method for years, and has never known it to fail. In this method, as in all others, it is, of course, necessary that the fowls should occupy coops protected from the cold, and kept perfectly clean and dry.

To impart a flavor to the flesh of fowls, such as constitutes the "game flavor" of the wild state, the Boston *Journal of Chemistry* recommends Cayenne pepper, ground mustard, or ginger, to be added to their common food.

Milk and Water. — It makes a great difference whether water is given to the cow or to the can. Dr. Dancel, in a communication to the French Academy of Sciences, adduces proof that the yield of milk can be considerably increased by giving salt to incite cows to drink large quantities of water, and by moistening their food, with very little if any of the peculiar effect produced by the experiments of milkmen at the later stage of the operation. According to Dancel's observations, when a cow begins to give milk she drinks from eleven to as much as forty-five quarts of water per day more than before. All cows that drink fifty quarts per day were found to be excellent milkers, yielding nineteen to twenty-three quarts per day. Less than twenty-seven quarts invariably marked a very poor milker. Of course the experiment of artificial stimulation by means of salt was intended only for scientific purposes. The importance of an abundant and convenient supply of pure water at all times, as much as the animal will take, is the practical deduction.

A Dog's Bed.—The best bed which can be made for a dog, consists of dry, newly-made deal shavings; a sackful of these may be had for a shilling at almost any carpenter's shop. The dog is delighted in tumbling about in them until he has made a bed to suit himself. Clean wood shavings will clean a dog as well as water, and fleas will never infest dogs that sleep upon fresh deal shavings. The turpentine and rosin in new pine soon drive them away.

Cooked or Raw. —Where it is possible to avoid it, meat should never be fed raw to dogs or fowls. It has the effect of making them quarrelsome. In addition to this, meat that is cooked is more nutritious than when fed raw.

"Morning Milk," says an eminent German philosopher, "commonly yields some hundredths more cream than the evening's at the same temperature. That milked at noon furnishes the least. It would therefore be of advantage, in making butter, etc., to employ the morning't milk, and keep the evening's for domestic use."

A little grated carrot, and a few lumps of white sugar, added to the cream in the churn, will add very much to the taste as well as the appearance of the butter.

Tanning Sheep-Skins. — For mats, take two long-wooled skins, make a strong suds, using hot water; when it is cold, wash the skins in it, carefully squeezing them between the hands to get the dirt out of the wool; then wash the soap out with clean cold water. Now dissolve alum and salt, each half a pound, with a little hot water, which put in a tub of cold water sufficient to cover the skins, and let them soak in it over night, or twelve hours; then hang over a pail to drain. When they are well drained, spread or stretch carefully over a board to dry. When a little damp, have one ounce, each, of salt-petre and alum, pulverized, and sprinkle the flesh side of each skin, rubbing in well; then lay the flesh sides together and hang in the shade for two or three days, turning the under skin upper-most every day until perfectly dry. Then scrape the flesh side with a blunt knife, to remove any remaining scraps of flesh, trim off projecting points, and rub the flesh side with pumice or rot-ten-stone, and with the hands; they will be very white and beautiful, suit-able for a door or carriage mat. They also make good mittens. Lamb-skins (or sheep-skins, if the wool be trimmed off evenly to about one-half or three-fourths of an inch long,) make most beautiful and warm mittens for ladies or gentlemen.

Furs may be taken from the first of October to the first of April. They are not good for furs the rest of the season, as the hair comes out.

To Remove the Taste of New Wood.

— A new keg, churn, bucket, or other wooden vessel, will generally communicate a disagreeable taste to anything that is put into it. To pre-vent this inconvenience, first scald the vessel well with boiling water, letting the water remain in it till cold. Then dissolve some pearlash, or soda, in luke-warm water, adding a little bit of lime to it, and wash the inside of the vessel well with this solution. Afterward scald it well with plain hot water, and rinse it with cold before you use it.

To Relieve Muscular Pain in Horses.

— The thorn-apple plant is a very excellent remedy, as an external application, for the treatment of mus-cular pain, ligamentary lameness, sprain of the fetlock, etc. It is a remedy of great efficacy in chronic pains and inflammatory tumors. Four ounces of the plant to one pint of boil-ing water, are the proportions. When cool the parts are to be bathed often; when practicable a flannel is to be sat-urated with the fluid, bound on the affected parts, the whole to be covered with oiled silk. Thorn-apple is a deadly poison; the bottle containing it should be so marked, that it may not be taken internally by mistake.

MANGE, OR SCAB. — This is denoted by the animal rubbing the hair off about the eyes and other parts. The skin is scaly or scabby, sometimes appearing like a large seed-wart.

Remedies. — Rub the spots with sul-phur and lard, after scraping and wash-ing with soap.

When the skin is cracked, take sul-phur, one pound; turpentine, quarter pound; unguentum (or mercurial oint-ment), two ounces; linseed oil, one pint. Melt the turpentine and warm the oil, and when partly cooled, stir in the sul-phur; when cold, add the unguentum, mixing all well. Rub this thoroughly with the hand on the parts affected.

To Cure Scratches in Horses.

— Scratches or grease may very often be cured by washing the legs with warm water and soap, and, after drying thor-oughly with a soft cloth, applying glycerine or lard perfectly free from salt. If this does not avail, a pound of "concentrated lye," or carbonate of potash, may be dissolved in two quarts of water, and put into a bottle. A quarter of a pint of this solution should be put into a pailful of cold water, and the horse's heels bathed with it night and morning. The legs should be dried immediately after the bathing, but considerable moisture will exude from the skin afterward. The stable must be kept clean, and no snow or ice allowed to remain on the legs.

To Clean Canary Birds.

— These pretty things are, like meaner objects, often covered with lice, and may be ef-fectually relieved of them by placing a clean white cloth over their cage at night. In the morning it will be cov-ered with small red spots, so small as hardly to be seen, except by the aid of a glass. These are the lice, a source of great annoyance to the birds.

To Prevent Moths.—In the month of April or May, beat your fur garments well with a small cane or elastic stick; then wrap them up in linen, without pressing the fur too hard, and put betwixt the folds some camphor in small lumps; then put your furs in this state in boxes well closed. When the furs are wanted for use, beat them well as before, and expose them for twenty-four hours to the air, which will take away the smell of the camphor. If the fur has long hair, as bear or fox, add to the camphor an equal quantity of black pepper in powder.

To Banish Moths. — Moisten a piece of linen with spirits of turpentine, and place it in the bureau, or wardrobe, or place where the clothes are kept, for a day or two; or sprinkle pimento (allspice) berries, or the seeds of the musk plant, among the clothes.

To Destroy Ants. — Drop quicklime on the mouth of their nest, and wash it in with boiling water; or dissolve some camphor in spirits of wine, then mix with water, and pour into their haunts; or tobacco water, which has been found effectual. They are averse to strong scents. Camphor will prevent their infesting a cupboard, or a sponge saturated with creosote. To prevent their climbing up trees, place a ring of tar about the trunk, or a circle of rag moistened occasionally with creosote.

To Destroy Bugs. — Spirits of naphtha rubbed with a small painter's brush into every part of a bedstead is a certain way of getting rid of bugs. The mattress and binding of the bed should be examined, and the same process attended to, as they generally harbor more in these parts than in the bedstead. Three pennyworth of naphtha is sufficient for one bed.

Bug Poison. — Proof-spirit, one pint; camphor, two ounces; oil of turpentine, four ounces; corrosive sublimate, one ounce. Mix.

CLEAN. — A gentleman writes:—"I have been for a long time troubled with bugs, and never could get rid of them by any clean and expeditious method, until a friend told me to suspend a small bag of camphor to the bed, just in the centre overhead. I did so, and the enemy was most effectually repulsed, and has not made his appearance since —not even for a reconnoissance!" We therefore give the information upon this method of getting rid of bugs, our informant being most confident of its success in every case.

To Destroy Flies in a room, take half a teaspoonful of black pepper in powder, one teaspoonful of brown sugar, and one tablespoonful of cream, mix them well together, and place them in the room on a plate, where the flies are troublesome, and they will soon disappear.

FLY PLASTER is made by mixing a cupful of molasses with a cupful of glue of the consistency used by carpenters; boil the two together a few minutes, then spread it on brown paper, or old newspapers,— place it about the house, the flies will come to it and will stick.

To Destroy Rats and Mice, place some chloride of lime at the entrance to their holes, then pour a little spirits of salt or other acid upon it; the gas disengaged being heavier than air, will descend into the holes and destroy them. Chloride of lime strewed about a cellar infested by rats will generally drive them away, but the above may always be depended upon.

A New Wheelbarrow. — We here

NEW WHEELBARROW.

give an illustration of a new wheelbarrow. It is so simple, the engraving fully explains itself. It makes a very strong, durable wheelbarrow, and almost any one can make it. No iron stays of any kind are required, and no mortices or tenons to make. The farmer can make a wheelbarrow of this kind, any wet day, at a less expense than he can repair one of the usual make. In fact it is easier, cheaper, and better, to make one than it is to borrow one.

To Drive Rats Away. — The following is said by a New York man to be a good plan to drive away rats: — "The floor near the rat-hole is covered with a thin layer of moist caustic of potassa. When the rats walk on this it makes their feet sore; these they lick with their tongues, which makes their mouths sore; and the result is that they shun this locality, not alone, but appear to tell all the rats in the neighborhood about it, and eventually the house is entirely abandoned by them, notwithstanding the houses around may be teeming with rats."

How to Catch Rats. — The following is said to be a cheap and effective way to catch rats: — Cover a common barrel with stiff, stout paper, tying the edge round the barrel; place a board so that the rats may have easy access to the top; sprinkle cheese parings or other feed for the rats on the paper for several days, until they begin to think that they have a right to their daily rations from this source; then place in the bottom of the barrel a piece of rock about six or seven inches high, filling with water until only enough of it projects above the water for one rat to lodge upon. Now replace the paper, first cutting a cross in the middle, and the first rat that comes on the barrel top goes through into the water, and climbs on the rock. The paper comes back to its original position, and the second rat follows the first. Then begins a fight for the possession of the dry place on the stone, the noise of which attracts the others, who share the same fate.

A New Rat Trap. — Take a smooth kettle, fill to within six inches of the top with water, cover the surface with chaff or bran, place it where the rats harbor, and it will drown all that get into it. Thirty-six were taken in one night by this process.

STREW wild mint where you wish to keep the mice out, and they will never trouble you.

To KILL cockroaches, take carbolic acid and powdered camphor in equal parts; put them in a bottle; they will become fluid. With a painter's brush of the size called a sash tool, put the mixture on the cracks or places where the "critters" hide; they will come out at once. It is wonderful to see the heroism with which they move to certain death. Nothing more sublime in history; the extirpation is certain and complete. While on this theme we would add that a mixture of carbolic acid with water — one-fourth acid three-fourths water — put on a dog, will kill fleas at once.

How to Make Good Cement Walks. — Having previously graded and rolled the ground, heat your tar very hot, and with a long-handled dipper begin at one end of a pile of quite coarse gravel, pouring on the tar, quickly shovelling over and over so as to mix thoroughly. Cover the ground two and a half or three inches deep with the tarred gravel, and then roll. Clean the roller with a broom as you proceed. Then put on a layer of finer tarred gravel one and a half inches thick, and roll. Then sprinkle the surface with hot tar, spreading the tar with a broom; finally, cover the surface with a light coat of fine sand, and your walk is complete, ready for use. It will improve in hardness by age. Provide portable tar kettles, screens, a roller not very heavy, and tools for systematic work, and you can hardly fail to derive satisfaction.

A Novel Mode of Pasturing Sheep. — A grazier has introduced the following singular method of economizing his green crops: — Over the whole field is placed a rack or fence, so made that the sheep cannot jump over it, but must feed between the bars; and when all the herbage within their reach is consumed, the rack is moved forward, so as to give them a fresh supply of forage. Regularity in cropping and great economy result from the employment of this singular system

Wheat for a Barrel of Flour.—

The question is often asked, how much wheat does it take to make a barrel of flour? Sixteen bushels of winter wheat yielded three barrels and one hundred and three pounds of flour—at the rate of four bushels and fifteen pounds of wheat to the barrel. Of spring wheat, fifty bushels yielded eleven barrels of flour, being four bushels and thirty-two pounds per barrel. The wheat used was of a fair average quality.

Whitewash for Stables.—

Take a clean water-tight barrel, or other suitable cask, and put into it half a bushel of lime. Slack it by pouring water over it, boiling hot, and in sufficient quantity to cover it five inches deep, and stir it briskly till thoroughly slacked. When the lime has been slacked, dissolve it in water, and add two pounds of sulphate of zinc, and one of common salt. These will cause the wash to harden, and prevent its cracking, which gives an unseemly appearance to the work. If desirable, a beautiful cream color may be communicated to the above wash, by adding three pounds of yellow ochre; or a good pearl or lead color, by the addition of lamp, vine, or ivory black. For fawn color, add four pounds umber — Turkish or American — the latter is the cheapest; one pound Indian red, and one pound of common lampblack. For common stone color, add four pounds raw umber, and two pounds lampblack. When applied to the outside of outhouses and to fences, it is rendered more durable by adding sweet milk, or some mucilage from flaxseed, — about a pint to the gallon will suffice. All stables should be whitewashed once or twice every year, as the increased white light which it

reflects tends to promote the health of animals. Hand round this information to every man who owns a horse or a cow; because for one stable that is whitewashed, there are a hundred on the walls of which no brush was ever laid.

PRESERVATIVE PROPERTIES OF WHITEWASH.—

A friend says: "Some twenty years since, I caused to be heavily whitewashed, with pure lime, the furnace-pipe in my cellar, it being exposed to the exhalations arising from tide-water, causing me to replenish the sheet-iron pipe each season. By whitewashing each year, the last one remained good for six years. Gas-pipes used under ground have been thus coated at my suggestion, and show no oxidation as yet. Last year I tried an experiment with peaches and pears, placed in boxes allowing but little ventilation, thoroughly coated with pure whitewash. They kept seventeen days without showing signs of decay, while those left in the crate all decayed in four days."

A New Whitewash for Walls.—

Soak one-fourth of a pound of glue over night in tepid water. The next day put it into a tin vessel with a quart of water, set the vessel in a kettle of water over the fire, keep it there till it boils, and then stir until the glue is dissolved. Next put from six to eight pounds of Paris white into another vessel, add hot water and stir until it has the appearance of milk of lime. Add the sizing, stir well, and apply in the ordinary way while still warm. "Paris white" is *sulphate of baryta*, and may be found at any drug or paint store.

Stone-Colored Wash for Outside of Wooden Buildings, or Fences.—

Cheap and very durable, and preserves the wood.—Take two pounds of flaxseed, and boil it in a common wash-boiler for an hour or more, in four pails of water; after thoroughly boiling, strain it into an old tight barrel; put in one peck, in bulk, of common land plaster, one peck of nicely sifted wood ashes, one quart of wheat flour, and one quart of salt. Put in your barrel a good stick as large as a hand-spike, and stir it till it is as thick as cream; let it stand in the sun for a week, and every time you go by the barrel, stir it thoroughly: at the end of the week it won't settle, but will remain incorporated, and is fit for use.

Substitute for Glass for Hot-Houses. — Apply, with a common painter's brush, boiled oil, or Canadian balsam, diluted with oil of turpentine, to the surface of white muslin previously stretched out, and fastened in the position it is intended to occupy. This is often used by the English in woodsheds and out-houses, where glass would be liable to frequent breakings.

Melted Alum mixed with burr stone reduced to the consistency of sand, is the cement used for filling holes in burr stones. If the holes are large, coarse pieces of burr stone may be used at first, finishing with the finer material.

Cement for Fastening Instruments in Handles. — A material for fastening knives or forks into their handles, when they have become loosened by use, is a much-needed article. The best cement for this purpose consists of one pound of colophony (purchasable at the druggist's) and eight ounces of sulphur, which are to be melted together, and either kept in bars or reduced to powder. One part of the powder is to be mixed with half a part of iron filings, fine sand, or brick-dust, and the cavity of the handle is then to be filled with this mixture. The stem of the knife or fork is then to be heated and inserted into the cavity; and when cold, it will be found fixed in its place with great tenacity.

Cement for Iron and Stone.— Glycerine and litharge stirred to a paste hardens rapidly, and makes a suitable cement for iron upon iron, for two stone surfaces, and especially for fastening iron to stone. The cement is insoluble, and is not attacked by strong acids.

Leaden Tobacco Boxes.--Dr. Mayer of Berlin, states that he has traced six cases of lead colic and paralysis to the use of tobacco held in leaden boxes. M. Chevallier has found, also, that tobacco wrapped in lead foil — improperly called tin foil — becomes impregnated in course of time with acetate of lead.

Time to Paint.—There are two objects in the use of paint — decoration and preservation, both of which are entirely defeated by painting out of doors in the summer months. Wood-work painted in October looks better at the end of four years than it would in two if painted in June. The heat of the summer sun extracts the oil (the only portion of paint that nourishes and preserves the wood from decay) before it has time to penetrate below the surface. If judiciously applied in the autumn, it accomplishes the object—*preservation*—and preserves its body and appearance a much longer period.

Flexible Varnish. — First, India-rubber in shavings, one ounce; mineral naphtha, two pounds; digest at a gentle heat in a closed vessel till dissolved, and strain. Second, India-rubber, one ounce; drying oil, one quart; dissolved by as little heat as possible, employing constant stirring, then strain. Third, linseed oil, one gallon; dried white copperas and sugar of lead, each three ounces; litharge, eight ounces; boil with constant agitation till it strings well, then cool slowly and decant the clear. If too thick, thin it with quick-drying linseed oil. These are used for balloons, gas-bags, etc.

VARNISH. — A very free flowing black varnish is made with one pint of Canada balsam, four of bitumen (Judea), and four of chloroform.

Shingle Roofs.—A thick wash composed of lime, some salt, a little molasses, and some fine sand, applied to shingle roofs, render them nearly fire-proof, and are more durable than others not so covered.

To Make Boots Water-tight.— It can be done in this way: In a pint of best winter-strained lard oil, dissolve a piece of paraffine the size of a hickory nut, aiding the solution with a gentle heat, say 130° or 140° F. The readiest way to get pure paraffine is to take a piece of paraffine candle. Rub this solution on your boots about once a month; they can be blacked in the meantime. If the oil should make the leather too stiff, decrease the proportion of paraffine, and vice versa.

Composition for Leather.—One of the very best compounds known to us for rendering leather boots and shoes almost perfectly water-proof, and at the same time keeping them soft and pliable, is composed of fresh beef tallow, half an ounce, yellow beeswax, one ounce, and one-eighth of an ounce of shellac. Melt the tallow first and then remove all the membrane from it; add the beeswax in thin shavings, and when it is melted and combined with the tallow, add the shellac in powder, and stir until it is melted. Beeswax is one of the best known preservatives of leather. This compound should be applied warm to the boot or shoe, and the soles should receive a similar application to the uppers. In using it a rag or a piece of sponge should be employed, and the boot or shoe held cautiously before the fire or stove until the compound soaks into it. Care must be exercised not to expose the leather too close to the fire. If the boot be blackened and brushed until it becomes glossy before the application of this preparation, it will remain black and shining for a long period after it is applied. A little vegetable tar mixed with the foregoing composition makes it more adhesive, and improves its quality for walking among snow. A liberal application of this composition every two weeks during winter will keep boots and shoes that are worn daily water-proof and soft.

How to Save Shoe Soles.—It consists merely in melting together tallow and common rosin in the proportion of two parts of tallow to one of rosin, and apply to the soles of the boots or shoes as much of it as they will ab-

sorb. Shoe soles thus treated will wear much longer than those not so treated.

French Polish for Boots and Shoes. — Mix together two pints of the best vinegar and one pint of soft water; stir into it a quarter of a pound of glue, broken up, half a pound of logwood chips, a quarter of an ounce of finely powdered indigo, a quarter of an ounce of the best soft soap, and a quarter of an ounce of isinglass. Put the mixture over the fire, and let it boil for ten minutes or more. Then strain the liquid, and bottle and cork it: when cold it is fit for use. Apply it with a clean sponge.

To Polish Enameled Leather. — Two pints of the best cream, one pint of linseed oil; make them each lukewarm, and then mix them well together. Having previously cleaned the shoe, etc., from dirt, rub it over with a sponge dipped in the mixture: then rub it with a soft dry cloth until a brilliant polish is produced.

Boots and Shoes should be cleaned frequently, whether they are worn or not, and should never be left in a damp place, nor be put too near to the fire to dry. In cleaning them, be careful to *brush* the dirt from the seams, and not to scrape it with a knife, or you will cut the stitches. Let the hard brush do its work thoroughly well, and the polish will be all the brighter.

Paste Blacking. — 1. Ivory black, two pounds; molasses, one pound; olive oil and oil of vitriol, of each, a quarter of a pound. Mix as before, adding only sufficient water to form into a paste. 2. In larger quantity: Ivory black, three hundredweight; common molasses, two hundredweight; linseed oil and vinegar bottoms, of each, three gallons; oil of vitriol, twenty-eight pounds; water, a sufficient quantity.

Note. — The ivory black must be very finely ground for liquid blacking, otherwise it settles rapidly. The oil of vitriol is powerfully corrosive when undiluted, but uniting with the lime of the ivory black, it is partly neutralized, and does not injure the leather, while it much improves the quality of the blacking.

Liquid Blacking. — 1. Ivory black and molasses, of each, one pound; sweet oil and oil of vitriol, of each, a quarter of a pound. Put the first three together until the oil is perfectly mixed or "*killed*;" then add the oil of vitriol, diluted with three times its weight of water, and after standing three hours add one quart of water or sour beer. 2. In larger quantity it may be made as follows: Ivory black, three hundred-weight; molasses, two hundredweight; linseed oil, three gallons; oil of vitriol, twenty pounds; water, eighty gallons. Mix as above directed.

Driving Nails. — Within a year we have seen it stated, as a new truth, that if a nail were wetted in the mouth, and if, in addition, the narrow edge was placed with the grain of the wood, it would seldom split the board into which it was driven.

A Cheap Ice-House. — An inexpensive ice-house may be easily made: any farmer can construct his own without any difficulty. Lay some rails or poles on a piece of ground, sufficiently inclined to carry off water, fill the crevices with sawdust, and cover with old boards or slabs. Get from the saw-mill a few loads of slabs; take four about twelve feet long, notch the corners as for a log-house, set them on the platform, and you have a crib about ten and a half feet square by the width of the slab deep; fill this crib with sawdust and pack it down hard. Cut your ice so that it will pack close, lay it on the sawdust, put on another crib of slabs, and fill up and pack hard with sawdust all around, and so go on until you get up six or eight feet; then put a foot and a half of sawdust on top. Over this put a shed roof of slabs — one end of the slabs nearly to the ice, raising the other three feet. Ice will keep in such a house as well as in a more elaborate structure.

Home-made Ice. — In some places remote from fresh water, or ponds, it is difficult to procure ice; a cheap and convenient way is as follows: Procure a number of barrels—old flour barrels answer well—place them in an exposed situation (if you have no rubber hose to conduct the water the barrels should be placed near the pump or the hydrant), put about six inches of water in each barrel, this will soon be frozen solid, when four or six inches more water may be added occasionally until the barrel is full. A few days of cold weather will give you all the ice you need for family use, the only limit being the number of barrels. It is not necessary that these barrels be water tight, for the water freezing in the joints will soon effect this. When the barrel is frozen full of ice it may be *rolled* into the ice-house or place where you intend to keep it. Eight barrels filled in this way will give a family ten pounds of ice each day for four months.

MEM. — *The barrels being round, it is easy to remove the ice to its storage place, and then, if preferred, the hoops of the barrels may be broken and the barrels taken off; but this is not necessary. We prefer to pack it away in the barrel, being careful to fill all the spaces between the barrels with shavings, sawdust etc., and remove a barrel and cut it into pieces as we want to use the ice.*

Strength of Ice. — As people are a little timid about travelling on the ice at times, we give the capacity of the ice as furnished by the U. S. Ordnance Department, which is correct. Ice two inches thick will bear infantry; four inches, cavalry with light guns; six inches, heavy field guns; and eight inches, the heaviest siege guns with one thousand pounds weight to a square inch.

CEMENTS. — The term cement includes all those substances employed for the purpose of causing the adhesion of two or more bodies, whether originally separate, or divided by an accidental fracture. A cement that answers admirably under one set of circumstances may be perfectly useless in others. A vast number of cements are known and used in the various arts, but they may all be referred to a few classes; and our object in this paper will be to describe the manufacture and use of the best of each class.

It is an important rule, that the *less* cement in a joint the stronger it is. Domestic manipulators usually reverse this, by letting as much cement as possible remain in the joint, which is, therefore, necessarily a weak one. A thick, nearly solid cement, which cannot be pressed out of the joint, is always inferior to a thinner one, of which merely a connecting film remains between the united surfaces.

Mouth Glue.—A very useful preparation is sold by many stationers under this title; it is merely a thin cake of soluble glue, which, when moistened with the tongue, furnishes a ready means of uniting papers, etc. It is made by dissolving one pound of fine glue or gelatine in water, and, adding half a pound of brown sugar, boiling the whole until it is sufficiently thick to become solid on cooling; it is then poured into moulds, or on a slab slightly greased, and cut into the required shape when cool.

PASTE is usually made by rubbing up flour with cold water, and boiling; if a little alum is mixed before boiling it is much improved, being less clammy, working more freely in the brush, and thinner, a less quantity is required, and it is therefore stronger. If required in large quantity, as for papering rooms, it may be made by mixing one quartern of flour, one quarter of a pound of alum, and a little warm water; when mixed, the requisite quantity of boiling water should be poured on while the mixture is being stirred. Paste is only adapted to cementing paper; when used it should be spread on one side of the paper, which should then be folded with the pasted side inwards, and allowed to remain a few minutes before being opened and used; this swells the paper, and permits its being more smoothly and securely attached. Kept for a few days, paste becomes mouldy, and after a short time putrid; this inconvenience may be obviated by the use of

PERMANENT PASTE — Made by adding to each half pint of flour paste without alum, fifteen grains of corrosive sublimate, previously rubbed to powder in a mortar, the whole to be well mixed; this, if prevented from drying, by being kept in a covered pot, remains good any length of time, and is therefore convenient; but unfortunately it is extremely poisonous, though its excessively nauseous taste would prevent its being swallowed accidentally; it possesses the great advantage of not being liable to the attacks of insects.

TO MAKE PASTE THAT WILL KEEP FOR A YEAR. — Dissolve slowly in water two square inches of glue and an equal quantity of alum. Mix and boil with flour as usual, and when nearly cold stir in two teaspoonfuls of oil of cloves or lavender, the whole to make a pint of paste. Keep in a well-covered vessel.

Liquid Glue.—Several preparations were much in vogue a few years since under this title. The liquid glue of the shops is made by dissolving shellac in water, by boiling it along with borax, which possesses the peculiar property of causing the solution of the resinous lac. This preparation is convenient from its cheapness and freedom from smell; but it gives way if exposed to long-continued damp, which that made with naphtha resists. Of the use of *common glue* very little need be said: it should always be prepared in a glue-pot or double vessel, to prevent its being burned, which injures it very materially; the objection to the use of this contrivance is, that it renders it impossible to heat the glue in the inner vessel to the boiling point; this inconvenience can be obviated by employing in the outer vessel some liquid which boils at a higher temperature than pure water, such as a saturated solution of salt (made by adding one-third as much salt as water). This boils at 224° Fahr., 12° above the heat of boiling water, and enables the glue in the inner vessel to be heated to a much higher temperature than when pure water is employed. If a saturated solution of nitre is used, the temperature rises still higher.

Diamond Cement. — Soak isinglass in water till it is soft; then dissolve it in the smallest possible quantity of proof-spirit, by the aid of a gentle heat; in two ounces of this mixture dissolve ten grains of ammoniacum, and while still liquid, add half a dram of mastic, dissolved in three drams of rectified spirit; stir well together, and put into small bottles for sale.—*Directions for Use.*— Liquefy the cement by plunging the bottle in hot water, and use it directly. The cement improves the oftener the bottle is thus warmed; it resists the action of water and moisture perfectly.

Rice Flour Cement.—An excellent cement may be made from rice flour, which is at present used for that purpose in China and Japan. It is only necessary to mix the rice flour intimately with cold water, and gently simmer it over a fire, when it readily forms a delicate and durable cement, not only answering all the purposes of common paste, but admirably adapted for joining together paper, cards, etc., in forming the various beautiful and tasteful ornaments which afford much employment and amusement to the ladies. When made of the consistence of plaster-clay, models, busts, bas-relievos, etc., may be formed of it; and the articles, when dry, are susceptible of high polish, and very durable.

The White of an Egg, well beaten with quicklime, and a small quantity of very old cheese, forms an excellent substitute for cement, when wanted in a hurry, either for broken china or old ornamental glassware.

Cement for Broken China, Glass, etc. --The following recipe, from experience, we know to be a good one; and being nearly colorless, it possesses advantages which liquid glue and other cements do not: — Dissolve half an ounce of gum acacia in a wineglass of boiling water; add plaster of Paris sufficient to form a thick paste, and apply it with a brush to the parts required to be cemented together. Several articles upon our toilet table have been repaired most effectually by this recipe.

Lime and Egg Cement is frequently made by moistening the edges to be united with white of egg, dusting on some lime from a piece of muslin, and bringing the edges into contact. A much better mode is to slack some freshly-burned lime with a small quantity of *boiling* water; this occasions it to fall into a very fine dry powder, if excess of water has not been added. The white of egg used should be intimately and thoroughly mixed, by beating with an equal bulk of water, and the slacked lime added to the mixture, so as to form a thin paste, which should be used speedily, as it soon sets. This is a valuable cement, possessed of great strength, and capable of withstanding boiling water. Cements made with lime and blood, scraped cheese, or curd, may be regarded as inferior varieties of it. Cracked vessels of earthenware and glass may often be usefully, though not ornamentally, repaired by white lead spread on strips of calico, and secured with bands of twine. But, in point of strength, all ordinary cements yield the palm to Jeffery's Patent Marine Glue. It is not affected by water. It is made as follows: — Take one pound of India-rubber, cut it into small pieces, and dissolve it in about four gallons of coal-tar naphtha, the mixture being well stirred for some time, till perfect solution has taken place. After ten or twelve days, when the liquid has acquired the consistence of cream, two parts, by weight, of shellac are added to one of the liquid. This mixture is put into an iron vessel having a discharge-pipe at the bottom, and heat applied, the whole being kept well stirred. The liquid which flows out of the pipe is spread upon slabs, and preserved in the form of plates. When required for use it is heated in an iron pot to about 248° Fahr., and applied hot with a brush.

The Red Cement, which is employed by instrument-makers for cementing glass to metals, and which is very cheap, and exceedingly useful for a variety of purposes, is made by melting five parts of black rosin, one part of yellow wax, and then stirring in gradually one part of red ochre or Venetian red, in fine powder, and previously *well dried*. This cement requires to be melted before use, and it adheres better if the objects to which it is applied are warmed. A soft cement, of a somewhat similar character, may be found useful for covering the corks of preserved fruit, and other bottles, and it is made by melting yellow wax with an equal quantity of resin, or of common turpentine (not oil of turpentine, but the resin), using the latter for a very soft cement, and stirring in, as before, some dried Venetian red. Bearing in mind our introductory remarks, it will be seen that to unite broken substances with a thick cement is disadvantageous, the object being to bring the surfaces as closely together as possible. As an illustration of a right and a wrong way of mending, we will suppose a plaster of Paris figure broken. The wrong way to mend it is by a thick paste of plaster, which makes, not a joint, but a botch. The right way to mend it is by means of some well-made carpenter's glue, which, being absorbed in the porous plaster, leaves merely a film covering the two surfaces; and if well done, the figure is stronger there than elsewhere.

Mastic Cement. — This is employed for making a superior coating to inside walls, but must not be confounded with the *resin mastic*. It is made by mixing twenty parts of well-washed and sifted sharp sand with two parts of litharge and one of freshly-burned and slacked quicklime, in fine *dry* powder. This is made into a putty, by mixing with linseed oil. It sets in a few hours, having the appearance of light stone; and we mention it, as it may be frequently employed with advantage in repairing broken stone-work (as steps), by filling up the missing parts. The employment of Roman cement, plaster, etc., for masonry work, hardly comes within the limits of domestic manipulation.

Cement for Leather and Cloth. – An adhesive material for uniting the parts of boots and shoes, and for the seams of articles of clothing, may be made thus : —Take one pound of gutta-percha, four ounces of India-rubber, two ounces of pitch, one ounce of shellac, two ounces of oil. The ingredients are to be melted together, and used hot.

BIRDLIME. — Take any quantity of linseed oil, say half a pint; put it into an old pot, or any vessel that will stand the fire without breaking. The vessel must not be more than one-third full; put it on a slow fire, stir it occasionally until it thickens as much as required; this will be known by cooling the stick in water, and trying it with the fingers. It is best to make it rather harder than for use. Then pour it into cold water. It can be brought back to the consistency required with a little Archangel tar.

MUCILAGE. — Take a quarter pound of gum arabic, put into a bottle with half a pint of water, stir it occasionally; next day it will be fit for use. This is the mucilage sold in bottles.

MUCILAGE FOR LABELS. — Macerate five parts of good glue in eighteen to twenty parts of water for a day, and to the liquid add nine parts of rock candy and three parts of gum arabic. The mixture can be brushed upon paper while lukewarm ; it keeps well, does not stick together, and when moistened adheres firmly to bottles. For the labels of soda or seltzer water bottles, it is well to prepare a paste of good rye flour and glue, to which linseed oil, varnish, and turpentine have been added in the proportion of half an ounce of each to the pound. Labels prepared in the latter way do not fall off in damp cellars.

To Make Paper Stick to White-washed Walls.—Make a sizing of common glue and water, of the consistency of linseed oil, and apply with a brush to the wall, being careful to go over every part; the top and bottom should have especial attention. Apply the paper in the usual way.

To Soften Putty and Remove Paint.

—To destroy paint on old doors, etc., and to soften putty in window frames, so that the glass may be taken out without breaking and cutting, take one pound of American pearlash, three pounds of quick-stone lime, slack the lime in water, add the pearlash, and make the whole about the consistence of paint. Apply it to both sides of the glass, and let it remain for twelve hours, when the putty will be softened so that the glass may be taken out of the frame without being cut, and with the greatest facility. To destroy paint, lay the above over the whole body with an old brush (as it will spoil a new one); let it remain for twelve or fourteen hours, when the paint can be easily scraped off.

To Remove Old Putty.

—Dip a small brush in nitric or muriatic acid, and with it anoint or paint over the dry putty that adheres to the broken glass and frames of your windows; after an hour's interval, the putty will have become so soft as to be easily removable.

Remedy for Smoky Chimneys.

—If a chimney is built near a wall, or any other obstruction to the passage of the wind when it is blowing from the side on which the chimney is erected, the compression of the air in the vicinity of the wall is such that it will seek every crevice, stove-pipe and chimney through which to escape, thus producing a draft the wrong way. To prevent this, raise the top of the chimney above surrounding objects; this is generally effectual.

How to Read a Gas Meter.

—The veracity of gas companies is often called in question by consumers of that article, though with how much justice is not, of course, for us to decide. The employés of the company maintain that they deal honestly by their customers, and the latter, knowing that they are in the power of the company, often pay their bills feeling dissatisfaction. The matter of dissatisfaction might be easily remedied. The process of reading a meter is almost as simple as telling the time of day by a clock, and may be acquired by any person of common intelligence in ten minutes. Below we give a brief explanation.

At the top of the meter is placed a small tin case, three or four inches long, which opens by means of a little door in front, and discloses a plate with three small dials, about an inch in diameter, which are furnished with one pointer apiece, moved by cog-wheels and pinions on the inside, which, in turn, are made to revolve by a large wheel propelled by the passage of the gas. The circle on the dial is divided into ten spaces, numbered around the edges with figures like the dial of a clock. The dial on the extreme right indicates, by means of its pointer, the burning of 100 feet of gas; the dial in the middle indicates the burning of 1000 feet; and the dial on the left the burning of 10,000 feet. For instance, the three pointers all stand at cipher. The pointer on the right hand dial having moved from cipher to figure one, indicates that 100 feet of gas have been consumed. If it move to the two, 200 feet, and so on, until the pointer has gone around the circle, and again reached the cipher, when 1000 feet have been consumed.

When this point has been reached, the eye will be directed to the next dial, when it will be found that the pointer has moved to the figure one, indicating that 1000 feet have been consumed. The pointer on the first dial continues on, and still marking the amount passing. Suppose that at the end of the first month the pointer on the first dial stands at eight, that on the second between one and two, it is easy to understand that 1800 feet have been consumed. When the pointer on the second dial reaches two, that on the first is again at cipher, indicating that 2000 feet have been consumed. Thus it goes on until the pointer on the second dial has made the circuit, which indicates that 10,000 feet have been consumed, when the pointer on the third dial will stand at one. This, in turn, with an entire revolution, indicates that 100,000 feet have been consumed. Taking the three dials in connection, the exact amount of cubic feet may thus be ascertained, commencing anew every time 100,000 feet have run through the meter and been consumed.

Now, to ascertain the exact amount of gas which will be consumed during the coming month, inspect the dials of the meter on the first of the month. The pointer on the left hand dial perhaps stands between the figures 6 and 7, indicating 60,000 feet. The pointer on the middle dial stands between 5 and 6, indicating 5000 feet, and the pointer on the right-hand dial stands between 7 and 8, indicating 700 feet. You thus have a total of 65,700 feet of gas previously consumed. Set the figures down, and at the end of the month again inspect the dial. The right-hand dial stands, perhaps, nearly as before, and still indicates 60,000 feet. The middle one has moved on, and stands between 7 and 8, indicating 7000. The right-hand one has made a number of revolutions, and stands between 1 and 2, indicating 100 feet. We then have a total of 67,100 feet. Subtract from this the number set down at the beginning of the month, and you have 1400 feet of gas consumed. Multiply this by the price per cubic foot, and you have your gas bill for the month. If housekeepers would take the trouble to do this themselves, they would satisfy themselves, and be sure to guard against mistakes.

How to Detect Escaping Gas. — If your gas bills seem too high, or you have the evidence of escaping gas by sense of smell, but not positively so, take a reading of the meter when no burners are in use, and after an hour or so repeat the reading, and if gas is escaping it will be shown. To detect the locality of the leak is often a more difficult matter. The first thing is to see that no burners have been left turned on by accident, which is often the case where the cock has no *stop*,

and is caused by the cock being turned partially round again so as to open the vent. Imperfect stop-cocks are, for this reason, dangerous, and should be at once removed.

The next thing to do in order to detect a leak is to try the joints of the gas-fittings. The sense of smell will frequently be sufficient by bringing the face near the suspected joint; a lighted taper or match held near the joint is a more certain plan. If gas is escaping, it will take fire at the leak, or if too little to burn steadily, it will momentarily catch and extinguish in little puffs.

Sometimes the gas escapes from the joints or imperfect piping between the ceiling and floor, or behind the walls or casings.

If beneath the floor, the sense of smell will generally detect the section of the floor under which the leak is, as it escapes owing to its levity upwards through the crevices of the floor, and penetrates the carpet, if there be one. If bracket or side burners are used, and the escaping gas is behind the walls or casings, the crevices in the casings, or the opening where the pipe enters the room, will let the escaping gas enter the room sufficiently at these points to indicate somewhat nearly the location of the leak.

In such cases, the proper way is *never* to apply a light to the crevices or casings, but to turn off the gas at the meter and send for a gasfitter, otherwise an explosion may occur, involving serious consequences. In ordinary leaks of gas-fixtures and pipes, whether at the joints or at the attachment of the burner, the fitting or burner should be unscrewed, and white lead or common bar soap rubbed in the threads, and then screwed home again. This can often be done without any aid from a gasfitter.

How to Detect Counterfeit Notes. — Examine the vignette and pictures on the note; see if the faces look natural. The eyes should be so perfect that the white is clear and the pupil distinct. The clothing should fit well, and show the folds clearly, and should have an easy, graceful appearance. The sky should be clear, or soft and even. This would indicate a genuine note. But if, instead of the above, the features are indistinct, the eyes dull, the clothing stiff and ill-fitting, a counterfeit may be presumed.

All circular ornaments, or rulings around or on which figures are printed, should be uniform and regular; the shading or parallel ruling and the fine lines and curves in genuine notes are perfect, but in counterfeit notes there 's an absence of uniformity and finish. The letters and figures should be uniform and regular, the lines and curves of which they are composed without breaks, and parallel with each other. All small figures and letters on a genuine note are always well executed, but in counterfeits not so.

The signatures should be well examined—the genuine has a free, smooth stroke. Counterfeits usually have a cramped appearance; and even when they are lithographed, they have to be traced over with ink; this gives a ragged edge to the lines and an irregular stroke.

Sometimes a note is altered by raising the amount; this is done by cutting out the genuine figures, and inserting or pasting in figures of a larger denomination. In such cases, the difference in the paper and the color of the ink may be seen; but the best and surest way to detect these altered notes is to hold the note up to the light; the parts pasted in can be seen.

As counterfeit money is generally taken in a hurry, and during a press of business, or through carelessness, all hurry and confusion when taking money should be avoided, for with ordinary care counterfeits may be detected.

Simple Method of Ascertaining Death.—Dr. Carrière, of St. Jean du Gard, in reply to the offer of the Marquis d'Orches, of a premium of twenty thousand francs for a practical method of determining death, furnished the

24

following, which he says he has practiced for forty years : Place the hand, with the fingers closely pressed one against the other, close to a lighted lamp or candle; if alive, the tissues will be observed to be of a transparent, or a rosy hue, and the capillary circulation of life in full play; if, on the contrary, the hand of a dead person be placed in the same relation to light, none of the phenomena are observed — we see but a hand as of marble, without circulation, without life.

To Light a Dark Room, in which the darkness is caused by its being situated on a narrow street or lane. If the glass of a window in such a room is placed several inches within the outer face of the wall, as is the general custom in building houses, it will admit very little light—that which it gets being only the reflection from the walls of the opposite houses. If, however, for the window be substituted another in which all the panes of glass are roughly ground on the outside, and flush with the outer wall, the light from the whole of the visible sky and from the remotest parts of the opposite wall will be introduced into the apartment, reflected from the innumerable faces or facets which the rough grinding of the glass has produced. The whole window will appear as if the sky were beyond it, and from every point of this luminous surface light will radiate into all parts of the room.

To Solder Lead Pipe.—It sometimes happens that lead pipes are accidentally cut in excavations and other places, and the water cannot be conveniently shut off to repair it. First stop the leak by a bandage around the pipe, or cut it in two, and drive a plug into each end of the pipe, then place a few quarts of powdered ice and salt around each end of the pipe. In a few minutes the water in the pipes will be frozen. Then remove the plugs, and solder the joint as quickly as you can; the ice will soon thaw out of the pipe, and the water flow through it as usual.

Pipe Joints *to Water - Closets, Wash-*

bowls, Sinks, etc. — The old plan of cementing the lead pipes to closet pans, etc., is very objectionable. Take about four inches of rubber tubing, insert the lead pipe in one end, and draw the other end over the arm or neck of the pan, and bind each end with a few turns of copper wire. In this way a cheap, durable, and water-tight joint is obtained.

Marking Cutlery.—Take a quarter ounce each of alum, blue stone (sulphate of copper), and common salt, pound all together and dissolve in a quarter pint of vinegar. Cover that portion of the article to be marked with wax, then draw the letters with a large needle through the wax down to the surface of the metal; now into the lines pour some of the above mixture, and allow it to remain half an hour, then clean all off, and the metal will be found permanently etched as marked with the needle.

To Soften Hard Water.—Professor Clarke of Scotland has obtained a patent for softening water obtained from chalk or lime formations, by means of quicklime itself, which precipitates the soluble carbonate by converting it into an insoluble—into whiting, in fact—and so deprives the water of its hardness.

To Cut Iron or Brass.—Take the steel spring from an old corset and hack it on the edge with an old chisel or knife, making the teeth as near together as possible, and uniform in size. This is easily done by placing the chisel on the edge of the spring and striking it lightly with a hammer; then place the chisel as near the cut so made as the ridge formed by the chisel will allow, again strike with the hammer, and continue the operation until you have three or four inches in length. With the saw so made and a little kerosene (oil) a bar of iron can soon be cut in two.

How to Bore Holes in Glass. — Any hard steel tool will cut glass with great facility when wet freely with camphor, dissolved in turpentine. A drill bore may be used, or even the

hand alone. A hole bored may be easily enlarged by a round file. The ragged edges of glass vessels may also be smoothed thus with a flat file. Flat window glass may be easily sawed with a watch-spring saw, by aid of this solution. In short, the most brittle glass can be wrought almost as easily as brass by the use of cutting tools kept constantly moist with the camphorized oil of turpentine.

To Cut Glass to any shape, without a diamond, hold it quite level under water, and with a pair of strong scissors clip it away by small bits from the edges.

Ventilating Waterproof Cloth. — India-rubber and oil-cloth capes and coats, although perfectly waterproof, are unfit for wearing during warm rainy weather, because they retain the perspiration and prevent the necessary ventilation required for the body. The best light capes for soldiers and travellers when marching during wet weather, are made of what is called "Tweed cloth," prepared as follows: Take two pounds and four ounces of alum, and dissolve it in ten gallons of water; in like manner dissolve the same quantity of sugar of lead in a similar quantity of water, and mix the two together. The cloth is immersed for one hour in the solution, and stirred occasionally, when it is taken out, dried in the shade, washed in clean water, and dried again. This preparation enables the cloth to repel water like the feathers of a duck's back, and yet allows the perspiration to pass somewhat freely through it, which is not the case with gutta-percha or India-rubber cloth.

The sulphate of lead is formed in this manner, and enters into the pores of the cloth. It is an insoluble salt; hence, the reason why it makes the cloth waterproof, while, at the same time, there is sufficient room in the interstices to allow the perspiration and heat from the body to escape.

Tweed cloth is light, and not expensive; it is also soft and pliable, and capable of being rolled up into small oulk without permanent wrinkles being formed in it. We have frequently prepared cloth in this manner, and have found it to answer an excellent purpose in rainy weather; while at the same time, in color and appearance, it does not differ from unprepared cloth.

A **Grindstone** should not be exposed to the weather, as it not only injures the woodwork, but the sun's rays harden the stone so much as, in time, to render it useless. Neither should it stand in the water in which it runs, as the part remaining in water softens so much that it wears unequally, and this is a very common cause of grindstones becoming "out of true." The grindstone is a self-sharpening tool, and after having been turned for some time in one direction (if a hard stone) the motion should be reversed. Sand of the right grit applied occasionally to a hard stone will render it quite effectual.

Permanent Ink for Writing in Relief on Zinc. — Bichloride of platinum, dry, one part; gum arabic, one part; distilled water, ten parts. The letters traced upon zinc with this solution turn black immediately. The black characters resist the action of weak acids, of rain, or of the elements in general, and the liquid is thus adapted for marking signs, labels, or tags which are liable to exposure. To bring out the letters in relief, immerse the zinc tag in a weak acid for a few moments. The writing is not attacked, while the metal is dissolved away.

Cure for Cold in the Head. — Inhale hartshorn through the nostrils six or eight times a minute until relief is obtained. Then after an hour or so repeat again. This remedy is used in France with good results.

Domestic Hints. — *Why is the flesh of sheep that are fed near the sea more nutritious than that of others?*—Because the saline particles (sea salt) which they find with their green food gives purity to their blood and flesh.

Why does the marbled appearance of fat in meat indicate that it is young and

tender? — Because in young animals fat is dispersed through the muscles, but in old animals it is laid in masses on the outside of the flesh.

Why is some flesh white and other flesh red? — White flesh contains a larger proportion of albumen (similar to the white of egg) than that which is red. The amount of blood retained in the flesh also influences its color.

Why are raw oysters more wholesome than those that are cooked? — When cooked they are partly deprived of salt water, which promotes their digestion; their albumen becomes hard (like hard-boiled eggs).

Why have some oysters a green tinge? —This has been erroneously attributed to the effects of copper; but it arises from the oyster feeding upon small green sea-weeds, which grow where such oysters are found.

Why is cabbage rendered more wholesome by being boiled in two waters? — Because cabbages contain an oil, which is apt to produce bad effects, and prevents some persons from eating "green" vegetables. When boiled in two waters, the first boiling carries off the greater part of this oil.

Why should horseradish be scraped for the table only just before it is required? — Because the peculiar oil of horseradish is very volatile; it quickly evaporates, and leaves the vegetable substance dry and insipid.

Why is mint eaten with pea soup? — The properties of mint are stomachic and antispasmodic. It is therefore useful to prevent the flatulencies that might arise, especially from soups made of green or dried peas.

Why is apple sauce eaten with pork and goose? — Because it is slightly laxative, and therefore tends to counteract the effects of rich and stimulating meats. The acid of the apples also neutralizes the oily nature of the fat, and prevents biliousness.

Why does milk turn sour during thunder-storms? — Because, in an electric condition of the atmosphere, ozone is generated. Ozone is oxygen in a state of great intensity; and oxygen is a general acidifier of many organic substances. Boiling milk prevents its becoming sour, because it expels the oxygen.

Why does the churning of cream or milk produce butter? — Because the action of stirring, together with a moderate degree of warmth, causes the cells in which the butter is confined to burst; the disengaged fat collects in flakes, and ultimately coheres in large masses.

What is the blue mould which appears sometimes upon cheese? — It is a species of fungus, or minute vegetable, which may be distinctly seen when examined by a magnifying glass.

Why are some of the limbs of birds more tender than others? — The tenderness or toughness of flesh is determined by the amount of exercise the muscles have undergone. Hence the wing of a bird that chiefly walks, and the leg of a bird that chiefly flies, are the most tender.

Why does tea frequently cure headache? — Because, by its stimulant action on the general circulation, in which the brain participates, the nervous congestions are overcome.

Why are clothes of smooth and shining surfaces best adapted for hot weather?— Because they reflect or turn back the rays of the sun, which are thus prevented from penetrating them.

Why is loose clothing warmer than tight articles of dress? — Because the loose dress encloses a stratum of warm air, which the tight dress shuts out; for the same reason, woollen articles, though not warmer in themselves, appear so, by keeping warm air near to the body.

Why should the water poured upon tea be at the boiling point? — Because it requires the temperature of boiling water to extract the peculiar oil of tea.

Why does the first infusion of tea possess more aroma than the second?— Because the first infusion, in which the water used is at the boiling temperature, takes up the essential oil of the tea, while the second water receives only

the bitter extract supplied by the tannic acid of tea.

Why does a head-dress of sky-blue become a fair person? — Because light blue is the complementary color of pale orange, which is the foundation of the blonde complexion and hair.

Why are yellow, orange, or red colors suitable to a person of dark hair and complexion?—Because those colors, by contrast with the dark skin and hair, show to the greater advantage themselves, while they enrich the hue of black.

Why is a delicate green favorable to pale blonde complexions? — Because it imparts a rosiness to such complexions —red, its complementary color, being reflected upon green.

Why is light green unfavorable to ruddy complexions?—Because it increases the redness, and has the effect of producing an overheated appearance.

Why is violet an unfavorable color for every kind of complexion? — Because reflecting yellow, they augment that tint when it is present in the skin or hair, change blue into green, and give to an olive complexion a jaundiced look.

Why is blue suitable to brunettes?— Because it reflects orange, and adds to the darkness of the complexion.

Why do blue veils preserve the complexion? — Because they diminish the effect of the scorching rays of light, just as the blue glass over photographic studios diminishes the effect of certain rays that would injure the delicate processes of photography.

A New Cure for Fever and Ague. -- Just as the chill is coming on, start at the top of a long flight of stairs and crawl down on your hands and feet, head foremost. You never did harder work in your life, and when you arrive at the bottom, instead of shaking, you will find yourself puffing, red in the face, and perspiring freely, from the strongest exertions made in the effort to support yourself. It will effect a cure, beyond a doubt; but whether from this cause or from that, we will never tell

Horn must be treated in the same manner as bone and ivory for the various colors given under that heading.

IMITATION OF TORTOISE-SHELL. — First steam and then press the horn into proper shapes, and afterward lay the following mixture on with a small brush, in imitation of the mottle of tortoise-shell : — Take equal parts of quicklime and litharge, and mix with strong soap-lees; let this remain until it is thoroughly dry, brush off, and repeat two or three times, if necessary. Such parts as are required to be of a reddish-brown should be covered with a mixture of whiting and the stain.

Iron. — *Black, for ships' guns, shots, etc.* — To one gallon of vinegar add a quarter of a pound of iron rust, let it stand for a week; then add a pound of dry lampblack, and three-quarters of a pound of copperas: stir it up for a couple of days. Lay five or six coats on the gun, etc., with a sponge, allowing it to dry well between each. Polish with linseed oil and soft woollen rag, and it will look like ebony.

Paper and Parchment. *Blue.* — 1. Stain it green with the verdigris stain, and brush over with a solution of pearl-ash — two ounces to the pint — till it becomes blue. 2. Use the blue stain for wood.

PAPER AND PARCHMENT. *Green* and *Red.* — The same as for wood.

PAPER AND PARCHMENT. *Orange.* — Brush over with a tincture of turmeric, formed by infusing an ounce of the root in a pint of spirit of wine; let this dry, and give another coat of pearl-ash solution, made by dissolving two ounces of the salt in a quart of water.

PAPER AND PARCHMENT. *Purple.* — 1. Brush over with the expressed juice of ripe privet berries. 2. The same as for wood.

PAPER AND PARCHMENT. *Yellow.* — 1. Brush over with tincture of turmeric. 2. Add anatto or dragon's-blood to the tincture of turmeric, and brush over as usual.

WOOD. — *Black.* — 1. Drop a little sulphuric acid into a small quantity of water, brush over the wood and hold to the fire; it will be a fine black, and receive a good polish. 2. Take half a gallon of vinegar, an ounce of bruised nut galls, of logwood chips and copperas each half a pound — boil well; add half an ounce of the tincture of sesquichloride of iron, formerly called the muriated tincture, and brush on hot. 3. Use the stain given for ships' guns. 4. Take half a gallon of vinegar, half a pound of dry lampblack, and three pounds of iron rust, sifted. Mix, and let stand for a week. Lay three coats of this on hot, and then rub with linseed oil, and you will have a fine deep black. 5. Add to the above stain an ounce of nut galls, half a pound of logwood chips, and a quarter of a pound of copperas; lay on three coats, oil well, and you will have a black stain that will stand any kind of weather, and one that is well suited for ships' combings, etc. 6. Take a pound of logwood chips, a quarter of a pound of Brazil wood, and boil for an hour and a half in a gallon of water. Brush the wood several times with this decoction while hot. Make a decoction of nut galls by simmering gently, for three or four days, a quarter of a pound of the galls in two quarts of water; give the wood three coats of this, and, while wet, lay on a solution of sulphate of iron (two ounces to a quart), and when dry, oil or varnish. 7. Give three coats with a solution of copper filings in aquafortis, and repeatedly brush over with the logwood decoction, until the greenness of the copper is destroyed. 8. Boil half a pound of logwood chips in two quarts of water, add an ounce of pearlash, and apply hot with a brush. Then take two quarts of the logwood decoction, and half an ounce of verdigris, and the same of copperas; strain, and throw in half a pound of iron rust. Brush the work well with this, and oil.

WOOD. *Blue.* — 1. Dissolve copper filings in aquafortis, brush the wood with it, and then go over the work with a hot solution of pearlash (two ounces to a pint of water), till it assumes a perfectly blue color. 2. Boil a pound of indigo, two pounds of woad, and three ounces of alum, in a gallon of water; brush well over until thoroughly stained.

IMITATION OF BOTANY BAY WOOD. — Boil half a pound of French berries (the unripe berries of the *rhamnus infectorius*) in two quarts of water till of a deep yellow, and while boiling hot give two or three coats to the work. If a deeper color is desired, give a coat of logwood decoction over the yellow. When nearly dry, form the grain with *black stain*, used hot; and when dry, dust and varnish.

WOOD. *Green.* — Dissolve verdigris in vinegar, and brush over with the hot solution until of a proper color.

WOOD. *Mahogany Color.* — *Dark.* 1. Boil half a pound of madder and two ounces of logwood chips in a gallon of water, and brush well over while hot· when dry, go over the whole with pearlash solution, two drams to the quart. 2. Put two ounces of dragon's-blood, bruised, into a quart of oil of turpentine; let the bottle stand in a warm place, shake frequently, and, when dissolved, steep the work in the mixture.

WOOD. *Light Red Brown.* — 1. Boil half a pound of madder and a quarter of a pound of fustic in a gallon of water; brush over the work when boiling hot, until properly stained. 2. The surface of the work being quite smooth, brush over with a weak solution of aquafortis, half an ounce to the pint, and then finish with the following: — Put four ounces and a half of dragon's-blood and an ounce of soda, both well bruised, to three pints of spirits of wine; let it stand in a warm place, shake frequently, strain, and lay on with a soft brush, repeating until of a proper color; polish with linseed oil or varnish.

WOOD. *Purple.* — Brush the work several times with the logwood decoction used for No. 6 *black*, and when dry give a coat of pearlash solution — one dram to a quart — taking care to lay it on evenly.

WOOD. *Red.* — 1 Boil a pound of Brazil wood and an ounce of pearlash in a gallon of water, and while hot brush over the work until of a proper color. Dissolve two ounces of alum in a quart of water, and brush the solution over the work before it dries. 2. Take a gallon of the above stain, add two more ounces of pearlash ; use hot, and brush often with the alum solution. 3. Use a cold infusion of archil, and brush over with the pearlash solution.

IMITATION OF ROSEWOOD. — 1. Boil half a pound of logwood in three pints of water till it is of a very dark red, add half an ounce of salt of tartar; stain the work with the liquor while boiling hot, giving three coats; then, with a painter's graining brush, form streaks with *black-stain;* let dry, and varnish. 2. Brush over with the logwood decoction *black*, three or four times; put half a pound of iron filings into two quarts of vinegar; then with a graining brush, or cane bruised at the end, apply the iron filing solution in the form required, and polish with beeswax and turpentine when dry, or varnish.

WOOD. *Yellow.* — 1. Brush over with the tincture of turmeric. 2. Warm the work and brush over with weak aquafortis, then hold to the fire. Varnish or oil as usual.

To Ascertain the Age of Cows.— A safe rule is afforded by the teeth. At birth, the two centre teeth (front) protrude through the gum; at the end of the second week the second pair appear; at the end of the third week the third pair, and at the end of the fourth week, the fourth and last pair. The wearing of these teeth now constitutes the only guide for the next three months, at the expiration of which time all these (which are called the "milk teeth") begin to diminish in size and shrink away from each other, which process continues until the animal is two years old, when the new teeth begin to push out slender remnants of the old and shrunken ones. At the end of second year, the first two permanent teeth appear in front; at three years, the second pair are well up; at four, the third pair; and at five years, the fourth and last pair have appeared, and the central pair are beginning to be worn down; at six years, the last pair are full-size; at seven years, the dark line with bony boundary appears in all the teeth, and a broad circular mark appears within the central pair; at eight years, this mark appears in all the teeth; at nine years, a process of shrinkage and absorption, similar to that which reduced the front teeth, begins to take place in the central pair; at ten, it begins with the second pair; at eleven, with the third pair; at twelve, with the fourth pair. The age of the animal, after this period is attained, is determined by the degree of shrinkage and wearing away of all the teeth in the order of their appearance, until the fifteenth year, when scarcely any teeth remain.

How to Prepare Sea - Water - There cannot be a question that by far the simplest plan would consist in the evaporation of the sea-water itself in large quantities, preserving the resulting salt in closely-stopped vessels, to prevent the absorption of moisture, and vending it in this form to the consumer; the proportion of this dry, saline matter being fifty-six ounces to ten gallons of water less three pints. This plan was suggested by Dr. E.

Schweitzer, for the extemporaneous formation of sea-water for medicinal baths. The proportion ordered to be used is six ounces to the gallon of water, and stirred well until dissolved.

Indelible Ink TO MARK LINEN WITH A PEN. — Twenty two parts carbonate of soda are dissolved in eighty-five of distilled water, and twenty parts of pulverized gum arabic are diffused through the menstruum. Eleven parts of nitrate of silver are then liquefied in twenty parts of ammonia. The mixed fluids are next warmed in a flask, by which they become grayish-black, and partly coagulated; subsequently brown and clear; then, when ebullition commences, very dark, and of such a consistence that it will flow readily from the pen.

INDELIBLE INK FOR MARKING LINEN WITH STAMPS OR STENCIL PLATES.—Five parts nitrate of silver, twelve parts distilled water, five parts powdered gum arabic, seven parts carbonate of soda, and ten parts ammonia. Mix the carbonate of soda and the gum arabic in the distilled water, then in a separate vessel, dissolve the nitrate of silver in the ammonia, then mix the two liquids and heat them in a flask, until it acquires a very dark tint. Both of these inks become blacker by washing.

EVERY ONE HIS OWN LAWYER.

REQUISITES OF A CONTRACT—NOTES, DRAFTS AND CHECKS—LANDLORD AND
TENANT—HOW TO DRAW A WILL—PARTNERSHIP AGREEMENTS.

"I wish every man knew enough law to keep out
of it." — *Lord Bacon.*

An **Agreement** is a contract between persons to do or refrain from doing certain things.

A CONTRACT, to be binding, must be mutually understood. If made under compulsion, or procured by fraud, it may be voided.

A CONTRACT may be orally, or in writing. If formally agreed to, either orally or in writing, it is special. If inferred from the acts of the parties, it is an implied contract.

A BOND is an instrument in writing under seal. The party giving the bond acknowledges his indebtedness to a certain amount, with a provision that if the party who gives the bond does some particular act (for which the bond was given as security) then the obligation is void, otherwise it shall remain in full force.

IDIOTS, LUNATICS, common drunkards, minors, and those incapacitated by age or infirmity, are not competent to make contracts.

THE SUBJECTS of contracts must be legal acts or transactions; but illegality will not be presumed, it must be shown.

CONTRACTS to do illegal acts are void. The law will not compel any person to break it, or enforce immorality.

THERE must be a valuable consideration in contract to make it valid—it may be relationship or affection. The consideration may not be adequate, but it must have some real value, and must

376

be stated.

A WRITTEN contract must contain the whole of the agreement; oral testimony will not be admitted to vary it.

GOOD FAITH is essential to a valid contract; fraud will make it void.

PARTIES to a contract are supposed to know the law; their ignorance in relation to a question of *law* will not invalidate a contract; but ignorance of the *fact* excuses an illiterate man who signs a deed which is read to him *falsely,* and will invalidate it.

Legal Principles. — AGREEMENTS are above the law.

A PERSON finding property, on which a definite reward has been offered, has a lien upon the property found for payment of the reward.

THE LAW compels no one to do impossibilities.

POSSESSION is a strong point in law.

IF a person in making a sale shows a specimen of the goods, it does not become a sale by sample, unless so agreed.

EVERY ACT between parties is to be taken most strongly against the maker.

CONTRACTS made on Sunday are void.

IT IS fraud to conceal fraud.

IGNORANCE of the law excuses no man.

HE WHO IS FIRST in point of time has the best title.

An **Assignment** is a transfer in writing of the title or interests of one party to another, and is only valid when made in good faith.

An assignment made with intent to hinder, delay, or defraud creditors, is void. If made for the benefit of creditors, it must be an absolute surrender of all the debtor's effects. If any effects are secretly held back, it is fraud and punishable.

An assignment, like any other conveyance of land and other property, must be acknowledged and recorded. No particular form is required. Any language showing an intention to transfer an interest is sufficient.

Know all men by these presents, That I, A. B., of Boston, in consideration of one hundred dollars, to me in hand, paid by C. D., have sold and assigned to C. D. and his assigns, all my right, title, and interest in the within written instrument, and to the proceeds thereof; and I do hereby authorize him, in my name or otherwise, but to his own use and at his own cost, to enforce the same according to its intents.

Witness my hand and seal, this seventh day of August, 187

A. B. [SEAL.]

Executed and delivered ⎫
in the presence of   ⎬

Arbitrations and Awards. — An agreement by parties to refer matters in dispute between them to other parties for a decision, is called a submission.

The persons to whom the point in dispute are referred, are called arbitrators. An award is the decision rendered by the arbitrators.

The submission may be withdrawn by either party from the arbitrators, any time *before the award is made*, the party so withdrawing paying the whole costs. But if the award is made in writing, it can be enforced.

While an award must not embrace any extraneous matter, it must embrace everything submitted; must not be uncertain in its character, but specific in its terms, and clear and distinct in language.

In ordinary cases of arbitration, it is usual for each party to name a person as his arbitrator, and for these arbitrators so appointed, *before considering the matter submitted to them*, to appoint a referee; this referee must be satisfactory to both arbitrators, and

he must consent to act in the matter. If the two arbitrators come to a decision, the referee is not called upon to act; but if they cannot come to a decision, the points in dispute between them are submitted to the referee, whose decision is final.

AFFIDAVITS. — An affidavit is a statement in writing, subscribed to by the party making it, and sworn to before a notary public, or other qualified officer.

RECEIPTS. — A receipt is a written acknowledgment of payment, but it is not absolute in its character. If error or fraud can be proven, the receipt will not stand.

A receipt given for money wherein the person signing it is to use the money for a certain purpose, is an agreement, and will bind the giver of the receipt to use the money as described in such receipt.

A receipt given in full of all demands, is only good for its face. If a larger amount is legally owing, it may be collected on proof. But it may be rendered good for the full amount by referring to it as a compromise, and stating that it is given as a settlement for the greater amount. Where it is intended to be a legal release of all demands, it is better to take a receipt in the form of a release, stating a consideration.

$50.   PHILADELPHIA, March 10th, 187

Received of A. B., fifty dollars on account.   C. D.

$100.   NEW YORK, February 8th, 187

Received of A. B. one hundred dollars, in full of all demands for labor to date.   C. D.

I, A. B., of Chicago, in consideration of one hundred dollars to me paid by C. D., the receipt of which is hereby acknowledged, do hereby release the said C. D. from all demands of any kind or nature which I may have against him. As witness my hand and seal, this tenth day of June, 187 .

A. B. [SEAL.]

A **Bill of Exchange** is an instrument in writing drawn by one person upon another, requesting him to pay a sum of money to a third person, or to himself, or to his order, absolutely and at all events.

When no time for payment is stated, they are payable on presentation.

When no place is named for payment, they should be presented at the place of business, or at the residence, of the acceptor.

$200.   PHILADELPHIA, May 2d, 187

Thirty days after date pay to the order of John Jones, *two hundred dollars*, for account of merchandise, February 2d, 187

Value received, and charge the same to account of   JOHN JONES.
To HENRY HARRIS, }
    Albany, N. Y.   }

$106.   BOSTON, March 4th, 187

At sight, pay to the order of George Davis, *one hundred and six dollars*, for balance of account to date.

Value received, and charge the same to account of
                    CHARLES PASCHAL.
To HENRY ASHMEAD, }
    New York.   }

A **Promissory Note** is much the same as a bill of exchange, being a written promise by one person to pay to another person a certain sum of money, absolutely and at all events. If made payable to order, it is negotiable.

$200.   FEBRUARY 24th, 187

Four months after date, I promise to pay to the order of A. B., *two hundred dollars*, value received.   C. D.

$300.   JULY 1st, 187

Ten days after date, I promise to pay to A. B., *three hundred dollars*, value received.   C. D.

A **Judgment Note** is a note with power of attorney attached, authorizing the holder to enter up judgment if it is not paid when due.

$700.   BOSTON, June 12th, 187

Four months after date, I promise to pay to Charles Coles, or order, seven hundred dollars, for value received, with interest.

And, in default of payment, I hereby appoint A. B., or any attorney-at-law, to appear in any court of record, at any time, to waive the service of process, and confess a judgment in favor of said Charles Coles, or his assigns.

Witness my hand and seal, this twelfth day of June, 187
                    PHILIP JONES. [SEAL.]
Attest, GEORGE AUSTEN.

A **Letter of Credit** is a letter written by one person to another, requesting him to advance money, or sell goods to the bearer or person named, and undertaking that the debt which may be thus contracted shall be paid.

PHILADELPHIA, August 3d, 187
Messrs. J. B. & Co., Fulton St., New York.

Gentlemen: Mr. Edwin James is coming to New York to buy goods for his business. Will you please deliver to him goods to any amount not over two thousand dollars, and I will hold myself accountable to you for the amount, if Mr. James does not pay you.

Please inform me of the amount you give him credit for, and, if he default in payment, advise me immediately.

I am, gentlemen, your obedient servant,   FRANKLIN J. WILLIAMS.

A **Promise** to pay something, not money, is not a promissory note, but an order.

When given for a certain amount of money, payable in merchandise, and the payment is not made within the time mentioned, the amount can be collected in money. It can be assigned to other parties by indorsement.

$300.   CHICAGO, July 20th, 187

Thirty days after date, I promise to pay Henry Miller, or order, three hundred dollars, in good merchantable hay, at market price.
                    JOHN D. HALL.

A Due Bill is simply a written acknowledgment by one person that a certain sum is due to the person named.

Boston, 8th June, 187 .
Due John Hall on demand, seventy dollars, value received.

FRANK SURE.

An Order is a written request from one person to another.

Boston, 9th June, 187 .
To Henry Jones & Co.
Please pay to John Hall, or order, one hundred and fifty dollars, and charge the same to my account.

FRANK SURE.

A Check presented at a bank where payable, for certification, and marked good by the proper officers of the bank, will bind the bank to pay it.

A person is not compelled to accept or pay the draft of another, although he may owe him as much, or a larger amount of money, unless he received such money for the purpose of protecting such draft, except he be a banker ; in this case, if he holds enough funds of the drawer, he must pay it.

An Agent is one authorized by others to act for them in transactions with other parties, and may be either special or general. Special is when the agent is authorized to act in certain cases, or capacity named.

The appointment may be in writing or orally, or implied from the action of the principal, without showing any express authority.

A Factor can sell goods, deliver them, and take payment therefor.

A Broker differs from a factor in that he only arranges the business for two principals, but his bought and sold notes bind both parties to a contract. He may receive the purchase money *only when authorized to do so.*

In contract for sale, the title does not pass to the buyer on delivery, if the condition be made that the title shall not pass until the goods are paid for, although they may be delivered at and remain in the store of the purchaser.

When goods are sold, and only require delivery to complete the con-
tract, if the person buying them refuse to receive them, the seller may retain them, and, first giving notice to the buyer, may sell them, and, if loss from it, he can recover from the refusor.

Landlord and Tenant. -- The person from whom houses or lands are holden, or rented, is the Landlord.

The person who holds, or rents, a house or land, is the Tenant.

A lease is a contract, by which a landlord empowers a person to take possession of a certain house or land in consideration of a certain rent.

A lease for a longer period than a year must be in writing.

PRECAUTION. — In taking a lease, the tenant should carefully examine the covenants, or if he take an under-lease, he should ascertain the covenants of the original lease, otherwise, when too late, he may find himself so restricted in his occupation that the premises may be wholly useless for his purpose, or he may be involved in perpetual difficulties and annoyances ; for instance, he may find himself restricted from making alterations convenient or necessary for his trade ; he may find himself compelled to rebuild, or pay rent in case of fire ; he may find himself subject to forfeiture of his lease, or other penalty, if he should underlet or assign his interest, carry on some particular trade, etc.

COVENANTS. — The covenants on the landlord's part are usually the granting of legal enjoyment of the premises to the lessee ; the saving him harmless from all other claimants to title ; and also for future assurance.

A tenant is not liable for taxes unless it is so stated in the lease.

ASSIGNMENTS. — Unless there be a covenant against assignment, a lease may be assigned, that is, the whole interest of the lessee may be conveyed to another, or it may be underlet ; if, therefore, it is intended that it should not, it is proper to insert a covenant to restrain the lessee from assigning or underletting. Tenants for terms of years may assign or underlet, but tenants at will cannot.

REPAIRS.— A tenant who covenants to keep a house in repair is not answerable for its natural decay, but is bound to keep it wind and water tight, so that it does not decay for want of cover.

NEGLECT OF REPAIRS BY LANDLORD. — If a landlord covenant to repair, and neglect to do so, the tenant may do it, and withhold so much of the rent. But it is advisable that notice thereof should be given by the tenant to the landlord, in the presence of a witness, prior to commencing the repairs.

RIGHT OF LANDLORD TO ENTER PREMISES. — A landlord may enter upon the premises (having given previous notice, although not expressed in the lease), for the purpose of viewing the state of the property.

TERMINATION OF LEASES. — A tenant must deliver up possession at the expiration of the term (the lease being sufficient notice), or he will continue liable to the rent as tenant by sufferance without any new contract; but if the landlord recognizes such tenancy by accepting a payment of rent after the lease has expired, such acceptance will constitute a tenancy; but previous to accepting rent, the landlord may bring his ejectment without notice; for, the lease having expired, the tenant is a trespasser. A lease covenanted to be void if the rent be not paid upon the day appointed, is good, unless the landlord make an entry.

NOTICES. — All notices, of whatever description, relating to tenancies, should be in writing, and the person serving the said notice should write on the back thereof a memorandum of the date on which it was served, and should keep a copy of the said notice, with a similar memorandum attached.

RECEIPT FOR RENT. — When an agent has been duly authorized, a receipt from him for any subsequent rent is a legal acquittance to the tenant, notwithstanding the landlord may have revoked the authority under which the agent acted, unless the landlord should have given the tenant notice thereof.

CARE OF RECEIPTS FOR RENT. — Be careful of your last quarter's receipt for rent, for the production of that document bars all prior claim. Even when arrears have been due on former quarters, the receipt, if given for the last quarter, precludes the landlord from recovery thereof.

NOTICE TO QUIT. — When either the landlord or tenant intends to terminate a tenancy, the way to proceed is by a notice to quit, which is drawn up in the two following ways:

Form of a Notice to Quit from Tenant to Landlord. -- Sir, — I hereby give you notice, that on or before the —— day of —— next, I shall quit and deliver up possession of the house and premises I now hold of you, situate at ——, in the town of ——, in the county of ——.

Dated the —— day of ——, 187 .
Witness, G. C.   L. O.
To Mr. R. A.

Notice from Landlord to Tenant. — Sir, — I hereby give you notice to quit the house and appurtenances, situate No. ——, which you now hold of me, on or before —— next.

Dated ——, 187 .
(Signed)   R. A. (landlord).
To Mr. L. O.

A Deed or Conveyance, is a contract in writing between parties who are legally competent to make them.

Deeds should be recorded in the office of the County Clerk, (or it will not stand against a subsequent purchaser in good faith, but it would stand as between the parties thereto.) Before a deed can be recorded, it must be signed by the parties thereto, and witnesses; if there are no witnesses, the deed should be acknowledged before a commissioner.

A Lien is a right or hold upon a property, as security for payment of a debt; or having agreed to sell property, he has a lien upon it until the purchase money is paid.

A Mortgage is a contract selling the property mortgaged to the buyer, with the condition that the buyer shall not take possession of the property if the mortgager perform the conditions of the contract, (the conditions of the deed generally are that the mortgager shall within a certain time pay a certain sum of money, and until that time he shall pay interest). All the conditions being performed, the contract becomes void.

He who gives a mortgage, is the mortgager; he who receives it is the mortgagee.

A Conveyance is an absolute deed of transfer of land.

A Trust Deed, is a conveyance for a special purpose, generally for the interest of a third party.

A Quit Claim, is a conveyance of the interest the party had at the time it was made.

Contracts for Labor for less than a year, need not be in writing. If for more than a year, they should be, and although it is implied that payment will be made, it is best to state the amount, and how and when it shall be paid, or the amount may be withheld until the completion of term of services.

In the absence of an agreement, the reasonable value of the services rendered may be recovered, but it must be shown that he was requested to perform the services.

APPRENTICE is one, either male or female, who is bound by agreement in writing, to serve or work for a certain specified time, in the interest of the person to whom he is bound. The employer engages to teach the apprentice, either by himself or his workmen, his trade, calling, or profession.

The agreement made is called an indenture, and should state all the particulars, such as the nature of the business, the duration of the apprenticeship; and if wages are paid, state them, etc.

If the master to whom an apprentice is bound for a particular trade changes that trade for another, the indenture binding the apprentice becomes null and void.

APPRENTICE'S INDENTURE. — This Indenture witnesseth that J. M., now of the age of sixteen years, son of C. M., of the town of ———, in the County of ———, of his own free will and accord, and with the consent of his father (or mother), places and binds himself apprentice to A. B. of ———, master carpenter, to learn the trade, or occupation of a carpenter, and to serve the said A. B. as an apprentice for the full term of four years from the date of this indenture. During which said term of four years, the said J. M. shall, and will well and faithfully serve, and demean himself, and be just and true to the said A. B., and everywhere willingly obey all his lawful commands: that he shall do no hurt or damage to his said master, in his goods, estate, or otherwise: that he shall not traffic, or buy and sell with his own goods, or the goods of others, during the said term, without his master's leave: that he shall not, at any time, by day or night, depart, or absent himself from the service of his said master, without his leave; but in all things, as a good and faithful apprentice, shall, and will, demean and behave himself, to his said master, during the said term.

And the said A. B. doth covenant, and agree, to teach and instruct the said apprentice, in the said trade of a carpenter, after the best way and manner that he can, and to find, and allow, unto his said apprentice, *meat, drink, washing, lodging, and apparel, including linen, and all other necessaries, in sickness and in health, meet and convenient for such an apprentice, during the term aforesaid; and at the expiration of the said term, shall, and will, give to his said apprentice an entire new suit of clothes, of a cash value of Thirty-five dollars, and a new set of carpenter's tools, of a cash value of Forty dollars;* and for the true performance of all, and singular, the covenants and agreements aforesaid, the parties hereto bind themselves, each unto the other, finally by these presents.

Witness our hands and seals, this day of in the year one thousand eight hundred and

Signed, sealed, and }   A. B. [SEAL.]
delivered in pres- }   J. M. [SEAL.]
ence of }   C. M. [SEAL.]

NOTE.—*If it is not intended to board and clothe the apprentice, then omit the part in italics, and insert the following: the sum of six dollars per week for the first year, eight dollars per week for the second year, ten dollars per week for the third year, and twelve dollars per week for the fourth year, in each case to be paid weekly.*

PARTNERSHIP is an association of two or more persons, to carry on a business, and to share the profits and losses. The contract may be oral, or in writing. It is always best to have it in writing, and state what the business is, what each person is to do, how the profits are to be paid, etc. Partnerships may be general or special.

General partnership may be carried on under the name of one or more of the partners; and although an old-established business may be carried on under the name of the former partners, a new business cannot be started in the name of a person not interested in the firm.

If no provision is made in the agreement, one partner cannot place another person as a partner in the firm without the consent of the other. If he should sell out his interest, the buyer would only be entitled to the amount which it would realize after the debts were paid.

A partner has no right to use the name of the firm in his individual business.

Special partners are those who furnish money for capital, and are not liable beyond the amount they agree to invest in the business. To form a special partnership, a certificate must be signed and acknowledged before a Notary Public (or other proper officer), giving the name of the firm, the nature of the business, the names and residences of all the partners, the amount of money contributed by the special partners, and the date at which the partnership is to begin and terminate.

A WILL is an instrument in writing, by which a person makes disposition of his property. The person making it should state fully and plainly his intention, describe property by its exact location, and persons by their proper names in full.

The person making a will is called the testator, who must write his own name in full at the end of the will, and must be attested by two witnesses, who should write their residences after their names.

If the testator is unable, from any cause, to sign his name, he may request some one to write it for him. The person so signing the testator's name must also write his own name, in the presence of two other witnesses.

A CODICIL is an addition to a will, either altering it or explaining, and must be signed in the same manner as a will.

No WILL IS VALID UNLESS IT IS IN WRITING, signed at the foot or end thereof by the testator, or by some other person in his presence, and by his direction. And such signature must be made or acknowledged by the testator, in the presence of two or more witnesses, all of whom must be present at the same time; and such witnesses must attest and subscribe the will in the presence and with the knowledge of the testator.

A WILL OR CODICIL ONCE MADE cannot be altered or revoked, unless through a similar formal process to that under which it was made, or by some other writing declaring an intention to revoke the same, and executed in the manner in which an original will is required to be executed, or by the burning, tearing, or otherwise destroying the same by the testator, or by some person in his presence and by his direction, with the intention of revoking the same.

No WILL OR CODICIL, or any part of either, that has once been revoked by any or all of these acts, can be revived again, unless it be executed in the manner that a fresh will or codicil is required to be.

ALTERATIONS IN WILLS OR CODICILS require the signature of the testator and of two witnesses to be made upon the margin, or upon some other part of the will, opposite or near to the alteration.

WHERE PROPERTY IS CONSIDER.-

BLE, and of different kinds,—or even where inconsiderable, if of different kinds—and to be disposed of to married or other persons, or for the benefit of children, for charities, or trusts of any description, it is absolutely necessary and proper that a qualified legal adviser should superintend the execution of the will.

WHEN A PERSON HAS RESOLVED UPON MAKING A WILL, he should select from among his friends persons of trust to become his executors, and should obtain their consent to act. And it is advisable that a duplicate copy of the will should be entrusted to the executor or executors. Or he should otherwise deposit a copy of his will, or the original will, in the office provided by the Probate Court for the safe custody of wills.

THE FOLLOWING IS A SIMPLE FORM OF WILL:—This is the last will and testament of J— B—, of Brooklyn, New York: I hereby give, devise, and bequeath to my wife, Mary B—, her heirs, executors, and administrators, for her and their own use and benefit, absolutely and forever, all my estate and effects, both real and personal, whatsoever and wheresoever, and of what nature and quality soever; and I hereby appoint her, the said Mary B—, sole executrix of this my will. In witness whereof I have hereunto set my hand this twentieth day of January, one thousand eight hundred and sixty-four. JOHN B—. [SEAL.]

Signed by the said John B— in the presence of us, present at the same time, who, in his presence, and in the presence of each other, attest and subscribe our names as witnesses hereto.
JOHN SMITH,
Brooklyn, N. Y.
JOSEPH WILSON,
New Haven, Conn.

OTHER FORMS OF WILLS give particular legacies to adults, or to infants, with direction for application of interest during minority; to infants, to be paid at twenty-one without interest; specific legacies of government stock;

general legacies of ditto; specific legacies of leasehold property or household property; immediate or deferred annuities; to daughters or sons for life, and after them their children; legacies with directions for the application of the money; bequests to wife, with conditions as to future marriage; define the powers of trustees, provide for and direct the payment of debts, etc. All these more complicated forms of wills require the superintendence of a professional adviser.

It should be remembered that a false economy in saving the amount which an honest and competent lawyer would charge for his services in drawing up and executing a will, results sometimes in the squandering of thousands of dollars in litigations, after the death of the testator.

A Power of Attorney is an authority given by one person to another to act in his behalf; such authority may be special, or general. When special, the particular matter or business is mentioned; when general, it is to act for the person in all matters or business that may arise.

The person to whom the power to act is given, is called an attorney.

An attorney cannot delegate his power without express permission from his principal. A power of attorney may be withdrawn by revocation at any time, but its effect as to third persons takes effect only from the time they have notice of it.

KNOW ALL MEN BY THESE PRESENTS, That I, A. B., of Boston, Mass., have made, constituted, and by these presents do make, constitute, and appoint C. D., of Worcester, Mass., my true and lawful attorney, for me and in my name, place and stead, to [here insert the particulars], giving and granting unto my said attorney full power and authority to do and perform all and every act and thing whatsoever requisite and necessary to be done in and about the premises, as fully, to all intents and purposes, as I might or could do if personally present, with full power of substitution and revocation, hereby ratifying and confirming all that my said attorney (or his substitute) shall lawfully do, or cause to be done, by virtue hereof.

In witness whereof, I have hereunto set my hand and seal, this fifth day of March, 187

A. B. [SEAL.]

Sealed and delivered }
in the presence of }
M. A. }

KNOW ALL MEN BY THESE PRESENTS, That whereas I, A. B., of Boston, Mass., by my letter of attorney bearing date of fifth day of March, 187 , did appoint C. D., of Worcester, Mass., my attorney to [*insert the particulars*], as by the said letter of attorney will appear : NOW KNOW YE that I, the said A. B., do by these presents revoke, countermand, and make void the said letter of attorney, and all power and authority thereby given, or intended to be given, to the said C. D.

In witness whereof, I have hereunto set my hand and seal, this tenth day of May, 187

A. B. [SEAL.]

Sealed and delivered }
in the presence of }
E. M. }

Common Carriers. — E x p r e s s companies, and persons who transport goods for others as a business, also railway companies, owners of steamboats, and stage coaches, who carry passengers, are common carriers, and as such are liable for the full value of goods entrusted to them, if not delivered by them as directed.

They are also liable for damage to goods while in their possession, unless such damage is caused by the elements, or the acts of the common enemy.

The liability of a carrier commences as soon as he receives them, and continues until he has delivered them.

A carrier may refuse to receive goods for transport, if the sender refuses to pay the usual freight charge; and if he takes them to be paid at the

destination, he may retain them there until the freight charge is paid. It is usual for carriers, on their bills, to declare their non-liability, but this will not exempt them from damage, loss, or fraud, caused either by omission or commission of themselves, or agents. But they may make a condition that they will not be answerable for any package (or personal baggage) beyond a certain value, unless such value is stated and paid for accordingly.

MARRIAGE. — Mutual consent is the basis of marriage; no particular form is necessary. The consent of the parties to a marriage given before a clergyman, a magistrate, or other reputable witnesses, is sufficient. Infants — that is, males under the age of fourteen, and females under the age of twelve—and persons of unsound mind, cannot legally marry; neither can a man who has a former wife living, from whom he has not been *legally* divorced. The consent of parents, or guardians, for persons under twenty-one years of age, is generally required by an officiating minister; but it is not *legally* necessary.

If a man and woman, who are living as man and wife, shall, in the presence of respectable witnesses, declare that they are man and wife, the declaration being made by one and assented to by the other, will constitute a marriage valid in law.

PAROL EVIDENCE of the purport of a written document will be admitted, if it is proven that the document is lost.

IN THE CONSTRUCTION of contracts the intent of the parties must be considered.

A MAN cannot take advantage of his own wrong.

IF A MAN CONTRACT to perform certain labor, and is prevented by sickness from completing, he can recover for the portion done.

PRINCIPALS are responsible for the acts of their agents.

WHEN CONTRARY laws come in question, the superior laws must

stand. A new law will stand before an old one.

Time and Distance Table.

NAMES OF CITIES.	*No. of miles from New York.*	*Time at each place.*
New York City	0	12·00
Philadelphia, Pa	87	11·56
Baltimore, Md	185	11·50
Washington, D. C	225	11·48
Richmond, Va	353	11·46
New Orleans, La	1597	10·56
Montreal, Canada	401	11·58
Louisville, Ky	934	11·14
St. Louis, Mo	1087	10·55
Cincinnati, Ohio	799	11·19
Indianapolis, Ind	825	11·44
Columbus, Ohio	650	11·24
Detroit, Mich	663	11·24
Buffalo, N. Y	422	11·41
Chicago, Ill	898	11·06
Cleveland, Ohio	581	11·30
Wheeling, W. Va	481	11·33
Pittsburg, Pa	431	11·36
Albany, N. Y	146	11·58
Boston, Mass	236	12·12

Legal Rates of Interest.

STATES.	LEGAL RATES.	Conventional not exceeding.
	Per cent.	
Alabama	8	....
Arkansas	6	as agreed.
California	10	....
Connecticut	6	as agreed.
Delaware	6	....
Florida	8	....
Georgia	7	as agreed.
Illinois	6	10
Indiana	6	....
Iowa	6	10
Kansas	7	12
Kentucky	6	10
Louisiana	5	8
Maine	6	as agreed.
Maryland	6	....
Massachusetts	6	as agreed.
Michigan	7	10
Mississippi	6	as agreed.
Missouri	6	10
Minnesota	7	12
Nebraska	10	12
Nevada	10	....
New Hampshire	6	....
New Jersey	7	....
New York	7	....
North Carolina	6	8
Ohio	8	....
Oregon	10	12
Pennsylvania	6	....
Rhode Island	6	as agreed.
South Carolina	7	as agreed.
Tennessee	6	10
Texas	8	12
Vermont	6	....
Virginia	6	8
West Virginia	6	....
Wisconsin	7	10
District of Columbia	10	as agreed.

Note.—In some States it is allowed to charge a higher rate of interest, if a written agreement is made; this is called the conventional rate. In those States where no agreement is made, the legal rate only is allowed.

To find the interest on a given sum, for any number of days, at any rate of interest:

At five per cent., multiply the principal by the number of days, and divide by 72
At 6 per cent., as above, and divide by 60
7 " " " 52
8 " " " 45
9 " " " 40
10 " " " 36
12 " " " 30
15 " " " 24
20 " " " 18

TABLE showing how many years it will take money to double itself at various rates of interest:

RATE OF INTEREST.	SIMPLE INTEREST.	COMPOUND INTEREST.
1 per cent.	100 years.	69 2/3 years.
1 1/2 " "	66 2/3 "	46 1/2 "
2 " "	50 "	35 "
2 1/2 " "	40 "	28 "
3 " "	33 1/3 "	23 1/2 "
3 1/2 " "	28 1/2 "	20 1/7 "
4 " "	25 "	17 2/3 "
4 1/2 " "	22 1/4 "	15 3/4 "
5 " "	20 "	14 1/4 "
5 1/2 " "	18 1/6 "	13 "
6 " "	16 2/3 "	12 "
6 1/2 " "	15 1/3 "	11 "
7 " "	14 1/4 "	10 1/4 "
7 1/2 " "	13 1/3 "	9 1/2 "
8 " "	12 1/2 "	9 "
8 1/2 " "	11 3/4 "	8 1/2 "
9 " "	11 "	8 "
9 1/2 " "	10 1/2 "	7 2/3 "
10 " "	10 "	7 1/4 "

Value of Foreign Coins in U. S. Gold.

Pound Sterling (Sovereign), England	$4 86
Crown, "	1 15
Shilling, "	22
Twenty Francs (Napoleon), France	3 84
Five Francs "	98
One hundred Reals, Spain	4 96
Pistareen (new) "	20
Doubloon, Mexico	15 61
Dollar, "	1 06
Ten Thaler, Germany, North	7 90
Crown, " "	6 64
Ducat, " South	2 27
Thaler (new) " North	73
Florin, " South	41
Ten Thaler, Denmark	7 90
Two Rigsdaler, "	1 10
Ten Guilders, Netherlands	3 99
Ducat, Sweden	2 23
Rix dollar, "	1 11
Ducat, Austria	2 28
Twenty Liri, Italy	3 84
Gold Crown, Portugal	5 80
Five Livre, Sardinia	98

Value of Foreign Money of Account in the U. S.

1 Florin, Amsterdam	$ 40
1 Thaler, Berlin	69
1 s. Daler, Bremen	79⅞
1 Rupee, Calcutta	44½
1 s. Daler, Christiana	1 06
1 Medjidii, Constantinople	3 35
1 s. Daler, Copenhagen	1 05
1 Florin, Frankfort	40
1 Lira, Genoa	18⁶/₁₀
1 m. Banco, Hamburg	35½
1 Milreis, Lisbon	$1 12
1 Pound, Loudou	4 86
1 Duro, Madrid	1 00
1 Ducat, Naples	80
1 Owza, Palermo	2 40
1 Franc, Paris	19⅕
1 Tael, Pekin	1 48
1 Milreis, Rio de Janeiro	51¼
1 s. Romano, Rome	99½
1 s. Rouble, St. Petersburg	75
1 Daler, Stockholm	1 06
1 Lira, Venice	16
1 Florin, Vienna	48½

A Table of the Number of Days from any Day of one Month to the same Day of any other Month.

FROM	Jan.	Feb.	Mar.	Apr.	May.	June.	July.	Aug.	Sept.	Oct.	Nov.	Dec.
To January	365	334	306	275	245	214	184	153	122	92	61	31
February	31	365	337	306	276	245	215	184	153	123	92	62
March	59	28	365	334	304	273	243	212	181	151	120	90
April	90	59	31	365	335	304	274	243	212	182	151	121
May	120	89	61	30	365	334	304	273	242	212	181	151
June	151	120	92	61	31	365	334	304	273	243	212	182
July	181	150	122	91	61	30	365	334	303	273	242	212
August	212	181	153	122	92	61	31	365	334	304	273	243
September	243	212	184	153	122	92	61	31	365	335	304	274
October	273	242	214	183	153	122	92	61	30	365	334	304
November	304	273	245	214	184	153	123	92	61	31	365	335
December	334	303	275	244	214	183	153	122	91	61	30	365

USE OF THE ABOVE TABLE.

What is the number of days from 10th October to 10th July?

Look in the upper line for October, let your eye descend down that column till you come opposite to July, and you will find 273 days, the exact number of days required.

Again, required the number of days from 16th February to the 14th August?

Under February, and opposite to August, is .... 181 days.

From which subtract the difference beween 14 and 16 .... 2 days.

The exact number of days required is .... 179 days.

N. B. — In Leap Year, if the last day of February comes between, add one day for the day over ½ the number in the Table.

When Gold is at	Currency is at	$100 Currency will buy
5 per ct. prem.	4·77 per ct. disc't.	In gold, $95 23
10 " "	9·10 " "	" 90 90
15 " "	13·04 " "	" 86 96
20 " "	16·67 " "	" 83 33
25 " "	20·00 " "	" 80 00
30 " "	28·08 " "	" 76 92
40 " "	28·58 " "	" 71 42
50 " "	33·33 " "	" 66 66
60 " "	37·50 " "	" 62 50
70 " "	41·18 " "	" 58 82
80 " "	44·45 " "	" 55 55
90 " "	47·37 " "	" 52 63
100 " "	50·00 " "	" 50 00

Avoirdupois Weight.

(*For groceries and heavy goods.*)

16 drams	equal 1 ounce.
16 ounces	" 1 pound.
112 pounds	" 1 cwt.
20 cwt., or 2240 pounds, 1 ton.	

Troy Weight.

(*For Jewellers.*)

24 grains	equal 1 pennyweight.
20 pennyweights	" 1 ounce.
12 ounces	" 1 pound.

Cloth Measure.

2¼ inches	equal 1 nail.
4 nails	" 1 quarter yard.
4 quarters	" 1 yard.

Dry Measure.

4 quarts	equal 1 gallon.
2 gallons	" 1 peck.
4 pecks	" 1 bushel.
36 bushels	" 1 chaldron.

Liquid Measure.

4 gills	equal 1 pint.
2 pints	" 1 quart.
4 quarts	" 1 gallon.
31½ gallons	" 1 barrel.
42 gallons	" 1 tierce.
63 gallons	" 1 hogshead.
84 gallons	" 1 puncheon.
126 gallons	" 1 pipe or butt.
252 gallons	" 1 tun.

Long Measure.

3 barleycorns	equal 1 inch.
12 inches	" 1 foot.
3 feet	" 1 yard.
6 feet	" 1 fathom.
5½ yards	" 1 rod or perch.
40 rods	" 1 furlong.

Long Measure (*continued*).

8 furlongs	equal 1 mile.
3 miles	" 1 league.
69¾ miles	" 1 degree.
360 degrees	the circumference of the earth.

Land (or Square) Measure.

144 square inches	equal 1 square foot.
9 square feet	" 1 square yard.
30¼ square yards	" 1 square rod.
40 square rods	" 1 rood.
4 roods	" 1 acre.
160 acres	" 1 qua'r section
640 acres	" 1 square mile.

Distance Measure.

7$\frac{92}{100}$ inches	equal 1 link.
25 links	" 1 rod.
4 rods	" 1 chain.
10 chains	" 1 furlong.
1 square chain	" 16 square poles.
80 chains	" 1 mile.
10 square chains	" 1 acre.

Cubic (Solid) Measure.

1728 cubic (solid) inches	=1 cubic foot.
27 " feet	equal 1 " yard.
16½ " feet	" 1 " perch.
40 " feet round timber	=1 ton.
50 " feet hewn	" =1 ton.
42 " feet	equal 1 ton shipping.
128 " feet	" 1 cord wood.

Jewish Long Measure.

A cubit	equals 1$\frac{824}{1000}$ feet.
A Sabbath day's journey	" 3648 "
A mile	" 7296 "
A day's journey	" 33⅓ miles

American mile	equals 5,280 feet
English "	" 5,280 "
Irish "	" 6,720 "
Scotch "	" 7,920 "
Russian "	" 8,300 "
Italian "	" 5,566 "
German "	" 26,400 "
Dutch "	" 21,120 "
Spanish "	" 21,120 "
Polish "	" 21,120 "
Indian "	" 15,840 "

SUNDRIES.

24 sheets of papermake 1 quire.
20 quires　　　"　　　" 1 ream.
Barrel of flour　contains 196 pounds.
Barrel of Beef or Pork "　200　"
Peck of salt weighs　　14　"
1 cubic foot of Anthracite coal weighs
　50 to 55 pounds.
1 cubic foot of bituminous coal weighs
　45 to 55 pounds.
1 cubic foot of charcoal 18 pounds.
28½ bushels of coal, or ⎫
43½ cubic feet,　　　⎬ 1 ton.
　　　　　　　　　⎭

Habits of a Man of Business. — A sacred regard to the principles of justice forms the basis of every transaction, and regulates the conduct of the upright man of business.

He is strict in keeping his engagements.

Does nothing carelessly or in a hurry.

Employs nobody to do what he can easily do himself.

Keeps everything in its proper place.

Leaves nothing undone that ought to be done, and which circumstances permit him to do.

Keeps his designs and business from the view of others.

Is prompt and decisive with customers, and does not over-trade his capital.

Prefers short credits to long ones; and cash to credit at all times, either in buying or selling; and small profits in credit cases with little risk, to the chance of better gains with more hazard.

He is clear and explicit in all his bargains.

Leaves nothing of consequence to memory which he can and ought to commit to writing.

Keeps copies of all his important letters which he sends away, and has every letter, invoice, etc., belonging to his business, titled, classed, and put away.

Never suffers his desk to be confused by many papers lying upon it.

Is always at the head of his business, well knowing that if he leaves it, it will leave him.

Holds it as a maxim that he whose credit is suspected is not one to be trusted.

Is constantly examining his books, and sees through all his affairs as far as care and attention will enable him.

Balances regularly at stated times, and then makes out and transmits all his accounts current to his customers, both at home and abroad.

Avoids as much as possible all sorts of accommodation in money matters, and lawsuits where there is the least hazard,

He is economical in his expenditure, always living within his income.

Keeps a memorandum-book in his pocket, in which he notes every particular relative to appointments, addresses, and petty cash matters.

Is cautious how he becomes security for any person; and is generous when urged by motives of humanity.

Let a man act strictly to these habits — ever remembering that he hath no profits by his pains whom Providence doth not prosper — and success will attend his efforts.

Taking a Store or Place of Business. — If you are about to take a place of business, you will do well to consider the following remarks:

SMALL CAPITALISTS. — Let us take the case of a person who has no intimate knowledge of any particular trade, but having a very small capital, is about to embark it in the exchange of commodities for cash, in order to obtain an honest livelihood thereby. It is clear, that unless such a person starts with proper precaution and judgment, the capital will be expended without adequate results; rent and taxes will accumulate, the stock will lie dead or become deteriorated, and loss and ruin must follow. For the least absorption acting upon a small capital will soon dry up its source; and we need not picture the trouble that will arise when the mainspring of a tradesman's success abides by him no more.

LARGER CAPITALISTS. — The case of the larger capitalist can scarcely be considered an exception to the same rule. For it is probable that the larger capitalist, upon commencing a business, would sink more of his funds in a larger stock — would incur liability to a heavier rent; and the attendant taxes, the wages of assistants and servants, would be greater, and, therefore, if the return came not speedily, similar consequences must sooner or later ensue.

LOCALITIES. — Large or small capitalists should, therefore, upon entering on a storekeeping speculation, consider well the nature of the locality in which they propose to carry on trade, the number of the population, the habits and wants of the people, and the extent to which they are already supplied with the goods which the new adventurer proposes to offer them.

NEW NEIGHBORHOODS. — There is a tendency among small capitalists to rush into new neighborhoods with the expectation of making an early connection. Low rents also serve as an attraction to these localities. We have found, however, in our experience, that the early suburban places seldom succeed. They are generally entered upon at the very earliest moment that the state of the locality will permit — often before the house is finished the store is tenanted, and goods exposed for sale — even while the streets are unpaved, and while the roads are as rough and uneven as country lanes. The consequence is, that as the few inhabitants of these localities have frequent communication with adjacent towns, they, as a matter of habit or of choice, supply their chief wants thereat; and the suburban dealer depends principally for support upon the accidental forgetfulness of his neighbor, who omits to bring something from the cheaper and better market; or upon the changes of the weather, which may sometimes favor him by rendering a "trip to town" exceedingly undesirable.

FAILURES. — " While the grass is growing the horse is starving; " and thus, while the new district is becoming peopled, the funds of the small tradesman are gradually eaten up, and he puts up his shutters just at the time when a more cautious speculator steps in to profit by the connection already formed, and to take advantage of the now improved condition of the locality. It seems, therefore, desirable for the small capitalist rather to run the risk of a more expensive rent, in a well-peopled district, than to resort to places of slow and uncertain demand; for the welfare of the small dealer depends entirely upon the frequency with which his limited stock is cleared out and replaced by fresh supplies.

PRECAUTIONS. — But should the small capitalist still prefer opening in a suburban district, where competition is less severe, and rents and rates less burdensome, there are certain precautions which he will do well to observe. He should particularly guard against opening a shop to supply what may be termed the superfluities of life; for the inhabitants of suburban districts are those who, like himself, have resorted to a cheap residence for the sake of economy. Or, if this be not the case — if they are people of independent means, who prefer the "detached villa" to the town house, squeezed up on both sides, they have the means of riding and driving to town, and will prefer choosing articles of taste and luxury from the best marts, enriched by the finest display.

NECESSITIES OR LUXURIES. — The suburban storekeeper should, therefore, confine himself to supplying the *necessities* of life. Hungry people dislike to fetch their bread from five miles off; and to bring vegetables from a long distance would evidently be a matter of considerable inconvenience. The baker, the butcher, the grocer, etc., are those who find their trade first established in suburban localities. And not until these are doing well should the tailor, the shoemaker, the hatter, the draper, the hosier, and others, expect to find a return for their capital and reward for their labor.

CIVILITY. — In larger localities, where competition abounds, the small dealer frequently outstrips his more powerful rival by one element of success, which may be added to any stock without cost, but cannot be withheld without loss. That element is *civility.* It has already been spoken of elsewhere, but must be enforced here, as aiding the little means of the small trader to a wonderful degree. A kind and obliging manner carries with it an indescribable charm. It must not be a manner which indicates a mean, grovelling, time-serving spirit, but a plain, open, and agreeable demeanor, which seems to desire to oblige for the pleasure of doing so, and not for the sake of squeezing an extra penny out of a customer's pocket.

INTEGRITY. — The sole reliance of the storekeeper should be in the integrity of his transactions, and in the civility of his demeanor. He should make it the interest and the pleasure of the customer to come to his place. If he does this, he will form the very best "connections," and so long as he continues this system of business, they will never desert him.

DUTIES OF A STOREKEEPER. — He should cheerfully render his best labor and knowledge to serve those who approach his counter, and place confidence in his transactions; make himself alike to rich and poor, but never resort to mean subterfuge and deception to gain approbation and support. He should be frugal in his expenditure, that, in deriving profits from trade, he may not trespass unduly upon the interests of others; he should so hold the balance between man and man that he should feel nothing to reprove his conscience when the day comes for him to repose from his labors and live upon the fruits of his industry. Let the public discover such a man, and they will flock around him for their own sakes.

Early Rising. — The difference between rising every morning at six and at eight, in the course of forty years, amounts to 29,200 hours, or three years one hundred and twenty-one days and sixteen hours, which are equal to eight hours a day for exactly ten years. So that rising at six will be the same as if ten years of life (a weighty consideration) were added, wherein we may command eight hours every day for the cultivation of our minds and the despatch of business.

FRUGALITY.—The great philosopher, Dr. Franklin, inspired the mouthpiece of his own eloquence, "Poor Richard," with "many a gem of purest ray serene," encased in the homely garb of proverbial truisms. On the subject of frugality we cannot do better than take the worthy Mentor for our text, and from it address our remarks. A man may, if he knows not how to save as he gets, "keep his nose all his life to the grindstone, and die not worth a groat at last. A fat kitchen makes a lean will."

" Many estates are spent in getting,
Since women for tea forsook spinning and knitting,
And men for punch forsook hewing and splitting."

If you would be wealthy, think of saving as well as of getting. The Indies have not made Spain rich, because her out-goes are greater than her incomes.

Away with your expensive follies, and you will not have so much cause to complain of hard times, heavy taxes, and chargeable families. "What maintains one vice would bring up two children."

You may think, perhaps, that a little tea, or superfluities now and then, diet a little more costly, clothes a little finer, and a little entertainment now and then, can be no great matter; but remember, "Many a little makes a mickle."

Beware of little expenses: "A small leak will sink a great ship," as Poor Richard says; and again, "Who dainties love, shall beggars prove;" and moreover, "Fools make feasts and wise men eat them."

Here you are all got together to this sale of fineries and nick-nacks. You call them goods; but if you do not take care they will prove evils to some of you. You expect they will be sold cheap, and perhaps they may, for less than they cost; but if you have no occasion for them they must be dear to you. Remember what Poor Richard says,

"Buy what thou hast no need of, and ere long thou shalt sell thy necessaries."

"At a great pennyworth, pause awhile." He means, perhaps, that the cheapness is apparent only, and not real; or the bargain, by straitening thee in thy business, may do thee more harm than good; for in another place he says, "Many have been ruined by buying good pennyworths."

"It is foolish to lay out money in the purchase of repentance;" and yet this folly is practised every day at auctions for want of minding the Almanack.

Cash and Credit.—If you would get rich, don't deal in bill books. Credit is the "Tempter in a new shape." Buy goods on trust, and you will purchase a thousand articles that cash would never have dreamed of. A dollar in the hand looks larger than ten dollars seen through the perspective of a three months' bill. Cash is practical, while credit takes horribly to taste and romance. Let cash buy a dinner, and you will have a beefsteak flanked with onions. Send credit to market, and he will return with eight pairs of woodcocks and a peck of mushrooms. Credit believes in diamond pins and champagne suppers. Cash is more easily satisfied. Give him three meals a day, and he doesn't care much if two of them are made up of roasted potatoes and a little dirty salt. Cash is a good adviser, while credit is a good fellow to be on visiting terms with. If you want double chins and contentment, do business with cash.

Don't Run in Debt.

"Don't run in debt;"—never mind, never mind
  If your clothes are faded and torn:
Scam them up, make them do; it is better by far
  Than to have the heart weary and worn.

Who'll love you the more for the shape of your hat,
  Or your ruff, or the tie of your shoe,
The cut of your vest, or your boots, or cravat,
  If they know you're in debt for the new?

There's no comfort, I tell you, in walking the street
  In fine clothes, if you know you're in debt;
And feel that, perchance, you some tradesman may meet,
  Who will sneer—"They're not paid for yet."

Good friends, let me beg of you, don't run in debt
  If the chairs and the sofas are old,
They will fit your back better than any new set,
  Unless they are paid for—with gold.

If the house is too small draw the closer together,
  Keep it warm with a hearty good will;
A big one unpaid for, in all kinds of weather,
  Will send to your warm heart a chill.

Don't run in debt—now, dear girls, take a hint,
  If the fashions have changed since last season,
Old Nature is out in the very same tint,
  And old Nature, we think, has some reason.

But just say to your friend, that you cannot afford
  To spend time to keep up with the fashion:
That your purse is too light, and your honor too bright,
  To be tarnished with such silly passion.

Gents, don't run in debt—let your friends, if they can,
  Have fine houses, and feathers, and flowers;
But, unless they are paid for, be more of a man
  Than to envy their sunshiny hours.

If you've money to spare, I have nothing to say—
  Spend your silver and gold as you please;
But mind you, the man who his bill has to pay
  Is the man who is never at ease.

Oh! take my advice—it is good, it is true!
  But, lest you may some of you doubt it,
I'll whisper a secret now, seeing 't is you—
  I have tried it, and know all about it:

The chain of a debtor is heavy and cold,
  Its links all corrosion and rust;
Gild it o'er as you will, it is never of gold,
  Then spurn it aside with disgust.

HOME AMUSEMENTS.

IN-DOOR AND OUT-DOOR GAMES—CHESS AND WHIST FULLY EXPLAINED—
THOUGHTS ABOUT CONUNDRUMS AND CHARADES.

Amusements Needed.—There can be no question that the mental and physical requirements of our people are almost wholly ignored; and although there has been a marked change in this respect within the last few years, there is ample room for improvement. Business and professional men take far too little recreation and exercise; and although the ban is somewhat removed which for so long was held over the clerical profession, some of the old prejudice remains which forbids recreation, especially field-sports, to that class. Chess and playing upon musical instruments, even the violin, is allowed to the minister. Indeed, the canons of propriety have been so far infringed as to allow him an occasional indulgence in the unorthodox game of checkers — but should he appear in shooting jacket, it is regarded as a thing, if not exactly wicked, that is "greatly to be deprecated on the part of our minister." It is to be feared also that our national game of ball, which, when first introduced, seemed to be exactly suited to the purpose for which it was designed, is fast losing its usefulness. Upon its first introduction it appeared to be just the thing. Clerks and employers could run out and take a hand at ball; but its very popularity soon defeated its original aims. Like the game of "cricket" in England, it has now become so scientific in its character that only those are willing to play it who have gone through a regular professional course of training.

392

Evening Pastime.—Among the innocent recreations of the fireside, there are few more commendable and practicable than those afforded by what are severally termed Anagrams, Charades, Conundrums, Enigmas, Puzzles, Rebuses, Riddles, Transpositions, etc. Of these there are such a variety, that they are suited to every capacity; and they present this additional attraction, that ingenuity may be exercised in the *invention* of them, as well as in their solution. Many persons who have become noted for their literary compositions may date the origin of their success to the time when they attempted the composition of a trifling enigma or charade.

Anagrams are formed by the transposition of the letters of words or sentences, or names of persons, so as to produce a word, sentence, or verse, of pertinent or of widely different meaning. They are very difficult to discover, but are exceedingly striking when good. The following are some of the most remarkable:

Transposed	*Forms.*
Astronomers............	...No more stars.
Catalogues..................	...Got us a clue.
Elegant	...Neat leg.
Impatient....................	...Tim in a pet.
Immediately................	...I met my Delia.
Masquerade.................	...Queen as mad.
Matrimony..................	...Into my arm.
Melodrama.................	...Made moral.
Midshipman...............	...Mind his map.
Old England...............	...Golden land.
Parishioners........... ...	...I hire parsons.
Parliament.................	...Partial men.
Penitentiary................	...Nay I repent.
Presbyterians..............	...Best in prayer.
Radical Reform............	...Rare mad frolic
Revolution..........	...To love ruin.
Sir Robert Peel............	...Terrible poser.
Sweetheart..................	...There we sat.
Telegraphs..................	...Great helps.

ENIGMAS are compositions of a different character, based upon *ideas*, rather than upon words, and frequently constructed so as to mislead, and to surprise when the solution is made known. Enigmas may be founded upon simple catches, like Conundrums, in which form they are usually called RIDDLES, such as—

"Though you set me on foot,
I shall be on my head."

THE ANSWER is, *A nail in a shoe.* The celebrated Enigma on the letter H, by Lord Byron, is an admirable specimen of what may be rendered in the form of an Enigma.

Rebuses are a class of Enigma generally formed by the first, sometimes the first and last, letters of words, or of transpositions of letters, or additions to words. Dr. Johnson, however, represents Rebus to be a word represented by a picture. And putting the Doctor's definition and our own explanation together, the reader may glean a good conception of the nature of the Rebus. Example:

The father of the Grecian Jove;
A little boy who's blind;
The foremost land in all the world;
The mother of mankind;
A poet whose love-sonnets are
Still very much admired;—
The *initial* letters will declare
A blessing to the tired.

ANSWER—*Saturn*; *Love*; *England*; *Eve*; *Plutarch.* The initials form *sleep.* **PUZZLES** vary much. One of the simplest that we know is this:

Take away half of *thirteen* and let *eight* remain. Write XIII on a slate, or on a piece of paper—rub out the lower half of the figures, and VIII will remain.

Laws of Chess.—The rules given below are based upon the code published in "Walker's Art of Chess Play." The word *piece* frequently includes the *pawn.*

If the board or pieces be improperly placed, or are deficient in number (except in the case of odds), the game must be recommenced, if the error is discovered before the fourth move on each side (the eighth move of the

game). If not discovered before this stage, the game must proceed.

If a player give odds, and yet omit to remove the odds from the board at the commencement, he may recommence the game, and remove the odds given, provided he discover his error before playing his fourth move. But if he has made his fourth move, the game must be played out; and should the player who agreed to give the odds win the game, it shall nevertheless be considered drawn.

When parties play even, they draw lots for the first move of the first game. The first move is afterwards taken alternately throughout the sitting, except when a game is drawn, when he who had the first move in that game still claims it, a drawn game being of no account. He who gains the move has also the choice of color.

Each player uses the same color throughout the sitting. When a match is made for a given number of games, the move passes alternately throughout the match. A player giving odds has the choice of men, and takes the move in every game, unless agreed to the contrary.

A player who gives the odds of a piece, may give it each game from the king's or queen's side, at his option. If he gives the odds of a pawn, he must give the king's bishop's pawn, unless otherwise stipulated. The player who receives the odds of a certain number of moves at the commencement, must not with those moves cross from his own half of the board.

If a player, in his turn to play, touch one of his men, he must move that piece, if it can legally move, unless, when he first touches it, he says aloud, "*J'adoube.*" No penalty is attached to touching a piece, unless it is your turn to move.

If the player touch his king, with the intention of moving him, and then find that he cannot do so without placing the king in check, no penalty can be inflicted on his replacing his king and moving elsewhere. [Otherwise?] If the player should touch a man which cannot be moved without placing his king in check, he must move his king instead.

If a player about to move touch one of his adversary's men, without saying "*J'adoube*" when he first touches it, he must take that piece, if it can be lawfully taken. Should it not be taken, he must, as a penalty, move his king; but should the king be unable to play without going into check, no penalty can be enforced. It is not allowed to castle upon a compulsory move of the king.

While you hold your piece you may move it anywhere allowed by the rules; but when you quit your hold the move is completed, and must be abided by.

If you inadvertently move one of your adversary's pieces instead of your own, he may compel you to take the piece you have touched, should it be *en prise;* or to replace it and move your king, or to leave it on the square to which you have moved it, and forego any other move at that time. Should you capture one of the adverse pieces with another, instead of one of your own, the capture holds good, if your opponent so decides.

If the player takes a piece through a false move, his adversary may compel him to take such piece with one that can lawfully take it; or to move the piece that has been touched, if such move does not expose the king to check; or he may be directed to move his king.

If you take one of your own men, instead of one of your adversary's, you may be compelled to move one of the two pieces touched, at the option of your opponent. Mr. Walker thinks that the penalty should be to lose the man you have improperly taken off.

An opponent has the option of punishing a false move, by claiming the false move as your move, by compelling you to move the piece touched, as you may think fit, or to replace the piece and move your king.

The king must never be exposed to check by any penalty enforced.

If you move twice running, you may be compelled to abide by both moves, or to retract the second.

Unlimited time is allowed for the moves [unless otherwise agreed]. If one player insists upon the postponement of the termination of a game, against the will of his opponent, the game is forfeited by him who will not play on.

When a pawn is moved two squares, it is liable to be taken, *en passant*, by a pawn, but not by a piece.

If you touch both king and rook, intending to castle, you must move one of the two pieces, at the option of your adversary; or he may compel you to complete the castling. You cannot take a piece and castle at the same time; nor does the rook check as it passes to its new position; but it may check on its position after castling.

False castling is liable to the same penalties as a false move.

When a player gives the odds of a rook, he does not relinquish the right of castling on the side from which the rook has been taken, all other conditions being lawful, as if the rook were in its place.

When you give check you must say so aloud. If check is not called on either side, but subsequently discovered, you must endeavor to recall all the moves back to the period when check first occurred.

You are not compelled to cry check when you attack the queen.

If you cry check, and afterwards alter your determination, you are not compelled to abide by the intention, provided you have not touched the piece.

When a pawn reaches the opposite side of the board it may be replaced by any piece, at the option of the owner, and irrespective of the pieces already owned by him.

Stall mate is a drawn game.

Drawn games count for nothing; and he who moved first in the drawn game, moves first in the following.

If you declare to win a game, or position, and only draw it, you are accounted the loser.

When you have either of the following advantages of force, you are compelled to give check-mate in fifty moves, or the game is considered drawn:

King and queen against king.
King and rook against king.
King and two bishops against king.
King, bishop, and knight against king.
King and queen against king and rook.
King and rook against king and minor piece.
King and pawn against king.
King and two pawns against king and pawn.

If you move after your adversary has made a false move, or committed other irregularity, you cannot claim the penalties.

Spectators are forbidden to make remarks.

Disputes to be referred to a third party.

Draughts or Checkers.—The laws for regulating the game of draughts are as follows:

Each player takes the first move alternately, whether the last game be won or drawn.

Any action which prevents the adversary from having a full view of the men is not allowed.

The player who touches a man must play him.

In case of standing the huff, which means omitting to take a man when an opportunity for so doing occurred, the other party may either take the man, or insist upon his man, which has been so omitted by his adversary, being taken.

If either party, when it is his turn to move, hesitate above three minutes, the other may call upon him to play; and if, after that, he delay above five minutes longer, then he loses the game.

In the losing game, the player can insist upon his adversary taking all the men, in case opportunities should present themselves for their being so taken.

To prevent unnecessary delay, if one color have no pieces, but two kings on the board, and the other no piece, but one king, the latter can call upon the former to win the game in twenty moves; if he does not finish it within that number of moves, the game to be relinquished as drawn.

If there are three kings to two on the board, the subsequent moves are not to exceed forty.

WHIST.—(*Upon the principles of Hoyle's games.*)—Great silence and attention must be observed by the players. Four persons cut for partners; the two highest are against the two lowest. The partners sit opposite to each other, and the person who cuts the lowest card is entitled to the deal. The ace is the lowest in cutting.

SHUFFLING. — Each person has a right to shuffle the cards before the deal; but it is usual for the elder hand only, and the dealer after.

CUTTING. — The pack is then cut by the right hand adversary; and the dealer distributes the cards, one by one, to each of the players, beginning with the person who sits on his left hand, until he comes to the last card, which he turns up, being the trump, and leaves on the table till the first trick is played.

FIRST PLAY. — The person on the left-hand side of the dealer is called the elder, and plays first; whoever wins the trick becomes elder hand, and plays again; and so on, till all the cards are played out.

MISTAKES.—No intimations, or signs of any kind, during the play of the cards, are permitted between the partners. The mistake of one party is the game of the adversary, except in a revoke, when the partners may inquire if he has any of the suit in his hand.

COLLECTING TRICKS. — The tricks belonging to each party should be turned and collected by the respective partners of whoever wins the first trick in every hand. All above six tricks reckon towards the game.

HONORS.—The ace, king, queen, and knave of trumps are called honors; and when either of the partners have three separately, or between them, they count two points towards the game; and in case they have four honors, they count four points.

GAME. — The *game consists of ten points.*

Terms Used in Whist. —*Finessing,* is the attempt to gain an advantage; thus: — If you have the best and third best card of the suit led, you put on the third best, and run the risk of your adversary having the second best; if he has it not, which is two to one against him, you are then certain of gaining a trick.

Forcing, is playing the suit of which your partner or adversary has not any, and which he must trump in order to win.

Long Trump, means the having one or more trumps in your hand when all the rest are out.

Loose Card, means a card in hand of no value, and the most proper to throw away.

Points. — Ten make the game; as many as are gained by tricks or honors, so many points are set up to the score of the game.

Quart, is four successive cards in any suit.

Quart Major, is a sequence of ace, king, queen, and knave.

Quint, is five successive cards in any suit.

Quint Major is a sequence of ace, king, queen, knave, and ten.

See-Saw is when each partner turns a suit, and when they play those suits to each other for that purpose.

Score is the number of points set up. The following is the most approved method of scoring:

1	2	3	4	5	6	7	8	9
					0	0	00	000	0
0	00	000	0000	00	000	0	0	0
								0

Slam is when either party win every trick.

Tenace is possessing the first and third best cards, and being the last player; you consequently catch the adversary when that suit is played:

as, for instance, in case you have ace and queen of any suit, and your adversary leads that suit, you must win two tricks, by having the best and third best of the suit played, and being the last player.

Tierce is three successive cards in any suit.

Tierce Major is a sequence of ace, king, and queen.

Rules for Playing Whist. — Lead from your strong suit, and be cautious how you change suits; and keep a commanding card to bring it in again.

Lead through the strong suit and up to the weak; but not in trumps unless very strong in them.

Lead the highest of a sequence; but if you have a quart or cinque to a king, lead the lowest.

Lead through an honor, particularly if the game is much against you.

Lead your best trump, if the adversaries be eight, and you have no honor; but not if you have four trumps, unless you have a sequence.

Lead a trump if you have four or five, or a strong hand; but not if weak.

Having ace, king, and two or three small cards, lead ace and king if weak in trumps, but a small one if strong in them.

If you have the last trump, with some winning cards, and one losing card only, lead the losing card.

Return your partner's lead, not the adversaries'; and if you have only three originally, play the best; but you need not return it immediately, when you win with a king, queen, or knave, and have only small ones, or when you hold a good sequence, have a strong suit, or have five trumps.

Do not lead from ace queen, or ace knave.

Do not lead an ace, unless you have a king.

Do not lead a thirteenth card, unless trumps be out.

Do not trump a thirteenth card, unless you be last player, or want the lead.

Keep a small card to return your partner's lead.

Be cautious in trumping a card when strong in trumps, particularly if you have a strong suit.

Having only a few small trumps, make them when you can.

If your partner refuses to trump a suit, of which he knows you have not the best, lead your best trump.

When you hold all the remaining trumps, play one, and then try to put the lead in your partner's hand.

Remember how many of each suit are out, and what is the best card left in each hand.

Never force your partner if you are weak in trumps, unless you have a renounce, or want the odd trick.

When playing for the odd trick, be cautious of trumping out, especially if your partner be likely to trump a suit; and make all the tricks you can early, and avoid finessing.

If you take a trick, and have a sequence, win it with the lowest.

Laws of Whist. — DEALING. — If a card be turned up in dealing, the adverse party may call a new deal, unless they have been the cause; then the dealer has the option.

If a card be faced in the deal, the dealer must deal again, unless it be the last deal.

If any one play with twelve cards, and the rest have thirteen, the deal to stand good, and the player to be punished for each revoke; but if any have fourteen cards, the deal is lost.

The dealer to leave the trump card on the table till his turn to play; after which none may ask what card was turned up, only what is trumps.

No person may take up the cards while dealing; if the dealer in that case should miss the deal, to deal again, unless his partner's fault; and if a card be turned up in dealing, no new deal, unless the partner's fault.

If the dealer put the trump card on the rest, with face downwards, he is to lose the deal.

PLAYING OUT OF TURN. — If any person play out of his turn, the adversary may call the card played at any time, if he do not make him revoke;

or if either of the adverse party be to lead, may desire his partner to name the suit, which must be played.

If a person supposes he has won the trick, and leads again before his partner has played, the adversary may oblige his partner to win it, if he can.

If a person lead, and his partner play before his turn, the adversary's partner may do the same.

If the ace, or any other card of a suit, be led, and any person play out of turn, whether his partner have any of the suit led or not, he is neither to trump it nor win it, provided he do not revoke.

REVOKING. — If a revoke happen to be made, the adversary may add three to their score, or take three tricks from them, or take down three from their score; and, if up, must remain at nine.

If any person revoke, and, before the cards be turned, discover it, the adversary may cause the highest or lowest of the suit led, or call the card then played at any time, if it do not cause a revoke.

No revoke to be claimed till the trick be turned and quitted, or the party who revoked, or his partner, have played again.

If any person claim a revoke, the adverse party are not to mix their cards, upon forfeiting the revoke.

No revoke can be claimed after the cards are cut for a new deal.

CALLING HONORS. — If any person call, except at the point of eight, the adverse party may consult, and have new deal.

After the trump card is turned up no person may remind his partner to call, on penalty of losing one point.

If the trump card be turned up, no honors can be set up unless before claimed; and scoring honors, not having them, to be scored against them.

If any person call at eight, and be answered, and the opposite parties have thrown down their cards, and it appear they have not their honors, they may consult, and have a new deal or not.

If any person answer without an honor, the adversaries may consult, and stand the deal or not.

If any person call at eight, after he has played, the adversaries may call a new deal.

SEPARATING AND SHOWING THE CARDS.—If any person separate a card from the rest, the adverse party may call it if he name it; but if he call a wrong card, he or his partner are liable, for once, to have the highest or lowest card called in any suit led during that deal.

If any person throw his cards on the table, supposing the game lost, he may not take them up, and the adversaries may call them provided he do not revoke.

If any person be sure of winning every trick in his hand, he may show his cards, but is liable to have them called.

OMITTING TO PLAY TO A TRICK.—If any person omit to play to a trick, and it appear he has one card more than the rest, it shall be at the option of the adversary to have a new deal.

RESPECTING WHO PLAYED A PARTICULAR CARD. — Each person ought to lay his card before him; and if either of the adversaries mix their cards with his, his partner may demand each person to lay his card before him, but not to inquire who played any particular card.

These laws are agreed to by the best judges.

Maxims for Whist. — LEADER. — Begin with the suit of which you have most in number; for, when the trumps are out, you will probably make several tricks by it.

If you hold equal numbers in different suits, begin with the strongest, because it is the least liable to injure your partner.

Sequences are always eligible leads, as supporting your partner without injuring your own hand.

Lead from a king or queen, rather than from an ace; for since the adversaries will lead from those suits which you do not, your ace will do them most harm

Lead from a king rather than a queen, and from a queen rather than from a knave; for the stronger the suit, the less is your partner endangered.

Lead not from ace queen, or ace knave, till necessary; for, if that suit be led by the adversaries, you have a good chance of making two tricks in it.

In all sequences to a queen, knave, or ten, begin with the highest, because it will frequently distress your left-hand adversary.

Having ace, king, and knave, lead the king; for, if strong in trumps, you may wait the return of this suit, and finesse the knave.

Having ace, queen, and one small card, lead the small one; for, by this lead, your partner has a chance to make the knave.

Having ace, king, and two or three small cards, play ace and king if weak, but a small card if strong in trumps: you may give your partner the chance of making the first trick.

Having king, queen, and one small card, play the small one; for your partner has an equal chance to win, and you need not fear to make king or queen.

Having king, queen, and two or three small cards, lead a small card if strong, and the king if weak in trumps; for strength in trumps entitles you to play a backward game, and give your partner a chance of winning the first trick; but if weak in trumps, lead the king or queen, to secure a trick in that suit.

Having an ace, with four small cards, and no other good suit, play a small card if strong in trumps, and the ace if weak; for strength in trumps may enable you to make one or two of the small cards, although your partner cannot support the lead.

Having king, knave, and ten, lead the ten; for, if your partner hold the ace, you have a good chance to make three tricks, whether he pass the ten or not.

Having king, queen, and ten, lead the king; for, if it fail, by putting on the ten, upon the return of that suit from your partner, you have a chance of making two tricks.

Having queen, knave, and nine, lead the queen; for, upon the return of that suit from your partner, by putting on the nine, you will, probably, make the knave.

SECOND HAND.— Having ace, king, and small ones, play a small card if strong in trumps, but the king if weak in them; for, otherwise, your ace or king might be trumped in the latter case, and no hazards should be run with few trumps but in critical cases.

Having ace, queen, and small cards, play a small one, for, upon the return of that suit, you will, probably, make two tricks.

Having ace, knave, and small cards, play a small one, for, upon the return of the suit, you will, perhaps, make two tricks.

Having ace, ten, or nine, with small cards, play a small one, for, by this method, you have a chance of making two tricks in the suit.

Having king, queen, ten, and small cards, play the queen; for, by playing the ten upon the return of the suit, you will, probably, make two tricks in it.

Having king, queen, and small cards, play a small card if strong in trumps, but the queen if weak in them; for strength in trumps warrants playing a backward game, and it is always advantageous to keep back your adversaries' suit.

If you hold a sequence to your highest card in the suit, play the lowest of it, for, by this means, your partner will be informed of your strength.

Having queen, knave, and small ones, play the knave, because you will, probably, secure a trick.

Having queen, ten, and small ones, play a small one, for your partner has an equal chance to win.

Having either ace, king, queen, or knave, with small cards, play a small one, for your partner has an equal chance to win the trick.

Having either ace, king, queen, or knave, with one small card only, play the small one, for, otherwise, your adversary will finesse upon you.

If a queen be led, and you hold the king, put that on, for if your partner hold the ace, you do no harm; and, if the king be taken, the adversaries have played two honors to one.

If a king be led, and you hold ace, knave, and small ones, play the ace, for it cannot do the adversary a greater injury.

THIRD HAND. — Having ace and king, play the ace and return the king, because you should not keep the command of your partner's strong suit.

Having ace and queen, play the ace, and return the queen; for, although it may prove better in some cases to put on the queen, yet, in general, your partner is best supported by this method.

Having ace and knave, play the ace and return the knave, in order to strengthen your partner's hand.

Having king and knave, play the king; and, if it win, return the knave, for same reason as preceding paragraph.

Always play the best when your partner plays a small card, as it best supports your partner.

If you hold the ace and one small card only, and your partner lead the king, put on the ace, and return the small one; for, otherwise, your ace will be an obstruction to his suit.

If you hold the king and one small card only, and your partner lead the ace, if the trumps be out, play the king; for, by putting on the king, there will be no obstruction to the suit.

FOURTH HAND. — If a king be led, and you hold ace, knave, and a small card, play the small one; for, supposing the queen to follow, you probably make both ace and knave.

When the third hand is weak in his partner's lead, you may often return that suit to great advantage; but this rule must not be applied to trumps, unless you are very strong indeed.

CASES IN WHICH YOU SHOULD RETURN YOUR PARTNER'S LEAD IMMEDIATELY. — When you win with the ace and can return an honor, for that will greatly strengthen his hand.

When he leads a trump, in which

case return the best remaining in your hand (unless you held four originally), except the lead be through an honor.

When your partner has trumped out; for then it is evident he wants to make his great suit.

When you have no good card in any other suit; for then you entirely depend on your partner.

CASES IN WHICH YOU SHOULD NOT RETURN YOUR PARTNER'S LEAD IM-MEDIATELY. — If you win with the king, queen, or knave, and have only small cards left; for the return of a small card will more distress than strengthen your partner.

If you hold a good sequence; for then you may show a strong suit, and not injure his hand.

If you have a strong suit; because leading from a strong suit directs your partner, and cannot injure him.

If you have a good hand; for, in this case, you ought to consult your own hand.

If you hold five trumps; for then you are warranted to play trumps, if you think it right.

LEADING TRUMPS. — Lead trumps from a strong hand, but never from a weak one, by which means you will secure your good cards from being trumped.

Trump not out with a bad hand, although you hold five small trumps; for, since your cards are bad, it is only trumping for the adversaries' good ones.

Having ace, king, knave, and three small trumps, play ace and king; for the probability of the queen's falling is in your favor.

Having ace, king, knave, and one or two small trumps, play the king, and wait the return from your partner to put on the knave, in order to win the queen; but, if you particularly wish the trumps out, play two rounds, and then your strong suit.

Having ace, king, and two or three small trumps, lead a small one; this is to let your partner win the first trick; but if you have good reason for getting out the trumps, play three rounds,

or play ace and king, and then proceed with your strong suit.

If your adversaries be eight, and you do not hold an honor, throw off your best trump; for, if your partner has not two honors, you have lost the game; and if he holds two honors, it is most advantageous to lead a trump.

Having ace, queen, knave, and small trumps, play the knave; for, by this means, the king only can make against you.

Having ace, queen, ten, and one or two small trumps, lead a small one, for it will give your partner a chance to win the trick, and keep the command in your own hand.

Having king, queen, ten, and small trumps, lead the king; for if the king be lost, upon the return of trumps you may finesse the ten.

Having king, knave, ten, and small ones, lead the knave, because it will prevent the adversaries from making a small trump.

Having queen, knave, nine, and small trumps, lead the queen; for, if your partner hold the ace, you have a good chance of making the whole suit.

Having queen, knave, and two or three small trumps, lead the queen, for the reason just mentioned.

Having knave, ten, eight, and small trumps, lead the knave; for, on the return of trumps, you probably may finesse the eight to advantage.

Having knave, ten, and three small trumps, lead the knave, because it will most distress your adversaries, unless two honors are held on your right hand; the odds against which are about three to one.

Having only small trumps, play the highest; by which you will support your partner all you can.

Having a sequence, begin with the highest; by this means, your partner is best instructed how to play his hand, and cannot possibly be injured.

If any honor be turned up on your left, and the game much against you, lead a trump the first opportunity; for, your game being desperately bad, this method is the most likely to retrieve it.

In all other cases it is dangerous leading through an honor, unless you be strong in trumps, or have a good hand; because all the advantage of trumping through an honor lies in your partner's finessing.

Supposing it hereafter proper to lead trumps, when an honor is turned up on your left, you, holding only one honor, with a small trump, play the honor, and next the small one; because it will greatly strengthen your partner's hand, and cannot hurt your own.

If an honor be turned up on the left, and you hold a sequence, lead the highest of it, because it will prevent the last hand from injuring your partner.

If a queen be turned up on the left, and you hold ace, king, and a small one, lead the small trump, because you will have a chance of getting the queen.

If a queen be turned up on the left, and you hold a knave, with small ones, lead the knave; for the knave cannot be of service, as the queen is on your left.

If an honor be turned up by your partner, and you are strong in trumps, lead a small one; but if weak in them, lead the best you have; by this play the weakest hand will support the strongest.

If an ace be turned up on the right, you holding king, queen, and knave, lead the knave; a secure lead.

If an ace be turned up on the right, and you hold king, queen, and ten, lead the king, and upon the return of trumps play the ten; for, by this means, you show a great strength to your partner, and will, probably, make two tricks in them.

If a king be turned up on the right, and you hold queen, knave, and nine, lead knave, and, upon the return of trumps, play the nine, because it may prevent the ten from making.

If a king be turned up on your right, and you hold knave, ten, and nine, lead the nine, and, upon the return of trumps, play the ten; because this method will best disclose your strength in trumps.

26

If a queen be turned up on the right, and you hold ace, king, and knave, lead the king, and, upon the return of trumps, play the knave, because you are then certain to make the knave.

If a queen be turned up on the right, and you hold ace, king, and small ones, lead the king; and, upon the return of trumps, you may finesse, unless the queen falls, for, otherwise, the queen will make a trick.

If a knave be turned up on the right, and you hold king, queen, and ten, lead the queen, and, upon the return of trumps, play the ten; for, by this means, you will make the ten.

If a knave be turned up on the right, and you hold king, queen, and small ones, lead the king; and, if that come home, play a small one, for it is probable your partner holds the ace.

If a knave be turned up on the right, and you hold king and ten or queen and ten, with two small cards, lead a small one; and, upon the return of trumps, play the ten, for it is five to four that your partner holds one honor.

WHEN YOU TURN UP AN HONOR IN WHIST. — If you turn up an ace, and hold only one small trump with it, if either adversary lead the king, put on the ace.

But, if you turn up an ace, and hold two or three small trumps with it, and either adversary lead the king, put on a small one; for, if you play the ace, you give up the command in trumps.

If you turn up the king, and hold only one small trump with it, and your right-hand adversary lead a trump, play the king.

If you turn up a king, and hold two or three small trumps with it, if your right-hand adversary lead a trump, play a small one.

If you turn up a queen or a knave, and hold, besides, only small trumps, if your right-hand adversary lead a trump, put on a small one.

If you hold a sequence to the honor turned up, play it last.

PLAYING FOR THE ODD TRICK. — Be cautious of trumping out, notwithstanding you have a good hand.

Never trump out, if your partner appears likely to trump a suit.

If you are moderately strong in trumps, force your partner, for by this you probably make a trick.

Make your tricks early, and be cautious of finessing.

If you hold a single card of any suit, and only two or three small trumps, .ead the single card.

CALCULATIONS OF WHIST. — It is about five to four that your partner holds one card out of any two.

It is about five to two that he holds one card out of three.

It is about four to one that he holds one card out of any four.

It is one to two that he does not hold a certain card.

It is about three to one that he does not hold two cards out of any three.

It is about three to two that he does not hold two cards out of any four.

CRIBBAGE.—The game of cribbage differs from all other games by its immense variety of chances. It is reckoned useful to young people in the science of calculation. It is played with the whole pack of cards, generally by two persons, and sometimes by four. There are also five different modes of playing—that is, with five, six, or eight cards; but the games are principally those with five and six cards. The rules vary a little in different companies, but the following are those most generally observed:

TERMS USED IN CRIBBAGE. — *Crib.* — The crib is composed of the cards thrown away by each party, and the dealer is entitled to score whatever points are made by them.

Pairs are two similar cards, as two aces or two kings. Whether in hand o- playing they reckon for two points.

Pairs-Royal are three similar cards, and reckon for six points, whether in hand or playing.

Double Pairs-Royal are four similar cards, and reckon for twelve points, whether in hand or playing. The points gained by pairs, pairs-royal, and double pairs-royal, in playing, are thus effected :—Your adversary having played a seven and you another, constitutes a pair, and entitles you to score two points : your antagonist then playing a third seven, makes a pair-royal, and he marks six ; and your playing a fourth is a double pair-royal, and entitles you to twelve points.

Fifteens.—Every fifteen reckons for two points, whether in hand cr playing. In hand they are formed either by two cards, such as a five and any tenth card, a six and a nine, a seven and an eight, or by three cards, as a two, a five, and an eight, etc. And in playing thus, if such cards are played as make together fifteen, the two points are to be scored towards the game.

Sequences are three or four or more successive cards, and reckon for an equal number of points either in hand or play. In playing a sequence, it is of no consequence which card is thrown down first; as thus:—your adversary playing an ace, you a five, he a three, you a two, then he a four, he counts five for the sequence.

Flush.—When the cards are all of one suit, they reckon for as many points as there are cards. For a flush in the crib, the card turned up must be of the same suit as those put out in the crib.

Noddy. — The knave of the suit turned up reckons for one point; if a knave be turned up, the dealer is to mark two; but it cannot be reckoned again; and when played it does not score anything.

End Hole.—The point scored by the last player, if he makes under thirty-one; if he makes thirty-one exactly, he is to mark two. To obtain either of these is considered a great advantage.

Last. — Three points taken at the commencement of the game of five-card cribbage by the non-dealer.

RULES OF CRIBBAGE.—The adverse parties cut the cards to determine who shall be dealer ; the lowest card has it. The ace is the lowest.

In dealing, the dealer may discover

his own cards, but not those of his adversary—who may mark two, and call a fresh deal.

Should too many cards be dealt to either, the non-dealer may score two, and demand another deal, if the error be detected previous to taking up the cards; if he do not wish a new deal, the extra cards must be drawn away. When any player has more than the proper number of cards in hand, the opponent may score four, and call a new deal.

If any player meddle with the pack after dealing, till the period of cutting it for the turn-up card, then his opponent may score two points.

If any player take more than he is entitled to, the other party should not only put him back as many points as are overscored, but likewise take the same extra number for his own game.

Should either party even meddle with his own pegs unnecessarily, the opponent may score two points; and if any one take out his front peg, he must place the same back behind the other. If any be misplaced by accident, a bystander may replace the same, according to the best of his judgment; but he should never otherwise interfere.

If any player neglect to set up what he is entitled to, the adversary is allowed to take the points so omitted.

Each player may place his own cards, when done with, upon the pack.

In five-card cribbage, the cards are to be dealt one by one; but when played with six cards, then it is customary to give three, and if with eight cards, four at a time.

The non-dealer, at the commencement of the game, in five-card cribbage, scores three points, called *three for last;* but in six and eight-card cribbage this is not to be done.

In what is called the Bath game, they reckon flushes upon the board; that is, when three cards of the same suit are played successively, the party playing the third scores three points; if the adversary play a fourth of the same suit, then he is to score four, and

so on for four, five, six, or as long as the same suit continues to be played in uninterrupted succession, and that the whole number of pips do not reckon thirty-one.

FIVE-CARD CRIBBAGE.—It is unnecessary to describe cribbage - boards; the sixty-one points or holes marked thereon make the game. We have before said that the party cutting the lowest card deals; after which, each player is first to lay out two of the five cards for the crib, which always belongs to the dealer; next, the adversary is to cut the remainder of the pack, and the dealer to turn up and lay upon the crib the uppermost card, for which, if a knave, he is to mark two points. The card turned up is to be reckoned by both parties, whether in showing their hands or crib. After laying out and cutting as above mentioned, the eldest hand is to play a card, which the other should endeavor to pair, or find one, the pips of which, reckoned with the first, will make fifteen; then the non-dealer must play another card, and try to make a pair, pair-royal, sequence, flush (where allowed of), or fifteen, provided the cards already played have not exceeded that number; and so on alternately, until the pips on the cards played make thirty-one, or the nearest possible number under that.

COUNTING FOR GAME. — When the party, whose turn it may be to play, cannot produce a card that will make thirty-one, or come under that number, he is then to say "Go" to his antagonist, who, thereupon, will be entitled to score one, or must play any card or cards he may have that will make thirty-one, or under; and if he can make exactly thirty-one, he is to take two points; if not, one: the last player has often opportunity this way to make pairs or sequences. Such cards as remain after this are not to be played; but each party having, during the play, scored his points gained, in the manner before directed, must proceed, the non-dealer first to count and take for his hand, then the dealer for his hand,

and also for his crib, reckoning the cards every way they can possibly be varied, and always including the turned-up card.

	Points.
For every fifteen...................	2
Pair, or two of a sort.............	2
Pair-royal, or three of a sort...	6
Double pair-royal, or four ditto	12
Knave of the turned-up suit...	1
Sequences and flushes, whatever number.	

MAXIMS FOR LAYING OUT THE CRIB CARDS. — It is always requisite, in laying out cards for the crib, that every player should consider not only his own hand, but also to whom the crib belongs, as well as the state of the game; for what might be proper in one situation would be highly imprudent in another. When any player possesses a pair-royal, it is generally advisable to lay out the other cards for crib, unless it belongs to the adversary, and they consist of two fives, a deuce, and a trois, five and six, seven and eight, five and any other tenth card, or that the game be almost finished. A player, when he does not thereby materially injure his hand, should for his own crib lay out close cards, in hope of making a sequence; or two of a suit, in expectation of a flush; or any that of themselves amount to fifteen, or such as reckoned with others will make that number, except when the antagonist be nearly up, and it may be expedient to keep such cards as probably may prevent him from gaining at play. The opposite method should be pursued in respect to the adversary's crib, which each person should endeavor to balk, by laying out those cards that are not likely to prove to advantage, unless at such a stage of the game when it may be of consequence to keep in hand cards likely to tell in play, or when the non-dealer would be either out by his hand, or has reason for judging the crib of little moment. A king is the best card to balk a crib, as none can form a sequence beyond it, except in some companies, where king, queen, ace, are allowed as a se-

quence; and either a king or queen, with an ace, six, seven, eight, or nine, are good ones to put out. Low cards are generally the most likely to gain at play; the flushes and sequences, particularly if the latter be also flushes, constitute the most eligible hands, as thereby the player will often be enabled either to assist his own crib, or balk that of the opponent, to whom a knave should never be given, if with propriety it can be retained.

THREE OR FOUR-HAND CRIBBAGE differs only from the preceding, as the parties put out but one card each to the crib; and when thirty-one, or the nearest approximating number has been made, then the next eldest hand leads, and the players go on again in rotation, with any remaining cards, till all are played out, before they proceed to show. For three-hand cribbage triangular boards are used.

THREE-HAND CRIBBAGE is sometimes played, wherein one person sits out, not each game, but each deal, in rotation. In this the first dealer generally wins. The chances in this game are often so great, that even between skilful gamesters it is possible, at five-card cribbage, when the adversary is fifty-six, for a lucky player, who had not previously made a single hole, to be more than up in two deals, his opponent getting no farther than sixty in that time; and in four-hand cribbage, a case may occur wherein none of the parties hold a single point in hand, and yet the dealer and his friend, with the assistance of a knave turned up, may make sixty-one by play in one deal, while the adversaries only get twenty-four; and although this may not happen for many years, yet similar games may now and then be met with.

SIX-CARD CRIBBAGE varies from that played with five, as the players (always only two) commence on an equality, without scoring any points for the last, retain four cards in hand, and all the cards are to be played out, as in three and four-hand cribbage, with five cards. At this game it is of advantage to the last player to keep as close as possible, in hopes of coming in for fifteen, a sequence, or pair, besides the end hole, or thirty-one. The first dealer is reckoned to have some trifling advantage, and each player may, on the average, expect to make twenty-five points in every two deals. The first non-dealer is considered to have preference, when he gains ten or more the first hand, the dealer not making more than his average number.

THE GREATEST POSSIBLE NUMBER that can be gained by the show of any hand or crib, either in five or six-card cribbage, is twenty-nine; it is composed of three fives and a knave, with a fourth five, of the same suit as the knave, turned up; this very seldom happens. But twenty-four is an uncommon number, and may be formed of four threes and a nine, or two fours, one five, and two sixes; add some other combinations that experience will point out.

EIGHT-CARD CRIBBAGE is sometimes played, but very seldom.

ODDS OF THE GAME OF CRIBBAGE. —The average number estimated to be held from the cards in hand is rather more than four, and under five; to be gained in play, two for the dealer, and one for the adversary, making in all an average of six throughout the game; the probability of the crib is five; so that each player ought to make sixteen in two deals; by which it will appear the dealer has somewhat the advantage, supposing the cards to run equal, and the players well matched. By attending to this calculation, any person may judge whether he be at home or not, and thereby play his game accordingly; either making a grand push when he is behind and holds good cards, or endeavoring to balk his adversary when his hand proves indifferent.

ALL-FOURS is usually played by two persons; not unfrequently by four. Its name is derived from the four chances, called *high, low, Jack, game,* each making a point. A complete pack of cards must be provided, six of which are to be dealt to each party, three at a time; and the next card, the thirteenth, is to be turned up for the trump by the dealer, who, if it prove a knave, is to score one point. The party who cuts the highest card is to deal first. The cards rank in the same manner as at whist, for whoever scores the first ten points wins.

LAWS OF ALL-FOURS.—A new deal can be demanded, if in dealing the dealer discovers any of the adversary's cards; if, to either party, too many cards have been dealt: in the latter case it is optional with the parties, provided it be done before a card has been played, but not after, to draw from the opposing hand the extra card.

If the dealer expose any of his own cards, the deal is to stand good.

No person can beg more than once in each hand, except by mutual agreement.

Each party must trump or follow suit if they can, on penalty of the adversary scoring one point.

If either player score wrong, it must be taken down, and the adversary shall either score four points or one, as may have previously been agreed.

When a trump is played, it is allowable to ask your adversary if it be either high or low.

One card may count all-fours; for example, the eldest hand holds the knave and stands his game, the dealer has neither trump, ten, ace, nor court-card; it will follow that the knave will be both high, low, Jack, and game, as explained by—

TERMS USED IN ALL-FOURS.—*High.* —The highest trump out, the holder to score one point.

Low.—The lowest trump out, the original holder to score one point, even if it be taken by the adversary.

Jack.—The knave of trumps, the holder to score one, unless it be won by the adversary; in that case the winner is to score the point.

Game.—The greatest number that,

in the tricks gained, can be shown by either party, reckoning—

Four for an ace. | *One* for a knave.
Three for a king. | *Ten* for a ten.
Two for a queen.

The other cards do not count: thus it may happen that a deal may be played without having any to reckon for game.

Begging is when the eldest hand, disliking his cards, uses his privilege, and says, "*I beg;*" in which case the dealer must either suffer his adversary to score one point, saying, "*Take one,*" or give each three cards more from the pack, and then turn up the next card, the seventh, for trumps; if, however, the trump turned up be of the same suit as the first, the dealer must go on, giving each three cards more, and turning up the seventh, until a change of suit for trumps shall take place.

MAXIMS FOR ALL-FOURS.—Always make your knave as soon as you can.

Strive to secure your tens ; this is to be done by playing any small cards, by which you may throw the lead into your adversary's hand.

Win your adversary's best cards when you can, either by trumping or with superior cards.

If, being eldest hand, you hold either ace, king, or queen of trumps, without the knave or ten, play them immediately, as, by this means, you have a chance to win the knave or ten.

DOMINO. — DESCRIPTION OF THE GAME.—This game is played by two or four persons, with twenty-eight pieces of oblong ivory, plain at the back, but on the face divided by a black line in the middle, and indented with spots, from one to a double-six, which pieces are a double-blank, ace-blank, double-ace, deuce-blank, deuce-ace, double-deuce, trois-blank, trois-ace, trois-deuce, double-trois, four-blank, four-ace, four-deuce, four-trois, double-four, five-blank, five-ace, five-deuce, five-trois, five-four, double-five, six-blank, six-ace, six-deuce, six-trois, six-four, six-five, and double-six. Sometimes a double set is played

with, of which double twelve is the highest.

METHOD OF PLAYING DOMINOES.- At the commencement of the game the dominoes are well mixed together, with their faces upon the table. Each person draws one, and if four play, those who choose the two highest are partners against those who take the two lowest ; drawing the latter also serves to determine who is to lay down the first piece, which is reckoned a great advantage. Afterwards each player takes seven pieces at random. The eldest hand having laid down one, the next must pair him, at either end of the piece he may choose, according to the number of pips, or the blank in the compartment of the piece; but whenever any one cannot match the part, either of the domino last put down, or of that unpaired at the other end of the row, then he says "*Go;*" and the next is at liberty to play. Thus they play alternately, either until one party has played all his pieces, and thereby won the game, or till the game be *blocked:* this is when neither party can play, by matching the pieces where unpaired at either end; then that party wins who has the smallest number of pips on the pieces remaining in their possession. It is to the advantage of every player to dispossess himself as early as possible of the heavy pieces, such as a double-six, five, four, etc. Sometimes, when two persons play, they take each only seven pieces, and agree to *play* or *draw, i. e.*, when one cannot come in, or pair the pieces upon the board at the end unmatched, he then is to draw from the fourteen pieces in stock till he find one to suit.

LOO.—DESCRIPTION OF THE GAME. — Loo, or Lue, is subdivided into limited and unlimited Loo; it is a game the complete knowledge of which can easily be acquired, and is played two ways, both with five and three cards, though most commonly with five dealt from a whole pack, either first three and then two, or by one at a time. Several persons may play together, but the great-cst number can be admitted when with three cards only.

METHOD OF PLAYING LOO. — After five cards have been given to each player, another is turned up for trump; the knave of clubs generally, or sometimes the knave of the trump suit, as agreed upon, is the highest card, and is styled pam; the ace of trumps is next in value, and the rest in succession, as at whist. Each player has the liberty of changing for others, from the pack, all or any of the five cards dealt, or of throwing up the hand, in order to escape being looed. Those who play their cards, either with or without changing, and do not gain a trick, are looed; as is likewise the case with all who have stood the game, when a flush or flushes occur; and each, excepting any player holding pam, of an inferior flush, is required to deposit a stake, to be given to the person who sweeps the board, or divided among the winners at the ensuing deal, according to the tricks which may then be made. For instance, if every one at dealing stakes half a dollar, the tricks are entitled to ten cents apiece, and whoever is looed must put down half a dollar, exclusive of the deal: sometimes it is settled that each person looed shall pay a sum equal to what happens to be on the table at the time. Five cards of a suit, or four with pam, compose a flush, which sweeps the board, and yields only to a superior flush, or the elder hand. When the ace of trumps is led, it is usual to say, " *Pam, be civil;* " the holder of which last-mentioned card is then expected to let the ace pass. When Loo is played with three cards, they are dealt by one at a time, pam is omitted, and the cards are not exchanged, nor permitted to be thrown up.

PUT. — The game of Put is played with an entire pack of cards, generally by two, but sometimes by four persons. At this game the cards have a different value from all others. The best card in the pack is a *trois*, or three; the next *deuce*, or two ; then come in rotation, as at other games, the ace, king, queen, knave, ten, etc. The dealer distributes

three cards to each player, by one at a time; whoever cuts the lowest card has the deal, and five points make the game, except when both parties say, "*I put*"— for then the score is at an end, and the contest is determined in favor of that party who may win two tricks out of three. When it happens that each player has won a trick, and the third is a tie — that is, covered by a card of equal value — the whole goes for nothing, and the game must begin anew.

TWO-HANDED PUT. — The eldest hand should play a card; and whether the adversary pass it, win it, or tie it, you have a right to say, " *I put*," or place your cards on the pack. If you accept the first and your opponent decline the challenge, you score one; if you prefer the latter, your adversary gains a point; but if, before he play, your opponent says, " *I put*," and you do not choose to see him, he is entitled to add one to his score. It is sometimes good play to say, "*I put*," before you play a card; this depends on the nature of your hand.

FOUR-HANDED PUT. — Each party has a partner, and when three cards are dealt to each, one of the players gives his partner his best card, and throws the other two away ; the dealer is at liberty to do the same to his partner, and *vice versa*. The two persons who have received their partners' cards play the game, previously discarding their worst card for the one they have received from their partners. The game then proceeds as at two-handed Put.

LAWS OF PUT. — When the dealer accidentally discovers any of his adversary's cards, the adversary may demand a new deal.

When the dealer discovers any of his own cards in dealing, he must abide by the deal.

When a faced card is discovered during the deal, the cards must be reshuffled, and dealt again.

If the dealer give his adversary more cards than are necessary, the adversary may call a fresh deal, or suffer the dealer to draw the extra cards from his hand.

If the dealer give himself more cards than are his due, the adversary may add a point to his game, and call a fresh deal if he pleases, or draw the extra cards from the dealer's hand.

No bystander must interfere, under penalty of paying the stakes.

Either party saying, "I *put*"—that is, "I play"—cannot retract, but must abide the event of the game, or pay the stakes.

SPECULATION is a noisy round game, at which several may play, using a complete pack of cards, bearing the same import as at whist, with fish or counters, on which such a value is fixed as the company may agree. The highest trump in each deal wins the pool; and whenever it happens that not one is dealt, then the company pool again, and the event is decided by the succeeding *coup*. After determining the deal, etc., the dealer pools six fish, and every other player four; then three cards are given to each, by one at a time, and another turned up for trump. The cards are not to be looked at, except in this manner: The eldest hand shows the uppermost card, which, if a trump, the company may speculate on, or bid for—the highest bidder buying and paying for it, provided the price offered be approved of by the seller. After this is settled, if the first card does not prove a trump, then the next eldest is to show the uppermost card, and so on—the company speculating as they please, till all are discovered, when the possessor of the highest trump, whether by purchase or otherwise, gains the pool. To play at speculation well, a recollection only is requisite of what superior cards of that particular suit have appeared in the preceding deals, and calculating the probability of the trump offered proving the highest in the deal then undetermined.

MATRIMONY.—The game of Matrimony is played with an entire pack of cards, by any number of persons from five to fourteen. It consists of five chances, usually marked on a board, or sheet of paper, as follows:

This game is generally played with counters, and the dealer puts what he pleases on each or any chance, the other players depositing each the same quantity, except one—that is, when the dealer stakes twelve, the rest of the company lay down eleven each. After this, two cards are dealt round to every one, beginning on the left; then to each person one other card, which is turned up, and he who so happens to get the ace of diamonds sweeps all. If it be not turned up, then each player shows his hand; and any of them having matrimony, intrigue, etc., takes the counters on that point; and when two or more people happen to have a similar combination, the oldest hand has the preference; and should any chance not be gained, it stands over to the next deal. *Observe*—The ace of diamonds turned up takes the whole pool, but when in hand ranks only as any other ace; and if not turned up, nor any ace in hand, then the king, or next superior card, wins the chance styled pool.

Pope Joan.—Pope, a game somewhat similar to that of matrimony, is played by a number of people, who generally use a board painted for this purpose, which may be purchased at most turners' or toy shops. The eight of diamonds must first be taken from the pack, and after settling the deal, shuffling, etc., the dealer dresses the board, by putting fish, counters, or other stakes, one each to ace, king, queen, knave, and game; two to matrimony, two to intrigue, and six to the nine of diamonds, styled Pope. This dressing is, in some companies, at the individual expense of the dealer, though, in others, the players contribute two stakes apiece toward the same. The cards are next to be dealt round equally to every player, one turned up for trump, and about six or eight left in the stock to form stops; as, for example, if the ten of spades be turned up, the nine consequently becomes a stop; the four kings and the seven of diamonds are always fixed stops, and the dealer is the only person permitted, in the course of the game, to refer occasionally to the stock for information what other cards are stops in their respective deals. If either ace, king, queen, or knave happen to be the turned-up trump, the dealer may take whatever is deposited on that head; but when pope be turned up, the dealer is entitled both to that and the game, besides a stake for every card dealt to each player. Unless the game be determined by pope being turned up, the eldest hand must begin by playing out as many cards as possible; first the stops, then pope, if he have it, and afterward the lowest card of his longest suit, particularly an ace, for that never can be led through; the other players are to follow, when they can, in sequence of the same suit, till a stop occurs, and the party having the stop thereby becomes eldest hand, and is to lead accordingly; and so on, until some person parts with all his cards, by which he wins the pool (game), and becomes entitled besides to a stake for every card not played by the others, except from any one holding pope, which excuses him from paying; but if pope has been played, then the party having held it is not excused. King and queen form what is denominated matrimony; queen and knave make intrigue, when in the same hand; but neither these, nor ace, king, queen, knave, or pope, entitle the holder to the stakes deposited thereon, unless played out; and no claim can be allowed after the board be dressed for the succeeding deal; but in all such cases the stakes are to remain for future determination. This game only requires a little attention to recollect what stops have been made in the course of the play; as, for instance, if a player begin by laying down the eight of clubs, then

the seven in another hand forms a stop, whenever that suit be led from any lower card; or the holder, when eldest, may safely lay it down, in order to clear his hand.

CASSINO. — The game of Cassino is played with an entire pack of cards, generally by four persons, but sometimes by three, and often by two.

TERMS USED IN CASSINO. — *Great Cassino*, the ten of diamonds, which reckons for two points.

Little Cassino, the two of spades, which reckons for one point.

The Cards is when you have a greater share than your adversary, and reckons for three points.

The Spades is when you have the majority of that suit, and reckons for one point.

The Aces : each of which reckons for one point.

Lurched is when your adversary has won the game before you have gained six points.

In some deals at this game it may so happen that neither party win anything, as the points are not set up according to the tricks, etc., obtained, but the smaller number is constantly subtracted from the larger, both in cards and points; and if they both prove equal, the game commences again, and the deal goes on in rotation. When three persons play at this game, the two lowest add their points together, and subtract from the highest; but when their two numbers together either amount to or exceed the highest, then neither party scores.

LAWS OF CASSINO. — The deal and partners are determined by cutting, as at whist, and the dealer gives four cards, by one at a time, to every player, and either regularly as he deals, or by one, two, three, or four at a time, lays four more, face upwards, upon the board, and, after the first cards are played, four others are to be dealt to each person, until the pack be concluded; but it is only in the first deal that any cards are to be turned up.

The deal is not lost when a card is

faced by the dealer, unless in the first round, before any of the four cards are turned up upon the table; but if a card happen to be faced in the pack, before any of the said four be turned up, then the deal must be begun again.

Any person playing with less than four cards must abide by the loss; and should a card be found under the table, the player whose number is deficient is to take the same.

Each person plays one card at a time, with which he may not only take at once every card of the same denomination upon the table, but likewise all that will combine therewith; as, for instance, a ten takes not only every ten, but also nine and ace, eight and deuce, seven and three, six and four, or two fives; and if he clear the board before the conclusion of the game, he is to score a point; and whenever any player cannot pair or combine, then he is to put down a card.

The tricks are not to be counted before all the cards are played; nor may any trick but that last won be looked at, as every mistake must be challenged immediately.

After all the pack is dealt out, the player who obtains the last trick sweeps all the cards then remaining unmatched upon the table.

VINGT - UN. — DESCRIPTION OF THE GAME. — The game of *Vingt-un*, or twenty-one, may be played by two or more persons; and, as the deal is advantageous, and often continues long with the same person, it is usual to determine it at the commencement by turning up the first ace, or any other mode that may be agreed upon.

METHOD OF PLAYING VINGT-UN. — The cards must all be dealt out in succession, unless a natural Vingt-un occur, and in the meantime the pone, or youngest hand, should collect those that have been played, and shuffle them together, ready for the dealer, against the period when he shall have distributed the whole pack. The dealer is first to give two cards, by one at a time, to each player, including him-

self; then to ask every person in rotation, beginning with the eldest hand on the left, whether he stands or chooses another card, which, if required, must be given from off the top of the pack, and afterwards another, or more, if desired, till the points of the additional card or cards, added to those dealt, exceed or make twenty-one exactly, or such a number less than twenty-one as may be judged proper to stand upon. But when the points exceed twenty-one, then the cards of that individual player are to be thrown up directly, and the stakes to be paid to the dealer, who also is, in turn, entitled to draw additional cards; and, on taking a Vingt-un, is to receive double stakes from all who stand the game, except such other players, likewise having twenty-one, between whom it is thereby a drawn game; and when any adversary has a Vingt-un, and the dealer not, then the opponent so having twenty-one wins double stakes from him. In other cases, except a natural Vingt-un happen, the dealer pays single stakes to all whose numbers under twenty-one are higher than his own, and receives from those who have lower numbers; but nothing is paid or received by such players as have similar numbers to the dealer; and when the dealer draws more than twenty-one, he is to pay to all who have not thrown up.

NATURAL VINGT-UN.—Twenty-one, whensoever dealt in the first instance, is styled a *Natural Vingt-un*, it should be declared immediately, and entitles the possessor to the deal, besides double stakes from all the players, unless there shall be more than one Natural Vingt-un; in which case the younger hand or hands having the same are excused from paying to the eldest, who takes the deal, of course. *Observe* — An ace may be reckoned either as eleven or one; every court-card is counted as ten, and the rest of the pack according to their points.

THE ODDS OF NATURAL VINGT-UN merely depend upon the average number of cards likely to come under or exceed twenty-one; for example, if those in hand make fourteen exactly, it is seven to six that the one next drawn does not make the number of points above twenty-one; but if the points be fifteen, it is seven to six against that hand; yet it would not, therefore, always be prudent to stand at fifteen, but as the ace may be calculated both ways, it is rather above an even bet that the adversary's two first cards amount to more than fourteen. A natural Vingt-un may be expected once in seven coups when two, and twice in seven when four people play, and so on, according to the number of players.

CROQUET.—This out-door pastime is of comparatively modern creation, and is every day becoming more in vogue. It may be played by persons of all ages and of either sex; but it is especially adapted for ladies and young persons, as it demands but trifling personal exertion, while it affords delightful and health-giving sport.

THE GROUND UPON WHICH CROQUET IS PLAYED is preferably a grass-plot of an oblong form; but an ordinary lawn or expanse of even turf will answer the purpose, so long as it is of sufficient extent for the operation of the game.

THE IMPLEMENTS FOR PLAYING Croquet are the balls, the mallets, the starting and turning-pegs, the croquet clips or markers, the hoops or arches. These may be obtained at the ordinary toy warehouses.

ARRANGEMENT OF THE HOOPS.— As much of the interest of this game depends upon the arrangement of the hoops, it is essential that they should be fixed in the ground on definite principles. In the first place, the starting-peg is driven in at one end of the ground, and the turning-peg is driven in at the other extremity. From each of these pegs a space of twelve feet intervenes; here a hoop is fixed; another space of ten feet intervenes, when a second hoop is fixed; a space of eight feet then succeeds,

and at this point is formed what may be termed the base, on each side of which, at a distance of twenty feet, and succeeding each other at intervals of ten feet, three hoops are driven in. By this arrangement a square is formed, the starting-peg leading into its centre, and the turning-peg leading from it. Where the ground is small, the distances may be contracted proportionally. Other arrangements of the hoops may be made at the discretion of the players, but the first-named plan will be found best worthy of adoption, as it affords the most excellent opportunities for the display of address and skill.

THE GAME CONSISTS in striking the balls from the starting-peg through the seven hoops to the peg at the opposite extremity. The balls are then driven back again to the starting peg.

THE GAME MAY BE PLAYED by any number of persons not exceeding eight. A larger number protracts the intervals between the several turns, and thereby renders the game tedious. The most eligible number is four. If two only play, each player should take two balls, and when as many as eight play, there should be two sides or sets.

IN PLAYING THE GAME each player takes a mallet, ball, and croquet clip of the same color or number, the clip being used to indicate the hoop at which, in his turn, he aims. The division into sides, choice of balls, mallets, etc., is determined by the players among themselves.

LAWS OF THE GAME.—In Croquet, as with many other sports when first established, there exist differences of opinion on certain points of practice. We have consulted numerous treatises on the game, and find Jaques's " Laws and Regulations of the Game of Croquet " to be one of the most practical and straightforward manuals extant. It is to this work that we are mainly indebted for the following laws of the game:

On commencing, each player must place his ball within a mallet's length of the starting-peg in any direction, and his opening stroke must be to pass through the first hoop.

The players on each side are to play alternately, according to the colors on the starting-peg, and the order in which they play cannot be altered during the game.

Each player continues to play so long as he plays with success, that is, so long as he drives his ball through the next hoop in order, or croquets another ball.

When a player strikes his own ball so as to hit another at a distance, he is said to roquet it; and, having thus hit a ball, he must then, as it is termed, "take the croquet," which is done as follows :—He lays his own ball against the other so that the two touch ; he then places his foot on his own ball, which he strikes with his mallet; this will drive the ball with a momentum and in a direction most desired. In doing this the player should press his foot on his own ball.

A player must move the ball he croquets. He is said to "take a stroke off" when he places his own ball to touch the croqueted ball very lightly, so as to leave it, when croqueted, in nearly the same position ; but in doing this the croqueted ball must be perceptibly moved.

No ball can croquet, or be croqueted, until it be passed through the first hoop.

Any player missing the first hoop takes his ball up, and, when his turn comes again, plays from the starting place, as at first.

A player may croquet any number of balls consecutively; but he cannot croquet the same ball twice during the same turn, without first sending his own ball through the next hoop in order.

Instead of aiming at his hoop or another ball, a player may strike his ball towards any part of the ground he pleases. When he has made a complete circuit from the starting-peg back to the starting-peg, he may either retire from the game by pegging, or, by not

doing so, remain in. In this case he is called a "rover," and will still have the power of croqueting consecutively all the balls during any one of his turns.

When a ball roquets another ball, the player's ball is "dead," and "in hand" until after the player of it has taken the croquet. Hence it follows that if it cannon from one ball to another, or from a ball through its own hoop, or from a ball on to either of the pegs, none of these subsequent strokes count anything. If, however, a player cannon off a ball which in the same turn he has croqueted, and then runs off it and makes a stroke, that stroke counts.

A player whose ball is roqueted or croqueted through its hoop in order, counts the hoop.

A player must hit his ball fairly— not push it. A ball is considered to be fairly hit when the sound of the stroke is heard. A ball is "pushed" when the face of the mallet is allowed to rest against it, and the ball propelled without the mallet being drawn back.

A player may play in any attitude, and use his mallet with his hands in any way he pleases, so that he strike the ball with the face of the mallet.

When the ball of a player hits the starting-peg, after he has been through all the hoops, whether by his own play, or by being roqueted (subject to the provisions in law 10), or by being croqueted, he is out of the game, which goes on without him, his turn being omitted.

The clip is placed on the hoop through which the player is next going. The clips are to be changed by the umpire, and are decisive as to the position of a player's ball ; but if the umpire forget to change a clip, any player may remind him before the next stroke. Should there be no clips, a player is entitled to ask any other player how he stands in the game.

A player stops at the peg; that is having struck the turning-peg in order, his turn is at an end, and even though he should roquet off the peg, it does not count. When his turn comes round again, he plays his ball from the spot it rolled to after pegging.

A ball is considered to have passed through its hoop if it cannot be touched by the handle of the mallet, laid on the ground from wire to wire, on the side from which the ball passed.

The decision of the umpire is final. His duties are — to move the clips; to decide when balls are fairly struck; to restore balls to their places which have been disturbed by accident; and to decide whether a croqueted ball is moved or not, in doubtful cases.

TERMS USED IN THE GAME.—*Roquet.* —To hit another ball with one's own. *Croquet.*— To strike one's own ball when in contact with a roqueted ball. *Wired.* — To have the ball in such a position that a hoop prevents the stroke which is wished to be made. *Peg.* — To " peg " is to strike either of the pegs in proper order. *Dismiss.* — To " dismiss " a ball is to croquet it to a distance.

Conundrums. — These are simple catches, in which the sense is playfully cheated, and are generally founded upon words capable of double meaning. The following are examples:

Where did Charles the First's executioner dine, and what did he take?

He took a chop at the King's Head.

When is a plant to be dreaded more than a mad dog?

When it's madder.

What is majesty stripped of its externals?

It is a jest. [The m and the y, externals, are taken away.]

Why is hot bread like a caterpillar?

Because it's the grub that makes the butter fly.

Why did the accession of Victoria throw a greater damp over England than the death of King William?

Because the King was missed (mist) *while the Queen was reigning* (raining).

Why should a gouty man make his will?

To have his legatees (leg at ease).

Why are brankrupts more to be pitied than idiots?

Because bankrupts are broken, while idiots are only cracked.

Why is the treadmill like a true convert?

Because its turning is the result of conviction.

When may a nobleman's property be said to be all feathers?

When his estates are all entails (hentails).

The Charade is a poetical or other composition founded upon a word, each syllable of which constitutes a *noun*, and the whole of which word constitutes another noun of a somewhat different meaning from those supplied by its separate syllables. Words which fully answer these conditions are the best for the purposes of charades; though many other words are employed. In writing, the first syllable is termed "*My first,*" the second syllable, "*My second,*" and the complete word, "*My whole.*" The following is an example of a poetical charade:

The breath of the morning is sweet;
  The earth is bespangled with flowers;
And buds in a countless array
  Have oped at the touch of the showers.
The birds, whose glad voices are ever
  A music delightful to hear,
Seem to welcome the joy of the morning,
  As the hour of the bridal draws near.

What is that which now steals on *my first*,
  Like a sound from the dreamland of love,
And seems wand'ring the valleys among,
  That they may the nuptials approve?
'Tis a sound which *my second* explains,
  And it comes from a sacred abode,
And it merrily trills as the villagers throng
  To greet the fair bride on her road.

How meek is her dress, how befitting a bride—
  So beautiful, spotless, and pure!
When she weareth *my second*, oh, long may it be
  Ere her heart shall a sorrow endure.
See the glittering gem that shines forth from her hair —
  'Tis *my whole*, which a good father gave;
'Twas worn by her mother with honor before —
  But *she* sleepeth in peace in her grave.
'Twas her earnest request, as she bade them adieu,
  That when her dear daughter the altar drew near,
She should wear the same gem that her mother had worn
  When she as a bride full of promise stood there.

THE ANSWER is *Ear-ring.* The bells *ring*, the sound steals upon the *ear*, and the bride wears an *ear-ring.* Charades may be sentimental or humorous, in poetry or prose; they may also be *acted*, in which manner they afford considerable amusement.

ACTED CHARADES. — A drawing-room with folded doors is the best for the purpose. Various household appliances are employed to fit up something like a stage, and to supply the fitting scenes. Characters dressed in costumes made up of handkerchiefs, coats, shawls, table-covers, etc., come on and perform an extempore play, founded upon the parts of a word, and its *whole*, as indicated above. For instance, the events explained in the poem above might be *acted* — glasses might be rung for bells — something might be said in the course of the dialogues about the sound of the bells being delightful to the *ear;* there might be a dance of the villagers, in which a *ring* might be formed; a wedding might be performed; and so on. Though for *acting* Charades there are many better words, because *ear-ring* could with difficulty be *represented* without at once betraying the meaning.

THE ART OF NEEDLEWORK.

LITTLE WAYS TO MAKE HOMES ATTRACTIVE—LESSONS IN WAX FLOWER-
WORK—INSTRUCTIONS ABOUT KNITTING AND EDGING.'

Anglo-Japanese Work.—This is an elegant and easy domestic art. Take yellow withered leaves, dissolve gum, black paint, copal varnish, etc. Any articles may be ornamented with these simple materials — an old tea-caddy, flower-pots, fire-screens, screens of all descriptions, work-boxes, etc. Select perfect leaves, dry and press them between the leaves of books; rub the surface of the article to be ornamented with fine sand-paper, then give it a coat of fine black paint, which should be procured mixed at a color shop. When dry, rub smooth with pumice-stone, and give two other coats. Dry. Arrange leaves in any manner and variety, according to taste. Gum the leaves on the under side, and press them upon their places. Then dissolve some isinglass in hot water, and brush it over the work. Dry. Give three coats of copal varnish, allowing ample time for each coat to dry. Articles thus ornamented last for years, and are very pleasing.

Ornamental Leather Work.—An excellent imitation of carved oak, suitable for frames, boxes, vases, and orna ments in endless variety, may be made of a description of leather called basil. The art consists in simply cutting out this material in imitation of natural objects, and in impressing upon it by simple tools, either with or without the aid of heat, such marks and character-istics as are necessary to the imitation. The rules given with regard to the imi-tation of leaves and flowers apply to ornamental leather work. Begin with a simple object, and proceed by degrees to those that are more complicated. Cut out an ivy or an oak leaf, and im-press the veins upon it; then arrange these in groups, and affix them to frames, or otherwise. The tools re-quired are ivory or steel points of vari-ous sizes, punches, and tin shapes, such as are used for confectionery. The points may be made out of the handles of old tooth-brushes. Before cutting out the leaves the leather should be well soaked in water, until it is quite pliable. When dry, it will retain its artistic shape. Leaves and stems are fastened together by means of liquid glue, and varnished with any of the drying varnishes, or with sealing-wax dissolved to a suitable consistency in spirits of wine. Wire, cork, gutta-percha, bits of stems of trees, etc., may severally be used to aid in the forma-tion of groups of buds, flowers, seed-vessels, etc.

Black Paper Patterns.— Mix some lampblack with sweet oil. With a piece of flannel cover sheets of writing-paper with a mixture: dab the paper dry with a bit of fine linen. When using, put the black side on another sheet of paper, and fasten the corners together with small pins. Lay on the back of the black paper the pattern to be drawn, and go over it with the point of a steel drawing pencil: the black will then leave the impression of the pattern on the under sheet, on which you may draw it with ink.

Patterns on Cloth or Muslin are drawn with a pen dipped in stone blue,

415

a bit of sugar, and a little water; wet to the consistence wanted.

Feather Flowers. — Procure the best white swan or goose feathers; have them plucked off the fowl with care not to break the web; free them from down, except a small quantity on the shaft of the feather. Get also a little fine wire, different sizes; a few skeins of fine floss silk, some good cotton wool or wadding, a reel of No. 4 Moravian cotton, a skein of Indian silk, the starch and gum for pastes, and a pair of small sharp scissors, a few sheets of colored silk paper, and some water colors.

HAVING PROCURED TWO GOOD SPECIMENS of the flower you wish to imitate, carefully pull off the petals of one, and, with a piece of tissue paper, cut out the shape of each, taking care to leave the shaft of the feather at least half an inch longer than the petal of the flower. Carefully bend the feather with the thumb and finger to the proper shape; mind not to break the web.

TO MAKE THE STEM AND HEART OF A FLOWER. — Take a piece of wire six inches long; across the top lay a small piece of cotton wool, turn the wire over it, and wind it round until it is the size of the heart or centre of the flower you are going to imitate. If a single flower, cover it with paste or velvet of the proper color, and round it must be arranged the stamens; these are made of fine Indian silk, or feathers may be used for this purpose. After the petals have been attached, the silk or feather is dipped into gum, and then into the farina. Place the petals round, one at a time, and wind them on with Moravian cotton, No. 4. Arrange them as nearly like the flower you have for a copy as possible. Cut the stems of the feathers even, and then make the calyx of feathers, cut like the pattern or natural flower. For the small flowers the calyx is made with paste. Cover the stems with paper or silk the same as the flowers; the paper must be cut in narrow strips, about a quarter of an inch wide.

TO MAKE THE PASTES OF THE CALYX,

HEARTS, AND BUDS OF FLOWERS. — Take common white starch and mix it with gum water until it is the substance of thick molasses; color it with the dyes used for the feathers, and keep it from the air.

TO MAKE THE FARINA. — Use common ground rice, mixed into a stiff paste with any dye: dry it before the fire, and when quite hard, pound it to a fine powder. The buds, berries, and hearts of some double flowers are made with cotton wool, wound around wire, moulded to the shape with thumb and finger. Smooth it over with gum water, and when dry, cover the buds berries, or calyx with the proper col·ored pastes: they will require one or two coats, and may be shaded with a little paint, and then gummed and left to dry.

FLOWERS OF TWO OR MORE SHADES are variegated with water colors, mixed with lemon-juice, ultra-marine, and chrome for blue; and to produce other effects, gold may also be used in powder, mixed with lemon-juice and gum water.

To Dye Feathers Blue. — Into ten cents worth of oil of vitriol mix ten cents worth of the best indigo in powder; let it stand a day or two; when wanted shake it well, and into a quart of boiling water put one tablespoonful of the liquid. Stir it well, put the feathers in, and let them simmer a few minutes.

YELLOW. -- Put a tablespoonful of the best turmeric into a quart of boiling water; when well mixed put in the feathers. More or less of the turmeric will give them different shades, and a very small quantity of soda will give them an orange hue.

GREEN. — Mix the indigo liquid with turmeric, and pour boiling water over it; let the feathers simmer in the dye until they have acquired the shade you want them.

PINK. -- Three good pink saucers in a quart of boiling water, with a small quantity of cream of tartar. If a deep color is required, use four saucers. Let the feathers remain in the dye several hours.

RED. — In a quart of boiling water dissolve a teaspoonful of cream of tartar; put in one tablespoonful of prepared cochineal, and then a few drops of muriate of tin. This dye is expensive, and scarlet flowers are best made with the plumage of the red ibis, which can generally be had of a birdfancier or bird-stuffer, who will give directions how it should be applied.

LILAC. — About two teaspoonfuls of cudbear into about a quart of boiling water; let it simmer a few minutes before you put in the feathers. A small quantity of cream of tartar turns the color from lilac to amethyst.

BLACK; CRIMSON. — Read the general instructions upon Dyeing.

BEFORE THE FEATHERS ARE DYED they must be put into hot water, and allowed to drain before they are put into the dyes. After they are taken out of the dye, rinse them two or three times in clear cold water (except the red, which must only be done once), then lay them on a tray, over which a cloth has been spread, before a good fire; when they begin to dry and unfold, draw each feather gently between your thumb and finger, until it regains its proper shape.

THE LEAVES OF THE FLOWERS are made of green feathers, cut like those of the natural flower, and serrated at the edge with a very small pair of scissors. For the calyx of a moss-rose the down is left on the feather, and is a very good representation of the moss on the natural flower.

Waxen Flowers and Fruit. — There is no art more easily acquired, nor more encouraging in its immediate results, than that of modelling flowers and fruit in wax. The art, however, is attended by this drawback — that the materials required are somewhat expensive.

THE MATERIALS REQUIRED for commencing the making of waxen flowers may be obtained at most fancy repositories in large towns. Persons wishing to commence the art would do well to inquire the particulars, and see specimens of materials; because in

this, as in every other pursuit, there are novelties and improvements being introduced, which no book can give an idea of.

THE PETALS, LEAVES, etc., of flowers, are made of sheets of colored wax, which may be purchased in packets of assorted colors.

THE STEMS are made of wire of suitable thickness, covered with silk, and overlaid with wax; and the leaves are frequently made by thin sheets of wax pressed upon leaves of embossed calico. Leaves of various descriptions are to be obtained of the persons who sell the materials for wax flower making.

LADIES WILL OFTEN FIND, among their discarded artificial flowers, leaves and buds that will serve as the base of their wax models.

THE BEST GUIDE to the construction of a flower — far better than printed diagrams or patterns — is to take a flower, say a tulip, a rose, or a camellia. If possible, procure two flowers, nearly alike, and carefully picking one of them to pieces, lay the petals down in the order in which they are taken from the flower, and then cut paper patterns from them, and number them from the centre of the flower, that you may know their relative position.

THE PERFECT FLOWER will guide you in getting the wax petals together, and will enable you to give, not only to each petal, but to the contour of the flower, the characteristics which are natural to it. In most cases, they are merely pressed together and held in their places by the adhesiveness of the wax. From the paper patterns the wax petals or other portions of the flowers may be cut. They should be cut singly, and the scissors should be frequently dipped into water, to prevent the wax adhering to the blades.

THE SCRAPS OF WAX that fall from the cutting will be found useful for making seed-vessels, and other parts of the flowers.

LEAVES OF FLOWERS. — Where the manufactured foundations cannot be obtained, patterns of them should be

27

cut in paper, and the venous appearance may be imparted to the wax by pressing the leaf upon it.

IN THE CONSTRUCTION OF SPRIGS, it is most important to be guided by sprigs of the natural plant, as various kinds of plants have many different characteristics in the grouping of their flowers, leaves, and branches.

TAKE A FLOWER AND COPY IT, observing care in the selection of good sheets of wax, and seeing that their colors are precisely those of the flower you desire to imitate.

FOR THE TINTS, STRIPES, AND SPOTS of variegated flowers, you will be supplied with colors among the other materials; and the application of them is precisely upon the principle of water-color painting.

FOR THE IMITATING OF FRUIT in wax, very different rules are to be observed. The following directions may, however, be generally followed:—The material of which moulds for waxen fruit should be composed is the *best* plaster of Paris, which can be bought from the Italian figure-makers at about a penny a pound, in bags containing fourteen pounds, or half-bags containing seven pounds. If this cannot be procured, the cheaper plaster from the oil-shops may be substituted, if it can be obtained *quite fresh*. If, however, the plaster is faulty, the results of the modelling will of course be more or less faulty also. It is the property of plaster of Paris to form a chemical union with water, and to form a paste which rapidly "sets" or hardens into a substance of the density of firm chalk. The mould must therefore be made by an impression from the object to be imitated, made upon the plaster before it sets.

THE USE OF AN ELASTIC FRUIT in early experiments leads to a want of accuracy in the first steps of the operation, which causes very annoying difficulties afterwards: and therefore a solid, inelastic body — an egg boiled hard— is recommended as the first object to be imitated.

HAVING FILLED A SMALL PUDDING

BASIN about three-quarters full of damp sand (the finer the better), lay the egg lengthways in the sand, so that half of it is above and half below the level of the sand, which should be perfectly smooth around it. Then prepare the plaster in another basin, which should be half full of water. Sprinkle the plaster in quickly till it comes to the top of the water, and then, having stirred it for a moment with a spoon, pour the whole upon the egg in the other basin.

WHILE THE HALF MOULD THUS MADE is hardening thoroughly, carefully remove every particle of plaster from the basin in which it was mixed, and also from the spoon which has been used. This must be done by placing them both in water, and wiping them perfectly clean. This is highly important, since a small quantity of plaster which has set will destroy the quality of a second mixing if it is incorporated therewith. In about five minutes the half mould will be fit to remove, which may be done by turning the basin up with the right hand (taking care not to loose the sand), so that the mould falls into the left hand. The egg should then be gently allowed to fall back on the sand out of the mould; if, however, it adheres, lightly scrape the plaster from the edge of the mould, and then shake it out into the hollow of the hand. If, however, the exact half of the egg has been immersed in the sand, no such difficulty will arise; this shows how important is exactness in the first position of the object from which a casting is to be taken. The egg being removed and laid aside, the mould or casting must be "trimmed ;" that is, the sand must be brushed from the flat surface of the mould with a nail-brush, very slightly, without touching the extreme and sharp edges where the hollow of the mould commences. Then upon the broad edge, from which the sand has been brushed, make four equi-distant hollows (with the round end of a table-knife), like the deep impression of a thimble's end. These are to guide hereafter in the fixing of the second half of the mould. The egg should now be replaced in the casting, and the edge of the cast, with the holes, thoroughly lubricated with sweet oil laid on with a feather, or what is better, a large camel-hair brush.

INTO THE SMALL PUDDING BASIN, from which the sand has been emptied, place, with the egg uppermost, the half mould, which, if the operation has been managed properly, should *fit* close at the edges to the side of the vessel; then prepare some more liquid plaster as before, and pour it upon the egg and mould, and while it is hardening, round it with the spoon as with the first half.

IN DUE TIME REMOVE THE WHOLE from the basin; the halves will be found readily separable, and the egg being removed, the mould is ready to cast in, after it has been set aside for an hour or two, so as to completely harden. This is the simplest form of mould, and all are made upon the same principle.

THE CASTING OF AN EGG is not merely interesting as the first step in a series of lessons, but as supplying a means of imitating peculiarly charming objects, which the natural historian tries almost in vain to preserve. We shall proceed, then, with the directions for the casting of an egg in the mould.

FOR THE FIRST EXPERIMENTS, common yellow wax may be used as the material, or the ends of half-burnt wax candles. The materials of the hard (not tallow) composition mould candles will also answer.

EVERY LARGE OBJECT TO BE IMITATED in wax should be cast *hollow;* and therefore, though the transparent lightness required in the imitation of fruits is not requisite in an artificial egg, we shall cast the egg upon the same principle as a piece of fruit. Firstly. The two pieces of the plaster of Paris mould must be soaked in hot water for ten minutes. Secondly. The wax should in the meantime be very slowly melted in a small tin saucepan, with a spout to it, care being taken not to allow it to boil, or it will

be discolored. As to the quantity of wax to be melted, the following is a general rule: If a lump, the size of the object to be imitated, be placed in the saucepan, it should be sufficient for casting twice, at least. Thirdly. As soon as the wax is melted thoroughly, place the saucepan on the hob of the grate, and, taking the parts of the mould from the hot water, remove the moisture from their surfaces by pressing them gently with a handkerchief or soft cloth. It is necessary to use what is called in some of the arts "a very light hand" in this operation, especially in drying moulds of fruits whose aspect possesses characteristic irregularities — such as those on the orange, the lemon, or the cucumber. The mould must not be *wiped*, but only *pressed*. If the *water* has not been hot enough, or if the drying is not performed quickly, the mould will be too cold, and the wax will congeal too rapidly, and settle in ridges and streaks; on the other hand, if the wax has been too hot, it will adhere to the mould, and refuse to come out entire. Fourthly. Having laid the two halves of the mould so that there can be no mistake in fitting the one in its exact place quickly on the other, pour from the saucepan into *one* of the half moulds nearly as much wax as will fill the hollow made by the model (egg), quickly fit the other half on the top of it, squeeze the two pieces tightly together in the hand, and still holding them thus, turn them over in every possible position, so that the wax, which is slowly congealing in the internal hollow of the mould, may be of equal thickness in all parts. Having continued this process at least two minutes, the hands (still holding and turning the mould) may be immersed in cold water to accelerate the cooling process. The perfect congealment of the wax may be known after a little experience by the absence of the sound of fluid on shaking the mould. Fifthly. As soon as the mould is completely cooled, the halves may be separated carefully, the upper being lifted straight up from the under, and if the operation has been properly managed, a waxen egg will be turned out of the mould. Lastly. The egg will only require *trimming*, that is, removing the ridge which marks the line at which the halves of the mould joined, and polishing out the scratches or inequalities left by the knife with a piece of soft rag, wet with spirits of turpentine or spirits of wine. It is always desirable to make several castings of the same object, as the moulds are apt to get chipped when laid by in a cupboard; and for this reason, as well as for the sake of practice, we recommend our pupils to make at least a dozen waxen eggs before they proceed to any other object. If they succeed in this *completely*, they may rest assured that every difficulty which is likely to meet them in any future operations will be easily overcome.

To COLOR THE WAX. — While the wax is yet on the hob, and in a fluid state, stir into it a little *flake white*, in powder, and continue to stir the mixture while it is being poured into the half mould. It will be found that unless the fixing and shaking of the moulds is managed quickly, the coloring matter will settle on the side of the half into which the mixture is poured; a little care in manipulation is therefore again requisite. The coloring of the wax is a matter which comes easily enough by experiment. Oranges, lemons, large gooseberries, small cucumbers, etc., etc., are excellent objects for practice.

To PRODUCE A GOOD IMITATION OF THE SURFACE. — It will be noted by the close observer that the shell of the common hen's egg has a number of minute holes, which destroy the perfect smoothness of its appearance. This peculiarity is imitated in the following simple manner :— In the first place, very slightly prick with a fine needle the surface of your waxen egg, and then, having smeared it with spirits of turpentine, rub the surface all over, so as *nearly* to obliterate the marks of the needle point.

DIAPHANIE. — This is a beautiful, useful, and inexpensive art, easily acquired, and producing imitations of the richest and rarest stained glass; and also of making blinds, screens, skylights, Chinese lanterns, etc., in every variety of color and design.

IN DECORATING HIS HOUSE, an American spends as much money as he can conveniently spare; the elegances and refinements of modern taste demand something more than mere comfort; yet though his walls are hung with pictures, his drawing-rooms filled with bijouterie, how is it that the windows of his hall, his library, his staircase, are neglected? The reason is obvious. The magnificent historical old stained glass might be envied, but could not be brought within the compass of ordinary means. Recent improvements in printing in colors led the way to this beautiful invention, by which economy is combined with the most perfect results. A peculiar kind of paper is rendered perfectly transparent, upon which designs are printed in glass colors (*vitre de couleurs*), which will not change with the light. The paper is applied to the glass with a clear white varnish, and when dry, a preparation is finally applied, which increases the transparency, and adds tenfold brilliancy to the effect.

THERE IS ANOTHER DESIGN, printed in imitation of the half-light (*abatjour*); this is used principally for a ground, covering the whole surface of the glass, within which (the necessary spaces having been previously cut out before it is stuck on the glass) are placed medallion centres of Watteau figures, perfectly transparent, which derive increased brilliancy from the semi-transparency of the surrounding ground. This is by far the cheapest method, though involving extra trouble.

To ASCERTAIN THE QUANTITY of designs required, measure your glass carefully, and then calculate how many sheets it will take. The sheets are arranged so that they can be joined together continuously, or cut to any size or shape.

PRACTICAL INSTRUCTIONS.—Choose a fine day for the operation, as the glass should be perfectly dry, and unaffected by the humidity of the atmosphere. Of course, if you have a choice, it is more *convenient* to work on your glass before it is fixed in the frame. If you are working on a piece of unattached glass, lay it on a *flat* table (a marble slab is preferable), over which you must previously lay a piece of baize or cloth to keep the glass steady. The glass being thus fixed, clean and polish the side on which you intend to operate (in windows this is the inner side), then with your brush lay on it very equably a good coat of the prepared varnish; let this dry for *an hour*, more or less, according to the dryness of the atmosphere and the thickness of the coat of varnish; meantime cut and trim your designs carefully to fit the glass (if it is one entire transparent sheet you will find little trouble); then lay them on a piece of paper, face downwards, and damp the back of them with a sponge, applied several times, to equalize the moisture. In this operation arrange your time so that your designs may now be finally left to dry for fifteen minutes before application to the glass, the varnish on which has now become tacky or sticky, and in a proper state to receive them. Apply the printed side next to the glass without pressure; endeavor to let your sheet fall perfectly level and smooth on your glass, so that you may avoid leaving creases, which would be fatal. Take now your palette, lay it flat on the design, and press out all the air-bubbles, commencing in the centre, and working them out at the sides; an ivory stick will be found useful in removing creases; you now leave this to dry, and after twenty-four hours apply a slight coat of the liqueur diaphanie, leaving it another day, when, if dry, apply a second coat of the same kind, which must be left several days: finally, apply a coat of varnish over all.

IF THESE DIRECTIONS ARE CARE-FULLY FOLLOWED, your glass will never be affected by time or any variations in the weather; it will defy hail, rain, frost, and dust, and can be washed the same as ordinary stained glass, to which, in some respects, it is even superior.

IT IS IMPOSSIBLE TO ENUMERATE the variety of articles to the manufacture of which diaphanie may be successfully applied, as it is not confined to glass, but can be done on silk, parchment, paper, linen, etc., *after they have been made transparent,* which may be accomplished in the following manner:

STRETCH YOUR PAPER, or whatever it may be, on a frame or drawing board, then apply two successive coats (a day between each) of diaphanous liquor, and after leaving it to dry for *several* days, cover it with a thin layer of very clear size, and when dry it will be in a fit state to receive the coat of varnish and the designs.

SILK, LINEN, OR OTHER STUFFS should be more carefully stretched, and receive a thicker coat of size than paper or parchment; the latter may be strained on a drawing or any other smooth board, by damping the sheet, and after pasting the edges, stretching it down while damp (silk, linen, and other stuffs require to be carefully stretched on a knitting or other suitable frame). Take great care to allow, *whatever you use,* time to dry before applying the liqueur diaphanie.

ALL KINDS OF SCREENS, lamp shades, and glasses, lanterns, etc., etc., may be made in this way, as heat will produce no effect upon them. The transparent pictures are successful, because they may be hung on a window frame or removed at will, and the window blinds are far superior to anything of that kind that have yet been seen.

INSTEAD OF STEEPING THE DESIGNS in the transparent liquor at the time of printing them, which was previously done *in order to show their transparency to the purchaser,* but which was practically objectionable, as the paper in that state was brittle, and devoid of pliancy, necessitating also the use of a peculiarly difficult vehicle to manage (varnish) in applying it to the glass, the manufacturer now prepares his paper differently, in order to allow the use of parchment size in sticking them on the glass. The liqueur diaphanie, which is finally applied, renders them perfectly transparent. In this mode of operation, no delay is requisite, the designs being applied to the glass immediately after laying on the size, *taking care to press out all the air-bubbles,* for which purpose a roller will be found indispensable. The designs should be damped before the size is applied to them.

DECALCOMANIE.—This recently discovered and beautiful art consists in transferring colored drawings to glass, porcelain, china, wood, silk, furniture, plaster of Paris, alabaster, ivory, paper, paper hangings, windows, tea trays, oilcloth, and all kinds of fancy articles; in short, materials of any kind, shape, or size, provided they possess a smooth surface, can be decorated with decalcomanie; the immediate result being an exact resemblance to painting by hand. The art itself is simple and ingenious, and while affording agreeable occupation to ladies, it may be made to serve many useful purposes, on account of the numerous objects which will admit of being thus ornamented.

THE MATERIALS EMPLOYED IN DECALCOMANIE are — 1. A bottle of transfer varnish for fixing the drawings. 2. A bottle of light varnish to pass over the drawings when fixed. 3. A bottle of spirit to clean the brushes, and to remove those pictures which may not be successful. 4. A piece of beaver cloth about nine inches square. 5. A paper-knife and roller. 6. Two or three camel-hair brushes. 7. A basin of water. 8. A bottle of opaque varnish.

INSTRUCTIONS. — Thoroughly clean and free from grease the article to be decorated; then, having cut off the white paper margin of the drawing, dip one of the brushes into the transfer varnish, and give it a very light coat, being especially careful to cover the whole of the colored portion, but

not to allow it to touch the blank paper; then lay the drawing, face downward, on the object to be ornamented, taking care to place it at once where it is to remain, as it would be spoiled by moving. If the varnish, on its first application, is too liquid, allow the picture to remain for about ten minutes to set. Moisten the cloth with water, and lay it gently on the drawing which has been previously laid in its place on the object to be decorated; then rub it over with the paper-knife or roller, so as to cause the print to adhere in every part; this done, remove the cloth, well soak the paper with a camel-hair brush dipped in water, and immediately after lift the paper by one corner, and gently draw it off. The picture will be left on the object, while the paper will come off perfectly white. Care must be taken that the piece of cloth, without being too wet, is sufficiently so to saturate the paper completely. The drawing must now be washed with a camel-hair brush, in clean water, to remove the surplus varnish, and then left till quite dry. On the following day, cover the picture with a light coat of the fixing varnish, to give brilliancy to the colors.

To ORNAMENT DARK-COLORED OBJECTS, such as the bindings of books, Russia leather, blotting-cases, leathern bags, etc., the picture must be previously covered with a mixture of opaque white varnish, taking care not to pass beyond the outline of the design. On the following day, proceed according to the instructions given in the preceding paragraph.

To ORNAMENT SILK PAPER, OR ARTICLES WHICH WILL NOT BEAR WETTING. — Varnish the picture with the transfer varnish, as previously explained, following the outline of the design, then allow it to dry for an hour or two; when quite dry, pass a damp sponge over the entire surface of the sheet, so as to remove the composition which surrounds the picture, and which may spoil the object. Let the paper dry once more, and varnish the picture again with the transfer varnish; in about ten minutes, place it face downward on the object to be decorated, and rub it with the paperknife or roller, over the whole of its surface. Finally, moisten the paper with a wet brush, allow it to remain sufficiently long to become moist, then strip the paper off. *To remove a spoiled picture from any object,* dip a soft rag in the essence, and rub it over the surface.

To INSURE A SUCCESSFUL RESULT, care must be taken to give a very light coating of varnish to the parts to be transferred. When the varnish is first applied it is very liquid, and must remain ten minutes, the best condition for transferring being when the varnish is only just sticky, without being too dry.

THE FOLLOWING DESIGNS WILL BE FOUND THE MOST ELEGANT AND APPROPRIATE. —Flowers of every variety, bouquets, tropical birds, flowers and fruits in imitation of aquatint, garlands with cupids after Watteau, and garlands with birds, domestic scenes, pears and cherries, apples and plums, white grapes and plums, black grapes and peaches, plums and mulberries, large bouquet of roses, bouquets of moss roses and pansies, bouquets of small camelias, bouquets of wall-flowers and poppies, bouquets of orange-blossom, medallions, various subjects, birds' nests, Gothic initials and monograms, fleursde-lis ; borders various.

FANCY NEEDLEWORK. — Instructions in Crochet. — Perhaps no kind of work has ever attained such popularity as *Crochet.* Whether as a simple trimming, as an elaborate quilt, or as a fabric, almost rivalling point lace, it is popular with every woman who has any time at all for fancy work, since it is only needful to understand the stitches, and the terms and contractions used in writing the descriptions of the different designs, to be enabled to work with ease the most beautiful pattern that ever appeared in crochet.

The crochet hook should be very smooth, made of fine steel, and fixed in handles. The *"Tapered Indented"* hook, which has the *size* engraved on the handle, will be found convenient, from its quality, and saving trouble of referring to a gauge.

The marks used in our crochet recipes are simple, consisting chiefly of printers' marks, such as crosses, daggers, asterisks, etc. They are used to mark repetitions. It will be seen that wherever a *mark* is used, another *similar* one is sure to be found ; the repetition occurring between the two.

Sometimes one repetition occurs within the other. For instance : + 2 Dc, 4 Ch, miss 4, * 1 Dc, 1 Ch, miss 1, * three times, 5 Dc, + twice, it would at full length be — 2 Dc, 4 Ch, miss 4, 5 Dc, 1 Ch, miss 1, 5 Dc, 1 Ch, miss 1, 5 Dc, 1 Ch, miss 1, 5 Dc, 2 Dc, 4 Ch, miss 4, 5 Dc, 1 Ch, miss 1, 5 Dc, 1 Ch, miss 1, 5 Dc, 1 Ch, miss 1, 5 Dc. There is another mode of abbreviating ; but this can only be used where a row has a centre, both sides of which are alike, the latter being the same as the former, worked *backwards.* In this case the letters *b, a,* are employed, to show that in the latter part of the row the instructions must be reversed :—*b,* 7 Dc, 3 Ch, miss 2, 1 Dc, 2 Ch, miss 1, *a,* 1 Dc (the centre stitch), would be 7 Dc, 3 Ch, miss 2, 1 Dc, 2 Ch, miss 1, 1 Dc, miss 1, 2 Ch, 1 Dc, miss 2, 3 Ch, 7 Dc. A knowledge of these abbreviations is easily acquired, and much space is saved by them.

The stitches used are *Chain, Slip, Single, Double, Treble,* and *Long Treble Crochet.*

Chain Stitch is made by forming a loop on the thread, then inserting the hook, and drawing the thread through the loop already made. Continue this, forming a succession of stitches.

Slip Stitch is made by drawing a thread *at once* through any given stitch, and the loop on the needle.

Single Crochet (Sc).— Having a loop on the needle, insert the hook in a stitch, and draw the thread through in a loop. You then have two on the hook ; draw the thread through both at once.

Double Crochet (Dc). — Twist the thread round the hook before inserting it in the stitch, through which you draw the thread in a loop. There will then be three loops on the hook ; draw the thread through two, and then through the one just formed, and the remaining one.

Treble Crochet (Tc), and *Long Treble* (long Tc),are worked in the same way ; in treble the thread is put *twice ;* in long treble *three times,* before inserting it into the stitch.

Square Crochet is also sometimes used. The squares are either open or clos An open square consists of one Dc, two Ch, missing two on the line beneath, before making the next stitch. A close square has three successive Dc. Thus, any given number of close squares, followed by an open, will have so many times three Dc, and *one over;* consequently, any foundation for square crochet must have a number that can be divided by three, having one over.

To Contract an Edge.— This may be done in Dc, Tc, or long Tc. Twist the thread round the hook as often as required, insert it in the work, and half do a stitch. Instead of finishing it, twist the thread round again, until the same number of loops are on, and work a stitch entirely ; so that, for two stitches, there is only one head.

To Join on a Thread. —Joins should be avoided as much as possible in open work. In joining, finish the stitch by drawing the new thread through, leaving two inches for both ends, which must be held in.

To use several Colors. — This is done in single crochet. Hold the threads not in use on the edge of the work, and work them in. Change the color by beginning the stitch in the old color, and finishing it with the new, continuing the work with the latter holding in the old. If only one stitch is wanted in the new color, finish one stitch, and begin the next with it ; then change.

To Join Leaves, etc.—When one part of a leaf or flower is required to be joined to another, drop the loop from the hook, which insert in the place to be joined ; draw the loop through and continue.

How to Make a Dress-body Fit Well. — All who attempt dressmaking should have as many as six different size paper patterns, with pleats already made in them, so that they can cut out the body by one, and then tack it together and place it on the figure. The shoulder and under the arm are the principal places to let a body out or take it in. You must measure your paper pattern on the party you are going to fit. No amount of pulling it will ever make it fit, neither will pinning it closely to the figure. Let the lady keep her dress on while you measure your pattern down the shoulder seam, under the arm seam, down front and back seams, and across the chest from arm seam to arm seam ; the same with the back. If one pattern is too large or too small, try another ; practice and industry will soon make you perfect. It is a good plan to keep two or three sizes made up ready to fit on. A clever dressmaker knows very nearly what body will fit before she puts it on. The taking the size of the waist is the least important part of your body. Most young beginners do not place the bosom pleats right ; the pleats should not be carried high over the bosom. It must be noticed whether the bosom be high or low ; if low, the length from the seam on the shoulder to the bosom pleats will be longer than for another body whose bosom lies high ; if this point was more attended to there would be fewer complaints of the dress being tight across the chest.

To Work over Cord.—Hold the cord in the left hand with the work, and work round it, as you would over an end of thread, working closely. When beads are used they must be first threaded on silk or thread, and then dropped, according to the pattern, on the *wrong* side of the work. This side looks more even than the other ; therefore, when bead purses are worked from an engraving, they are worked the reverse of the usual way, viz., from right to left.

Gothic Edging, in Crochet.

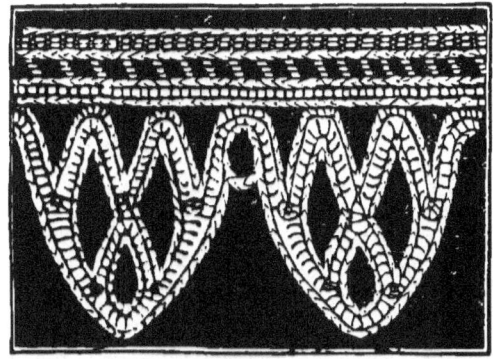

Materials. — Cotton of any size suitable for the work to be trimmed. — For Petticoat, No. 16 — with Crochet-hook, No. 20. For coarser articles, No. 4, or No. 8, with a Hook proportionably large.

Make a chain of the length required, the number of stitches being divisible by 17: if a straight piece, add five more chains; but if intended for trimming drawers, or similar articles, close into a round, without adding any extra stitches.

1st Row. — Sc.

2d Row. — + 1 Dc, 1 Ch, miss 1, + repeat.

3d Row. — Sc.

4th Row. — 5 Sc, putting the hook through both sides of the Ch of the previous row at every stitch, + * 11 Ch, miss 2, 3 Sc (under both sides of the Ch), * 3 times, 2 Sc, + repeat for every pattern.

5th Row. — 5 Sc, on 5, then on the first loop, 6 Sc, on the first 6 of 11 Ch, + 1 Sc, 2 Dc, 1 Sc on next, 4 Sc, on next 4, 1 Sc, on centre of 3 Sc. On the next loop, 5 Sc, on 5 chain ; 1 Sc, 2 Dc, 1 Sc, on the 6th Ch ; 5 Sc, on the next 5 ; 1 Sc, on centre of 3 Sc. On the next loop, 4 Sc, on 4 Ch ; 1 Sc, 1 Dc, on next Ch. Turn the work on the wrong side : — 8 Ch, 2 Sc, on the point of the 2d loop ; 8 Ch, 2 Sc, on 2 Dc, at the point of the 1st loop. Turn the work on the right side : — 4 Sc, on 4 Ch ; 3 Sc, on the next ; 1 on each of the last 3. Miss the 2 Sc, at the point of the 2d loop ; and on the other chain of 8, 3 Sc, on the 1st 3, 2 Sc on the next. Turn the work on the wrong side : — 6 Ch, 2 Sc, at the point of the loop. Turn on the right side : — 2 Sc, in the 1st ; 2 Ch, 2 Sc, in each of the next 2 ; 2 in the next 2. Sc down the chains of the half loops, taking care not to contract the edge at all. 5 Sc, on 5 Sc ; 3 Sc, on chain of the next loop ; 3 Ch, draw the loop through the corresponding part of the Sc of last loop. Slip back on the 3 Ch ; 3 Sc on 3 more chains of the loop. + repeat as often as may be required for the number of patterns.

Crochet Border, 1. — This

border is suitable for a great variety of purposes, according to the size of the cotton employed ; in coarse cotton it will make a trimming for couvrettes and berceaunette covers ; with fine cotton it can be used for children's clothes, small curtains, etc.

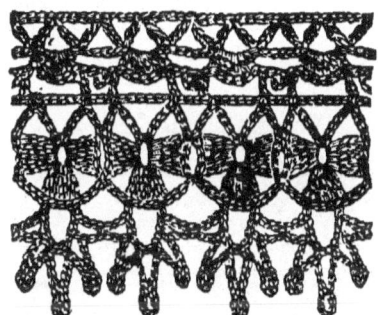

Material. — Crochet cotton of any size.

Make a sufficiently long foundation chain, and work the 1st row : * 2 treble divided by 3 chain in the 1st foundation chain stitch, miss 3 ; repeat from *. 2d row : * In the first scallop of the preceding row, 1 double, 5 treble, 1 double, then 1 chain, 1 purl (4 chain, 1 slip stitch ·in the 1st of the four), 1 chain, miss under these the *next* chain stitch scallop; repeat from *. 3d row: 1 treble in the chain stitch on either side of the purl in the preceding row, 5 chain. 4th row: * 2 double divided by 7 chain in the two first treble of the preceding row (insert the needle underneath the upper parts of the stitch), 10 chain, 1 slip stitch in the 5th of these 10 stitches so as to form a loop, 4 chain; repeat from *. 5th row: * 1 slip in the middle-stitch of the scallop formed by 7 chain in the preceding row, 4 treble, 3 chain, 5 treble, 3 chain, 4 treble, all these 13 stitches in the loop of the preceding row, so as to form a clover leaf pattern; repeat from *, but fasten the 4th treble with a slip stitch on the 10th treble of the preceding figure 6th row. In the first and last stitch of the 5 middle treble of the clover leaf 1 double, 7 chain between. 7th row: * 1 double in the 2d chain stitch of the scallop which is above the 5 middle treble of the clover leaf, 2 chain, 1 purl (5 chain, 1 slip stitch in the first), 2 chain, 1 double in the next chain stitch of the same scallop, 2 chain, 1 purl, 2 chain, miss 1 chain of the scallop, 1 double, 2 chain, 1 purl, 2 chain, 1 double in the next chain stitch, 3 chain, 1 double in the middle stitch of the following scallop, 0 chain; repeat from *.

Crochet Border, No. 2.

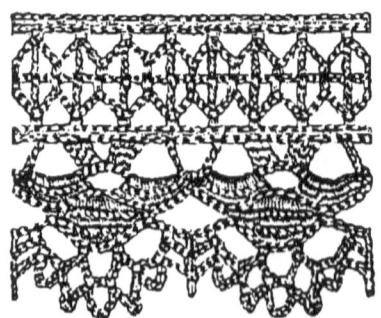

Material. — Crochet cotton.

On a sufficiently long foundation chain work the 1st row: 1 double in each chain stitch. 2d row: Alter-

nately, 1 double, 7 chain, miss under the latter 3 stitches of the preceding row. 3d row: 1 treble in each double of the preceding row, 1 double in the middle stitch of each scallop, 2 chain between. 4th row: 1 double on each double of the preceding row, 1 treble on each treble, 3 chain between. 5th row: 1 double on each treble of the preceding row, 3 chain between. 6th row: 1 double in each stitch of the preceding row. 7th row: * 1 treble in the 1st stitch of the preceding row, 4 chain, miss 1, 3 treble in the following 3 stitches, miss 3 stitches, 3 treble in the following 3 stitches, 4 chain, miss 1 stitch, 1 treble, 2 chain, miss 4; repeat from *. 8th row: Repeat regularly 8 treble in the scallop formed of 4 chain in the preceding row, 1 double in the middle of the following 3 chain. 9th row: * 1 double in the 4th treble of the preceding row, 2 treble, 1 long treble in next treble but 2, 2 long treble in each of the 2 following treble, 1 long treble, 2 treble in the next treble, 1 double in the next treble but 2, 3 chain, 1 purl (4 chain, 1 slip), 3 chain stitch; repeat from *. 10th row: * 1 double in the 4th treble of the preceding row, 2 chain, 1 purl, 2 chain, miss 2 under them, 1 double, 2 chain, 1 purl, 2 chain, 1 double in the next chain but 1 of the next scallop, 2 chain, 1 purl, 2 chain, 1 double in the 2 chain stitch after the purl of the preceding row, 2 chain, 1 purl, 2 chain; repeat from *. 11th row: In each scallop of the preceding row 2 double (they must meet on either side of the purl); they are divided alternately by 5 chain, and by a scallop formed of 2 chain, 1 purl, and 2 chain, only in the chain stitch scallops which join the two treble figures work no double, but 2 chain, 1 purl, 2 chain.

Wheel and Shamrock Antimacassar.

— As this antimacassar is made in separate pieces, it will suffice to thread a few rows of beads on the cotton at a time. For the same reason, it may be made of any required dimensions, and it may or may not have a border: but if one is desired, it should be of close crochet, with the pattern in beads, and a deep fringe beyond it.

A WHEEL.—Make a chain of 8, close it into a round, and work under it 16 Sc stitches. + 9 Ch, dropping a bead on every stitch, miss 1 of the 16, and Sc under the next + 8 times. Slip stitch on 4 of the first 9 Ch. Sc on the next 2 of the 9 * 3 Ch, Sc on the

Materials.
Crochet cotton, No. 10, and Turquoise beads, No. 1.

4th, 5th, and 6th of the next 9 chain * all round. End with slip stitch on the 1st and 2d of the first 3 chain. † 8 Ch, Sc under the next chain of 3. † 7 times. 8 Ch, Sc on 2d slip stitch. To complete the wheel, do under each chain of 8, 1 Sc, 10 Dc, 1 Sc, dropping a bead on every stitch.

A SQUARE. — 6 Ch, close it into a round. + Sc under chain, 5 Ch, + 4 times, † 1 Sc on 2d Sc, 4 Dc under chain, with a bead on each, 5 Ch, 4 Dc with a bead on each, under the same Ch * 4 times. Slip stitch up the first 4 Dc. † 5 Ch, Sc under 5 Ch of last round, 6 Ch, Sc under same 5 Ch, Sc under same; 8 Ch, Sc under the next chain of 5.

Last Round. — 1 Sc, 4 Dc under the chain of 5, 2 *Ch*, 4 Dc, 1 Sc under same. 1 Sc, 4 Dc under chain of 6, 2 *Ch*, 4 Dc, 1 Sc under same, 1 Sc, 4 Dc under chain of 5, 2 *Ch*, 4 Dc, 1 Sc under same. 1 Sc under chain of 8. Do this

all round, dropping a bead on every stitch. The two chains which are printed in italics are those places where the squares are to be connected with the other pieces. It will be seen that the last round forms four shamrocks. The centre leaf of each shamrock (coming at the point of the square) is to be united to the point of another square; while those at the side are to be joined to the rounds.

A bead is dropped on every Dc stitch.

Jewelled d'Oyley—The Ruby.—Begin by threading all the beads on the cotton; then make a chain of 8 stitches, and close into a round. All the d'oyley is done in Sc, except the edge.

1st Round.— +1 Ch, 1 Sc on Sc, + 8 times.

2d Round. —+1 Ch, 2 Sc on 2 Sc, + 8 times. It will be observed that instead of the usual way of increasing by working two stitches in one, a chain-stitch is made, and one Sc only is worked on each Sc.

3d Round. —+1 Ch, 3 Sc on Sc, + 8 times.

4th Round. —+1 Ch, 4 Sc on Sc, + 8 times.

5th Round. — +1 Ch, 5 Sc on Sc, + 8 times.

6th Round. —+1 Ch, 6 Sc on Sc, + 8 times.

7th Round. —+1 Ch, 7 Sc on Sc, + 8 times.

1st Bead Round.— +2 cotton, 6 beads, + 8 times.

2d Round.— + 4 beads, coming over 2 cotton, and 1 bead at each side, 5 cotton over 4 beads, + 8 times.

3d Round. — + 2 beads over the centre of 4, 8 cotton, + 8 times.

4th Round. —+3 beads, the first 2 over 2, 3 cotton, 1 bead, 4 cotton, + 8 times.

5th Round. —+7 beads (the first over first of last round), 5 cotton, + 8 times. End with one bead on the last stitch.

6th Round. —+ 6 beads (1st on 1st), 6 cotton, 1 bead, + 8 times.

7th Round. —+ 3 beads, 10 cotton, 1 bead, + 8 times. End with 2 beads.

8th Round. — + 3 beads, 10 cotton, 2 beads, + 8 times. End with 3 beads.

9th Round. — + 3 beads, 11 cotton, 3 beads, + 7 times, 3 beads. This round is not perfect.

10th Round. — + 3 cotton over cotton, 1 bead, 4 cotton, 4 beads, 1 cotton, 3 beads, + 8 times.

11th Round. — + 2 cotton, 9 beads, 3 cotton (over 1 bead, 1 cotton), 3 beads, + 8 times.

12th Round. — + 3 cotton over 2, + 7 beads, 5 cotton, 4 beads, 2 cotton, + 8 times.

17th Round. — + 9 beads, 1 cotton, 4 beads, 2 cotton (last over 1 cotton), 3 beads, 4 cotton over 3, + 7 times. Eighth time, 3 cotton on 2.

18th Round. — + 9 beads, 1 cotton, 5 beads, 2 cotton, 5 beads, 2 cotton on 1, + 7 times. Eighth, 1 cotton.

19th Round. — + 5 beads, 5 cotton, 5 beads, 10 cotton (over 9 stitches), + 8 times.

20th Round. — + 3 beads, 8 cotton (over 7 stitches), 5 beads, 5 cotton, 1 bead, 4 cotton, + 8 times.

21st Round. — + 3 beads over 3, 10 cotton (making 1), 5 beads (beginning

Materials.—1 oz. ruby-colored beads, No. 2, and one reel No. 16 crochet cotton.

13th Round. — + 1 cotton, 5 beads, 5 cotton, 3 beads, 1 cotton, 2 beads, 1 cotton, + 8 times.

14th Round. — + 4 cotton (over 1 cotton, 2 beads), 3 beads, 5 cotton, 4 beads (the last on last of 3), 4 cotton, + 8 times.

15th Round. — + 2 cotton, 5 beads (the last on last of 3), 3 cotton, 6 beads, 5 cotton, + 8 times.

16th Round. — + 13 beads, 1 cotton, 2 beads, 6 cotton on 5, + 7 times. Eighth time, 4 cotton only on 3.

on the 2d of 5), 3 cotton, 2 beads, 4 cotton, + 8 times.

22d Round. — + 3 beads on 3, 12 cotton (making 1), 9 beads, 4 cotton, + 8 times.

23d Round. — + 3 beads on 3, 6 cotton, 4 beads, 3 cotton, 7 beads (on centre 7 of 9), 5 cotton, + 8 times.

24th Round. — + 3 beads on 3, 6 cotton on 5, 6 beads, 14 cotton, + 8 times.

25th Round. — + 4 beads (beginning over 1st of 3), 7 cotton (on 5 and 1 bead), 5 beads, 14 cotton, + 8 times.

26*th Round.* — + 1 cotton over 1 bead, 4 beads, 3 cotton, 1 bead, 3 cotton, 4 beads (over last 4 of 5), 13 cotton, + 8 times.

27*th Round.* — + 2 cotton on 1 cotton, 8 beads, 3 cotton, 4 beads, 13 cotton, + 8 times.

28*th Round.* — + 3 cotton over 2 C and 1 B, 6 beads, 3 cotton, 4 beads, 14 cotton, + 8 times.

29*th Round.* — + 4 cotton, 3 beads (the 1st over 2d of 6), 3 cotton, 5 beads, 16 cotton, + 8 times, 5 cotton.

30*th Round.* — + 9 beads, beginning on 2d of 3, 21 cotton, + 8 times.

Do one round of cotton only, and then one of beads.

BORDER. — + 2 Sc cotton, 15 beads, 2 cotton, 13 chain with a bead on each, miss 12, + 8 times.

2*d Round.* — 2 slip on 2 cotton, + 2 Sc with cotton on the first 2 beads, * 1 bead, 1 cotton, * alternately 6 times, 1 cotton, 5 Ch, with beads, 1 Sc with bead on 4th of 13, 7 Ch with beads, miss 5 of 13, Sc with bead on next, 5 Ch with beads, + 8 times.

3*d Round.* — + 2 Sc with cotton on 2d Sc and 1 bead, * 1 bead, 1 cotton, * 5 times, 1 cotton, 5 Ch with beads. 1 Sc with bead on 4th of 5, 6 Ch with beads, 1 Sc on 4th of 7 with beads, 6 Ch with beads, Sc with bead on 2d of 5 Sc, 5 Ch with beads, + 8 times.

4*th Round.* — + 2 Sc cotton as before, * 1 bead over cotton, 1 cotton over bead, * 4 times. 1 more cotton, 5 Ch with beads, 1 Sc with bead on 4th of 5, 6 Ch with beads, 1 Sc with bead on 4th of 6, 6 Ch with bead, 1 Sc with bead on 3d of next 6, 6 Ch with beads, 1 Sc with bead on 2d of 5, 5 Ch with beads, + 8 times.

These D'Oyleys must be washed with white Windsor soap and soft water only. When quite clean rinse them in fresh water, and hang them before a fire, or in the air to dry. When nearly dry, pull them out into shape. On no account use any starch, nor an iron. Beads, when of good quality, and properly washed, will remain for years uninjured.

HINT ON D'OYLEYS. — Experienced workers often find a difficulty in knowing the exact termination of a round in D'Oyley's, and frequently the pattern is destroyed by an error in the calculation. This difficulty may be remedied at once, by attention to the following rule: — Take a thread very opposite in color to that of your work, and only a few inches long. When only two or three rounds are done, and it is still perfectly easy to see the end of the round, draw the needleful of thread through the chain of the last stitch. Do the same with every other round, so that the colored thread finally runs in a straight line from the centre to the edge. It will save much trouble and many blunders, especially when working the Jewelled D'Oyleys.

Crochet à Tricoter. — Take rather a long crochet hook, with a button on the end. Make a chain as for ordinary crochet, leaving the last made stitch on the hook to form the first stitch of the next row; this kind of crochet being worked backward and forward.

2*d Row.* — Put the hook through the next loop on the chain to the loop already on the hook, and draw the thread through, leaving this last made loop on the hook. Continue till you have taken up on the hook as many loops as there were in the original chain.

3*d Row.* — Put the thread once round the hook and draw it through the two first loops on the hook. Thread once round the hook and through the last loop made and the one next to it on the hook. Repeat till all are worked off.

4*th Row.* — Put the hook through the first long perpendicular loop, draw the thread through, leaving the last made loop on the hook. Repeat till all the long loops have been worked, keeping all the loops on the hook and taking always the loop at the edge.

5*th Row.* — Same as 3d.

This stitch is only suitable for straight work. To narrow, leave out the edge loop.

A chain of 30 makes a pretty scarf for a lady. It should measure a yard and half long, with fringe four or six inches long at each end.

Ladies' Comforter in Crochet.

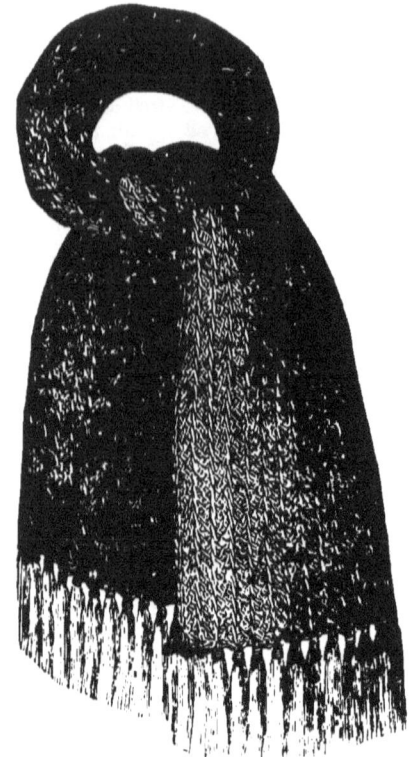

PART OF COMFORTER
(FULL SIZE).

Materials.— 2½ ounces white double Berlin wool, ½ ounce lilac filoselle.

This comforter is worked with white wool in ribbed stitch, a variety of crochet *à tricoter ;* it is edged all round with some rows of chain and double stitches. These, as well as the fringe at both ends of the scarf, can be made with white wool and lilac filoselle, or only with wool. The pattern is 20 stitches wide and 120 double rows long. Begin the scarf at one end on a foundation chain of 20 stitches, and work as follows : 1st part of 1st double row (forwards). Take up 1 loop in every other stitch.

2d part of the 1st double row (backwards). Alternately cast off 1 loop, 1 chain.

1st part of the 2d double row : Take up alternately one loop in the pre-viously missed stitch of the foundation chain, working at the same time round the top chain of the stitch in the preceding row, and one loop in the next long chain of the preceding row.

Second part of the second double row : Cast off together the next loop taken up in the foundation chain with the following loop, 1 chain.

First part of the third double row : Take up alternately one loop underneath the next chain stitch of the double row before the last, and one loop in the next long chain of the preceding row. Miss the following long stitch. Work back as in the second double row. This third double row is repeated till the scarf is sufficiently long. Work all round the outer edge one row of double stitch with lilac filo-selle, then one row of double stitch with white wool; the third row is worked again with filoselle, alter-nately one double, one chain stitch, missing one under the last; in the last two rows insert the needle into the two upper chains of the preceding rows.

The comforter is ornamented at both ends with fringe in white wool, the upper edge of which may be covered with lilac filoselle.

Instructions in Netting. — The beauty of netting consists in its firm-ness and regularity. All joins in the thread must be made in a very strong knot; and, if possible, at an edge, so that it may not be perceived.

The implements used in netting are a netting-needle and a mesh. In fill-ing a netting-needle with the material, be careful not to make it so full that there will be a difficulty in passing it through the stitches. The size of the needle must depend on the material to be employed, and the fineness of the work. Steel needles are employed for every kind of netting except the very coarsest. They are marked from 12 to 24, the latter being extremely fine. The fine meshes are usually also of steel; but, as this material is heavy, it is better to employ bone or wooden meshes when large ones are required. Many meshes are flat; and in using them the *width* is given.

The first stitch in this work is termed *diamond* netting, the holes being in the form of diamonds. To do the first row, a stout thread, knotted to form a round, is fastened to the knee with a pin, or passed over the foot, or on the hook sometimes at-tached to a work cushion for the pur-pose. The end of the thread on the needle is knotted to this, the mesh being held in the left hand on a line with it. Take the needle in the right hand; let the thread come over the mesh and the third finger, bring it back under the mesh, and hold it be-tween the thumb and first finger. Slip the needle through the loop over the third finger, under the mesh and

the foundation thread. In doing this a loop will be formed, which must be passed over the fourth finger. With-draw the third finger from the loop, and draw up the loop over the fourth, gradually, until it is quite tight on the mesh. The thumb should be kept firmly over the mesh while the stitch is being completed. When the neces-sary number of stitches is made on this foundation, the future rows are to be worked backwards and forwards. To form a *round*, the first stitch is to be worked immediately after the last, which closes the netting into a circle.

ROUND NETTING is very nearly the same stitch. The difference is merely in the way of putting the needle through the loop and foundation, or other stitch. After passing the needle through the loop, it must be brought out, and put *downwards* through the stitch. This stitch is particularly suitable for purses.

SQUARE NETTING is exactly the same stitch as diamond netting, only it is begun at a corner, on one stitch, and increased (by doing two in one) in the last stitch of every row, until the greatest width required is at-tained. Then, by netting two stitches together at the end of every row, the piece is decreased to a point again. When stretched out, all the holes in this netting are squares.

Square and diamond netting are the most frequently used, and are orna-mented with patterns darned on them, in simple darning or in various point stitches. In the latter case it forms a variety of the sort of work termed *guipure*, now so fashionable.

GRECIAN NETTING. — Do one plain row. First pattern row. Insert the needle in the first stitch, and, without working it, draw through it the second stitch, through the loop of which draw the first, and work it in the ordi-nary way. This forms a twisted stitch, and the next is a very small loop formed of a part of the second stitch. Repeat this throughout the row. The second row is done plain. The third like the first; but the first and last stitches are to be done in the usual manner, and you begin the twisting with the second and third loops. The fourth is plain. Repeat these four rows as often as required.

Use No. 20 mesh for the fancy rows, and No. 14 for the plain.

Stitches in netting are always counted by knots.

Oriental Table-Cover.

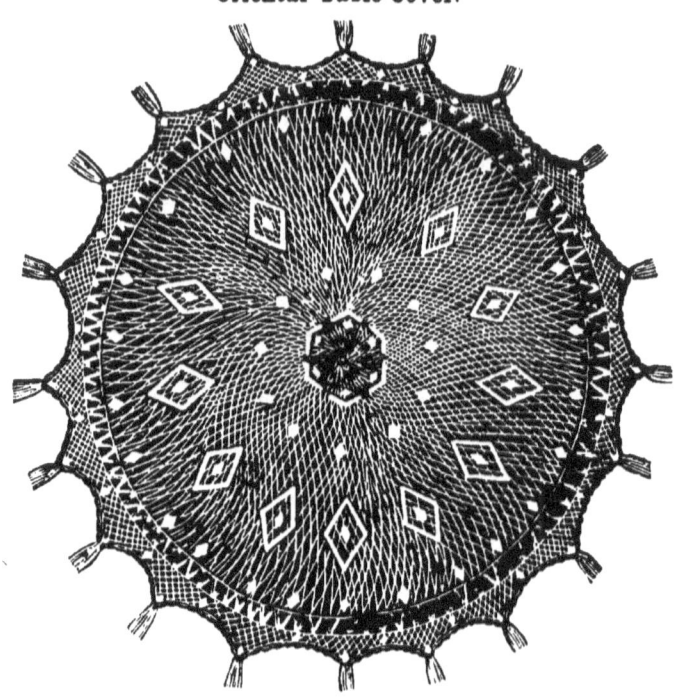

Materials. — Knitting Cotton, No, 4; three Meshes, 2 flat, half an inch wide, the other an inch and a half; and one round Mesh, No. 14; 27 skeins Berlin Wool; three of each of the following colors — peach, green, plum, yellow, claret, dark blue, pink, light blue, and scarlet; a large rug needle, and a netting-needle.

On a round foundation of 23 stitches with the half-inch mesh, net 2 plain rounds.

3d Round. — Round mesh, plain netting.

4th, 5th, and 6th Rounds. — The same.

7th Round, half-inch mesh. — 2 stitches in each.

8th Round. — Same mesh, 1 stitch in each, missing the first, netting the next stitch, and returning to the missed one all round.

9th Round, round mesh, 1 stitch in each.

10th, 11th, 12th, and 13th Rounds. — The same.

14th Round. — Half-inch mesh, 3 stitches in each.

15th Round, and 21 succeeding Rounds. — Round mesh, 1 stitch in each.

37th Round. — Wide flat mesh, 3 stitches in each.

38th Round, round mesh. — Net 3 stitches together, missing the first 3, netting the 3 next, and returning to the missed 3, continue all round.

39th Round, round mesh. — 1 stitch in each.

40th Round, and 4 succeeding Rounds. — The same.

The top part of the cover is now netted, and there remain but the points to net.

With round mesh net 13 stitches, and instead of continuing the round, return on the 13 stitches, missing the last. Continue backwards and forwards on these, always missing the last till you have but one stitch left on the mesh. Cut the cotton and fasten the end; take up the next 13 stitches, and make another point, and continue the same all round the cover.

Now commence the darning. Thread the rug needle with green wool, and insert it in the 5th mesh from the centre (which is where the two knots are visible in one mesh), and darn 3 meshes upwards to the right, filling the meshes closely with wool; then in a line with the first of these 3 and upwards to the left darn 2 meshes, each separately, in order that all the darning may lean to the right.

Having done this there will be one mesh left in the middle of the green vandyke, which darn in plum color. Darn 6 of these round the centre of the cover. Between the lower points of each vandyke there will be 3 diamonds, darn the middle one in dark blue.

Now in 12th mesh (where the 3 knots are seen in one mesh), with scarlet darn a diamond of 4 meshes to the right; do the same in every 5th mesh all round.

As before, there will be 3 vacant meshes between the lower points of each scarlet diamond, the centre one of which fill with dark blue, and above the dark blue spot darn a vandyke of 4 meshes in claret.

In the 36th round of netting darn close diamonds of 9 meshes (leaving a space of 3 meshes between the lower points of each), of different colors, in the following order : — peach, green, plum, yellow, claret, dark blue, pink, light blue. There are 33 diamonds required in the round; it will there-

28

fore be necessary to work these 8 colors 4 times, which will leave one still vacant; this one may be darned in scarlet.

Miss 3 meshes upwards from one of these closely darned diamonds, and darn 6 meshes to the right, then 4 meshes in an opposite direction from each point of the 6 already darned, thus three sides of a diamond are formed; complete the 4th side by darning 6 meshes.

There will be 17 diamonds, which may be darned thus : — yellow, dark blue, scarlet, green, peach, claret, light blue, pink. Repeat these colors twice, which will leave one to do; this may be done in plum color.

This will leave an open diamond of 16 meshes (4 each way), the centre 4 of which darn in 2 colors, the two opposite each other in one, and the other two in a good contrasting color.

There is always a slight irregularity in round netting, which will cause the first diamond to appear scarcely even with the last. This, however, cannot be avoided, and is not discernible except on very close examination, and does not at all affect its appearance when on the table. It will also be found necessary to lessen the space between the open diamonds, one mesh in two instances, as if there were two more meshes it would cause an irregularity in the close diamonds.

The top part of the cover is now finished, and the points only remain to be darned.

Between each point darn a close diamond of 9 meshes, the lower point of which will hide the fastening of cotton at the commencement of the netted point.

At the end of every point darn an open diamond of 4 meshes, and knot a tassel in the last mesh of each point composed of 4 strands of each color used in darning.

This cover is quickly done, and has a very foreign and elegant appearance.

Netted D'Oyley.

Materials.—One skein Knitting Cord, No. 16 ; one reel of Mecklenburgh Thread, No. 5, and one No. 80; three rows of blue Beads (large) ; two Meshes, one flat, nearly half an inch wide, and the other round, steel No. 16 ; one Netting Needle, and one coarse Sewing Needle.

On a foundation of 18 stitches net one plain round with flat mesh.

2d *Round.*— Flat mesh, two stitches in each except the last, in which net only one.

3d *Round.* — Small mesh, 1 stitch in each.

4th *Round.*—Same as 3d.

5th *Round.* — Flat mesh, 2 in each, except the last, in which net only one.

6th *Round.*—Small mesh, 1 stitch in each, missing 1 stitch, netting the next, and returning to the missed one all round.

7th *Round.*—Small mesh, 1 stitch in each.

Net 12 rounds more, the same as 7th round.

20th *Round.* — Flat mesh, net 2 stitches in each.

21st *Round.* — Small mesh, same as 6th round.

22d *and* 23d *Rounds.*—Small mesh, 1 stitch in each.

Fasten off, cut away the foundation, draw up the stitches tightly, and with the Mecklenburgh No. 5 darn the first round of meshes closely. Then in the 13 rounds of small netting darn 1 line of diamonds the entire depth of small netting, which will be 13 diamonds, with Mecklenburgh No. 5, miss 6 meshes, darn the 7th line of diamonds; continue thus all round the D'Oyley. Now miss 2 meshes from the top of a darned line, and darn 4 with the same thread. Miss 3 meshes downward from this, and darn 4 more. Miss 3 again and darn 4, repeat all round.

Thus there will be 3 darned diamonds of 4 meshes between every darned line of diamonds. Thread a needle with No. 5, and insert it in the mesh at the right-hand corner of the centre darned diamond, pass a bead into the mesh and slip the needle under the thread to the next mesh; before putting in another bead, take a back stitch over the thread under which you just passed the needle, then slip on another bead, and so on all round the close diamonds.

Now with No. 80 do a row of loose buttonhole stitch all round the beads, taking each stitch in a bead mesh;

then do another row of buttonhole stitches in the same meshes, reversing the stitches, taking one in each mesh opposite the one already done, and passing the needle every time through the loop made in the last row. This will fill the entire space between the darned lines.

Darn every mesh of the 21st round with No. 5 closely, and in the last row knot a fringe about an inch in depth.

Care must be taken that all the darning runs the same way, and the beads may be omitted if desired.

Lady's Watch-Pocket, in Netted Embroidery.

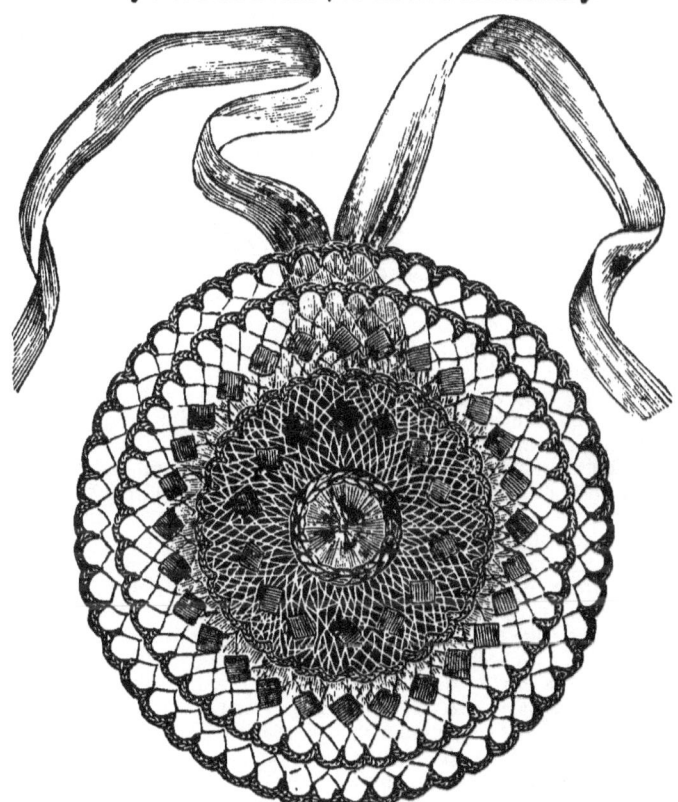

Materials.—One reel Crochet Cotton No. 16; two Meshes, the same as those used in the Netted D'Oyley; a Netting Needle; one skein of colored Wool, of any color to suit the drapery of the room; a yard of inch-wide Sarcenet Ribbon; a round of Cardboard; and a small piece of Silk the same color as the Wool.

On a foundation of 28 stitches net one round with wide mesh.

2d *Round.*—Small mesh, 1 in each. 3d, 4th, 5th, and 6th.—Same as 2d.

7th *Round.*—Large mesh, 2 in each.

8th *Round.*—Small mesh, 1 in each.

9th *and* 10th *Rounds.*—Same as 8th.

Fasten the thread, and with the wool cover the entire outside round of meshes with loosely-wrought button-hole stitches. This forms the first round of the pocket.

On the same foundation, with wide mesh, net 1 plain round.

2d *Round.*—Wide meshes, 2 stitches in each.

3d *Round.*—Small mesh, net 2 stitches together all around.

4th *Round.*—Small mesh, 1 in each. Do 6 more rounds the same.

11th *Round.*—Small mesh, 2 stitches in each.

12th *Round.*—Small mesh, 1 in each. 13th, 14th, 15th, and 16th *Rounds.* — Small mesh, 1 stitch in each.

Fasten off and work the edge as before. In the 14th round darn every alternate diamond with the wool.

On a foundation of 18 stitches with wide mesh net 1 round.

2d *Round.* — Small mesh, 2 in each.

3d *Round.* — Small mesh, 1 in each. Do 5 more rounds the same, and work the edge as before; darn every alternate diamond in 6th round.

Take a round of cardboard the size of a *large* watch, leaving about an inch above the round at the top, cover it with the silk, lay the first piece of netting flat on it, and stitch it round.

Now take the second piece and stitch the 5th round of diamonds down tightly, rather more than half round, so as to make the edge come to the 7th round of the first piece. This will leave it loose in the centre to form the pocket. Stitch the other piece of netting to the middle of this, and finish with a knot of ribbon in the centre. Attach a piece double, about three inches long, to the top, and add a ro-sette and ends.

Instructions in Tatting, or Friv-olité. — The only necessary imple-ments for tatting are a shuttle or short netting-needle, and a gilt pin and ring, united by a chain. The cotton used should be strong and soft. There are three available sizes, Nos. 1, 2, and 3. Attention should be paid to the man-ner of holding the hands, as on this depends the grace or awkwardness of the movement. Fill the shuttle with the cotton (or silk) required, in the same manner as a netting needle. Hold the shuttle between the thumb and first and second fingers of the right hand, leaving about half a yard of cotton unwound. Take up the cot-ton, about three inches from the end, between the thumb and first finger of the left hand, and let the end fall in the palm of the hand; pass the cotton round the other fingers of the left hand (keeping them parted a little), and bring it again between the thumb and forefinger, thus making a circle round the extended fingers. There are only two stitches in tatting, and they are usually done alternately ; this is there-fore termed a *double stitch.*

The first stitch is called the *English stitch*, and made thus :— Let the thread between the right and left hands fall towards you ; slip the shuttle under the thread between the first and second fingers ; draw it out rather quickly, keeping it in a horizontal line with the left hand. You will find a slipping loop is formed on this cotton with that which went round the fingers. Hold the shuttle steadily, with the cotton stretched tightly out, and with the sec-ond finger of the left hand slip the loop thus made under the thumb.

The other stitch is termed *French stitch ;* the only difference being, that instead of allowing the cotton to fall *towards* you, and passing the shuttle *downwards*, the cotton is thrown in a loop over the left hand, and the shuttle passed under the thread between the first and second fingers *upwards.* The knot must be invariably formed by the thread which passes round the fingers of the *left* hand. If the operation is reversed, and the knot formed by the cotton connected with the shuttle, the loop will not draw up. This is occasioned by letting the cotton from the shuttle hang loosely instead of drawing it out and holding it tightly stretched. When any given number of these double stitches are done, and drawn closely together, the stitches are held between the first finger and thumb, and the other fingers are withdrawn from the circle of cotton, which is gradually diminished by drawing out the shuttle until the loop of tatting is nearly or entirely closed. The tatted loops should be quite close to each other, unless directions to the contrary are given.

The pin is used in making an ornamental edge, something like purl edging, thus: — Slip the ring on the lefthand thumb, that the pin attached may be ready for use. After making the required number of double stitches, twist the pin in the circle of cotton, and hold it between the forefinger and thumb, whilst making more double stitches; repeat. The little loops thus formed are termed *picots*.

Trefoil Tatting is done by drawing three loops up tightly, made closely together, and then leaving a short space before making more. The trefoil is sewed into shape afterwards with a needle.

To Join Loops. — When two loops are to be connected, a *picot* is made in the *first*, wherever the join is required. When you come to the corresponding part of the *second* loop, draw the thread which goes round the fingers of the left hand through the picot with a needle, pulling through a loop large enough to admit the shuttle. Slip this through, then draw the thread tight again over the fingers, and continue the work. In many patterns a needle is used to work over, in buttonhole stitch, the thread which passes from one loop to another. A long needleful of the same cotton or silk used for the tatting is left at the beginning of the work, and a common needle used to buttonhole over bar wherever they occur.

Picots are also sometimes made with

the needle and cotton in working over these bars.

Edging in Tatting. — No. I.

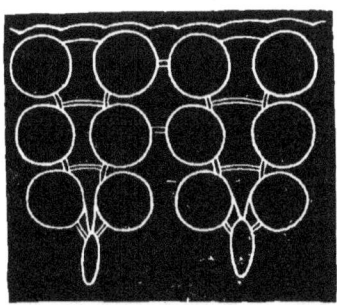

Materials. — Tatting cotton, steel shuttle, and a purling pin. The size of the cotton must depend upon the nature of the article which the edging is designed to trim. As a general rule, No. 1 is suitable for ladies' jupes, children's drawers, and other articles made in calico. No. 2 is a medium size, and will do for finer drawers, and generally for things made in jaconet or cambric muslin. No. 3 is very fine, and fit for infants' robes, caps, ladies' collars, etc.

1st Pattern. — Begin by threading the end of the cotton with a sewing needle. Double the cotton, allowing a long needleful on the needle; and holding the doubled end between the finger and thumb, do 14 buttonhole stitches with the needle. The thread can then be drawn up tight, so as not to leave a loop. Now begin with the shuttle.

1st Loop.—12 double stitches, 1 picot, 4 double, draw up the loop, but not tightly, and work with the needle on the bar of thread 10 buttonhole stitches.

2d Loop. — With the needle, do 2 buttonhole stitches on the thread before beginning this loop. 4 double, join to the picot of the last; 8 double, 1 picot, 4 double. Draw this up like the first, and work on the bar 10 buttonhole stitches. 2 more on the thread before the

3d Loop. — 4 double; join to the picot; 9 double, 1 picot, 3 double. Draw up this loop rather tighter; work on it 7 buttonhole stitches, and 2 on the thread afterward.

4th Loop.—(At the point.) 2 double, join to the picot, 12 double, 1 picot, 2 double. Draw this loop up *quite tightly*.

Work 2 buttonhole stitches on the thread afterward.

5th Loop. — 3 double, join, 9 double, 1 picot, 4 double, draw up this like the third. Work on it 7 buttonhole stitches, and 1 on the thread afterward. Slip the needle through between the two buttonhole stitches after the second loop, and draw the thread through, allowing for a bar on which 6 buttonhole stitches can be worked. By doing these the thread is brought back to the fifth loop; do one more buttonhole stitch on the thread, and proceed to the

6th Loop. — 4 double, join; + 4 double, 1 picot, + twice, 4 double. Draw it up and work it with 10 stitches. Then join across to between the first and second loops, as after the fifth.

7th Loop.—4 double, join,+4 double, 1 picot, + twice, 4 double. Take the needle across to the commencement of the first loop, and on the bar do 10 buttonhole stitches, 9 more buttonhole on the thread, join to the last picot, 9 buttonhole on the thread, make a picot, 9 more buttonhole. This completes one pattern.

1st Loop of the 2d Pattern. — 4 double, join to the picot on the thread, 4 double, join to the picot of the 7th loop, 4 double, 1 picot, 4 double. Draw it up and work on the bar 10 buttonhole stitches, and 2 after.

2d Loop.—4 double, join to the picot, 4 double, join to the picot of the 6th loop, 4 double, 1 picot, 4 double. Draw it up, and work it like the last.

The remaining 5 loops are to be worked exactly like those of the first pattern. All subsequent ones are done like the second.

It may, perhaps, be permitted to us to observe that tatting (or frivolité), besides being very pretty, has the merit of wearing extremely well. It requires far less eyesight than crochet, and is much stronger than knitting, and is also (as we trust we prove) susceptible of great and elegant variations of design.

Infant's Cap Crown in Tatting. — MATERIALS. — *Tatting Cotton, No.* 2; *Steel Shuttle, No.* 14; *a very fine Purling Pin; and a Reel of Mecklenburgh, No.* 12, *for the Mechlin wheel in the centre.*

The pattern consists of five loops, ten patterns being required to form the circle.

1st Pattern. — *1st Loop.* — 3 double stitches, 1 picot, 4 double stitches, 1 picot, 2 double stitches, 1 picot, 6 double stitches, 1 picot, 3 double stitches. Draw it up, leaving a bar of thread, on which 8 buttonhole stitches can be worked.

2d Loop. — 3 double stitches ; join to the last picot of former loop, + 5 double stitches, 1 picot, + twice, 3 double stitches. Draw it up a little tighter than the last.

3d Loop. — 3 double stitches, join to the last picot of 2d loop, + 6 double stitches, 1 picot, + twice, 3 double stitches. Draw it quite tight.

4th Loop. — Same as 2d loop.

5th Loop. — 3 double stitches, join to the last picot of 4th loop ; 6 double stitches, 1 picot, 2 double stitches, 1 picot, 4 double stitches, 1 picot, 3 double stitches. Draw it up, but not tighter than 1st loop.

To work the buttonhole stitches, take a common sewing needle, with a very long piece of the same cotton ; slip the needle through the picot, after the two double stitches of the first loop, draw it out, leaving a short end, on which do four common buttonhole stitches ; catch up the next picot ; make 6 buttonhole stitches, 8 buttonhole stitches on the bar of the 1st loop, 2 between that and the bar of 2d loop, 6 on 2d bar, 2 between that and bar of 4th loop, 6 on bar of 4th loop, 1 before the next : now slip the needle through the two stitches after the 1st loop, thus forming a bar, on which work back 6 buttonhole stitches, then 1 more between 4th and 5th loops, and 8 on the bar of 5th loop. Take the needle across to the base of the 1st loop, and work back 10 stitches ; now work 6 buttonhole stitches on the thread connected with the shuttle.

catch up the picot, work 8 buttonhole stitches, catch up the next picot, 4 buttonhole stitches, catch up 3d picot, 4 buttonhole stitches; make a picot, 8 buttonhole stitches; make another picot, 6 buttonhole stitches.

Now resume the shuttle, leaving the needleful of cotton attached to the work.

2d Pattern.—1st Loop.—Three double stitches, join to the last picot made with the needle and cotton; 4 double stitches, join to the other picot made with the needle, 2 double stitches join to picot in centre of the 5th loop of 1st pattern (which has already been caught up in working with the needle), 6 double stitches, 1 picot, 3 double stitches.

2d, 3d, 4th, and *5th Loops* to be done as in the 1st pattern.

Then work the buttonhole stitches with the needle and cotton as before.

For the centre do ten loops thus:

1st Loop. — Four double stitches, 1 picot, 6 double stitches; join to the picot at the point of the 3d loop of a pattern, 6 double stitches, 1 picot, 3 double stitches.

2d Loop.—Four double stitches; join to the last picot of 1st loop 6 double stitches; join to the picot at the point of 3d loop of a pattern; 6 double, 1 picot, 3 double stitches.

3d, 4th, 5th, 6th, 7th, 8th, 9th, and *10th,* same as 2d. These loops must not be drawn very tightly. The bars which connect them must be buttonholed, as those of the patterns.

These ten loops will form a small circle, within which a Mechlin wheel should be worked with the Mecklenburgh, No. 12. The crown when completed should be trimmed with the following narrow edge:

1st Loop. — Four double stitches,+1 picot, 2 double stitches, + 4 times. Draw it up to form a semicircle.

2d and all following Loops. — Two double stitches; join to the last picot of former loop 2 double stitches, + 1 picot, 2 double stitches, + 4 times.

Draw up as 1st loop, and sew neatly round the crown.

Edging in Tatting. — No. II.

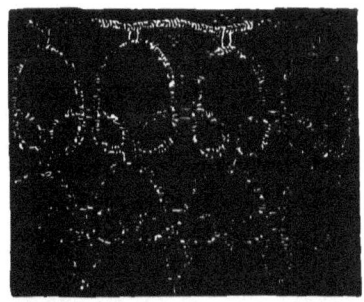

Fill the shuttle *without* cutting off the thread from the reel, as the *reel thread* is required for working the connecting bars; begin at the edge and make the

* 1st Oval of Trefoil.—Work 4 double stitches, 1 picot, 4 double, 1 picot, 4 double. Draw up tight.

2d Oval.—5 double, join into last picot of former oval, 4 double, 1 picot, 4 double, 1 picot, 5 double. Draw up tight.

3d Oval.—4 double, join into last picot of former oval, 4 double, 1 picot, 4 double. Draw up tight. This completes one trefoil.

Now put the thread attached to the reel over the left hand, and on it work 6 double, 1 picot, 6 double, this forms the connecting bar between each trefoil; begin again as at ***, joining each trefoil by the picots. To form the upper part of the pattern, work 4 double, join into the picot in the centre of connecting bar, 4 double, draw up tight, then with the reel thread over the left hand work 7 double, 1 picot, 7 double. With the shuttle thread next work 4 double, join to the same picot as the last made small oval, 4 double, draw up tight, repeat from ***.

To form the heading, work a crochet chain of seven stitches into each of the picots of the bars last made with the reel thread.

Edging in Tatting. — No. III. —

The edge half of this pattern is worked with the single thread.

1st large Oval. — 6 double, * 1 picot, 1 double, * 6 times, 6 double, draw up tight. Leave about the sixth of an inch between each oval, and work the small oval the reverse way of the large one, 4 double, 1 picot, 3

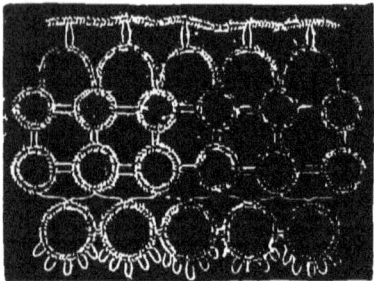

double, 1 picot, 3 double, 1 picot, 4 double, draw up tight; this forms the small oval. Leave the thread as before, and work the second large oval, joining it into the last picot of the preceding large oval. Join the smaller ones in the same manner to each other.

To form the upper half of pattern, fill the shuttle from the reel without cutting off the thread, work 3 double, 1 picot, 3 double, join into the lower picot of the small oval in preceding row, 3 double, 1 picot, 3 double, draw up tight; with the reel thread work 6 double, 1 picot, 6 double, to form connecting bar; make a small oval with the shuttle thread as before, joining it into the last picot of the former small oval in this row. Repeat: make a crochet heading as in the former pattern.

Edging in Tatting. — No. IV.

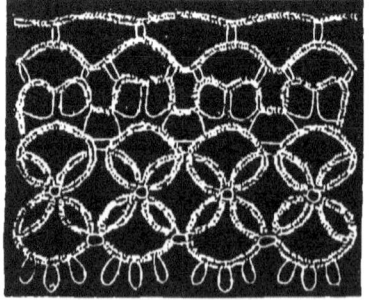

This pattern is worked in four rows, all with the double thread, i. e., the

shuttle filled without cutting off the thread.

1st Row. — Begin at the small oval, * 5 double, 1 *large* picot, 5 double, draw up. With the reel thread work 3 double, 1 picot, 2 double, 1 picot, 2 double, 1 picot, 3 double; then with shuttle thread work a second small oval, 5 double, join into the *large* picot of the first oval, 5 double, draw up. Repeat from *.

2d Row is exactly the same process reversed.

1st Small Oval. — * 5 double, join into the *large* picot of the first oval in the former row; 5 double, draw up. With the reel thread work 3 double, 1 picot, 2 double, 1 picot, 2 double, 1 picot, 3 double.

2d Oval. — 5 double, join into the same large picot as last small oval, 5 double; there are now 4 small ovals joined into the same large picot. Repeat from *.

3d Row is worked with the reel thread. Begin by joining the thread into the first picot of last row. Work * 3 double, 1 picot, 3 double, join into second picot of last row, 3 double, 1 picot, 3 double, join into third picot, 2 double, join into next picot. Repeat from *.

4th Row. — Join reel thread into 1st picot of last row. Work * 4 double, 1 picot, 4 double, join into second picot, 2 double, join into third picot. Repeat from *. Crochet heading as in former patterns.

Tatting Insertion.

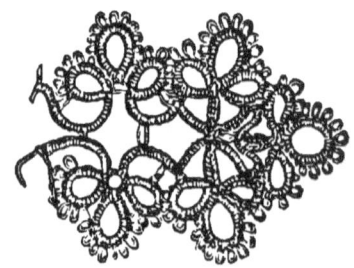

Join your two threads together and make 2 stitches in *long* tatting, then a loop and 6 stitches, a loop and 6 stitches; all in *long* * tatting.

Then you commence the trefoil in *round* † tatting: — 5 stitches, join it to the loop after the 2 stitches in *long* tatting, 1 stitch, 1 loop, till there are 6 loops, then 5 stitches, and draw it together.

5 stitches, join it into the 6th loop of last round; 1 stitch, 1 loop, till there are 10 loops, then 5 stitches and draw it up.

5 stitches, join it into 10th loop of last round, 1 stitch, 1 loop, till there are 6 loops, then 5 stitches and draw it up. Now take the *long* tatting thread and join closely 6 stitches, 1 loop, 6 stitches, join it into the last loop of the last *round* of the trefoil; 2 stitches, 1 loop, 6 stitches, 1 loop, 6 stitches, and then leave the *long* tatting and begin the trefoil again.

The other side of the insertion is worked in the same way, only instead of *making* the loops between the different 6 stitches of the *long* tatting, you join it into the loops on the opposite side.

To turn the corner you finish a trefoil and make your 6 loops of *long* tatting, then draw your thread through all the 5 loops of the *three* last trefoils.

Instructions in Knitting. — Although the art of knitting is known perhaps more generally than almost any other kind of fancy work, still, as the knowledge is not universal, and there have been of late years great improvements in many of the processes, we hope that a short account of all the stitches, and the elementary parts of the craft, will be welcomed by many of our friends; and most seriously would we recommend them to attain *perfection* in this branch of work, because, above all others, it is a resource to those who, from weak eyes, are precluded from many kinds of industrial amusement, or who, as invalids, cannot bear the fatigue of more elaborate work. The fact is that knitting does not require eyesight at all; and a

* Worked with the reel thread.
† Worked with shuttle thread.

very little practice ought to enable any one to knit while reading, talking, or studying, quite as well as if the fingers were unemployed. It only requires that the fingers should be properly used, and that one should not be made to do the duty of another.

The implements used for knitting are rods or pins of ivory, bone, or steel. The latter are most commonly used, and should have tapered points, without the least *sharpness* at the extremity.

The first process is Casting On.—Hold the end of cotton between the first and second fingers of the left hand, bring it over the thumb and forefinger, and bend the latter to twist the cotton into a loop; bend the needle in the loop; hold the cotton attached to the reel between the third and little fingers of the right hand, and over the point of the forefinger; bring the thread round the needle by the slightest possible motion; bend the needle towards you, and tighten the loop on the left-hand finger, in letting it slip off to form the *first* stitch.

Now take that needle with the loop on it in the left-hand, and another in the right. Observe the position of the hands. The left-hand needle is held between the thumb and the second finger, leaving the forefinger free, to aid in moving the points of the needles. This mode of using the forefinger, instead of employing it merely to hold the needle, is the great secret of being able to knit without looking at the work, for so extremely delicate is the sense of touch in this finger, that it will, after a little practice, enable you to tell the sort of stitch coming next, in the finest material, so that knitting becomes merely mechanical. Insert the point in the loop, bringing it behind the other needle, slip the thread round it, bring the point in front, and transfer the loop to the left-hand needle, without withdrawing it from the right hand. Repeat the process for any number of stitches required.

Plain Knitting. — Slip the point of the right-hand needle in a loop, bring the thread round it, and with the fore-finger push the point of the needle off the loop so that the thread just twisted round forms a new one on the right hand.

Purling. — The right-hand needle is slipped in the loop *in front of* the left-hand one, and the thread, after passing between the two, is brought round it; it is then worked as before. The thread is always brought forward before beginning a purled stitch, unless particular directions to the contrary are given.

The Mode of making Stitches. — To make one, merely bring the thread in front before knitting, when, as it passes over the needle, it makes a loop; to make two, three, or more, pass the thread *round the needle in addition*, once for 2, twice for 3, and so on.

To Decrease. — Take one stitch off without knitting; knit one, then slip the point of the left-hand needle in the unknitted stitch and draw it over the other. It is marked in receipts d. 1. To decrease 2 or more, slip 1, knit 2, 3, or more together, *as one*, and pass the slip stitch over.

The way to Join a Round. — Four or five needles are used in round work, such as socks, stockings, etc. Cast on any given number of stitches on one needle, then slip another needle in the last stitch, before casting any on it; repeat for any number. When all are cast on, knit the first 2 stitches off on to the end of the last needle. One needle is always left unused in casting on for a round.

The way of Joining the Toe of a Sock, or any similar thing.—Divide all the stitches on to two needles, hold both in the left hand, as if they were one, and in knitting take a loop off each one, which knit together.

To cast off.—Knit 2 stitches; with the left-hand needle draw the first over the second; knit another; repeat. Observe that the row before the casting off should never be very tightly knitted.

To knit three stitches together, so that the centre one shall be in front.—Slip 2

off the needle together, knit the third, and draw the others over together.

To raise a stitch is to knit the bar of thread between the two stitches as one.

The abbreviations used are : — K, knit ; P, purl ; D, decrease ; K 2 t, knit two together; P 2 t, purl two together ; M 1, make one.

Take care to have needles and cotton or wool that are suitable to each other in size. The work of the best knitter in the world would appear ill done if the needles were too fine or too coarse. In the former case the work would be close and thick; in the latter it would be too much like a cobweb.

Shells for a Knitted Counterpane. — Fine knitting cotton and steel needles. Cast on 45 stitches. Knit 2 plain rows.

3d Row. — 5 plain, thread forward and 2 together, 17 times, 5 plain.

4th Row. — Plain knitting.

5th Row. — 5 plain, forward 2 together, purl 1, till there are only 7 left 2 together, 5 plain.

6th Row. — Plain.

7th Row. — Same as 5th.

8th Row. — Plain.

9th Row. — 5 plain, 2 together, plain 1, till 7 are left. 2 together, 5 plain.

10th Row. — Purl all.

Continue 9 and 10 alternately until four ribs are formed, there will then be only 10 stitches on the needle; narrow these in the centre one till only one remains. Fasten off.

Brioche Stitch. — This stitch is extremely elastic, and is very suitable for comforters, polka jackets, as well as for the Turkish cushion properly called a Brioche. Cast on any number of stitches that can be divided by 3, knit backwards and forwards. Thread forward, slip 1, knit 2 together, and repeat.

Vase Mat. — Having cut the round in cashmere, line it with strong white linen ; procure a small ivy leaf, by which cut nine leaves of velvet; brush the backs over with thin gum and lay them on the cashmere in the form seen in the engraving, then lay the gold cord all round each leaf, fastening it down with the sewing silk, and passing the ends through the cashmere.

button. Now line the mat with the green sarcenet, and sew the cord all round.

This mat may, of course, be made

Materials. — A piece of white Cashmere large enough to cut a round of 30 inches in circumference; a small piece of ivy green velvet; one skein of gold cord; nine skeins Berlin wool, different colors (all light); two rows of pearls, No. 2; netting-needle and mesh (half an inch wide); a little gold-colored sewing silk; a piece of green sarcenet for lining the mat; and thick green silk cord sufficient to go round it.

Now on a strong thread net 120 stitches of one color wool, which will be nearly the skein, thread a needle with white cotton, lift 8 stitches on it, pass a pearl on it and tie it, making the knot come inside the stitches, so as to be hidden when finished. Do the same with each skein of wool, then cut rounds of buckram one inch in diameter, on each of which tack one of the skeins of wool already prepared, commencing at the outer edge, and finishing in the middle with a velvet of a color if preferred to white, but care must be taken that it is a color which will harmonize well with the green leaves — pale, pink, maize, or peach would look equally well; and if durability be an object, a rich light brown may be employed with good effect, when the wools chosen must also be darker.

This mat, when made of light colors, forms a very acceptable and elegant little gift to a bride, its beauty consisting in its simplicity.

Toilet Cushion.

Materials. — A piece of very fine white Swiss muslin nine inches square; a little rose-colored Shetland wool; a very fine rug needle; a half yard of narrow white braid, and one yard of white silk fringe.

The design (which consists of sprays of leaves in the centre, surrounded by vandykes, having a single leaf in each), must first be drawn on paper, thus:

Draw a circle 5 inches in diameter, in which draw 4 sprays of three leaves, each spray occupying the space of one quarter of the circle. Let the stems incline toward the centre, as seen in the engraving. Now draw 8 vandykes round the circle, in each of which draw a single leaf to correspond with those in the sprays — the leaf running to the point of the vandyke, which should be about two inches deep.

The design being thus prepared, place it under the muslin, on which trace it with a fine black lead pencil, or a brush, and indigo mixed with thin gum-water.

Now remove the paper, and with the Shetland wool chain stitch the sprays and single leaves in the vandykes very finely. Take a piece of white braid sufficient to go round the circle, and with the wool slightly and loosely work a row of open buttonhole stitches on one edge of it, and run it neatly round the circle, taking the two ends through the muslin, as it is difficult to fasten braid invisibly. Cut away the muslin between the vandykes, leaving sufficient outside each to form a narrow turning, which must be made on the right side of the cushion. On this turning lay the white silk fringe, and run it neatly round each vandyke, making the edge exactly cover the mark forming the outline of the vandykes. Now make a cushion of strong white linen, sufficiently high to allow the fringed points to touch the table. The bottom of it may be covered with rose-colored silk, and the top and sides with white silk or satin. Fill it tightly, but not too hard, and tack the circle round which the braid is sewn to the top of the cushion, allowing the points to fall over. Make a pretty knot of rose colored and white ribbon mixed, tack in the centre, and the cushion is complete.

It is impossible to describe the chaste and elegant appearance of this simple cushion when made; and we feel sure our fair young friends will acknowledge it to be a pretty specimen of the many ornamental and useful articles which may be made at very trifling expense, both of money and time.

The cushion may, of course, be made to suit the drapery of any room by substituting any other colored wool, ribbon, etc.

MADAME KELLOGG.

TAILOR DRESSMAKING SYSTEM.

The Art of Dressmaking.—Advantages of Doing One's Own Sewing. —Old-Fashioned Methods Superseded by Practical Systems.— How to Cut and Fit.—Useful Charts.

The sewing-machine has found its way into every household, and in nearly every family either the mother or one of the daughters has become an adept in its use. The advantages of doing one's own sewing are so marked that nearly every woman desires to make at least a portion of her own garments. The detailed instructions given in this department will give any intelligent woman an insight into dressmaking which will enable her to follow it as a business, or to save enough in the making of her own wardrobe to provide her with rich fabrics and costly trimmings, the luxury of which she might otherwise have to forego.

Advice About Shopping.—A few words about the selection of materials for dressmaking will not be inappropriate. Buy everything needed before the work of dressmaking is begun, and be sure to get a sufficient quantity of dress goods, for the patterns may not be easily matched afterwards. It is much better to have enough goods left over for mending than to run short of material, and experience delay and inconvenience in efforts to make additional purchases. Thread, linings, buttons, trimmings and needles, while easily duplicated, never come amiss, if a quantity is left over for the scrap-basket.

Tailor-made Gowns.—Tailor-made garments are now in vogue. The remarks upon this system, and the instructions and diagrams which follow, are by permission reproduced from a treatise on the subject by Madame Kellogg, of Philadelphia, Pa., and Battle Creek, Mich.

The cutting and making of garments for gentlemen have, for many years, been regulated by exact systems and mathematical laws, while the same work for ladies has almost entirely been done by charts and patterns, based on the idea that the only substantial difference in the bodies of women was in the "size." The radical difference between the two systems will become apparent on a moment's consideration. While the former is scientific, and founded on the adjustment of varying dimensions and measurements in one harmonious whole, the latter is subject to being constantly thrown "out of balance" by the change of a single dimension relatively to any or all of the rest.

French Tailor System.—The inventor, after years of practice, in dress-cutting by all the old methods, was forced to the conclusion that the "tailor's square" was the true basis of accurate work in the cutting of garments for ladies as well as for gentlemen, and accordingly has perfected a system by combining its use with graded scales, by means of which a perfect fit is assured at the hands of any intelligent dressmaker, and in the most expeditious manner.

This system of cutting is as much superior to the "chart" method of dress-cutting as the work of the artistic tailor is to "ready-made" clothing. Indeed, the relation is very much the same, while the ratio of importance is vastly greater, inasmuch as the variation in the female form has a much wider range, and the demands of fashion and good taste require a better fit in the garments of ladies than in those of gentlemen.

A dress "well made" means something more than good sewing, fine stitching,

447

or elaborate trimming. All these may exist, and a misfit will spoil the whole. In fact, no amount of good work will atone for this one defect. Hence no dressmaker, however perfect her taste and judgment in other respects, can give complete satisfaction unless her work is based on a correct system of cutting; for herein lies the secret of success.

In introducing the **French Tailor System** to the public, the inventor claims that it meets every demand for simplicity, accuracy, economy of time and material, and ease of comprehension. It is adapted to all irregularities of form, and is unaffected by any change in fashion. It is therefore a means of saving time, labor and money—three points which entitle it to the careful consideration of all who would be successful in business. Those who have used this system are surprised to find in it such a combination of accuracy with simplicity, the idea being very prevalent that absolute accuracy requires a very complicated system of details, which is too true of many other systems of cutting; but in this case, accuracy is secured by conforming to scientific principles, and these, when rightly applied, are exceedingly simple.

Few who call themselves *cutters* realize the true meaning of the word, especially with reference to the cutting and fitting of ladies' garments. The degree of tightness or looseness is no indication of the fit, as a lady may have a dress which is very snug, and another which is very loose, and yet both may be excellent fits. On the other hand, she may have a tight dress which is a *misfit* in every sense, while the same may be true of a loose dress.

The art of dress-cutting and fitting, therefore, does not consist merely in regulating the tightness or looseness of a garment, nor even the relative length of waist, shoulder or sleeve; but in so cutting and combining the different parts that when made into a garment it shall conform to the shape of the person who is to wear it, whether loosely or otherwise, without wrinkles or the distortion of its various parts. That this requires talent of no mean order, any observing person must be ready to acknowledge, and any system of principles that will assist in perfecting such an art will be hailed with gladness by those who desire its development and cultivation.

However perfect a system of cutting may be, its use can never produce uniformly successful results unless the cutter is uniform in taking measurements. Two cutters, using the same system in the same establishment, will produce varying results if one takes loose measurements and the other draws the tape tightly. In this particular, more than any other branch of dressmaking, the exercise of good judgment plays a leading part. The varying dimensions of the human form, the hardness or softness of the tissues, the character of the material to be used, and the purpose for which the garment is to be especially adapted, must all be carefully considered, and should enter into the calculations of the one who is to apply the tape line, before a figure is put down as the basis of the work. Unless this is done, success cannot be expected with any system of cutting, however excellent it may be.

In regard to the claims of many of the so-called tailor systems, we will simply remark that any method which does not employ the *tailor's square and scales* cannot properly be called a tailor system. A plan of cutting by diagrams and pasteboard patterns is not and cannot be a tailor system, at least until tailors adopt such a method and throw away the square, which they are too wise to undertake in the present advanced state of their art.

The **Kellogg French Tailor System** combines the use of the tailor's square with the graded scales, and the methods of drafting being the result of long study and experience, are fully protected by

29

United States patents, and cannot be infringed upon without violation of law.

How to Measure.—Measurements here given are for a well-proportioned form, and used only as a guide for beginners : Bust measurement, 36 inches; chest measurement, 13½ inches ; length of waist in back, 16 inches ; under arm, 8 inches ; length of waist in front, 13¼ inches ; width of back, 13 inches ; length of shoulder, 5½ inches ; around the waist, 23½ inches ; skirt measure, 40 inches.

Arm Measure.—From neck to shoulder, 5½ inches ; from shoulder to elbow, 18½ inches ; from elbow to wrist, 25½ inches ; around the arm between elbow and shoulder, 10½ inches ; around the elbow when bent, 10 inches ; around wrist, 8 inches.

1. To obtain the bust measurement, place the tape line around the person close under the shoulder blades, and over the largest part of the bust. Take a snug but not tight measurement. Great care should be used in taking this measurement. If taken too tight, the whole waist will be too tight ; if taken too loose, the garment will be too loose.

2. In taking the chest measurement, have the lady stand perfectly natural, then measure straight across the chest from armpit to armpit.

3. To obtain length of front, place tape line at point of neck and down to bottom of waist.

4. To obtain length of waist in the back, place tape line at prominent neck bone and to bottom of waist. (This is a measure that plays a very important part.)

5. Take under arm measurement by placing tape directly under the arm, bringing it straight to bottom of waist. This is one of the most important measures to be taken. If taken too long, it will cause the dress to wrinkle under the arm, and bring top of darts too high.

6. To take measurement for width of back apply the tape line in the same manner as for the chest.

7. To obtain length of shoulder, place tape line on neck about the same height as prominent neckbone, carrying a little back from top of shoulder. The length of shoulder can make or mar the beauty of a dress.

8. Take the waist measurement *next to corset*, around the smallest part of the waist. Take this measurement rather tight.

9. To obtain size of hips, measure around the hips about 7 inches below waist measurement.

10. To obtain length of sleeve, place tape line same as in taking the shoulder measurement. Take length of shoulder, from length of shoulder to elbow, and from elbow to wrist. To take measurement around the arm, close the hand and bend the arm. Take measure around arm between elbow and shoulder. Take this measurement as tight or loose as you wish the sleeve. Apply tape at elbow and wrist in same manner. If you wish the sleeve loose at wrist, take the measure over the hand.

To take measurement for a Princess Polonaise, or a tight-fitting wrapper, take same measurements as for a basque, and the same rule will apply in taking measures for cloaks, except that the measures should be one or two sizes larger.

In taking measures for a tight-fitting walking jacket, take same as for basque, excepting in the waist measure, which should be taken over the dress. In drafting, use one scale larger. If bust measure is 34, use 35 inches.

Hip Measurement.—Measure around the hips 7 inches below waist. Measure each piece of the front and back draft, 7 inches below line G in diagram A.

If the pattern is not as large as the hip measure, add part of the surplus on line V, and the remaining part on lines T and W. The measure is necessary only in tight-fitting garments, where no plaits are used in the back.

To Draft Front of Tight-fitting Basque.— *See Diagram A.*—In drafting, we select scale by the bust measurement. (In this draft we use scale 36.) The top of scale is where bust measurement is printed. The side, numbering from 1 to 26, is used in laying out the waists and sleeves. The reverse side of scale, where a portion of the alphabet is printed, is used only in the back on line G, in obtaining space for centre of back and waist measurement. In beginning to draft, have the corner of square to your left hand. To obtain lines E and F, place square one inch from front and top edges of paper, drawing line F, length of short arm of square, and line E, length of long arm of square, dotting on line E length of back of waist, 16 inches. To obtain line G, place corner of square at the 16-inch dot. keeping long arm of square on line E, and draw line G, dotting on line E length of

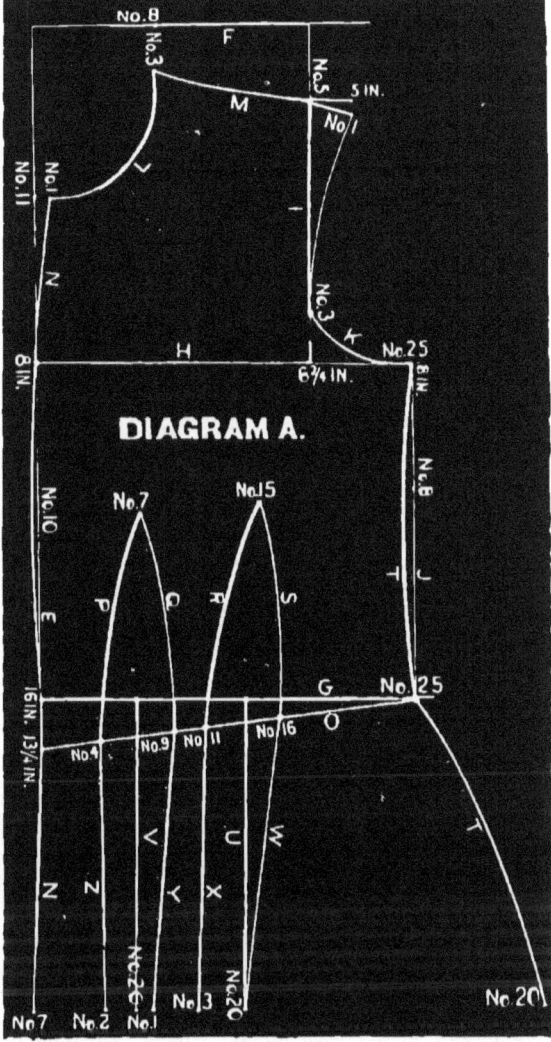

DIAGRAM A.

under arm measurement, 8 inches. To obtain line H, place corner of square at the 8-inch dot on line E, keeping long arm of square on line E, and draw line H, dotting on line H half the width of chest measurement, 6¾ inches. To obtain line I, place corner of square at the 6¾-inch dot on line H, keeping short arm of square on line H, and draw line I. To obtain No. 11 for front of neck, place scale on line E with top of scale at line F, and dot at No. 11. Place top of

scale at No. 11, and dot at No. 1.   To obtain No. 8 for side of neck, place scale
on line F with top of scale at line E, and dot at No. 8.   Place top of scale at
No. 8, and dot at No. 3.   To obtain No. 5, place scale on line I with top of
scale at line F, and dot at No. 5.   To obtain No. 3, place scale on line I with
top of scale at line H, and dot at No. 3.   To obtain No. 25, place scale on line
II with top of scale at line E, and dot at No. 25.   Place scale on line G with top
of scale at line E, and dot at No. 25.   To obtain line J, place corner of square
at No. 25 on line G, and at No. 25 on line H, and draw line J.   To obtain the
curve portion of line K, place inside curve of short arm of square at top of line
J, with inside curve of long arm of square at No. 3 on line I, and draw curve
part of line K.   To obtain line L for neck, reverse square, placing inside of short
arm of square at No. 1 on line E, with inside of long arm of square at No. 8,
and draw line L from No. 1 to No. 3.   To obtain line M for shoulder, place
point D on dart rule at No. 3, with rule side of dart rule at No. 5 on line I, and
draw length of shoulder required, 5 inches.   (In this draft we are using 5½
inches.   We usually make front of shoulder from ⅛ to ¼ inch shorter than the
back.)   Place top of scale at the 5-inch dot, and dot at No. 1.   Place point R
on dart rule midway on line M and No. 1, and draw sloping curve for shoulder.
To finish line K, place B on dart rule at No. 3 on line I, with rounded or convex
side at No. 1, and finish drawing line K.   To obtain line N, place 19 on dart
rule at the intersection of lines E and G, with rule side at No. 1, and draw line
N.   To obtain line O for bottom of darts, place tape line at No. 1 on line N,
and measure down on line N, length of front, 13½ inches.   Place corner of
square at the 13½-inch dot and at height of lines G and J, and draw line O.   To
obtain the length and top of darts, place scale on line E, with top of scale at
line H, dotting on line E at No. 10.   Place scale on line J, with top of scale at
line H, dotting at No. 8 on line J.   Place top of scale at No. 10 on line E, with
end of scale at No. 8 on line J, dotting at Nos. 7 and 15.   Place scale on line
O, with top of scale at line E, dotting at Nos. 4, 9, 11 and 16.   To obtain lines
P, Q, R and S, place point D on dart rule at No. 7, with rule side of dart rule
at No. 4 on line O, and draw line P.   Reverse dart rule, and place point R at
No. 7 and at No. 9, and draw line Q.   Draw lines R and S in the same manner.
To obtain line T, place 3 inches on dart rule at No. 25 on line H, and at No. 25
on line G, and draw curved line T.   To obtain lower part of darts, dot midway
on line G from lines R and S, placing corner of square at this dot, keeping short
arm of square on line G, and draw line U.   Place scale on line U with top of
scale at line G, and dot at No. 20.   Place top of scale at No. 20 on line U, dotting
at No. 3.   Place corner of square at No. 16 on line O, and at No. 20 on line U,
and draw line W.   Place corner of square at No. 11 on line O, and at No. 3,
and draw line X.   Dot midway on line G from lines P and Q, placing corner of
square at this dot, with short arm of square on line G, drawing line V.   Place
scale on line V, with top of scale at line G, dotting at No. 20.   Place top of
scale at No. 20, and dot at No. 1.   Place top of scale at No. 20, and dot at Nos.
2 and 7.   Place corner of square at No. 9 on line O and at No. 1, and draw line
Y.   Place corner of square at No. 4 on line O, and at No. 2, and draw line Z.
Place corner of square at the 13½-inch dot and at No. 7, and draw line N.   To
obtain hip curve, place top of scale at No 20 on line U, keeping scale parallel
with line G, and dot at No. 20.   Place point R on dart rule at No. 25 on line
G, with concave side of rule at No. 20, and draw line T.

To Draft Back of Tight-fitting Basque.—*See Diagram B.*—Place square
one inch from top and front edge of paper, drawing line F length of short arm

of square, and line E length of long arm of square, dotting on line F length of back measurement, 16 inches. Place corner of square at the 16-inch dot, with long arm of square on line F, and draw line G, dotting on line E, length of under arm measurement, 8 inches. Place corner of square at the 8-inch dot, with long arm of square on line E, and draw line H, dotting on line H half the width of back measurement, 6½ inches. Place corner of square at the 6½-inch dot, keeping short arm of square on line H, and draw line I. Place scale on line E, with top of scale at line F, and dot at No. 3. Place scale on line F with top of scale at line E, and dot at No. 4. Place top of scale at No. 4, and dot at No. 2. Place scale on line E, with top of scale at line H, and dot at No. 10. Place scale on line I, with top of scale at line H, dotting at Nos. 4, 8 and 11. Place scale on line H, with top of scale at line E, and dot at No. 24. Reverse scale, placing scale on line G, with top of scale at line E, dotting at A, D, and at the waist measurement, 23½ inches. To obtain line J, place corner of square at the 23½ scale, dot on line G, and at No. 24 on line H, and draw line J, length of under arm measurement, 8 inches. Place the inside curve on short arm of square at top of line J, with inside curve of long arm of square at No. 4 on line I, and draw curved part of line K. Place point D on dart rule at No. 3 on line E, with rule side at No. 2, and draw line L. Place point D on dart rule at No. 2, with rule side at No. 11 on line I, and draw line M, 5½ inches. Place B on dart rule at No. 4 on line I, with rounded or convex part at 5½ inches, and finish line K. Place B on dart rule at letter A on line G, with rounding part to No. 10 on line E, and draw line N. Place A on dart rule at No. 8, with rounded part at letter D on line

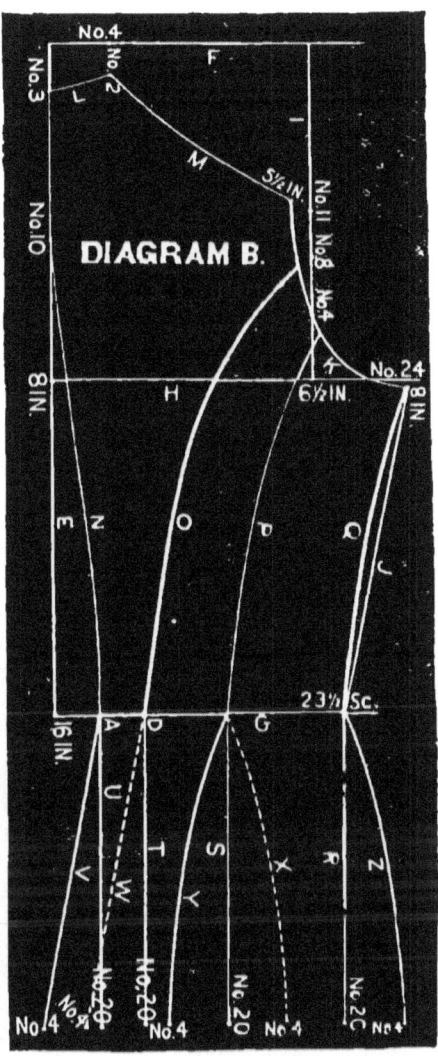

DIAGRAM B.

G, and draw line O. To obtain line P, dot midway on line G from lines O and J. Dot midway on line K from lines O and J. Place point D on dart rule at this dot on line K, with rule side at this dot on line G, and draw line P. Line

P may be drawn to or from line O, to change width of back.　(See **Diagram B.**) Place 3 inches on dart rule at top of line J, with rule side at the intersection of lines J and G, and draw line Q.　Place corner of square at the intersection of lines J and G, and draw line Q.　Place corner of square at the intersection of lines J and G, with short arm of square on line G, and draw line R.　Place scale on line R, with top of scale at line G, and dot at No. 20.　Place top of scale at No. 20, and dot at No. 4.　Place point R on dart rule at intersection of lines J and G, with concave side to No. 4, and draw line Z.　Place corner of square at intersection of lines G and P, with short arm of square on line G, and draw line S.　Place scale on line S with top of scale to line G, and dot at No. 20.　Place top of scale at No. 20, and dot at No. 4.　Place point D on dart at intersection of lines P and G, with rule side at No. 4, and draw line Y. Place top of scale at No. 20 on line S, and dot at No. 4.　Place point R on dart rule at intersection of lines P and G. and at No. 4, and draw line X.　Place corner of square at intersection of lines O and G, and draw line T.　Place scale on line T, with top of scale at line G, and dot at No. 20.　Place top of scale at No. 20 on line T, and dot at No. 4.　Place corner of square at intersection of lines O and G, and at No. 4, and draw line W.　Place corner of square at intersection of lines N and G, with short arm of square on line G, and draw line U.　Place scale on line U, with top of scale at line G, and dot at No. 20.　Place top of scale at No. 20 on line U, and dot at No. 4.　Place corner of square at intersection of lines N and G, and at No. 4, and draw line V.

To Draft Tight-fitting Sleeve.—*See Diagram C.*—Draw line A length of long arm of square, and line B length of short arm of square. Place scale on line B, with top of scale at line A, dotting at Nos. 8 and 16. To obtain length of sleeve, place 5¼ inches on tape line (this being the length of shoulder used in this draft) on line B, midway from Nos. 8 and 16, bringing tape line at line A, dotting at length of elbow measurement 18½ inches, and at length of wrist 25½ inches. Place corner of square at the 18½-inch dot, keeping long arm of square on line A, and draw line C. Place square at the 25½-inch dot, and draw line D. Place scale on line A, with top of scale at line B, and dot at No. 11. Place scale on line C, with top of scale at line A, dotting at No. 4. Place scale on line D, with top of scale at llne A, dotting at No. 2. Place point E on dart rule at No. 11, with rounded or convex side at No. 8, and draw part of line E from No. 11 to No. 8. Reverse dart rule, placing letter A at No. 11, with convex side at No. 16, and draw line F. Place D on dart rule at No. 4 on line C, with rule side at No. 11, drawing upper part of line G. Reverse dart rule, placing R at No. 4, with concave side at No. 2, finishing line G. Place scale on line F, with top of scale at line A, dotting at No. 15 on line F. To obtain the size around the top of the sleeve, measure the arm seye of waist pattern, adding to the measurement two inches to give fulness for sleeve (in this draft we use 16 inches for sleeve). Measure with tape line from No. 15 on line F to No. 11, and from No. 15 on line F to No. 11, and from No. 11 to No. 8 on line E, and from No. 8 the length of line B, dotting on line B at top of sleeve measurement, 16 inches. Measure with tape line on line C from line G, dotting on line C one-half of elbow measurement, 5 inches. Measure on line D from line G, dotting on line D one half of wrist measurement, 4 inches. Place scale on line C, with top of scale at the 5-inch dot, dotting at No. 3. Place top of scale at the 5-inch dot on line C, dotting at No. 3. Place scale on line D, with top of scale at the 4-inch dot, dotting at No. 3 on scale side of 4-inch dot. Place F on dart rule at No. 3 on line C, with convex side at No. 3 on line D, drawing lower part of line II. To give more fulness over the muscle of the arm, drop F on dart rule 1½ inches below line C. (See Diagram C.) Draw lower part of line I in the same manner. Place B on dart rule at No. 3, with convex side at No. 15, drawing upper part of line H. (In drawing upper part of lines H and I, B on dart rule may be moved above or below line C, to form a true curve). Place B on dart rule at No. 3, with convex side at the 16-inch dot, and finish upper part of line I. Place scale on line H, with top of scale at line F, dotting at No. 2. Place scale on line I, with top of scale at line B, dot-

DIAGRAM D.

ting at No. 6. Place point C on dart rule at No. 6 on line I, with convex side at No. 16 on line B, drawing part of line E. Finish line E with curve on square from Nos. 8 and 16. Place A on dart rule at No. 11, with convex side at No. 2, drawing running line. Measure with tape line from line G to line H, midway from lines C and F, placing the amount, 4¼ inches, at line G, measuring across to line I, dotting at arm measurement, 11 inches. Dot midway from the 11-inch dot to line I, placing the amount on the inside of line II. Place B on

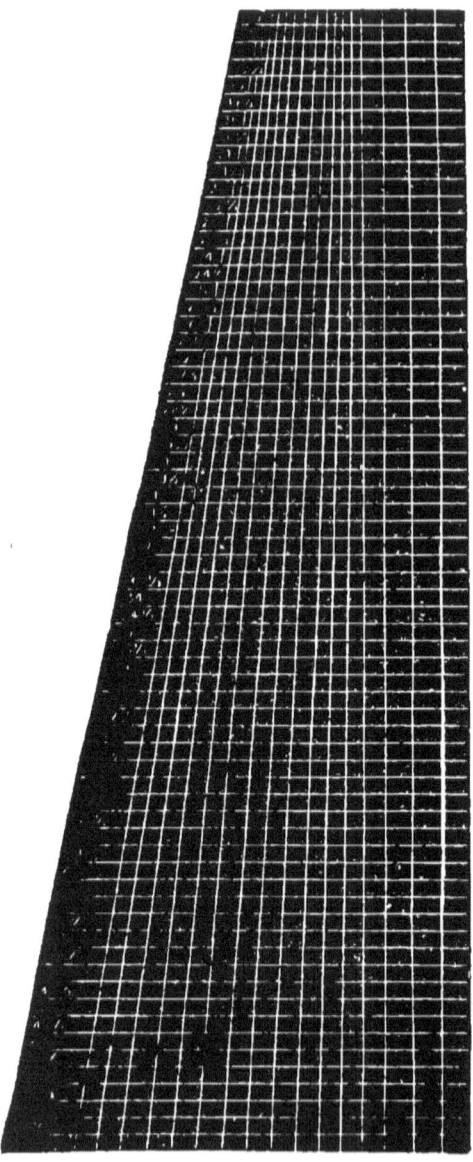

DIAGRAM E.

dart rule at No. 3 and at this dot, and draw part of line K. Place 3 inches on dart rule at No. 2, and at upper part of line K, and finish drawing line K. Draw line J in the same manner.

Hints for Basting.—In placing the lining on the dress goods, be sure the threads on the lining at bottom of waist run parallel with the threads in the dress goods. Pin the lining firmly. Do not put your poor help at basting. This, above all work, should be the most carefully done. We consider a dress well cut and basted as being half made. Use if possible thin whale bone, having them shaved thin at the top. The *modiste* should use her greatest skill in making up a deficient figure. Much padding is often required, and should be so arranged as to look perfectly natural and not inconvenience the wearer. No dress should go from the hands of a skilful dressmaker without an inside belt firmly secured to the back seams. This will prevent the waist from becoming twisted and working upward from the bottom of the waist. To prevent the dress from wrinkling over the point of bust, you should full the lining slightly. Always cut out the darts, and *commence at the top of darts in basting.*

The Worth and French dart is especially adapted for fleshy persons, as it prevents any fulness around the arm seye. French dressmakers use this dart for all figures. It cannot be used for an extended garment except where drapery is used, as it gives too much fulness below the waist. To prevent the darts' bulging at top, before placing lining on dress goods, draw the top of darts together in the lining, taking out about one-fourth of an inch

In cutting a polonaise, which is draped high over the hips, join the side body to the front at about 5 inches from bottom of waist, and for a pelisse or wrapper, join at 7 inches from bottom of waist.   In drafting for a polonaise, to prevent too much fulness in front, lap one side of the lining at bottom of the dart over the other side all you can, without drawing the upper part of the waist.   Use plaits in the back.   If you wish plaits to come below the waist line, cut as for a plain basque, placing the plaits where desired.

In using the **French Tailor System,** *no seams are allowed,* as we draft from actual measurement, and ALL SEAMS MUST BE ALLOWED except in neck and arm scye.   All using this perfect system of dress-cutting should use in connection one of our *double adjustable tracing wheels,* as you can trace the seams for cutting and basting at the same time, thus giving a uniform width of welts, which in basting is invaluable.

The rule made use of in the Kellogg French Tailor System is represented in Diagram D, on page 455.

The scale used by Madame Kellogg is illustrated in Diagram E, on page 456.

The Divided Skirt.—This garment is becoming better known, and many ladies are anxious to know something of it, as its promoters declare it to be easier to walk in than the ordinary drawers and skirts ; and at the present day women eagerly seize upon any help in the way of lighter skirts.   The garment has been issued by three pattern houses, and is for sale at all of the large underwear establishments under the name of " divided skirt " or " bifurcated skirt." At the Dress-Reform Association—who really brought it into notice—persons are advised to make the first garment, worn in place of drawers, of muslin, cambric or surah—the two former finished with lace or embroidery, and the latter having a feather-stitched hem.   It requires four yards of 27-inch goods, and consists of two pieces shaped similarly to drawer legs, only each is 50 inches around at the lower edge, and slopes very little to the yoke, which has a deep point in front and is narrow in the back, fastening in front.   The top of the seam may be closed or left open, as desired.   Over this skirt, or drawers, the originators advise one of flannel and one of surah, both sewed to one yoke, made just like this, only longer, to act as the petticoats ; then comes the dress skirt. Ready-made, the two latter are $12, and the first one, if of surah, is $7. Another reform garment combines the divided skirt and corset-cover.   Any one wishing to try this mode of dress will find the garment easy to make, with a pattern as a guide, and whether the style is a comfortable one to wear is a question that each lady may easily determine for herself.

Remodeling Gowns.—The making over of old dresses is an important part of household economy, and it requires even more tact to make a partially worn dress appear well when made over, than to fashion a new gown.   Half-worn skirts after being put in order should be worn in summer with loose blouses or fancy jacket basques.   Brighten dull, black dresses with full sleeves, collar and yoke of red or blue tartan surah, cut on the bias.   A tapering V-shaped vest will become short-waisted people.

Dresses for Children.—Let the clothes of the little ones be plain, but of as durable material as your purse will warrant.   Do not make a sad-faced child look more sorrowful by putting on too sombre colors.   Give tapering effects to a stout little figure.   Blouse suits of outing flannel will be appropriate for summer attire.   The dry goods stores abound with pretty patterns of cheap light-weight goods for summer wear, and with a small sum of money a mother by doing her own sewing may provide a child with many dainty gowns.

The winter dresses need not be so numerous, as they will not be so quickly soiled.

Neatness in Dress.—The most perfect neatness in dress is that of the demure Quakeress or the gentle Sister of Charity. They have made the cleanliness, next to godliness, possess a certain coquetry that is as attractive as it is quiet. The most beautiful dress in the world becomes, when out of order, unbeautiful. And the finest lace in a ragged condition is on a par with the commonest of cottons that is whole. Neatness is one of the leading feminine virtues, and an untidy girl need never expect to be treated with as much consideration as is she who is always just right. Dress undoubtedly has a great influence on the mind, and as the poor little Russian girl wrote in her diary, "I cannot understand how a woman who goes about with her hair in papers, cold cream on her face and a dirty gown can expect to keep her husband," so it may be taken for granted that the girl whose skirt is torn, whose unmended bodice is hidden under a fancy wrap, whose bonnet is just pinned together and whose ripped gloves are hidden in the muff, can never be quite right at heart. She is a deception in one way and she is very apt to become one in another. It only takes a minute to sew on the loose braid, not all of an hour to mend the bodice, a half an hour to brush the American soil from the skirt, a little time to sew up the gloves and behold a feeling of security comes over your body and extends itself to your manners. No woman can be at her ease mentally whose clothes have reached the rag-tag and bobtail condition. And no woman can wear dirty finery and be self-respecting. Better a thousand times just have the one neat dress, wear it day in and day out, know that it is brushed and in good order, and be happy. If I were a man I would pick out for my wife the woman who understood the value of personal neatness, which is personal sweetness.

A BRIEF AND PRACTICAL
TREATISE UPON THE HORSE.

ARRANGED AND WRITTEN IN SO SIMPLE A MANNER THAT THE
MOST UNSKILLED PERSON MAY SUCCESSFULLY TREAT AND
OVERCOME MANY OF THE COMMON COMPLAINTS
THAT ARE LIABLE TO ATTACK THAT MOST
USEFUL OF ANIMALS — THE HORSE.

POINTS WHICH SHOULD BE REGARDED IN BREEDING.

THIS very important subject is too often neglected. In breeding, a common mistake is often made, that mares are bred from after they become useless for work, regardless of hereditary diseases which may be transmitted to their offspring. It should be remembered that one of the characteristic laws of life is the reproduction in kind, — "like begets like."

Both parents should be selected with reference to their individual points of excellence, and also that the points of one are adapted to the points of the other; although both may be excellent individually, the points which characterize one may actually counteract those of the other; but if defects exist, the breeder should be sure that it is merely accidental, and not natural.

None but sound parents should be bred from (accidents, of course, are not to be regarded as unsoundness). Both parents should be free from any infirmity relative to a vicious temper or bad disposition; although the points of excellence in one may sometimes counteract the points in the other relative to that defect. Great care should be exercised that the same defect does not exist in both.

Some knowledge of the parentage of the sire and dam is therefore indispensable.

For ordinary business purposes, the best form of a mare to breed from is a short-legged beast, with a deep and roomy chest, wide hips, and so built in every way as to indicate a robust animal, with a strong constitution. Always avoid, when possible, selecting a mare for breeding purposes which has ringbone, spavin, or any disease which will render the offspring liable to be afflicted with the same by hereditary descent.

The "breed" should be taken into consideration, also. If it is desired to raise a carriage-beast, select a mare with a good animated countenance, sprightly, not too nervous nor too sluggish, but with a general muscular structure. The head of the brood-mare is a point which should be always regarded; for a mare that has a large head, with a dull, stupid countenance, will not breed a good foal, unless it might be from a very sprightly, ambitious horse. The shoulder-blade should be wide and long, extending nearly to the top of the withers, and so well covered with muscle as not to present any undue prominence. The neck should come out from the top of the withers, and not low down; the fore-leg should be perpendicular, so that the point of the shoulder and the toe will be in a right line; the foot should be sound, and of good, symmetrical shape.

The hips should be long, oval, and broad; the hock-joint should be well formed, and not of the "cow-hock" or "sickle-hock" kind.

In selecting a stallion, the rules which we have already given should be observed, remembering that compactness is quite essential, so that much goodness and strength are condensed into a small space. The shoulder should be well back, with the shoulder-blade lying obliquely; but

when it is desired to raise a slow, draught-horse, a large stallion should be selected, with upright shoulders.

In summing up the whole matter, we would say, if you would be successful in breeding, do not breed into the same family and blood, but select a horse of different blood, unless it should be eight or ten generations removed.

Avoid using a horse which is defective in any particular, when the mare has the same defect, but select one as near perfect as possible in that point. Do not breed small mares with very large horses, for there should be mutual adaptation in size and form, as we have before stated.

PRACTICAL POINTS IN REGARD TO FOOD.

No doubt, the majority of diseases contracted by the horse are due to the improper manner of feeding; no attention being paid to the age, variety of work, or constitution. The impropriety of such a course is readily to be seen.

Bad Hay is always dear, no matter at what price it is purchased; not containing the proper nourishment, the horse soon loses its vitality.

An old horse would do better fed on chaff than on hay, being better able to masticate and digest it.

A horse should not be fed upon grass or hay alone, especially while under hard work. Never give damaged corn, as it is very apt to produce inflammation of the intestines.

Chopped hay containing a teaspoonful of salt dissolved in a little water, renders it more digestible, and is very acceptable to the horse.

For an ordinary coach-horse, from four to six quarts of good oats, with seventeen to nineteen pounds of good hay, are sufficient. For extra work, he

should have more of each; for less, in like proportion.

Corn and oats are the very best food for a horse when he is worked hard; but if not, more hay should be given, on account of the corn and oats supplying more material for muscular force than any other kind of food; hay supplies very little.

The horse should be given a pailful of water morning and evening; yet, what is much better, a half pailful four times during the day.

A horse should never be worked nor driven hard directly after eating or drinking, as it interferes with digestion.

Never drive a horse, after he refuses food or drink, until he gets rested.

Never feed nor water the horse when he is overheated. Walk him about until he is cooled off; then groom him down with a handful of straw, and then with comb and brush; rub the legs well with the hand. When cool, give him his grain.

DISEASES OF THE HORSE.

Abdominal Dropsy is due, in most cases, to an existing inflammation of the bowels of a chronic character.

Symptoms.— A hard, wiry pulse, dry

mouth, pale condition of the membranes, drooping head, great thirst, no appetite, is weak, a constant disposition to lie down, great depression.

Sudden turning around or upon pressing the abdomen causes the animal to groan; the abdomen large, yet the horse is very thin in flesh, constipated and hide-bound, and one of the legs is sometimes swollen.

Treatment.— Make no delay. After deciding the condition, administer the following, night and morning: Sulphate Quinine, 10 grains; Extract of Belladonna, 20 grains; Iodide of Iron, 35 grains; Strychnia, ½ grain. Mix altogether, and give at a single dose. Then take 5 ounces of Tincture of Iodine, 2 ounces of Croton Oil; mix together, and apply by rubbing upon different parts of the abdomen, changing your position when the parts become sore. Many cases are incurable.

Bots.—The stomach of the horse appears to be a natural incubator of the Bot-Fly. The .eggs, after having made their abode in the stomach for a year, then suddenly let go, for they have undergone a change known as the chrysalis (that is the form of the butterfly just previous to the development of its wings). Being thrown off with the dung, in a few days it will have wings, and begin at once to fly around, depositing its eggs upon the horses, to undergo the same change. There seems to be two varieties of the fly infesting the stomach and fundament; the Bots that affect the stomach is caused by the eggs laid upon the fore-legs of the horse whilst the horses are out at pasture during the summer months.

Symptoms.— The horse looks lean, with a poor, unhealthy looking coat, soon after being turned to pasture.

The condition of the horse should be attended to at once. The animal must be toned up in order to overcome the exhausting effects of the fly. To expel the Bot or destroy the egg seems to be almost impossible. The best tonic to give the horse is the following; it greatly improves the general condition: Powdered Gentian, ¼ pound; Powdered Copperas, ¼ pound; Powdered Fenugreek, ½ pound; Powdered Elecampane, ¼ pound. Mix all

thoroughly together; give a heaping tablespoonful once a day.

The Fundament Bot.—This is caused like the Stomach Bot; but instead of the eggs being deposited on the legs, they occur upon the lips, also around the rectum, occasionally around the root of the tail and anus.

Treatment.— Linseed Oil injections, or tobacco smoke, have a good effect.

Bowels, Inflammation of.—The prominent symptom is great pain in the belly. Unlike colic, the pain does not seem to have any intermission whatever, but one continued pain. The animal rolls or paws with an appearance of general nervous disorder, and continually moving about. Among the more prominent features are cold legs and ears, belly painful and tender on pressure, the nose and upper lip are thrown upward in a singular manner.

Common Causes.— Drinking cold water when the body is overheated, exposure, hard driving, diarrhœa, etc. In a horse predisposed to the disorder, any of the above conditions would be liable to bring it on.

Treatment.— If due to constipation, give about a quart of raw Linseed Oil, with 5 or 6 drops of Croton Oil if necessary. If due to severe or too much purging, give an ounce and a half of Laudanum in half a pint of water.

Bronchitis.— This disease is due to an inflammation of the air-passages of the lungs. It is very common among horses, and is often mistaken for inflammation of the lungs, distempers, and colds.

General Symptoms.— The disease begins with a chill, then fever, harsh cough, labored breathing, mouth hot and dry, with loss of appetite. In the course of a day or so a discharge from the nose will be noticed.

Treatment.— Give 15 or 20 drops of Tincture of Aconite Root; repeat this dose every four hours until six doses have been taken, which will in most cases have removed the fever. The horse should be allowed plenty of cold water to drink. I do not like the idea of bleeding, as it is more likely to do harm than good. The fever having subsided (generally about the second day), the following powders will do a great deal of good: Take Powdered Licorice Root, Powdered Fenugreek, and Powdered Gentian, 2 ounces of each. Mix, and divide in six powders; give in feed two or three times a day.

Colic is a very common and dangerous disorder. It is divided into two varieties — spasmodic and flatulent, or wind colic. Spasmodic colic, as its name implies, is of a spasmodic character, and will, in severe cases, or when not suddenly checked, run into inflammation of the bowels, causing speedy death. It is caused by drinking cold water while in a heated condition, improper or unwholesome food, costiveness, undue amount of food, etc.

Symptoms. — The horse evinces great pain, shifting his position almost constantly, manifesting a great desire to lie down. In a few minutes these symptoms pass off, and the horse is easy for a short time, when they return with greater severity than at first, and so increasing until the horse is unable to be kept upon his feet. Turning around in a bewildered condition, he looks around to his flank, generally at the right side, as though to indicate the seat of the disease; he scrapes the ground with his forward foot, and will almost strike his belly with his hind foot. The horse kicks and rolls and heaves at the flanks, seeming greatly excited, acting as though he wanted to make water, which he cannot do on account of the spasm of the urethra. This symptom need not be treated, for, as soon as the animal is relieved of the colic, he will pass his water all right, therefore follow the treatment prescribed, and relieve the colic as soon as possible. As the disease advances, the horse will frequently throw himself down with force, look around at his sides, and sometimes snap with his teeth, striking upward with his hind feet, as they do in cases of intestinal inflammation of the bowels.

DIFFERENCE OF SYMPTOMS BETWEEN COLIC AND INFLAMMATION OF THE BOWELS.

Colic. — The attack is sudden; intervals of rest; the pulse nearly the same in the early stage of the disease; rubbing belly gives relief; ears and legs of an even motion gives relief· strength scarcely affected.

Inflammation of Bowels. — Symptoms come on gradually; the pain is constant; the pulse small and quickened, and too feeble to be felt in many cases; belly quite tender and sore to the touch; ears and legs cold; motion increases pain; strength rapidly failing.

Treatment. — Relieve the pain by giving one ounce of Sulphuric Ether, two ounces of Tincture of Opium (Laudanum), and a pint of raw Linseed Oil; and if not relieved in an hour, repeat the dose. If there is not relief after the second dose is given, some recommend bleeding from 6 to 10 quarts of blood from the neck vein. But I think that it is rarely necessary to do this. Walk the horse about occasionally in order to excite the bowels to action.

The following is a very good mixture: Take Aromatic Spirits of Ammonia, 1 pint; Sulphuric Ether, 1 pint; Sweet Spirits of Nitre, 1 pint and a half; Gum Opium (in fine powder), 4 ounces; Gum Camphor, 4 ounces; Assafœtida, 4 ounces. Mix altogether and shake frequently for a fortnight; strain through flannel and it will be ready for use. Dose — a tablespoonful in a little water every half hour. In very severe cases, a larger dose may be given. In certain cases of acidity, a tablespoonful of saleratus mixed with a pint of milk is an excellent remedy.

Flatulent or Windy Colic. — In this form of the affection, the animal is quite uneasy. His head droops, exhibiting some of the general symptoms of spasmodic colic before there is any enlargement of the belly, and particularly after; for as soon as the belly becomes swollen, pawing commences, although not so violent as in the spasmodic variety. There is not so much rolling and kicking. The horse is not so apt to move about. If the disease is not checked, the belly increases in size, the animal becoming very restless.

Treatment. — A horse should not be bled in flatulent colic; always use an injection first. If any gas or wind come away, the animal soon recovers; but if there be no relief from the injection, give remedies as recommended for spasmodic colic. Let the horse be kept moving around quietly until the medicine has time to act, in order to prevent the horse falling, which might cause a rupture of the diaphragm; an action which would prove certainly fatal.

Debility. — *Debility* is a condition induced by many causes; it usually follows other diseases. For this reason, anything which has a tendency to reduce the power or strength of the horse should be avoided, especially in disorders of the chest and lungs.

The *General Symptoms* of debility are, thickening or swelling of the legs, sheath, abdomen, and breast; the horse being weak, and staggering as he walks.

Bleeding in treating disease, insufficient or improper food given to the sick horse when it should have been supported by wholesome and nourishing food, will induce the disease.

Treatment. — Rest, and give tonic powders recommended under the head of Bots once or twice a day, with a liberal amount of good feed, and allow the animal to fully recover before putting to hard work.

Diarrhœa. — When the disease is not attended with pain, griping, or pawing, as in colic, no treatment becomes necessary; but should it continue, and the horse show signs of pain or colic, there are reasons to suspect the presence of some irritating poison retained in the bowels, which does not pass off with the excrement.

Treatment. — The first thing to do is to relieve the pain. Give 20 drops of Tincture of Aconite Root in a little water; then follow with a powder, as

given below, every three hours until the horse is better. Take prepared Chalk, 5 drachms; Catechu pulverized, 1 drachm; powdered Opium, 10 grains. Mix, and give as stated above, and allow the horse to have plenty of good cold water to drink. When diarrhœa is better, give bran mash for a few days; add a little ground flaxseed, if convenient.

Dysentery (Acute). — Owing to the extreme length and size of the intestines of the horse, any disease within them becomes a very serious affair.

Cause. — Dysentery of the acute form is usually produced by taking some irritating substance into the stomach, such as croton oil and aloes, which produces an inflammatory purgation, or from improperly applied poisonous drugs, such as tartar emetic, arsenic, etc., any of these substances being readily eaten with the grain. Persons not knowing the doses of poisonous drugs should never venture to give them.

The Symptoms are rather obscure at the commencement, as is usual in nearly all the disorders of the intestines. There is pain in the abdomen. The pain may be slight at first, or it may be so violent as to be confounded with the pains of colic. The animal is always thirsty, with an offensive stench.

Treatment. — Near about the same as for Diarrhœa, with larger doses of opium when pain is violent. Keep horse and stable clean; do not be concerned about the bowels if they do not move at all for a few days.

Distemper. — *Distemper*, sometimes called Strangles, is a peculiar form of sore throat, characterized by swelling between the bones of the lower jaw, terminating in an abscess, caused by a specific poison in the blood; few horses escaping its baneful ravage.

Treatment. — A great difference of opinion prevails regarding the treatment of this affection, some recommending poultices, while others forbid it, etc. The following plan is said to be as good as any. Give grass or soft feed (very little medicine should be given); hasten suppuration with warm poultices, or some prefer blistering; the appetite returns when the abscess breaks or is opened.

Epizootic. — An epidemic disease affecting many animals at the same time. Originates in one common cause. Without going into any further details upon the disease, I will here lay down a remedy which experience has proved to be the very best. Take of Powdered Licorice, 1 pound; Elecampane, 1 pound; Powdered Fenugreek, 1½ pounds; Powdered Gentian, ½ pound; Powdered Anise Seed, ¼ pound; Ginger, ¼ pound; Black Antimony, ¾ pound; Saltpetre, ½ pound; Sulphur, ½ pound; Epsom Salts, ½ pound; Rosin, ¼ pound; Hard Wood Ashes, ½ pound; Copperas, ¼ pound. Mix altogether well, and give a tablespoonful three times a day at first, and then only twice a day. This cured every horse to which it was administered.

Founder. — This disease arises from an inflammation of the sensitive lamina of the foot, of which there are two kinds, acute and chronic; the latter being a long continued condition of the former. The acute form is readily cured, if properly treated; but the chronic variety is generally considered incurable; yet it can be relieved very much.

Causes. — Permitting the horse to drink when overheated and tired from overwork; standing in draughts while warm; long and hard drives over hard, dry roads, etc.

Symptoms. — The horse may be noticed standing upon his heels, with forefeet and legs stretched apart as far as he can get them, in order to throw the weight off them as much as possible; and he can scarcely be made to move. There is fever and considerable disturbance in the acute variety of the disease.

Treatment. — Give the horse a good clean bed of straw in a large, well ventilated room or stall, so as to encourage him to lie down, thus, by re-

moving the weight from the inflamed parts, relieve his sufferings and hasten the cure.

As soon as his bed is fixed, give him 20 drops of Tincture of Aconite Root in half a pint of cold water, poured into his mouth from a bottle having a strong neck. Repeat this dose every four hours until six or eight doses have been taken; keep the pain down with wet cloths applied to the feet. Give plenty of cold water to drink. The above treatment should be adopted as soon as the horse has been attacked with founder. Let the horse remain quiet until he has fully recovered; give grass or mashes for two or three days, and then give a good and fair amount of hay.

Heaves. — This disease is due, usually, to an enlarged, and occasionally, a ruptured, condition of the air cells of the lungs, which lessens the value and usefulness of the horse.

The disease exists in every degree of intensity, from the slight case to the one which finds the horse almost powerless to breathe.

Causes. — In cases of heaves, horses are always enormous eaters. It has generally been found that horses over-fed on hay are liable to this disease. Heaves are never found in the racing-stable, where horses are properly fed.

Treatment. — Restrict the amount of hay and increase the grain feed, which will allow more room for the lungs to act.

RECEIPTS FOR THE CURE OF HEAVES.

First. — Powdered Assafœtida, 1 ounce; Powdered Camphor, ½ ounce. Mix, and make four powders. Feed one every other night for a week.

Second. — Capsicum, 1 ounce; Rosin, 1 ounce; Tartar Emetic, 1 ounce; Carbonate of Iron, 1 ounce. Mix altogether thoroughly, and give two teaspoonfuls twice a day in the feed.

Third. — Heaves has been cured by administering the Oil of Tar. By pouring it upon the tongue, and then giving some grain, which carries it into the stomach. In bad cases it may be given in tablespoonful doses. It is an excellent remedy for coughs, improving the appetite and body in general.

Hide-Bound. — *Hide-Bound* is a condition easily recognized by an adherence of the skin to the ribs, arising generally from an insufficient quantity or poor quality of food, and is a usual attendant of an exhausting or lingering disease.

The Treatment consists in giving mixed feed, bran, corn-meal, cut hay, etc., moistened with just sufficient water to keep the mass together; then take ·;Powdered Gentian Root, 3 drachms; Powdered Sulphate of Iron, 2 drachms. Mix, and give at one dose.

Kidney Diseases. — *Disease of the Kidneys* is usually known by a peculiar straddling gait, indicative of some disordered condition of those glands, as gravel, stony or gritty matter formed within them, which passes off in the urine, causing an irregular flow of the water.

Treatment. — 30 drops of Hydrochloric Acid should be given in a pail of water twice a week.

Kidney troubles in old horses can generally be relieved by giving soft feed. Boiled or steamed feed, flaxseed tea, cut grass, etc. Plenty of cold water should be allowed.

Inflammation of the Kidneys is usually brought on by hard work, improper food, sudden colds, or by an indiscriminate use of diuretic medicines.

General Symptoms. — Quick breathing, indicative of pain; hard, quick pulse, with more or less fever; unwilling to move hind legs, which he straddles apart when he walks; the water is scanty and of a deep color, at times bloody. Great tenderness on pressure over region of kidneys; refuses to move about or lie down.

Treatment. — Never give diuretic medicines. They will do harm. In the first stage administer about 40 grains of Opium with 15 grains of Cal-

30

omel sprinkled on the tongue. Repeat every two hours during the *acute* stage of the disease. If there be a hard, quick pulse, give 20 drops of Tincture of Aconite Root. Repeat until the pulse becomes slow and soft. Give plenty of rest.

Lungs, Diseases of. — *Pneumonia* (inflammation of lungs). A diseased condition of the lungs' structure, characterized by a discharge from the nostrils, following a sudden exposure to cold after being in a warm stable. The disease starts by a sudden chill, followed by a fever; cold ears and legs; hard, quick pulse, with labored breathing; pain in the chest, with cough; the animal stands with drooping head, does not care to move about; the nostrils are widely distended; a peculiar crackling noise is heard, if the ear is applied to the side of the chest.

Its Cause. — One of the most frequent causes is a hard drive in a cold wind, after coming out of a warm, comfortable stable.

Treatment. — Keep animal comfortable in well-ventilated, roomy stable. Keep dry. Give 25 drops of Tincture of Aconite Root every 4 hours in a cup of cool water, until 5 or 6 doses have been administered. Most likely the horse will now begin to perspire freely, care being taken that no draught of air strikes the horse. After taking sufficient of the Aconite Root and as soon as the appetite returns, thoroughly scald a pint of crushed oats, and give during the day. Care must be taken not to give much food at one time, as a return of the disease might ensue; the food must be increased gradually. No hay should be given for a week or two. If the horse is very weak, give *raw* eggs or other nourishing food in as concentrated a form as possible.

Loss of Hair or Baldness. — This disorder is produced by imperfect digestion. When small watery blebs occur, the horse should be turned to grass. If caused by blisters, burns, or sores, etc., apply the following lotion once a day: Tincture of Cantharides

1 ounce; Aqua Ammonia, 1 drachm; Glycerine, 2 ounces. Mix. The following is also recommended: Iodine, ⅓ drachm; Iodide Potassium, 15 grains; Lard, 2 ounces. Mix all together thoroughly, and rub down to the skin three times a week.

Skin Diseases OF MANGE, ITCH, ETC. — A group of contagious diseases caused by an insect burrowing in the skin.

Symptoms. — The horse is continually rubbing himself against everything he can. Small, red, elevated points may be seen upon the skin of the head and neck. The hair falls off, leaving the skin bald and fissured, with intense itching.

Treatment. — The horse must first have a good scrubbing with a stiff brush, and then with Castile soap and water containing a small quantity of soda (a tablespoonful to the quart). Wipe dry, and after thoroughly drying, apply the following ointment: Take Lard, 10 ounces; Sulphur, 4 ounces; Carbolic Acid, ½ ounce; Oxide Zinc, 2 ounces. Mix.

Owing to the contagious character of this disease, great care should be taken that all articles used about the horse should be cleaned, and subjected to great heat or the vapor of water containing carbolic acid, in order to destroy the insect which has caused the disease.

Tape-Worm. — The presence of the *tape-worm* is generally indicated by checked or retarded growth, a large head and abdomen, long ears, voracious appetite, rough coat, thin and emaciated body, with fetid breath. The colt pecks and bites its sides, and rubs its nose forcibly against the walls and fence posts.

Treatment. — Turpentine is a very effectual remedy.

For a *colt three months old*, from a ½ to a tablespoonful.

For a *colt six months old*, from 1 to 2 tablespoonfuls.

For a *colt one year old*, 2 to 3 tablespoonfuls.

For a *colt two years old*, 2 to 4 tablespoonfuls.

For a *horse four years old*, 3 to 4 ounces. Mix the turpentine with a ½ pint of infusion of Quassia Bark; add from ¼ to ½ a drachm of Powdered Camphor, and with the yolks of 3 eggs; shake well, and give early in the morning. Feed well, and give the medicine below every morning until the coat becomes glossy: Tincture of Chloride of Iron, 1 teaspoonful to an ounce; also Fowler's Solution, from 15 drops to 2 drachms, according to the age.

Pin-Worms. — *Pin-Worms* are a variety of worms infesting the rectum, causing great irritation to that part of the body; the horse rubbing its hair off, in order that it may stop the intolerable itching.

Treatment. — Give an injection composed of Catechu, 1 ounce, in a quart of water; and when dissolved, give an injection, and repeat for seven mornings, and on the eighth morning give a mash. At night, follow with a ½ ounce of Aloes, with a drachm of Calomel; it may be repeated if necessary.

SPECIAL FORMULAS

For Colic. — Take Laudanum, 1 ounce; Essence Peppermint, 2 ounces; Sulphuric Ether, 1½ ounces; Water, 16 ounces. Mix, and shake well before giving.

For Heaves. — Take Balsam Copaiba, 1 ounce; Spirits of Turpentine, 2 ounces; Balsam of Fir, 1 ounce; good Vinegar, 16 ounces. Mix; give a tablespoonful once a day.

An Excellent Liniment. — Take Oil of Spike, 1 ounce; Oil of Origanum, 2 ounces; Alcohol, 16 ounces. Good for lameness from any cause.

For Cuts and Sores. — Take Tincture of Aloes, 1 ounce; Tincture of Myrrh, ½ ounce; Tincture of Opium, ½ ounce; Water, 4 ounces. Mix. Apply night and morning.

Condition Powders. — Take Gentian, 2 ounces; Fenugreek, 2 ounces; Sulphur, 2 ounces; Saltpetre, 2 ounces; Cream of Tartar, 2 ounces; Rosin, 1 ounce; Black Antimony, 1 ounce

Ginger, 3 ounces; Cayenne, 1 ounce; Licorice, 3 ounces. Powder and mix all together. *Dose*, a tablespoonful once or twice a day for the cure of coughs and colds, distempers, etc., and in all diseases where condition powders are indicated.

For Galls and Bruises. — Take Laudanum, 2 ounces; Tannin, 2 drachms. Mix, and apply twice a day.

Eye-Water. — Take Laudanum, 1 drachm; Sugar of Lead, ¼ drachm; Soft Water, 8 ounces. Mix, and apply to the eye two or three times a day.

Diabetes. — Take Catechu, ¼ dr.; Laudanum, 2 drachms; Sugar of Lead, 5 grains; Alum, 15 grains; Water, 8 ounces. Mix.

Fever-Balls. — Take Tincture of Aconite, 10 drops; Saltpetre, 1 drachm; Tartar Emetic, ¼ drachm; Ginger, 2 drachms; Linseed Meal, 1 ounce. Mix, and make a ball. Repeat three or four times a day, if necessary.

Diuretic and Tonic Ball. — Take Copperas, 1 drachm; Saltpetre, 3 drachms; Rosin, 4 drachms; Fenugreek, 2 drachms; Flax-seed Meal, 1 ounce; Castile Soap, 2 drachms. Mix, and make a ball.

For Galled Shoulders. — Take Tincture of Arnica, 1 ounce; Vinegar, 6 ounces; Brandy, 4 ounces; Sal Ammonia, 2 ounces; Water, 1 pint. Mix; bathe the parts frequently.

For Thrush. — Take White Vitriol, 2 ounces; Water, ½ pint. Mix. After cutting away the diseased parts and thoroughly cleaning, apply to the diseased structure. Pack with lint to exclude dirt.

THE DOSES OF MEDICINE REQUIRED FOR THE HORSE

Name of Drug.	Action and Use.	Dose.	Antidote.
Arsenic...............	Alterative and Tonic, used for Paralysis, Mange, etc.	1 to 5 grs.....	Magnesia and Oil.
Carbolic Acid..	Externally and Disinfectant...............	....	Eggs, Soap, Gruel.
Tannic Acid........	Astringent.......................	20 to 40 grs.	
Alum................	Astringent...........................	2 to 3 drs.	
Aloes................	Laxative and Tonic...................	½ to 1 oz.	
Ether................	Anti-spasmodic.......................	½ to 2 ozs.!	
Anise Seed.........	Aromatic and Stomachic...............	½ to 2 ozs.	
Tartar Emetic......	Sedative and Alterative...............	½ to ½ dr...	Tannic Acid.
Assafœtida	Anti-spasmodic, Coughs, etc...............	1 to 3 drs.;	
Bismuth	For Chronic Diarrhœa, etc...............	½ to 1 oz.	
Camphor	Anti-spasmodic.......................	½ to 1 dr.	
Cantharides.........	Diuretic and Stimulant................	3 to 6 grs.	
Cayenne............	Stimulant and Carminative...............	5 to 25 grs.	
Prepared Chalk.....	Antacid.......................	½ to 1 oz.	
Blue Vitriol.........	Astringent and Tonic................	½ to 1 oz.	Eggs, Milk, etc.
Copperas............	Tonic and Astringent................	½ to 1½ drs.	
Digitalis Leaf.......	Sedative and Diuretic................	10 to 20 grs..	Stimulate.
Gentian Root.......	Tonic.............................	1 to 2 drs.	
Calomel	Cathartic.......................	10 to 40 grs.	Eggs and Milk.
Aqua Ammonia.....	Stimulant and Antacid................	1 to 4 drs.	Vinegar.
Fowler's Solution..	Used for Skin Diseases. See Arsenic, a preparation of.	1 to 4 drs.....	Hydrated Peroxide of Iron.
Solution of Lime...	Antacid, used as an Antidote to Poisoning by Acids.	4 to 6 ozs.	
Magnesia............	For Colts, as an Antacid and Laxative.	¼ to 1 oz.	
Epsom Salts........	Cathartic and Febrifuge................	2 to 8 ozs.	
Nux Vomica.........	Nervous Stimulant — used for Paralysis.	15 to 25 grs.	Saleratus followed quickly by Copperas, both dissolved in water
Linseed Oil.........	Cathartic and Nutritive	1 to 2 pts.	
Castor Oil...........	Cathartic.......................	½ to 1 pt.	
Croton Oil..........	Powerful Purgative................	10 to 15 d'ps	Opium.

THE DOSES OF MEDICINE REQUIRED FOR THE HORSE

(CONTINUED.)

NAME OF DRUG.	ACTION AND USE.	DOSE.	ANTIDOTE.
Opium	Anodyne and Anti-spasmodic. Given in Colic, Inflammation of Bowels, Diarrhœa, etc.	¼ to 1 dr.....	Belladonna, Strong Coffee, Brandy and Ammonia. Dash cold water on and keep the horse moving.
Bicarbonate of Potash.	Diuretic and Antacid. Good for Rheumatism.	3 to 5 grs......	Vinegar and Linseed Oil.
Chlorate of Potash.	Diuretic. Given for Bloating, etc.	1 to 2 drs.	
Saltpetre..............	Diuretic and Febrifuge	1 to 3 drs.	Linseed Oil largely.
Iodide of Potassium.	Diuretic and Alterative. Used for Rheumatism, Dropsy, Enlarged Glands, etc.	½ to 1½ drs.	Give freely Starch or Flour, with water largely.
Black Antimony...	Promotes the Secretions	¼ to ½ dr...	Infusion of Oak Bark. Give also Linseed Oil.
Quinine	Tonic given during Convalescence........	15 to 50 grs.	
Soda Bicarb..........	Similar to Bicarb. Potash......................	3 to 8 drs.	
Glauber-Salts........	Cathartic..	6 to 12 ozs.	
Soda Sulphite.......	Antiseptic and Alterative, used for Blood Diseases.	½ to 1 oz.	
Sweet Spirits of Nitre.	Diuretic and Diaphoretic.	½ to 1½ ozs.	
Spirits of Chloroform.	Anodyne and Anti-spasmodic.	1 to 2 ozs.	
Strychnia..............	Tonic and Stimulant. Used for Paralysis.	½ to 1 gr.....	Tobacco.
Sulphur................	Alterative and Laxative. Used for Skin Diseases and Rheumatism.	½ to 2 ozs.	
Tincture of Aconite Root.............	Sedative. Used for Lung Fever, etc.	15 to 35 d'p's	Give small doses of Nux Vomica and stimulants largely, and keep moving.
Tincture of Cantharides.	Stimulant and Tonic.	1 to 2 ozs.	
Tincture Ergot......	Parturient..	1 to 2 ozs.	
Tincture Iron........	Tonic and Astringent. Used for Typhoid Diseases.	½ to 1 oz.	
Tincture Iodine....	Used Externally		
Tr. Nux Vomica....	Tonic Stimulant in Paralysis and Dyspepsia.	2 to 4 drs.....	See Nux Vomica.
Tincture Opium....	Anodyne and Anti-spasmodic	1 to 2 ozs.....	See Opium.
Mercurial Ointment.	Used for Mange, Itch, Lice, and other Parasites.	....	Whites of Eggs with Milk given freely.
White Vitriol........	Astringent. Used for Cuts, Wounds and Sores in solution	5 to 15 grs...	Milk, Eggs, and Flour.
Ginger..................	Tonic, Stimulant and Stomachic. Used for Flatulent Colic, Dyspepsia, etc.	2 to 5 drs.	

For a colt one month old, give one twenty-fourth of the full dose for an adult horse as given above; three months old, one-twelfth; six months old, one sixth; one year old, one-third; two years old, one-half; three years old, three-fourths.

APPENDIX.

YOU ASK!—I'LL TELL!

INDEX.

ABSCESSES, 92.
Acetate of Ammonia, 130.
Acetate of Potassa, 129.
Acid, Citric, 132.
Acid, Tartaric, 132.
Accidents, to Prevent, 153-155.
Affidavits, 377.
Agents, 379.
Agreements, 376.
Alabaster, to Clean, 283.
Alcohol, 122.
All Fours, Game of, 405.
Aloes, 129.
Alum Whey, 270.
Ammonia, 124.
Ammoniacum, 130.
Amusements, 392.
Anagrams, 392.
Anchovies, to Make, 206.
Anchovy Toast, 252.
Antacids, 132.
Antalkalies, 132.
Anthelmintics, 132.
Antimacassar, 426.
Antimony, 130.
Antispasmodics, 124.
Ants, to Destroy, 358.
Apparatus, 140.
Appetite, 148.
Apple Dumplings, 242.
Apple Jelly, 257.
Apple Marmalade, 257.
Apple Sauce, 210, 215.
Apple Water, 271.
Apples, to Keep, 254.
Apples, Stewed and Roasted, 258.
Apprentices, 381.
Apoplexy, 42.
Apricots, to Dry, 254.
Arbitration and Awards, 377.
Arrowroot, Blanc Mange, 258.
Artichokes, to Boil, 233.
Artichokes, to Pickle, 226.
Articles of Food, 159.
Asiatic Cholera, 73.
Asking Papa, 333.
Asparagus, 233.
Assafœtida, 124.
Assignments, 376.
Asthma, 60.
Astringent, 126.
Attorney, Power of, 383.

BACON and Eggs, 196.
Bacon, to Boil, 183.
Bacon, English Breakfast, 183.
Bacon, to Cure, 293.
Baked Meats, 173.
Baking, 170.
Balls and Parties, 330.
Bandages, 138.

Bark, Peruvian, 125.
Bark, Angostura, 126.
Barley Water, 270.
Barometers, 297.
Basting, 170.
Bathing, 144.
Beans, French or String, 233.
Beans, Baked, 236.
Beds, Cheap, 279.
Beds, Feather, 16.
Bed-Rooms, 279.
Beds, to Tell if Aired, 279.
Beds, to Heat, 156.
Beef, Baked, 175.
Beef, Boiled, 176.
Beef, Cold Cookery, 176.
Beef, Dried, 294.
Beef, Extract of, 203.
Beef, Extra, 294.
Beef Gravy, 215.
Beef, Hashed, 176.
Beef, Heart, to Dress, 174.
Beef, Minced, 177.
Beef, Potted, 176.
Beef, Shin of, 178.
Beef, Sirloin, to Roast, 173.
Beef-Steak, Broiled, 174.
Beef-Steak, Fried, 174.
Beef-Steak Pie, 177.
Beef-Steak Pudding, 178.
Beef Stew, 177.
Beef Stewed with Oysters, 176.
Beet Root Coffee, 269.
Beet Root, to Pickle, 226.
Bicarbonate of Ammonia, 124.
Bilious Colic, 68.
Bills of Exchange, 378.
Birds, to Clean, 357.
Biscuit, Hot, 271.
Biscuits, Ginger, 250.
Biscuits, Sugar, 250.
Biting the Nails, 303.
Blackberry Cordial, 264.
Blackberry Jam, 256.
Blackberry Wine, 264.
Blacking, 362.
Black Paper Patterns, 415.
Bladder, Inflammation of, 76.
Blanc-Mange Arrowroot, 258.
Blanc-Mange Lemon, 258.
Blankets, to Wash, 287.
Bleeding, 141.
Bleeding at Nose, 117.
Blistered Hands and Feet, 348.
Blood, The, 147.
Bluestone, 132.
Boiling, 167.
Boiling Vegetables, 230.
Boils, 95.
Bologna Sausage, 197.
Books, Grease and Stains from, 287.

Boot Polish, 362.
Boots and Shoes, to Make Fit, 348.
Boots, to Blacken, 349.
Boots, Watertight, 361.
Borders, Crochet, 425.
Bottles, to Clean, 283.
Bottling and Fining, 280.
Bottling Fruits, 253.
Bowels, Diseases of, 68.
Boys, 304.
Boy Wanted, 305.
Brain, Diseases of, 41.
Brandy Sauce, 243.
Bread, Boston Brown, 274.
Bread, Corn, 272.
Bread, Economical, 272.
Bread, French, 274.
Bread, Graham, 272.
Bread, Home-made, 272.
Bread, Rye, 274.
Bread, Unfermented, 272.
Bread, Wholesome, 274.
Breakfast Rolls, 272.
Breasts, Inflammation of, 82.
Bricoli, to Boil, 236.
Bridesmaids, 336.
Bright's Disease, 76.
Brioche Stitch, 442.
Broiling, 170.
Broken Breasts, 82.
Broken Bones, 101.
Brokers, 379.
Bronchitis, 57.
Bruises, 104.
Brussels Sprouts, 233.
Buckthorn, 129.
Bugs, to Destroy, 358.
Bunions, 105.
Buns, Bath, 250.
Buns, Plain, 251.
Burgundy Pitch, 131.
Burns and Scalds, 97.
Burr Stones, Holes in, 361.
Business and Legal Information, 376.
Business, Localities for, 388.
Business, Men of, 388.

CABBAGE, to Boil, 234.
Cabbage, to Pickle, 203.
Cake, Butter, 249.
Cake, Banbury, 250.
Cake, Children's, 247.
Cake, Common Seed, 248.
Cake, Drop, 249.
Cake, Fruit, 249.
Cake, Ginger, 250.
Cake, Gingerbread, 249.
Cake, How to Ornament a, 248.
Cake, Icing for, 248.
Cake, Mixed Fruit, 249.

Cake, Plum, 247.
Cake, Plum, a Rich, 248.
Cake, Pound, 247.
Cake, Short, 249.
Cake, Snow, 251.
Cake, Soda, 248.
Cake, Tea, 249.
Caledonians, 338.
Calf's Head Boiled, 184.
Calf's Head Soup, 201.
Calfs Liver and Bacon, 184.
Calico, to Wash, 287.
Calomel, 125.
Camomile, 126.
Camomile Tea, 271.
Camphor, 122.
Cancer, 106.
Candies, to Make, 259.
Candy Drops, 259.
Canker of Mouth, 109.
Cantharides, 131.
Caper Sauce, 211.
Capitalists, Small, 388.
Carbuncle, 96.
Carditis, 62.
Carpets, to Choose, 276.
Carpets, to Clean, 282.
Carpets, Stair, 282.
Carriage Accidents, 154.
Carriage and Express Companies, 384.
Carrots, 234.
Carving, the Art of, 218.
Carving, Arrangements for, 219.
Carving Beef, 220.
Carving Ducks, 223.
Carving Fish, 219.
Carving Fowls, 223.
Carving Goose, 223.
Carving Ham, 223.
Carving Lamb, 221.
Carving Mutton, 221.
Carving Partridge, 224.
Carving Pork, 222.
Carving Tongue, 224.
Carving Turkeys, 223.
Carving Veal, 222.
Carving Venison, 220.
Cash and Credit, 391.
Casks, to Sweeten, 281.
Cassino, Game of, 409.
Castor Oil, 128.
Catarrh, 51.
Catechu, 126.
Cathartics, 128.
Cauliflowers, to Boil, 234.
Cause and Effect, 371.
Caustic, 132.
Cautions, 155.
Celery, 234.
Cement, 363, 365.
Cement for Iron and Stone, 361.
Chairs, Cane, to Clean, 283.
Chalk, 127.
Champagne, English, 263.
Champagne, Mock, 266.
Champagne, Summer, 267.
Change of Life, 83.
Charades, 392-413.
Charcoal, 171, 154, 264.
Checks, 379.
Cheesecakes, 247.

Chemical Remedies, 131.
Cherries, to Preserve, 256.
Chess, How to Play, 393.
Chestnut Sauce, 214.
Chicken, Boiled, etc., 188.
Chicken Pie, 189.
Chicory, 270.
Chilblains, 106.
Chimneys, Smoky, 280, 367.
Chocolate, 270.
Choice of Food, 159.
Chloride of Zinc, 132.
Cholera, Asiatic, 73.
Cholera Infantum, 28.
Cholera Morbus, 73.
Cholera, to Prevent, 153.
Chow-Chow, 228.
Chowder, Fish, 209.
Chutney Sauce, 216.
Cider, Mulled, 268.
Cider Wine, 268.
Cider, to Keep Sweet, 268.
Cider Vinegar, 214.
Civility, 389.
Clams, to Cook, 209.
Cleaning Dresses, 288-290.
Cleaning Furniture, 281.
Cleanliness, 145.
Clocks, Family, 280.
Clothes, Old, to Clean, 287.
Clothes, Black Cloth, to Clean, 290.
Cloth, Water-proofing, 370.
Cocoa, 270.
Cocoa-nut Candy, 259.
Codfish, 204.
Coffee, to Clear, 270.
Coffee, to Make, 269.
Coffee, Turkish, 269.
Coffee, Milk, 270.
Coffee a Disinfectant, 150.
Coins, 385.
Colds, 49.
Cold in the Head, 371.
Colds, to Avoid, 352.
Cold Meat Sauce, 212.
Colic, Bilious, 68.
Colic, Infant's, 29.
Colic, Painter's, 69.
Colocynth, 128.
Color of Dresses, to Preserve, 289.
Coloring Outbuildings, 360.
Comforter, Ladies', 430.
Complexion, The, 343.
Composition, 320.
Compresses, 137.
Confectionery, 257.
Congestive Headache, 39.
Conveyance, Deed of, 380.
Constipation or Costiveness, 69.
Consumption, 58.
Contract, 376.
Contracts for Labor, 381.
Conundrums, 413.
Conversation, 307.
Cooking Processes, 164.
Cordial, Blackberry, 264.
Corks from Bottles, 352.
Corn, Sweet, 236.
Corns, 105.
Correct Speaking, Rules for, 308.
Correspondence, 330.

Cotillion, 339.
Coughs, 50.
Cough, Whooping, 26.
Counsels for the Young, 303.
Counterfeit Notes, 368.
Country Dance, 341.
Cowage, 132.
Courtship, 332.
Cows, Age of, 374.
Cows, How Much Water, 356.
Cranberry Sauce, 212.
Crape, Stains from, 289, 291.
Cream Candy, 259.
Cream of Tartar, 129.
Cream, Substitute for, 269.
Credit, Letter of, 378.
Cribbage, How to Play, 402.
Crochet Border, 425.
Crochet Edging, 425.
Crochet Instructions, 423.
Crochet Tricoter, 429.
Crockery Wear, to Anneal, 285.
Croquet, Game of, 411.
Croup, 24.
Cucumbers, to Dress, 235.
Cucumbers, to Pickle, 225.
Cupping, 141.
Cure for Drunkenness, 41.
Currants, Red Jam, 255.
Currants, Red Jelly, 255.
Currants, Red Wine, 265.
Currants, Black Jam, 257.
Currants, Black Jelly, 257.
Curry Powder, 215.
Cushion, Toilet, 444.
Custard, Baked, 242, 247.
Custard, Boiled, 258.
Cutlery and Children, 155.
Cutlery, Marking, 370.
Cutting Iron or Brass, 364.

DAMP Walls, 279.
Damsons for Winter use, 256.
Dancing and Dances, 337.
Daughters, 303.
Deafness, 54.
Death, to Ascertain, 369.
Decalcomanie, 422.
Deed, 380.
Delirium Tremens, 40.
Demulcents, 133.
Devil'd Turkey, 198.
Diabetes, 78.
Diaphanie, the Art of, 420.
Diaphoretics, 130.
Diarrhœa, 70.
Diarrhœa in Consumption, 59.
Dictionary of Terms, 133.
Diluents, 133.
Dinner Table, 325.
Diphtheria, 32.
Diseases of Bladder, 76.
Diseases of Bowels, 68.
Diseases of the Brain, 41.
Diseases of the Chest, 57.
Diseases of Children, 24.
Diseases of the Ear, 54.
Diseases of the Eye, 112.
Diseases of Females, 79.
Diseases of the Heart, 62.
Diseases of Infants, 16.

INDEX. 487

Diseases of the Kidneys, 75.
Diseases of the Liver, 65.
Diseases of the Nerves, 40.
Diseases of the Stomach, 67
Disengaged, 332.
Disinfecting Fluid, 149.
Dislocation, 101.
Distance and Time-table, 385.
Disturbed Sleep, 49.
Diuretics, 129.
Dogs' Beds, 356.
Domestic Hints, 295, 371.
Domestic Measures, 118.
Domestic Surgery, 136.
Domestic Yeast, 271.
Dominoes, to Play, 406.
Door, to Keep Open, 279.
D'Oyley, Jewelled, 427.
D'Oyley, Netted, 434.
Draughts or Checkers, 395.
Dredgings, 170.
Dress, Night, 16.
Dress, Visiting, 324.
Dresses, to Clean, 288.
Dresses, Faded, to Bleach, 291.
Dressings, 136.
Dressmaking, 424–447.
Drinking in Warm Weather, 153.
Dripping Crust, 244.
Drunkard's Cure, 41
Dry Cupping, 141.
Dry Warmth, 141.'
Ducks, Care of Young, 355.
Ducks, Hashed, 190.
Ducks, Raising of, 354.
Ducks, Stewed, and Peas, 190.
Ducks, Wild, Roast, 192.
Due Bills, 379.
Dumpling, Apple, Baked, 242.
Dumpling, Apple, Boiled, 242.
Dutch Oven, 172.
Dysentery, 72.
Dyspepsia, 67.
Dyspepsia Bread, 273.

EARACHE, 55.
Early Rising, 148–390.
Economy, 296.
Edging, Crochet, 425.
Eels, to Cook, 205–210.
Effect and Causes, 371.
Effervescent Drink, 271.
Egg Flip, 267.
Egg Omelet, 196.
Egg Sauce, 211.
Eggs for Winter Use, 294.
Eggs, to Cook, 195.
Eggs, to Pickle, 227.
Eggs, to Poach, 196.
Eggs, to Tell if Good, 197.
Elderberry Wine, 265.
Emetics, 127.
Emolients, 133.
Engaged, 334.
English Champagne, 263.
English Mixed Pickle, 228.
Enigmas, 393.
Epispastics, 131.
Epsom Salts, 129.
Erysipelas, 36.
Escharotics, 132.
Essence of Mushroom, 213.

Ether, 123.
Etiquette, 324.
Evening Pastime, 392.
Exercise, 15, 146.
Expectorants, 130.
Extract of Beef, 203.
Eyelashes, 343.
Eye, Diseases of the, 112.
Eyesight, to Preserve, 115.

FACTORS, 379.
Failures, 389.
Fainting, 48.
Family Soup, 200.
Family Wine, 266.
Fancy Needlework, 415.
Farm Recipes, 353.
Fat, 170.
Feather Beds, 16.
Feather Flowers, 416.
Feathers and Beds, to Clean, 290.
Feathers, to Dye, 416.
Feet, Care for the, 349.
Feet, Wash, 348.
Felon, 116.
Female Disease, 79.
Fences, to Color, 360.
Fern Root, 132.
Fever and Ague, 85.
Fever and Ague, New Cure for, 372.
Fever, Causes of, 83.
Fever, Hay, 61.
Fever, Lung, 60.
Fever, Milk, 82.
Fever, Typhoid, 84.
Fever, Yellow, 87.
Finger Nails, 347.
Finger Nails, Biting of, 303.
Finger Ring, to Remove, 350.
Fire, Precautions in Case of, 155.
Fire Screens, 280.
Fires, to Prevent, 155.
Fish, to Cook, 204.
Fish Cakes, 209.
Fits, 29.
Flannel, Effect on the Skin, 349.
Flannel, to Wash, 285.
Flannel, to Shrink, 289.
Flannel, to Scour, 284.
Flies, to Destroy, 358.
Floors, to Scour, 284.
Flowers, Feather, 416.
Flowers and Fruit, Wax, 417.
Flowers, Language of, 342.
Food, 15.
Food, amount of, 164.
Food, Choice of, 159.
Forcemeat, 209, 217.
Fowls, to Boil, 188.
Fowls, to Roast, 187.
Fowls, Fricasseed, 188.
Fractures, 101.
Freezing with and without Ice, 261.
French Beans, to Boil, 233.
French Beans, to Pickle, 226.
Fricassee Rabbits, 193.
Fried Oysters, 219.
Frost Bite, 118.
Frugality, 390.
Fruits, to Preserve, 253.

Frying, 170.
Frying Fish, 208.
Frying Pan, 172.
Funerals, 336.
Furnishing a House, 275.
Furniture, Care of, 281.
Furniture, Scratched, 283.
Furniture, Stains out of, 286.
Furs, to Clean and Preserve, 290.

GALBANUM, 124.
Gamboge, 132.
Garden Walks, 359.
Garnishes, 216.
Garters, 348.
Gas Escaping, to Detect, 368.
Gas Meter, to Read, 367.
Gentian, 126.
Gentleman, A, 327.
Gherkins, to Pickle, 227.
Giblet Pie, 191.
Giblets, to Stew, 191.
Gilt Frames, 279.
Ginger, 130.
Ginger Beer, 266.
Ginger Bread, 251.
Ginger Cakes, 250.
Ginger Candy, 259.
Ginger Snaps, 251.
Ginger Wine, 265.
Giving Medicines, 120.
Glass, to Break any Shape, 280.
Glass and China Cement, 365.
Glass, Ground, to Imitate, 280.
Glass, Holes in, to Bore, 370.
Glass Stopples, to Loosen, 281.
Glass, Substitute for, 361.
Glassware, to Anneal, 285.
Glassware, to Wash, 283.
Glauber's Salts, 129.
Glossary of Terms, 133.
Glue, Liquid, 364.
Glue, Marine, 365.
Gooseberry Sauce, 213.
Goose, to Roast, 187.
Grapes, to Keep, 257.
Grape Wine, 265.
Gravel, 78.
Gravy, Beef, 215.
Gravy Soup, 200.
Green Peas, 225.
Gridiron, 172.
Grindstone, 371.
Grouse, Roast, 192.
Grubs, or Worms on Face, 38.
Guinea Fowl, Roast, 192.

HADDOCK, 205.
Hair Dye, 344.
Hair, Preparations for the, 344.
Hair Brushes, to Clean, 347.
Halibut, 209.
Ham, to Bake, 181.
Ham, to Boil, 182.
Ham, to Cure, 243.
Ham, Skippers in, to Prevent, 294.
Ham and Veal Pie, 183.
Hand, Management of the, 347.
Hashed Goose, 187.
Hashed Venison, 194.
Hashed Turkey, 186.

Hat, to Take Care of, 347.
Hay Fever, 61.
Head, Protection for the, 150.
Headache, Congestive, 39.
Headache, Periodic, 40.
Headache, Rheumatic, 40.
Headache, Sick, 39.
Health, to Preserve, 143.
Hearing, 54.
Heart, Diseases of the, 62.
Heartburn, 64, 271.
Hearth Rugs, 278.
Heaters and Stoves, 285.
Hens' Eggs, to Choose, 355.
Hens, to Fatten, 355.
Hens, to Make Lay, 355.
Hernia, 111.
Herbs, 163.
Herring, Potted, 229.
Hiccough, 48.
Hints, Domestic, 277.
Hints upon Dress, 372.
Hints upon Spelling, 322.
Home, 11.
Home Comfort, Hints for, 277.
Home-made Bread, 272.
Hominy, 236.
Honey, to Keep, 295.
Hops, 123.
Horseradish Powder, 216.
Horses, 459.
Horses, Age of, 353.
Horses, to Feed, 353.
Horses, Flies, to Keep Off, 354.
Horses, Pain in, to Remove, 357.
Horses, Scent, 354.
Horses, Scratches in, to Cure, 357.
Horses, Stumble, 354.
Hot Biscuit, 271.
Hot Cakes, 273.
Hot Sauce, 213.
House, to Furnish, 276.
House, Taking a, 276.
Household Management, 278.
Housewife, 170.
Husbands, Hints for, 298.
Hydrophobia, 46.

ICE CREAM, Flavoring, 262.
Ice Cream, to Make, 261.
Ice, Home-made, 363.
Ice House, Cheap, 363.
Ice Pitcher, Cheap, 298.
Ice, Strength of, 363.
Ice Water, 263.
Icing for Cakes, 248.
Incontinence of Urine, 78.
Indigestion, 67.
Infant's Cap, 438.
Infants, Diseases of, 21.
Infants, Management of, 18.
Indian Pickle, 226.
Inflammation of Bladder, 76.
Inflammation of Bowels, 68.
Inflammation of Breasts, 82.
Inflammation of Heart, 62.
Inflammation of Kidneys, 76.
Inflammation of Liver, 65.
Inflammation of Spleen, 66.
Inflammations, 92.
Influenza, 66.
Ingrowing Toe Nail, 105.

Ink, Indelible, for Linen, 375.
Ink, Marking, to Take Out, 286.
Ink, to Take from Paper, 286.
Ink, to Write on Zinc, 371.
Ink, to Remove Stains, 284.
Integrity, 390.
Interests, Legal Rates of, 385.
Interest, Tables, 385.
Intermittent Fever, 85.
Ipecacuanha, 127.
Ironing without Heat, 293.
Iron Rust from Linen, 286.
Itch, 35.

JALAP, 128.
Japanese Work, 415.
Jaundice, 66.
Jellies, Bottled to Mould, 259.
Juniper, 130.
Joints, 161.

KETCHUP, Mushroom, 213.
Ketchup, Oyster, 214.
Ketchup, Tomato, 212.
Kettles, to Clean, 257.
Kidneys, to Cook, 198.
Kidneys, Diseases of, 75.
King's Evil, 90.
Kino, 126.
Knife Handles, to Fasten, 361.
Knitted Counterpane, 442.
Knitting, Instructions in, 441.

LACE VEILS, etc., 291.
Ladies, 326.
Ladies' Comforter, 430.
Lamb Chops, 180.
Lamb, Leg of, Roast and Boiled, 180.
Lamp Chimneys, 285.
Lamps, to Fill, etc., 286.
Lamps, to Prevent Smoking, 279.
Lancers, The, 338.
Landlord and Tenant, 379.
Language of Flowers, 342.
Larder, The, 279.
Large Stoves, 285.
Laughter, Power of, 151.
Lead Pencils, to Sharpen, 352.
Lead Pipe, to Solder, 369.
Leases, 380.
Leather, Composition for, 362.
Leather Work, Ornamented, 415.
Leeches, 141.
Legal and Business Information, 376.
Legal Principles, 376.
Lemons, 131.
Lemonade, 267.
Lemon Peel, Tincture of, 271.
Lemon Sauce, 242.
Lemon Sherbet, 267.
Letter of Credit, 378.
Letter Writing, 320.
Liens, 380.
Life, Turn of, 151.
Life Belts, 154.
Light, a Dark Room, 309.
Linen, Care of, 281.
Linen, Incombustible, 292.
Linen, Stains Out of, 286, 287.
Linseed, 133.

Lint, 137.
Liquorice, 133.
Liver, Diseases of, 65.
Lobsters, 206.
Local Stimulants, 127.
Logwood, 127.
Loo, How to Play, 406.
Looseness of Bowels, 70.
Loss by Boiling, 169.
Loss by Roasting, 167.
Lozenges, to Make, 260.
Lumbago, 90.
Lunar Caustic, 132.
Lung Fever, 60.
Lungs, to Ascertain State of, 352.

MACARONI SOUP, 203.
Mackerel, 206.
Madeira Wine, 265.
Magnesia, 128.
Management of Infants, 19.
Mania-a-Potu, 40.
Man of Business, 388.
Manna, 128.
Marble, to Clean, 283, 284.
Marketing, 163.
Marking Cutlery, 370.
Marmalade Apple, 257.
Marmalade Orange, 256.
Marriage, 335.
Marriage with Blood Relations, 152.
Marriage, Legal, 384.
Marsh Mallow, 133.
Mat for Vase, 442.
Matrimony, Game of, 408.
Matting, Straw, 282.
Mattrasses, Stains from, 286.
Mazurka, 339.
Measles, 29.
Measures, Domestic, 119.
Meats, to Cure in Hot Weather, 294.
Meats, to Hang, 293.
Meats, to Pickle, 293.
Meats, to Dry-Salt, 293.
Mechanical Remedies, 132.
Medicine, Terms Used in, 133.
Medicines, Precautions, 120.
Medicines, their Properties, 122.
Medicines, to Make, 119.
Melons, to Pickle, 225.
Melted Butter, 211.
Mending, 281.
Menstruation, 79.
Milk Fever, 82.
Milk Lemonade, 267.
Milk, to Keep Sweet, 295.
Milk, Morning, 356.
Milk and Water, 356.
Mincemeat, 244.
Mint Sauce, 211.
Mirrors, to Clean, 285.
Mixed Pickle, English, 228.
Mock Turtle Soup, 201.
Molasses, Boil your, 243.
Molasses Candy, 259.
Money of Account, 386.
Money, to Double Itself, 385.
Money, Foreign, Value of, 385.
Mourning Dresses, Stains, 289.

Mortgages, 380.
Mothers, Model, 302.
Moths from Closets, 287.
Moths, to Prevent and Banish, 287.
Mucilage, 366.
Mulled Cider, 268.
Mulled Wine, 268.
Mushrooms, 162.
Mushroom, Essence of, 213.
Mushroom Ketchup, 213.
Mushroom, to Pickle, 226.
Mushroom, to Stew, 233.
Mustard, 127.
Mutton, Breast of, Stewed, 179.
Mutton, Broiled, and Tomatoes, 180.
Mutton Chops, Boiled, 179.
Mutton, Hashed, 179.
Mutton, Leg, Boiled, 179.
Mutton, Leg, Roasted, 178.
Mutton, Loin, Roasted, 179.
Mutton, Minced, Baked, 181.
Mutton Sausages, 197.
Mutton, Shoulder of, Roast, 180.

NARCOTICS, 122.
Nasturtions, 228.
Nausea, 67.
Needlework, Fancy, 415.
Nerve Diseases, 39.
Nervous Palpitation, 63.
Netted D'Oyley, 434.
Netting, Instructions in, 431.
Neuralgia, 47.
Neuralgia of the Head, 40.
New Neighborhoods, 389.
Night-dress, 16.
Nightmare, 49.
Night Sweats, 59.
Nitrate of Silver, 132.
Nitre, 129.
Nitric Ether, 123.
Nose Bleeding, 117.
Notes, Promissory, 378.
Notes, Judgment, 378.
Notice to Quit, 380.

OAK Bark, 127.
Oil Cloths, to Clean, 282.
Oil Paintings, 281.
Oil of Turpentine, 130.
Omelets, 196.
Onion Sauce, 212.
Onions, Baked, 235.
Onions, Pickled, 225.
Onions, Stewed, 235.
Operations, Minor Surgical, 136.
Opium, 123.
Orange Marmalade, 256.
Oranges, 131.
Orders for Merchandise, 378.
Organic Headache, 40.
Ostrich Feathers, to clean, 290.
Ovens, New, to Temper, 285.
Oxford Sausages, 197.
Oxide of Zinc, 125.
Oxtail Soup, 202.
Oysters, 210.
Oyster Ketchup, 214.
Oyster Powder, 215.

Oyster Sauce, 211.
Oyster Soup, 202.

PAINT, to Clean, 279-283.
Paint and Putty, to Remove, 367.
Paint, Smell of, 279.
Paint, Time to, 361.
Painters' Colic, 69.
Palpitation of Heart, 63.
Pancakes, 252.
Paper Hangings, to Clean, 282.
Paper on Whitewash Walls, 366.
Paper, to Remove Grease, 287.
Paralysis, 44.
Paralysis of Bladder, 78.
Parsley and Butter, 212.
Parsnips, Boiled, 235.
Parsnip Wine, 264.
Partnerships, 382.
Parties, Evening, 330.
Partridge, Roast, 192.
Paste, 370.
Pastils, for Burning, 280.
Pastry, 243.
Patterns on Cloths or Muslin, 415.
Peaches, to Preserve, 254.
Peas, Green, Boiled, 235.
Pea Soup, 202.
Pepperpot, 203.
Periodic Headache, 40.
Peruvian Bark, 124, 125.
Pheasant, Roast, 192.
Piccalilli, 228.
Pickled Salmon, 208.
Pickling, 225.
Pie, Apple, 245.
Pie, Apple, Open, 246.
Pie, Beef-Steak, 177.
Pie, Cherry, 246.
Pie, Chicken, 189.
Pie, Cocoanut, 247.
Pie Crusts, 244.
Pie Dish, Cup in a, 246.
Pie, Fish, 205.
Pie, Giblet, 191.
Pie, Gooseberry, 246.
Pie, Ham and Veal, 183.
Pie, Lark or Sparrow, 195.
Pie, Mince, 245.
Pie, Oyster, 205-210.
Pie, Potato, 232.
Pie, Rabbit, 194.
Pie, Rhubarb, 246.
Pie, Veal, 185.
Pie, Venison, 195.
Pigeon, Jugged, 191.
Pigeon, Roast, 191.
Pig's Liver, Baked, 182.
Piles, 69.
Pimples on the Face, 38.
Pipe Joints to Sinks, etc., 370.
Pitch, 131.
Plasters, 137.
Plated Ware, to Clean, 283, 284.
Pleurisy, 59.
Plums, Preserved, 254.
Pneumonia, 60.
Poisoning, 100.
Politeness, 324.
Polka, 342.

Polypus, 110.
Polypus of the Ear, 56.
Pomades, to Make, 345.
Pope Joan, Game of, 408.
Pork Cutlets or Chops, 181.
Pork from a Bushel of Corn, 354.
Pork, Leg of, Boiled, 182.
Pork, Leg of, Roast, 181.
Pork, Pickled, to Boil, 182.
Pork, Spare-rib, Roast, 181.
Portable Soup, 203.
Position for Sleep, 16.
Potash, Sulphate of, 129.
Potassa, Acetate of, 130.
Potatoes, to Cook, 231.
Potato Yeast, 271.
Pot Pie, 189
Potted Herring, etc., 229.
Poultices, 137.
Poultry, Cooking, 167.
Powders, Ginger Beer, 266.
Powders, Soda Water, 267.
Powders, Seidlitz, 267.
Power of Attorney, 383.
Preservation of Health, 143.
Preserving Fruits, 253.
Prevention of Cholera, 153.
Pronunciation, Rules for, 314, 316.
Proposing, 333.
Provincialisms, 316.
Pudding, Apple, 237.
Pudding, Batter, Baked, 238.
Pudding, Beef-Steak, 178.
Pudding, Bread, 237.
Pudding, Bread and Butter, 240.
Pudding, Currant, 240.
Pudding, Custard, Baked, 241.
Pudding, Damson, 241.
Pudding, Hasty, 239.
Pudding, Huckleberry, 239.
Pudding, Jam, Roly-Poly, 240.
Pudding, Lemon, Boiled, 241.
Pudding, Oatmeal, 240.
Pudding, Peas, 240.
Pudding, Plum, Christmas, 239.
Pudding, Plum, English, 239.
Pudding, Potato, 240.
Pudding, Rabbit, 194.
Pudding, Rhubarb, 238.
Pudding, Rice and Apple, 242.
Pudding, Rice and Tapioca, 242.
Pudding, Sauces for, 242.
Pudding, Suet, 238.
Pudding, Suet, with Roast Meat, 241.
Pudding, Yorkshire, 238.
Puddings, Baked and Boiled, 237.
Puff-paste, 243.
Pulse, The, 64.
Punch, Whiskey, 268.
Punctuation, 320.
Put, How to Play, 407.
Puzzles, 393.

QUACKERY, 13.
Quadrilles, 337.
Quassia, 126.
Quinsy, 31.

RABBIT, Boiled, 193.
Rabbit, Economical, 194.

Rabbit, Pie and Pudding, 194.
Rabbit, Roast, 193.
Radishes, to Boil, 233.
Raspberry Jam, 256.
Raspberry Vinegar, 268.
Raspberry Wine, 265.
Rats and Mice, 358, 359.
Razors, 349.
Rebuses, 393.
Receipts for Money, 377.
Reel, the Highland, 342.
Refrigerants, 131.
Refusal, 335.
Relishes, 217, 251.
Rheumatic Headache, 40.
Rheumatism, 88.
Rhine Wine, 266.
Rhubarb, 128.
Rhubarb, to Preserve, 254.
Ribbons, to Smooth, 288.
Rice, Boiled, 242.
Rice Sauce, 212.
Ringworm, 35.
Roasting, 165.
Roast Duck, 190.
Roast Fowls, 187.
Roast Goose, 187.
Roast Grouse, 192.
Roast Partridges, 192.
Roast Pheasant or Guinea Fowl, 192.
Roast Turkey, 186.
Roast Wild Duck, 192.
Roast Woodcock, 193.
Room, Dark, to Light, 369.
Rooms, to Beautify, 276.
Rose Leaves, 127.
Rubefacients, 131.
Running up Stairs, 349.
Rupture, 111.

SAGE and Onion Seasoning, 215.
Salad, Lobster, 206.
Salads, 229.
Saleratus, 271.
Salmon, 207.
Salt Rheum, 36.
Samphire, to Pickle, 226.
Sandwiches, 204.
Sarsaparilla, 130.
Saucepan, The, 173.
Sauce for Puddings, 242.
Sauces, 210.
Sausages, to Make and Cook, 197.
Savory Omelet, 252.
Scalds and Burns, 97.
Scammony, 129.
Scarlatina, 30.
Scent Bags for Linen, 292.
Schottische, 341.
Scollops, 209.
Scotch Punch, 268.
Scouring, 284.
Scouring Drops, 287.
Scrofula, 90.
Scurvy, 91.
Seidlitz Powders, 267.
Senna, 128.
Servants, 300.
Seville Oranges, 131.

Shad, 208.
Sheep, to Find the Age of, 353.
Sheep, to Pasture, 359.
Sheep, to Make Own a Lamb, 353.
Sheepskin Mats, 356.
Sherbet, Lemon, 267.
Shingles, 36.
Shingle Roofs, 361.
Shoe Soles, to Save, 362.
Sialagogues, 130.
Sick Headache, 39.
Sickness of Stomach, 67.
Silks, to Clean and Keep, 288.
Silks, to Wash, 288.
Silver Plate, to Clean, 283.
Singing, Utility of, 147.
Skin Diseases, 35.
Sleep, 15.
Sleep, How to Get, 147.
Sleep Walking, 49.
Sleeping Together, 149.
Small-pox, 33.
Smelts, 208.
Smoky Chimneys, 280, 367.
Soap, to Make, 292.
Soda Water Powders, 267.
Sofas and Ottomans, 283.
Soldering, 280.
Somnambulism, 49.
Sore Nipples, 83.
Sore Throat, 33.
Sounds and Tongues, 209.
Soups, 198.
Spanish Dance, 338.
Spanish Flies, 131.
Spasmodic Croup, 25.
Speaking, Errors in, 307.
Spectacles, When Required, 116.
Speculation, Game of, 408.
Spelling, Hints upon, 322.
Spit, 172.
Spleen, 66.
Spirits of Mindererus, 130.
Sprains, 104.
Squashes, to Cook, 236.
Squills, 130.
Squinting, 28.
Squinting, Cause of, 352.
Staining, the Art of, 351, 373.
Stains from Silver, 284.
Stains, Fruit and Wine, 286.
Stairs, Why Run up, 349.
Starch, Gum Arabic, 292.
Stewed Duck, 190.
Stewed Giblets, 191.
Stewed Mushroom, 233.
Stewed Oysters, 210.
Stewed Tomatoes, 213.
Stimulants, 122.
Stock for Soups, 199.
Stockings, Mending, 289.
Stomach, Diseases of, 67.
Store, Location of, 389.
Storekeepers, Duties of, 390.
Stoves, Economy of, 285.
Stoves, to Temper, 285.
Strawberry Jam, 257.
Straw Bonnets, to Clean, 291.
Strength of Man, 157.
St. Vitus's Dance, 46.
Styes, 114.
Substitute for Cream, 269.

Succotash, 236.
Suet Crust for Pie and Pudding, 244.
Sulphate of Copper, 132.
Sulphate of Potash, 129.
Sulphate of Zinc, 127.
Sulphur, 128.
Sulphuric Ether, 123–125.
Sunstroke, 45.
Surgery, Domestic, 136.
Sweetbreads, 198.
Sweet Corn, 236.
Sweet Sauce, 243.
Swimming, the Art of, 156.
Syrup, to Make a, 253.

TABLE Cover, Oriental, 432.
Table, Dining, 283.
Table, to Preserve, 279.
Tables of Weights and Measures, 387.
Taffy, Everton, 259.
Taffy, Plain, 259.
Taking a House, 275.
Taking a Store, 388.
Tamarinds, 128.
Tartar Emetic, 130.
Tarts, Fruit, 246.
Taste of New Wood, to Remove, 357.
Tatting Edging, etc., 437.
Tatting Infant's Cap, 438.
Tatting, Instructions in, 436.
Tea, Camomile, 271.
Tea, Economy of, 268.
Tea Loaves, 273.
Tea, Making, 268.
Teapot, China, 281.
Teeth, The, 52, 343.
Teeth Set on Edge, 152.
Teething, 23.
Temperance, 148.
Tenant, Rights of, 379.
Terms Used in Medicine, 133.
Tetter, 36.
Throat Diseases, 31.
Thrush, 24.
Time and Distance Table, 385.
Tincture of Lemon Peel, 271.
Tired Mothers, 302.
Toast, Anchovy, 252.
Toast, Buttered, 252.
Toasted Cheese, 252.
Tobacco, Effects of, 152.
Tobacco in Lead Wrappers, 361.
Toe-Nail, Ingrowing, 105.
Toilet Cushion, 444.
Toilet Requisites, 343.
Tolu, 130.
Tomatoes, to Keep, 295.
Tomato Jam, 256.
Tomato Ketchup, 212.
Tomato Sauce, 212.
Tomato Soup, 202.
Tomatoes, Stewed, 213.
Tomatoes, to Can Whole, 256.
Tonics, 125.
Tool Chests, Family, 278.
Toothache, 53.
Tooth Powder, 344.
Tragacanth, 133.
Trout, 209.
Tumors, 110.

Turkey, Boiled, 186.
Turkey, to Choose and Roast, 186.
Turkey, Hashed, 186.
Turkeys, Raising, 355.
Turnips, Mashed, 236.
Turpentine, Oil of, 130.
Turpentine, Venice, 129.

ULCERS, 94.
Urine, Inability to Hold, 78.

VACCINATION, 35.
Valerian, 125.
Varicose Veins, 110.
Varnishing, Flexible, 361.
Varnishing Maps, etc., 280.
Vase, Mat for, 442.
Veal Cutlets, 183.
Veal, Fillet of, 183.
Veal and Ham Pie, 183.
Veal, Knuckle of, Stewed, 184.
Veal, Minced, 185.
Veal Pie, 185.
Veal, Ragout of, 185.
Veal Sausages, 197.
Vegetables, to Prepare and Cook, 230.
Vegetable Soup, 203.
Velvet, to Restore, 289.
Venice, Turpentine, 129.
Venison, Haunch, etc., 194.
Venison Pasty, 195.
Ventilation, 15, 151.
Vinegar, Raspberry, 268.
Vinegar, Cider, etc., 214.
Vingt-un, or Game of Twenty-one, 410.

Visits, 297.
Visiting the Sick, 155.
Volatile Salt, 124.
Vomiting, 67.

WALKS of Cement, 359.
Walking, 147.
Walnuts, to Pickle, 225.
Waltz, 339.
Warts, 104.
Washing, Hints About, 291.
Watch, How to Take Care of, 350.
Water Brash, 67.
Water Cress, to Stew, 233.
Water, Hard, to Soften, 280, 370.
Water Ices, 263.
Waterproof Cloth, 370.
Water, Sea, to Prepare, 375.
Wax in the Ear, 56.
Wax Flowers and Fruit, 417.
Weather, Signs and Precautions, 297.
Welsh Rare Bit, 251.
Wen, 110.
Wheat for a Barrel of Flour, 360.
Wheelbarrow, a New, 358.
Whist, How to Play, 395.
Whites, 81.
Whitewashing, 360.
Whitelow, 116.
White Vitriol, 126, 127.
Whooping Cough, 26.
Wife's Power, 299.
Wild Duck, Roast, 192.
Wills, 382.
Wine, Blackberry, 264.
Wine, Champagne, 264.

Wine, Champagne, Mock, 266.
Wine, Cider, 268.
Wine, Currant, 265.
Wine, Elderberry, 265.
Wine, Family, 266.
Wine, Ginger, 265.
Wine, Grape, 265.
Wine, Madeira, 265.
Wine, Making, 263.
Wine, Mulled, 268.
Wine, Parsnip, 264.
Wine, Raspberry, 265.
Wine, Rhine, 266.
Wine, Sauce, 212, 243.
Wine, Turnip, 264.
Wine Whey, 267.
Winter Salad, 229.
Wives, Hints for, 300.
Woodcock, Roast, 193.
Woollen Dresses, to Clean, 288.
Woollens, to Wash, 287.
Worcestershire Sauce, 213.
Worms, 74.
Wormwood, 125, 126.
Wounds, 99.
Wow Wow Sauce, 216.
Wristlets, 348.
Writing, Faded, to Restore, 352.
Writing Letters, 320.

YEAST, Making, 271.
Yellow Fever, 87.
Young Ladies, Advice to, 303.
Youth, Health in, 149.

ZINC, 125.
Zinc, Chloride of, 132.
Zinc, Sulphate of, 127.

Index to Treatise Upon the Horse.

	PAGE
Antidotes, etc.	454
Baldness,	452
Bots, Fundament	448
Bots, Stomach	448
Bowels, Inflammation of,	448
Breeding	446
Bronchitis	448
Bruises, Liniment for,	454
Colic, Flatulent	449
Colic, Spasmodic	449
Condition Powders	453
Cuts and Sores, Cure for,	453
Debility	450
Diabetes, Cure for,	454
Diarrhœa	450

	PAGE
Distemper	450
Diuretic and Tonic Ball	454
Doses, etc.	454
Dropsy, Abdominal	447
Dysentery	450
Epizootic	451
Excellent Liniment	453
Eye-Water	454
Fever-Balls	454
Food	447
Galled Shoulder	454
Galls and Bruises, to Heal	454
Heaves	451
Heaves, to Cure	451

	PAGE
Hide-Bound	452
Horse, Diseases of	447
Itch	453
Kidney, Diseases of	452
Loss of Hair	452
Lungs, Diseases of	452
Mange	453
Pin-Worms	453
Skin, Diseases of	453
Special Formulas	453
Tape-Worm	453
Thrush	454

THE END.